Shorter Views

Other Books by the Author

Fiction

The Jewels of Aptor (1962)
The Fall of the Towers:
   Out of the Dead City (formerly Captives of the Flame, 1963)
   The Towers of Toron (1964)
   City of a Thousand Suns (1965)
The Ballad of Beta-2 (1965)
Empire Star (1966)
Babel-17 (1966)
The Einstein Intersection (1967)
Nova (1968)
Driftglass (1969)
Equinox (formerly The Tides of Lust, 1973)
Dhalgren (1975)
Trouble on Triton (formerly Triton, 1976)
Return to Nevèrÿon:
   Tales of Nevèrÿon (1979)
   Neveryóna (1982)
   Flight from Nevèrÿon (1985)
   Return to Nevèrÿon (formerly The Bridge of Lost Desire, 1987)
Distant Stars (1981)
Stars in My Pockets Like Grains of Sand (1984)
Driftglass/Starshards (collected stories: 1993)
They Fly at Çiron (1993)
The Mad Man (1994)
Hogg (1995)
Atlantis: Three Tales (1995)

Graphic Novels

Empire Star (1982)
Bread & Wine (1999)

Nonfiction

The Jewel-Hinged Jaw (1977)
The American Shore (1978)
Heavenly Breakfast (1979)
Starboard Wine (1984)
The Motion of Light in Water (1988)
Wagner/Artaud (1988)
The Straits of Messina (1990)
Silent Interviews (1994)
Longer Views (1996)
Times Square Red, Times Square Blue (1999)

Shorter Views

Queer Thoughts &

The Politics of the Paraliterary

Samuel R. Delany

Wesleyan University Press

Published by University Press of New England • Hanover and London

Wesleyan University Press
Published by University Press of New England, Hanover, NH 03755
© 1999 by Samuel R. Delany
Printed in the United States of America
5 4 3 2 1
CIP data appear at the end of the book

For Patrick Merla & Marc Shell

The following works in this collection were previously published:

"The Rhetoric of Sex / The Discourse of Desire" was initially delivered as a lecture at MIT; it first appeared in print in *Heterotopias: The Body Politic*, ed. Tobin Siebers, Ann Arbor: University of Michigan Press, 1995.

"Street Talk / Straight Talk" appeared in *Difference*, eds. Naomi Shor & Elizabeth Weed, special issue on Queer Theory: Lesbian and Gay Sexualities, guest edited by Teresa de Lauretis, vol. 3, summer 1991, Providence.

"On the Unspeakable" first appeared in *Everyday Life*, eds. George and Chris Tysh, Detroit, 1987; subsequently it appeared in *Avant Pop: Fiction for a Daydreaming Nation*, ed. Larry McCaffery, Fiction Collective-2, Boulder, Colorado, 1993.

"Coming / Out" appeared first, in slightly different form, in *Boys Like Us*, edited by Patrick Merla, New York: Avon Books, 1997.

"A Bend in the Road" first appeared in the *Yale Journal of Criticism*, eds. Esther da Costa et al, vol. 7, no. 1, spring 1994; New Haven.

"The 'Gay' Writer / 'Gay Writing' . . . ?" first appeared in the *AWP Journal*, 1993.

"The *Black Leather in Color* Interview" first appeared in *Black Leather in Color*, edited by Antoinette, Lidell Jackson, and S. Guy Giumento, no. 3, fall 1994, New York City.

continued on page 458

Contents

Preface: On Creativity and Academic Writing   vii

Part One: Some Queer Thoughts

1   The Rhetoric of Sex / The Discourse of Desire   3

2   Street Talk / Straight Talk   41

3   On the Unspeakable   58

4   Coming / Out   67

5   A Bend in the Road   98

6   The "Gay" Writer / "Gay Writing" . . . ?   111

7   The *Black Leather in Color* Interview   115

8   The Thomas L. Long Interview   123

Part Two: The Politics of the Paraliterary

9   Neither the First Word nor the Last on Deconstruction,
    Structuralism, Poststructuralism, and
    Semiotics for SF Readers   141

10 The *Para•doxa* Interview: Inside and Outside the Canon   186

11 The Politics of Paraliterary Criticism   218

12 Zelazny/Varley/Gibson—and Quality   271

13 Pornography and Censorship   292

14 The Making of *Hogg*   298

15 The Phil Leggiere Interview: Reading *The Mad Man*   311

16 The Second *Science-Fiction Studies* Interview:
    Of *Trouble on Triton* and Other Matters   315

Part Three: Some Writing / Some Writers

17 Antonia Byatt's *Possession: A Romance*   353

18 Neil Gaiman, I, II, and III   359

19 A Tribute to Judith Merril   373

20 Michael Perkins's *Evil Companions*   377

21 Now It's Time for Dale Peck   384

22 *Othello* in Brooklyn   388

23 A Prefatory Notice to Vincent Czyz's *Adrift in a
    Vanishing City*   396

24 Under the Volcano with Susan Sontag   399

25 Some Remarks on Narrative and Technology *or*:
    Poetry and Truth   408

Appendix:

Some Notes for the Intermediate and Advanced
Creative Writing Student   433

Index   461

Preface

On Creativity and Academic Writing

For twenty-five years I've taught more creative writing classes than any other sort—I've been *asked* to teach more creative writing classes than any other sort. Creative writing is also the class that has given me the most pause. When I arrive at a new university, some form of the following conversation almost always occurs:

Them: "Oh, you will teach a creative writing class, won't you?"

Me: "I'd rather not."

Them: "But you seem so eminently *qualified* to teach creative writing. You've written so many novels and short stories."

Me: "Novels, yes. Stories, no. But I really don't know if I have anything to *teach* in terms of creative writing."

Them: "Oh, but I'm sure you do . . ."

I'm being somewhat disingenuous. As I said, creative writing is the class I *have* taught the most, and I suspect it will be the class I shall go on teaching the most. (I am scheduled to teach one such workshop this coming summer.) Certainly it's an easy class to fill with pleasant comments, pleasing pastimes, and passably interesting exercises. The problem is, however, philosophical—specifically, ontological. I'm just not sure if "creativity"—as it is presupposed, as it is hypostatized, as it is commodified and reified in endless writing workshops and the brochures they send out to attract writing students—exists. And I feel the same discomfort teaching a class in "creative" writing as I would were I a physicist assigned to teach a class in "phlogiston" physics—assigned to teach it not as a historical reaction of a vanished and discredited theory, but as a modern enterprise all my eager students believed was the latest scientific dope on the realest of real worlds.

In his various notes on nineteenth-century Paris, Baudelaire, and the Arcades, Walter Benjamin makes a most intricately suggestive observation: When, in the ninteenth-century marketplace, industrial products passed a certain number, it became a practical impossibility to know all the relevant facts about each product's manufacture, the quality of the materials that went into it, the care and craft with which it had been made, and thus its durability and functionality. To compensate for this general loss of empirical knowledge, the more generalized notion of "good taste" arose to occupy the interstices, override the positivities, and finally sublate the material interplay of the known and the unknown— all that was left of the empirical knowledge about care, quality, manufacture, and efficiency that had gone by the name of quality.

It is, then, in the same sense that I might say that good taste has no ontological status that I suggest a similar denial of ontological status to creativity. That is, while it is a social reality, it is reducible—like a chemical compound—to its constitutive elements. But, unlike a compound, its fundamental properties are also reducible (as in a chemical mixture) to the properties of its constitutive elements.

Having located this so important relationship between empirical knowledge and good taste, we can fix a number of other concepts that bear the same necessarily mystified relation one to the other. Most important for us today is, I suspect, the relation between individual strength and institutional power; for I would maintain that it is interesting, even necessary if we wish to be effective political citizens, to consider that strength bears the relationship to power that empirical knowledge bears to good taste. Use value and exchange value are another, more classical pair that bear a like relation (and the complexities of *their* mutual and forever interdependent analyses suggest just how complex this relationship—however simple it may look at first—actually is). The relationship of technology to science is one more such relationship. And the relationship of craft to art is still another and—in this discussion—the one that most concerns us.

What is problematic about these relationships is that in the second, reified, mystified term from all these pairs—from good taste to exchange value to power to science to art—lies all possibility for both guided and unguided growth, for unconscious response, for both evolutionary and entropic change. That such change and growth have been present in the human universe since caves and chipped flints is the reason that the earlier, positive, and seemingly pure terms—knowledge, strength, use value, craft, technology—are never *really* pure. The mystified nimbus always inheres in them, glimmers like an aura about them, flickers as their afterimage, however brief or restricted, waiting only till material forces conspire to make it theoretically necessary to name these later and more problematic developments.

Craft is something produced by skill.

Art is something produced by creativity.

I don't think the suggestion is terribly profound that the "creativity effect" in art is an indeterminate interplay of skill and originality in a field in which it is empirically impossible to know in some exhaustive manner which is which. It is impossible for the audience of the art work to know. And while the artist may be a bit more on top of certain aspects of the problem than some members of the audience, finally and for the same reasons it is also impossible for the artist to know. What makes it impossible to know is the virtually infinite number of repetitions that must sediment implicitly—and the extraordinary effect small perturbations make on the overall perception of the results.

This is also, of course, what makes the teaching of anything where creativity (rather than skill) is involved problematic: for the modern notion of creativity, through its reliance on the ideas of skill and originality, comes to mark out, just like Benjamin's notion of "good taste," an area of human endeavor and everyday semiosis based largely, as it were, on ignorance.

In practical terms:

I have had the rather disconcerting experience of having taught a creative writing workshop from which five of the twenty students went on to become respected and regularly publishing writers. After winning a Hugo Award for her first novel and basing another on a passing exercise I'd given in class (and then going on to set up a successful workshop of her own at her own university based on the one I had given), one told me she'd found the workshop I'd taught extremely helpful and liberating for her. Another young man at the same session who went on to publish three novels that I personally respect greatly explained to me that, for him, the same workshop was one of the most destructive and painful experiences of his life and that, if anything, it accounted for his delay in writing his books. And the three others who went on to write and publish their novels claimed that they found the same workshop moderately helpful but helpful in the way that—they suggested—all their life experiences more or less contributed to their writing.

While it is the statistics—the five out of twenty who went on to become professional (and in one case, award-winning) writers—that justify to the administration, however long after the fact, the workshop's existence, it is the same writers' individual responses that make me question the efficacy and, indeed, the ontological status of what, after all, it is that's supposed to be taught.

The assumption has always been that creativity, like good taste, can be acquired by guided exposure. But, as with language learning, the exposure is far more important than the guidance. Doubtless this is why, for myself, I've always felt that I do far more to foster creativity (of the creative writing variety) in the courses I've taught in the *reading* of novels, poems, and short stories, than I have when I was actually assigned to "teach creative writing." Certainly there is the habit of writing; and it *is* a habit. But what I have been saying up until now is simply another way of saying that, for all the ignorance on which it is founded, for all its minuscule energy and paltry glow, what creativity I have seems to me to be far more contoured, fueled, and even constituted by reading in a political and material world than it does by the actual practice—whether one reads practice in the sense of tradition or repetition—of writing, as hard and as energy- and time-consuming as it is.

Perhaps the conscious mind and the unconscious mind are another pair to which our exemplary Benjaminian relationship obtains. It certainly would explain why so many of us feel so right before Lacan's assertion that the unconscious is structured (as are good taste, power, exchange value, science, and art) as a language.

But here we are at the verge of our titular topics: creativity and *academic* writing.

The theoretical problem of creativity *in* academic writing—if there is one—is finally a rhetorical one. As in the other paraliterary writing practices (comics, science fiction, pornography, mysteries . . .), in academic writing some people are far more comfortable with what they assume to be a purified rhetoric: "Let's speak here only of writing skills and scholarly crafts," they often say. "In terms of academic writing, art and creativity make me uncomfortable, thanks to a host of problems that run the gamut from institutional to ideological."

But that particular rhetorical element of the problem is solved through reminding ourselves that, as I said before, the terms *are* never pure. The aura of creativity and art inheres in the very notion of skill and craft whether we want it to or not. The difference is one of connotative emphasis, not denotative ontology. Semantic purity is not ours for the having.

But I don't think it should come as any surprise that for me the most comfortable way to promote creativity—or skill, if you are more comfortable with the false purity of the term—in academic writing is the same way I feel most comfortable promoting it among creative writing students: guided exposure.

In the field of academic writing, I want to see creative writing (for example) students reading John Livingston Lowe, Erich Auerbach, and Ian Watt; I want to see them reading Barbara Johnson, Stephen Greenblatt, Chris Baldick, Francis Barker, and William Gass; they should read

Shoshana Felman on James and Freud; they should read Jane Gallop on Sade and Lacan. They should read Arnold Rampersad on Hughes and Hayden. They should read E. J. Dijkterhuis on the history of science and Owen Barfield on Coleridge and Peter Hulme on the Caribbean. They should read Pater and Popper and Ryle on Plato and Arthur O. Lovejoy on the Great Chain of Being. They should read Marc Shell on money and art. They should read J. Dover-Wilson and Bernard Grebanier and A. C. Bradley and G. Wilson Knight and Leonard Knights and Stephen Orgel on Shakespeare. They should read Pears on Wittgenstein and Goldmann on the intellectual ferment in the seventeenth century at Port Royal and Philippe Ariès on childhood and Fernand Braudel on history. They should read W. E. B. DuBois on black reconstruction in America and David Levering Lewis on DuBois. (And certainly I have my writerly allegiances to Foucault, Derrida, and Barthes.) They should read Charles Rosen on Schoenberg and classical style and Moldenhauer on Webern and Paul Robinson on opera. They should read Kenner on Pound and Ellingham and Killian on Jack Spicer and Edna Kramer on the nature and growth of modern mathematics and Mary-Claire van Leunen on how to write scholarly writing. But good criticism (however you define it; and, as an insistently paraliterary field, academic criticism remains an idiosyncratic rhizome of multicanonical discourses)—good criticism as it is *read*—will do a great deal more to further creativity in academic writing than all the exhortations to "be creative" any department or university or workshop can proffer.

Limit cases are always problematic, but I will wind up with another anecdote. When I was first a visiting professor in the English department of the State University of New York at Buffalo (1975), I found myself with three graduate students to advise who were in the process of preparing thesis proposals. Faced with the mélange of early outlines and their sprawling non-limited topics leaping about between genres and centuries, I asked if any of them had ever *read* a Ph.D. thesis in English. Blank stares. The notion that, in order to write one (not to mention write a good one—or, heaven help us, write a creative one), they might actually *read* one (or possibly even read five or six, if not a few dozen) had never entered their very creative minds.

But I can assure you that these same bright and enthusiastic young people, if I had described to them someone who tried to write a sonnet, who had never read one but had only the rhyme scheme to go on, would have chuckled as much as you just did.

For both creative writing and academic writing, I believe that if the reading takes place, the writing—given any chance at all—will take care of itself. (I also believe that the most meaningful change, where individuals can triumph over both entropy and evolution as it were, comes when people use empirical knowledge *against* good taste, use strength *against* power, skill *against* art, and technology *against* science in their easiest and unthinking modes. Invariably this means allying them *to* those same fields in their broader, theoretical modes, in terms of intelligence, tradition, and those questions of taste that are not immediately exhausted by simpleminded notions of good and bad—within the largely unknown fields the second terms constitute.) But this means reading widely in the best (and, alas, in the worst) that is currently being written. It means reading widely in the tradition. The workshops and the courses in academic writing—or even God help us—in "How to Be More Creative in Our Academic Writing" are exhortatory, supplementary, even, on occasion, a wonderful help. Like all supplements, inherent within them is the possibility for any number of power reversals. Do not slight them. But without the reading, there is no possibility of writing worth the name, skillful, creative, or otherwise.

—*Amherst*
May 1989

Part One

Some Queer Thoughts

1

The Rhetoric of Sex / The Discourse of Desire

1. Apples and Pears. In the two dozen years between 1488 and 1512, Leonardo da Vinci produced a series of fascinating anatomical drawings that strike the modern viewer as highly realistic and rich with the texture and look of the bodies whose dissections he observed or, no doubt, took part in, as he drew from life—or more accurately, from death—his schemas of the blood vessels, the workings of the heart, the bladder and urinary system, the womb and the fetus inside it.[1] These drawings are clearly and carefully observed, detailed, and rich in layerings and representations of tissue texture—and practically useless to a modern anatomist.

For as we look closer, we find there are no atriums or auricles in his depiction of the human heart; rather, he shows a two-chambered affair with only ventricles; and while here and there we can recognize the aorta and the esophagus, as well as the larger organs, the circulatory system and the alimentary system are depicted in gross form; there are no articulations shown between the stomach and the intestines (mostly absent from his drawings, though not his writings). And in an early anatomic depiction of heterosexual copulation, a "wholly fictitious piece of plumbing" (to use the commentator's term from the 1989 catalogue of the Haywood Gallery da Vinci exhibition in London)[2] runs from the man's penis, bypassing the testicles, to the small of the back, where many during the Italian Renaissance believed "the seed of life" was manufactured. Indeed, hardly any vessel shown in any of Leonardo's anatomic interiors connects up to what, today, we are fairly certain that it does.

And what are we to make of Leonardo's depiction of the womb? For the modern anatomist, the uterus is traditionally described as pear-shaped, small end down, and connected by means of the cervix to the vaginal cavity. The pear-shaped bulge at the upper end is largely a product of the entrance into the uterus of the fallopian tubes, which, left and right, lead back from the outer ends of the ovaries to conduct the egg to the wall of the uterine cavity.

Leonardo's womb, however, whether it is engorged with a "four month old fetus" as in the pen and ink drawing with wash over traces of black and red chalk from 1510-12, "The Fetus in the Womb," or whether it is without child, as it is in the 1507 drawing of pen and ink and wash on washed paper, "The Principal Organs and Vascular and Urino-Genital System of a Woman," is as round as an apple. In "The Fetus in the Womb," while an ovary is indeed shown, only the vascular connection about the base is drawn; there is no connection at all from the business end of the ovaries to the womb proper. The fallopian tubes and all the muscular protuberances of the upper end are omitted as tissuey irrelevancies to the womb's presumed perfect, Renaissance sphericality. Nor is this surprising.

The assumption of the times was that the material relation obtaining between a man and his offspring was that between seed and plant. The relation between a woman and *her* offspring, however, was that of contiguity, sympathy, resemblance through imposed distortion—of *environment* to plant. Certainly, people had noticed that a child was as likely to resemble its mother or people in its mother's family as it was to resemble its father or people in its father's family. But the assumption was that paternal resemblances and maternal resemblances were of two different orders. You resembled your father because you were grown from his seed. You resembled your mother, however, because you spent so much time in her womb that you picked up her traits—because her food had been your food, her pains your pains, her sorrows your sorrows, her soul your soul.

In one of the notes on the drawing "The Fetus in the Womb," in da Vinci's famous mirror writing, we find Leonardo's clear expression of the maternal sympathy between the body of the mother and the body of the child:

> In the case of the child the heart does not beat and . . . breathing is not necessary to it because it receives life and is nourished from the life and food of the mother. And this food nourishes such creatures in just the same way as it does the other parts of the mother, namely the hands feet and other members. And a single soul governs these two bodies, and the desires and fears and pains are common to this creature as to all the other animated members. And from this it proceeds that a thing desired by the mother is often found engraved upon those parts of the child which the mother keeps in herself at the time of such desire and sudden fear kills both mother and child.
>
> We conclude therefore that a single soul governs the two bodies and nourishes the two. (McCurdy 173)

On the same drawing, fascinatingly enough, there is talk of a *female seed*:

> The black races of Ethiopia are not the product of the sun; for if black gets black with child in Scythia, the offspring is black; but if a black gets a white woman with child the offspring is gray. And this shows that the seed of the mother has power in the embryo equally with that of the father. (McCurdy 173)

But from what one knows of the range of Renaissance writings, the maternal seed, for all its presumed equality with the male, was a highly metaphorical one—just as the male "seed" was to become mere metaphor upon discovery of sperm and egg reproduction. But in the common course of things, it was generally not given much credence as long as one was within the country, the family, the race.

Leonardo died in France during the late spring of 1519.

Four years later in 1523 at the tiny town of Modena, Italy, Gabriello Fallopio was born. Soon Fallopio became canon of the Modena cathedral. He studied medicine at Ferrara, then embarked on a world tour, during which he spent a while working with the great Belgian anatomist, Andreis Vesalius. He returned to Ferrara, where he now taught anatomy, having long since switched his name to the Latin form that befit a Renaissance scholar and under which he is more widely known today: Fallopius. Thence he removed to Pisa, and from Pisa, on the installation of the new grand duke of Tuscany, Cosimo I, to Padua, where, besides the chairs of anatomy, surgery, and botany, he was also created superintendent of the new botanical garden. It was Fallopius who discovered the opening of the ovarian tubes of the human female into the abdominal cavity. As well, he named both the vagina (after the Latin for scabbard) and the placenta (after the Greek for pancake). He died in Padua in 1562, a year after publishing (in Venice) his single treatise. The fallopian tubes (which retained a capital *F* desultorily into the 1830s but lost it by the 1870s) have borne his name ever since.

With Fallopius's anatomy, the spherical womb of Leonardo gave way to the pear-shaped womb we are familiar with from the modern anatomical vision. But what I have tried to dramatize in this little narrative is the force shaping the very sight itself of a visionary as great and as revered as any in our culture, Leonardo da Vinci. It is the till-now-in-our-tale unnamed structuring and structurating force that can go by no better name than "discourse." For what has metamorphosed between Leonardo and Fallopius is the discourse of the body itself—medical discourse, anatomical discourse—and that force seems strong enough to contour what is apparent to the eye of some of the greatest direct observers of our world. We find it at work in Leonardo's anatomy, as we find it at work in Gray's.

2. Interlogue One. I pause here to say that, thanks to my title, I feel somewhat like the man who shouts, "Sex," then continues on to say, "Now that I have your attention . . ."

For we have come to the real, i.e., the political, topics of my essay, which are rhetoric and discourse. Sex and desire—while they may now and again provide some of the more dramatic narratives through which we shall endeavor to show how discourse can manifest and problematize itself through rhetoric—will in my essay remain largely occasions for the exploration of rhetoric and discourse themselves.

And though we will return to sex and desire again and again, and even try to plumb them for the secrets of the misfiring of so many relations called "sexual" between men and women, men and men, women and women, we shall stray from them again and again—to areas as diverse as children's picture books and children's games around a fountain in Central Park, to tales told over a calabash of beer in the rainy season of the West African Tiv, to very similar-sounding criticisms of writers as different as Ursula Le Guin and Toni Morrison, to dimly perceived objects in a house in Amherst at the edge of dawn, to the lack of operationalism in AIDS research.

But now we ask: What is this "discourse" that has for so long protruded its rhetorical stumbling block into the jargon-heavy realms of literary theory, either since the Middle Ages or World War II, depending on whose account you read?

Well, here's a tale of a tale.

3. Pictures and Books. I have an eighteen-year-old daughter. And fifteen years ago, when she was three and just beginning to read (and, even more, enjoying being read to), like so many parents of those years I noticed that there were precious few children's picture books with female protagonists. Somehow, with the exception of Frances the Hedgehog, the illustrated bestiary in these books was overwhelmingly male. This struck me as ridiculous as well as unfair—and even, perhaps, dangerous.

Who knew what happened to children whose only identificatory objects resided outside their race, their class, their sex, their gender—not to say their kind?

Indeed, having proved itself powerful enough to stabilize the process by which the nation's schools had been desegregated, an entire discourse from the fifties was already in place with its unpleasant suggestions precisely about the answers to that seemingly rhetorical question.

What was a parent to do with such books when little girl animals were simply not extant?

One book that fell into my hands, back then, was a charming and well-drawn affair, about a little bear called Corduroy.[3] What's more, Corduroy wore a pair of denim Oshkosh overalls—as did my three-year-old on most of her days at playschool. Certainly, *there* was a point of correspondence. Why couldn't I simply up and change Corduroy's sex in the telling? With white-out and felt-tip pen, I went so far as to remove the *he*'s and change the pronouns to *she*'s—in case Iva's reading had actually progressed further than I suspected.

Then I sat down, with my daughter.

I began the story—and at the first pronoun, Iva twisted around in my lap to declare: "But Daddy, it's a *boy* bear!"

"I don't think so," I said. "The book says 'she' right there."

"But it's *not!*" she insisted.

I was sure of my argument. "How do you know it's a boy bear?"

"Because he's got pants on!"

Surely she had fallen into my trap. "But *you're* wearing pants," I explained. "In fact, you're wearing the *same* kind of Oshkosh overalls that Corduroy is wearing. And you're a little girl, aren't you?"

"But Daddy," declared my three-year-old in a voice of utmost disdain at my failure to recognize the self-evident, "that's a *book!*"

During the same three or four months' reading in which I was learning of the rhetorical failure of the discourse of children's picture books to provide an egalitarian array of multigendered protagonists, my daughter, of course, had been learning that discourse itself.

And the fact was, she was right—I was wrong. Corduroy *was* a boy. No matter how unfair or how pernicious it was or might prove, the discourse of children's books *made* him a boy. And that discourse was so sedimented that a single instance of rhetorical variation, in 1977, registered not as a new and welcomed variant but, rather, as a mistake self-evident to a three-year-old.

"Well," I said, "let's *make* Corduroy a 'she.' We'll pretend she's a girl, just like you."

Iva had also learned the discourse of "let's pretend"—surely from the same books that had taught her pants (in books) meant male. She settled back in my lap and seemed satisfied enough with the revised story.

Today, in the shadow of its shelf, *Corduroy* has dust on its upper edge. But days ago I phoned Iva in the city where she was getting ready to go off to college next year, and—in preparation for this essay—I asked her whether she had any memory of the incident.

No, she didn't. "But once I was looking through some of my old picture books, and I remember finding *Corduroy* and realizing someone had taken a pen and changed all the *he*'s to *she*'s. I remember wondering why they'd done it."

4. Interlogue Two. Perhaps here is the place to state some principles, then, of discourse. Discourses are plural and are learned, with language, where they function as a particular economic level in the linguistic array. They are not a set of criteria that are to be met or missed by a text. Rather, they lodge inchoately in the processes by which we make a text make sense—by which we register a text well-formed or ill-formed. They are revisable, often from within themselves. The maintenance of a discourse, like the revision of a discourse, always involves some violent rhetorical shift—though the final effects of that violence may well be in some wholly unexpected area of understanding that the discourse affects. And most discourses worth the name have complex methods—starting with simple forgetfulness—for regularly healing themselves across such rhetorical violences. And this is also the place to recall a comment by my fellow science-fiction writer, Ursula Le Guin: Only adults confuse fantasy and reality; children never do.

From this anecdote of a parent, a child, and a picture book, it is not too great a leap to the suggestion that wherever the world appears (in Plato's phrase) "illuminated by the sun of the intelligible," the light that does the illuminating is discourse.

But what our earlier tale of Fallopius and Leonardo reminds us is just how powerful a light that is. For it may make a pear look like an apple—or, indeed, an apple look like a pear.

5. Text and Text. Here are two texts that I think might have been much clarified by the notion of discourse:

For here is a young woman, who signs herself J. R. Dunn,[4] writing a critique of a recent article by Ursula Le Guin in a letter to *Monad*, an informal critical journal devoted to science fiction:

> In her opening pages, Le Guin stated that: ". . . in the European tradition the hero who does great deeds is a white man . . . human women were essentially secondary, taking part in the story only as mothers and wives of men, beloved by or the seducers of men, victims of or rescued by men. Women did not initiate action, except passively . . . the great deeds were men's deeds."
>
> I don't think I'm mistaken in taking this as the essay's key premise. That being so, it's unnecessary to go on any further: My argument with Le Guin lies right there.
>
> That passage represents the standard feminist historical model in action:

that before the modern era women were victims at best, a mute inglorious mass marked by biology, allowed no contribution to any branch of human endeavor, the history of the female sex is a vast boneyard of oppression, suffering and degradation. This interpretation has been institutionalized for two decades and it's late in the day to pick a fight over it. But I believe that it is in error, and those adhering to it are seriously contradicted by the record.

Dunn then goes on to give a catalogue of great women of accomplishment in the West, from warrior queens such as Telesilla of Argos, Zenobia of Palmyra, and Boadicea of Great Britain, on to women cultural figures, such as Sappho, Anna Comnena, Juliana of Norwich, Christine de Pisan, Vittoria Colonna, and Anne Bradstreet, punctuated with a list of the great tragic heroines from Greek drama.

And toward her conclusion (I abridge), Dunn writes:

> I'm not suggesting that Le Guin doesn't know any of this. I'm sure she does. It just doesn't connect. I won't speculate on why except to note that ideology tends to restrict critical thinking. This happens to the best of us. It's happened to me. . . .
>
> I accept the proposition that feminism is divided into egalitarian and various radical branches. I strongly support the egalitarian position on grounds of logic and common sense. The other variants, "gender" or "radical" feminism, what have you, I can only reject, seeing the nature of the "facts" they're based on. I object to any contention that the two streams are in any way one and the same.
>
> I'll go on to say I can picture few greater social tragedies than egalitarian feminism collapsing in the wreckage of the weirder varieties.

I hope it will not simply be a jejune exercise to point out that, in her pursuit of logic and common sense, Dunn has misread Le Guin and accomplished a truly astonishing rewrite of history—a misreading and a rewriting that can be pried apart by the careful insertion of a notion of discourse that will, perhaps, yield us its analytical fruit.

But before I do so, I want to offer another text, this time on racial matters, that seems ripe for the same sort of misreading that Le Guin's text has fallen victim to in Dunn.

From Toni Morrison's recent book-length essay, *Playing in the Dark: Whiteness and the Literary Imagination*:

> For some time now I have been thinking about . . . a certain set of assumptions conventionally accepted among literary historians and critics and circulated as "knowledge." This knowledge holds that traditional, canonical American

literature is free of, uninformed, and unshaped by the four-hundred-year-old presence of, first, Africans and then African-Americans in the United States. It assumes that this presence—which shaped the body politic, the Constitution, and the entire history of the culture—has had no significant place or consequence in the origin and development of that culture's literature. . . . There seems to be a more or less tacit agreement among literary scholars that, because American literature has been clearly the white male views, genius, and power, those views, genius, and power are without relationship to and removed from the overwhelming presence of black people in the United States.[5]

It is all too easy to see, at some not-so-distant point, such a paragraph from Morrison taking its place within a critique of some fancied radical liberation movement much like Dunn's critique of "radical" feminism; and some young reader, straight from a perusal of the paperback shelves of his or her local college bookstore, bringing out the currently available paperback editions of Phillis Wheatley's *Poems* and the slave narratives from Olaudah Equiano and Frederick Douglass and Harriet E. Wilson's *Our Nig* and Martin Delany's *Blake* and the stories of Charles W. Chesnutt and novels of Iola Harper and Zora Neale Hurston and Richard Wright and Chester Himes and William Demby, and citing the National Book Award to Ralph Ellison and McPherson's and Johnson's and even Morrison's own Pulitzer Prize, in order to declare: "How can you say that there's a conspiracy to keep centuries of black American writers from being considered a literary presence . . . ?"

The sanest place to begin to answer either Dunn's criticism of Le Guin or my hypothetical critic of Morrison is with the historical truism: Things as they are today are not necessarily the same as they were even ten or fifteen years ago, much less twenty-five or thirty, much less fifty or seventy-five years gone. We can only hope *that* point will hold the arguments stable long enough to look in more detail at both Le Guin's and Morrison's initial statements. For they share a number of rhetorical features.

On the one hand, "white males" are the putative villains of both passages. (Are they heterosexual? But of course. We do not even have to ask—for there is a discourse already in place that makes that at least as inarguable as the sex of Corduroy in 1977.) On the other hand, the words "tradition" and "traditional" in both take a deceptively *en passant* role among the opening sentences of each. And it is within the notion of tradition that what we call discourse—traditionally—hides. Articulating it might have avoided some of these subsequent problems. Had Le Guin or Morrison been able to foreground it clearly, instead of leaving it implicit under the "traditions" both are citing and for which the "heterosexual white male" more than anything else stands as a marker, a name, an indicator of a dominant current in the ideology of the present century, their passages might be less subject to such accusations and misrepresentations.

I'd like to think that if, instead of, "In the European tradition, the hero who does great deeds is a white man" Le Guin had written, "In traditional European discourse, the hero who does great deeds is a white man," Dunn's subsequent confusions might have been less inevitable.

Or if Morrison had written, "This knowledge holds that in the traditional discourse of canonical, American literature, that literature is free of, uninformed, and unshaped by the four-hundred-year-old presence of, first, Africans and then African-Americans in the United States," then perhaps my hypothetical critic might have been less confused.

Of course, discourse is a strong and meaningful concept for me. It represents an economic order of language that is apart from tradition itself as it is apart from doctrine and ideology, though it leans on aspects of all of them, as all of them lean on aspects of discourse. But I am aware that possibly what characterizes Dunn or my other hypothetical spoil-sport critic, is that the concept of discourse may be what they themselves lack.

For what discourse does above all things is to assign import. Discourse, remember, is what allows us to make sense of what we see, and hear, and experience. Yes, the Zenobias and the Christine de Pisans, the Wilsons and Chesnutts and Hurstons were there. But discourse is what tells us what is central and what is peripheral—what is a mistake, an anomaly, an accident, a joke. It tells us what to pay attention to and what to ignore. It tells us what sort of attention to pay. It tells us what is anomalous and therefore nonserious. And till very recently "anomalous and nonserious" is how the accomplishments of women, whether in the arts or in the world, were judged. And the writings of blacks in this country were, until very recently, considered even more of an accident.

The rewriting of history I've spoken of is simply that it would be hard to make a list of the works that have done more to change the discourse of gender so that, today, Dunn or I can walk into our local bookstores and buy a copy of Christine de Pisan's *City of Ladies*, that did not include Le Guin's works, such as *The Left Hand of Darkness* (1969) and *The Dispossessed* (1974). It would be hard to make a list of those works that had helped change the discourse of race so that we can now walk into the same bookstore and buy any of the paperback volumes in the Schomberg Library of nineteenth-century black women writers, that did not include Morrison's own novels *Sula* (1973) and *Song of Solomon* (1977).

What it is necessary to remember, in order to make discourse a strong concept, is that it is the materialist side of reason and ratiocination, of understanding and history. It is all very well to explain that electric lights were simply not very common seventy or eighty years ago. Or that, even in my own early childhood in the 1940s, our perfectly comfortable country house, which we drove to every summer, was lit by kerosene lanterns. Or that, at the same time, the country house of my uncle, a fine and upstanding judge in the Brooklyn Domestic Relations Court, had no indoor toilet facilities but only an outhouse in the back.

It is another thing, however, to explain to people today, whether they remember kerosene lamps or not, that, in a pre-electric light era, the creation of illumination always meant an expenditure of time and physical energy at least as great as that of lighting a match (which is already several times more than turning on a light switch)—and the vast majority of times meant an expenditure of physical energy far greater than that, an expenditure, which, to be efficient, was embedded in a social schema that involved getting candles, fuels, regularly trimming wicks and cleaning the glass chimneys, chopping wood and stoking fires, so that even the casual creation of light in such an age was an entirely different social operation from what it is today. One might even say that, in such an age, light could not *be* casually created. Light was at the nexus of a great deal more physical energy and daily planning. Thus, because of our vastly different relation to it, light itself was a different social object from what it is today. And thus, every mention of light, in any text from that period, whether it be in the deadest of hackneyed metaphors or in the most vibrant and vivid poetry, is referring to a different order of object.

What we have begun to explore here, of course, is the discourse of light. It is the discourse that, explored in enough detail, can revivify the evil, distant, flickering lights that haunt American writers from Nathaniel Hawthorne to Ambrose Bierce, even as they turn into clichés in the later writings of Lovecraft; we must remember that initially such lights usually meant fires in the distance—forest fires or homes caught from some light source (got out of control), which, at the time, was always a flame source too.

In the discourse of sexual roles, certainly the greatest material disturber of traditional roles was the spread, after World War II, in the late forties and early fifties (even more so than the Pill), of the home washer-dryer combination. Until that time, in any family of more than two people, the washing, hanging out by hand, and ironing of clothes took up a minimum of two full days a week; and that was what made it a foregone conclusion, as self-evident to women at the time as it was to men, that in order to have any sort of family, someone would have to have at least two days a week in a small family (of four, say), and three or more in a large one, to devote to this task.

The reduction of the week's laundry from two or three days to two or three hours was as traumatic to the discourse of sexual roles as the introduction of electricity and the light switch was to the discourse of light.

We can say, of course, that things have changed—and have specifically changed in terms of race and sex. But I hope we have some way now of perceiving the extremely strong statement we are making when we say, for example, that the discourse of sex and the discourse of race have changed far more—catastrophically more—since 1956 (to pick as an arbitrary date the year when the nation's schools were, by law, desegregated) than has the discourse of light since World War II.

6. Interlogue Three. Etymologically, the term "discourse" is a Latin word that refers to an old, oval, Roman race track.

At a modern race track, spectators sit in seats on the outside of the track and look in on the runners. At a discourse, however, the spectators entered the central section of the track before the race, took their seats—or more often simply walked about from one side to the other—while the racers coursed around and around them.

With such an object at its origins, it is hard to avoid metaphorizing. One entered the discourse and left it only at specified positions. The discourse encircled one; it surrounded the spectator, moving around and around him or her.

It is also hard not to speculate on the nature of its initial shift into metaphor. Though it's anyone's guess as to how the discourse became a metaphor for reason, understanding, and ratiocination, since discourses were places of much betting, it's probable that the kind of head scratching, the touting up of odds, and the endless speculative conversation on the merits of the racers characteristic today of horse-racing tracks were a part of daily life at the discourse and thus prompted the metaphoric shift.

But even that's speculation.

No one knows for sure.

Today, however, the *OED* gives us under "discourse":

1. Onward course; process or succession of time, events, actions, etc. Obs.
2. "The act of the understanding, by which it passes from premises to consequences," (Johnson); reasoning, thought, ratiocination; the faculty of reasoning, reason, rationality.
3. Communication of thought by speech; "mutual intercourse of language," (Johnson).

And again:

1. To run, move, travel over a space, region, etc.
2. To reason. (To turn over in the mind; to think over.)
3. To hold discourse, to speak with another or others, talk, converse; to discuss a matter, confer.
4. To speak or write at length on a subject; to utter or pen a discourse. (To utter, say, speak or write formally.)

But we are basically interested here in meaning number two within the cloud of rhetorical connotations meanings three and four have set in motion—around and around it.

That arbiter of seventeenth-century prose, Sir Thomas Browne (1605–1682), wrote "Hydroitaphia or a discourse of the sepulchral urns lately found in Norfolk" (1658)—that is to say, a discourse *of*, not a discourse on. The forty-seven–page essay represents Browne's understanding, his reasoning around, his comprehension of the urns; it presents the information from life and letters the wise doctor possessed (or that possessed him) to bring to bear upon them that made the urns make sense—and, in its concluding thanatopsis, the sense that then soared from them.

But, as I hope my brief example of Dunn has already shown, without the notion of discourse—or something that stands in its stead—there can be no sophisticated idea of history.

7. Discourse and Desire. To explore a discourse is inevitably to tell a story: At such and such a time, people did this and that; thus they thought and felt one thing and another.

One of my favorite storytellers is a Frenchman named Raymond Roussel. The method he used to tell a number of extraordinarily far-ranging and imaginative stories, as he outlined it in an essay published shortly after his death in 1934, *Comment j'ai écrit certains de mes livres*,[6] involved taking two phrases, word for word identical or different only by, say, one letter of one word, in which every word had at least two distinct meanings, and thus had two distinct meanings as phrases. His most famous example is: *Les lettres de blanc sur les bandes du vieux billard* and *Les lettres du blanc sur les bandes du vieux pillard*, which mean, respectively, "The white letters inscribed on the cushions of the old billiard table," and "The white man's letters written about the troops of the old bandit." (Needless to say, the *vieux pillard*—the old bandit—in Roussel's story is black.) Roussel saw his various tales as attempts to maneuver logically from one phrase, which we would find in the first sentence of his tale, to the second, which we would find in the last. En route, again and again, Roussel constructed incidents around phrases that had a more or less self-evident meaning but that could be reread to mean something else ("What do you do with a stiff neck?" "What do *you* do with a stiff . . . neck?"); I have always taken the fact that the tales of this wealthy French homosexual eccentric—when freed from the constraints of ordinary narrative discourse by the systematicity of his eccentric method—again and again swooped into the subject of race, of blacks, of Africa *(Parmi les noirs, Impression d'Afrique)* as a cultural index of just what a pervasive discourse race was for Europe—just as you will find, if you try the exercise in English, the secondary meanings so often have a sexual side.

The discourse of race is intimately tied to the discourse of sex; the term *race,* until the late eighteenth century, meant family—specifically a large, ancient, powerful family, such as the Sforza race, the Medici race. When Leonardo wrote of the "Ethiopian races" in the notes he made on "Foetus in the Womb" sometime between 1510 and 1512, one of the reasons for the plural, *races,* is that, within the discourse of the time, what he was saying, denotatively, was "the Ethiopian families." The notion of "race" as we know it would seem to begin in an anxiety to locate a unit, still mediated by heredity, larger than the family yet somehow within its conceptual economy, but not coextensive with the nation. And there is no way to have heredity without sex.

But even while we have spoken of the rhetoric of sex, and explored some of the relations of those rhetorical figures, we have stayed, till now, purposefully away from the idea of desire.

Desire is a very scary and uneasy notion. Its mark is absence. Accordingly, a positivistic culture frequently finds itself at a loss to explore it or elaborate its workings.

The two doctrinal principles that most of us have access to come respectively from Freud and his most astute reader, Lacan:

Said Freud: Repetition is desire.

Said Lacan: What one desires is the desire of the Other.

There are, of course, other ways to tell stories besides Roussel's. Roussel expended extraordinary imaginative energy to make sentences that were phonically all but identical mean different things.

But suppose we tell two apparently different stories—and try to elaborate a discursive structure in which they can be seen as one.

Despite having a daughter, I come to you as a gay black male. But it is a reasonable assumption that some straight white males linger somewhere in my heredity. I find straight white males interesting—and sometimes, personally, sympathetic. A few years ago, I wrote a book, *The Motion of Light in Water*,[7] an autobiography that tried to delineate for me what it meant to grow up in an American city as a black, gay, male writer of paraliterary fictions. In the book I talked very openly about my own particular sexual experiences and sexual fetishes.

I assumed that the book would be most interesting to others in marginalized positions, vis-à-vis those straight white males who demonize so much of marginal discourse. The book received its share of approbation from black readers (female and male), white readers (female and male), and gay readers (female and male). Nevertheless, by far the largest number of people who have come up to talk to me about it or—on more than one occasion now, after one or another lecture such as this—have grabbed me by the shoulder, dragged me into a corner, sat me down, and begun to tell me their problems, then asked me, with great concern, what, from my marginal position, I thought they ought to do about them, are straight white males.

One would almost think they felt empowered to take anything the society produced, no matter how marginal, and utilize it for their own ends—dare we say "exploit it"?—certainly to take advantage of it as long as it's around. And could this possibly be an effect of discourse? Perhaps it might even be one we on the margins might reasonably appropriate to our profit; or perhaps some of us already have.

Most of their problems, of course, involved their relations with females—some white, some black, some gay, some straight. I have heard an extraordinary range of stories—and what these fellows are attracted to, oh my women friends, is amazing. Some want women of one race, some want them of another, some want women with glasses and some want women who are overweight, some want women with high IQs and some want women with narrow shoulders set slightly forward—indeed, the range of tales I have heard from these fellows since 1988 when my book was published is enough to make the variety of vanilla heterosexual male desire seem a seething pit of perversions quite as interesting as any to be found in any S&M bar, lesbian, gay, or straight.

But despite that range, I find myself again and again making the same rhetorical intervention. For here we are centrally sunk in the Discourse of Desire.

What again and again I find myself saying to these men is: Can you utter the simple statement to the troublesome object of your desire:

"I like you. Do you like me?"

And what is this terror of rejection that is so strong that it almost invariably drives one half, the other, or both of these enunciations out of the realm of articulation?

Doubtless you can understand why both paired clauses are essential. If you cannot say, "I like you," she will simply never know. If you cannot follow it with, "Do you like me?" *you* will never know. More to the point, if you cannot say, "I like you," she will never know you have any emotions. And if you can't say "Do you like me?" she will be sure, probably rightly, you are unable to evince any interest, care, or concern with hers. This alone is why, "I like you. Let's fuck," does not accomplish the same communicative ends.

In three out of four cases, these fellows will eventually ask: "But why doesn't *she* say it to *me?*"

To which I answer: "That is not the point. You're the one who claims to be in pain. What are *you* going to do about it—for what I tell you is as likely to get you out of it as anything else you can do. It is certainly more effective than waiting in silent agony or clowning about in over-energetic exuberance for her to see through your sedimented silences or eruptive vulgarities your central yearning self."

I say this rather gently, of course. For one thing one learns in fifty years is that, though most of us eventually learn to ask, more or less, for what we want, it is always more or less impossible to ask for what we need. (If we could ask for it, by definition we wouldn't *need* it.) That can only be given us. Finally, we are left to conspire, inarticulately and by our behavior alone, to make sure there is as much of it available in the landscape as is possible, in the hope that, eventually, we will be fortunate enough to receive some.

But I have known a number of women who, when a man became interested in her (when he manages to communicate the first part of that oh so important diptych), wait around through whatever number of dates and get-togethers they feel are reasonable, for the second part—for the other shoe, as it were, to drop. And, when it doesn't, they break off the relationship secure in the fact that they are leaving a situation where, for whatever reasons (at this point, the why is no longer her concern), their own feelings will never *really* be solicited—probably about anything.

I recall one young man, deeply in love with a woman who seemed, certainly, fond enough of him to accept dates with him and TV viewings with him. He asked my advice on several occasions. "But does she like me?" he wanted to know.

"Why don't you ask?" I suggested.

"I mean, I know she likes me. But does she *like* me?"

"Again, if you don't ask, you may never find out."

"I've told her that I liked her," he complained.

"The magic words," I said, "are: 'I like you; do you like me?' Of course," I added, "if you ask, you risk the possibility of being told, 'No.' But isn't that better than having to wait and wonder and not know for who knows how long?"

When, after much rhetoric, he allowed as how it was, I thought the problem finally reduced to that never simple matter of gritting one's teeth and indulging in that terrible bravery that has to be breached in one form or another in every situation of desire.

But a few days later, he was back.

"I can't ask her," he declared.

"You're that frightened of being told, 'No'," I asked, "that you would give up the possibility of being told 'Yes'?"

"It's not that. It's because of what it would *mean* if I asked her."

"What *would* it mean?" I asked.

"It would mean, like, well"—and here, I hope what becomes clear is the structure of the discourse in which we have been involved all along— "it would mean, somehow, that I was insulting her. That she was the kind of girl who was used to guys asking her, all the time, if she wanted to go to bed with them, if she *liked* them—it would mean like, well, I thought she was some kind of whore. And I couldn't stand that."

"You mean," I said, "that if she had any sexual feelings for you of the sort that you have been regaling me with for the past six weeks, that have been destroying your sleep and plaguing your dreams, she would be a whore."

"Well, like, no."

"What about," I said, "like, yes."

"Well, like it," he said. "But not exactly it."

"Like it, close enough," I said.

The young woman broke off the relationship after another week. And wisely, I suspect. But I hope this tale alone is enough to suggest what a violent rhetorical intervention in the discourse of patriarchy, with its saints and whores (for that of course is the discourse we speak of here), the simple bipartite statement and question, "I like you. Do you like me?" represents.

The discourse of desire, at work throughout the discourse of patriarchy, maintains such a situation, with its nebulous orders—want, need, and desire itself—notoriously impossible to pin down. For as soon as one systematically relates them (say, in the provisionally brilliant Lacanian schema: When *all* the elements of need are satisfied in the situation of *want*, the *remainder* is desire), ordinary language, with its italics and special emphases, manages to displace them soon enough so that all we are left is a memory of a momentary bit of rhetorical brilliance.

Well, that is the first story I tell.

But sometimes I tell a second story. Though I assure you, for all its radically different sound, it is as close in meaning to "I like you. Do you like me," as the opening and closing phrases of a tale by Roussel are close in sound.

That tale is the dark knowledge my own life in the margins provides. Very simply, that second story runs: "The desire to be loved is sadism. The desire to love is masochism."

To unravel the track from one to the other in the complex Discourse of Desire—to show that both inhabit a single discourse—is to evoke the Freudian notion that the realm of desire is the mirror realm of ordinary motivations. Freud told us that a perversion was the opposite of a neurosis: In the childhood machinations of psychic development, *either* we sexualize something *or* it becomes a neurotic character trait.

To take pleasure from imposing your emotions on another person is sadism—a much easier translation to follow. But then, what else is the open, pleasurable, sincere, and aboveboard statement: "I like you"? Isn't that, if it's sincerely stated, a pleasurable imposition of one's emotions on another, and thus, when it is shot through with desire, a terrifyingly difficult enunciation?

To take pleasure from the emotions of others over and above your own is masochism—an equally easy translation. What else then is the open, pleasurable, sincere, and aboveboard request: "Do you like me?" Again, when such a question is shot through with desire, isn't its asking equally terrifying?

For you must have noticed—by now, certainly—that while some people are *afraid* of saying one, they are *terrified* of speaking the other—terrified to the point of sweating, heart-pounding, dry-tongued paralysis.

And the difference between ordinary fear and terror is the difference between the social fear of sexual rejection and the totality of the universe-obliterating failure of both the self and the other that homes among desire's ancient and hideously deep foundations.

Certainly we would stop our interrogations and discursive translations with the glib observation that every relation to start pleasurably, then, requires a little healthy sadism, a little healthy masochism—on everyone's part. But it is that notion of pleasure, and its dark relation to desire, that completes the identification of the tales. For, again, we all know—and know that the assignment has no necessary relation to who has what genital configuration—that there are simply too many people who, though they can manage to handle either one of those paired clauses, are absolutely broken before the other.

There are too many people who can tell you what they want but who are constitutionally incapable of responding to what someone else might want. There are too many people who are endlessly concerned with what others want but seem to have the same constitutional inability to articulate their own wishes.

Again, the mark of desire is lack—and (and *pace* Freud) repetition. So that once again, if you want to be loved to the intensity of desire—

so that you seek that situation out again and again, so that the love of someone else inflames you, so that even another's miming of the emblems of such a situation is enough to excite, so that the form of another's love is a lack in you that, no matter how many times it is fulfilled by whatever act of love, it can never be finally and wholly sated, because it is the form of your desire itself, then your behavior in the world to acquire what you seek must fall, one way or the other—to the extent that it is in excess of any real possibility—into the forms of sadism.

And if what you want is to love another, again to the point of desire— so that you seek out opportunities to do so again and again, so that the possibility of another to love is what inflames you, so that another's miming that she or he approves, deserves, demands that love is enough to excite, that the form of love expressed in you is a lack, that, no matter how many times it is repeated by your behavior, can never be finally and wholly exhausted, because it is the form of your desire itself, then your behavior in the world to acquire what you seek must fall, one way or the other—to the extent that it is in excess of any real possibility—into the forms of masochism.

"I like you; do you like me?"

But the darker and more dangerous tale revealed beneath it is a clash of sadistic and masochistic imperatives: "The *desire* to be loved is sadism; the *desire* to love is masochism."

For what are both these tales finally about?

Power. Power is what distinguishes the psychic discourse of desire from the social rhetoric of sex. The rhetoric of sex commands enough strength to make a man or a woman walk the streets of the city for hours, to drive alone or in groups, searching for a proper gap in the communicative wall through which desire may somehow show. But desire, to the extent that it is a material and social discourse, commands power enough to found and destroy cities, to reform the very shape of the city itself, laying down new avenues and restructuring whole neighborhoods within it. And desire—paradoxically—is what holds erect that barrier to sex that so much of our rhetoric, as well as our actions of which finally rhetoric is a part, breaks against and crumbles.

The power involved in desire is so great that when caught in an actual rhetorical manifestation of desire—a particular sexual act, say—it is sometimes all but impossible to untangle the complex webs of power that shoot through it from various directions, the power relations that are the act and that constitute it:

You're having sex with someone. Very well.

Whose scenario is it?

Who is exerting the most physical energy to bring it off?

What is the social value assigned to each player in the particular act? What sorts of energy, action, and articulation are needed to transform or reverse any one of these?

During such power analyses we find just how much the matrix of desire (the Discourse of Desire and the matrix of power it manifests here and masks there) favors the heterosexual male, even if there is no such actor involved. Whoever is doing what the heterosexual male *would* be doing usually comes out on top. Though his 1915 footnote makes perfectly clear that, by the use of the word "masculine" he simply meant "active," this may nevertheless have been part of the thrust of Freud's statement: "that libido is invariably and necessarily of a masculine nature, whether it occurs in men or in women and irrespective of whether its object is a man or a woman."[8] It is a statement that, if taken in the biological sense (which the same footnote excludes from the reading), is precisely as ridiculous as "the urge to sneeze is invariably and necessarily of a masculine nature, whether it occurs in men or women."

What we on the margins have been most able to appropriate of this discourse is the power analysis that so much of the discourse of patriarchy is structured precisely to mystify.

In many cases, its demystification is precisely what has allowed us to survive.

8. Discourse contra Discourse. Rich with its materiality and explicative force, the idea of discourse that I have been putting forward is an exciting one and a seductive one to those first coming to history.

In 1840 the postage stamp was introduced in England. Before that date, when a letter was sent, the *recipient* paid the postman on delivery. After that date, the *sender* paid—and suddenly letter writing became a species of vanity publishing.[9] To know this is to be able to make sense of a range of sentences found in dozens of early nineteenth-century novels that often appear as some form of "From then on, she would longer receive his letters." Specifically what that means is: she refused to *pay* the postman for the letters—and they were returned to the sender. At once, we have an explanation for questions ranging from why so many letters from before that date were preserved (what you paid for you kept), to why there was no junk mail before then (who *would* pay for it?), to why the correspondents themselves were often so witty (if you knew you had to make your letters worth the three or four pennies your recipient had to shell out—eighty or ninety cents at today's prices—you were likely both to write at length and to try to have something to say). We begin to see such letters fitting into the social matrix very differently from the way our mail does, and we begin to develop a postal discourse.

In 1851, the lead paint tube was introduced, which meant that suddenly artists could keep with them amounts of paint much smaller than in the pig-bladders full of hand-ground pigments, traditional since *before* Leonardo. With the invention of the metal ferrule in the same few years, which held the bristles to the brush and flattened them, it became far easier for artists to travel from their studios and paint nature; the average size of the canvases suddenly shrank; the possibility of an amateur painter became real. Hordes of painters now descended across the landscape—and Impressionism was the result, as dependent on that bit of soft lead foil as on any aesthetic considerations. The relation of the artist to society, through all the economic changes from that technological development, which, through that change, changed the relation of society to art, resulted in a major reformation of the discourse of art.

In the early 1870s at Bayreuth, Richard Wagner, at the opening of that concert hall, so as not to break the atmosphere created by the music, for the first time in Western concerts initiated the convention that audiences not applaud between movements of symphonies or string quartets; now, as the Bayreuth Festspielhaus moved on to the production of operas, he put up signs in the lobby that no talking was to occur during the performance; and, to help the audience concentrate on the music and stage action, he turned the house lights off during the performance of an opera, so that the audience watched the performance enveloped in the dark, with light only on the stage.[10] Elizabethan theaters had performed under sunlight at the open-roofed Globe and Blackfriars; Jacobean theater, as well as the theater of Racine and Molière, the later theater of Mozart and Beaumarchais, were all theaters of light. But when, under Wagner's direction, the house lights were lowered—and the tradition spread from Bayreuth through all the opera houses and finally all the theaters of the West—a different relation was marked between art and audience, a change in the relationship, which had been growing throughout the rise of Romanticism, a change that we can read in metamorphoses of theatrical discourse.

The initial excitement from the discovery of material changes controlling discourse (these changes are often so total we do not realize they render one side or the other of a cultural discontinuity set in place by money and technology: the new and modern gas lamps, say, by which Wagner's Festspielhaus was lighted and darkened, as well as the great steam curtain that produced the billows of effective stage fog, which, as George Bernard Shaw noted in his recollections of the Ring performances of the late 1890s, "made the theater smell like a laundry") at first produces a kind of vertigo in the young intellectual newly alert to the complexities of history.[11]

It is perhaps, then, time to cite the example of the intellectual figure most responsible for the current spread of the notion of discourse as a historical modeling tool, Michel Foucault. When we have been considering the problems raised by our own studies of discourse, nothing is more exciting than the essay he published at the end of his methodological study of the problems of discursive study (*The Archaeology of Knowledge,* where he tears down his own former notion of *"épistèmès"* and replaces it with a theory of discourses, utterances, genealogies, and apparatuses), *"L'Ordre du discours"* ("The Form of Discourse"), rather flightily translated as "The Discourse on Language."[12] In the course of this essay, while he exhorts us to look for chance, discontinuity, and materiality, Foucault warns us away from the idea of founding subjects, originating experiences, universal mediation, and the tyranny of the signifier.

I think Foucault would be the first to remind us that, in the midst of that most anxious paragraph on our Leonardo drawing, concerning the paradox of Africa as Italy had to see it, there is that anomalous "female seed." Look at it, research it, seek it out in a range of synchronous and diachronous texts, before deciding precisely *what* kind of anomaly it is.

And the current discourse of patriarchy and the Discourse of Desire that suffuses it, and—now and again, here and there at its several points—seeks to subvert it, is just as materially grounded as any of the historical ones I have cited. Similarly, and perhaps more importantly, none of the historical ones, when studied in their specificity, their discontinuity, their exteriority, are any less complex than we know from our first-hand experience the discourse of desire and patriarchy to be.

9. Interlogue Four. From the array of voices with which discourse addresses us, one insists:

"Return a moment to the homilies with which, at the end of section seven, you effected your utopian turn, and allow me to ask: Why is it necessary for sadism to be about all these *emotions*? Why can't it simply be about pain? Does it take an active anticipation of your argument on my part to provoke you to the cool reason that your text keeps putting forward as your stance? Soon you will be explaining that the analogical relation between the sexual and the social that is mistaken for causal is, most generously, the structure of superstition and most oppressively the structure of oppression itself. Why, then, must you make this spurious analogy between the psychological and the sexual? You yourself have argued that *The Authoritarian Personality* by Adorno and the Frankfurt Group first validated the notion of the causal relation between the behavior of the Nazi bureaucracy of the thirties and forties and sexual sadism, and thus functions on exactly the same level as the discursive origin of an oppressive structure as political as the medical institution of homosexuality that allows heterosexuality itself to come into existence. Would you actually argue that I am, whether with my breasts thrust into black leather or basket heavy in a studded jock, the One Always There, who, when everyone else is redeemed, can be thrown to the dogs, at the eye of the patriarchal cyclone you've already located as the straight white (need I add?) vanilla male? As you make your accusations of appropriation, surely you've noticed the totality of the structure you excoriate: with Jung, he steals, in the form of the anima, whatever from the straight female; with the rhetoric of 'latent homosexuality,' he appropriates all he could possibly use from the real thing; in the emergent rhetoric of transsexualism, as the center of discourse, as he learns that most transsexuals are lesbians anyway, he takes over lesbianism for himself (as he has had it already in any number of lesbian scenes in any number of pornographic films); and now you'd toss him my whip and chains, along with that Freudian reduction that claims, in a patriarchally produced scarcity field of sexually available females, the only way he can get by is with a little 'healthy' sadism. Ha! I'll take the sick kind, thank you very much. No wonder he comes out on top. That's simply where you've placed him! Would you settle for some argument in which everyone, even your straight white vanilla male, needs his very own Other—and claim that is, somehow, something new? The discourse—your privileged term—has been contoured for generations: Jew, forget the insults that lace its text, and look at *The Merchant of Venice*. Woman, forget the insults and look at *Madame Bovary* ("sitting like a toadstool on a dung heap," writes Flaubert in his novel). Sadist, forget the insults, and look at Hitchcock's *Frenzy*. Gay black male, look at Mapplethorpe's Man in Polyester Suit. There's something there (haven't we all been told?), universal, transcendent, aesthetic—good for you. Just swallow; and always insist to yourself that what must be swallowed is something other than the self-respect that is not, of course, his. Well, neither my sadism nor my masochism runs in that particular direction. But even by talking for me this much, you exile me to the position of that dark and eccentric figure lurking at the horizon of Romanticism, speaking all you dare not resist. Well, your cowardice is not masochism. And my articulation is not sadism. Don't think because you speak, or rather mumble, in my stead, I can somehow be silent or you can silence this rhetorical fusillade.

"What would happen if you *really* (i.e., politically) extirpated that metaphoric idiocy from your proposed discourse of desire—idiot not because metaphors are themselves the idiot things Western philosophers have been claiming since Plato, but because metaphors badly formed are the discursive elements that mystify and stabilize oppressive systems. Describe for me the picture book about the little bear who discovers the pleasures of pain, of degradation, and who learns the delights of giving it, receiving it. (Let's get *really* radical with your white-out and your felt-tip!) You and I might even suggest, one to the other, it teaches that you must make sure to exercise such pleasures only with someone else who appreciates it, complete with 'safe words' for ending sessions and 'talking out periods' at the start (you can find such in any reasonable manual of S&M practices with which, today, I must vouchsafe my social reason). There's your role model, you'll say. There's your certificate declaring you a member of the greater society of sexual variation. And, my friend, when such picture books are neither laughable nor politically correct, but as common as *Corduroy*, then, rest assured, I shall tell you *not* that I accept your Discourse of Desire in all its utopian naïveté; rather, that will be the very moment I shall at least and at last be able to hold up both and demand why *my* desires must be policed in the one, while *his* are still so untrammeled, unmarked, and free that they need not even be mentioned in the other—the reticence creating the margin across which he creates himself by creating me but across which, yes, I plunder him regularly. (Oh, sing it, honey: 'Not only is it a boy bear, Daddy! It's a straight, white, heterosexual, vanilla, boy bear—in case you hadn't noticed.') That will be the moment when at last and at least I can prove to you that precisely at the point I would seize my desire in its freedom, there *you* would name my particular form of it the core and kernel of *all* policing: the embarrassing Hegelian wish to rule and be ruled. As Freud and Marx gave you tools to analyze this on its own terms, you insistently equivocate one set of causes with the other and leave democracy a consumer travesty of itself through the people's ignorance of what this ruling and being ruled is really about—then you demonize it by claiming that, whenever it rises into articulation clear enough to signal conflict, somehow its courting political torture is itself one with sexual torture, and lay it at my terrifying, cloven foot.

"Well, I'll tell you. Anyone who believes your vaunted power relations in a session of consensual sexual torture are the same as those in a session of imposed political torture is simply and brutally ignorant of both—and deserves (the political discourse of the time demands—as 'shave and a haircut' demands 'two bits') whatever happens . . . ?

"Him or her, my friend, no more than I.

"No one *deserves* 'whatever happens.' That deserving can only be *enforced.*

"Ruling and being ruled, the very deployment of political power, the walls of reality and every attempt to scale, breach, or reposition them— that is the material ground and limit of your discourse. Who speaks now is precisely the devil that discourse has placed here to frighten you off the very question—who lied to you that ruling and being ruled are causally entailed with my desires, just as you lied to him that, in his cowardice, he is as strong as I. But learn, *mon semblable, mon frère,* not that I am you; rather that you are *not* me—even while the organization of our oppressions may be the same. Learn, too, by so learning, how different what all your patriarchal logic tells you is an identity is from the cored out, resonant hollow of our differences.

"Those discursive identities are there to kill me, not you—whoever you, the privileged speaking subject who allows me only to function as your ventriloquized puppet, are."

10. Interpretation and Perception. In the discussion of discourse a concept eventually must arise. It seems to be a part of the modern discourse of discourse itself. It is given by the phrase, "Interpretation precedes perception." To understand it, we might start with an alternate narrative as to how humans perceive things. This alternate narrative of perceived meaning commences something like this.

We begin by perceiving abstract colors, shapes, sounds; eventually, by relating them to one another, to other sets of abstract colors, shapes, and sounds both temporally and spatially, we build up a picture of objects, events, and finally of reality. Once we have an objective model, we interpret it and ask what we can understand of it.

The problem with this story of perception is that, from both neurological study and introspection, it just doesn't seem to be the way the brain—or the mind—is set up. Interpretation of vision begins, for example, as soon as light hits the retina. Cats see horizontal lines and vertical lines with different nerve bundles. And some nerve cells in the frog's eye respond to small, dark moving dots, which might be any one of the range of edible bugs, while other nerves respond to broad patches of general color, which might be land, lily pad, or whatever. There may, indeed, be electrical impulses moving around the brain that are signs for abstract colors or even shapes. But by the time they register in anything like "mind," interpretation of what they are has well begun.

Introspectively, we humans can supply our own evidence for the priority of interpretation over perception. I recall waking up last autumn in my Amherst apartment, in that dim period when the sky beyond the bedroom and bathroom windows was still deep blue. Looking for my hairbrush, I wondered if for some reason I'd left it in the kitchen. And so I stepped in through the kitchen door—

Ah, there it was, across the room on the small triangular table by the sink, its black plastic handle sticking out behind the edge of a colander left there from last night's spaghetti.

I took a step across the linoleum floor—

But now I saw all this dust on the handle's edge. Gray fluff was visible in three small heaps generally spread from one end to the other.

I took another step, and what I'd seen as a black plastic handle with the long, three-peaked mound of dust on it, became the handle of one of my kitchen knives. The handle was black bakelite. What I'd seen as dust was the light glinting off the three steel bolts that, level with the bakelite, held the blade in place . . .

The point here is that often we do not have enough perceptual information to make out what something is; but in such situations, we do not perceive—at first—that we have only partial information. We perceive some *thing*; then, sometimes only a moment later, we perceive some *other* thing that contradicts the first. *Those contradictions* are the sign that we eventually learn to interpret *as* incomplete perceptual information. Eventually, if the contradictions go on long enough and will not resolve, we perceive an abstract color or shape, whose substance or full form we cannot know. But such a perception represents an even *higher* order of interpretive complexity than the perception of concrete objects and events—rather than a simple and atomic element on which perception itself is grounded.

Abstract entities are a discourse. The person or the small dog we catch out of the corner of our eye when we know no person or dog is there becomes, when we look at it fully, an overcoat hanging from a hook on the inside of the open closet door, the overturned shoe box fallen from the chair beside the bed. Though, faithful to that other story, we might even say, "I saw something that, a moment later, resolved into a coat, or a shoe box," the truth is that, however fleeting, the something was probably something fleeting but specific—not something in general.

To become aware of this process is to become aware that some, if not all, of these mistaken perceptions relate to, if they are not controlled by, preëxisting discourses. (Reason, memory, and desire told me I might find my hairbrush in the kitchen.) Once we accept the notion that we cannot perceive without already having interpreted what we perceived, however mistakenly, as *something*, even if our interpretation finally settles on the one we call the *fact* that we are seeing does not provide enough information to draw a solid conclusion about the object (and thus must remain in the realm of unresolved abstraction), directly we find ourselves asking such questions as:

Did Leonardo really *see* a round womb?

And, by extension, was that round womb of the order, say, of my black plastic hairbrush handle that I thought I saw across the room—or perhaps of the dust piled on the piece of black plastic that replaced it?

This is certainly the commonsense place where opponents of theories of discourse find themselves banding together to look for commonsense weaknesses.

The answer is, I think, that we cannot know for sure—though there are other possibilities that, in this case, seem more probable than this one.

You cut open a fresh chicken to clean it. What is the shape of the chicken liver?

There was, of course, a Renaissance discourse in place that spoke of the womb as the center and sun of the body, that talked of its necessary perfection in terms of the perfect geometrical form, the sphere. Did da Vinci just draw from an uncharacteristically spherical womb? Or did he see the pear shape but dismiss it as an anomaly of his particular cadaver and silently correct it in his picture? Or did he know the pear shape as well as Fallopius would come to but simply pandered to current prejudices? Or did the womb look round? We don't know. That is precisely the knowledge that the discourse itself excludes.

That is what discourse does: it excludes—information, distinctions, differences . . . and similarities.

That is its precise and frightening power—the mark, the trace, of its one-time presence.

That "interpretation precedes perception" is supported by and supports a theory of discourse is not to say that the two notions—discourse and the priority of interpretation—are one. But that is the equivocation that those who raise the objections are finally making.

11. Interlogue Five. Laura Bohannan's amusing 1966 essay, "Shakespeare in the Bush," is a charming parable of discourse.[13] After an argument with an Oxford friend, who tells her, "You Americans . . . often have difficulty with Shakespeare. He was, after all, a very English poet, and one can easily misinterpret the universal by misunderstanding the particular," Bohannan protests "that human nature is pretty much the same the whole world over," and, upholding the universality of such great and classic Western works as *Hamlet*, she goes off, with her friend's copy of the play as a gift, on her second field trip to the West African Tiv and with an exhortation from him to lift her mind above its primitive surroundings: Possibly, by prolonged meditation, she might achieve the grace of correct interpretation.

An extremely wet rainy season, however, interrupts Bohannan's research. The elder tribesmen whom she hopes to observe at their various cultural rituals have nothing to do but sit around in the reception hut and drink calabash after calabash of beer, brewed by the women, and tell tales.

Bohannan sought solace awhile with *Hamlet*. But finally she found herself in the reception hut as well, faced with the request that she tell a story. And so it is the story of Hamlet that she decides to tell, sure that its universal resonance will sound out as clearly in the Tiv as it might in an Oxford seminar room.

But problems of interpretation, perception—and discourse—arise immediately.

While the tribe has an evolved and subtle concept of magic, knowledge, madness, and the relations among them all, Bohannan's tribe has no concept of ghosts.

In the tribe, there simply *were* no stories of the dead returning—either believed or accepted as fantasy. Thus, the very first scene of Hamlet's father's ghost on the battlements registers with Bohannan's hearers neither as a frightening event nor as an emblem of the supernatural simply to be accepted—but as a narrative mistake. Obviously what she must mean, they explain, is that it is an omen sent by a witch. Because if you see a dead person actually walking around, you can be pretty sure that's what it is. But as for its being the soul of the dead, that's just silly and obviously, then, narrational error. ("But, Daddy, it's a *boy* bear . . . !") The tribe's term for "wise man" and "witch" were the same. Thus, establishing Horatio's position as a benign scholar was rather difficult. In that tribe there were strict proscriptions about what was appropriate to the various generations—proscriptions that served to determine what jobs as well as what topics of concern were appropriate to each; as well, those proscriptions served equally to discourage intergenerational violence:

Parents did not strike children.

Children did not strike parents.

If, in that tribe, someone had problems or complaints about you, from childhood on they presented them, either up or down the scale, to your age mates, by whom you were then judged and, if necessary, punished. Intergenerational conflicts there were likely to be the stuff of mild irony or appalling vulgarity. But the same proscriptive institutions prevented them from being the center of comedy or tragedy. Thus, the whole Oedipal scenario so much fiction in the West depends on—the conflict between generations—had for Bohannan's hearers a somewhat sleazy air; and certainly no tale that appealed seriously to them could resonate as the major conflict behind all cultural progress, somehow—in this story—gone awry and gotten terrifyingly and tragically out of control. Rather, it seemed an unnecessary nastiness that ordinary social institutions ought to have obviated. Hamlet's status as a hero was immediately in question by all the village auditors.

Finally, the borderline incest Claudius and his sister-in-law Gertrude indulge to Prince Hamlet's consternation was, in this tribe, *de rigueur*. No, certainly you didn't go around murdering your brothers. But if your father died, then simple politeness said his brother should marry his surviving wife or wives. And if he was suspected of such a murder, it's for your father's age mates to decide—not for you to do anything about.

Hamlet's madness caused equal problems—since every one knows that madness is always the result of a witch at work somewhere. What's more, the witch has to be a male relative on the victim's father's side. (Everybody knows that.) Since he was Hamlet's only male relative in the story, obviously Claudius was to blame—

Well, yes, Bohannan had to agree. He was. But with that as the explanation for why, did any of the Western tale really remain at all . . . ?

Polonius's murder behind the arras was also completely revalued in this tribe of ardent and experienced hunters, where, just before you throw your spear, you must call out, "Game!" whereupon anyone in the vicinity who can't see where you're throwing shouts out so that you don't hit them. When he sees the arras move, Hamlet calls out: "A rat!"

As one of the hearers commented to Bohannan: "What child would not know enough to shout out, 'It's *me!*'"

As the tale goes on, to turn it into a "good story," a logical story, a story where the actions were believable, where the motivations made sense to them, Bohannan's auditors distort the tale into a comic cascade whose humor for us is only subverted by its endless intricacy: Hamlet's forging of the letter that gets him out of trouble with the King of England and gets Rosencrantz and Guildenstern beheaded in his place sounds particularly suspect from Bohannan, since she, having already acted as the scribe for the tribe in its relations with the outside world, has already had to tell many of the same listeners, when they'd come to ask her to change various amounts on various bride-price documents, that such forgery is impossible and would immediately be detected.

If Bohannan can't forge a letter, how come Hamlet can?

But it is only by taking over the tale and turning it into an unrecognizable concatenation of unrecognizable people in unrecognizable situations operating through unrecognizable motivations, and finally of a significance wholly incomprehensible to us, that Bohannan's tribesmen can make any sense of the tale at all. (Laertes *must* have driven Ophelia mad and killed her, of course, since he's the only male relative of her generation mentioned in the tale. His attempt to avenge her death? Obviously a cover-up for deeper, more logical reasons.) And when their interpretation does manage to offer a recognizable evaluation, it is for such a different web of reasons that the similarity is really an accident rather than any shared cultural resonance.

An old man, gathering his ragged toga around him, finally tells Bo-hannan: "That was a very good story. You told it with very few mistakes. . . . Sometime you must tell us some more stories. We who are elders will instruct you in their true meaning, so that when you return to your own land your elders will see that you have not been sitting in the bush, but among those who know things and have taught you wisdom."

What Bohannan has learned, of course, is that the universal is noth-ing but an intricate relation of specificities. And what's more, the "uni-versal" is quite different and distinct, cultural locale to cultural locale. The discursive wisdom that Bohannan's tale can teach us today concerns what Foucault, in "*L'Ordre du discours,*" calls "the tyranny of the signifier." That is the notion, all too easy to fall into if one has not moved about among radically different discursive structures, that a single recogniz-able event, a single recognizable object, or a given rhetorical feature will have the same meaning no matter what discourse it is found in. This is the notion that impels the so well-intentioned cultural imperialism of symbol explicators such as Jung or Joseph Campbell, who again and again seem to feel that when they find a dragon or a mandala in two widely separated cultures, somehow they have discovered the "same" or a "shared" symbol.

For me this notion exploded on my first trip to Greece, in 1965, where I quickly learned that the palm-up beckoning gesture by which North Americans say, "Come here," there meant, "Good-bye." The palm-down flapping of the hand by which we indicate "So long," there meant, "Come over here." The sideways movement of the head by which we in-dicate negation there meant, "Yes." And the single up-and-down move-ment of the head, which here is very close to our nod of agreement, there meant, "No." If the very signifiers for *yes, no, come here,* and *good-bye* could all reverse between, say, Paris and Athens, then the apprehension of the "same" signifier in China and Mexico, in Texas and Thailand, in India and Guatemala, must *mark* the existence of cultural specificity, of discursive difference, rather than some biculturally obliterating, transcendent "universality"—almost always functioning in the service of some structure of economic exploitation.

Bohannan's tale is structured to throw into relief a limit of discursive disjuncture.

And that, as we have noted, is what we experience when we read Roussel.

That both use Africa as their background is, itself, controlled by the racist discourse of the West. We must not, for a moment, ever think, therefore, that our exploration of discourse is free, complete; rather, those explorations are always policed by discourses already set in place.

12. Observation and Articulation. One day in a Central Park playground in the summer of the same year in which my daughter had learned the discourse of children's books, around the fountain and having shed all clothing an hour back, a handful of kids in my daughter's play school group all clustered around a three-and-a-half-year-old girl named Mischkatel, who enthusiastically proposed a game to Sascha and Iva and Nord and Aiesha (this was, recall, the seventies): "Let's see who can pee-pee the farthest!" And while I looked on—I confess, surprised—the five of them stood to the ankles in the water at the fountain's edge—and let whiz.

The girls, of course, without exception, won—since, in general, the urinary track exits from the body proper horizontally, or even with a slightly upward tilt. And since every one was just standing there, letting fly, the little boys, who dangled a bit, had not thought to use their hands to guide their stream and so generally watered in a downward slant rather than straight out. Mischkatel, Iva, and Aiesha all more or less tied and left the two little boys, Nord and Sascha, frowning down at their self-evident lack and symbol of powerlessness, marking the male site of greatest physical vulnerability.

In a society where children play regularly naked with one another, this can *not* be an anomaly. But I had to ask myself, sometime later, if I was empowered—as it were—to *see* this by a situation from not a full decade before, when, in 1969, I had lived in San Francisco, and a nude sunbathing and beer fest had started on the tarred-over roof of our Natoma Street flat. Eight or half a dozen of us were sitting around, naked, drinking bottle after bottle of beer, when, as several of the men had already done, one young woman got up, went to the back of the tar-paper roof, and proceeded to urinate off the edge with as high-flying an arc as anyone might want.

I remember how cool we were all being—in what, I suspect for most of us, was some astonishment. A young woman was about to speak, when a young man asked (another white male appropriation, no doubt): "How did you *do* that?"

Her answer was classic: "You aim, stupid."

Then she proceeded to demonstrate how, with two fingers of one hand in a V, turned down over the upper part of the vaginal crevice, one could control the direction of one's stream.

I am a writer.

Needless to say, I incorporated the scene (or rather one based closely on it) in my next novel. Some months after the book appeared, I received a letter, signed by a group of five women in Vancouver, that said, in brief: "Thanks."

But the tale has its converse. In the late sixties a cheap series of char-
tered buses ran back and forth between New York and San Francisco, generically called "the Gray Rabbit." By the end of its run, the restroom at
the back of the coach had long since lost its door. In general, with the
rather free-wheeling young men and women who availed themselves of
the $45 one-way fare, this was not a large problem in itself. What became
a problem was that, after the first day of the trip, because of the lack of
springs and the back roads, thanks to the men on the bus the restroom
became pretty foul.

And the women on the bus didn't like it.

The problem was eventually solved by a woman driver, who took a
length of a two-by-four, a hammer, and some nails and fixed it into the
doorway at little above chest height; she put another one behind it so
that there was simply no way to approach the commode in a fully upright
position. On the first of the two-by-fours she hung a sign:

YOU DON'T SIT,

YOU DON'T PISS!

The problem was more or less solved.

But the point is that women can, and some do, urinate standing up;
and men can, and some do, urinate sitting down. As to arcs and distances, well, in the same conversation in which I asked my daughter
about *Corduroy*, I asked if she remembered her infantile peeing contest.
No, she didn't, any more than she remembered the female *Corduroy*. But
was that exclusion from her memory chance? Was it because that memory had not been stabilized by a pre-extant discourse?

Men and women do what they do—what they're comfortable doing.
But the constraints on that comfort, on who does what and when, are
material, educational, habitual—feel free to call them social.

And where all three—material, education, and habit—are stabilized
in one form or another by language, we have a discourse.

From such memories I turn to others that are so like the experiences
that prompted Freud to his theory of "penis envy," when my daughter, at
age four, a year after her forgotten triumph in the park peeing contest,
in imitation of me, would stand at the commode with her hands on her
genital region and make hissing sounds. In another series of stories I
wrote about that time, you will find the detritus—and pretty much my
thinking—on all the incidents above.

But is the reason such incidents as this are not usually talked of—speculated over, theorized, included in our traditional elaborations of the
way our culture works—because of some massive discursive exclusion?
Are they simply not seen by most people because they take the form of
the pear-like bulge in the upper part of the uterus—or are they simply

misperceived as something else, like the mistake of a knife for a brush? Again, that is precisely the information the structure of the discourse that has prevailed up till now means that we can never have with any real certainty about the past.

Again, that is what discursive exclusions *do.*

But I also asked my adult daughter, not too long ago, if she remembers ever wanting a penis. "No," she said, with some consideration. "But I certainly remember, when I was four, wanting to urinate standing up. It seemed so much more convenient."

A reasonable thought for a four-year-old who, at three, could—and had won a contest by doing so.

13. Interlogue Six. The material fact that has made it desperately important for people, when writing about sex, to write about what they have done and experienced and seen themselves, is, of course AIDS. This disease, which by February 1993 (this year), according to the always conservative statistics of the CDC, has killed more than 135,000 people in the United States, out of the more than 210,000 reported cases (1,800 of whom are children under the age of thirteen and 11,000 of whom are women), is certainly the largest material factor in the transformation of the discourse of desire and that transformation's manifestation in the rhetoric of sex.

It is painfully ironic that Foucault, who wrote in his 1970 lecture, *"L'Ordre du discours,"* "We are a very long way from having constituted a unitary, regular discourse concerning sexuality; it may be that we never will, and that we are not even traveling in that direction" (233), died of AIDS in 1984—for AIDS has come as close to unifying certain strands of sexual discourse as it has come to fraying certain others.

Foucault also said, in a 1980 lecture at Stanford on political and pastoral power: "We must get rid of the Freudian schema. You know, the schema of the interiorization of the law through the medium of sex."

He did not say we must get rid of Freud but only that we must get rid of a certain reduction—and I would add, distortion—of Freud's critique of society that is too often justified by citations of Freud, usually at his most speculative: "the interiorization of the law through the medium of sex. . . ."

Well, what does this mean? It means an intellectual move in which the thinker notes some analogy between some aspect of a given sexual act, usually the tritest and most common one in a given culture (often our own), and some form of the culture itself or the usual psychology of those in it. At that point, the thinker claims the former as a cause for the latter, and this causal relationship is elevated to a transcendent affirmation of the universal and unchangeable nature—the law—of the social (or the psychological) through the power of the sexual. Nor does it matter whether the argument is: "Because men lie on top of women during sex, men will forever dominate women during . . . badminton tournaments," or "Because a fatal disease is now transmitted sexually, the whole of society itself must somehow be psychologically sick and doomed to destroy itself." Sex has become the medium through which someone declares a form of the social to be "natural" law rather than considering sex itself simply another social form. At this point, we should be able to recognize the same discursive structure—and the same misapplied logic—in them all. For this is the discourse, the reasoning, of sympathetic magic, pure and simple; it is as much superstition today as it was when in 1890 Sir James George Frazer described its practice in the initial chapters of *The Golden Bough*. And it mystifies and distorts any study of the material realities (i.e., the politics) to which both the sexual and social actually respond.

But with that exhortation (a position implied in Foucault's work, again and again) Foucault becomes easily identifiable as the enemy of all sexual spectators who would take refuge behind such superstitions, with their ideas entailed by the notion, as we usually characterize them today, that biology equals destiny. (The most recent and vociferous is, perhaps, Camille Paglia.) Similarly, Foucault had already been identified as the clear and present enemy by those who claim history is over, and that we have entered some posthistorical period (often designated postmodernism), where all discourses are homogenized and there are no discursive articulations to be found any more, thanks to the current invisibility of power; I mean, of course, the author of *Forget Foucault*, Jean Baudrillard.[14]

Well, Foucault also said: "While we sit discussing the word, power works in silence." But the idea that there is a nature—or a culture—outside of history, before history, or after history, to which somehow we have a clear access, partakes of a single discursive form.

There seem to be at least two ways to highlight some of the structures of a given discourse. Both may boil down to the same thing. One is the critical observation of what is around us, precisely while on the alert for things that contravene what we expect. The other way is to suffuse one discourse with a systematically different discourse and watch the places where strain and tensions result. This, in effect, is what Bohannan does with her story of the story of *Hamlet*, and it is what Foucault does again and again in the range of his work, with his insistent systematicity that grids and grills and constantly tries to locate objects schematically within them, even while, as much as Derrida, Foucault himself eventually throws off his own gridding systems as too loose, too lax, improperly positioned, and necessarily displaced.

This is what Roussel does in his fiction; his eccentric linguistic method, by which he arrives at his progression of preposterous machines, incidents, and relations, always gives us the feeling that narrative discourse as we know it is strained, near to the point of breaking, and thus becomes a palpable object in our experience of his texts. It is no wonder that Roussel was also a favorite storyteller of Foucault's and that his early study, published in English as *Death and the Labyrinth*, is certainly—and systematically—the best single study of Roussel currently available.[15]

14. Conclusion. The last thing I want to speak about is a place where, indeed, the homogenization of discourses has produced an angering, murderous sexual rhetoric that fights the Discourse of Desire at every point—a social locus where two discourses that already suffuse one another must be separated out. I have already cited the mortality statistics; and, if we do not separate these discourses, those statistics may be a long, long time in leveling off their horrendous upsurge.

For it was as far back as 1987 when I realized that AIDS had become, among my friends and acquaintances, the single largest killer, beating out cancer, suicide, and heart attacks combined.

To my knowledge there have only been two monitored studies to date on the sexual transmission vectors of AIDS—certainly no more than two that have received anything approaching visible coverage. More accurately, there have been only one monitored study and one semimonitored study. That the studies agree as much as they do in their outcome is, then, surprising and heartening. But in my own informal survey, fewer than one out of ten AIDS educators knows either of the studies, of their results, or where to direct people to these studies who ask about AIDS.

What is a monitored study?

Well, other than intentionally experimenting with humans and the AIDS virus (which is illegal), a monitored study is the only way we can obtain information about AIDS transmission vectors that can in any way be called scientific.

In a monitored study of sexual transmission vectors for HIV, a number of people, preferably in the thousands, who test sero-negative are then monitored, in writing, at regular intervals, as to their sexual activity: from the number of times, to the number and sex of partners, to the specific acts performed, oral (active and passive), anal (insertive or receptive), vaginal (insertive or receptive), anal-oral (active and passive), and what have you. At the end of a given period, say six months or a year, the same people are tested for sero-conversion. The status of various

HIV positive and HIV negative people is then statistically analyzed against their specific sexual activity.

Of the two studies that have been done of this sort, one by Kingsley, Kaslow, Rinaldo, et al., was published in *The Lancet* of 14 February 1987; it involved 2,507 gay men. The other, The San Francisco Men's Health Study, involving 1,035 men picked at random from a neighborhood having the highest AIDS rate in the city, was reported and described in a letter to *The Journal of the American Medical Association* of 4 April 1986. I call this last a semimonitored study because there the monitoring was done only twice, once at the beginning and once at the end of the study, and was in the form of a general survey, asking "What do you do in bed and what do you not do?" rather than the specific and regular tracking of Kingsley, Kaslow, Rinaldo, et al.

Both of these studies report, quite interestingly, a statistical correspondence of 0 percent—not 1 percent, not 3 percent, not ½ of 1 percent—0 percent of sero-conversions to HIV positive for those gay men who restrict themselves to oral sex, unprotected, active or passive (147 men in Kingsley, Kaslow, Rinaldo, et al.; an unspecified number in the *JAMA* letter describing The San Francisco Men's Health Study). The statistical correlation between sero-conversions and receptive anal intercourse in both studies was devastating. Nor was there any statistical indication that repeated sexual contact had anything whatsoever to do with transmission. Kingsley, Kaslow, Rinaldo, et al. reported eight sero-conversions to HIV positive among men who reported only a *single case* of anal-receptive intercourse for the duration of the study.

Should I have to point out that this renders the rhetoric of "repeated sexual contact," so much a part of AIDS education both before the 1987 study and since, murderous misinformation? Well, then, I hear an apologist for the status quo of (lack of) AIDS information say, maybe it applies to some other areas of sexual behavior besides anal intercourse? To which I can only say: "Tell me where." No: Many men who believed such rhetoric applied to anal intercourse and based their sexual behavior on it are now dead. It's that simple.

There has been no dissemination of information of any monitored studies for sexual transmission of the HIV virus from and/or to women. I can only assume, after three years' research, that such a study has not been done. And with an epidemic that has caused more than 135,000 deaths in ten years, and 11,000 cases among women, this situation is a crime whose statistics are reaching toward the genocidal.

A monitored study is a powerful discursive machine for producing a set of highly operationalized rhetorical figures—of the sort we call evidence in situations such as this. In a monitored study, is there room for mistake, or lying, or distortion? Certainly. But the knowledge obtained is still preferable to the alternative.

There is, of course, another discourse that produces its own rhetorical array. A person is diagnosed HIV positive or with full-blown AIDS, and the doctor asks: "Any idea how you got it?"

And the patient, possibly trying to think what he or she was doing sexually six months or so ago, possibly relying on what he or she already "knows," gives an answer. Logically, however, this cannot be evidence in an attempt to find out how AIDS is transmitted, if only because it presumes the answer is already known to the question we are trying to learn the answer *to.* Is it necessary here to stress that people, especially in sexual situations, will lie, will forget, or will misremember pears for apples or even hairbrushes for knife handles—for any number of discursive reasons, in a discourse that has undergone catastrophic changes without cease over the last ten years? Nevertheless, the information gleaned from this second discourse is regularly overlaid, called fact, and used to displace information from the first. Otherwise responsible publications regularly report that now 8, now 16, now 12 percent of men have gotten AIDS from oral sex, now 1, now 2, now 3 percent of men have gotten AIDS from prostitutes, when the most they can mean is that this is what a certain percentage of men, when diagnosed with AIDS, have *said when asked,* in a discursive field whose precise discursive form is that we do not know about these vector possibilities (because they have not been adequately researched) and, thus, almost anything may be said and be believed. This, then, is the discourse of popular belief.

Purposely leaving needle transmission aside, we "know" (that is, the studies that have been done strongly suggest) only two facts about the sexual transmission of AIDS: that it is not transmitted by oral-genital sex between men. And that it is transmitted easily and effectively through anal sex.

Anything else we might say about its sexual transmission is all in the realm of superstition. Sometimes superstitions turn out to be true. But in a situation of such mortal concern, what can be gained for the Discourse of Desire through this appalling and institutionally supported ignorance? Please: If you—heterosexual or homosexual, man or woman— are concerned about the sexual transmission of AIDS, demand with me that monitored studies be initiated, be rigorously overseen, and their results be widely disseminated.

For the rhetoric of sex is complex; and the discourse that organizes it, that makes it make sense for our culture, is patriarchy. Study it, know it, critique it, cut it up and anatomize it any way you would like. The Discourse of Desire in its contemporary form, as it here and there subverts patriarchy, is a good deal younger than the oldest of my readers. The rhetoric of desire's discourse has only begun to sediment in the course of such personal and political intervention. Encourage it through your own discussions. Thank you.

—Amherst
1993

NOTES

1. Edward McCurdy, ed. and intro., *The Notebooks of Leonardo da Vinci, The Definitive Edition in One Volume* (New York: George Brazillier, 1939). Subsequent page references appear parenthetically in the text.

2. *Leonardo da Vinci: Artist, Scientist, Inventor,* catalogue of an exhibition held at the Haywood Gallery, by the South Bank Center, London (New Haven: Yale University Press, 1986).

3. Don Freeman, *Corduroy* (New York: Viking Books, 1968).

4. J. R. Dunn, "Letters," *Monad: Essays on Science Fiction* 2 (March 1992).

5. Toni Morrison, *Playing in the Dark: Whiteness and the Literary Imagination* (Cambridge: Harvard University Press, 1992).

6. Raymond Roussel, *How I Wrote Certain of My Books,* trans. with notes and a bibliography Trevor Winkfiend (New York: Sun, 1977).

7. Samuel R. Delany, *The Motion of Light in Water: Sex and Science Fiction Writing in the East Village* (1988; rpt. New York: A Richard Kasak Book, Masquerade Books, 1993).

8. Sigmund Freud, *Leonardo da Vinci and a Memory of His Childhood,* trans. Alan Tyson (New York: W. W. Norton, 1964), 85.

9. Samuel Taylor Coleridge, *Selected Letters,* ed. H. J. Jackson (New York: Oxford University Press, 1988). From the introduction by the editor: "The introduction of the postage stamp in 1840, six years after Coleridge's death, significantly altered the situation of correspondents. Until then, recipients paid postage; the writers themselves were responsible for making letters worth paying for. As objects paid for, letters had a certain status: they were shared with family and friends; in most households they were preserved and periodically reread; and on the death of the letter-writer, they were customarily returned to the family as part of the estate."

10. Samuel R. Delany, *Wagner/Artaud: A Play of 19th and 20th Century Critical Fictions* (New York: Ansatz Press, 1988).

11. George Bernard Shaw, *The Perfect Wagnerite: A Commentary on the Niblung's Ring* (London: G. Richards, 1898).

12. Michel Foucault, *The Archaeology of Knowledge & The Discourse on Language*, trans. A. H. Sheridan Smith (New York: Pantheon, 1972). Page references appear parenthetically in the text.

13. Laura Bohannan, "Shakespeare in the Bush," in *Ants, Indians, and Little Dinosaurs*, ed. Alan Ternes (New York: Scribner, c. 1975). (I would like to thank Margaret Minsky, who is responsible for my having my most recent copy of this delightful piece.)

14. Jean Baudrillard, *Forget Foucault* (Paris: Editions Galilee, 1977; New York: Semiotext(e), 1987).

15. Michel Foucault, *Death and the Labyrinth: The World of Raymond Roussel*, trans. Charles Ruas (New York: Doubleday & Company, 1986).

2

Street Talk / Straight Talk

1. Discourse—an order of response, a mode of understanding, for which various rhetorical features may function as symptoms. Yet rhetoric is never wholly coextensive with discourse. Discourse and rhetoric control one another, yes—but precisely because of that control, neither is wholly at one with the other.

Nevertheless—the relation of discourse to rhetoric is not the arbitrary relation, negotiable by introspection, of signified to signifier; it is the determined relation, negotiable by analysis, of the unconscious to the enunciated.

2. According to the discourse of "Discourse," rhetoric is quantifiable, particular, arrives in delimitable units, while meanings, to quote Quine (8), cannot be "individuated." Consider, then, four modes of rhetoric:

Street talk: Brutal, repetitious, vulgar, it marks a subdiscourse of ignorance, rumor, misunderstanding, and outright superstition. It is fixated—now on the aggressive, now on the sexual, now on the cupidinously acquisitive. The rhetoric of an underworld, its *raison* is lying; in the pursuit of myriad dishonesties and selfishnesses, "getting over," as it most recently characterizes a major factor of its own enterprise. It arises in sexually high dimorphic idiolects: But whether we move in the realm of gossip or of braggadocio, whatever its topic, the very banality of its endlessly repeated circuits makes it the mark of the limited, the illicit, a moment away from brute dumbness in one direction, a moment away from the linguistic zero of pure chatter in another.

Straight talk: Indicating it with the rhetorical mark reserved for it by "street talk," it is mellifluous, precise, sophisticated: The subdiscourse it takes for itself is "the learned," the characterization of itself it employs in the acknowledgement of its own truth. It functions to mediate between truth and knowledge, and thus is saturated by both. It functions to resolve disorder, to clarify confusion, to calm and commingle the diverse and the disparate, "to inform"—as it often says of itself—where formal differences and divisions have become unclear, violently erased, violated. Supposedly it is sexless—though this is the same as saying that it is un-marked, male, and materially wealthy. It takes all topics to itself and en-chains them in a limitless legitimacy that everywhere displaces them and replaces them, now in the shadow, now in the light, of its articulation.

Yet both these rhetorical modes cast shadows.

Straight talk: Indicating it with linguistic marks drawn from its own rhetoric, it is awkward, obscurantist, and often crashingly irrelevant. It refuses to remain within the recognizable discursive fields of the hearer and, by so doing, fulfills—more or less badly—only the function of in-timidation. It uses knowledge to hide the truth. Thus it exists as an op-pressive violence in a field in which articulation itself forever strives to mystify the very violence of its own enterprise. In its privileging of specu-lation, it excludes all action and consigns all reference to the exile of the illegitimate. Thus the very hollowness with which it resonates is one with the lies of a sermon delivered in a church without a god.

Street talk: Indicating it with linguistic marks drawn from its own rheto-ric, it is clear, concrete, and honest. If it is often unfair, it is factual and calls a spade a spade. Its specific vulgarity is the stuff of poetry—in the sense that good taste is the enemy of great art. Within its compass, you know where you stand. Used with clarity, its wisdom rivals the ancients'. Used with economy, it becomes song. The local inscription of its logic (among the "streetwise") is far more powerful than the vagaries of that "common sense" that it and straight talk both have abjured. And the endlessness of its blasphemies is, finally, both defense against and ac-knowledgement of the suffering that is the lot of all, but especially the poor, that straight talk has put—along with action—outside the precinct of what may be legitimately articulated.

3. Imagine a discourse, flung down on our coordinate system, traversing all four of the rhetorical quadrants outlined above: To one side of it rises the axial of death. Any utterance within that discourse is on a continuous and uninflected curve that shoots across a deadly locus; it is stopped by and absorbed by death at that terrifying and totalized point of unity. From there, the curve flows toward the axial of life—but a life that is wholly and ideally secure, rich in pleasure, close to immobile: That is to say that, above all things, this particular biotic axial is "safe." The axis of death cleaves its space, bearing with it a mythology similar to that with which the axis of the real cleaves the plane of complex numbers. The axis of life carries across *its* space an equally rarefied mythology suggesting nothing so much as the axis of the imaginary that transects the complex plane. The discourse approaches that lively, that imaginary axis asymptotically, yearningly, steadily, endlessly. . . .

4. A rhetorical moment abstracted from an undergraduate paper, turned in two-and-a-half years ago by a student at Hampshire College writing about a prime-time saga of money and power that had recently introduced a gay male character, more or less visibly, more or less sympathetically: "A gay male who does not think about AIDS is, for most gay males of this country, an other" (Sean Holland).

5. But of course the gay male character that Holland's rhetorical figure puts so strongly into question lies directly on the line of our discourse as we have just sketched it out; he is simply far along the road to an ideal life, to "safety," to the idealized world that television presents us—much farther along the road than you, than I. Indeed, to locate him on that line—"within that discourse," as many of us have learned to say—is to draw Holland's own rhetorical flourish that tries so staunchly, so violently, to position itself away from that line, ultimately closer to it. Holland, and presumably all the other gay males in this country with their presumed AIDS anxiety, are simply too far behind, not well enough advanced in the endless career toward life, pleasure, and safety: They are simply closer to death, and their anxiety, even as it masquerades as critique, is merely a rhetorical symptom of their position.

6. Discourses are pervasive, rapacious, hungry—they control, as we have said, rhetoric: Holland's, mine. . . .

7. It is possible that, for a while, a reasonable amount of the theoretical priority of any field such as gay studies, lesbian and gay male, in a social field where there is simply so much to *do*, may fall under that rubric where we traditionally find those theoretical articulations that work in the relation of theory to practice. But that—perhaps—is not what this paper is about.

8. Almost precisely a year ago, in February 1989, the *New York Times* and the *Daily News* both featured pieces in the same week stating that the *New England Journal of Medicine* (320.4, 26 Jan. 1989) had reported the first "confirmed" case of the "transmission of HIV infection from a woman to a man by oral sex." If you pull that issue of the *New England Journal* off the back-issues shelf in the periodical room of your library and page through it, checking the table of contents, you will find no article listed whose title would suggest such information, discussed, confirmed, or

otherwise. Indeed, it is only when you turn to the correspondence column that you find any mention of AIDS and oral sex at all. Let me read you the substantive section, paragraphs two and three, of a four-paragraph letter to the editor, that is the source of this "confirmed" case.

> Our patient, a 60-year-old uncircumcised man with insulin-dependent diabetes mellitus, was hospitalized because of fatigue, abnormalities of mental status, and pancytopenia. On examination, he was found to have subcortical dementia and diabetic peripheral neuropathy. His workup included a lumbar puncture, which revealed no abnormalities, and a normal brain computed tomographic scan, performed with and without iodinated contrast material. The man's evaluation included HIV antibody testing, and serum was reactive for HIV antibody on enzyme immunoassay (EIA) testing and Western blood analysis.
>
> On further questioning, the patient reported no homosexual encounters or intravenous drug use. He had never received a transfusion of blood products. Although he was living with his wife of more than 30 years, he had had no sexual contact of any sort with her for many years. (His wife's serum was nonreactive for HIV antibody EIA testing.) For the previous several years he had experienced erectile impotence, which had been attributed to his diabetic neuropathy. The patient's only extramarital affair had occurred over the course of the preceding two years, when he frequented a single female prostitute with whom he engaged in exclusively oral sex (both fellatio and cunnilingus). On one occasion he had seen her use intravenous drugs. He never performed cunnilingus during her menstrual periods and did not remember ever coming into contact with any of her blood. He reported that he had not engaged in deep French kissing with her. He did not remember her ever having oral or genital ulcers. The patient himself reported that he had never had oral ulcers. He described an occasional ulcer on his penis in the past, yet said he had never had sexual contact with his partner at a time when such an ulcer was present. Further laboratory testing of the patient resulted in a nonreactive serologic test of syphilis (rapid plasma-reagin) and revealed a peripheral-blood T-lymphocyte helper/suppressor ratio of 0.1, with an absolute T-helper (CD4) cell count of 36 per cubic millimeter. (Spitzler and Weiner)

But as I too yearn after a life on that forever inaccessible and wholly "safe" axis, let me violate my own rhetorical declaration and here read the first and final paragraphs of this letter, in a move that at once suggests a restoration of totality to the four-paragraph document under my gaze at the same time that it severs it in a moment of violence to this dis-

course which, I admit, even as I try to characterize it by Cartesian metaphors with Lacanian connotations, I do not fully comprehend; finally,
my rhetorical move is vouchsafed only by my contention that, as discourse controls rhetoric, so rhetoric *may*, at times, influence discourse.

Transmission of HIV Infection from a Woman to a Man by Oral Sex

To the Editor:
    In the United States, female-to-male sexual transmission of HIV has been
reported infrequently. (Friedland, GH. Klein, RS. Transmission of the human
immunodeficiency virus, N Engl J Med 1987: 317:1125–35.) Until now, oral
sex alone has not been proved to be a mode of transmission of HIV from
women to men. We now report what appears to be a case of HIV transmission
from a woman to a man exclusively by oral sex. . . .
    This case report suggests that oral sex alone can transmit HIV, even when
there is no coincident exchange of blood. In the light of this, public health
education about safer sexual practices must not only advocate the use of barrier contraceptives such as condoms during vaginal and rectal intercourse,
but also caution against the exchange of bodily fluids during oral sexual practices, such as oral sex.

                                                Peter G. Spitzler, MD
                                                Neil J. Weiner, MD
    Burlington, MA 01805   *Lahey Clinic Medical Center*

I can only say that, to me, what this suggests is that the paragraphs contained between these two, which I quoted above, should be moved
higher, that is nearer to death, on the line of discourse—and, by extension, that their importance, implied by the entire contextualization of a
medical journal, should be raised, implying a mobility back and forth
along the discursive slope that we will meet with again and again in the
course of our examination; though I think it is equally important to
point out that all logic tells us that there is nothing in the least *confirming*
in this letter (which is just that—a letter to the editor and not a reviewed
study); just as all reason tells us that a sixty-year-old man, married for
thirty years, still living with his wife and suffering from diabetes and de-
mentia, in Burlington, Massachusetts, would have every reason to lie
about either homosexual encounters or intravenous drug use—or, to
put it more strongly, can we think of any reason for such a man, come
down with AIDS, to tell the *truth* in today's climate, however much his
doctors might like to confirm it?

9. Some street rhetoric here: About three years ago, I picked up a telephone repairman named Tom in a gay bar on Eighth Avenue, called Cats, who was, frankly, drunk. But he was coherent enough to explain that he was out celebrating the birth of his first granddaughter. He was forty-two years old, and his nineteen-year-old daughter had just given birth to her first child. He had been married three times, and was currently separated from his third wife, but living with his sixteen-year-old son at his sister's house, in Brooklyn. The next morning, after a very satisfactory night of sex, when he was substantially soberer, Tom told me that, since his seventeenth year, he had found that for seven or eight months in a row he never considered sex with men, not even in passing. But once or twice a year, since that time, he would find himself going out to get drunk and, in the course of it, would usually get fucked by anywhere from three to ten men, sometimes more.

He found the experience deeply satisfying; and the result was that, again, for the next six months or so he did not even contemplate sex with men—until the same thing happened. He used to worry about it; but now, in his own words: "I guess it's just part of who I am." Since it averaged out at less than a twice-a-year occurrence, and in most places the urge was easily satisfied, he had never mentioned this "tendency" to any of his three wives.

I mention that I had not fucked him, although at one point he had very badly wanted me to. But after I insisted, for about five minutes, that I just was not going to do that (we had no condoms), we both ended up doing just about everything *else* two men can with one another—several times—before we fell asleep. Taking his quite soberly offered account at face value, I can only note that Tom is a prime target for AIDS. Also, I suspect that, should he contract it, we can be fairly sure that, for convenience's sake, he will likely go down in the books as having picked it up from a female prostitute.

Recalling Tom put me in mind of a young man of about twenty-five or thirty whom, for several years, perhaps fifteen years back, I used to run into and have sex with at about three- to five-month intervals. We met in a movie house on Eighth Avenue. The first time we did anything—mutual masturbation and fellatio—he began by confessing to me shyly that this was the first time he had done anything like this. All his other sexual experiences, he explained, had been with women.

Thus I was a little surprised when, three months later, I encountered him again, and—again—he explained that this was the first time he had done anything like this. All of his other sexual experiences, he explained, had—again—been with women. And, on our third encounter, though clearly he seemed to remember having met me and talked to me before, he once again explained that he had never done *anything* like this before. All of his other sexual experiences . . . Again, I suspect that, should this young man ever come down with AIDS, it is highly likely that he will be one of the people who have acquired the disease "heterosexually."

So much for street rhetoric.

A little street discourse analysis, however: These and many like experiences, some involving gay activity, some involving intravenous drug users, are the only ones I have that allow me to read the account in Doctors Spitzler and Weiner's letter quoted from the *New England Journal of Medicine* so that it makes anything like sense to me, whatsoever.

10. A moment from a novel I wrote in 1984, *The Tale of Plagues and Carnivals*:

> . . . while I was on the subway, I decided just to drop in on a public john at the Seventy-ninth Street subway stop—a rather active New York sexual congregating spot in those days—just to see how all this [the proliferation of AIDS rhetoric in 1983] was affecting things. . . . [W]ith all the brouhaha, the scientist in me was curious. Well, would you believe that, between the first and the second day I looked into that shabby hole with its peeling walls and asbestos covered pipes, the blue and ivory paint soiled almost to one hue, the filthy incandescent bulbs in their wire cages from another era, and only metal partitions between the stalls, someone came in and filled both the commodes and the urinals with plaster of paris, which hardened and bulged up over the porcelain rims, making the facilities wholly unusable—except for the industrial-sized sink in the corner, which, a day later, was fouled with urine, feces and soggy paper by the desperate?
>
> Irate straights attempting to render inoperable a well-known cruising spot? Social-minded gays trying to put the place out of operation, assuming they were lowering the chances of AIDS contact?
>
> No, there's no way to know for sure. But from the men who still stood around in it, it didn't stop the cruising—nor, from the condition of the floor and the sink, people using it for a toilet.
>
> But a few days later, the inoperable bathroom was permanently locked.

(451)

The question arises immediately: What status do I claim for this passage of declared fiction? Even lifted from its fictive context as I have done, abridged as I have abridged it, and placed here, I will always and forever claim it to have the status of a journal account, a text for which I might make the claim of truth appropriate for that genre: What I described, I saw. (Moreover, in half a dozen or more New York subway johns since, now locked up for good, I have seen the same again—when maintenance workers opened the doors briefly over the next years to put in a pail, to take out a mop. Indeed, the entire public bathroom system of New York men's and women's rooms, was put out of operation over that week or two period and has not been functional since.) What I speculated, I believed to be true—though, certainly, other evidence might someday conceivably convince me otherwise.

But the violence I still feel constrained to perform on my own text (not far from the violence I have performed on the medical letter above) is to point out, indeed to insist, that for you it is—presumably—just a text. What is more, it is in the margin between claims of truth and the claims of textuality that all discursive structures (that which allows us to read rhetoric) are formed. And this is as much a fact for my text as it is for the text of Doctors Spitzler and Weiner's letter.

11. A rhetorical moment from 1983 that did not make it into the same novel: While I sat in the balcony of the Variety Photoplays Theater in New York, a tall, muscular white man in his mid-thirties, in combat boots, Air Force flight jacket, with a military crew, finished sucking off one black guy in a paint-stained jacket, only to climb over the back of the seats of the row between us and, steadying himself on my shoulder, grinned at me with the wet-lipped delight of the satisfied. I grinned back, but felt constrained to say, softly, to this stranger who, until a minute before, had only been a head bobbing up and down between the legs of the man in the row in front of me, "Aren't you worried about AIDS?"

"Naw," he said. "You can't get it suckin' dick—unless you got cuts in your mouth or something like that."

I grinned back. "You're probably right—'cause if you weren't, we'd both have it." And, though we exchanged no more words, a minute later, he was crouched down between my knees and the back of the theater seat in front of me, his head between my legs.

12. A rhetorical moment from the same week that came from a letter written me from California by a concerned and sensitive heterosexual woman friend that struck me enough so that I found myself returning to it in thought day after day: "AIDS has now put gay men in the position that straight women have always been in with sex: Any unprotected sexual encounter now always carries with it the possibility of life or death."

13. I thought, indeed, about both this street level (balcony level?) exchange and this very powerful epistolary observation a good deal. Was I anxious about AIDS? Constantly, continuously. The first exchange, however, was—more or less—the one around which I structured my behavior. The second was the one around which I—more or less—structured my intellectual analysis of the situation.

What I can say at this distance, however, is that I doubt I ever thought about them both at the same time. At least in 1983. They belonged to two different discourses, and it was probably not till the summer of 1988, till just after a conference of the Marxist Summer Institute at Carnegie Mellon, not primarily on AIDS but on theory, when, from one of the most marginal participants, I received an offprint of a *Lancet* article by Kingsley, Kaslow, Rinaldo, et al. (14 Feb. 1987), that I was even able to consider the two together.

14. In 1984 The Mine Shaft, a gay bar near New York's Village expanse of waterfront, sandwiched between various meatpacking companies, was closed down by the city. In the same month, the St. Mark's Baths, on St. Mark's Place between the then-Valencia Hotel (whose lobby up into the early 60s had housed the Five Spot, though now it was a hotdog stand) and the old site of the Strait Theater (where once, as a teenager, I had acted in a New York–based summer stock company, and where, a few years later, Allen Ginsberg and the Fugs had performed, though more recently it had become a vintage clothing store), was permanently shut. I was never a regular at either institution, though I had been to each more than ten times in somewhat more than twice that number of years. Sex was just as constant in both places as at the Variety, if not more so. There was, however, this difference—and the factor was a prime one in the closing of each establishment: The managements of both places, in their last months, allowed concerned gay male groups to institute safe sex demonstrations at both. I never saw them, but I certainly talked to friends who did; and there were reports of them in the *Village Voice* newspaper. These demonstrations were hands-on, explicit, and active—and by report very effective in changing the behavior of the men who went there.

Many people who have not directly encountered situations where sex is public and persistent assume that, because the activity is marginal, it must somehow take place outside all social constraints and cultural order. I would hazard, however, that the exact opposite is true. In a situation where one must deal, publicly and repeatedly, with the fear and the reality of rejection (and however dionysiac the situation gets, there is still, for almost everyone, more sexual rejection than acceptance involved), such behavior becomes almost immediately and insistently constrained, if not ritualized. These are intricate and multiple patterns of politeness—and indeed, ritualized rudeness—which I have never yet seen formally given the Irving Goffman treatment, but which are nevertheless firmly and formally in place.

But you must imagine the effect of a group of people in such a highly and responsively social field where sex is actually occurring all around them, explaining and demonstrating: If you do this, you will die; if you do this, you will live. I point out that it was from this time and these demonstrations that we get our current emphasis on condoms and the lack of exchange of body fluids. The demonstrations were murderously effective, nevertheless.

The response of the city was to close both institutions.

15. Need I point out that the safe sex demonstrations at the Baths and at The Mine Shaft were *not* in agreement with the street level of discourse: They encouraged the use of condoms during fellatio as well as during anal intercourse. Rimming was out. All three practices were viewed and discussed in these demonstrations as if their fibrillating distance from the axis of death was a real and material consideration against which a latex barrier must be erected at all costs.

16. By 1986 we had moved into a period when anal intercourse had shifted its rhetorical slot and was now discussed repeatedly as "high risk" behavior, often in a rhetorical context of "repeated sexual encounters." Let me also point out, in passing, that in 1984, when I was writing my novel, *any* suggestion at all that one mode of bodily sexual behavior was safer than another was considered totally irresponsible.

It is into this rhetorical field that a letter was published in JAMA (*Journal of the American Medical Association*) on April 4, 1986:

> *To the Editor:*
> The San Francisco Men's Health Study is a prospective study of a population-based random sample of single men 25 to 54 years of age residing in the 19 census tracts of San Francisco with the highest incident of acquired immunodeficiency syndrome. One thousand thirty-five eligible men were recruited. Participants visit the study clinic at six-month intervals, where they undergo a detailed medical and life-style interview and physical examination and provide specimens for laboratory study. Serological testing for AIDS-associated retrovirus (ARV) is performed on the cohort using the indirect fluorescent antibody technique. . . . Compared with men who had no sexual partners in the prior two-year period, the men who continued to engage in oral-genital contact only did not have an increased rate of infection by ARV. . . . Moreover, we found in a more detailed sexual practices interview at subsequent clinic visits that all of the 14 seropositive men had engaged in receptive

anal intercourse prior to June 1982. In contrast, only 24 of the 50 seronegative men in these two groups had engaged in previous receptive anal intercourse. . . . These results may not completely exclude the possibility of transmission of ARV infection by oral-genital contact because they are based on a
small number of observations. They do, however, show no excess risk of infection by this route and support the theory that anal-genital exposure is the
major mode of infection. An extended report describing the distribution of
sexual practices and ARV serology is in preparation.

David Lyman, MD
Univ. of California at Berkeley   *Warren Winkelstein, MD*

And eight months later, in February, the aforementioned Kingsley, Kaslow, Rinaldo, et al. study was published in *The Lancet.* The study is too
long to quote in full, though I recommend anyone interested in the correlation of sexual behavior to seroconversion to HIV positive read it. If I
may summarize and condense: Twenty-five hundred and eight homosexual men, who, at the beginning of the study tested negative for antibod-
ies to HIV, were monitored as to their sexual activity for six months. The
study states: "On multivariate analysis receptive anal intercourse was the
only significant risk factor for seroconversion to HIV . . ." (345) in the
ninety-eight men who, in the course of the study, developed HIV anti-
bodies. It also states:

> The absence of detectable risk for seroconversion due to receptive oral-
> genital intercourse is striking. That there were no seroconversions detected
> among 147 men engaging in receptive oral intercourse with at least one part-
> ner, but not receptive or insertive anal intercourse, accords with other data
> suggesting a low risk of infection from oral-genital (receptive semen) expo-
> sure. It must be mentioned that we were unable to determine the infection
> status of the sexual partners to whom these men were exposed. Perhaps these
> 147 men who practiced receptive oral intercourse were never or rarely ex-
> posed to HIV seropositive men. However, this explanation seems improbable.
> (348)

The question quickly becomes why this information has not been disseminated with anything like the intensity of various claims for heterosexual transmission such as the one quoted, or another one-time report, again from a letter, this time to *The Lancet* (15 Aug. 1987) rather
than to JAMA, about a one-time case (though nevertheless referred to
in several general readership newspapers as a "well documented case")
of woman-to-woman transmission through oral sex (Greenhouse) —

which sometimes seems the only use the medical establishment has for the lesbian community, a dismissal we can sadly recognize as typical.

Need we point out that one-time cases are not, by definition, well documented? We can only talk about meaningful documentation in the case where we begin with seronegativity and then, over a period of time, sexual behavior is carefully monitored, until seropositivity occurs; nor can such cases be meaningful until they are carried out at a reasonable statistical range, since there is always the possibility of error in monitoring even when the establishment of seronegativity occurs.

Last year, in the three months before the Variety Photoplays Theater was closed down by the city, I seriously contemplated xeroxing up several hundred copies of the Kingsley, Kaslow, Rinaldo, et al. study and leaving them in a pile in the lobby. That I did not is, I suspect, a procrastination I shall forever feel guilty about. When the *Daily News* reported the closing, it claimed that inspectors, over a two-day period, had observed "158 acts of unsafe sex."

I will attest, from personal experience, that the only sexual acts occurring in the theater at that time were fellatio and the varieties of mutual and solo masturbation. But the discursive structure that controls this rhetoric, the *Daily News'* and mine, is characterized precisely by its ability to move acts anywhere and everywhere along that uninflected line, sometime within days, sometime within hours, or even minutes. . . .

17. At some point, the mavens of straight talk must realize that there are two discourses: Their findings can be expressed in both street talk and straight talk—which are, after all, merely rhetorical expressions, and thus multi-discursive.

The first is a discourse for which the individual rhetorical figures that constitute it and are manipulated within it are generated by a series of operationalized procedures before they are admitted within its compass as "evidence." The second is a discourse of experience, where all is evidence though it does not depend on operationalized rhetorical sifting. An individual diagnosed with AIDS, who is then asked, "How did you get it?" or "What has your sexual behavior been over the last year or year and a half?" is, in his or her answer, speaking from and to the second discourse. Only a group of seronegative men and/or women who are asked to monitor in writing, daily, their sexual activity, and who are then tested for seropositivity, and whose monitored reports are compared with the results, can contribute evidence to the first.

Is there room for mistake—or for lying—in the operationalized discourse? Of course. But the operationalizing of its rhetoric is nevertheless an effective means of steering a course closer to what both you and I are probably more willing to stake our lives on, in terms of its findings.

If these discourses are not kept separate, then we must be forever cursed with the murderous contradiction, in official discourse (or straight talk) so far, that all the monitored studies strongly suggest that it is difficult or impossible to transmit AIDS orally, while perfectly learnéd statements flood society, all stating, equally unequivocally, that AIDS can be transmitted by any and every sexual act involving an interchange of bodily fluids—all of them based on individual, after-diagnosis requests for origins, even though street rhetoric ("You can't get AIDS from sucking dick") has already polluted the concepts of all "high risk" behavior (i.e., anal sex and needle sharing), so that practically no one on the street will admit to any interest in either at all anymore, with or without a condom, with or without sterilization.

To the official question, "What has your sexual activity been for the past few years?" straight talk takes the myriad answers given by persons with AIDS, in all their discomfort or certainty—

"Mostly sucking, I guess."

"I only suck. Why do I have it?"

"Let's see—all I remember is sucking dick."

"No, I'd never take it up the ass. That's dangerous, I know that. Everybody knows that. I won't even suck: And if I do, I spit out and wash my mouth out right afterwards with Scope."

"Nothing that ought to make me come down with this shit!"

"It doesn't really matter, since I got it—probably getting head from some prostitute."

—and the myriad answers given by men and women who often inhabit a world of borderlines, lines laid out very differently from where the straight world might place them, and conflates these answers into an official statement, "AIDS can be passed through fellatio," complete, in many cases, with statistics on the number of people who have so caught it.

The law of discourses, like the law of genres, is that "Discourses are not to be mixed." (It is, of course, the same law.) And, as with the law of genres, the truth of the law is that it can never be obeyed: like genres, discourses never arrive pure. The problem with individuating discourses and genres is simply the macro-version of the problem of individuating meanings. The signified can only—at times—appear to be unitary.

Yet the conflation of discursively operationalized rhetoric with unoperationalized rhetoric, both taken as equally weighted evidence, has produced the current discourse of AIDS—provisionally, locally, and at this historical moment, a demonstrably murderous discourse, vigorously employed by the range of conservative forces promulgating the anti-sexual stance that marks so much of this era, a discourse of "high risk" and "low risk" behavior, rather than the dicta of street talk: "Don't get fucked up the ass without a condom. Don't use anyone else's works." Today, instead, the range of chatter and disinformation moves through all the modes of street talk and straight talk ("Use a condom for all sexual acts"), obscuring and occluding precision, articulation, and the possibility for life.

18. The range of discourses—and the rhetoric that falls out of them—must be listened to, and listened to carefully, if only to suggest further operationalized studies. But to give conclusions drawn from unoperationalized rhetoric the same weight as such studies, while lacking their outcomes, is a discursive crime at one with murder. And the range of our society, from highest to lowest, is guilty of that crime, on the grounds of what we say about AIDS.

19. Are we speaking of something that can, if one wishes, simply be called the scientific method? No. We are speaking, rather, of what happens to such a "method" in a field ripe with and riddled by despair and terror and prior political agendas that flagrantly, at all levels, abnegate that method, in a kind of wager far more immediate, if not more desperate, than the one Pascal so famously conceived: "If 'Don't get fucked up the ass without a condom' is safe, perhaps 'Don't do anything without a condom' is safer." But because the latter is far harder to follow, it militates instead for laxness; and to the extent that the two are perceived as somehow the same, the laxness finally infects the former.

But—to borrow an always already impure rhetoric—unless these discourses can be kept separate long enough to do more studies and to disseminate their results, nothing officially said about AIDS can be accepted as straight. All is twisted—and is deadly.

20. Which brings us to the ticklish question of women and AIDS. There is a kind of utopian desire to see AIDS as equally dangerous to women as to men. And without question, in its transmission through the use of IV needles, it is. Without question, in receptive anal intercourse, women are just as susceptible to AIDS as men. Whether AIDS can or cannot be passed to women vaginally, I, personally, have never heard discussed on the street, nor have I yet seen a monitored study to find out. The notion that AIDS is unlikely to be passed on by women in ordinary heterosexual vaginal intercourse sounds like another anatomical decree or gender powerlessness.

Do we really need another one?

What I have found in an informal survey of books on women and AIDS is that one can peruse volume after volume purportedly addressing women and AIDS in which anal intercourse is not mentioned; volume after volume in which *no* inflection in the contagion rates between oral and anal intercourse is suggested. The assumption would seem to be that women's bodies in sexual terms are nothing but vaginas—and that these totally vaginated bodies can never be looked at, monitored, or tabulated. We simply have another major situation of sexual/gender oppression to deal with, its thrust overwhelmingly toward heterosexually active women.

Although there is a discourse, controlling vast amounts of AIDS anxiety among gay males, in which, yes, my California friend's association still resonates, there is also a level of street discourse that has more or less wrestled with that anxiety from 1983 onward, and through which the straight rhetoric of the medical journals only now and again transpares.

It is of course straight discourse that is wholly entailed in the model I began this paper by describing. I shall repeat that description here: At one side of it rises the axis of death. The discourse is a totally continuous and uninflected curve that shoots across that deadly locus at "one"; that is, it is stopped by and absorbed by death at that terrifying and totalized point of unity. From there, the curve flows toward the base axis of life— but a life that is wholly and ideally secure, rich in pleasure, close to immobile: That is to say that above all things, this particular biotic axial is "safe." The axis of death cleaves the space bearing with it a mythology similar to that with which the axis of the real cleaves the plane of complex numbers. The axis of life carries across its space an equally rarefied mythology suggesting nothing so much as the axis of the imaginary that transects the complex plane. The discourse approached that lively, that imaginary axis asymptotically, yearningly, steadily, endlessly. . . .

For by now I hope we can recognize the rhetorical symptoms of this discourse: "High risk behavior" and "low risk behavior" define a discursive substratum where *all* sexual behavior becomes more or less dangerous, and all is subject to endless displacement and slippage along that discursive slope, now nearer to, now further from, death; in "repeated sexual encounters," a kind of inflation of pleasure brings one somehow more and more mysteriously close to infection and annihilation (in Kingsley, Kaslow, Rinaldo, et al., at least eight of the men who seroconverted had only a single anal receptive encounter). Symptoms include such phrases as "AIDS is everybody's problem," from the latest circular from my own university's so well-intentioned AIDS committee, a circular that does not go on to distinguish what *kind* of problem it is for different people—a tax problem here, a whole range of medical problems for a whole range of other people there; a whole range of specifically sexual problems, both for people who are in bed with each other and who are wondering what to do next, as well as for people who are wondering if they are ever going to end up in bed with anyone again. In short, the rhetorical symptoms of this discourse are not a set of political intentions but rather the signs of a discourse that, from whatever political position, homogenizes the problem instead of inflecting it; that assigns people and actions, sexual and social, positions on that unproblematic and uninflected line running from life to death—until the establishment of quarantines, curfews, and deathcamps. And I am convinced that a later age will look back on this one and respond to these rhetorical moves that scatter so many of our texts today; it will read them with the kind of mute horror with which we read the anti-semitic rhetoric that proliferated through Germany in particular and Europe in general all through the '30s and '40s.

21. Let me conclude with another piece of street rhetoric, another bit of street discourse.

Because, in various talks, I have been saying much what I am saying here for two years now, I felt it was incumbent upon me to have an HIV test and check out my own, aging body. Since I have been at the University of Massachusetts for a bit over a year and a half now, with only occasional visits to New York, my sexual encounters, in the city, all of them oral (semen receptive), without condoms, and the vast majority among strangers (I last got fucked well over twelve years ago), have certainly fallen off: A conservative estimate would be three hundred a year between 1977 and 1983; that falls down to about a hundred-fifty a year till I left for Massachusetts in 1988; that has then a bit more than halved, to somewhere between forty and sixty-five a year since. Four months ago, on a visit to the city, I availed myself of the city's HIV testing facilities. Four months ago, I was seronegative.

But now we must move to a discursive analysis of this very classically rhetorical ploy, for—despite its truth claims—it is nothing more.

In no way am I asking anyone to change his or her behavior on the strength of ways I have or have not behaved. What I am asking is that all of us begin to put forward the monumental analytical effort, in whichever rhetorical mode we choose, needed not to interpret what we say, but to say what we *do*. That requires first and foremost speaking with others *about* what we do. That is the only way that we can destroy the discursive disarticulation that muffles and muddles all, that drags all into and within it, that represses and suppresses and lies and distorts and rereads and rewrites any and every rhetorical moment within its field.

Rhetoric *can* control discourse—but only if it is insistent, accurate, analytical, and articulate.

—Amherst
February 19, 1990

WORKS CITED

Delany, Samuel R. "The Tale of Plagues and Carnivals." 1984. *Flight From Neveryon.* New York: Bantam, 1985.

Greenhouse, Peter. Letter. *The Lancet* 15 Aug. 1987: 401-02.

Kingsley, Lawrence A., Richard Kaslow, Charles R. Rinaldo, Jr., et al. "Risk Factors for Seroconversion to Human Immunodeficiency Virus Among Male Homosexuals: Results from the Multicenter AIDS Cohort Study." *The Lancet* 14 Feb. 1987: 345-48.

Lyman, David, MD, and Warren Winkelstein, MD. Letter. "Minimal Risk of Transmission of AIDS-Associated Retrovirus Infection Oral-Genital Contact." *Journal of the American Medical Association* 4 Apr. 1986. Rpt. in *The AIDS Reader: Documentary History of a Modern Epidemic.* Ed. Loren K. Clarke and Malcolm Potts. Vol. 1. Boston: Branden, 1988. 261.

Quine, W. V. *The Philosophy of Logic.* Engleside Cliffs, NJ: Prentice, 1970.

Spitzler, Peter G., MD, and Neil J. Weiner, MD. Letter. "Transmission of HIV Infection from a Woman to a Man by Oral Sex." *New England Journal of Medicine* 320.4 (1989): 251.

3

On the Unspeakable

[The Capri Theater, Times Square, 1987]

the positioning of desire that always draws us to "The Unspeakable" in the first place.

It is an area, a topic, a trope impossible to speak of outside (it is at once evil and extralinguistic) that range, equally difficult to describe, to define: "The Everyday." (*It* is at once banal and representationally difficult.) Both are terribly localized. Both are wholly and socially bounded. The division between everyday and unspeakable, difficult and extralinguistic, banal and evil may just be the prototype for all social division.

We need something from the everyday, then, of a 45-year-old black, gay male who cruises the commercial porn theaters along Eighth Avenue above 43rd Street in New York City (the "Author") in the middle and late 1980s: Why not this?

Rose is a pudgy, white, working class prostitute, maybe twenty-six, from Upstate New York; she's also a cracker—which means that for

to clear away the pre-cum leakage, raise his thumb to his mouth, and suck it clean. After three minutes, his hips began to lift in little twitches. He had both hands on his cock now. He shot in a couple or three four-inch spurts that fell, shiny as snot from a November sneeze, down the knuckles of both hands. He raised one and thrust the backs of three fingers into his mouth, turned them over, and sucked away the cum. Then he lifted the other, to lick more off, this time delicately. His tongue reached out pointed, but became broader, slugging slowly between one and the next knuckle, bright with saliva and semen in the video's flicker he still stared at.

That's when the old P.R. beside him woke up long enough to give him a frown.

The white kid jumped a little, rearing to the side, in a hyperbolic moment of fear. (Hyperbole is the figure of the everyday; euphemism is the figure of the unspeakable.)

the last few months she's seldom gone for more than ten dollars a trick, since her interests have dwindled pretty much to the next bottle of rocks—a hyperbole if there ever was one: the "bottle," a plastic capsule a shy centimeter long, stoppered at one end with something like they put in the top of Bic pens; the "rocks," about half a crystal of rock salt's worth of cooked-down coke broken up into smaller bits. Cost per bottle anywhere from six to ten dollars. Eight is average. The long-time professional hookers working the winter Strip outside have lost all patience with the new breed of "ten dollar whore" crack has created— many of them only fifteen, sixteen, and seventeen years old.

(The meaning of the following exterior urban portrait is entirely in terms of what it tells us of this momentary travesty of theatrical interiority.)

The last three years have seen a radical atmospheric and economic shift along the Strip from the fallout of the cocaine trade—crack, base, eightballs. It's part of the slowly gathering economic devastation of the entire neighborhood, which is presumably preparing the way for the brave new rebuilding as a large shopping mall, with a few theaters and business towers, scheduled to begin next year: grocery stores, comic-book stores, shoe repair shops, drugstores, barbershops, bookstores, theatrical lighting and make-up stores, the magic

But he gave the guy a look that said, "Say something to me, motherfucker, and I'll bust you!" There was a wholly macho aspect to his exhibitionism.

The old guy shook his head, leaned back against the wall, and closed his eyes again.

The kid went back to licking, moved to the inside of his wrist. With the edge of one thumb he squeegeed up some clam of cum that had fallen on his denim thigh, ate that, and examined his lap and green workshirt for any he'd missed. With a few more tugs he milked his cock of its final freight; then, with the hugely circular tongue maneuver five-year-olds reserve for dripping cones, he lapped the last from his first.

(The above, observed purely as information—his actions and his dress and his bearing, from politeness to belligerence—tell only of what is exterior to this tightly conventionalized and wholly contained commercial, public space.)

Watching him, I found it easy to see the entire non-white audience around him—macho, male, a scattering of prostitutes, of transsexuals, of faggots, and largely there for drugs and the safest of safe sex—as an analogue for the whole of American (if not of Western) civilization. I found it equally easy to see the trio of whites—Rose, Red, and the young worker (again sucking one finger and the next, now on his left hand, now on his right, for any lingering taste)—as

shop, souvlaki and hotdog and pizza stands, hardware stores, liquor stores, drugstores, cafeterias, coffee shops, and the second story rehearsal studios and the dry cleaners—the human services that, along the ground-floor fronts of the two- and three-story buildings (now deemed wholly unprofitable for the Towering City), scattered among the porn shops, peepshows, sex palaces and fuck-film houses, once kept the area alive and livable for a considerable residence—have been boarded up or shut down.

"The crackers are drivin' out the cookies," has been the call on the street for a year, now. ('Cookie' refers to the bent spoon or bottlecap in its hairpin holder—the cooker—with which heroin users traditionally boil up a fix, as 'crack' refers to the faint Rice Krispie crackle of the burning rocks as they heat to an orange glow in the screened-off end of the sooty glass tube through which the drug's inhaled.) But the crack trade, far vaster, cheaper, more visible, and more visibly damaging than the heroin traffic once was, is only part of the general decline.

This is the Strip: this is the neighborhood that, like numerous neighborhoods before it (Cannery Row, Farrell's or Bellow's Chicago, Runyon's Broadway) yearns to become a metaphor for the whole great American outside. There is no retreat/advance except within.

Rose was dozing in the ninth row of the balcony of the Capri

an analogue of whites and white culture within that American/ Western complex. Perhaps the major appeal of the analogy was that the reversal, the subversion, the overturning of more usual analogical alignments of primitive and sophisticated, of white and non-white, initiated (at least momentarily) its own critique of precisely the failures of such racially analogic thinking (the overriding characteristic of the culture it symbolized) in the first place.

The kid watched the movie a few more minutes; finally he pushed his cock back into his jeans and zipped up. A minute later, he stood and wandered to the balcony door to go down.

"Man," Rose was saying to Red (she'd already said it now as many times as she'd said "Huh?" before), "what the fuck is he gonna come bother me for if he ain't got no money? That ain't right. I gotta get me some money. What does he think I am?" Still half asleep, Red was rubbing between Rose's legs now—his reparation for sitting beside her, offering what protection he can while she sleeps or works. "Man, what the fuck is he gonna come bothering me for if he ain't got no money, you hear what I'm saying . . . ?"

This interior?

All three whites there—or perhaps just the relationship between them (its cultural, analogical richness)—I found, on one level or another, sexually attractive: both guys

porno theater on Eighth Ave. just below 46th Street, beside Red, one-time pimp, now wino and cracker, a scrawny guy with a medicine ball of dirty red hair, his winter-burned hands alight with the translucent bloat of the permanently under-nourished alcoholic.

Red was half asleep too, but now and again he'd scratch himself, pawing down inside the front of his jeans, clawing at his hip, bending to get at an ankle inside the double pair of sweaty tube socks I can smell from where I'm sitting a row in front of them to the left, now thrusting a hand through the neck of his sweater to rake out an armpit. Rose and Red were the only two whites visible among the young to middle-aged black and Hispanic men; here and there, long, forbidden flames from red, blue, and yellow Bic lighters, turned up high, played along glass stems. The smell of the drug—a burnt plastic stench, besides which the spicy odor of pot seems healthy and organic—welled here, fell away there, or drifted across the flickering video projection at the front of the narrow theater.

Three rows down from Rose and Red, a guy in a black and white checked scarf with tassels was giv-ing a blowjob to another guy, who leaned back staring through wire-framed glasses more at the ceiling than at the porn movie. Someone else was bending down between the seats, looking around with his lighter—and had been for ten min-

physically so, Rose intellectually so. But that, of course, is where I find myself at the particular boundary of the everyday that borders the unspeakable, where language, like a needle infected with articulation, threatens to pierce some ultimate and final interiority—however un-clear, as we approach it, that limit is (if not what lies beyond it) when we attempt analytic seizure.

The lack of clarity is, of course, what is there to be analyzed, artic-ulated.

The unspeakable.

The unspeakable is, of course, not a boundary dividing a positive area of allowability from a com-plete and totalized negativity, a boundary located at least one step beyond the forbidden (and the forbidden, by definition—no?—*must* be speakable if its proscriptive power is to function). If we pursue the boundary as such, it will recede before us as a limit of mists and va-pors. Certainly it is not a line drawn in any absolute way across speech or writing. It is not a fixed and locable point of transgression that glows hotter and brighter as we approach it till, as we cross it, its searing heat burns away all pos-sibility of further articulation.

Rather it is a set of positive con-ventions governing what can be spoken of (or written about) in general; in particular, it comprises the endlessly specialized tropes (of analysis, of apology, of aesthetic distance) required to speak or write about various topics at vari-

utes now—for any rocks that might have fallen on the floor between the cigarette butts and the soda bottles and the beer cans and the spit and the trickles of urine from the guys four and three and nine rows back, too lazy or too frustrated to go down to the john (which was always filled with five or six guys in the middle of a drug deal, anyway), and the dried and not-yet-dried cum puddles. Someone else pushed his rolled screen from one end of his stem to the other with a wooden stick to collect the melted residues from the glass sides for another impoverished hit.

The effects of the drug are kind of like a popper that lasts four minutes instead of forty seconds. Though it has no long-term withdrawal effects, it's got the worst come-down—between three and six hours of depressed headache, nausea, and achiness—this side of airplane glue. And its addiction schedule is fierce. Intermittent use over three months will hook you. And, as far as I can see, use on six consecutive days will make someone an addict.

Someone else was moving up and down in his seat, quickly, rhythmically, shoulders shaking in a masturbatory frenzy. I'd passed him five minutes back: He'd pulled his pants off, balled them up, and put them and his coat in the seat beside him, so no one would sit next to him while he beat off.

In a man's down jacket clutched

ous anomalous places in our complex social geography—places where such topics are specifically not usually (or ever) spoken of: What is speakable between client and accountant is unspeakable between newly introduced acquaintances at a formal dinner party. (What about the unspeakable as drug? Its history comprises laudanum, opium, heroin, and now crack. The unspeakable as drug becomes the epoch's romantic metaphor.) What is speakable between client and prostitute in the balcony of a 42nd Street porn theater is unspeakable between man and wife of thirty years. What is speakable between lovers of three weeks is unspeakable between best friends of a decade—and vice versa. What is speakable between a magazine essayist and an audience concerned with art and analysis is unspeakable between a popular journalist and an audience concerned with "everyday" news.

And there are a dozen people I—or you—might tell the story of Red, Rose, and the unnamed semenophage.

"Unspeakable," then, is always a shorthand for "unspeakable unless accompanied by especially pressing rhetorical considerations" (The unspeakable is as much about cruelty as it is about sexuality. Indeed, for many of us it is where they meet): I don't know how to tell you this, but . . . (The unspeakable comprises the wounds

around her with folded arms, an anorexically thin black woman with missing teeth leaned over me to smile: "You want company . . . ?" Then, recognizing me for gay, she grinned, shrugged, and whispered, "Oh . . . !" and hurried on. Oblivious, Rose opened her eyes. "Man, I'm itchin', too," she told Red: "You wanna scratch my back . . . ?"

Red finished his own clawing and turned to Rose with a grunt and a couple of bewildered sighs. Without really looking up, he rubbed the side of Rose's navy sweatshirt.

"No," Rose said. "Underneath."

So Red put his hand under the frayed cloth and rubbed. Rose twisted in the seat. "Hard, man. Yeah, there. Hard. Like that. This is killin' me!"

Not looking any more awake, Red leaned his full hundred-thirty pounds (five of which is hair) into her, rubbing, raking.

"That's it," Rose said, her back toward him. "Go on. Keep it up, man."

In down jacket and knitted watch cap, another white guy pushed through the fellows hanging around the balcony door. Husky, good-looking, between eighteen and twenty-three, he could be an apprentice starting at one of the construction sites further up, in from Long Island and just off work—or he could be a working-class student from one of the city's outlying colleges. Look-

on the bodies of abused children, their mutilations and outrageous shrieking or tight-lipped murders at the hands of parents); I have something I really have to explain to you . . . (It is certainly any pleasure at such abuses, even private, pornographic, onanistic); Allow me to make a special point here . . . (It is civil or political prisoners tortured or slowly slaughtered by ideologues or their hire); You mustn't take it personally, but . . . (It is the uncritical conjunction in the mind of certain social critics of pornography and such pleasure— a conjunction that dissolves with any real experiences of the range of current, commercial pornography or the real practices of practicing sadists and masochists—that makes the pornographic unspeakable, beyond any rhetorical redemption, impossible to apologize for); Now, this may sound very cruel, but I feel I just have to say . . .

Quotability always allows, at least as a limit case, the everyday journalist to quote the unspeakable artistic and/or analytic text. (What he cannot do—what remains, for the journalist, unspeakable, save through an analytical raid among the esthetic figures of analysis, of apology, esthetic distance—is tease apart for his everyday audience the boundary, the gap between probe and presentation, between interpretation and representation, between analysis and art.) It is as if we must establish two columns, with everything

ing around the aisle, he made toward Rose and Red as only one white can seek out another in the dark sea. Sitting two seats away from where Rose still swayed under Red's rubbing, for a minute the new guy looked at the dull, near colorless picture down on the screen; now and again he glanced at the pair to his left.

Finally, he turned in his seat, smiled openingly, leaned toward rocking Rose, and asked: "Can you use another hand?"

Not looking from under the bronze blades of her hair, Rose said: "Huh?"

"Can you use another hand?"

"Huh?" Rose still didn't look up.

"Can you use another hand?"

She looked now. (Red went on scratching.) "What'd you say?"

The kid was good-natured, pleased with himself:

"I said, 'Can you use another hand?'"

Because there were new words in the sentence, Rose was back to the beginning of her befuddlement. "Huh?" She grimaced, with eyes already pretty much swollen closed.

(This much repetition is, of course, narratively unacceptable, aesthetically unspeakable: Its only excuse is accuracy of transcription; its only meaning is the patient persistence of it: Repetition, said Freud, is desire.)

The guy repeated: "Can you use another hand?"

"Huh?"

of one mode relegated to one side and everything of the other relegated to the other.

It's as if we had to figure the impossibility of such a task, such a split, such a gap—figure it in language—rather than write of it, speak of it.

To speak the unspeakable without the proper rhetorical flourish or introduction; to muff that flourish, either by accident, misjudgment, or simple ignorance; to choose the wrong flourish or not choose any (i.e., to choose the flourish called "the literal") is to perform the unspeakable.

Many of us are not taught the proper rhetorical flourishes that allow us to say anything anywhere: How to tell your parents you're gay. How to tell your boss you want a raise. Having said any of these unspeakable things, that's no guarantee it will produce the effects we want. But the fear of reprisals (or failure) becomes one with the ignorance of how to say it. This is a form of oppression.

The history of the unspeakable descends most recently from the unprintable—from forties and fifties America when certain words would render a text "outside the law"—an interesting metaphor, as what the metaphor's exclusionary force actually once indicated was that, upon containing such words, a text became a privileged object *of* the law.

The metaphor was the underside of a system whose major thrust

"Can you use another hand?" His tone of whispered goodwill did not vary.

Rose pulled herself up, tugged the front of her sweat shirt down (it rode up from her belly right away because behind her Red was still rubbing). "You got any money?" she asked, finally, voice raucous and bitter.

The kid shook his head, laughing a little, not as a negative answer but just to acknowledge the suggestion's preposterousness. She can sell the niggers and spics around them ten dollar blowjobs, he was thinking, but not him. (Even he is unaware that Rose will go for five.) He turned back to look at the movie. Then, after another minute, he stood. Feeling along where foam rubber pushed between the metal backs, with their chipped maroon paint the color of his knitted cap, and the torn corduroy of the seat cushions, he edged to the aisle.

A few rows down, on the other side of the balcony, were three sets of two chairs apiece, all occupied except one at the front, before the iron balcony rail. Beside the free seat, in a black bomber jacket, fur collar up and white hair awry, an older Puerto Rican slept against the wall. The white kid moved down the aisle, looking left and right, like the eyes of a reader sweeping back and forth in their descent along the columnar text. (The unspeakable is always in the column you are not reading. At any

was protective. That which was within the law—people, actions, texts, property—were protected by the law. What was outside the law was attacked, detained, impounded, exploited, and punished by the law. The boundary was between a passive surveillance in the name of protection and an active aggression in the name of retribution.

The notion that anyone should clearly and committedly believe in the absolute locatability of such a boundary is, for many of us (if not most of us), unspeakable. Yet we function as if such a boundary were lucid, absolute, and unquestionably everyday.

The everyday and the unspeakable are only the linguistic—the 'social,' in its most limited sense—shadows of this legalistic system: the passive surveillance and the aggressive attack of the law spoken of, written of (figured) as an inside and an outside.

In many cases, desire lies like a bodily boundary between the everyday and the unspeakable. In some circles it is unspeakable to call men feminists: they may be "feminist sympathizers," but a "male feminist" is as much a contradiction in terms (as well as a sign of the most naive political co-optation on the part of any woman who accepts the term) as a "white black-militant." In other circles—American academe, for example—it is common parlance. In some circles it would be unspeakable to

given moment it is what is on the opposite side of the Möbius text at the spot your own eyes are fixed on. The unspeakable is mobile; it flows; it is displaced as much by language and experience as it is by desire.) Reaching the empty chair, the guy hesitated, pushed his lower lip over his upper a moment in thought; but the Puerto Rican really seemed out of it.

So he sat down beside him and unzipped his coat.

Tugging his belt open (like a text that loops and seals upon itself, without commencement or termination, the unspeakable lies in the silence, beyond the white space that accompanies the text, across the marginal blank that drops opaquely beside the text toward a conclusionary absence that finally is not to be found), unsnapped his jeans, pulled down his fly, and parked his Reeboks on the lower metal rail. Tugging his cock out from the side of his briefs, he moved it from one fist to another and back a few times, before he began to jerk. From where I sat, across the aisle and a row behind, the head above thumb and forefinger looked like a Barbie-doll hard-hat. His upward tug was clearly the business one; downward was just to get his fist back to where he could pull up. Now and again he'd rub the thumb of his free hand across his cock's crown

suggest that commercial pornographic films are relatively less sexist than the commercial non-pornographic cinema. Yet this is certainly the way in which they strike me. (However minuscule their plots, they have a higher proportion of female to male characters; they show more women holding more jobs and a wider variety of jobs; they show more women instigating sex; they show a higher proportion of friendships between women; and they show far less physical violence against women than do the commercial films made for the same sociological audience. Their particular didactic message about the sexual act *per se* is that "the normal sex act" should include cunnilingus, fellatio, male superior, and female superior position; anything else is perceived as a diversion from this norm.) But it is precisely this rhetorical frame that makes such an analysis—here—speakable, precisely as it makes speakable the analysis of the sociology of pornography (in the literal sense of writing about prostitutes) that is to follow. The positioning of desire is a result of social power. But the content of desire does not contain—the way a mirror contains—social power, in image or in reality. (What it contains, if anything other than itself, is that tiny part of the freedom of language associated with abjection.) Indeed, it is

4

Coming / Out

In the twenty-seven years since the 1969 Stonewall riots, "coming out" has acquired extraordinary significance in the gay community—so much significance that many of us might even say coming out "defines" the difference between being gay and an older, pre-gay notion of being homosexual. Through much of that quarter-century-plus, when, if you hadn't "come out of the closet," many gay men and lesbians felt you had somehow betrayed them, that you couldn't really "define yourself as gay," that you had not "accepted your gay identity," I found myself faced with a paradox: Much of my critical enterprise over that same period had been devoted to showing that such "defining" or "identifying" events (when, as a reader, you first became aware of science fiction; when, as a child, you realized you were black, gay, or an artist) simply did not "define" anything.

In the gradual, continual, and constantly modulating process of becoming who we are, all events take their meanings, characteristic or uncharacteristic, from the surrounding event field in which they occur. While certainly they contribute to what we are or are becoming, single events simply do not carry the explicative strength "definition" and "identity" denote. This is not to say some events aren't more important than others.

Recently I had a discussion with a woman who, some years back, had been a catcher in a circus aerial act. "Well," she said, "I see what you mean. But I remember the moment my partner fell. It completely changed my life. We were in the middle of a performance in Las Vegas. I didn't drop her—I'm rather touchy about that. She was swinging around, hanging from a hand-loop attached to the trapeze. To steady her, I was fronting the bar—my term for balancing horizontally on my pelvis on a still trapeze. We were just getting ready for the finale. The loop broke and she flew out, still on her side—and went down. She landed on the concrete, almost thirty feet below. No, she wasn't killed.

But she shattered her elbow, broke her arm, and bruised herself from head to foot. From that moment on, I just couldn't be an aerialist again. I formed another act with my boyfriend immediately, where he was the catcher this time. I guess it was to prove to myself that I *hadn't* changed. But three weeks later, after three more performances, I quit." She sighed. "I missed the circus for the next ten years. But my life just wasn't the same after the accident as it was before."

"I didn't say that what happens in a single moment can't *change* your life," I told her. "I said that it doesn't *define* your life. What made that moment have the meaning for you that it did was your previous years of training as an acrobat, as an aerialist, the circus tradition; it was the medical emergency that followed, the severity of your partner's injuries, the response of the people around you—all that makes such an occurrence as overwhelmingly significant as it was. The fact that you did go up again, and also that you missed the circus for so long, once you left, shows how much *wasn't* changed in spite of the very real change that *did* occur."

It's a subtle but important difference.

My friend agreed.

All the incidents I am going to recount—none so dramatic as my aerialist friend's adventure—changed my life. But they changed it in small, distinct ways. None of them marked a before or after point, distinguishing absence from presence. Rather, each is notable because it *was* a point of change, a point where what was present before was still present, only in rearranged form.

I

My second summer camp was as wonderfully rich and pleasant (I was ten) as my first had been nightmarish. The boys in the senior camp area were housed just beyond a small hill, the Knoll, in a clearing in the trees, the Tent Colony. To one side was a plank-walled, black-brown shack with a slant roof: the boys' john. Inside were two wooden-stalled showers, two wooden-stalled commodes, sinks, and urinals. Outside, just left of the door, against the creosoted planks and above a splatter of gravel, the steel basin (that let the water fall out the bottom onto the stones) leaned askew. A water fountain's rusted spigot thrust up from it, with an ancient spring-knob to turn it on.

Around a twenty-five- or thirty-yard clearing, set in pairs, were the wooden platforms and frames over which, for the summer, orange or olive drab canvas tents were put up to house the young male campers: two tents for Bunk Five, two tents for Bunk Six, two tents for Bunk Seven, two tents for Bunk Eight, and, finally, completing the circle on the other side of the john—two for storage of extra beds and mattresses. At least that was the ideal arrangement, but sometimes the vagaries of enrollment moved things around. The other interruption to this pattern was geographical: The far corner of the colony dipped steeply, so that the Bunk Seven tents were practically out of sight of the others.

1953, the summer the Korean War ended and my second summer at Woodland (I was eleven now), began with a major disappointment. I and some of my friends from the previous summer were assigned the same tents beside the john for Bunk Six as we had been in, the year before, for Bunk Five. The camp's logic and folklore was that the younger you were, the closer they wanted you to the bathroom. The extra eight- or nine-yard walk across the worn grass and gravel was to be a mark of our one year's seniority, our new maturity—and now it had been denied. We sulked as we put away our clothes in the wooden cubbies beside our beds, newly made up with olive drab army blankets.

Two days after our arrival, however, on a windy and rainy July 3, after we'd hiked down the cindery road in our rain gear to the recreation and dining hall for breakfast, while we were eating our oatmeal and pancakes, the weather blew up into a windstorm. In our green ponchos and yellow slickers, we crowded to the door to stand at the top of the high wooden steps and gaze out, laughing and daring each other to descend to the cinders and gravel, on each side of which branches snapped and quivered as torrential gusts slated the wading pool–sized puddles before the deluge salted them over with froth.

The rain stopped. The wind lessened.

But when we got back to the Tent Colony and the six of us Bunk Sixers (in the old Bunk Five tent) started across the clearing, we saw something wrong.

A tree had blown down, to fall across the tent's roof and smash the two-by-four that held up the peak. Our counselor, Roy, announced that we should stay a good twenty feet away from it. One small, angry camper, Noah, began to argue that he had valuable things in there that needed to be taken out. Now! Though I did not say it, I felt much the same. My violin was in there. The rest of us argued with Noah: Suppose the tent collapsed further while he was inside? No one *should* go in, at least till the fallen tree was removed.

"Now *don't* go in there!" were Roy's last words as he sprinted away toward the Tent Colony entrance to get some assistance. The moment he was gone, little Noah uttered a harsh, "Fuck *him!*" marched up to the half-collapsed tent, and pushed within the skew orange flap, to emerge a few moments later with his microscope, a box of slides, and his camera.

"You're crazy," a stolid camper named Dave declared. "You know that? You're really crazy."

"Well, I just didn't want anything to happen to *this*," Noah declared, "while they were fooling around with the tree."

Once the order was breached, however, we all drifted closer to check things out.

Bathtubs of rainwater filled the bellied-down canvas. Leaves floated in it. The tree itself had lodged securely. None of the tent canvas was actually torn, save a six-inch rip at one corner where weathered wood thrust through. A heavy, sensible kid named Billy shoved first at this part, then leaned on another. Nothing budged. Beneath the canvas, the shape the broken two-by-fours had fallen into was stable.

"I'm going to look inside, too," I said.

I stepped up through the front flap. Inside, weighted with all that water, the canvas pressed my bed, held up by my cubby beside it. Through canvas, a watery light deviled the shadows. The fabric smell was far more intense than it had been in the past two nights we'd slept there. Flush with the weighted tent, part off and part on my cubby, was my violin case.

Crouching and holding the edge of one, I squat-walked between two beds to see that the cubby corner had punctured the case's bottom. I tried to tug the case free. With hundreds of gallons of water above it, however, it wouldn't move.

In what condition, I wondered, was the violin?

Outside I went back down the platform steps. In minutes, Roy came back with the camp director and Mr. Herdmen, from the farm down the hillside.

Over the next hour, with block and tackle, the tree was removed from the tent roof, and it was decided that our group would relocate, along with one of the other bunks. We would get what, last year, had been the Bunk Seven tents, down in the depression at the Tent Colony's corner— even *further* from the john than the Bunk Six tents! The remaining Bunk Five tents would be used for storage; the old storage tent would now become the counselors' "day off" tent. It was a vindication and a reward Nature had engineered to compensate us for the indignity of the camp's shortsightedness.

Throughout the rest of the morning, we dragged trunks and remade beds. In the collapsed tent, the water was pushed out of the canvas, so that it roared and splattered over the tent ropes. I got my violin case out, took it down to my new tent, and, on my new bed, opened it.

The bridge's feet had stamped two tiny rectangular holes through the face—as the bridge itself had snapped. The strings lay loose. A seven-inch crack split the face.

I lifted the instrument from blue plush and turned it over. The cubby corner had gone through the black case bottom and punctured a right-angle crack in the back of the varnished wood. Short of major repair, it was unplayable.

The day's relocation meant Roy had to be down at the camp office a lot. The wind settled. The sun came out. The morning grew warmer. And, in our new tent out of sight in the dell, we were left unsupervised.

It was stolid Dave who suggested, "Hey, let's all gang up on somebody—and have a fight!"

"Yeah, sure!" declared Noah. We all felt the thrill of possible victimization—like a great Russian roulette game.

"Yeah, but who's it gonna be?" I asked.

"We're gonna gang up on . . ." In the middle of the tent floor, between the bunk beds, Dave turned slowly. ". . . *him!*" He pointed to short, heavy Billy.

Who cried out, ". . . *Hey!*"

Relieved, the rest of us threw ourselves on Billy, who began to shout: "Come on—cut it out! Now, *stop* it! Stop!"

It was also Dave who yelled: "Let's make him suck our dicks!"—a camper who, before or afterwards, I never had any reason to think was other than straight.

"Yeah!" agreed Joel, another big camper, in the midst of the fray.

Like me, Joel wore glasses. Like me, Joel was black. Like me, Joel was light enough that you might not have noticed it. It was signaled only by the broad nose and the tight curl to his brown hair, above a bony, even horse-like face, that, on someone older, could have spoken of a truly interesting character. Also Joel was a bad nail-biter.

Once Dave had articulated the game's goal, over the first thirty seconds I noticed the increased avidity, a level or two higher than anyone else's, with which Joel threw himself into it. In the crush of the six of us, pushing protesting Billy to his knees between the iron-frame steads, without even looking Joel grabbed first Dave's hand, then mine, to thrust it against his grey khaki crotch. Within, his penis was hard. Dave just yanked his hand away, and went on struggling with Billy, but I squeezed—and rubbed. And kept rubbing, till first Dave, then Joel, then Noah, then I pulled our flies open to push our cocks at Billy's grimacing face as he tried to twist away. Joel's and mine were the only two erect.

Quickly it was over. Billy was released, with all—except Billy—laughing. I remember watching him carefully. More than anything else, his attitude was annoyance. There was no major distaste, horror, or degradation. But, then, the "cocksucking" had only been a ritual touch of our penises to his mouth. Only Joel and I had tried to push within his pursed and tightened lips.

"That was really *stupid!*" Billy said—three times.

Moments later, Roy was coming up the tent steps, and the incident—like several during those first days—simply vanished in all its bodily traces, as much from Billy as it did from Dave, Joel, and the rest of us.

I don't know when I determined to speak to Joel about it, but sometime in the following ten days I decided to, next time we were alone.

Joel and I both loathed baseball: After a week, we were regularly chosen last for the baseball teams. Finally, in despair at our lack of enthusiasm for his underhand pitches, Roy put the two of us to tetherball—a "girls' game" set a dozen yards into the baseball field's foul area: A twelve-foot pole was driven into the ground in the center of an irregular concrete circle, a rope fixed to its top, a net at the rope's end, holding a soccer ball. Joel and I batted it back and forth, each trying to get it past the other, till finally the rope wrapped the post and the ball banged the wood. By the game's end, we were often in hysterics over our shared clumsinesses; and when Roy called, "Okay—athletics is over! Time for your swim," often we got to leave for the pool (at the upper end of a hundred-yard field, beside a muddy, man-made lake called the Ushy-Gushy), a minute or so before the others, who clustered around home plate with Roy, to demand if they threw like Pee-Wee Reese, if they hit like Mickey Mantle. One afternoon, thirty or forty yards ahead of Noah, Dave, Billy, and the others, Joel and I were walking to the pool.

"Joel," I said, "do you remember when we had the fight where we all made Billy suck our cocks?"

"Yeah," Joel said. "Sure."

"We really *liked* that, didn't we? I mean, I could tell—you and me, we liked it a lot more than the others did."

"Huh? Yeah, I guess we did."

"I could see it. I mean, I liked it too." Then I said: "I think that's because we're homosexual."

Though I had read it, looked it up in the dictionary, and searched it out of the indexes of any number of books, this was the first time I'd spoken the word "homosexual" to another person.

"Oh," Joel said. "Yeah. I guess so . . . I figured that." He let out a sigh.

I sighed too. "It's funny," I said. "You and me. We're both homosexual. We're both Negro . . ."

"Well," Joel said, after a considered moment. "I'm only *half* Negro. It's just my father."

I was a little surprised. A shade or so lighter than Joel, I'd never thought of myself as anything other than black. But then, he'd been raised by a white mother. I'd seen them together the previous year's Visiting Day. From some chance conversation, when I'd asked him why his father hadn't been able to come up, I'd learned Joel's dad had left the family so long ago Joel didn't even remember him.

"Yeah," I said. "But in this country, that doesn't mean anything. Legally, you might as well be all Negro."

"Yeah," Joel said. "I thought about *that*, too."

"We should probably be friends," I said. "'Cause we may have a very rough time. A lot of people don't like people like us, when they find out."

"Yeah," Joel said, "I know."

It sounded as though that came from experience.

Before we reached the pool, we had agreed to be friends—then had practically nothing to do with each other for the summer's remainder.

Three years later, when I entered the Bronx High School of Science, I learned that Joel had also arrived there as a freshman. None of our courses overlapped, though, and a certain anxiety connected largely to what I was learning about what society thought of such sexual pursuits kept me from seeking him out. By my junior year, however, experience had sedimented within me both more self-consciousness and more social awareness. I decided to find Joel—if only to say hello again, to see how he was doing, and, yes, to reminisce about old times at summer camp. I asked a girl named Maddy if she remembered him. She did. But after three or four days, it became clear that Joel no longer attended the school. I asked a number of students if they had any idea what had happened to him. I even hunted up people who'd gone to elementary school with him. None had any news.

In the years since, I've run into dozens of people from my high school days; now and again I've heard news of dozens more: But, though I've often asked after him, I've never encountered Joel—or any information about him.

II

There's a reason heterosexuals do not usually ask each other, "What was the moment you realized you were straight?" That's because the fixing of such a moment would mean that there was a whole block of time, prior to it, when you *didn't* know you were straight. To know you are straight is to know you are normal. Thus, to the extent that such ignorance is itself a form of knowledge, not to know you were straight would signify a time when you were dangerously close to *ab*normal. Not only is that an uncomfortable idea for homophobic reasons, also it's intuitively "off." One learns one is attracted to whatever attracts one—males, females, whatever—more and more over a period of time. And the only times straight men are asked, "When did you first become interested in girls?" or straight women asked, "When did you first become interested in boys?" are when the overarching rhetorical enterprise is to trivialize and delimit male heterosexuality vis-à-vis some other social field, such as labor or familial relationships, or to trivialize female heterosexuality, often vis-à-vis male heterosexuality.

The rhetoric of singular discovery, of revelation, of definition is one of the conceptual tools by which dominant discourses repeatedly suggest that there is no broad and ranging field of events informing the marginal. This is true of science fiction versus the pervasive field of literature; art as compared to social labor; blacks as a marginal social group to a central field of whites; and gay sexuality as marginal to a heterosexual norm. That rhetoric becomes part of the way the marginal is trivialized, distorted, and finally oppressed. For what is wrong with all these seemingly innocent questions—which include, alas, "When did you come out?"—is that each tends to assume that the individual's subjective field is one with the field of social statistics.

Sexual interests, concerns, and observations form a broad and pervasive field within every personality, as broad a field in me as it is in you, as broad within the straight man as it is in the gay woman. When we speak of burgeoning sexuality, that's the internal field we speak of—not the social field defined by what percent of us are gay or straight, male or female. The discourse behind that same rhetoric of singularity is, of course, the discourse which stabilizes the belief that a single homosexual event can make an otherwise straight person turn gay—or that the proper heterosexual experience can "cure" someone gay and turn him or her straight.

As a prelude to more incidents, then, that preceded my "coming out," I've put together a list of some twenty-two incidents involving sex that happened to me between age seven (1949) and age fifteen (1957), including the 1953 incident with Joel. The twenty-two are not exhaustive. They are the ones I remember. A reason I remember them is because each taught me some specific lesson. (Possibly I've forgotten the sexual incidents that only repeated or confirmed these lessons.) Together they limn the *range of sexual events* against which any *individual event* among them signifies; thus they delineate at least part of the field of my childhood sexual awareness.

To help them register *as* a field, however, I'll speak about them for a few paragraphs in statistical cross sections, rather than as specific occurrences, or even as particular meanings drawn from them:

Only one of the twenty-two—the earliest, during my second year at my first summer camp, with a somewhat older girl, herself wildly misinformed about sex—involved anything like pain or physical abuse.

Eight of these twenty-two events occurred in rural settings.

Three occurred in suburban locations.

Eleven occurred in New York City, where I lived the vast majority of my life throughout those years—far more than the fifty percent the statistical deployment suggests.

Seventeen involved bodily contact with other youngsters.

Seven of them were fundamentally heterosexual.

Finally, fifteen of them were fundamentally homosexual, so that, with experience to back me, I was fairly sure by the age of eleven my own sexuality was largely gay—though I was curious enough about the other kind.

Virtually all specifically sexual behavior for the pre-fifteen-year-old lies outside socially acceptable—but by no means outside socially determined—boundaries. Freud, Foucault, and Ariès have all reminded us that the family *is* the social unit that most confines and constrains children's sexual behavior. The "normal" model for all of us in the West, even the most resolutely heterosexual, is to begin our sexual life *outside* the socially acceptable, as children, and only with time to enter it more and more.

Immediately and absolutely I bow to the assertion that the various meanings I took from those early incidents were determined by a range of intersecting and intercritiquing preëxisting discourses—discourses which allowed me to read, which stabilized in my memory, which constituted for me the events themselves. But because of that "intercritique" one of the important meanings I quickly inferred from my experiences was that often what is said about sex does not cover the case.

But now we can proceed with some sense of an informing field to the following incidents—prologue, as I have said, to "coming out."

Generally summer camp was a constant series of sexual surprises. My very first evening in Bunk Five, a young camper named Kenroy from Florida explained to the bunk that the way to have the best summer was if the big boys (like him) regularly fucked the asses of the smaller boys (like me)—and proceeded to use an interested and willing me to demonstrate how it was done. Five years later, on my very last night, half a dozen of us were cavorting about, in the altogether after lights out in the bunk next to our own, when the flashlight of the returning counselor flickered across the porch screening. To my astonishment, big, rough Berny, whose foreskin was as long as his four-syllable Italian last name, lifted up his covers and whispered, "Quick, Delany! Get in!"—and I slid in to be enfolded by his arms, my naked body pulled against his, where his cock, already rigid, began to rub against my belly.

In that same landscape, between those first last days, fell some half-dozen of those twenty-two incidents that constituted the field of my childhood sexuality. One of the oddest was when, in my third year of senior camp, I noticed a boy, Tom, hanging toward the outside of the circle of campers and counselors that we formed every morning around the flag pole before breakfast for Flag Raising. When he thought himself unobserved, Tom would dig in his nose repeatedly with one thick finger or the other and feed himself the pickings. Watching him gave me an erection. There was little specificity to the desire, neither to emulate nor to share, though if he had offered me some, I would have accepted, wonderfully pleased by the bold self-confidence and inclusion of his gesture. (Aged five, in school, I'd been roundly embarrassed out of the same habit by public ridicule, led by Miss Rubens: "If you are hungry, young man, I'm *sure* we can arrange for you to get something to eat. But *stop* that!") My response was to make every effort to befriend Tom and, once that friendship had been secured, to explain to him that I had no problems with the habit I knew must have caused him, now and then, at least *some* social pain. He should feel free to indulge it whenever we were alone together. He did, at first with some trepidation, though less and less as time went on. We ended up taking long walks through the woods, holding hands (another nail-biter, he), talking of this and that. While he dug and ate, I wandered along beneath the leaves, pushing aside brush, crunching twigs, and climbing over logs in a haze of barely presexual ecstasy.

The same years contained three fairly enduring (for weeks in each case) heterosexual experiments which, while they were physically pleasant enough (all three involving everything, as they say, except penetration), nevertheless registered with a complete emotional flatness and lack of affect, save the immediate *frisson* of trying something new—a flatness and lack whose prevailing sign is the lack of detail with which I recount them here. (The four girls' bunks occupied two bunkhouses outside the Tent Colony on the other side of the Knoll, across from a red and white barn—gray inside and housing a Ping-Pong table and upright piano—called, rather eccentrically, "Brooklyn College.") Although the word "love" was spoken repeatedly—and, I suspect, sincerely—by the young women (and even a few times by me, to see how it tasted on my tongue), silent judgment was that if this was all that accrued to these "normal" adventures—very much socially approved of by both the male and female counselors—they just weren't worth it. In two cases, the lessons learned were among the more negative ones I took from these early explorations. One affair ended with a fight between me and a rival named Gary over the affection of one girl who could not, or would not, make up her mind.

"You decide which one of us you like better," Gary and I agreed, "and the other one will go away."

"But I can't! I don't want to hurt anybody's *feelings!*" the young woman insisted, then lamented, repeatedly behind Brooklyn College, while Gary and I growled, repeated our request, then shoved, repeated our request once more, then—finally, to avoid any hurt feelings—bloodied each other's noses.

A feminist critic, to an earlier account of this incident once suggested: "Perhaps she wanted you both and was as stymied in her ability to get outside the status quo response as either of you were." It's quite possible. Probably we were all social dupes: My rival, Gary, was fat and had long dirty fingernails—and thus held *no* sexual interest for me. The other girl (Karen), the other boy—both may have been acting under the impetus of an always-excessive [hetereosexual] desire. But if some idealized social norm *is* the villain in the piece, then I represent it—since, though I sincerely *liked* the girl and (equally sincerely) disliked the boy, I found both without sexual interest: My actions were determined purely *from* my knowledge of social norms, and had none of the creative energy, enthusiasm, or invention that sexual desire can sometimes lend—which may well be why the incident was the particular (and not greater or lesser than the) disaster it was.

I've no clear memory of what any of us did afterward. I don't think much of it was with each other. (Possibly she wanted neither of us—and this was the only socially acceptable way to get rid of *me*.) Leave such pursuits to the girls and boys, I decided, who got some sense of soaring, of safety, of security—or at least got the rewards from creative social manipulations that honest sexual interest always adds to a situation. But all my heterosexual experiences have grown from opposite-sex friendships that have gotten out of hand, spurred on by a vague sense of social expectations, whether at summer camp or in the dozen years after.

Another incident returns me to New York City, the spring in which I went from fourteen to fifteen (though today I don't recall which side of my birthday it fell on). By that time, I'd learned (again, I don't remember how) that New York's 42nd Street and Broadway area was one of the centers of the city's furtive homosexual activity. Sunday morning, when I was expected to go to church and then choir practice, I decided to visit.

I'd contemplated the journey for days. But how or why, that particular Sunday, when I woke, I knew that *this* was the day I would make the trip down from Harlem, I couldn't tell you—though I recall the silent, tingling excitement, all morning, through breakfast down in the kitchen, through shaving at the upstairs bathroom mirror, through putting on my white shirt and tying my red tie.

In gray suit and tan overcoat, I left my Harlem house to walk up Seventh Avenue, turn left at 133rd Street, stop for a shine at Lewy's sagging green-painted plank stall, then continue down the street, even angling across the macadam between the cars toward St. Philip's back entrance, now and again wondering if any of the three horse bettors chatting with Lewy inside his "shoeshine parlor" would notice that, this morning, I did not turn in to the Parish House that would let me into the church basement, but continued down the street toward Eighth Avenue. No, I figured, they would all be too busy speculating on the track events that went into the day's "number"—at least, I hoped so.

There were three or four Harlem blocks I knew to every inch, but my father was strict about where I was and where I was not allowed to go. As little as a block away from my own house lay vast areas of the neighborhood I'd simply never seen. At the unfamiliar corner of Eighth Avenue and 133rd Street I turned north, thankful for my knowledge of the city's grid. Though I traveled to high school every morning using the 135th Street/St. Nicholas Avenue subway stop, this morning's decision had sent me there by a wholly new route, by new barbershops, new eating places, new accountant offices, new record shops, and new funeral parlors (far smaller than my father's or Mr. Sterritt's back on Seventh Avenue). Finally, at the familiar 135th Street subway station, across from the rising slope of St. Nicholas Park and under a sky without cloud, I took the steps to the downtown side (instead of the uptown kiosk across the street—as I would have done on a school morning).

I came up, some few minutes before nine, at 42nd just in from Eighth Avenue. In those days, 42nd Street was an all-night affair, with its dozen-plus movie houses open till four o'clock in the morning and reopening four hours later at eight. On weekdays, that is. Opening time was ten o'clock on Sundays, I found out when I wandered up to a closed ticket window. Across the street and up at the other end of the block, Grant's (where one could get hot dogs, hamburgers, and fresh clams at the sidewalk counter) had a few people lingering before it. Directly across from me, someone wandered into the Horn & Hardart Automat, while someone else wandered out. But there was certainly not the constant and lively flow of pedestrians that I'd seen on my last Saturday afternoon or Friday evening visit with whatever friend or cousin.

It was my first visit alone.

Across the street, its neon lights wan in the chill spring daylight, Hubert's Museum was open. I went to the corner, crossed, and decided that might be as good a place as any to explore. On the front window, hand-painted letters declared: Hubert's Flea Circus—a sign that easily could have been twenty years old.

I went inside—was the Sunday morning admission fifty cents?—and down the black stairwell, at the bottom pushing through the orange curtain. In the little room, someone else was already waiting. When two other people joined us, the guide/guard (wearing a uniform cap, but otherwise in street clothes) said they usually waited for six customers before they started. But it didn't look as if they were going to get six any time soon. So we four were ushered out to see, first, behind a rail up on a kind of stage, the Fat Lady, who told us how heavy she was, how much she ate daily. Then, grinning, she leaned over the rail to hand us her statistics on little paper slips. We went on to see the Alligator Man and the Dog-Faced Boy. The guide apologized that the Siamese Twins were off that morning.

I don't remember which exhibition we were watching, but, with my overcoat open, I was standing at the front, both my hands on the wooden bar, when, on my left hand, I felt something warm.

I looked down—and up.

A young black man in a sports jacket and a cap, perhaps just twenty, had slid his dark fingers over mine and was smiling at me. I knew that this was exactly what I had come here for. But I was too surprised to smile. I pulled my hand from under his, turned back to whatever was on stage, but did not step away.

Moments later, we were ushered into the room with the flea circus—a round, glass-covered table, beneath whose transparent pane the fleas pulled a small cart, jumped over a hurdle, wore odd little bits of colored paper that were their "costumes." Maybe six people could fit around it at any one time. I made a big show of watching, deciding quietly that, when we went upstairs, I would speak to the young man—that is, once the others had left.

Only when I looked up—the show was over, we were asked to go upstairs—he was gone. Apparently because I had not responded, he'd decided he'd better leave.

Back on 42nd Street, I looked about for him. But he'd hurried away—perhaps gone into the Automat, or just sprinted across to the subway.

It was almost an hour till the movies opened. After walking up and down the block another twenty minutes, I went to the subway and rode home.

* * *

By my last year of high school, my friends were divided into two categories: those who knew I was "queer"—the working-class term in general use back then—and those who didn't.

Those who knew included Marilyn, Judy, Gale (friends of mine now in college, a year or so ahead of me in their education), and a young man in a number of my high school classes named Murray. Blond and gray-eyed, Murray had been born in the Bronx. But his hair was *extremely* long, as if he were some European or South American—a half or even three-quarters of an inch longer than any other boy's in the school. In the pre-Beatles fifties, that was as good as having a two-foot ponytail. There were always whispers about how Murray looked like a girl. His features were delicate. He was very smart. Like me, he enjoyed music and the arts. I was certain he must be queer.

There was *nothing* about him I found sexually attractive.

But I'd also realized that, since entering high school, the easy, polymorphous bisexuality that had been rife among my friends in elementary school and summer camp had dried up almost completely. I had moved into a space where a stricter and stricter code of heterosexuality was taking over. If I wanted to have any sort of satisfying sexual outlet for myself, I'd have to work at it.

Several times I'd invited Murray to my house. A couple of times I'd gone over to his. On his next visit to my place, after a few minutes of moody silence, during which he asked me what was the matter, I told him that I was homosexual—and wanted to go to bed with him.

I was very surprised when he explained to me (1) he just wasn't *like* that, (2) this was the second time, not the first, that someone had felt this way about him, and (3) though he liked me and wanted to be my friend, he really hoped I wouldn't find it too upsetting or frustrating if he didn't share my sexual feelings. But (4) knowing how serious the matter was, he promised that he would not reveal my secret.

To which I said, "Yeah . . . sure. Okay," actually with some relief.

We remained friends. And I did have—though oddly acquired—a straight male friend with whom, however guardedly, I could mention, now and again, my desires for other men, which—intellectually, at least—he seemed to find interesting.

III

I first heard the words "camp," "closet," and "coming out" all on the same afternoon in July of 1959. I was seventeen and had gotten a juvenile role in an aspiring summer stock company whose directors had had the ingenious notion of basing the company in New York City. They'd rented a little theater one building to the west of the St. Marks Baths, on the south side of St. Marks Place near the corner of Third Avenue. (The iron steps that led up to the lobby are still there today, though the space is now a secondhand clothing store.) After our theatrical company was long gone, the theater became the performance space for Ed Sanders, Allen Ginsberg, and the legendary Fugs. When we got it, however, the performance space and lobby were in appalling condition. In true summer stock style, cast members were requisitioned by the set designer, his assistant, and the two directors/producers to paint the entire theater— lobby, auditorium, and stage—once some minimal carpentry work had been done.

The set designer and his male assistant were lovers—had been lovers, they told us all, that afternoon, for some ten years. I was the only person in the volunteer paint crew under twenty-one, and much was made of it, to my embarrassment. I'd been taking ballet lessons for the previous three months and had a hopeless crush on the only straight student in the class, a twenty-three-year-old aspiring actor with a wonderful bear-like body who had been instructed by his acting coach to study dance to "learn how to move." We were becoming friends, but I'd taken a lesson from Murray: There was as much chance of our becoming lovers as there was of this thick-thighed, stout-bellied fellow's becoming a dancer. But I'd never gone back to 42nd Street, and, despite the banter and repartee in the Ballet Theater men's changing room (and, frankly, there wasn't much), in many ways I was as naïve about the social side of homosexuality as it was possible for a New York City youth to be.

From the joking that went on among the actors painting the theater lobby that afternoon, I learned that "coming out" meant having your first homosexual experience. And what you came out *into*, of course, was homosexual society. Until you had a major homosexual experience, you could be—as many younger, older, straight, gay, male or female folk have always been—a kind of mascot to homosexual society. But it took some major form of the sexual act itself to achieve "coming out." And fooling around with your bunk-mates after lights out, I was informed, was *not* major.

The origins of the term were debutante cotillions, those sprawling, formal society balls where, squired by equally young and uncomfortable cousins, brothers, or schoolmates, young ladies of sixteen or so "came out" into society. By now I had been an escort at a couple of those, too— Harlem variety: the presentation march down the hall's red central carpet, two seventeen-year-old or eighteen-year-old gentlemen on the arms of each sixteen-year-old young lady, the listless rehearsals in echoing ballrooms, the quivering orchid petals, the nervous parents, the rented tuxedos.

During that afternoon's painting session, I first learned what "a camp" was—the color scheme the directors had chosen for the theater, for one: peach, gold, and azure. I also learned that "to camp" and the gerund "camping" denoted dressing up in drag and, by extension, acting in a particularly effeminate manner, either in private or in public—flouting the notions of the straight world by flaunting the customs of the queer one. The noun form was the base form: "Oh, my dear, she is such a camp!" ("she," in such cases, almost always referring to a male). Etymologically, of course, "camp" was an apocopation of "camp follower." Camp followers were the women, frequently prostitutes, who followed the armies across Europe from military camp to military camp. Since the military have always had a special place in homosexual mythology, and presumably because the advent of a large group of young, generally womanless men was as good an excuse as any for cross-dressing among the local male populace so inclined, the then-new meaning of the term—"to go out and camp it up"; "to have a mad camp" (and "*mad* camp" was the phrase most commonly in use)—gained currency in England during World War I and had been brought back to the United States by American soldiers. Calling something "a camp" followed the same linguistic template as calling a funny experience "a riot." Indeed, the two were often synonymous.

That same afternoon, I learned that ordinary day-to-day homosexual argot had a far more analytic way of dividing up people by sexual preferences than any but the most detailed psychiatric jargon: There were queers interested exclusively in "seafood" (sailors); there were "toe queens" (foot fetishists) and "dinge queens" (white men interested only in blacks) and "snow queens" (from a popular brand of ice cream, black men interested only in whites) and "speed queens" (this last, taken from the name of a common clothes washing machine: It meant a gay male addicted to amphetamines). There were "leather queens" (the S&M crowd) and "size queens" ("There are two kinds of queers, my dear. There are size queens—and there are *liars!*") and "chubby chasers" and "chicken queens" (those who went after young children) and "closet queens."

However mildly pejorative each was, each represented an active perversion. A closet queen was someone who *liked* doing it in the closet— that is, who enjoyed the fact that friends and others didn't know.

I don't know how much my discovering a group of gay men who used these terms and expressed themselves with this slang had to do with it, but four months later, in October, when the plays and playfulness of the summer were over, I "came out."

In many ways it was a repeat of something I'd already done, though not for three years. Once more, alone, I went down to 42nd Street—on a Saturday afternoon. This time I walked directly to the largest theater on the strip, the New Amsterdam, and, inside, took a seat midway back in the orchestra. It was a busy day, and soon people were sitting on both sides of me. The film was a western in which I had no interest, but which I made myself watch.

After fifteen minutes, on my right I felt a leg move against mine. I remembered what had happened to the guy in Hubert's Museum and resolved not to let this one get away, no matter who it was.

I pressed back. Soon a hand was on top of mine; it moved over to my crotch. I felt around between *his* legs. He was stubby and hard. When I looked, he was a dumpy guy in his middle or late forties, with glasses and white hair. Finally, tentatively, he leaned over to speak. "Can you come home with me . . . ?" He had a strong accent.

"Yes!" I declared.

We got up together and left the theater. He lived in Brooklyn, he explained.

Brooklyn was a long way; but I was determined.

On the subway, sitting inches apart, we had a spare conversation. The man was Israeli. He'd been in the country not quite a year. I also realized, as we rode over the Manhattan Bridge, he was nervous.

A block from his house, I listened to his complicated instructions. He would go in first and leave the door open for me—if it was all right. If someone was around, he would lock the door—he was sorry. But if the door was locked, then I would simply know the coast was not clear and I had to go home.

If the door was *not* locked, I was to come up to the third floor and knock—softly—on the apartment door there. Even inside his apartment we had to speak quietly. . . .

The door was open. In a stairwell covered with cracked, yellow paint, I walked up to the third floor. I knocked—softly. The door opened, wide enough to show half his face. For a moment he looked as though he was not sure who I was. Then, the quick whisper: "Come in . . . !"

He lived in two grungy rooms, the first of which was both kitchen and living room (with *very* blue walls). He took me into the second. We sat on his bed and put our arms around each other. I was excited enough by the whole situation of doing it with a stranger that I came the moment we lay down. (It remains my single experience of premature orgasm.) Because I felt guilty for coming so fast and because I still had an erection, I tried to be obliging while we took our clothes off—he never removed his undershirt—and we labored to an orgasm for him.

"Okay," he whispered, as soon as he finished. "You gotta go now."

"Couldn't we rest just a little?" I asked, even as I slid on my pants. I'd worked hard to make him come, and I was tired.

He took a deep breath. "You wanna rest a little . . . ?" He didn't sound happy. "But I don't think it would be good in the same bed." He got up and, carrying the clothes I hadn't yet put on, took me back into the living room/kitchen. "I rest in there. *You* rest in here—on the couch."

"Okay . . ." I said, sat on the sagging yellow sofa, and stretched out.

He hurried back inside. A moment later, I heard a kind of *ratchet* and looked up. There was a full key-and-lock mechanism on the bedroom door.

I stretched out again, possibly even tried to sleep. After a little while—it may have been only minutes—I got up, went back around the couch, and knocked.

There was no answer. I tried the knob—yes, he'd firmly locked the door against me.

Suddenly I got a sense of the despairing idiocy of the whole thing. "Hello . . . !" I called, through the door. "Look, I'm going to go home now."

He didn't answer. Maybe *he'd* fallen asleep.

"I'm going to leave now. Good-bye."

I put on my shirt and my shoes, got on my jacket, and went outside into the hall and down the stairs.

A year later, I'd had many more sexual experiences, many of them on 42nd Street, many of them on Central Park West. If you'd asked me to evaluate my "coming out" experience against these others on a scale of one to ten, where five was average/acceptable, I'd have given it a two. Frankly, it doesn't often get much worse than that. But the unpleasant ones are the most informative; I'd learned from it how much anxiety certain men could connect with the sexual encounter—and how much anxiety people were willing to put up with to have sex in spite of it.

Eventually I described the experience in a long letter, complete with an attempt to sketch the man's face, intended for my friend Gale, which I never sent her. Rather, I kept it. A year later, when I read the letter over, I was astonished by how many stock phrases of despair and disgust I'd used, as though the entire vocabulary for describing the incident had been lent me by some true-confessions magazine (that didn't exist) devoted to degrading homosexual encounters. The experience had *only* been a two, after all—not a one or a zero!

Another bit of fallout from the whole business is worth mentioning.

I talked about the experience endlessly to Marilyn, to Judy, to Gale. I also talked with them of the much more pleasant encounter, only a few weeks later, with a Puerto Rican pharmacist who picked me up on Central Park West and gave me detailed instructions on how to give and take anal sex, and who lived in a friendly brownstone off the park, all of whose tenants were gay and most of whom I met over a three-day stay. I told them about the twenty-three-year-old postal worker, who drove me back to his apartment in Brooklyn. Quite as anxiety ridden as the Israeli, at least he was one of the most physically gorgeous men I've ever been to bed with, before or since. I told them about the odd experiences with Cranford and Peter and the incredibly hung black man, just out of jail, who took me back to the Endicott Hotel. ("He came walking up to me, where I sat on a bench on Central Park West, stopped right in front of me, with a big, friendly smile, and said, 'Hi, there. What you out lookin' for?' And I said, 'I don't know! What do you . . . have?' And he said, "Oh . . . 'bout eleven inches—'!" Gale threw her hands over her face and cried, "No! No—*really*? Oh, my God. Really? No, don't tell me this. Yes, *tell* me . . . !")

Other friends—mostly male—I simply didn't even consider broaching the subject with. One of those was my good friend Bob.

I don't think I've ever known anyone who had more hostility toward his parents, both of whom were fairly elderly—his father a doctor, his mother an administrator in the New York public high school system. A grandmother lived with them, who reputedly had quite a bit of money (millions was the rumor among the tenants at Morningside Gardens housing cooperative where we'd both lived throughout my high school years). Bob claimed that his parents' only interest in letting his grandmother live with them was her wealth. From what I'd seen of his parents and his grandmother, that sounded patently unfair. But to visit their apartment with Bob was soon to witness a shouting match between child and parents of a vicious intensity I've never encountered, before or since, at *any* social level.

Bob's sexual history was equally strange. The first time he'd masturbated, he explained to me, he'd been twelve or thirteen, sitting in the tub finishing a bath. The orgasm had occurred underwater. Soapy bath water had backed up his urethra and spermduct; within a day or two, infection had ensued. Afraid to tell his parents about it, he'd let it go till it reached an incredibly painful state. He'd had to be hospitalized and come near having to be castrated. He'd never masturbated again.

Almost exactly a year after the October I came out, my father died.

And at the same month's end (it was 1960), I moved into Bob's 113th

Street apartment, in the St. Marks Arms (no, it had nothing to do with St. Marks Place) and immediately—unbeknownst to Bob—started a low-key, pleasant, desultory affair with a white guy from the South who lived down the hall from us, named Leon.

At about the same time, Judy and Bob had gone out on a few dates together—and Judy finally told him of my 42nd Street adventure. Today, I'm not sure if he realized how long ago it had been. But one evening, when I came in and stepped into the living room full of Bob's ham-radio equipment, where both of us slept, he switched off his microphone, turned around and stood up somewhat uncomfortably, his blond hair awry, his bare feet on the cluttered rug. Pulling at his T-shirt, he began: "I've got something very important to say to you, Chip. You don't have to say anything back. Judy told me that you . . . did something. Down on 42nd Street. You know what I'm talking about. We don't have to say exactly what it was—no, don't say anything now . . ."

I was dumbfounded. I had no idea *what* he was talking about. The incident I'd told Judy about had occurred almost a year ago; and there'd been a goodly number of others since, on 42nd Street and elsewhere. I began to realize that it must have had to do with sex—and probably homosexual sex. Only as he went on, did I realize it was last year's "coming out" that he was talking about.

". . . But I don't want you to do anything like that ever again! That's very important. You have to promise me—no, we're not going to talk about it. But you have to promise me that—see? I don't want you to try to explain it. I don't want you to say anything about it at all—except that you promise me you'll never do it again. And now I've accepted your promise—" (All I'd done was raise an eyebrow, when finally I'd realized what he was referring to.) "—and now it's over. We'll never mention it anymore. It's all been taken care of. I won't—I promise you. And you won't. Because you've promised me. That's all there is to it." Nodding his head, he turned back to sit at the radio.

I was left to get a soda from the icebox, sit for a while, read, then finally leave the little apartment we shared to go off down the hall, drop in on Leon, and, between bouts of lovemaking, tell him about what Bob had said, decry how self-righteous he'd been, but suggest that we'd better be careful, the two of us. . . .

One night seven years later, I was leaving my mother's house and ran into Bob, who was now married to a pleasant young black woman with whom I had gone to elementary school. With a surge of old friendship he invited me to come up and say hello. He and his wife were living in another Morningside Gardens apartment filled with strange contraptions: mechanical gypsy fortune-telling booths of the sort that had lined the walls of Hubert's Museum; old musical instruments contained in glass booths, such as the Tango Banjo or the Duo Arts Player Piano or the Violano Virtuoso (a player violin built in 1916 with mechanical stops and an automatic bow that played songs programmed into it). Bob had restored them all and had become an expert on them—though they made his apartment look like the back storage room in a bizarre carnival. The notes I took on the evening, right afterward, provided a scene in the novel I was then writing, *Nova*.

A year or so later, Bob took his own life somewhere in the Caribbean.

IV

When I was seventeen and my friend Judy was eighteen, one evening I left my parents' Morningside Gardens apartment to visit a coffee shop around on Amsterdam Avenue and settle into the phone booth, so Judy and I could have an uninterrupted hour-and-a-half conversation. Judy had been a child actor and was now a dancer. She knew lots of gay men, some of whom (Freddy Herko, Vincent Warren, James Waring) she'd introduced me to. I remember my surprise when she said (the first of half a dozen women who would later tell me the same), "I always wanted to be a man so I could go to bed with other men. I've often wondered why *anyone* would want to go to bed with a woman, anyway!" The comment was offered as support from a young woman to a younger gay man. But even in 1959—pre-Stonewall; pre-Women's Liberation; pre-Martin Luther King—I could hear in it a profound and troubling dissatisfaction with the *whole* situation of woman in this country.

Marilyn, Judy, and Gale are a trio of names anyone who has looked at my memoir, *The Motion of Light in Water* (1988), will remember as repeatedly sounding out, singularly and together, through the course of my late adolescence and early manhood. Marilyn, in August 1961, became my wife; we lived together for thirteen years and have a wonderful daughter who has always known her parents were gay. (In 1984, when she was ten, my daughter sat on a panel of Children of Gay Parents at the Lesbian and Gay Community Services Center in New York, discussing the situation and answering questions. All those children agreed that it's best to let your child know as early as possible. The sooner they know, the less traumatic it is.) When we were first married, I remember how, at eighteen, Marilyn seemed to delight in using gay terms and gay slang in front of our straight friends, to make jokes or to pass comments to me behind their backs or over their heads. Several times when we were alone, I asked her not to. It seemed as though she wondered what was the fun of being gay if it wasn't a special club that allowed you to have it over the ordinary people. But in that need to be special, I sensed the same dissatisfaction with the ordinary situation of women that I had in Judy's statement on the phone a year or so before.

Racism, anti-Semitism, sexism, and homophobia are intricately re-lated—only secondarily because of the overlapping categories of op-pressors. Despite their vast range of specific differences, so many of their mechanics follow the same pattern, from the direct inflicting of eco-nomic and social damages, to blaming the victim and the transcendental mythicizing of the victim's "world." Immediately our marriage brought that analysis (the tale is told in *Motion*) to articulation.

If only as a gloss, I must mention here all the help, support, and friendship I've had from women, over these same periods, in learning to understand these mechanisms—from hours, months, years of personal discussion, questions, and insights, to the (at the institutional level) many volumes of feminist and social analysis I've been lucky enough to have them push at me, without which my understanding of the mechan-ics of oppression, from racism to homophobia, would have remained in another, far more impoverished ballpark.

Judy and Marilyn remain my friends to this day. And happily I would welcome a reunion with Gale.

All three eventually took greater or lesser joy in lesbianism. But being gay is not a matter of being in a special club. In this country it's a belea-guered situation that one must learn to negotiate as best one can.

I don't think I've ever been that much into control—as an earlier gen-eration might have put it. But I did want to be in control of who knew and who didn't know I was gay. In the homophobic social field that ob-tained pre-Stonewall (and, indeed, since), it was still—as it had been with Bob—a little too disorienting when people found out on their own. As our current society is discursively constituted, that is still one of the things that creates tension in the relations between some gay men and a range of women.

It's a philosophical paradox:

Differences are what create individuals. Identities are what create groups and categories. Identities are thus conditions of comparative sim-plicity that complex individuals might move toward, but (fortunately) never achieve—until society, tired of the complexity of so much individ-ual difference, finally, one way or the other, imposes an identity on us.

Identities are thus, by their nature, reductive. (You do not need an identity to become yourself; you need an identity to become *like* someone else.) Without identities, yes, language would be impossible (because categories would not be possible, and language requires categories). Still, in terms of subjects, identity remains a highly problematic sort of reduction and cultural imposition.

Through the late sixties the sensation-hungry media began rummaging through various marginal social areas for new and exciting vocabulary. In almost every case, however, once a new term was found, an almost complete change in meaning occurred as it was applied to more or less bourgeois experiences and concerns. "Rap" had already been appropriated from the world of down-and-out amphetamine druggies ("rapping" was initially the term for the unstoppable, often incoherent cascade of talk from someone who'd taken too much of the drug); "camp" had already been borrowed from gay slang, largely in the wake of a popular 1964 *Partisan Review* essay by Susan Sontag, "Notes on 'Camp,'" after which it all but lost its meaning of "cross-dressing" and became a general synonym for "just *too* much." With Sontag as quotable source, "camp" became an adjective, driving out "a camp" and "campy"—as though "riot" were to be used as an adjective, displacing both "a riot" and "riotous." (To ears my age, adjectival "camp" *still* sounds like a usage error.) Spurred on by Stonewall and the rapid formation just after it of an organized Gay Liberation Front, the term "coming out" over the next eighteen months changed its meaning radically.

Gay liberation proponents began to speak about "coming out" *of* "the closet"—the first time either the words or the concepts had ever been linked. (Till then no one would have thought of asking the closet queen to give up his closet any more than of asking the toe queen to give up his toes—save in the smug, peremptory tone in which all perversion was decried.) In the media this metaphorical extension soon completely displaced the denotative meaning ("coming out *into*" gay society: having one's first major gay sexual experience). A good number of people—myself included—who were under the impression we had come out ages ago, now realized we were expected to come out yet again in this wholly new sense.

The logic of "coming out"—in this new sense—was impeccable. Sixteen and seventeen years before, the House Un-American Activities Committee, along with its hounding of communists, had been equally vigilant in its crusade against homosexuals: Its logic was that homosexuals were security risks because we were susceptible to blackmail. Said the Gay Liberationists, if we're "out," nobody *can* blackmail us and nobody can accuse us of being blackmailable. So let them all know who we are, how many of us there are, and that we're proud to be what we are!

Like many gay men, I found myself seriously asking, "Just how out am I?"

In 1961, I'd gotten married.

As far back as 1964, I'd decided—when I'd a spent a few weeks in Mt. Sinai Hospital's mental ward—that if anyone ever asked me was I queer or not, I would never even consider lying. Was that a kind of "coming out"? Only it was five years before Stonewall and in a wholly pathologized situation. And though I'd made the decision (and stuck to it), years had passed without my having to confront such a question directly and test my resolve.

In 1967 I'd published a story, "Aye, and Gomorrah . . . ," in which the basic situation dealt with a future perversion, clearly an analogue of current homosexuality. The story won a Nebula Award for best SF story of its year. I was sure most of the tale's readers would assume I was gay. In 1968, I'd written "Time Considered as a Helix of Semi-precious Stones," a story about homosexual S&M which went on to win both a Nebula and a Hugo. I was pretty sure any reader who'd had doubts about my sexuality after the first story would have them cleared up with the second. Was I afraid of being found out? Yes. In no way do I mean to imply I partook of some particularly heroic social bravery. The fact that I was gay had been one of the greatest factors in determining me to commit myself seriously to writing and the arts in the first place: Even in my early teens I knew the worlds of theater, dance, and literature were far more tolerant of such deviancy as mine, whereas what happened to get men and women in more "central" areas of endeavor were the sort of tragedy and social ostracism portrayed in Lillian Hellman's *The Children's Hour*, a play I'd read in high school.

At least one straight science fiction scholar, who did not meet me till more than a decade later, has told me: "I knew you were gay by 1968, though I don't know *how* I knew. Nor do I remember who told me." I'm sure he did too. The only people in America who wrote even vaguely sympathetic portrayals of gay men and women were—it was a foregone conclusion—gay themselves. In science fiction, the only gay characters *not* written by gay authors were those like the evil Baron Harkonnen and his equally evil nephew, Feyd Rautha, in Frank Herbert's *Dune*, monstrous villains who Died Horribly in the End.

By 1969 it was common knowledge throughout the science fiction field that I was gay. Marilyn and I were living together about half the time. (When Stonewall occurred, we were together in San Francisco.) The other half we were following our own amatory pursuits, with neither one of us really set on establishing any sort of permanent relationship— which was not proving to be an easy solution for either of us.

As a result of Stonewall and the redefinition of "coming out," I had to consider that, while I approved vigorously of "coming out" as a necessary strategy to avoid blackmail and to promote liberation, there seemed to be an oppressive aspect of surveillance and containment intertwined with it, especially when compared to the term's older meaning. Before, one came out *into* the gay community. Now, coming out had become something entirely aimed at straights. Its initial meaning had been a matter of bodily practice. (It involved *coming . . .*) Now it had become a purely verbal one. Despite its political goals, *was* this change really as beneficial as it was so often touted to be? Since it had been a case of displacing a term, rather than adding a term, hadn't we perhaps lost something by that displacement?

We heard the phrase more and more. It became almost a single word. The straight media began to take it over. (That was the time when the "silent majority" was now "coming out" of the closet of its silence. A few months later, fat people were "coming out" of the closet of their fat, and smokers were "coming out" of the closet of their smoking.) I found myself wanting to stop people, every time they began say the phrase—to slow them down, startle them with a slash struck down between the words, make them consider what each meant separately, and remind them of all the possible meanings—historical, new, and revolutionary—that the two could be packed with, either apart or joined.

There was a closet of banality, overuse, and cliché I wanted to see "coming out" come out of!

In 1975, I taught my first university class. I told my students I was gay within the first two weeks. In the gay press the fact had appeared often enough that there seemed no reason to let it move through a new group of young people as a more or less confirmed rumor. I'd heard too many horror stories about gay teachers who did *not* come out to their students, accused by neurotic young men or women (who knew, of course, their teacher's secret) of playing favorites because of sexuality. The problem is taken care of when everything is aboveboard, when they know, when I know they know, and when they know I know they know—because I've told them.

In the middle seventies I received a harsh criticism from a gay friend because a biographical paragraph that appeared in the back of a number of my books mentioned that I was married to the poet Marilyn Hacker, that we had a daughter, and that Marilyn had won the National Book Award for Poetry. Not only was I trying to gain prestige through Marilyn's reputation (ran my friend's accusation), I was falsely presenting myself as a straight man, happily married, with a family, even though in those years Marilyn and I no longer lived together. The paragraph had been written perhaps a month before we'd last separated. I'd used it, first, because it was true when I wrote it. My reason for mentioning the

National Book Award I'd felt to be wholly altruistic. Though it's the highest, or one of the highest, awards for poetry in the United States, the fact is, a year after you've won it, hardly anyone can remember—even people presumably concerned with such things. (Can *you* name the last three years' recipients?[1]) I'd thought by putting it in my biographical squib I might keep the fact of Marilyn's award before a *few* people's eyes just a *little* longer than usual.

That's how I'd intended it, and that's how Marilyn had taken it. (At about that time, Marilyn applied for an interim job teaching at Columbia University. When the junior professor who was interviewing her mentioned the range of possible salaries and asked how much she would seek, she named the highest figure. He laughed. "For us to give you that much," he said, "you would have to have won a National Book Award or something." Recounting it to me later, she said: "It was so much fun to be able to smile at him demurely and say, 'Well, actually . . . I have.' He turned quite red.")

I'd already made one desultory attempt to change the paragraph even before my friend objected, but it had gone astray in the Bantam Books office. Now, true, Marilyn and I *were* living apart. I had a permanent male lover. I wrote a new biographical paragraph and turned it in to my publisher, only to learn that a new run of my science fiction novels had just been ordered mere days before—with the *old* squib! It was another year and a half before I could correct it. However innocent my transgression, my friend's criticism had its point, though, and I felt I should respond to it.

V

In 1977 for the first time, at the World Science Fiction Convention in Phoenix, Arizona, a panel on "gay science fiction" was placed on the official World Con Program. I was asked to sit and agreed readily.

The four panelists included Frank Robinson (author of the 1956 science fiction classic *The Power*), Norman Spinrad (our token straight), and me. When the program committee asked for permission to tape the proceedings, I was surprised when the young woman on the panel flatly refused. She would not participate if there were any chance of its getting back to her family. A week before the panel, however, I too was electrically aware that it was the first time I'd sit in front of an audience and talk about being gay. To our surprise, that audience turned out to be standing room only and comprised of more than three hundred people.

It was wonderfully invigorating. For me its high point was when Robinson told us what Theodore Sturgeon, already a personal hero of mine, had had to go through in 1953, during and after writing his ovular story on a gay theme, "The World Well Lost." When Sturgeon submitted it to *Fantastic*, editor Howard Browne not only refused to publish it but launched a telephone campaign among all the field's editors never to publish anything by Sturgeon again, and, further, threatened to see that anyone who published *that* particular tale would be ostracized from the SF community. Feisty little hunchbacked editor Ray Palmer broke the nascent boycott and published the story in *Universe Science Fiction*, where it became an immediate classic.

After the panel had taken place, I was astonished how quickly I became "Samuel R. Delany, the black, gay science fiction writer" in the straight media. (Though my 1967 and 1968 stories had gotten me invited to *sit* on the panel, they had produced no such effect!) An interview in the *Advocate* followed, and several articles appeared in the *Village Voice*. Any newspaper mention of me—even in the *New York Times Book Review*—seemed obliged to tag me as gay (and black), and if the article was by a straight reporter, usually the tag appeared in the first sentence. After only a little while, the situation began to seem vaguely hysterical, as if, through an awful oversight, someone might *not* know I was gay. I didn't mind. But, from time to time, it got a bit tired.

In the late seventies, when my daughter was about four, I helped establish a Gay Fathers group with two other men—a bank vice president and a musician teaching at Columbia. Over the next two years the group expanded to include more than forty fathers and twice that number of children. I was surprised to learn that, just as I had, all of us had told our wives-to-be that we were gay well before the wedding; though often neither husband nor wife was quite sure what, exactly, that would mean once marriage took place.

In those same years, a collection of gay businessmen put on a program at an East Side gay club in which they asked three gay male "role models"—Quentin Crisp, and an openly gay policeman on the New York City police force who had been much in the news of late, and me—to take part. During the fresh-faced blond cop's presentation, I remember, he said, "You know, there've been half a dozen articles about me in the *New York Times* in the last year—but the truth is, I'm not out to my mother."

Frankly, I wanted to hug him. I'd never spoken about being gay to anyone in my immediate family, either.

I remember visiting my mother in 1985, while her downstairs neighbor, Mrs. Jackson, having dropped up for a visit, enthused to me over a recent *Village Voice* article, in which, yes, I'd been identified as gay in the first sentence. Did my mother herself know? I don't see how, during those years, she could have missed it!

Still, we'd never talked about it to each other.

Perhaps a year later, my mother took me to see William M. Hoffman's moving AIDS play, *As Is*, which she'd already seen once and had been impressed with enough to see again. She'd wanted me to see it. Was this her way of letting me know she knew? We talked only about the play, not about ourselves.

Along with the burgeoning tragedy of AIDS, I was reading many articles by gay men about the problems they had getting their families to accept their gay lovers. My family, however, was always immediately and warmly accepting of any man *I* ever lived with.

My problems began when we broke up; *my* folks seemed unable to accept that such a relationship was finished. "Why don't you ever bring over X, these days?"

"I told you, Mom. He moved out. We don't live together anymore."

"Oh, well where *is* he living? Maybe I'll call him up and invite him over for dinner next Sunday. He always used to enjoy my Sunday biscuits so much . . ."

Would my "coming out" to my mother really solve such a problem? (In later years, several times I'd had to speak to my mom to remind her that Marilyn and I really *were* divorced.)

In the mid-eighties, I was giving lectures regularly in which the personal examples I cited came from my life as a gay man. One November evening I was lecturing to a large audience at the main branch of the New York Public Library. Halfway through it, I realized my sister was sitting some rows back—next to Mrs. Jackson. When the question period afterward started, I saw among the audience a dozen other well-tailored black women, also close friends of Mom's, who'd come to the lecture together and were sitting to one side.

When the lecture was over, Mrs. Jackson brought my sister up and explained, "I realized that Peggy had never heard you talk. You've always been such an eloquent speaker, I decided to bring her here to the Library to hear you lecture as a birthday present!" A minute later, my mother's friends had gathered, each of them congratulating me on one or another of my points.

I was truly happy to see them.

But I left the library that night thinking, "Well, if I wasn't out before, I am now!"

In 1987 I began writing a memoir, focusing specifically on changes in attitudes toward sex—gay sex at that—from 1955 through the sixties. I resolved that, once I finished the text, I *would* have the by-now-fabled "coming out" talk with Mom.

Since our separation Marilyn had been exploring her own lesbianism; she had finally opened the subject with my mother, only to find—to her surprise (but not really to mine)—that it had *not* gone well. My mother felt such things were better left behind closed doors and not spoken of.

But because of the nature of the book I was writing, I felt that such a direct conversation—the first and most important that so many advocates of "coming out" encouraged—was imperative.

Some two weeks before I finished the manuscript, in a Village restaurant on the way to the Public Theater with two old friends, my mother suffered a major stroke, as a result of which she lost all powers of language, both of speaking and of understanding. She survived in that state, wheelchair bound for the next eight years.

Once the book was finished, I did have a conversation with my sister: It turned out to be easy, brief, and all but superfluous.

I never did get the chance to come out to my mother.

The truth is, though, it's not a major regret.

Many times I've asked myself, just when and if (in the post-Stonewall sense) I *did* come out?

Although I approve of coming out and believe it's imperative at the statistical level, it's still not a question I can answer easily.

Did I do it when I was eleven, walking from the athletic field with Joel?

Is it what I did at nineteen when, on the platform of the D-train, I asked pregnant Marilyn, whom I would shortly marry, if she was *really* aware that I was homosexual, and that even if we married, I didn't see how that was going to change. (She laughed and said, "Of course I am! You've taken me cruising with you, for God's sakes!")

Did I do it in the mental hospital when I spoke to the group of psychiatric residents interviewing me and explained I didn't think my homosexuality had anything to do with any problems that had brought me there?

Did I do it when I took my three-, four-, then five-year-old daughter on outings with the Gay Fathers and our kids to the Upper Central Park ice-skating rink, where she laughed and had fun with the other children? (As I wobbled across the ice, a large black woman in a sweeping purple coat, far steadier on her blades than I, asked, "Excuse me, but who *are* you all?" I explained, "We're a group of gay men, here with our . . . children!" and *fell* into her arms.) Or did I do it at the Staten Island Zoo, where I answered the same question for the young woman taking the kids around on the donkey ride?

("When are we going with the *daddies* again?" my four-year-old de-manded, just before we left. Everyone laughed. And "The Daddies" be-came the group's unofficial name.)

Did I do it the first time I sat on the gay panel in Phoenix and spoke about the realities of being a gay SF writer?

Will coming out be something I shall do in three weeks, once I start teaching again at the University of Massachusetts, and (again) I tell the anonymous hundred-fifty faces in my lecture class that I have to look at this tale or that from the point of view of a gay man—because, after all, I *am* gay?

Or, finally, is it something that I, like the gay policeman written about so widely in the *Times,* can *never* really do, because I never came out to Mother?

I wonder today if, instead of considering "coming out"—in the new sense *or* the old—a point-effect that separates a *before* (constituted of si-lence, paralysis, and fear) from an *after* (constituted of articulation and bodily, emotional, or linguistic freedom), the discontinuity between the absence and presence of an identity, it might be better to consider com-ing out an aware attitude, a vigilant disposition, an open mood (or even a discursive apparatus) that could beneficially inform all our behavior and discussions involving the sexual, and even, at some points, for any number of considerations, contain its presumed opposite—*not* coming out to someone—as long as the reason involved choice and not terror, not intimidation, not victimization, nor any of the range of attitudes that fall under the umbrella of oppression. (For those, I'm afraid, we *still* have to come out; and if it's too scary to do it by yourself, organize a full-scale demonstration: That's one of the things they're for.) But the fact is, coming out (in the post-Stonewall sense) was something that many of us had begun to do, here and there, without the name, years before Stone-wall: Stonewall only focused and fixed its statistical necessity as a broad political strategy. We need to remember that if the human material—not to mention the simple bravery so many have shown and continue to show in our still homophobic society—had not already been there, the strategy would not have been anywhere near as successful as it was.

Many people have made the point: One does not come out once. Rather, one comes out again and again and again—*because* the dominant discourse in this country is still one of heterosexist oppression and be-cause it still controls the hysteria to *know* who's gay and who's not. Heterosexuals do not have to come out—indeed cannot come out—be-cause there is no discursive pressure to deny their ubiquity (and, at the same time, deny their social contribution and the sexual validity of their growth and development, the event field–effect of their sexuality) and to penalize them for their existence. This is the same discourse that constrains "coming out," for all the act's utopian thrust, to a condition of heterosexist surveillance. And though perhaps my "coming out" with the anxious Israeli was an incident that my interested friends could subsequently use to define the fact that I had, indeed, actually come out, or though my "coming out publicly" in Phoenix meant that the straight media could now define me, regularly, as a "gay science fiction writer," though I would not relinquish either experience, and value what both taught me (for both are part of the *field* of experiences that have articulately demonstrated to me that the human boundaries of sexuality can be far more humanely placed than they have been: Both of them changed me, and changed me for the better), though both showed me much and changed my life in ways I can only celebrate, I cannot claim that either *identified* or *defined* anything of me but only illuminated parts of my endlessly iterated (thus always changing) situation.

Firmly I believe that's how it should be.

—New York City
January 1996

NOTES

1. A. R. Ammons, 1993; James Tate, 1994; Stanley Kunitz, 1995.

5

A Bend in the Road

"We're having a conference on postcolonialism. We'd like you to take part."

"But it's not my field. I'm a science fiction writer—a black science fiction writer, who dabbles in gay studies."

"Well—we thought we'd put you on the panel called 'The United States'."

"Oh—then, I suppose so. All right."

Why do I feel that, somehow, I have been recolonized?

Why do I feel, in line with Gayatri Chakravorty Spivak's definition (provisional description?) of postcolonialism ("Postcolonialism represents the failure of recolonization"), that if what I have to say this morning bears any relation at all to questions of postcolonialism or postcoloniality, as we have undertaken them in their multiplicity during yesterday's two panels, it will indeed be through that recolonization's failure?

I

"More than three-quarters of the people living in the world today have had their lives shaped by colonialism," begins the introduction to a book bearing a science-fiction inspired title and containing a collection of fascinating fictions about fiction, *The Empire Writes Back*. What a vast topic, then, our conference title covers! And only a page later, we find the first mention of the subject of our particular panel:

> So the literatures of African countries, Australia, Bangladesh, Caribbean countries, India, Malaysia, Malta, New Zealand, Pakistan, Singapore, South Pacific Island countries, and Sri Lanka are all post-colonial literatures. The literature of the U.S.A. should also be placed in this category.[1]

That last, singular sentence, in which the United States falls outside the brotherhood that—for the USA—defines the exotic, might give any number of readers pause.

But our *Empire* authors, Ashcroft, Griffiths, and Tiffin, immediately explain their singularizing the USA in its very own sentence:

> Perhaps because of its current position of power, and the neo-colonizing role it has played, its post-colonial nature has not been generally recognized. But its relationship with the metropolitan centre as it evolved over the last two centuries has been paradigmatic for post-colonial literatures everywhere.[2]

It is moot whether the next sentence includes the United States—or excludes it, as a special case, already covered in the previous two sentences. That sentence reads:

> What each of these literatures has in common beyond their special and distinctive regional characteristics is that they emerged in their present form out of the experience of colonization and asserted themselves by foregrounding the tension with the imperial power, and by emphasizing their difference from the assumption of the imperial centre.[3]

Let me note here the most fleeting, historically bounded ideolectal difference in my own, very marginal ideolect of written American English, with its local, historically prescribed, and outmoded notion of proscriptive grammar: In that fast-fading ideolect I write, the singularity of "each" would control the rest of the nouns in the sentence more tightly than this particular academic ideolect (which so easily encompasses "different than") allows. In my outmoded and all but superseded American ideolect (and let me stress, perhaps as an invented Unity, that it is an American ideolect our three Australian-based writers seem to me to write—an ideolect that has been the recipient of much translated post-structuralism and Marxian rhetoric), *I* might have written: "What each of these literatures has in common beyond its special and distinctive regional characteristics is that it emerged in its present form out of the experience of colonization and asserted itself by foregrounding the tension with the imperial power and by emphasizing its difference from the assumption of the imperial centre." What I hope we can hear in what sits so uneasily between a rewriting and a translation is an uneasiness with such specificity that begins with the first notion of "regional characteristics" as applied to the countries involved, an uneasiness that resonates all the way to the end.

The special and distinctive "regional characteristics" of Indian literature, as a hypostatized whole, are certainly as problematic as the special
and distinctive regional characteristics of "American" literature as a
whole—not to mention Australian literature, Caribbean literature, or Pacific Island literature. And would the described template really cover all
postcolonial literatures in the list—including the American? What about
that postcolonial writing—however embarrassing, it is there—that *supports* the imperial centre? More to the point, isn't that what a good deal
of postcolonial literature is polemicizing with, defining itself against? Especially if one is to include, however uncomfortably, the United States?
Is it perhaps allegorical of something we might find useful that this particular pluralized blindness to the problems of specificity occurs precisely in a sentence in which it is undecidable whether that sentence
does, or does not, include the United States as postcolonial?

And while we hold onto that notion, certainly we should note as well
that, in the pause we spoke of above, there is certainly room for a good
deal of questioning of the whole assertion. That argument extended,
British literature itself is a form of postcolonial literature, since at some
point in the age of the blue-painted Picts, Britannia itself was under
Rome . . .

II

This is where I'd gotten, when I asked myself: What, from my own, marginal, contemporary position, do I see in these postcolonial discussions?
What, indeed, is that position?

I am, of course, first and foremost a writer, a teller of tales.

I am, coequal with that, a black man, in America, who, although six
out of eight of his great-grandparents were slaves in this country, is nevertheless, in the current debates—in which melanists contest with cultu-
ralists, who contest with Afro-centrists, over just what black means—at a
rather problematic position.

And quite as subjectively important as either of the previous two, I am
a gay man—which is to seize only another marginal and problematic
index in the discussion around so sexually and hereditarily laden a notion as race—and I am a gay man, let us not forget, who has had a wife
and a child.

From such a position, fixed only through so many intersecting margins, if I were to choose to tell a tale, what would it be?

Like the teller, it would be marginal.

Its relation to the discussion could be only indirect.

And, yes, it would chronicle a certain play between blindness and a singular vision.

Certain margins we envision as safe, practicing a sort of safe sex, as it were: my tales will all come from at least twenty years ago or more—though, I hope, the points drawn from them will not.

III

In 1965, when I was twenty-three, I took off to Greece with a friend. I wanted to go because the country was cheap. I wanted to go because the culture, both ancient and modern, was of historical interest. It had never occurred to me that Greece was a colonial, or postcolonial, country—and certainly not a colony of the United States. The Greco-Turkish War, that, in 1897 Stephen Crane had reported on so vividly in the New York press, for me was a dateless ghost. But World War II's Greco-German hostilities, as novelized by John Fowles in *The Magus*, I'd read of only months, if not weeks, before my trip. And Fowles's smoky tableaus of the embattled islands were burned through by the bright images from Lawrence Durrell's *Bitter Lemons*, *Prospero's Cell*, *Reflections on a Marine Venus*, and Henry Miller's *Colossus of Maroussi*. Also, my own marginal genre, science fiction, had marked the same geographic area of the imagination with Roger Zelazny's novel of a devolved Greece, *And Call Me Conrad*—as interesting a novel about life in an occupied country as *Ulysses*. That novel—*And Call Me Conrad*—looking back on it, should have warned me. But it didn't.

Understand:

I wanted to visit Paris.

Understand:

I wanted to visit Venice.

But—understand—I wanted to *live* in Greece.

The specific channels through which I'd gotten the sexual samizdat information that Greece, as a Mediterranean country, would likely be . . . well, a land not of sexual boredom but of sexual pleasure, I can no longer recall. But it was part of the image, with which I took off from the States.

Two of us left; another young man, a Canadian, joined us on the plane, so that when we set down in Luxembourg, we were a group of three. My companions were straight and white. And our trio persisted, in an uneasy coherence, through ten days in Paris at a then inexpensive hotel on the Isle St.-Louis, and ten days in Venice at a pensione near Ferovia, and finally, after a night on the ferry from Brindisi, through the Corinth Canal and into the Piraeus.

Paris and Venice had both provided generous sexual encounters within the first twenty-four hours of my stay, so that I was, at this point, rather blasé about the possibilities of pleasure in general. Athens lived up to its reputation, however. Within the first twenty *minutes* we were there, while Ron went in to see if any mail had collected for us at American Express, and Bill, as was his wont, went to check the prices in hotels that were obviously beyond our means, I was sitting in Syntagma Square, when a Greek in his early thirties started a conversation with me in English, and after a few looks, a few not particularly subtle questions, suggested I come with him to the men's room. When we were finished, I asked him my usual question: "But where do . . . people—*go* in Athens?"

He mentioned several park areas, gave me the names of two movie houses in a street just off Oimoineia Square (one, the Rosyclaire, he told me, I should watch out for, as it could get a little rough), and the names of some clubs. "But, really," he said, "in Athens, if you're looking for it, you'll find it practically anywhere."

Then he left.

That night we three spent the first of four days at the dingy Hotel Oimoineia. That evening we ate in a restaurant near Syntagma, recommended—sign of an earlier age—in Hope and Arthur Fromer's *Europe on Five Dollars a Day.*

Pale, pleated curtains stretched over the lower parts of the window and down the glass in the door's dark wooden frame. We sat at a white-clothed table, eating avgo-lemono soup and discussing our travel plans. *And Call Me Conrad* had scenes set on the isle of Kos—and so, with no more reason than that, Kos was our destination.

Just then, from the table diagonal to ours, a Greek businessman in his forties, wearing a staid suit and tie, with a horseshoe of black hair around a prematurely bald head, coughed and said to us in very good English: "Excuse me—I couldn't help overhearing you. But the three of you are planning to go to Kos, for six weeks you were saying? Does one of you have relatives there?"

No . . .

"Then I just don't think that's where you want to go. I understand, you don't want a heavily touristed island. But, at this time of the year, *none* of the islands are heavily touristed. You could even go to Mykonos, and still be quite private. But Kos—you have to understand. There's nothing there at all! No hotel. No guest houses. I don't think there are three hundred people living on the island! A boat will make a special stop there—perhaps once a month, if there's a particular reason to. You'll be going to an island where the people have simply never *seen* tourists before. Really, with only your best interest in mind, may I make some suggestions . . . ?"

His suggestion was an island called Mílos. There were two towns on it, an old city, Plaka, and a harbor town, Además. In the old city, there were some catacombs and also some Hellenistic ruins. And three days later found us on the weekly boat to Mílos. (Only after we arrived did we realize the island housed the site of the discovery of the Venus di Milo.) Knowing how isolated we were on Mílos, where, indeed, in the first afternoon we rented a small house on the edge of the harbor town that could be traversed, end to end, by a sharply hurled pebble, we realized how right our restaurant acquaintance had been about the more mountainous and even more remote Kos. But two and a half months later, with a notebook full of seaside tales about our local baker, butcher, *cafeneon* owner, fishermen, and landlady, and finally, yes, a month on Mykonos, we returned to Athens.

I had not forgotten the locations of the movie theaters given to me on my first afternoon in Athens, so many weeks ago now. And on a warm day in a month that, in New York would have been in the dead of winter, I went to visit them.

A single narrow marquee with wrought-iron decorations hung over both. Both screened Steve Reeves-style Italian muscle epics, alternating with American westerns. (At one, I recall, I saw Anjelica Huston's first film, *A Walk with Love and Death*.) To say that the Rosyclaire was the rougher simply meant that there were more young Greeks there, often from the army or the navy, actively hustling the procession of middle-aged businessmen, in and out, many of whom could easily have been cousins to the man who had diverted us from rock-shot Kos.

I would move from one theater to the other, simply to vary the faces that, even in the flickering darkness, grew, after a week or two, fairly familiar fairly quickly. An afternoon there began with some quip exchanged with the prim and aging gentleman with his black bow tie who took your money through the bars of the Rosyclaire's ticket window, or it would involve some whispered tale—in my inventive Greek—to another patron about the thickly bespectacled, blue-smocked, iron-haired, woman attendant of the incredibly sexually active men's room, who reigned over the first three feet of those facilities with lordly hauteur, while maintaining magisterial obliviousness to what went on in the remainder of that dripping, white-tiled hall. As far as I could tell, no one ever tipped her after their first visit. In that rougher setting, then, I was surprised, one afternoon, when I saw a young man, about eighteen, sitting in the balcony in a suit and tie—rare among the work clothes, military uniforms, and slouch jackets most of the patrons wore. He seemed a bit too proper for this milieu. But, after observing him for twenty minutes, I saw he knew a number of the people moving about from seat to seat in the balcony—and, a bit later, once we had passed each other on the narrow stairway up to the balcony, he came over to talk to me! Petros was a student—and turned out to be extraordinarily intelligent. Committed to being a doctor, he was nevertheless a lover of literature. At the movies—and, later, back at the Boltetziou Street room my two friends and I were renting—we had sex some three or four times. "Are you really black?" he wanted to know.

And I explained as best I could that, according to American law and culture, I was. His response was to leap on me for another session of lovemaking, which merely confirmed what I'd already learned, really, in France and Italy: that the racial myths of sexuality were, if anything, even more alive in European urban centers than they were in the cities of the United States.

Almost as soon as we finished, Petros asked me would I give him English lessons—though he already spoke the language fairly well. In return, he said, he would help me with my Greek.

Could he take one of the novels I had written home with him to try to read it? Certainly, I said. The four or five sessions over which I helped Petros unscramble the syntax of various paragraphs in my fifth novel, *City of a Thousand Suns*, were some of the most useful lessons in the writing of English *I* have ever had!

And for my first Greek lesson, a day or two later, Petros came over to my rooms after his university classes with a pamphlet copy of Yanis Ritsos's 1956 *'O Sonata Selinophotos (The Moonlight Sonata)*. In that high-ceilinged room, with its three cot beds and tall, shuttered windows, we sat down and began.

"If you are going to learn Greek, you start with very good Greek—very great Greek poetry," Petros explained. "You know Ritsos? A great modern poet!"

In some ways reminiscent in both tone and matter of Eliot's "Portrait of a Lady," *'O Sonata Selinophotos* is a good deal longer, however, and—finally—more complex. The speaker, an old woman in a house (which may, after all, be empty), keeps looking out the French window, wanting to go with someone in the moonlight just as far as "the bend in the road"— *"'o streve tou dromou."* No literary slouch, Petros spent an hour and a half explicating the phrase, "let me come with you," which tolls repeatedly through the poem, each time modulated in its nuance—the phrase with which he had invited himself to my room, as he reminded me with a grin.

By the end of two weeks, sex had fallen out of our relationship: Poetry had taken its place. Then, with a burst of warm weather, now at my excuse, now at his, even the language lessons dropped off. But the friendship endured. A brief trip I took to Turkey (I was deported for a week, but that's another story), at about this point, established a few of its own postcolonial insights. Some of the things I'd suspected were now confirmed: With its white skirt and fez, the Greek national costume was largely Turkish in origin. The Greek custom of having the kitchen in the front of the restaurant seemed to be basically Turkish. And a good many Greek foods were very similar to Turkish foods—only the Turks ate them in much smaller quantities and much more varied combinations. On my return, I mentioned these insights to Petros.

To appropriate a phrase directly from the imperial centre: We were not amused.

One evening after my return, Petros and I decided to go for dinner down to the Piraeus—a few stops out on the subway that began at Oimoineia Square, with its dozens of lottery salesmen and their sticks and streaming ticket strips, strolling about the underground concourse.

Along the docks, as the clouds striped the east with evening, we hunted out the smallest and most pleasant of places we could find: A wooden structure, it was built out over the dockway. Inside, it was painted green, with screening at the windows rather than glass. At places you could look down between the floorboards and see water flicker.

At a picnic-style, or perhaps barracks-style, table, we set out our beer and a plate of *mezei*—hors d'oeuvres. As we sat, talking, jabbing toothpicks into oily bits of octopus, artichokes, and stuffed grape leaves, somehow we got onto the politics of Greek and American relations.

What pushed us across the transition from the amiable converse of two young, gay men out in the purple evening to something entirely other, I've never been able to reconstruct. But suddenly Petros was leaning across the table toward me, both his hands in fists on the boards. "Even this place—" he was saying. "What could be more Greek than this place—eh? You think, yes? Here on the Piraeus docks? Eh? Well, I tell you—everything you see here is American! The paint on the walls—American! The screening in the windows—American! The nails in the boards—American! The fixture on the sink over there—American. Even the calendar on the wall, there—even you can see that's American!"—he pointed to a pin-up calendar, in Greek, advertising Coca-Cola. "The blades that cut the paper mats we're eating on! The machinery that puts the electroplating on this knife and fork. None of that is Greek! Look out the windows at the boats in the harbor. Even if some of them are Italian-built, their hull paint is American! Everything, the floor, the ceiling, everything you look at, every surface that you see—in this Greekest of Greek places—is American! I have no country! You—you Americans—have it all!"

To say I was taken aback just does not cover my response.

But somehow Petros, then I, recovered. We finished eating. Then we went for a walk outside by the water. But it was, indeed, as if I had come so far along an evening road, only to round a certain bend—to discover a waterfall or an ocean or a mountain range beyond, that I had never seen before, so that, even on the return trip, nothing looked quite the same. Soon, however, we were more or less amiable.

I told Petros where I had to go the next afternoon—a street that made him raise an eyebrow, then laugh.

It was famous in the city for its cross-dressers. But I explained to Petros: "No—there's an English-language school down there, where a British friend of mine is teaching. Because I write books, he's asked me to come and visit his class. He wants me to read them something of mine. And to talk about writing English with them."

"Will you talk to them about some of the things you spoke to me about, in your book that we read?"

"Probably," I told him.

"Good!" Petros pronounced.

We caught the subway back to Athens, and I walked up steep 'Ippocratou to 'Odos Boltetziou, trying to keep hold of the fact that what I was seeing—much of it, at any rate—was simply not what I had thought I was seeing when I'd left.

IV

The next afternoon at twenty-to-four, I threaded my way out from Oimoineia Square to the glass door with the venetian blinds inside it, hurried up to the second floor of what was called something very like the *Panipistemiou Ethnike Anglike;* and my British friend John let me into the room, where his fourteen pupils—two girls and twelve boys, all about seventeen or so—had been in session for twenty minutes of their hour-and-a-half English lesson.

The pages I read them from one of my science fiction novels and our discussion of them were nowhere near as interesting as Petros's exegesis of Ritsos. But the students made a brave attempt to question me intelligently about it. ("How much money you make from writing of a book in America?" At the time, I made a thousand dollars a novel—seven hundred and fifty, if it was under sixty thousand words. "Are writers very rich in America—they are not so rich in Greece, I think.") Then my part in the lesson was more or less over, and John moved on to other material. Whether it was one of the students or John, at some point, who made a joke about the cross-dressers who, outside, would soon be strolling up and down the evening street, I don't remember. But I recall how one thick-set, dark-eyed youngster leaned forward now. "I must say . . ." he began three times: "I must say . . . I must say, because we have a guest today, I must say—must explain: There is *no* homosexuality in Greece!" In concentration, his fists knotted on the small table before him, as he leaned with an intensity that mirrored Petros's from the night before—though this young man was a year taller, and weighed, I'm sure, half again as much. "There is *no* homosexuality in Greece! The Greeks must not—*can* not do that. It is dirty. It is bad. It is bad and disgusting they who do that. The Greeks do not do that. There is homosexuality only from foreigners. They make homosexuality in Greece! It is not us—the Greeks! It is the bad and dirty foreigners! It is all the bad and dirty tourists that make—that bring homosexuality in Greece. The Englishmen. The Americans. The Germans. The tourists! Not Greeks—you know, now!"

John knew that I was gay—though I doubt the students did. Perhaps, as someone who had invited me to his class, he felt he had to defend me, though I would have been perfectly happy to let it ride. "That just doesn't make sense to me, Costa. When you all go home from here, the people you see on the street, most of them are pretty obviously Greek. You hear them talking with one another, joking. That's Greek I hear, downstairs."

"You don't *see* that!" Costa insisted. "You don't *see* that! Not Greeks! If Greeks do that, it is only because of the foreigners. They do it, sometimes, maybe for need money—maybe, that the foreigners pay them. But Greeks not do that. It is bad, it is very bad. *Why* would Greeks do that? It—how you say, doesn't make sense!"

I watched this impassioned young man. I looked at the other youngsters around the room: One girl in a dark sweater rubbed the edge of a book with her foreknuckle. A boy with a bush of light hair slouched back, one hand forward over the front edge of the table. Some smiled; some just looked uncomfortable without smiling. The room's walls were gray. A ceiling fan hung from the center, not turned on. Blinds were raised halfway up the windows. Costa's white shirt was open at the neck; his sleeves were rolled up his forearms. Beneath his desk, he wore dark socks beneath broad-strapped sandals, which now he slid back under his chair. I wondered what surfaces of Greece, if any, I was seeing.

After the class, I walked home with English John—who was rather breezy about it all, though even he seemed troubled. "You know, he manages to make that speech to us almost every other week! I wasn't expecting it today, though, but—like he said—we had a guest."

Over the next days, I found myself thinking about both experiences. What was particularly bothersome to me was the way the second seemed posed to obliterate the first—to impugn the very social conduit by which my new vision had been gained. If, indeed, as Costa insisted, I "didn't *see* that," what was I to make of what I did see?

The way to "untrouble" such conflicting visions is, of course, to shrug off—as daily, in those months, I'd found myself having to do—the notion of some hypostatized, monolithic entity called "modern Greece" and its constitutive necessity, "the modern Greek." The country I was in was as various and multifaceted in its play and counterplay of ideas as anywhere else. And what I was seeing when I looked at Costa, I now know—this side of Stonewall—was just a good deal of Petros's problems to come.

For better or for worse, the experiences that we actually have form the models by which we interpret all situations that we encounter, verbally or pictorially, in the abstract.

(And a situation presented to us only in film or video is as abstract as one presented in words.)

V

Today, however, when I hear discussions of heterosexual AIDS in Zaire, say (and AIDS is certainly the most postcolonial of diseases), it is impossible for me not to remember a thirty-four-year-old black African from Nairobi (one of two carpenters whom I had regular, casual sex with in those months; the other was white, named John, and lived in a furnished flat south of the Thames), who told me he wanted to be called Willy because his real name I would probably be unable to negotiate. For several months, during the two years I lived in London almost two decades ago now—a city where I lived with my wife, where my daughter was born, where my homosexuality was at its most marginal— I would meet him near Baker Street. Willy was missing an eye from a childhood accident and lived in Earls Court in a slightly uneasy truce with his numerous Australian neighbors; and he explained to me that, between the time he was eighteen and the time he was twenty-five, when he'd left Nairobi, his sexual partners had included, in his own words, "Pretty much every black African in the Nairobi police department. They would pick me up on their motorbikes. Then we'd go off— then they'd drive me home." And I can also remember Willy saying: "Are you *really* black? You are? That's very exciting! Come here, let's do it again!"

Though I am perfectly aware that Zaire is not Kenya, though I'm perfectly aware people like to exaggerate their sexual conquests, I also remember Willy saying: "No, it is not like here. There is no homosexuality in Africa: There you don't talk about it at all. You just do it!" But though his words were closer to Costa's, his inflection was closer to Petros's.

My story of Greece belongs, of course, to the neocolonialism that Ashcroft, Griffiths, and Tiffin described in their opening paragraphs. If there is a point to draw from it, it is that neocolonialism can so easily masquerade as postcolonialism that they are often indistinguishable.

And my story of Willy. . . ?

Understand, I do not tell any of these as a tale of *the* homosexuals or *the* homophobes of Greece. I do not tell them as a tale of *the* homosexuals of Africa, representing some happy Hegelian synthesis of, for better or worse, the Greek opposition, say. And although I think Willy's story offers at least a partial *explanation* for what I heard in Athens eight years before, that is still not the direction I hope you will take the stories' exemplarity in. I want my tales to trouble with the same trouble that was pluralized out of the opening sentence of *The Empire Writes Back* about what is common to all postcolonial literature—possible exception, the United States's, which of necessity must contain, for better or worse, these tales. And as they trouble, I hope they remind us of the differences in the world that have come about since they occurred. (I have since read accounts of celebrations of Gay Pride Day in Athens.) I hope they call into question certain assumptions about the world that is not the United States for those who, here at this panel, are considering the United States as a topic of examination, study, and interrogation—for those who, here, in this conference, are considering venues where (sometimes) there is homosexuality and, sometimes, there isn't.

Equally I hope that none of these tales suggests a centered answer to any question of homosexuality, certainly not of AIDS, nor—heaven forefend—of postcolonialism itself. But when we hear heterosexual statistics for AIDS in Africa, I should simply like to know what happened to the homosexual statistics, which, from all I've been able to find, don't exist—though such nonexistence should not be terribly surprising for a country in which, as Willy informed me, between bouts of vigorous lovemaking, there is no homosexuality; nor should it be surprising that, in such a country, the heterosexual statistics are as high as the homosexual statistics are low. But should even these—let's face it, very American—tales I have told eventually stand revealed as ventriloquized by the imperial centre itself, against which other marginal subjects have to polemicize and define themselves, I hope only that their side of the polemic is carried on at the level of direction *and* indirection, of statement *and* suggestion, which is where, alone I think, they can be of any use.

—*New York City*
April 1993

NOTES

1. Bill Ashcroft, Gareth Griffiths, and Helen Tiffin, *The Empire Writes Back: Theory and Practice in Post-Colonial Literatures* (London: Routledge, 1989), 2.
2. Ashcroft et al., *The Empire Writes Back*, 2.
3. Ashcroft et al., *The Empire Writes Back*, 2.

6

The "Gay Writer" / "Gay Writing"...?

It's too easy to reduce the problem of "the gay writer" to the split between those gay writers (like myself) who, on the one hand, feel that all art is political one way or the other and that all they write is from a gay position—and, in my case, from a black and a male position as well—and those writers who, on the other hand, feel that all they write is fundamentally apolitical, even if it involves gay topics; that they are just writers who happen to be gay, or, indeed, black, or female, or male, or Jewish or what-have-you. Whatever one's knee-jerk reaction to either stance, the truth is that a tally of what writers from both groups actually write in their fictions, in their poetry, in their plays would show that, outside of direct statements on the matter, there's no simple way to tell from their creative work—for *certain*—which ideological theme each espouses. Writers who believe that art is fundamentally apolitical often produce extraordinarily socially sensitive works. And it is an endless embarrassment to us who believe in the fundamentally political nature of all human productions that, simply from the plot reductions of their stories, or even from the expressed sentiments of their poems, measured against whatever notion of "political correctness" they believe in (and, like the rest of us, I believe in mine), writers who express the most "correct" political sentiments can produce the most politically appalling work.

If we are ever to solve our problems, I believe the opposition between the two—the belief in the fundamentally apolitical nature of the *best* art and the belief in the fundamentally political nature of *all* art—needs to be carefully undone. Personally I suspect that more important than which of these positions a particular writer adopts is whether that writer sees his or her own position as opposing the majority opinion around, or whether the writer sees his or her position as merely an extension of what most other intelligent people think. In the academy, for instance, there's a tendency to see everything as politicized: Thus writers who have longstanding academic connections can assert their oppositional stance by upholding art to be fundamentally apolitical.

I've lived most of my life outside the academy, in a society and at a time where and when the notion that there might be any political aspect to any work not announcing itself as propaganda is hardly entertained or is wholly pooh-poohed. Thus my oppositional belief in total politicization. But, if I'm honest, when I read with great care, say, much of Harold Bloom, or even Paul de Man, not to mention Milan Kundera, in *The Art of the Novel* (three critics who uphold that art is fundamentally apolitical), it seems that much of what they mean by "apolitical" is precisely what I mean by "political." I just don't know if they'd give me as generous a reading as I give them. And, indeed, the generosity of their readings, one way or the other, would be controlled, I suspect, by their perception of what each saw as the major abuses of the position he polemicizes against.

What I hope we can do this afternoon is to switch the scene of the debate from that of how the gay writer perceives her- or himself (engaged in a fundamentally political or apolitical endeavor) to how the gay writer is perceived at large. That, I think, is where the debatable problems lie.

Two examples come to mind that dramatize a range of perceptions and their problematics. My first example is Martin Duberman.

Prizewinning playwright and noted academic historian, Duberman is the biographer of James Russell Lowell and the author of the definitive history of Black Mountain College as well as a recent biography of Paul Robeson. And he is an outspoken defender of gay rights. For several years Duberman was also a regular reviewer for the *New York Times*. Once Duberman became established as a commentator on gay rights, he found the *Times* sending him nothing but books on gay topics to review. After several years of this, he finally asked them, first informally, then formally, to send him books on historical or dramatic topics to review as well. When they didn't, with much soul searching, he finally asked them to send him no more books on gay topics. He would be glad to review for them anything on history or theater, two areas in which he had demonstrated clear and pointed authority.

The result? Duberman has not reviewed for the *Times* since.

My second example is the career of the writer Guy Davenport. I start by saying I have no notion what Davenport's sexual persuasion might be. For many years he has closely associated with a woman in his hometown of Lexington. Even ten years ago, such a claim as mine might have been taken here as polite disingenuousness, a protective gesture toward prejudice and the law. But in this case, my disclaimer is sincere.

I don't know.

Nor do I care.

Certainly Davenport is among the most elegant writers at the sentence level to work in American prose. Only William Gass currently comes near him. And Davenport's erudition is occasionally *almost* beyond following . . . His short stories (in *Tatlin!, Da Vinci's Bicycle, Eclogues,* and *The Jules Verne Steam Balloon*) dramatize both my claims. His essays (in *The Geography of the Imagination* and *Every Force Evolves a Form*) confirm the facts behind the drama. He is also a superb translator from the Greek. His are simply the finest versions done of the prose and poetic fragments of Herodotus and Sappho, Alkmen, Archelogos, Anakreon, or of the mimes of Herondis. Some years back, it was rewarding to see Davenport now introducing Nabokov's posthumously published notes on *Don Quixote,* now writing the odd sidebar for the *Times,* now reviewing this or that work on classicism for a general audience whom his writerly color, range, and precision charmed.

But, as one book followed another, it became clear that one of Davenport's fictive themes was boys masturbating, singly or in groups, now alluded to in passing, now described in electric, limpid, endlessly inventive language. Masturbation surfaces in half a dozen of the twenty-six or so stories of his I've read. Whatever Davenport's own sexual leanings, the homoerotic charge on these onanistic celebrations is undeniable; the homophobic margin generated around them is inescapable—in a homophobic society. And Davenport's name becomes rarer and rarer in the better quality general readership magazines.

The last time I asked anyone literary about Davenport's work, I was given a small *mou* and a little shake of the head. "No, his work is too perfect. It's too studied—too polished; not first-rate art at all."

But the truth is that it is too homophobically embarrassing. And since it is always embarrassing to admit embarrassment, this silly judgmental judo is positioned to cover over a topic it does not even begin to tease at, much less touch on.

But these two examples—Duberman, the openly gay writer pigeonholed and stripped of one critical platform, and Davenport, the writer who, whatever his sexual fixes, nevertheless produces work saturated with pederastic resonances (only compare the relative ease with which Nabokov's far more legally and morally disturbing, and certainly as esthetically intense, pedophilia was assimilated: because it happened largely in the sixties and because the transgression was heterosexual) — are, for me, the best characterizations of the problem, not of the gay writer (such a topic finally dissolves before the impossibilities of definition), but of the problems accruing to the production of writings perceived to be gay.

Though you may accuse me of switching the scene of the debate once again—and once too often—I'd like to leave us with this question.

Not what would we advise Duberman or Davenport to *do* as writers. Presumably they will continue to write and to put whatever energies they do or do not put into that most impossible of objects, the writerly career, according to their wonts and temperaments.

My question is rather: Do we, gay, straight, or otherwise, as readers apprised of the situation, have any responsibility to Duberman, Davenport, or their texts?

—Philadelphia
February 1989

7

The *Black Leather in Color* Interview

Questions by Thomas Deja

BLIC: When you started writing science fiction, it was still basically a white, male heterosexual preserve. As a gay, black man, how did you feel about being the odd man out? Do you think it may have changed the way your career progressed in any way? Why does it still seem to be a community of white guys?

Samuel R. Delany: Of course, there *are* no "heterosexual" male preserves. There are social groups where gay or bisexual men feel safe acknowledging themselves—first to one another, then to pretty much everyone. And there are other social groups where they don't. By heterosexual preserve, you simply indicate the latter. The gay and bisexual men are there. But the homophobia in the group is high enough to make them wary of acknowledging their presence—sometimes even to themselves.

Possibly because I had an extremely supportive and wide-ranging extended black family, I've rarely felt myself the odd man out in any group I've entered—even though I probably was. Again and again. Or, possibly, because of my sexuality and because of my interest in writing as an art (I didn't come out sexually in my family at all when I was a youngster, and would have been scared to death to, but they all knew I wanted to write and thought that was great) I'm so used to being the odd man out I just don't notice it anymore.

You decide where, on the spectrum between the two, the explanation lies.

Certainly it's changed my career. The artist is always the odd woman or odd man out in any group—even in a group of other artists. (That last is the most painful lesson we always learn and then relearn.) If that's an anxiety-producing situation for you, and you're an artist—then you're bound to have an unhappy life; and that's certainly going to influence how you present yourself, how you're perceived, and how you're treated by those around you.

Why is SF still so overwhelmingly white? I wish I knew. There're lots of African-American SF readers—many more today than there were when I entered the field in '62, by hundreds of percent. I meet them at conventions. I meet them at academic conferences. I meet them at bookstore signings. Why haven't the writers followed? (They're four of us writing regularly in English: Octavia Butler, Steven Barnes, Charles Saunders, and myself—and most recently Nalo Hopkinson. In the related field of Horror there's Tananarive Due. And, writing in French, out of Canada, there's Haitian-born Jean-Claude Michel.) Again, I don't know. I know what it's not, though; it's not editorial bias. If anything, the white editors I've talked to today are aware enough of the black readership that they'd jump at the chance to sprinkle some good SF stories with a black perspective around their magazines or book lists.

Am I over-optimistic? Perhaps. But not by much, I'd wager. When submissions by black writers hit the twenty percent mark—or get above that—then we may well have some problems. But right now they're nowhere near that number.

BLIC: How did you discover the leather culture?

SRD: The leather world has always been the most visible part of the gay male world, next to the area that laps—or overlaps with—the world of cross-dressers. The real question for many if not most gay men might better be: How did you manage to find the *rest* of the gay world, once you found the world of leather and/or drag queens?

Among the first three of four times I got picked up and taken home, back when I was eighteen or nineteen (nine years before Stonewall), a guy in his thirties started talking to me on Central Park West and invited me back to his place, a few blocks away. Clearly, he explained, he was into sadomasochism and thus things would be somewhat unusual once we got there. But since I was new to the whole cruising scene, I wasn't all that clear on what the usual was. So I went with him. At his place, he had some leather lying around, a jacket on his coat hook, a vest over the back of one chair; he himself had gone cruising, I recall, in a brown, three-piece suit. He told me to strip, then—while he remained dressed—he started to put me through an instruction routine: "All right! Put your hands on your knees! Now your toes. Now reach around—and spread your buttocks!"

I went along with it with what I thought was perfect goodwill. What I wanted to do was suck and get sucked, cuddle some, and maybe do some fucking—in about that order of preference. But if this was a necessary prelude, I was willing to cooperate. After about ten minutes, though, he sat back and laughed: "You're not really into this," he said, "are you?"

I confessed: "Not really."

"Get your clothes on," he said, good-naturedly, "and get on out of here. You go back to Central Park and maybe you'll find somebody else more into what you're looking for."

So I did. We shook hands at the door. And I left, thinking he was a pretty nice guy.

That was my introduction to the leather world. A perfectly pleasant Mr. Benson, if you will—who knew what he wanted, and that I wasn't it. But in the way that first impressions often do, this one formed a pretty good basis for most of what I've found in that world since: a certain amount of common sense, a certain amount of goodwill.

BLIC: How has leather influenced your writing? Will it influence your writing further?

SRD: I first started writing about S/M—in a tale called "Time Considered as Helix of Semi-Precious Stones"—pretty much the way most people do. I saw S/M as a limit case for human sexuality. That is to say, initially S/M had been presented to me as sexuality straddling some border, beyond which we were outside of the "acceptable," the "human," the "civilized." I wrote about it in the typical way that one tends to when one is writing about a sexuality that one perceives as fundamentally "not mine." I offered explanations for it. (Whoever tries to explain his or her *own* sexuality, once society has allowed you to be comfortable with it? It's just you; it's what you enjoy doing!) I saw it permeating every aspect of the young character's (Hawk's) life—in dangerous, even suicidal ways. It functioned largely as a mark of doom, a scar of Cain. This is what's often called the "Romantic" view; and it's perfect nonsense. This is the view that says that somehow perfectly decent, ordinary guys, like the one who picked me up by the park when I was a kid, are at heart secret Jeffrey Dahmers or John Wayne Gacys—at least on the S side. And, conversely, anyone on the M side is somehow on some suicidal roller coaster that must lead to self-immolation. But because I'd had as many real and practical experiences as a sexually active gay man that I had (and of course there were, later, many more than the one I've just recounted), some of them leaked over into my description of things like actual meetings and real conversations.

The story won both a Hugo Award and a Nebula Award for 1968

from the Science Fiction Writers of America—probably for all the wrong reasons.

When I thought about taking on the topic again, I realized I could go on with the romantic view. Or I could go more deeply into the material that made up my own experiences.

But the reader reaction to the story—including the awards it won, from a largely straight readership after all—alerted me that there was a reality (and for me, "reality" is a synonym for "politics") to be explored here; and there was also a myth to be cut through.

My 1974 novel *Dhalgren* features a leather man—Tak Louffer—as an important secondary character. As Virgil guided Dante, Tak guides my nameless hero, as he explores the ins and outs of the burned-out city of Bellona. But the stories in which I turned to examine some of the real (i.e., again, I mean political) problems that the idea of S/M brings up was in a project I began in 1976—my series of stories set in the ancient land of Nevèryön.

Nevèryön is a land where the majority of the good citizens, the majority of its aristocracy are brown or black—which is to say the majority of the *money* is in the hands of people who are brown or black. Thus it represents an unsettling reversal of the American power structure. It's also a land that employs slavery as an economic system—many of the slaves are blond and blue-eyed "barbarians" from the south. And that of course takes the reversal one step further. In the course of the eleven stories and novels that make up the series, the background tale that holds them all together is that a green-eyed black man called Gorgik is himself taken—uncharacteristically—as a slave when he is sixteen. Over the course of the series, which covers some thirty-five years, Gorgik gains his freedom, foments a slave revolt, finally manages to be appointed a minister of state, from which position, after much work, he eventually abolishes slavery from the land.

The problematizing factor, however, is that Gorgik is not only gay, but he is also sexually attracted to the accoutrements of slavery—whips, chains, and the iron slave collars that, traditionally, slaves in Nevèryön were made to wear. He himself is not a blond barbarian—but he is clearly racially mixed; and he also finds the barbarians sexy. For a while, in the first half of the series, he has a barbarian for a lover . . . a relationship that comes to a rather bad end, by the bye.

But what paradoxes do these situations create for Gorgik? Does his own desire somehow contaminate his political project of abolishing slavery? Does it intensify it?

How is the relation between desire and politics perceived by his followers, by his adversaries—and by the ordinary people in the society who don't think of themselves as really involved in the question? For Gorgik is very much "out" about his preferences.

The stories have a lot both to interest and to disturb black readers, gay readers, S/M readers—and, probably, white, straight readers of both sexes. If you want to watch a writer trying to solve some of these problems, succeeding at some and failing at others, then these books might interest you. This past year, Wesleyan University Press rescued them from mass-market oblivion and has just reprinted them as handsome, trade paperbacks. Should you really want to know what this weird Delany guy is all about, *these* are the books to wrestle with.

BLIC: You've been on record as saying that *Starship Troopers*' color-blind society was one of the things that influenced you to embrace science fiction. Considering that, thirty years after Martin Luther King, the racial situation is as bad—if not worse—in this country, do you feel that such a society is still obtainable? What would we have to do to obtain it?

SRD: First of all, to say things are just as bad or worse than thirty years ago is absurd. Only someone who wasn't here thirty years ago could possibly say that. Things need to get a lot, lot better, certainly. But there are no restaurants in Manhattan, at least, which, if you're black, will stop you—assuming you're dressed properly—at the door and say, "I'm sorry. We can't serve you here. Why don't you try some place else?" I just came back, a couple of weeks ago, from a Black Arts Festival in Atlanta—a festival which had taken over the entire city. The whole public park had been turned over to black and white vendors and people exhibiting African fabrics, jewelry, pottery, and art. The guests at the motel I stayed at were about fifty percent African-Americans. There were both white and black waitpersons in the dining room.

Well, if you think that's what Atlanta was like thirty years ago, you're out of your mind!

Atlanta, New York City, Washington, Los Angeles have all had black mayors. There were *no* black mayors thirty years ago, my friend, and more to the point if you suggested that there ever might be, you'd have been laughed out of the room.

Thirty years ago it was 1964—and less than ten years before that schools were desegregated by law for the first time!

The paradox today, though, is that we actually seem to have achieved not Heinlein's "color-blind" world by any means, but something distressingly close to it: a world that's color-deaf. By that I mean a world where, with very few exceptions, such as now and again in the academy and in a few newscasts focusing particularly on a racial incident, there's little or no talk of racial matters at all. And there's absolutely no talk of the class matters—of money, politics, and power—that underlie them.

And—no—until that happens, we probably won't make much more progress than we've made. And that's a criminal situation.

What do we have to do to make things better? Shift around a lot of money; do a lot of politicking; and redeploy a lot of power.

But I don't see how that can be done—and done with intelligent goals—until we start talking about it, loudly and articulately, first.

BLIC: What influence do you think your work, and the work of the other 'New Wavers,' has had on more recent trends in science fiction? What's your opinion of such styles as cyberpunk?

SRD: Talking about your influence on those who've come after you is the quick way to sound like a pompous clown. That's for those who've been influenced to say—not me.

I enjoyed the cyberpunk phenomenon back when it was happening—between 1982 and 1987. That, seven years later, people are still talking about it, and that it's still seen as an active force in some people's minds, seems a little strange to me, I confess—like people talking about New England Transcendentalism as if, a hundred-forty years later, it was still going on. But I'm very pleased for the writers involved because it keeps them in the spotlight. I like Gibson's work. I'm always glad when a talented writer gains some serious attention.

The downside is, however, that a lot of people now think that once they've read Gibson, Stirling, and Cadigan, they've read all there is of interest in the whole science fiction field for the last fifteen years or so. They know nothing about the exciting work of Kim Stanley Robinson, or Karen Joy Fowler, or Lucius Shepard, or Connie Willis—not to mention Octavia Butler. But there are an incredible number of fine writers in the SF field right through here. It seems idiotic to penalize them simply because they weren't involved with one particular fanzine that flourished in Texas for a couple of years in the early eighties—*Cheap Truth*—which, when all is said and done, is really all the cyberpunks have in common.

BLIC: It is possible to write effective fiction without putting something personal into it? How much does your identity shape your fiction and vice versa?

SRD: Of course you can't write effective fiction without putting something of yourself in it—but I'd hate to leave this discussion with that as an end note. Because you can't write dreadful, wooden, lifeless fiction without putting something of yourself in that, either.

The sad fact about fiction is that the autobiographical element, which, more or less transformed, is always there, has nothing to do with effectiveness—or lack of it.

Fiction exists as an extraordinary complex of expectations. Texts that fulfill all these expectations register as moderately good or mediocre fiction: the sort one reads, more or less enjoys, but forgets immediately. What strikes us as extraordinary, excellent, or superb fiction must fulfill some of those expectations and at the same time violate others. It's a very fancy dance of fulfillment and violation that produces the "Wow!" of wonder that greets a truly fine piece of writing—a truly wonderful story. Those expectations have to do with everything from the progression of incidents that, in the course of the story, will register as plot, to the progression of sounds in the course of its sentences. And those expectations cover many other things at all levels—and often between levels.

No one sits down and teaches you what these expectations are— much less which ones you should conform to and which ones you should violate.

I've never seen a creative writing class yet that even talks about them at any length.

You learn them from reading other fiction—other truly good fiction; and also from reading bad fiction.

Because violation has as much to do with success as fulfillment does, there can never be one story, or even a group of stories, that can teach you all the expectations at once. Also, we learn those expectations not as a set of rules to follow or break—though, after a while, some writers can actually list a number of them. Rather we learn them in the same way we learn a language when we go to that country—learn its grammar and syntax; learn what is expected of a competent speaker of that language.

And just to up the ante, languages change—and the language of fiction changes as well. What was perceived as a violation yesterday is a sedimented expectation today. What was once an expectation is now to be honored only in the breach—or people will just giggle. The language of fiction is not quite the same today as it was eighteen or twenty years ago. And it's certainly not the same as it was sixty or seventy-five years ago. And it's almost entirely different from what it was a hundred or a hundred-fifty years ago. So while it's always good to know the history of the language you're speaking, and while that history will often tell you the reason why certain expectations are (or are not) still in place today, the great stories of the past hold the key to writing the great stories of today no more than an oration by Cicero will tell a contemporary politician the specifics of what to mention in his next sound bite.

Perhaps that's where your "personal identity" comes in, if we remember that identity is what we share with other people—again in the language sense: the infinite play of differences that make up our specific lives, whose patterns, when they become complex enough, start to register as similarities with the patterns the play of difference among other people make.

Your sense of the expectations is always filtered through that play of differences that is each of us. But, in terms of the text on the page—and in the reader's mind—their fulfillment (*and* violation) is everything.

—New York City
1994

8

The Thomas L. Long Interview

At the time of this interview, Thomas L. Long was a graduate student working at the University of Virginia on questions of AIDS and American apocalyptic imagery.

THOMAS LONG: What work does your writing perform in regard to HIV/AIDS? Would I be on track by thinking that §11.4 in *The Tale of Plagues and Carnivals* represents a summary of your self-understanding of all your writing?

SAMUEL R. DELANY: In general, what I hope at least part of my work performs—or helps to perform—is a necessary deformation of an older, pre-AIDS discourse, which privileged sexual reticence, into a discourse that foregrounds detailed sexual honesty, imagination, and articulation. AIDS makes such a discursive adjustment imperative. (Today, anything else is murder.) But such a deformation also has other benefits, in terms of the liberation of a range of subjects frequently marginalized under the rubric of "the perverse."

As an artist I (I want to add, "of course") resist the idea of my work containing any summary of itself. As I understand it, such a summary would make—or at least take steps toward making—the rest of the work superfluous. But especially I resist the notion of summary in terms of §11.4! That, yes, is the climax of my 1984 novel about AIDS, *The Tale of Plagues and Carnivals*. As such, it's a piece of writing that would be meaningless without all that has gone before in the novel—and that can only finish its reverberations as the reader reads the sections that come after it. Alone, it is particularly flat and dead. By itself, it is almost incoherent. Taken out of context, rather than summarize anything, it would strike most readers unacquainted with the rest of the book, I suspect, as lunatic babble. It's a piece of writing specifically crafted to be *without* any of the explanatory excess that, at least to my understanding, such a summary section would demand.

If I were going to choose a summary section from that novel, I would choose any and *every* section before I would choose that one!

Particularly, I would choose—as a summary—section §9.82 and the other sections circling around the Master's attempt at a biography of Belham. At least those sections dramatize what I see as the problem of the subject-for-another-subject—and do so in general summary terms. Their constituent microdramas allegorize the problems we have apprehending any other subject, whether that subject be the socially acclaimed great man, the most ordinary person on the street, or the particularly marginalized and oppressed: someone whom society urges us at every turn to see as oscillating between the state of "dangerous" and the state of "victim"—someone who is, say, HIV positive.

Thus they generalize the overall problems of fiction writing as I see them, whether about AIDS or about anything else involving human beings.

The faltering and all but impossible attempts of the "author" to describe a specific moment in the life of the ill "Pheron" in section §11.4 constitute a specific, non-summary example of the general problems that the Master has describing the life of Belham throughout section §9.82 (and has, equally, trying to find a recognizable reflection of his own life in §9.83).

I would hope it's clear that §9.82 and §9.83 dramatize the general case while §11.4 is a specific case (a specific narrative case effective as it *recalls* and *evokes* the generality, certainly)—but *not* the other way around!

The general is the resonance to the specific. This is the "law" controlling the rhetoric of Proust and James. And, for better or for worse, it controls my fictive rhetoric as well.

Indeed, my apprehension of the text—more than a dozen years after writing it, true—is so far from yours, at least in terms of this point, I suspect we may simply have different notions of the meanings of such terms as "summary," "understanding," and even (or especially) "writing."

TL: What can you tell me about your role as both writer-educator and writer-advocate (i.e., your inclusion of specific biomedical discourse on HIV infection and your persistent message that adequate research into vectors of transmission have not been undertaken)?

SRD: The message is persistent—and, yes, it still is—*because* the situation is persistent.

My general sense is that in an anti-sex society such as ours, everywhere we turn, whether it be to a group of the most well-intentioned women (in a demonstration I watched in Knoxville, less than two months ago) swathing themselves and their partners' bodies in rubber—gloves, dental dams, and condoms—so as to prevent literally all contact between bodies in the name of "safe sex," or whether it is the admonition to teenagers from advertisement cards along the tops of subway cars in New York City that "abstinence is the best protection," I think people are trying to use AIDS as an excuse to armor the body in silence, ignorance, and rubber—even as they proclaim this a form of education.

This is *why*, I think, so little work has been done in establishing transmission vectors. AIDS is currently at its most powerful as a "cultural tool" against sex within the dominant heterosexist discourse, to the extent we are in the greatest ignorance about it. The more we actually know of it, the less we can use it in such an anti-sex agenda as we have been.

I have actually heard people argue that it's *good* to use to AIDS to scare teenage girls away from becoming unwed mothers! This represents such a basic misunderstanding of the psychology of sex as to leave one reeling. The fear of AIDS is no more likely to scare teenage girls away from sex than it scared away the four-hundred-thousand-odd folk who have, or have died from, the disease already!

TL: Outside of writing, what role have you played in your neighborhood or local community with respect to HIV/AIDS?

SRD: Outside of writing and writing-related activities (lecturing to and talking with various groups, usually in colleges around the country), I've done very little.

I am not a member of any organization.

And when I wrote *The Tale of Plagues and Carnivals* back in 1984, I had done a great deal less! As I say in the book, at that point I hadn't even known anyone with AIDS. Since then (as I've written in subsequent editions), AIDS has become the largest killer among my personal circle of friends and acquaintances. (I learned of my friend poet Essex Hempell's death only a week ago. He died while I was teaching out at Minneapolis.) What *have* I done?

Well, I've had a lot of sex—without condoms. And I am always ready to talk and discuss the situation with the people I have sex with, especially those (very rare) folk who are more comfortable doing things with rubber. (I'm fifty-three, now, so that's down to about seventy-five to a hundred times a year. Up until 1992, this was closer to three hundred times a year. But then I established a permanent [open] relationship.) I get an HIV test every year.

And I remain HIV negative.

TL: What work do you see your "Benjaminesque montage" and "Bakhtinian polylogue" performing in both *The Tale of Plagues and Carnivals* and *The Mad Man?*

SRD: I go along a good bit with S. L. Kermit's internal critique of that sort of thing, as expressed in §10 of ToPaC. I think the only thing such techniques can do (and you have to remember that a "Bakhtinian polylogue" is what any novel worth the name, after all, *is*) is *invite* a certain richness of reading. But they cannot *assure* such a reading. That is something that can only be supplied by the radical reader.

(And, I might suggest, a search for summary points does not strike me as the most powerful of reading strategies to generate a radical reading—of my texts, or of anyone else's.)

TL: How have writings like *The Tale of Plagues and Carnivals* and *The Mad Man* been received by non-professional readers (i.e., people who aren't book reviewers, academics, or critics)? Are readers of paraliterary texts more communicative "fans" than the readers of literary texts, and how would you characterize your relation with them? In noting that "[t]he audience's performance is always more or less stochastic" (ToPaC, 345), do you mean conjectural (in the sense of "imaginative") or random or both or neither?

SRD: It is the rare, rare person who writes to a writer who doesn't harbor some ambition to write him- or herself. Often it is politely withheld until the third or fourth letter, but it is almost always there, somewhere. Thus, the distinction between professionals and/or academics on the one hand and non-professionals on the other is a bit hard to make. Where does one put, for example, enthusiastic students (graduate or undergraduate) who are *not* currently writing about *you?*

But I shall try to do my best.

When, in the summer of 1984, my editor finished reading the ToPaC manuscript, he called me up to tell me. His words stayed with me. I recount them now not to boast, but only because of what was to happen later. On the phone, he said: "When I finished the book, I was in a daze. I got up, walked out of my house, down the hill, and—kind of like a robot—turned in at my neighbor's yard. He was out there, working, and he asked me what was the matter. I told him, 'I think I've just read the finest book I've ever read, in my life—about anything. Period.'"

Realize, when he said this, I had no illusions about editorial hyperbole. It's a necessary fact of commercial publishing. The only reason, as I say, to cite this at all is not to appeal to any objective judgment on the novel, but only to suggest that there probably was at least *some* enthusiasm, if only on an emotional level, on that editor's part—unless he was simply an unconscionable liar. He also said (to be fair): "And I haven't the vaguest idea how to market it."

Flight from Nevèrÿon appeared in the early months of 1985. It received only two reviews: the obligatory paragraph in *Publishers Weekly* (which devotes one to every professionally published trade book as it appears) and another equally brief mention (by Marta Randall) in the *San Francisco Chronicle* (in which—Ahem—she called it a "masterpiece").

The book went through two paperback printings—the first, seventy-five thousand copies, the second fifteen thousand copies, putting eighty-five thousand paperback copies in print.

For a book printed in such numbers, this is an unusually small number of reviews.

An ordinary paperback original with only a twenty-five-thousand-copy print run, can usually count on anywhere between eight and a dozen reviews. In my files *Tales of Nevèrÿon, Neveryóna,* and *The Bridge of Lost Desire (Return to Nevèrÿon)*, have upwards of two *dozen* reviews a piece!

Volumes I, II, and IV—that is to say, the two volumes preceeding it and the volume following it—were all reviewed favorably in the *New York Times Book Review*. But a year after *Flight from Nevèrÿon* appeared, I happened to run into the reviewer (Gerald Jonas) who had been so generous to the first two and the last of the series. He was unaware that the third volume even existed!

The novel did elicit one hate letter from a Canadian reader. In substance, as I remember, it boiled down to, "You think you're so smart pulling all these literary tricks! Well, *I* think it's *boring!*" This was blurted with a spattering of four-letter words over three pages handwritten in red ballpoint. Neither AIDS nor sexuality was mentioned. I can only assume the writer was fairly young, and may not have gotten very far into the book.

No book I've ever published has received less attention than *Flight from Nevèrÿon*. Whether it was by the publishers' accident or by design, I have no way of knowing. Even at eighty-five thousand, the sales of the third volume were less than half the sales on either of the first two *Nevèrÿon* books. But even if it was an accident that the book was not sent to the usual reviewers, it's an accident that falls into a system, that functions as part of a repressive discourse.

While, from time to time, people have written to tell me that they disliked one book of mine or another (has it happened a dozen times in what now must total some three or four hundred fan letters I've received over thirty-five years?), the letter from Canada was certainly the most violent, if not energetic, in its negative expression.

To complete the story, when I turned in the manuscript of the fourth volume, *Return to Nevèrÿon*, three days later I received a brief note from the same editor who'd claimed to have been so taken with volume three. The note said he was returning the manuscript, unread. Bantam Books was no longer interested in pursuing the series; perfunctorily he wished me good luck with the book elsewhere.

The fourth volume was brought out by Arbor House, its name changed from *Return to Nevèrÿon* to *The Bridge of Lost Desire*: Editorial researches discovered that, now, in the minds of book distributors and book buyers across the country, the series was perceived to be contaminated, infected, sick in some strange and dangerous way, so that it seemed advisable to dissociate it *from* the series (of which it was the concluding volume)!

Since its hardcover appearance in spring 1994, *The Mad Man* has had a much more ordinary history of reviews. I've revised the book substantially, however, in preparation for a mass-market paperback edition. This week, actually, that mass-market edition appears. There are still a few mistakes—and, yes, even some minor additions to be made (I've prepared errata sheets)—but basically I'm very happy with it.

The *Mad Man* reviews, as you have seen, are overwhelmingly positive. If I do say so, the intelligence behind the Reed Woodhouse piece ("Leaving No Button Unpushed") and the Ray Davis overview ("Delany's Dirt") are at a level any writer must be grateful for. *Lambda* waffles. But the only truly dissenting voice was Candace Jane Dorsey's "On Being One's Own Pornographer."

The other responses to the book I've gotten are some six fan letters, all received in the first month after *The Mad Man* appeared. All were praiseful. Four are, indeed, from other academics at other universities than mine—thus they may fall outside your purview. Still another is from a gentleman who wrote to make me an honorary member of "The Soiled Sole Society," a group of twenty-five men and women who find dirty feet sexually attractive. Another invited me to a sex party, somewhere on the other side of the country in the Oregon woods.

I suspect, Tom, that people who do not enjoy such works as these simply don't get far enough into them to make writing the author a reasonable possibility.

You ask what I meant by "stochastic" on page 345. The word, you'll recall, is part of a two-pronged rhetorical attack and recovery, the first part of which is at the beginning of that same section: "The artist's performance is always more or less aleatory. . . . The audience's performance is always more or less stochastic." I would accept as a paraphrase: "The artist's performance is always more or less a scatter-shot affair . . . the audience's performance is always more or less guess work."

TL: In both *The Tale of Plagues and Carnivals* and *The Mad Man*, characters have encounters with a monstrous beast, though in both cases the manifestation is sufficiently hallucinatory or dreamlike as to seem imagined, not real. In both cases this manifestation is also not absolutely central to the narrative and seems to go against the grain of other realistic features of the narrative. Where in your own imagination does this beast come from? Are these beasts symbols or do you understand them to be performing other functions as well?

SRD: You might find it interesting that, until you pointed it out, I was unaware of the beasts as shared elements between the books!

The key to such a revelation is, I think, Freud's dictum: "Repetition is desire."

Both beasts are just that—figures of (and even for) desire.

(My novel *Equinox* contains a similar encounter with an hallucinogenic beast. *Hmmm* . . .)

Now that you have made the point, immediately I can see other features they share. Both are collage monsters, formed of fragments and disparate traits, held together only by the desire of a reader to make them into a whole, to form them into a coherent entity. In *The Tale of Plagues and Carnivals* it is, of course, the evil monster of desire who is figured in the text. In *The Mad Man*, the monster's function is more complex: I associate him both with Leaky *and* with Mad Man Mike—as well as with the death of Mike Bellagio, which death, in effect, brings the monster into being for Marr as something other than the question of Hasler's own death.

In his 1992 book *Donner la mort*, Derrida suggests that a religion comes into being when the experience of responsibility extracts itself from some interplay of the animal, the human, and the divine. (That is to say, the wings of the angels and the horns, hooves, and tail of the devil may just have a good deal more to do with marking Christianity as a religion than do the wounds of Christ.) Without the extraction or the divine, however, what is produced is the monstrous. The monstrous thus may just be a presupposition for the religious.

Part of the problem with such symbols, however, is that the author can usually negotiate them only within a specific text.

That's certainly true for me.

TL: What more can you tell me about the connection between the erotic and the mystical in both stories?

SRD: Alas, nothing. I've always felt that any "mystical" experience falls somewhere between a logical and a psychological breakdown. That goes for the one the letter to Sally Mossman describes in *The Mad Man*. That seventy-page letter is, as a matter of fact, a combination of three actual letters I wrote in the early eighties, two to women and one to a man, the three of them cobbled together into a single, fictive document.

Save a few dream moments, the one recounted there is the only mystical experience I've ever had. And, after all, what brought it on was thinking nonstop for two or three hours about matters of my own life and death. Mystical experiences are certainly rare, different, and interesting. But I don't think they are privileged, as it were, over any other sort. In fact I think it's best to interrogate them even *more* carefully than most. Certainly I don't believe they occur outside the constraints of discourse, say, however difficult it might be to articulate their content. As I said, I am much more likely to rack them up to (psycho)logical breakdown than I am to assume they imply any sort of access to a transcendental reality—though, certainly, when you *have* one, you can understand why people might assume them to be such.

TL: Apocalypse is an explicit theme in *The Mad Man*, where Tim Hasler has scrawled *"ekpyrosis"* in shit before his death, after which Mad Man Mike defiles the apartment. The Greek root of the term "apocalypse" means literally revelation or unveiling. Do you see a relationship between these two senses?

SRD: At the level of plot, what I'd intended the reader to assume is that most of the defilement was done *before* Tim and Mike left Tim's apartment—likely in a scene, possibly even involving several of Mike's friends, similar to the "turn-out" that fills up the second half of part IV and the first half of part V. And, yes, it's before they leave that *"ekpyrosis"* is daubed on the mirror and the window. Once, down at The Pit, Tim has been killed and Mike has been wounded, Mike *returns* to the apartment to wreck it. Thus the destruction—of furniture, books, and the like—is overlaid on top of the defilement. Defilement and destruction *surround* the murder of Hasler—as they do its replay, the murder of

Joey. It's important for the allegory that the murder neither climaxes (nor initiates) both defilement *and* destruction.

(But all this may be much clearer in the revised paperback version.)

There's a history, of course, of apocalyptic imagery used not only as a symbol of the end of things but also as a symbol for the beginning of things. (Genesis, and the Big Bang both, *begin* with apocalyptic moments.) One of the most famous such users, of course (about which I've written, in my monograph *Wagner/Artaud* [1988]), is the apocalypse that ends Wagner's *Götterdämmerung*—the ending of the Ring. That tripartite apocalypse (in one cataclysmic event, the fall of the Gibichung castle, the burning of Valhalla, and the flooding of the Rhine) is at once the *end* of divine, cyclic, mythical time and the *beginning* of human, developmental, historical time.

(This double reading of apocalypse I trace back to Wagner's association with Bakunin, as an account of the friendship begins, before the Dresden Uprising, in Wagner's *Mein Leben*.)

Certainly in *The Mad Man*, I wanted the apocalyptic imagery to function in both ways. But, again, that is much clearer in the revised paperback version—which spends more time portraying John and Leaky's life together *after* Joey's death—than in the earlier hardcover version.

TL: I am convinced that apocalyptic discourse is America's chief structure for constructing social identity, which it does by means of binary oppositions (Us/Other), usually predicated on sexual anxieties, particularly in terms of physical defilement. Both of your narratives explicitly seem to resist and dismantle such binarisms and so are in these respects anti-apocalyptic. Is this observation accurate in your view and how might you qualify it for me?

SRD: Basically I think you're on the right track. But I think that the apocalyptic discourse you have located is part of a larger discursive phenomenon—what Donna Haraway calls "salvationist rhetoric" of which apocalyptic imagery is an integral part.

Anthropologist Mary Douglas's work on dirt and defilement is also relevant here—though, I am trying to answer these questions quickly. I have forty cartons of unpacked books currently in a storage room, containing more than half my library—including the Douglas. So I'm afraid I can't give you the exact citation.

Etymologically, an apocalypse is a "dis-covery" or an "un-veiling." By tradition, what is uncovered or unveiled in an apocalypse (thanks to the Revelation of St. John) will initially appear more confusing than not, and will be seen to need interpretation. Often, in what is discovered, the news will not be good. In that sense an apocalypse is something of an exposé. To the extent I am writing in detail about people and practices that are not usually portrayed in fiction, I suppose you could call *The Mad Man* (if not *The Tale of Plagues and Carnivals*) apocalyptic. But, yes, in general, I try hard to resist the salvationist rhetoric that awaits to force such material into its well-worn grooves. That means resisting traditional apocalyptic imagery—in search, perhaps, of a more rigorous and productive sense of the apocalyptic.

In the sense that the books are anti-salvationist, they are also anti-(traditional) apocalyptic.

Certainly dismantling Us/Them oppositions is one way to resist salvationist rhetoric.

TL: Defilement is a cultural (and therefore, relative) category. (My mother, for example, once told me that she thought French kissing was disgusting. I didn't ask her what she thought of sucking cock, getting fucked, or rimming.) In *The Mad Man* particularly you seem to be carving out a discursive space or stretching our boundaries by graphic descriptions of what is possible or what can be imagined, a "pornotopic fantasy" which you (disingenuously) declare "never happened and could not happen." HIV/AIDS public discourse has found defilement issues difficult to talk about (e.g., "Cum, spit, piss, shit, etc." become "bodily fluids"). The religious right is fascinated/horrified by images of homosexual defilement. (I'm having a hard time defining a specific question here.) I'd like to know your observations, experiences of defilement and its relationship to bliss, the sacred (the *mysterium tremendum et fascinans*, terrifying and fascinating), identity, sense of self and other . . . What more can you tell me about "pornotopia"?

SRD: That's a lot of question, especially to come so late in the game. As far as my own experiences, suffice it to say that, without reproducing any of them photographically (the closest I come to that is the "Sleepwalkers" letter), *The Mad Man* covers a great enough range of them so that a reader who bears in mind that it is written by a fifty- and fifty-one-year-old man about a twenty- to thirty-five-year-old man, and thence allows for the necessary novelistic exaggeration and foregrounding, would probably not be too far off in most of his or her assumptions about my own sex life.

I do not have very much to say about bliss. I am much more comfortable talking about pleasure. (I quote John Marr: "Without being blown away by it, I liked it. And wanted to do it some more." That's been my reaction to most of the sex in my life, one way or another.) Bliss tends to function (for most of us?) as a point effect, and a point we perceive/

approach asymptotically, rather than encounter directly. Though I agree with what I take to be the polemical thrust of Barthes's discussion of *jouissance* in matters literary, I suspect his point finally *is* polemical and only signifies as a counter to those who would argue that reading is a purely Apollonian activity, with no Dionysian side at all.

As far as its relation to the mystical, again, while the mystical may (or may not) be a part of one's personal liberation into whatever one gets pleasure out of doing (with bliss seen as the ultimate point of pleasure), I don't think it is in any way a *necessary* part. To use a more Derridian formulation, the mystical is a structural possibility of any aspect of human experience—thus it can never be discounted, barred, or expelled from the Material City. But precisely because it is (potentially) inherent in everything, that's what makes it so uninteresting—at least to me. It does not work in any *strong* manner to differentiate. And difference for me is still the source of information, of interest, or, indeed, of pleasure.

"Pornotopia" is not the "good sexual place." (That would be "Upornotopia" or "Eupornotopia.") It's simply *the* "sexual place"—the place where all can become (apocalyptically) sexual.

"Pornotopia" is the place where pornography occurs—and that, I'm afraid, is the world of *The Mad Man*. It's the place where any relationship can become sexualized in a moment, with the proper word or look— where every relationship is potentially sexualized even before it starts. In *The Mad Man* I try to negotiate pornotopia more realistically than most —in much the same way that *À la recherche du temps perdu* and *Ulysses* negotiate the universe of comedy. But, though our lives are packed with the comedic, most of which we ignore day to day, the universe of comedy is still not the day-to-day world we inhabit—nor is it the same as what is called "realism."

The comedic universe has many correspondences to the world we live in—just as pornotopia has many such correspondences. But the two worlds are still not the same as the world of realism. They *feel* different. They are signed by discrete rhetorical markers. *Ulysses* and *À la recherche* are serious comedies. As such, they *are* often confusable with realism. But it *is* a confusion, nevertheless.

A critic who *completely* misses the comedic aspects of *À la recherche* and *Ulysses* would probably be taken to be misreading the texts—at least by most knowledgeable readers.

The Mad Man is a serious work of pornography. I suppose I ought to be flattered by some readers' confusing it with realism. But, finally, it *is* a pornographic work. Its venue is pornotopia, not a realistic portrayal of life on New York's Upper West Side, for all I have used that as the basis for what I wrote. Those who say it is not a pornographic work (and that I am being disingenuous by saying that it is) are, however well-intentioned, just wrong.

TL: In addition to "pornotopias" both narratives suggest a Whitmanian idea of affection between men that crosses class lines. How would you characterize your own utopics? Do you believe that revolution is possible or only resistance (Sara Schulman's position in "Why I'm Not a Revolutionary")?

SRD: Again, questions like revolution or resistance strike me as semantic haggling—possibly of a necessary order. (I don't know Ms. Schulman's essay.) A resister becomes a revolutionary when the perceived danger to her or to those she loves is great enough for her to go get a gun. Very possibly it is also a way of acknowledging that there *are* many situations out there where people have to and *are* fighting for their lives.

In a theory class of mine last year, a tall, soft-spoken young woman from Iran took a firm objection to the notion that everything was political. Some things, she maintained, were just private discussion, with no political aspect at all.

We asked her for an example.

This is what she came back with. "When my friend and I used to sit around in our room and argue for hours about who was going to be elected, or what the outcome of some new government policy was going to be, that seems to me purely private speculation. When, later the same week, I was crossing the street with my friend and she was shot dead beside me by a sniper on the roof across the street, and I had to run and take cover in a doorway so *I* wouldn't be shot, *that* was political!"

Given the shock all of us in that room underwent at the apocalypse of her experience in her homeland, if you wanted to start distinguishing between who was resisting and who was a revolutionary, I think all of us would have said: Sure. Go ahead.

But I also point out, the young woman was just as startled as we had been when someone pointed out that a social structure of laws, behavior, and customs that *prevents* people from being shot in the street was *also* political. To the young Iranian woman, all politics was evil. Anything that was not evil was private. The notion that politics could be good, and could be used to preserve a space of freedom and choice was as astonishing (and, finally, as liberating) a notion to this young woman as the necessity for greater distinction among levels of resistant political involvement had been to us, when we contemplated her experience of crossing the street and losing a friend to a bullet in her native city.

As gays, in the U.S. we do not yet—most of us—live in such a city.

But others do: Three years ago, at a conference on postcoloniality at Yale University, I delivered a paper "A Bend in the Road" (subsequently published in *The Yale Journal of Criticism*, Spring 1994, Volume 7, Number 1). My paper hinged on accounts of two conversations with two men, a young Greek student and a Kenyan carpenter, both of whom I'd met, years apart, while cruising. One of the other participants was Egyptian novelist and psychiatrist Nawal El Saadawi. When all the participants had adjourned for pizza, Dr. Saadawi commented to me, rather offhandedly: "You know, if you'd given your paper in my country, at the University of Cairo, say, before the afternoon was over you would have most certainly been arrested—and quite possibly killed before the week was out."

It behooves us to remember that the strides made in gay liberation have *not* occurred every place in the world. And if that is the sort of insight that accompanies Ms. Schulman's distinction between revolution and resistance, more power to her.

But, right now, Cairo is *not* the place *most* of the U.S. gay community lives—AIDS notwithstanding. Which is probably why there's a good deal more resistance here than revolution.

As to the relation of sex to the crossing of class lines, I've answered the question at some length in my book *Silent Interviews* (Wesleyan University Press: 1995), in the section entitled "Sword and Sorcery, S/M, and the Economics of Inadequation." You might pursue the topic there.

TL: What is the connection between "Joey" in *The Tale of Plagues and Carnivals* and "Crazy Joey" in *The Mad Man*.

SRD: None—that I'm aware of.

Joey was modeled on a homeless junky hustler whom I knew during the early eighties. I described our last meeting, in Spring of 1988, in "Postscript 3." Part of the task I set myself in that book was to remain as accurate as possible to the aspects of it that were reportage.

Crazy Joey was a composite portrait of several more or less deranged young men, met here and in San Francisco many years before, with a goodly dollop of fantasy added—which suits the creation of a denizen of pornotopia.

What is important about Joey is that he lives—and lives AIDS free, at least as far as I was able to determine.

What is important about Crazy Joey is that he dies.

As such, the two characters occupy different pivotal points in their respective novels.

TL: What are your thoughts on erotic transgression, sexual dissidence, embracing the role of pariah? How are these roles related to carnival? Are you aware of the sexual antinomianism often associated with millennial movements, particularly during the Reformation?

SRD: I am, of course, a great fan of the "antinomianism" of Anne Marbury Hutchinson, which inspired Hawthorne to his *Scarlet Letter.* (What American is not?) Of course, they were not really "antinomianists" ("persons against all Church laws") at all. That was simply how they were perceived and what they were dubbed by their Puritan church enemies. What they believed (before they were all slaughtered by Indians off in Pelham Bay in 1643, if that indeed is what really happened) was that there were enough intersecting social discourses in a caring and nurturing society to constrain its members' behavior to the good so that society did not *need* official Church law and official Church punishments. If anything, they were the country's first die-hard utopian social constructionists.

Are you familiar with Scott O'Hara's public sex journal *Steam?* O'Hara is an HIV-positive former sex worker in the gay porn industry turned writer and publisher. I find myself greatly drawn to what he has to say. (*Steam* published excerpts from *The Mad Man* just before it first came out.) In the most recent issue (Volume 3, Issue 3, Autumn 1995), O'Hara has all but repudiated the "Safe Sex" movement (although not all his writers have, by any means), with an article called "Good-Bye to the Rubberman," in a way that I am deeply in sympathy with. Says O'Hara quoting a positive friend: "I'm so sick and tired of these Negatives whining about how difficult it is to stay safe. Why don't they just get over it and get positive?" Though I am HIV negative myself and would like to stay that way, I'm not and never have been—at least not since my good old "mystical" experience at the Variety in '84—one to whine about it.

You'd have to read the whole article to follow what he's saying. But I agree with him: Not that we negatives should become positive (which is lunatic) but we should stop whining and take responsibility for learning to negotiate the sexual landscape that exists.

The millennial context comes close to forcing the elements you're discussing into a "salvationist rhetorical" context—and that's precisely the context that they have to be kept out of, if they are to function in a positive manner. Transgression, sexual dissidence, and the role of the pariah (not to mention carnival itself: a church-licensed celebration of a "farewell to the flesh" before a Lenten period of prolonged abstinence) must be removed from salvationist discourse if they are to be anything more than a return to orthodoxy.

The Tale of Plagues and Carnival had its title as early as 1980, four years before it had a topic. When I read Bakhtin's *Rabelais and His World* in 1984, I associated (and contrasted) his notion of carnival with Bateson's notion of the New Guinea custom of the Iatmul naven (*Naven*, 1958), which had already been at work in the Nevèrÿon tales. I wondered if this new disease, then still being referred to as the "Gay Plague," was what my story was about.

To find out, I wrote it . . .

By 1986, David Black's Science-in-Society Journalism Award-winning *The Plague Years: A Chronicle of AIDS, The Epidemic of Our Time* (Simon and Schuster, 1985) was being pilloried in the gay press, because people were beginning to realize that the constraints metaphors such as "plague" and "victim" imposed had much farther-reaching effects than had been heretofore supposed. Susan Sontag's very weak book on AIDS (*AIDS and Its Metaphors*, a follow-up to her extremely strong *Illness as Metaphor*) locates the range of military metaphors as the fall guy in AIDS rhetoric—and totally misses the boat. I know that she never saw my novel. If she had, she might have noticed that the *controlling* metaphoric structure for AIDS from the very beginning was: "*What* metaphor shall we use for it?" AIDS has been from the beginning a term-in-search-of-a-metaphor—and, in that sense, both her book and mine fall right *into* the controlling, dominant metaphoric structure.

Black happened to be a straight acquaintance of mine. I'd known him on and off for a number years before his book (or mine) appeared. It was quite an experience for him to go from being an award-winning science writer, receiving a good deal of praise from gays in the course of it, deeply in sympathy with the gay community and appalled by the ravages of the early years of AIDS to, a year later, finding himself pilloried in the gay press as an insensitive pander of plague and victim stereotypes. But it could just as easily have happened to me. By 1986, I couldn't possibly (nor could anyone else with a shred of social responsibility) have used the term "plague" in the title of anything having to do with AIDS.

But, by purging the disease of still *another* metaphor, we were all furthering the *dominant* discourse of the disease-with-*no*-fixed-metaphor. I hope your own "anti-apocalyptic" efforts don't fall into the same trap.

It's one of the tropes that still keeps so much of the disease literally "unspeakable."

But if there is a truth to be learned here, it is that dominant discourses are just that: the discourses that dominate. The dominant structure doesn't particularly care who adds to it, or how smart—or even well-intentioned—the ones who add to it are.

To conclude: At the beginning of the letter containing your list of questions here, you mention a range of works, a few of which (e.g., *Angels in America* and *The Mystery of Irma Vep*) I'm familiar with but most of which I'm not.

Let me refrain from comment on any of them. I don't quite see how, for your purposes, that would be useful—especially since I don't have the time (or the energy) to return to any of them for a closer look that alone would give such comment the energy or accuracy that might render it so.

Yes, I've read Professor Jackson's *Strategies of Deviance* and find the whole book quite an extraordinary performance. I'm honored by his attentions. Would you mind if I sent him a copy of our interchange here? He might find it of interest, if not of use.

—New York City
February 1996

Part Two

The Politics of the Paraliterary

9

Neither the First Word nor the Last on Deconstruction, Structuralism, Poststructuralism, and Semiotics for SF Readers

. . . to dissolve the introductory problem, to search out a common vocabulary among the debates' discussants, to pinpoint common ideas or presuppositions they share, to locate common centers for argument, or to describe the general rubric of language-as-model-for-all-meaning-processes that many of the dialogues have taken place under might well be construed by a number of the dialogues' participants as an aspect of a totalizing urge, a will to knowledge-as-power, a desire for mastery which has come under severe criticism and intense analysis at numerous points in these very debates. We might even say that a recurrent "theme" of the poststructuralist wave of these dialogues is that all such urges are distorting, biasing, untrustworthy, ideologically loaded, and finally blinding, so that they must be approached with continuous oppositional vigilance.

What you, my hearers, however, cannot see is the quotations marks around "theme" in the paragraph fragment above. As easily I could have put a line through the word, placing ~~theme~~—to take a figure from Derrida's 1967 book *Of Grammatology*, a figure that Derrida borrowed from the German philosopher Martin Heidegger—"*sous rature*," or "under erasure." A reason for this move is that this same critique of the totalizing impulse to mastery holds that even the social process of constituting a ~~theme~~ is, itself, an example of the same totalizing urge. The critique holds: A "theme" has the same political structure as a prejudice.

Both the words "theme" and "thesis" derive from the Greek word τίθε-ναι, to place, to pose, to posit, to position, or to let stand. Thus the idea of a ~~theme~~ is etymologically grounded in the idea of having, or holding to, a position. Indeed, as my semantically sensitive listeners will hear as we progress, the idea of positivity, of posing, of positionality is packed into—is impacted throughout—the entire discourse around (that is, posed or positioned around) the notion of theme/position itself.

No matter how much we talk as if ~~themes~~ were objects we found present in, or positioned by, a text, this critique maintains that ~~themes~~ are actually patterns that we always impose *on* a text (i.e., the position is always a position we position)—and always for reasons we cannot fully understand, that we can never fully master, that we remain blind to. We will confuse them just the way we confuse the "positions" within the parentheses in the last sentence. No matter how much we claim to have found objective evidence of one or another ~~theme~~ present in one or another text, the constitutive elements of that "theme" have already been politically in place, i.e., posited, before we made the blind move of recognizing it.

"The theme is already in place before the text is read."

"The text reads, if you like, the theme is us."

"The theme is historically sedimented: It is not an aesthetically privileged ground for the text."

. . . to use some locutions characteristic of the rhetoric associated with structuralist/poststructuralist discourse.

Paradoxically, if this criticism is correct—and I feel that it is—one of its inescapable consequences is that, really, we can never escape *from* thematics. Thus we must always maintain an alert and severe analytical stance *toward* them. This is why you will frequently hear, in discussions of "deconstruction" vs. "thematic criticism," people speak of the opposition between the two—or talk about a basic and essential antagonism between them. (Latin: position and opposition. Greek: thesis and antithesis.) The thematic critics' oppositional argument sees the searching out of themes (along with their sisters and their cousins and their aunts: symbols, allegories, and metaphors) as the primary activity of the critic, with a bit of semantic analysis, a bit of historical rereading—i.e., a bit of deconstruction—as a supplementary activity to complete the job, perhaps to add a critical form to the search, to give it closure at the end, to provide a sense of commencement at its opening. The proper critical position for "deconstruction" (which is, after all, *almost* a synonym for analysis), say the thematic critics, adding their own ironic quotes to the term, should be as an adjunct to thematics. Deconstruction should be used to trace out themes from particularly hazy passages, should be used to complete themes, to elide one theme to another, to fix a theme's autonomy, to do, in general, what deconstruction seems to do best and often even boasts of: ". . . to see relationships," (to use the words of Thomas Disch's parodic critical essay, by Burdie Ludd, in his short story "The Death of Socrates") "where none exist."

But for the poststructuralist critic, this oppositional tale between thematics and deconstruction is an old story. It is the story of two opposing forces whose right and proper relation is one of hierarchy, of subordination, of supplementarity. It is the story of the battle of the sexes, the antagonism between man and woman whose right and proper positionality is for woman to stand beside, behind, and to support man. It is the story of the essential opposition between white and black whose proper resolution is for black to provide the shadows and foreground the highlights for white, for black to work for white. It is the story of evil that finds its place in adding only the smallest of necessary spices to a pervasive, essential good. It is the story of nature and her cup-bearer, the primitive, posing a bit of relief for the rigors of civilization and its flag-waver, culture. It is the Other as the locus, as the position, as the place where the all-important Self can indulge in a bit of projection (i.e., can throw something forward into the place of the Other—or simply hurl things at the Other). It is the story in which the frail, fragile, and erring body is properly (as property, as an owned place) a vessel for the manly, mighty, and omnipotent mind; where masturbation (or, indeed, homosexuality or any of the other "perversions") is a fall-back only when right and authentic heterosexuality is not available; where the great, taxing, but finally rich literary tradition, with its entire academically established and supported canon, occasionally allows us to give place for a moment to those undemanding (because they are without power to demand) diversions (those objects we find when we turn from our right place of traditional responsibility) of paraliterary production—mysteries, comics, pornography, and science fiction. It is the story where the conscious and self-conscious subject occasionally discovers (i.e., uncovers the place of) certain inconsequential, or even interesting, slips of the tongue or sudden jokes that can be explained away by an appeal to an unconscious that is little more than a state of inattention. It is the story of the thinking, speaking, acting subject for whom the way to consider objects is as extension, property, tool; of presences merely outlined and thrown into relief by the otherwise secondary absences about them; of the authoritative voice that knows and speaks the truth, prompted by a bit of suspect writing whose proper use is only as an aid to memory; of primary creative work that, from time to time, may rightly, if respectfully, be approached through some secondary critical act; of the mad who can be heard to mention as they shamble past a few amusing or even shocking truths, here and there among their mutterings—truths that, alas, only the sane can really appreciate.

Male/female, white/black, good/evil, civilized/primitive, culture/ nature, self/other, literature/paraliterature, mind/body, conscious/un- conscious, subject/object, presence/absence, voice/writing, artist/critic, sanity/madness—these seeming conceptually egalitarian oppositions that cover vast socially exploited hierarchies are, themselves, a theme; perhaps, till fairly recently, they were the great theme of the West.

So when I point out first the opposition between thematics and de- construction, then point out the hierarchy that is assumed to be the proper thematic (i.e., positional) resolution to the opposition between them; and when I go on to point out that neither that opposition nor the subordination the opposition can be so easily shown to mask really an- swers the needs of criticism, I am engaging in a very old move—a move that will be familiar to those who have followed the structuralist/post- structuralist debates of the last years. The point is, the poststructuralist critic more so than the thematic critic must be aware of just how mired in themes we already are. What has changed for the poststructuralist critic is the state, the status, the ontological position of the theme.

When an object's ontological status changes, it is no longer the same object—possibly it is no longer an object at all: Hence (which means, after all, *from here*) the quotation marks around it; hence the line through it; hence the barrage of de-positioning rhetoric placed on all sides of it—hence, indeed, whatever ironic mark we need to tell us that, for a while at least, it is undecidable what our response to it should be— a description of irony courtesy of the historian of criticism, René Wellek.

A theme is now no longer one among many components of a text that we can locate here or there (a component sometimes present, some- times absent); it is not a component that, as we trace it through the text, as we map it between texts, explains the texts it occurs in; it is not the component that confers on texts unity and coherence, nor does it give them their status as objects worthy of analysis; it is not a component that lets us master texts, allows us to dispose of them (or dispose of the parts of the texts in which we read them), either those texts we like (put safely into our personal canon) or those texts we don't like (left safely outside it). Instead a theme becomes a sign, a political marker, a place to start the analysis that dissolves the border that allows us to recognize it in the first place. For the fact is, in the traditional notion of theme (as in the traditional notion of fact) there are too many things left out: Too many tacit presuppositions, too many historical pressures, too many stabilizing situations are just missing. To recognize an array of elements with this many gaps as a unified, coherent theme is only to mark the place where we have been made analytically blind, where we have been rendered ideologically passive. Under such an analytic regime, with their (old?

new?) ontological status, themes lose their specificity, their individuality, their structure, their critical privileges.

They no longer exist as objects, as property, as tools with which the subject-as-critic can mark out a clear and bounded territory, can solve the problems of the text. (Themes are no longer presences in the texts. They are no longer objects.) Themes are now demoted to the status at least of states (which can be overthrown) or of kings (who can be deposed), and removed from that position which claims that they are, as content, absolutely and irrevocably allied to their position, grounded in it and part of it. They dissolve, rather, into specific, decentered galaxies of problems—a problematic, as some poststructuralists might say. They are disposed of as themes and begin to be dispositions (i.e., moods).

Almost an Analysis. What I have done here, I mention in passing, is attempt to sketch out a brief and rather tentative deconstruction of the notion of "theme," i.e., of the opposition often cited between two modes of criticism, "old-fashioned thematics" and "new-fashioned deconstruction." One of the inescapable consequences of this argument, were we to take it from the level of generality at which we have been discussing it to the specific level of particular examples, is that we'd begin to see that much of the "old-fashioned" criticism looks nowhere near as old-fashioned as it might have when we started, and that much in the "new-fashioned" criticism will begin to look all too familiar. But I have started with this example—however sketchy—*of* a deconstruction because this is one of the most discussed, and thus one of the most troublesome, terms associated with poststructuralist discourse.

What deconstruction does, if I can hazard such a declarative statement in an area noted for its insistent verbal multivalences, is dissolve oppositions: I have said that "deconstruction" is almost a synonym for "analysis." But here is where that "almost" must come home. To analyze (cognate, after all, with Lysol) is "to dissolve from above," while deconstruction unbuilds throughout. It unbuilds oppositions by unmasking the hierarchies that hide behind them. Often, as an interim strategy, it overturns the hierarchy to reveal the contradictions and interdependencies the hierarchy rests on in order to maintain its positionality, its coherence, its unity. I must stress, however, that the reversal of the hierarchy can only be an interim move to highlight the positionality under (over?) the content. But when the hierarchy fixes in its reversed form—which all too frequently happens—nothing changes in the oppositional structure's characteristic organization. (Such reversals are, indeed, one way in which such hierarchical "oppositions" recoup themselves and heal themselves against various attacks.) To deconstruct, then, is to de-position without repositioning. Deconstruction sets the oppositional terms in motion—and retains its force only as long as the terms remain in motion.

With an example before us (the deconstruction of the opposition between thematics and deconstruction), we can perhaps say a few more things about it—about deconstruction—that might make this most troublesome and troubling term hold still enough to . . . to master? to thematize? to totalize?

Certainly not.

But does our ellipsis—our silence—leave us silent?

The inflation of language that characterizes poststructuralist rhetoric, for better or for worse, both as a style of thought and of discourse (i.e., response, understanding), should make it clear that silence is rarely our problem.

I iterate: A synonym of the verb to deconstruct is to analyze—with the rider that what is most often analyzed in deconstruction are those conflicting and self-subverting elements that suggest that for whatever we are analyzing to maintain itself, it must fight the very notions that it seems to be putting forth in order for that meaning to remain readable at all.

To deconstruct a text is to unpack the meanings that history and the language have packed into it, with particular attention to those meanings that challenge those elements that ideology has made appear self-evident.

The problem arises, however (it has always-already arisen), when we are no longer "doing it"—when we are not, right now, deconstructing some theme—but are talking *about* deconstruction . . . when language itself has transformed deconstruction from an analytical process we are involved in to an object we are discussing, analyzing, thematizing, an object that . . .

I have said that "deconstruction" is *almost* the same as an "analysis." But I should point out that in a 1983 letter to his Japanese translator, who was searching for a Japanese equivalent for "deconstruction," the French philosopher Jacques Derrida (with whom the term is associated) explained that he first took up the word to translate a German term in Heidegger: *Destruktion.* He chose the French term, "*déconstruction,*" which, though rare, has a number of legitimate French meanings. At least one, from the *Littré* dictionary, is: "Grammatical term. Disarranging the construction of words in a sentence." (Construction, as a grammatical term, is, of course, the noun from "to construe," and means "to understand.") In his letter to the translator, Derrida writes:

[I]n spite of appearances, deconstruction is neither an *analysis* nor a *critique* and its translation would have to take that into consideration. It is not an analysis in particular because the dismantling of a structure is not a regression toward a *simple element*, toward an *indissoluble origin*. These values, like that of analysis, are themselves philosophemes subject to deconstruction. No more is it a critique, in a general sense or in a Kantian sense. The instances of *krinein* or of *krisis* (decision, choice, judgment, discernment) is itself, as is all the apparatus of transcendental critique, one of the essential "themes" or "objects" of deconstruction.

Deconstruction is not an analysis, then, because the analytical fallout is *not* simpler and more fundamental than what is analyzed; deconstruction is an unpacking of meanings that, rather, problematize. Deconstruction is not a critique because its aim is not therapeutic: The crisis (κρίσις —as well as the κρίνειν or "cutting through") that originally gave us the notion of critique and criticism was initially, in Greek, the medical crisis of a disease that had to be gotten through before the body could return to health. And this sense lingers in the various cognates: thus one criticizes to correct, to restore, to make whole and healthy. And this is not what deconstruction does.

Derrida has also stressed that deconstruction is not an object (which can be the basis of an elaborated discipline). Neither is it a methodology (which can presumably be applied promiscuously to any object). His most rigorous commentators, Gayatri Chakravorty Spivak, Barbara Johnson, Rodolph Gasché, and Paul de Man (who, before his death, initiated a mode of deconstruction that—to many—seemed even more promiscuously radical and rarefied in the ways it overturned all thematic grounds)—all of them, in the ways of strongly disagreeing agonists— have stressed it as well. And, in an intensely funny survey of "American Deconstruction" (which, he claimed, several of his supporters had urged him not to present [*Memoirs for Paul de Man*, Columbia University Press, 1986]), Derrida seems willing to accept, in the most promiscuous move of all, the notion that any truly rigorous analysis might be deconstruction, if only because what deconstruction is in America is now radically undecidable.

In that same letter to his translator, however, Derrida wrote also:

It is not enough to say that deconstruction could not be reduced to some methodological instrumentality or to a set of rules and transposable procedures. Nor will it do to claim that each deconstructive "event" remains singular or, in any case, as close as possible to something like an idiom or a signature. It must also be made clear that deconstruction is not even an *act* or an *operation*. Not only because there would be something "patient" or "passive" about it . . . Not only because it does not return to an individual or collective subject who would take the initiative and apply it to an object, a text, a theme, etc. Deconstruction takes place, it is an event that does not await the consciousness, or organization of a subject, or even of modernity. *It deconstructs itself. It can be deconstructed. [Ça se déconstruit.]* The "it" *[ça]* is not here an impersonal thing that is opposed to some egological subjectivity. *It is in deconstruction* (the *Littré* says, "to deconstruct itself [*se déconstruire*] . . . to lose its construction"). And the "*se*" [itself] of "*se déconstruire*," which is not the reflexivity of an ego or of a consciousness, bears the whole enigma. I recognize, my dear friend, that in trying to make a word clearer so as to assist in its translation, I am only increasing the difficulties: "the impossible task of the translator" (Benjamin). This too is what is meant by "deconstructs."

The happiest rhetorical foray into the problem that I know of, by Gayatri Chakravarty Spivak (who translated Derrida's *Of Grammatology* into English, and who is the author of *In Other Worlds*, Methuen, New York and London, 1987), talks about deconstruction as a mode (i.e., a mood, a disposition) of vigilance—which is fine, de Man might well have added, as long as we take that to be an interim description and not *the* deconstructive theme . . .

SF: Seizing the Critical Imperative. The practical reason I have not started off with definitions of "signs," "fictions," or "texts" (or even worse, tried to define "structuralism," "poststructuralism," or "semiotics") is the same reason I would not start off a discussion of science fiction with some impossible, fruitless, and time-wasting d̶e̶f̶i̶n̶i̶t̶i̶o̶n̶ of our genre. (I place the notion of "genre definition" under erasure to remind us that, for perfectly logical reasons accessible to any bright fourteen-year-old, a "genre definition" is a wholly imaginary object of the same ontological status as unicorns, Hitler's daughter, and the current king of France. "Definitions" of science fiction are impossible for the same reason that "definitions" of poetry, the novel, or drama are impossible; though it is interesting to speculate on the historical and political reasons "definition" has persisted as a theme, if not the major symptom, of thematic SF criticism.) What we are dealing with here is a dialogue, a collection of dialogues, a set of debates, a range of ideas and a range of thinkers, of which only a larger or smaller fraction can be of interest to any particular person.

This is perhaps also the place to address the question: Why should science fiction readers be interested in such debates?

I have three answers.

The first is simply temperamental. I think many of us would find ourselves an interested audience to the books and journals some of these debates take place in for the same reason we are an interested audience for books such as Steven Weinberg's *The First Three Minutes*, Richard Feynman's *QED*, David Raup's *The Nemesis Affair*, Davis and Brown's *Superstrings*, or Gleick's *Chaos*. A great many very intelligent people are doing some very exact and interesting thinking in these fields. While each of the many debates requires its own preparation, many of them have, at this point, their own popularizers. And it is comparatively easy (as hard as, say, learning a new computer program: i.e., it can't necessarily be done in an afternoon, but frequently it can be done in a few weeks[1]) to arrive at the point where you can enjoy the works of the principal contenders themselves and you no longer have to depend on commentators. (Many of the popularizers for one debate are, as well, principal contenders in others.) Let me conclude this reason by noting that the first version of this article was requested in place of a Guest of Honor Speech at the Readercon Science Fiction Convention in 1988, in Lowell, Massachusetts, where, as far as I could tell, the interest in these topics was both high and sincere.

My second reason is strategic. In the course of a number of these debates, literature, philosophy, and the political aspects of both have come under a radical critique. Although deconstruction is not the same as demystification (and you will still find people with a faint knowledge of the one confusing it with the other), a good deal of demystification has, indeed, gone along with that critique. Everything from the effects of phrenology and popular science newspaper articles in the early nineteenth century on the novels of Charlotte Brontë to the hidden political agenda in the formation of the literary canon, when, after World War I, literature first became an academic discipline, have, among these debates, been teased apart in great detail. When it is put back together, literature will not be the same object that it was. (More accurately "Literature" *can* not be put back together.) The "literary" will no longer be a single, unified theme autonomously placeable in the greater text of Western culture. Marginality and marginalizations have been of primary concern through a number of these debates. The ways in which black writing, women's writing, Third World writing, and gay writing have been marginalized and kept marginal have been and still are being explored.

Now, the traditional thematic critical stance of the SF academic critic has been (if I may be forgiven such a crude characterization) to shout, "Look! Look! We're literature too!" These critics have been as responsible as anyone for the near thousand classes in SF currently taught in

1. [This paper was first drafted in 1988. Parts of it have been updated, but others have been left alone for historical interest.]

American universities. Is it simple ingratitude, then, to question just how much understanding of our history, our practices, our traditions, and our texts the majority of these classes are producing—or can produce under a thematic program that presents SF as exhausted with and mastered by not half a dozen themes that, in my opinion, terrorize our genre: "New Worlds," "The Alien," "Technology," "Time," "Space," and "Utopia/Dystopia"? However you judge it, I know that when I have discussed science fiction and its marginal status, how it has used its marginal status as a position from which to criticize the world, how it has organized itself differently from literature in everything from its material practices of publication and printing to the semantic conventions that govern the reading of the sentences that make up its texts, and when I have suggested SF has a philosophical worth and an esthetic beauty that can be valorized by intensive analysis, among critics with more recent allegiances, I've often felt that I am being heard, that the ideas I am putting forth are familiar to them. When I talk with thematic critics, however, frequently their response is: "But surely you too want science fiction to be literature too . . ." To which my answer is (surprising as some still find it) I don't and never have.

I don't even want literature to be literature.

I love them both too much.

My third answer is also, finally, a personal one—though it is positioned at the very interface of my first two. I would like to see a debate about our own practices of equal interest grow up, here, within the precincts of science fiction—a debate informed by the same disposition toward analytic vigilance, with the same willingness to historify and demystify the vast range of sediments, unquestioned self-evident positions, and givens under which our genre, its fandom, its readership struggle, along with energetic attempts to deconstruct those oppositions at which so much discussion of science fiction stalls: "technology" vs. "science," "reviewing" vs. "criticism," "pro" vs. "fan," "commercial" vs. "quality," and "craft" vs. "art."

For these are the oppositions on which the current and practical production of science fiction rests. These oppositions and the tensions they generate create the boundaries the SF text must cross and recross, not only after it leaves the writer to make its way through the publication and distribution machinery, but which it must negotiate even at its inception and at every stage of its execution. The endless and stifling contradictions, economic and ideological, of which these oppositions are constructed, are the ones that all of us in science fiction, readers, writers, editors, and critics, can only whisper of in the very margins of our respective productive efforts, practically in fear of expulsion from the field: Because if we spoke in any other way, no one in the field, we fear, would even understand us. These are the contradictions all of us—in the field—must declare ourselves blind to at every formal station as we negotiate our way about in it.

The debate I would like to see will occur when that marginal whisper is spoken out and is made accessible and articulate, through the function, the field, and the discourse of science fiction. And it would be warming to see such a debate informed by an awareness of the larger field of critical debates in which any critical discourse is embedded today. Though I am contributing editor to *Science Fiction Studies* and a regular reader of *Extrapolation* (the two American academic SF journals), I don't believe that such a debate can grow up within them. The material exigencies of academia preclude it—or assure that such an analytic vigilance will be half-hearted at best. But I think by seizing the critical imperative for ourselves, interested and informed readers of SF have the best chance to take as much intelligent charge of our history as possible.

At any rate, to make the smallest gesture toward implementing the last part of my tripartite suggestion ("... an awareness of the larger field of critical debate in which, today, any critical discourse is embedded ..."), we shall leave science fiction for a while—although, in a while, we shall return.

The Archaeology of Structuralism. For this introduction to be of use, we must now turn to history—take up the problem of origins, the problem of filiation (that is, the theme of sources and influences), that traditionally makes up what we assume to be history.

Writers characterized as structuralists include the structural anthropologist Claude Lévi-Strauss, the psychoanalyst Jacques Lacan, and the Marxist theoretician Louis Althusser, along with lesser known names, such as Gerard Genette (author of *Narrative Discourse: A Study of Proust*), Algirdas Greimas (author of *On Meaning*), and Michel Serres (author of *Hermes* and *The Parasite*). In 1980 at their apartment in the *École Normale Supérieure,* Althusser strangled to death Hélène Legostien (*née* Rytman), a woman seven years his senior who had been his companion since 1946 and his wife since 1976. After that, he lived back and forth between mental hospitals and an apartment in the north of Paris, till his own death in 1990 at age 72, having meantime written an autobiography, *The Future Lasts a Long Time [L'Avenir dure longtemps]* (1993). Lacan died in 1981, leaving behind a lengthy series of seminar transcripts that are still being edited and translated. Lévi-Strauss is still alive, though his last book to be translated into English (1985) is a collection of essays that appeared in 1983 in France, *The View from Afar [Le Regard Eloingné].* But all these thinkers are associated—along with the great linguistics scholar

Roman Jakobson (and his realization that in living language metonymy is a more fundamental process than metaphor)—with the structuralist phase of the dialogue.

If you will take the following statements of similarities among them not as a package to put them in, but rather as a place to start further inquiries that will reveal profound differences among them, differences time precludes us from pursuing here, then I can say that, for all three, Lévi-Strauss, Althusser, and Lacan, language was a privileged object in terms of their own discipline. Anthropologist Lévi-Strauss, after a monumental study of kinship patterns in primitive tribes, *The Elementary Structures of Kinship* (1949), which posed that primitive societies were held together by the exchange of women among men: father, brother, or uncle to husband, much the way signs are exchanged in language. After that he undertook a four-volume "Introduction to the Science of Mythology," with the overall title *Mythologique* ('64, '66, '68, '71), in which the elements of many South American Indian myths are compared and tabulated as if they were phonetic patterns in a language, in order to decode various deferred messages that might stand revealed behind their staggering variety.

One of the more *en passant* concepts that Lévi-Strauss introduced that proved extremely useful for a while was that of *bricolage*, as contrasted specifically with "engineering." The French *bricoleur* is a figure who is not really a part of the American landscape. The closest translation we can make is "handyman." But he is also a plumber, a carpenter, and an electrical repairman as well. His job is to solve whatever problems arise. His tools are available materials. The engineer takes a problem and, applying overarching principles to it, works down to the specific, well-formed solution. Contrastingly, the *bricoleur* starts with the local problem, solves one part, then the next, until often rather quirky, Rube-Goldberg-style structures arise, which nevertheless can be both stable and efficient. Lévi-Strauss's observation that, in spite of all the diagrams and the dense rhetoric, the efforts of the modern theorist (such as his own in *Mythologique*) were better understood as conceptual bricolage than as grand-plan engineering (*à la* Hegel) came to many academics working in the area of theory as a useful and liberating notion.

For psychoanalyst Lacan, "the unconscious" was "structured as a language." Lacan was responsible for a re-emphasis on psychoanalysis as "the talking cure," with a concomitant emphasis on language—the patient's, the analyst's—by means of a massive theoretical interrogation of how language forms and informs our entire social being, in a register he called the Symbolic, as distinct from the Imaginary—which is how the world appears as a series of images. (Imaginary comes from "image" here, not "the imagination.") The Symbolic has been described as the critical register in which, alone, the Imaginary can understand how it functions *as* the Imaginary. Writers who have provided particularly interesting explanations of this and other of Lacan's difficult concepts include Jane Gallup, Shoshana Felman, and Juliet Flower MacCannell.

Lacan was also responsible for a "return to Freud," that involved paying meticulous attention to the language of Freud's own writings. One of his most popular and stimulating pieces (though much of it can at first seem daunting) is his "Seminar on 'The Purloined Letter'" (that, in French, opens his thousand-page collected writings, *Écrits* [Paris: Seuil, 1966], and which, in translation, has been taken as the centerpiece for a book all its own: *The Purloined Poe: Lacan, Derrida, and Psychoanalytic Reading*, eds. John P. Muller and William J. Richardson, Baltimore: Johns Hopkins, 1988), in which Lacan traces out the structure of the psychoanalytic relation that arranges itself around any "signifier," as it forms, reforms, then forms once more about the letter whose contents we never learn as it moves among the characters in Poe's story. After reading Lacan's meditation on Poe's tale, William Gibson's 1982 story "Johnny Mnemonic" begins to look particularly interesting, in terms of both its similarities to and its differences from the Poe.

Another Freudian concept that Lacan reinvigorated (like Lévi-Strauss's *bricolage*, in passing: There is only one 1958 essay directly on the topic ["The Signification of the phallus," included in *Écrit*] and various other *en passant* mentions and discussions) was that of the phallus. For Lacan the phallus was specifically *not* the penis or clitoris that can symbolize it. Rather it was a structure of meaning that, like the narrative structures that form and reform around the purloined letter as it journeys on its way through Poe's tale, any "signifier of desire" must inhabit—and the signifier of desire (that is, the structure that creates such a signifier) is what the phallus *is*.

Unlike the clitoris or the penis, the phallus functions only through castration. Freud gives an account of the establishment of male heterosexuality that runs something like this: The little boy uncritically assumes that his mother is anatomically identical to himself—the pre-phallic stage. At a certain point, he learns or notices she does not have a penis as he has. This conceptual violence represents for him the maternal castration. Frequently little boys will assume, Freud noted, that their mothers have lost their penises or had them somehow cut off. The image/concept of the penis-that-is-not-there, this perceived absence, this difference-from-the-self, which organizes his fixation on the female genital region and eventually helps sexualize it, *is* the phallus—that is, the all-important "maternal phallus" in Freud's theoretical elaboration.

Another example of the phallus as a structure of meaning might be the traditional progress of the argument of feminists and feminist sympathizers (such as myself) against the whole Freudian theory of phallic symbols. In the pre-critical period there is the blanket assumption that Freud's theory of phallic symbols associates the various manifestations of male power with the having of a penis—the pre-phallic stage of the argument. Through logic and analysis we realize that there is no *necessary* connection between those powers men have and any particularity of male anatomy, the penis or any other part. This represents the castration of the pre-critical version of the theory. Further analysis of the powers that are associated with men proceed so that we can maintain a vigilant critique of the powers men *do* exercise, as well as eschew those powers when we don't like their results, or appropriate those others that we desire—an enterprise organized around a relationship-with-the-male that is important precisely because it is *not* there in any absolute or necessary way. This absolute-relationship-that-is-not-there is just as much the phallus as the unquestioned maternal penis-that-is-not-there: And thus, this is precisely the *phallic* stage of the argument—that is to say, the relationship between these powers and men is now specifically phallic, rather than pre-phallic. But some people are still surprised, and even troubled, to learn that Freud's theory of the phallus was not a theory of strength but rather a theory of strength subverted, contained, tamed, symbolized (for the phallus *only* functions through castration), i.e., a theory of power.

Further thought will show that the phallic structure of meaning is finally the structure through which *any* signifier operates, starting with the moment as toddlers, straining after the apple, the piece of candy, the toy just out of reach, we repeat and repeat ". . . apple . . . candy . . . toy," thus learning that the word is not the thing—a learning that is the "castration" or splitting of the concept of any verbally empowered concept. Thus, in its essence, the phallus not only has nothing necessarily to do with men, it has nothing to do with sex. Yes, it passes *through* sex; but it passes through *all* the processes of meaning we can locate. Realizing this is the necessary castration, or de-metaphorization, of the term that *is* necessary for it to function. That the process was first noted and named in a consideration of male desire is itself only an accident of the political fact that, since the tale of Adam distributing names in the garden (which, if I can indulge in a bit more castration/demetaphorization/demystification, is *not* the beginning of civilization but only a comparatively recent tale *about* its beginnings, and has been theorized by critic Harold Bloom to have been written by a noble woman in the court of King David, the "J Writer" of biblical exegesis), we *do* live in a sexist society that privileges men as presumed centers of meaning production. Had things been different, however, what Freud and Lacan designate as "phallus" and "castration" might have been called "mung beans" and "harvesting"; or "sunrise" and "blindfolding"; or "refuse-placement" and "removal"—and all would be equally prone to being misunderstood. For real mung beans and real refuse are not the same as "mung beans" and "refuse" in the psychoanalytic sense, since—in the psychoanalytic sense—"mung beans" and/or "refuse" can only function through "harvesting" and/or "refuse removal." And to the extent that, in their respective societies, the idea of mung beans and/or refuse is an exploited and mystified conceptual node of power, desire, and meaning, psychoanalytic mung-beans or psychoanalytic refuse becomes an important, vital, and clarifying symbol. For the same reason, so many feminists (e.g., Luce Irigaray, Julia Kristeva) have found the phallus a useful concept for analyzing the workings of the patriarchy in our society.

Lacan's theory of the phallus is a theory of desire, but not of desire as a force or power located in one subject that impels that subject toward another subject or an object. Rather it is a theory about the relationship between the subject and the category that includes desire's object, which must be established between subject and object-category if the relationship we recognize as desire is to obtain. And because it atomizes power into its constitutive anterior relationships, it can be a useful factor in a theory *of* power.

After resigning (along with four other distinguished colleagues) from the orthodox *Société psychanalytique de Paris* over a disagreement arising from personalities and finally fixing on how young psychoanalysts were to be trained, Lacan and his associates formed their own *Société Française de Psychanalyse*, which the older organization steadily refused to acknowledge—although, by the new organization's First Congress, in Rome in 1953, the *Société Française de Psychanalyse* had the support of almost half the student analysts. At the end of Lacan's address to colleagues and students at Rome, presented on September 26 and 27, "The Function and Field of Speech and Language in Psychoanalysis" (the dense and difficult lecture is often called by the nickname "The Discourse of Rome"), toward the end of his lengthy discussion of the transference mechanism, in an attempt to present an example of transference at its most beneficent Lacan rereads a text familiar to many English speakers: The referent text is, of course, "What the Thunder Said," section 5 of T. S. Eliot's *Waste Land.*

To the younger and older analysts attending him, Lacan concluded:

The psychanalytic experience has rediscovered in man the imperative of the Word as the law that has formed him in its image. It manipulates the poetic function of language to give to his desire its symbolic mediation. May that experience enable you to understand at last that it is in the gift of speech[2] that all the reality of its effects resides; for it is by way of this gift that all reality has come to man and it is by his continued act that he maintains it.

If the domain defined by this gift of speech is to be sufficient for your action as also for your knowledge, it will also be sufficient for your devotion. For it offers it a privileged field.

When the Devas, the men, and the Asuras were ending their novitiate with Prajapâti, so we read in the second Brahmana of the fifth lesson of the Bhradâranyaka Upanishad, they addressed to him this prayer: "Speak to us."

"*Da,*" said Prajapâti, god of thunder. "Did you hear me?" And the Devas answered and said: "Thou has said to us: *Damyata,* master yourselves"—the sacred text meaning that the powers above submit to the law of speech.

"*Da,*" said Prajapâti, god of thunder. "Did you hear me?" And the men answered and said: "Thou has said to us: *Data,* give"—the sacred text meaning that men recognize each other by the gift of speech.

"*Da,*" said Prajapâti, god of thunder. "Did you hear me?" And the Asuras answered and said: "Thou hast said to us: *Dayadhyam,* be merciful"—the sacred text meaning that the powers below resound in the invocation of speech.[3]

That, continued the text, is what the divine voice caused to be heard in the thunder: Submission, gift, grace. *Da da da.*[4]

For Prajapâti replied to all: "*You have heard me.*"

Even as it suggests that language has no meaning of its own, but only the meanings we hear in it, the projection onto the thunder of the moral imperative to treat ourselves and our fellows with respect and compassion is, for Lacan, Freudian transference at its best. For the three Sanskrit terms, Eliot so famously provided the meanings: control, give, sympathize. But however one reads them (whether we read them as moral imperatives or as demonstrations about language itself), certainly they mark out the field in which the intricately and endlessly complex recomplications of Lacan's later elaborations on the subject that is always split, that is never whole, and that is itself constituted of the illusion of its own existence will strive to function.

Certainly the structuralist thinker who turns out to have had the most lasting influence, the thinker who is least known outside the debates

2. Let it be understood that it is not a question of those 'gifts' that are always supposed to be lacking in novices, but of a gift that is in fact lacking to them more often than they lack it. [Notes outside square brackets are Lacan's; those inside are the translator's or SRD's.]

3. Ponge writes it: *réson* (1966) [In his *Pour un Malherbe*. 'Resound' is '*résonner*' in French: *réson* is a homonym of *raison*.]

4. '*Soumission, don, grâce*'. The three Sanskrit nouns (*damah, dânan, dayâ*) are also rendered "self-control"; "giving"; and "compassion" (Rhadhakrishnan), the three verbs, "control", "give", "sympathize" (T.S. Eliot, *The Waste Land*, Part V; "What the Thunder Said").

themselves, is Louis Althusser. Althusser was a Marxist theoretician. For Althusser, Marx was primarily a reader of other writers' texts. In *Lire le Capital* ("To Read *Das Capital*," a collection of five near-book-length essays by Balibar, Rancière, Macherey, Establet, and Althusser, which first appeared in two volumes in Paris, 1965: the Balibar and Althusser contributions have been translated by Ben Brewster as *Reading Capital* [NLB, London, 1972]), Althusser argued that Marx developed a new level of analytical reading: According to Althusser, earlier economists and political theorists read each other only in terms of what each said. Each then proposed his own ideas against that reading. But Marx's writings on earlier theorists presented a "double reading," Althusser maintains, in which Marx reads what the other economist said, then proceeds to read what he left out, his tacit presuppositions, the historical pressures on him, the stabilizing institutions he was involved with, the aspects he repressed or was blind to, thus allowing Marx to go on to show the contradictions within the "restored" text, and to speculate on the significance of the two texts of the way one comments on the other—a vigilant, analytic enterprise in which I hope you can recognize the similarities to the deconstruction of the notion of theme as I've already presented it.

Another idea from Althusser's 1969 essay "Ideology and Ideological State Apparatuses" (*Lenin and Philosophy and Other Essays*, Monthly Review Press, New York, 1971) that has received more and more consideration of late is the idea of "interpellation"—and the question of how we are interpellated as subjects by the people, institutions, and objects around us. "To interpellate" is an archaic verb that means (in both English and French) "to break in on" in the sense of "to interrupt." As well, it means "to petition," or as Althusser suggests, "to hail." The process of "interpellation" or "hailing," claims Althusser, creates us as subjects. Althusser writes:

[T]hat very precise operation which I have called interpellation or hailing . . . can be imagined along the lines of the most commonplace everyday police (or other) hailing, "Hey, you there!"

Assuming that the theoretical scene I have imagined takes place on the street, the hailed individual will turn around. By the mere one-hundred-and-eighty-degree physical conversion, he becomes a *subject*. Why? Because he has recognized that the hail was "really" addressed to him, and that "it was *really him* who was hailed" (and not someone else).

The quotation marks around "really" and the italics of *really him* suggest the *sous rature* marking with which we began. Indeed, Althusser uses them precisely because the only "reality" we have access to at any given moment is built up from myriad previous hailings, not only from individuals but from advertisements, institutions, and even objects in the landscape, so that, in effect, we are "always-ready" (another common structuralist/poststructuralist location used by Althusser) interpellated by our society at any given point. (Fritz Leiber's 1949 SF story "The Girl With Hungry Eyes" was taken up by Marshal McLuhan in his 1951 *Understanding Media* as a dramatic instance *avant la lettre* of the way in which advertisements "hail" us. It is equally interesting today for the same reason.)

The assumption of a reality beyond our personal, always-mediated experience of it—whether it be a reality of matter and energy that science suggests or a reality purely of ideas and relationships that philosophers from Plato to Berkeley and some contemporary philosophers of mathematics still believe in—is *the* leap into metaphysics. And because we cannot negotiate the world without assuming it is really one thing or the other, we are always within one metaphysical system or another.

Later commentators on Althusser have pointed out that the way in which we have always-already been hailed has a great deal to do with any individual instance of hailing: On the streets of New York, for example, a well-off and well-dressed white male will be/become a very different subject from a homeless black woman in a tattered coat, when hailed by the same, "Hey, you there!" from the same policeman.

But for all three of these thinkers, Claude Lévi-Strauss, Jacques Lacan, and Louis Althusser, in their separate disciplines, language is the model they use to describe what is meaningful in that discipline.

One of the insights most bruited about from these debates is that "the origin is always a construct." That is equally true for my suggestion of Althusser's reading of Marx's reading methods as it is true as a model for Derrida's deconstruction—though you will find it suggested by a number of other critics as well, including Fredric Jameson, whose early books and papers (*Marxism and Form* [1971], *The Prison House of Language* [1972], and the two-volume collection of his essays, *The Ideology of Theory* [1988]) are still a fine introduction to the first wave of thinkers in the debate if we can separate them from those thinkers like Max Weber, Emile Durkheim, Vladimir Propp, and Marcel Mauss—not to mention Marx and Freud—who came before them and from whom they learned (and on whom they built) and whose *Political Unconscious* (1981) has become recognized as an important continuation of the debates.

But all that I can really do here is point out other origins that have been constructed for deconstruction, with the clear suggestion that each of these origins has, indeed, its own ideological nuance, and various participants in the debates have frequently embraced more than one, and that from time to time antagonisms in the debates might be illuminated, at least for a period, in terms of a particular origin chosen.

The Geneva-born linguist, Ferdinand-Mongin de Saussure (1857–

1913), and the notes on his *Course in General Linguistics* that some of his students took during his classes at the University of Geneva between 1907 and 1911 and, after his death, published in 1916 have frequently been cited as a source for structuralism/poststructuralism.

Saussure, Peirce, and Semiotics. Saussure is cited most frequently for a number of important ideas as well as for privileging half-a-dozen-plus terms fundamental to the debate's rhetoric: *parole* (language as a set of possible utterances), *langue* (language as the syntactical and semantic rules that make utterances comprehensible), sign (that which consists of a signifier and its signified, an idea and terms Saussure borrowed from the Stoic philosophers of ancient Greece), signifier (the perceptible part of the sign), signified (the intelligible part of the sign: the concept the signifier is a sign *of*), synchronic (the mutual relation of elements [or signs] at the same historical moment), diachronic (the successive relation of elements [or signs] over the course of time).

Here are four of Saussure's most frequently cited ideas:

(1) The linguistic sign is arbitrary—that is, the relation between the signifier and the signified in words (Saussure called them "sound-images") is such that any sound combination can be assigned to any meaning and that relation will obtain until something comes along and makes a reassignment (either of the signifier or of the signified).

(2) Philology should be separate from linguistics. The separation should be the separation of synchronic elements (linguistics) from diachronic elements (philology).

(3) Language is a play of pure differences—this last is a notion hard to convey in a single phrase or a few sentences. Generally, however, Saussure's point was that what characterizes the sound "b" is its differences from the sounds "c," "d," and "f"—and, in general, its differences from all other possible sounds. Thus, differences in sounds become meaningful if one can establish "minimal pairs" for them: e.g., in spoken American English the difference between the voiced and unvoiced "th" is meaningful because that difference alone distinguishes the minimal pair "ether/either," with their different meanings.

(4) Human language is a subset of a more general system of signs by which nature's creatures communicate with each other or read the world to be laid out in a certain way. The study of this more general system of signs is semiotics.

All four of these ideas have held center stage for various periods in the structuralist/poststructuralist debates. It was the last of them, however, that was to prove most fertile when it was radically reversed by Roland Barthes in his brief book *The Elements of Semiology* (1964).

The American philosopher Charles Sanders Peirce (1839–1914), who spent many years, by the bye, living in Milford, Pennsylvania, the social and esthetic center of science fiction during the fifties and sixties, did a great deal of work on semiotics in the tradition of Saussure—without ever having encountered Saussure's very brief remarks on the topic from the *Course.* In his search for a generalized semiotics, of which human language was only a subset, Peirce divided signs into three categories: icons (in which the signifier, however abstractly, pictures the signified, as in various road signs for turnoffs and merging highways), indices (in which the signifier has a measurable relation to what is signified, such as the height of the mercury in a thermometer to the air temperature or the position of the hands on a clock to the time), and symbols (in which the relation of the signifier to the signified is arbitrary, such as in non-onomatopoeic spoken words or written Arabic numerals: Onomatopoeic words Peirce considered ironic).

For all the initial seeming elegance of his semiotic trichotomy, Peirce found as he pursued it that there was so much of the arbitrary lurking in both the iconic and the indexical sign, or that so many indexical or iconic elements could enter into the more complex organization of symbolical signs (such as Arabic numbers higher than ten, or in the rhetorical figures of poetry and literature), that, after generating several different subsystems of semiotic taxonomies (again, frequently divided in three) he found the whole process dissolving into what he called "unlimited semiosis"—*semiosis* meaning roughly "the interpretation of signs," and "unlimited semiosis" being his term for "signs used to interpret other signs that are used to interpret other signs that are used to interpret . . ."

The point was, however, that Peirce's exploration (carried out sporadically until his death) took place under what I've called Saussure's fourth assumption: Human language is a subset of a more general semiotic system. But it was not until the advent of Roland Barthes that substantial progress was made in this till-then rather marginal field of speculation.

The Advent of Barthes. In 1960 Roland Barthes published a long and exciting essay as an introduction to a new edition of the most famous and most academically revered classical French playwright, Jean Racine (1639–1699). But instead of talking about characters, motivations, psychological subtleties, and stylistic refinements of language, Barthes wrote about the plays as if they were geography, architecture, or geometry:

> [O]ne might say that there are three tragic sites. There is first of all the Chamber: Vestige of the mythic cave, it is the invisible and dreadful place where Power lurks . . . the Chamber is contiguous to the second tragic site, which is

the Antechamber, the eternal space of all subjection, since it is there that one *waits*. The Antechamber (the stage proper) is a medium of transmission; it partakes of both interior and exterior, of Power and Event . . . Between the Chamber and the Antechamber stands a tragic object which expresses both contiguity and exchange: the Door. Here one waits, here one trembles. To enter it is a temptation and a transgression . . . The third tragic site is the Exterior. Between Antechamber and Exterior there is no transition; they are joined as immediately as the Antechamber and the Chamber. This contiguity is expressed poetically by the "linear" nature of the tragic enclosure: The palace walls plunge down into the sea; the stairs lead down to the ships ready to sail; the rampants are a balcony above the battle itself . . .

In effect, Barthes superimposed all Racine's dozen plays one on the other, then dealt primarily with those patterns that were reinforced by the superimposition. When this essay, along with two others on Racine, was published as a book (*On Racine* 1960), Barthes was the subject of a newspaper attack by a leading French philologist from the Sorbonne, Raymond Picard, who decried Barthes's approach as mechanistic, scientistic, and, in all its over-intellectualism, without feeling or sensitivity to the great French plays. But in 1964 Barthes published a brief book that seemed to operationalize the very scientism of his approach, *The Elements of Semiology*, as well as, in 1966, an answer to Picard, called *Criticism and Truth*. Meanwhile, a scholar excited by Barthes's semiotic concerns, Gilles Deleuze, published a book that remains twenty-five years later one of the most brilliant and penetrating studies from the period, *Proust and Signs* (1964).

While French academic circles were being polarized by the Barthes/Picard debate, others were busy pointing out that, save for the particular flavor of the rhetoric, the sort of geometrical criticism Barthes was practicing on Racine was not very far from what various mavens of French academic criticism such as George Poulet had been doing in his essays for many years, in which he had analyzed "the space" of Baudelaire, Mallarmé, and Valéry. As well, it bore a number of rhetorical resemblances to the work of some of the more eccentric, if still established, critics, such as Gaston Bachelard (*The Poetics of Space, The Psychoanalysis of Fire*). In short, the philosophical split between the old and the new was largely manufactured by the older critics. Though the rhetorical split was certainly encouraged in all ways by the newer ones—a pattern that continues through the current deconstruction/thematic split, as I've already suggested.

The same year Deleuze published his Proust study, Barthes released (as I mentioned) *The Elements of Semiology* (1964). *Elements of Semiology* made the first major advance on Peirce's work through a reversal of Saussure's fourth assumption: Human language is a subset of a more general semiotic system.

That reversal more or less hinged on the following argument. Instead of making the conceptual field geographical and zoological, let's move the argument (Barthes suggests) to the theoretical plane. Human language is the most complex sign system that nature/culture has produced. Let us assume for the purposes of argument that all the simpler semiotic systems that one finds throughout human cultures and throughout the animal world utilize semiotic principles that, somewhere or other, can be found within—and can be described with—that richest of sign systems, language. Even if humans do not indulge in birdcalls or leave chemical scents behind them, the abstract principles that make these signs intelligible to the birds, lower mammals, insects, and plants who employ them, however blindly, must be contained somehow in human language for language to be able to describe the process at all.

So for Barthes, instead of linguistics residing as a subset of a more generalized and complex semiotics, "semiology" (Barthes's term) now existed as a subdiscipline of linguistics. Under this reversal, a number of the problems that had undermined Peirce's various trichotomies now seemed negotiable—most famously and successfully, by the Italian medievalist philosopher and contemporary social critic, Umberto Eco, in his *A Theory of Semiotics*, first translated into English in 1976. But once again for Barthes (and for Eco), language is the primary model for the particular area of meaning each explores—areas that for Barthes would range from the captioning system of French *haute coûture* photography (*The Fashion System* 1967) to his impressions of a visit to Japan (*Empire of Signs* 1970), to the writing of his own autobiography (*Roland Barthes by Roland Barthes* 1975) and his reflections on the organization of discourse and behavior during a love affair—certainly, we begin to suspect by the end of the book (*A Lover's Discourse* 1977), one of his own.

But to jump straight from Barthes to Eco is to abridge the debate far too violently.

History Intervenes. 1966 marks an important year for structuralist/poststructuralist debates in America. At Johns Hopkins University, in October, an international array of scholars, many of them French, met for what was to be the first of two years of eight international seminars on The Language of Criticism and the Sciences of Man, selections of which were eventually published as *The Structuralist Controversy* (eds. Macksey & Donato, Johns Hopkins, Baltimore and London, 1972).

The margin is frequently a privileged position in these debates. Much of interest goes on in the margins of a seemingly more centered discussion.

For those turning from popularizers to primary statements by Derrida, Lacan, Lucian Goldman, and René Girard, this volume (along with the special 1966 issue of *Yale French Studies*, republished as a Doubleday Anchor Book, *Structuralism*, edited by Jacques Ehrmann, New York & Garden City, 1970), with its illuminating discussion by the debate participants, is both invaluable and indispensable early reading. Certainly these conferences began to bring an awareness of these otherwise primarily European discussions to America.

Earlier that year, Michel Foucault (a former student of Althusser's) had published his fourth book in Paris, *Les Mots et les Choses* (*The Order of Things*, Vintage, New York, 1968). The book was both dense and lyrical—as well as profoundly systematic. It presented itself as a general "archaeology" of the concept of representation and a study of the changes representation underwent during the age of French Classicism, i.e., the seventeenth and eighteenth centuries. In the course of it, Foucault traced out an intricate shift in the general concept of the sign (representation must occur by means of signs), through a tripartite archaeology of three different fields: the transformation of the early Science of Wealth into the modern idea of economics, the transformation of the old notion of Natural Philosophy into the modern idea of biology, and the transformation of the General Grammar of Condillac and the seventeenth-century grammarians

"While we sit discussing the word, power works in silence." (Foucault)

of Port Royalle into the modern idea of philology and linguistics.

By placing this account of Foucault here, by starting not with his earlier work, but with his fourth book (and third major contribution), I am very conscientiously trying to produce the effect that Foucault's position in the overall debate was, and remains since his death from AIDS in 1984, that of a dauntingly erudite intervention in what, for all the internal disagreements, is otherwise all too easily reduced to a kind of thematic—yes, I can use the word too—a thematic that, at least without Foucault, centers almost entirely on language, literature, and primitive, "exotic" cultures, and very little on history and the current practices of Western men and women.

Immediately Foucault was called a structuralist.

Immediately he claimed, at length and with conviction, that he was no such thing.

His next book, *The Archaeology of Knowledge*, was a wholly theoretical, extended "position paper" on the principles of his work till then; it concluded with an outline of where these principles might take him in the future. And one thing became, with this book, very clear: For all Foucault's lucid apprehension of the debates up till now, the semiotic thrust of *The Order of Things* was a necessary accident, rather than his own central concern.

The impressive and lucid development of Foucault's work is such a compelling narrative that it was finally able to replace the simpler narrative many were tempted to tell about it, i.e., that he was the latest, most impressive contributor of a new chapter to an old story.

The Double Text. The story that replaces it was, in fact, a double story. The first part is simply the systematic progression of his subject matter. Foucault's first major book, *Madness and Civilization* (1961), attempted to trace, in those same classical centuries, the way the mad changed their position in society, as well as the changes in the way madness itself was perceived. The "origin," the "theme," of Foucault's story has been recounted many times. If we can keep in mind that the second part of the story—the theoretical progression of Foucault's work—develops precisely to analyze, to deconstruct if you will, to show the illusions and presuppositions and assumptions we blindly follow (and that presumably he once followed) that make it such an appealing story, such an easy narrative, then that story is worth recounting both for its seductions and for its insights.

Endemic throughout Europe during the Middle Ages, leprosy underwent a spontaneous (and to this day, largely unexplained) remission at the end of the fourteenth century. In most major cities, the largest buildings by far were the leper hospitals—Bicêtre and Charrington in Paris, Bedlam in London. But with these great buildings now all but empty, we come to the seventeenth century's "Great Confinement," where the government rounded up all the unsightly of Paris—the poor, the homeless, the drunk, the unemployed, the mad—and imprisoned them in these same, huge, dank buildings. Over the

Centered around Moorcock's *New Worlds*, the British New Wave of the 1960s was largely anti-theory, which, in retrospect, seems only a continuation of the generally anti-intellectual current that has run through the history of science fiction—as well as an expression of the gentlemanly British distrust of anything too abstract (a classist attitude toward the sciences, which were associated with the rising education of the nineteenth century English working classes), an attitude shared today, however much headway some of these debates sometimes seem to have made, by the majority of American university English departments, incidentally. Nevertheless, in 1967, while I was in London I received a report of a meeting that Langdon Jones, then assistant editor of *New Worlds*, held of *New Worlds* writers, in which the program of the magazine was discussed.

Three conventions of science fiction were located.

(1) The Generous Universe: In a world where no one survives a plane crash, in a solar system with only one oxygenated planet, science fiction was still full of spaceships crash landing

next years, one by one, the various categories of indigent were returned to the streets and to freedom. New laws were passed either to provide for, or to constrain them. The only ones to remain confined were the mad—who, until the Confinement, had been allowed to wander free, often to starve, occasionally to be sent by boat from city to city, but still out as a visible part of the social tapestry.

With the new situation, however, the insane asylum was now socially in place—as well, the modern concept of "madness" was posited, a concept that had as much to do with assumptions about medieval leprosy associated with the buildings in which the mad were now housed (their new position) as it did with the work ethic, with visibility, and with all the themes of the Confinement: Madness, like medieval leprosy, was both an illness and a punishment from God; madness, like medieval leprosy, was a price paid for a certain behavior, a behavior that could just as easily have been our parents' behavior as our own in childhood; madness, like medieval leprosy, held an ambiguous status between illness, sin, and crime—all ideas that are slightly displaced, but not fundamentally changed, by Pinel's great humanitarian move, when in the nineteenth century he took the chains from the mad at Bicêtre; ideas we can still trace in Freud's own theories of psychoanalysis as well as in the common prejudices of common people.

on planets in which everyone walks away unscarred from the wreck into a landscape with a breathable atmosphere, with amenable flora and fauna, and civilized beings . . .

(2) Linear Intelligence: In a world where the reigning math genius at any given university is eighty pounds over- (or under-) weight and can't keep his shirt buttons in their right holes, science fiction presents a world where a genius in one field is invariably a genius in all, often has a black belt in karate, and can negotiate with total suavity any social situation whatsoever . . .

(3) History Responds to the Individual: In a world where no social progress seems possible unless groups of people work long and hard together, science fiction continually presents a universe where one man is capable of changing the course of history . . .

These were the conventions of science fiction, of course, that *New Worlds* was *not* interested in promulgating in its pages.

As praiseworthy and productive as that program was twenty-five years ago, I would propose, however, that a meaningful theoretical reading of science fiction begins when we start looking at such works as Asimov's *Foundation* series, Brunner's *The Whole Man,* and Russ's *We Who Are About to . . .* as at once accepting of, and at the same time rigorously critical toward, these conventions, an examination that will reveal both the acceptance and the critique as intricately related, so that these conventions are not allowed to sediment into "themes" but are opened up into the complex and serious problematics these and other SF writers treat them as.

This is the story, as I said, many people still tell of Foucault's first major work. It is certainly a wonderful, clarifying story. But it is precisely

Since deconstruction frequently deals with oppositions, the texts it tends to privilege are philosophical or argumentative texts. While deconstructions of poetry or fiction have been done, clearly it works best when even these texts—or elements of these texts—are considered as enunciative rather than suggestive or descriptive. We might say, then, that deconstruction begins in the area of nonfiction. Paradoxically, though, the result of deconstruction is almost always to highlight the fictive nature of the nonfictive text deconstructed. the story that the rest of his work analyzes with great vigilance, that the rest of his work dissolves and deconstructs. The story, of course, is too simple; it leaves out too much. It must be read carefully and historically for its repressions and its gaps.

A former student of Foucault's, Jacques Derrida, wrote a thirty-three page examination of what he took to be the philosophical underpinnings and limitations of Foucault's book, "The Cogito and the History of Madness" (*Writing and Difference*, trans. Alan Bass, Chicago, 1978); and in the next edition of his own book, Foucault took on Derrida's critique as a philosophical challenge.

Foucault had argued (in pp. 56–59 of the French edition of *Madness and Civilization*, a passage not included in Richard Howard's translation and abridgement) that there was a discursive system in place by the end of the seventeenth century that excluded madness in a particular way, and that, in the formation of his famous *cogito ergo sum* as a decisive step in the pursuit of truth, the great French philosopher René Descartes (1596–1650) was entailed in that exclusion. Descartes is glibly but insightfully characterized by a child's encyclopedia from the fifties in my possession (*The World Book Encyclopedia*, vol. 4, p. 1959 [Chicago, 1953]) as follows: "Descartes asserted, first, that, as all existing knowledge rests on an unstable foundation [the evidence of the senses], the first step is to doubt everything that can be doubted. The only fact that he could not doubt was the fact that he was doubting. He reasoned that to doubt is to think, and to think is to exist. He expressed his conclusion in the saying *Cogito ergo sum* [I think, therefore I exist].")

In "The Cogito and the History of Madness" Derrida turns to a passage from Descartes' first *Meditation*, in which the hallucinations of madmen, the dreams of the philosopher himself, and, in another passage, the imaginative images of painters are considered as models for doubtful reality. He argues that there is a rhetorical level (though Derrida does not call it this) entailed with the working of language itself in which any exclusion is always-already based on an inclusion, which is alone what allows the exclusion to take place—and that this, in effect, both redeems Descartes and sabotages Foucault's project of speaking for the other. By failing to acknowledge that the other is already a part of us, precisely in the rhetoric of the sentences that we speak to banish the other, Foucault (claims Derrida, by the end of his lengthy exegesis) is simply denying the inclusion of the other in the same way that those he accuses of excluding the other, Descartes among the accused, are doing.

In his response, "My Body, This Paper, This Fire," which he appended to the new French edition of *Madness and Civilization* in 1972, Foucault argues persuasively: No, there really *is* a discursive level at which such an exclusion was in effect in the seventeenth century. Because it is not in effect in the same way today, we (and Derrida) miss the rhetorical details that betray it. What's more, Derrida's reading of the passage from the first *Meditation* does not *just* ignore those details but rather hinges on misreading *precisely* those details—as well, the reading remains blind to many other such details: Derrida's reading of Descartes, Foucault argues, confuses Descartes' presumed thoughts about an extravagant demonstration (madness) with his very different thoughts about the need for an accessible demonstration (dreaming); it hinges on Derrida's failure to appreciate subtleties in the original Latin (the difference, for example, between *insani* [the insane/"lunatics," who hallucinate] and the *amentes/dementes* [the out-of-their-mind/"madmen," who have no judicial rights]; it hinges on the failure of the translation to preserve the rupture impelling the phrase "but then these are madmen" ("*sed amentes sunt isti*"— perhaps closer to: "but wait a moment—these are madmen"); and it hinges on, in one case (when both are talking about another passage dealing with painters), a phrase only extant in the translation and not in Descartes' Latin.

> There are many other facts to which doubt is plainly impossible, although these are gathered from the same source [the senses]: e.g., that I am here, sitting by the fire, wearing a winter coat, holding this paper in my hands, and so on. Again, these hands and my whole body—how can their existence be denied? Unless indeed I likened myself to some lunatics, whose brains are so upset by persistent melancholy vapours that they firmly assert that they are kings, when really they are miserably poor; or that they are clad in purple, when really they are naked; or that they have a head of pottery, or are pumpkins, or are made of glass; but then they are madmen, and I should appear no less mad if I took them as precedent for my own case.
>
> —René Descartes, *First Meditation*

Foucault writes: "[I]n erasing these differences" between the *way* in which Descartes could think about madness and the *way* in which he could think about dreaming by the conventions of the time, rather than simply looking at, as Derrida seems to be, "what" "Descartes" "writes" about both, Descartes and his ideas are stripped of their historically specific discursive formations. "[I]n bringing the test of madness and that of dreaming as close together as possible, in making the one the first, faint failed draft of the other, in absorbing the insufficiency of the one in the universality of the other, Derrida is continuing the Cartesian exclusion."

What Foucault is giving us is the discursive structure, the historical forms, and the metaphoric system through which, specifically in seventeenth century France, such notions as madness, dreaming, and doubt could be thought; this is the discourse that constrained Descartes from doubting (to recall the *World Book*) that he doubted. (That is what madmen are extravagant enough to do; *that* is why the mad must be *excluded* as valid examples of doubt.) It was a discourse that involved specific relationships between states that dislocate the fixes of certainty: dreaming, madness, truth, doubt, and (later) artistic (painterly) imagination.

Derrida's attempt to deconstruct the opposition here between exclusion and inclusion not only ignores the historically demonstrable form of that exclusion but, in this case, directly mystifies and obscures it.

In the face of such an argument as historically and textually grounded as Foucault's, the extraordinarily wide range to which Derrida has applied what are often highly similar arguments begins to look like those arguments' greatest weakness. The force of Foucault's argument makes us, I think, not question whether Derrida's is right (yes, language *does* work the way Derrida has repeatedly demonstrated that it does), but rather question to what extent his argument can remain interesting in a case where precisely that discursive economy Foucault is seeking to unearth has been ignored/repressed. In such a situation, isn't any reading, even one as patient as Derrida is often willing to undertake, more or less doomed to become implicated in the repression itself?

Derrida had already claimed that there is nothing *hors du text* (outside the text), in an attempt to begin to encourage readers to consider the most distant and distinct material still to be related to any given text by relations of intertextuality.

By a rather suspicious revoicing of Derrida's text (suspicious for one who, as does Foucault, in the same paragraph, claims Derrida is caught in a system that reduces discursive practices to textual traces, elides events produced by those discursive practices, and invents voices behind texts to avoid having to analyze the way subjects are implicated in those discourses), Foucault revoices Derrida's exhortation that nothing is *hors du text*. Derrida used the phrase in the sense that there is nothing that cannot be related to the text by an inclusive web of intertextuality, a phrase that has served his students as an exhortation to examine the history around texts almost as much as the followers of Foucault.

Writes Foucault, Derrida is currently the most glorious representative of a well-determined pedagogic system that "teaches the pupils there is nothing outside the text, but that in it, in its gaps, its blanks, and its silences, there reigns the reserve of the origin; that it is therefore unnecessary to search elsewhere, but that here, not in the words, certainly, but in the words under erasure, in their *grid*, the 'sense of being' is said. A pedagogy that gives, conversely, to the master's voice the limitless sovereignty that allows it to restate the text indefinitely."

No one who has read Derrida carefully could say that any such New Critical-like reduction of texts has been the general form of Derrida's own work; no one who has read carefully the work of the best critics inspired by his example (Barbara Johnson, Gayatri Chakravorty Spivak, Rodolph Gasché, Neil Hertz . . .) could say that has been the result of Derrida's enterprise; rather, just the opposite. Nor could anyone seriously think that Derrida or his arguments were somehow blind to the fact that in the discourse of Western philosophy the origin is a traditionally privileged concept, privileged because, in that tradition/discourse, something of being is presumed to be immediately and transcendentally present at *the* origin. (As often happens in these debates, in one respect the scholars here are talking past each other.) Foucault's argument is, nevertheless, an extraordinary reminder of just how this can, indeed, happen, if only provisionally, the moment one's historical vigilance slips.

This was one of the great moments of the debates. But it sidesteps what is, I believe, an even more important critique that Foucault had already leveled against himself in 1963, two years after *Madness and Civilization* first appeared in France. This critique was, however, historical, rather than philosophical: One could not explore the idea of the "mad" and the "mentally ill" until one had a good handle on the development of the idea of "illness" itself.

Foucault's next book, *The Birth of the Clinic* (*Naissance de la Clinque*, 1963), was about precisely that concept, as it underwent its own changes over the same classical period. How, asks Foucault, did illness shift from a geographical organism (an entity that moved through countries, invaded cities, fixed itself on neighborhoods, an entity with a life cycle of youth and strength and declining weakness), to an entity that centered on, and finally located itself wholly within, the body?

The opening passages of Foucault's books tend to be as arresting as the hooks commencing the James Bond films of the sixties and seventies. *The Birth of the Clinic* begins by quoting a mid-eighteenth-century doctor named Pomme, who describes his treatment of an hysterical woman by making her "take baths ten or twelve hours a day, for ten whole months." The results of such a ghastly regimen? Pomme saw "membranous tissue like pieces of damp parchment . . . peel away with some slight discom-

Psychoanalytic criticism in these debates has generally been conservative—tending to bring conflicting criticisms in line with each other, tending to show how the text anticipates its own criticism. It seems only to have been used with any force for texts where authoritative readings have already sedimented—making it

fort, and these were passed daily with the urine: the right ureter also peeled away and came out whole in the same way." The same thing occurred with the intestines, which, at another stage, "peeled off their internal tunics, which we saw pass from the rectum. The oesophagus, the tongue, and the arterial trachea also peeled in due course; and the patient either had rejected different pieces by vomiting or by expectoration."

somewhat problematic for use in science fiction. Feminists have particularly espoused this mode of critical discourse, however. Certainly it remains open to exploration. But it seems to me that too little of this criticism has borne in mind what I've often considered the most important of Foucault's exhortations: "We must get rid of the Freudian schema. You know, the interiorization of the Law through the medium of Sex."

A modern medical reader of this report must find it some bizarre concoction of wild fantasy and impenetrable misapprehension. Yet, from a hundred years later, Foucault gives a medical report that, by most modern standards, *reads* like a medical report. What, asks Foucault, happened between the two? What were Pomme and the many, many respected doctors of the time who wrote similar reports, seeing? He does not ask, you understand, what *we* would see were we gazing on the patient in their stead. What, he asks, constituted *their gaze*—a term Foucault, as did many film theoreticians, borrowed from Lacan.

But even at the end of this study, for all the questions that were resolved, more were left open.

Economics, biology, and the foundations of language study, as each had undergone its own changes, had to be taken into account so that even the expanded argument, and certainly the original one, were simply vacuous without such considerations . . .

This was *The Order of Things*—which is where we came in. And the dazzling opening here is a luminous consideration of representation in Velázquez's painting, *Las Meninas* (*The Maids-in-Waiting*, 1656; also known as *The Royal Family*), a painting which, despite its deceptively untroubled surface (unlike the self-referential play rampant in modern works, no thing *and* its representation are simultaneously shown), is a nearly Escher-like visual construct; a painting of a painter painting a painting of animals and humans, noble and common, whole and deformed, while a king and a queen (Philip IV and Mariana, the reflected subjects of the painting) and courtiers and commoners observe him and what he observes from mirrors, through doors, from the darkened frames of other paintings, and presumably from the small "cabonet" of the Prado castle, where the ten-and-a-half by nine foot portrait of the Infanta Margarita in a studio of the Escorial was finally hung, the several positions collapsed one into the other before a frame containing an image the artist alone could never have observed.

The next book, *The Archaeology of Knowledge*, the "position paper" we have already mentioned, was purely theoretical. It repeated from the earlier books why Foucault had found it necessary to look not only at the history of the accumulation of right knowledge (i.e., knowledge currently still acceptable) but had to pay as much attention to historical writings that strike us today as lunatic (the aspect of his work that makes it an archaeology rather than a history): This was the only way he could discern the range of the system—the *épistème*—which is the synchronic organization of thought in a given period. More important, Foucault now expressed his dissatisfaction with the archaeological metaphor—and the idea of an *épistème* that went along with it—abandoning it here for a new theoretical battery of genealogies, enunciations, discourses, and *disposatifs* (which means both dispositions and apparatuses). In the terminal chapters he announced a set of possible future projects he might undertake.

The traditional notion of the sign is that of "the signifier of the signified," a signifier that leads to a signified, a word that connects to a thought, a sign that cleaves to a meaning. Derrida has suggested that we take the model for the sign, however, from writing: "the signifier of the signifier," a signifier that leads to another signifier, a written word that leads to a spoken word, a sign that leads to another sign. Thus our object of analysis always becomes some form of Peirce's unlimited semiosis.

Under such an analytic program, the beginnings and ends of critical arguments and essays grow particularly difficult. The "natural" sense of commencement and sense of closure the thematic critics consider appropriate to, and imminently allied throughout, the "naturally" bounded topic of his or her concern now is revealed to be largely artificial and overwhelmingly ideological.

Thus the beginnings and endings (as well as the often easier middle arguments, once we are aboard) of our criticisms must embody conscientiously creative and political strategies.

The next book turned, as he'd suggested it might at the close of *The Archaeology*, to historify another institution: jails.

Conceived by the English philosopher Jeremy Bentham, the Panopticon (the building in which all can be observed, usually from a central tower or station) had been modified for the construction of hospitals. Foucault had touched on their significance in *The Birth of the Clinic*. But the Panopticon had been used in a much purer form for the construction of jails—including our most famous penitentiaries in America (for the detention of penitents, of course), Alcatraz and Sing Sing.

Tracing the shift from public torture to hidden detention (i.e., from punishment inflicted on the body of the criminal and observed by the common public to the disciplines inflicted on the "soul" of the presumably penitential prisoner and observed by only the prison officials), *Discipline and Punish* was Foucault's next and generally most popular book. But with it, the original story of the detention/ constitution of the mad was now so thin and emended as to be unrecognizable.

In *Discipline and Punish* the opening move is a devastating eyewitness account of a public drawing and quartering, complete with melted lead, hot wax, and eventual burning at the stake—much of which, with ropes breaking, arms refusing to part from the still-conscious body, as the torturers with their pincers simply were not strong enough to strip the tendons from the criminal, didn't work or was even more cruelly inefficient. The victim was a sixteenth-century noble who had attempted regicide. Against this account, Foucault poses, from not a hundred years later, the pious and sanctimonious busywork that was by then the daily schedule for prisoners in French jails. How, Foucault tries to answer, does one practice give way, or transform, into the other?

The traditional model for art is that of the central practice of a Great Tradition (variously defined) to which there are many other marginal practices—political art, paraliterary art, popular art, women's art, black art, gay art, regional art, Third World art . . .

Today *all* art is marginal; and a far more appropriate model for any art work is that which takes place in the margin of another margin. Thus the paraliterary arts, such as science fiction, may become a privileged model for analyzing the ways in which all art is produced, is disseminated, and functions.

A subsidiary volume, *I, Pierre Riviere, Having Slaughtered My Mother, My Sister, My Brother* . . . , which Foucault edited and contributed to, grew out of a seminar Foucault conducted around the first case in France where psychiatric evidence was effectively brought in to commute a death sentence to life. The compilation brings together numerous documents around a murder in 1835, in which a "near-idiot" eighteen-year-old French peasant wiped out his mother and her children, whom he believed were destroying the quality of his father's life. The book includes depositions from doctors, lawyers, and various witnesses in the small community, testimony from the trial, and various newspaper accounts of the time. Various participants in the seminar, including Foucault, contribute seven terminal essays in which they discuss the range of problems surrounding this tragic dossier—the central document of which is the forty-page pamphlet the young "near-idiot" murderer wrote, explaining his situation, his motives, and his conviction that he'd performed his act aware that death would be his retribution. Shortly after completing the piece, Riviere committed suicide in jail, when his death sentence, over his protest, was commuted.

Now Foucault turned to still another project, also mentioned at the end of *The Archaeology*, a five-volume history of sexuality. Only the introductory volume appeared in the form initially outlined. The end of the introductory volume, *The Will to Knowledge*, promised that the remaining four volumes of the work would deal with the medical invention of "perversion," the "hysterization" of women's bodies (i.e., the prioritizing of women's reproductive function), and the control of children's sexuality.

It was a loaded list. It was a work that promised insights, if not inspiration, for feminists, for gay activists, and even for much harassed groups like NAMBLA (the North American Man-Boy-Love Association). At one point, leaving his university in Paris, Foucault was set on by some young men, thrown to the ground, and beaten—a sobering experience for a professional scholar who wrote of Nietzsche and Heidegger, Raymond Rousell, Margritte, Blanchot, and Bataille, who delivered lectures on the difference between political and pastoral power . . .

The signifier of the signifier . . . The margin of the margin . . . Can a discussion of such topics as we are reviewing here take place anywhere in the SF precincts *other* than at its margins? *The New York Review of Science Fiction,* where this piece now appears, is itself—like all fanzines—marginal to the science fiction genre. Yet, as has been noted, the margin is frequently the strongest position from which to deposit/deposition a strategic program, to set it in motion.

The next two books (all Foucault lived to complete) do not fulfill the promise raised at the end of *The Will to Knowledge.* While, in their prefaces, Foucault provides telling reasons for his decision to abandon his original scheme, the easy story to tell is that, in the years just prior to his death, the Foucauldian enterprise collapsed under the pressure of fame, his own recomplicated theoretical elaborations, possibly the repeated threats to his life—or even his waning intellectual powers, a waning of which the books he *did* write, or the many interviews he gave, I must say, show no sign.

I will conclude with the observation that the story of Foucault's decline (before the final collapse on June 2 from the opportunistic infection that killed him on June 25, 1984) is far too easy a tale—as much in need of critique as the tale of the social origins of modern madness he first attracted our attention with.

The Ends of the Beginnings. The slippery and elusive change between structuralism and poststructuralism in the thirty-year debate is often characterized by a change in an attitude we have already cited: The daunting and massively systematic organization in which the thought of the early thinkers was couched, as well as the belief in the scientificity of their enterprises by Lévi-Strauss, Althusser, and Lacan, in retrospect, certainly marks a sort of style. And that was what the next wave, characterized as poststructuralist, turned to critique in its examination of totality, of mastery, of closure, in a philosophical and historical examination of the metaphysical grounding of absolute knowledge as Plato had aspired to it and as Hegel claimed to have attained it.

But as usual we are progressing too quickly.

In 1967, among three books that he published that year, Derrida presented his study, that we've already mentioned, *Of Grammatology*. In it he analyzes—a near synonym, recall, for deconstructs—the opposition between voice and writing that runs, in general, through Western philosophy since Plato, and specifically through the work of Lévi-Strauss and, in the second half of Derrida's study, the eighteenth-century French philosopher of the noble savage, Jean Jacques Rousseau. In a brief section between the opening moment and the closing body of the book, however, he traces and analyzes the same use of voice and writing in Saussure's own work on the sign. What lies under them all—it should be old news to us by now—is a nostalgia for self-presence, for authority, for unity, for a metaphysical grounding on which the concepts of man, the sign, the self, the primitive, and the civilized might stand. All some of us might be provisionally content to know here is that in the context of Barthes's work and Foucault's from the same years, this seemed certainly another important contribution to the analysis of the sign.

The year after Derrida's first triple "biblio-blitz" (Barbara Johnson's term), on April 4 of 1968, Martin Luther King was assassinated by James Earl Ray in Atlanta. Days later, Valerie Solanis, a radical feminist, attempted to assassinate artist Andy Warhol as an example of an exploiter of women. A day after, that was knocked off the front page by the assassination of Robert Kennedy in Los Angeles by Sirhan Sirhan. In response to the racial situation, black students by now were sitting in at Columbia University. The whole situation in New York erupted days later in April, when the police decided to remove the students, after first jamming the Columbia University radio station through which the students were organizing and directing their protests and demonstrations.

WBAI-FM, a public radio station with hundreds of thousands of listeners, volunteered its services to the demonstrators. Very soon, the police actions exploded in horrendous, night-long police brutality and violence—which, because the whole evening was being broadcast on WBAI, was heard by hundreds of thousands of people throughout the night, across the city and the state.

The French academic system within which (and in reaction to which) much of this critical discourse arose is far more rigorous—and in a word, hidebound—than the American academy. But this means that many of the moves associated with it, such as the bringing to bear of vast analytic attention on some insistently marginal text (often by great writers) has an effect both of playfulness and scandal that is lost, or at least mitigated, when brought across the sea. One of Derrida's most interesting books,

Student eruptions over political inequities between pro-Palestinians and Israeli supporters had already broken out on the streets of Tunis, where Foucault was teaching that year—exacerbated by a visit from American Vice President Humphrey in March. For his support of the students, Foucault was pulled from a car and beaten (and tortured, claimed his long-time lover, Daniel Defert) by anonymous thugs. In France, student demonstrations at the University of Nanterre over sexual politics expanded to Paris and went on to encompass other causes, including French involvement in Vietnam and the rights of French workers, who showed astonishing solidarity with the students. The actions of students in one country served as major inspiration for the actions of the students in others. Though he missed some of the fighting on May 10, 11, and 12, Foucault returned to Paris for a few days that included a May 17 gathering of 50,000 at the Cherléty stadium in support of the students and workers, then again returned to Tunis. Unlike U.S. workers, French workers joined with the students. The result, in France, was what has been referred to ever since as "May '68," when students and workers came near to seizing control of the entire nation. Very little of the French intellectual horizon was left unchanged by this momentous event. Certainly one change was that what had generally been referred to as "structuralism" before was, in the light of the new, radical political consciousness, now spoken of as "poststructuralism." The general critique of totality, of power, of mastery, and of marginality, focused by the events of May '68, burgeoned with the new and exciting theoretical work. One text here that can be read as a response to the new sense of freedom and expanded possibilities growing up over the decade in France after '68 is Derrida's 1977 book, *Glas*, a two-column examination of, respectively, Genet and Hegel, a daunting Möbius strip of a book, where a consideration of the German philosopher, the family, and legitimacy runs along by (till finally it circles around to become one with) its darker side, an inquiry into the criminal novelist, crime, bastardy, and marginality (each critique written, as it were, in the margins of the other), each of which starts and stops in the middle of a sentence, each of which, at its beginning and end, seeming—almost—to join with the other.

Anyone who has looked at the text of *Glas* (which means the tolling of a bell), with its double columns, multiple type faces, marginal inserts, the

Spurs: Nietzsche's Style, turns, for instance, on a massive analysis of a notebook jotting by the German philosopher that says, simply, "My umbrella." What does such intellectual playfulness mean, however, when transferred to the far more relaxed American academic landscape? These questions of *Institution and Interpretation* have been discussed with some precision by Samuel Weber (U. of Montana Press, 1987).

deployment of white space and general typographic complexity, can see that by now the very coherence and unity of the critical page has broken down, as well as the quest after facility and clarity of expression traditionally associated with classical French criticism. This "family romance" of absolute knowledge [*savoir absolu, Sa*], the Immaculate Conception [IC], and its marginal subversion is a very beautiful book, both to look at and to read.

"Every educational system is a political means of maintaining or modifying the appropriation of discourse, with the knowledge and the powers it carries with it." (Foucault) [That goes for fanzines too—SRD]

One of the best kept secrets of poststructuralism is that Derrida's next work, *The Postcard* (1980), is actually a rather dry, experimental 253-page novel (*Envois*) about a man trying to make a phone call from a phone booth at Oxford. For those of you who enjoy the work of Harry Matthews or James McElroy, let me recommend it to you. It has certainly got to be one of the most remaindered books in the whole debate. The other aspect of this book that recommends it is that it brings together many of Derrida's writings on Freud. (But not all— "Notes on the Mystic Writing Pad" is a notable exception.)

Totality seems figured in the very metaphysic that grounds the fiction of "the systematic." (For Barthes, a fiction was "anything that partakes of the systematic.") But closer examination shows that all through Lévi-Strauss, Lacan, and Althusser, you find them warning their readers against the totality of their apparent systematicness. It is only as this warning ceases to be presented as passing comment and becomes, with some of the later commentators—dare we say it? (Yes, if we accept the analytical imperative)—a theme, that it distinguishes, however briefly, mistily, and finally inadequately, a poststructuralist leaning away from the dense, massive, systematic enterprises that might, if squinted at enough, seem to be at least one of the things structuralism was about.

I have already cited May '68 in France as a historical nodal point. But if one book was perceived as a *transition* between the two, structuralism and poststructuralism, it was Roland Barthes's write-up of his 1970 seminar on Balzac, *S/Z*. In this famous book, Barthes reads a till-then-almost-ignored thirty-six-page novelet by Balzac, "Sarrasine," about a young sculptor of that name who comes to Paris from the provinces and falls in love with a castrato, Zambinella, whom he initially believes to be a woman. As a result of intricate plottings, deceptions, cross purposes, and—yes—self-deceptions, Sarrasine dies-in-the-end. Balzac's story is indubitably interesting for a whole range of attitudes, both of license and of repression, it reveals about a number of topics ordinarily associated neither with Balzac nor with the nineteenth century. But as indubitably, its sentimentality and general artificiality make the tale, among such a sprawling *opera omnia* as Balzac's, all too easy to overlook or ignore. At any rate, in *S/Z*, Barthes shatters Balzac's story into 512 sections—or lexias—each of which he shows is controlled by one or more of five codes: the semic code, which covers what we might accept as ordinary signs, such as grammatical signs on the ends of words, or quotation marks to signal dialogue; the symbolic code, which covers artistic and cultural allusions; the referential code, in which the text appeals to what might be called knowledge of the social; the hermeneutic code, in which the text suggests there is some mystery to be solved "and thus covers the 'unfolding/discovery' of the plot"; and the proairetic code, in which the text indicates directly or indirectly that some action is occurring.

These codes, and these five codes alone (explains Barthes), exhaust what is going on in the story's 512 successive lexias. The sheer operationalism of assigning each lexia its appropriate code(s) seems rather a parody of what an unsympathetic observer of the structuralist dialogue till then might have found all structuralism to have been good for. But the enterprise is redeemed by the 93 divagations on reading, all more or less brief essays (most of them on reading this particular story), with which Barthes punctuates the otherwise near-mechanical progression of codic assignments. These divagations range from thoughts on the readerly—or "lisible"—text (the text we have all learned to expect a story to be, a story in which every readerly unit is exhausted by just such a limited set of codes—the well-made, well-plotted, and eminently forgettable story, such as "Sarrasine") to the writerly—or "scriptible"—text (the text that produces no notable reading experience without active participation by the reader, as though the reader *were* the writer—the text that even so thin a tale as "Sarrasine" becomes when subjected to a certain analytical pressure) to notions about castrations and psychoanalysis. With them, Barthes moves us into a critique of system, into a consideration of the excesses that outstrip even his own schema, and finally into a distrust of precisely the totality his pentagraphic codic exhaustiveness would seem to set in place.

And in Barthes's next book (not a full seventy pages long), *The Pleasure of the Text*, the systematic has been reduced to the alphabetic ordering of the key words in a set of similar divagations, in which any particular text as the occasion for these highly charged, meticulously written, and finally poetic meditations on the boredom of reading,

We find no more monolithically positive (or negative!) an attitude toward popular and/or marginal culture among the poststructuralist and semiotic debates (the discussions there that obtain most directly to SF) than we do toward anything else. Critics such as the late Theodore Adorno and the currently popular Terry Eagleton do not believe popular culture can be any more than a conservative reification of the *status quo*, or, in Eagleton's case, that such a

the pleasure of reading, and the ecstasy of reading (Barthes uses the French word *jouissance,* which is both "bliss" and "orgasm") has disappeared.

Perhaps the only thing to say after this in the discussion of semiotics *per se* (rather than about semiotics as it must endlessly aid and abet any discussion of representation)—to say it both for the provocation and for the implied criticism—is that semiotics seems to me to persist, beyond this point, as that which, in the face of the poststructuralist critique of the systematic, retains its systematic allegiances, even as it tries to take into account that critique.

But then semiotics is not a branch of the dialogue I have followed with any real care for the last few years. For an accessible and

"culture" could have any effect on any branch of thought whatsoever. But critics such as Fredric Jameson and Umberto Eco feel that popular culture is the site of some of the most important thinking that occurs in any society at all. (Eco's 1962 essay, "The Myth of Superman," in *The Role of the Reader* [Indiana U. Press, 1979], is one of the most sensitive, informed, and insightful things ever written on comic books—a judgment I do not hand easily to an academic.) And in a discourse that has already produced sensitive discussions of film and television, we will not find ourselves all that lost. The usual situation of the SF reader, confronted with criticism in general, is to discover, after whatever initial period of critical enthusiasm the critic claims for the genre, only the genre's lacks. In the poststructuralist mode of critical discourse, however, there is a good chance for us to forge a dialogue in which to speak with both passion and precision about our strengths.

And that seems worth the risk.

sensitive overview of recent semiotic developments, I recommend Marshal Blonsky's anthology *On Signs.*

The Deluge After. I hope some things are clear: Not only have we not given a definition of semiotics, poststructuralism, or structuralism so far, we have not given any functional descriptions of them either. (While "structuralism" was a French term, "poststructuralism" began, it should be pointed out, as an American one.) What I hope I've implied instead is that—with the possible exception of some of the work of Lévi-Strauss (who titled an early collection of papers *Structural Anthropology* [1958] and thus decanted the term)—structuralism and poststructuralism both, besides having no clear boundaries (even if, here and there, as the debates progress, you will find discussions of structure), have no more *necessary* relation to the idea of structure than Dadaism has a *necessary* relation to the idea of the hobbyhorse.

We are not defining our object of inquiry here because it is not an object; it is a vast and sprawling debate (or, better, a collection of debates), a great and often exciting dialogue, a wrangle between many voices, many writers, in which now and again certain events are agreed to have been of importance by certain people with certain intellectual interests.

Some of these I have tried to point out.
Some I have not mentioned are nevertheless high points in my own reading.
Some of the latter include:
Lévi-Strauss's dazzling eight-page description-*cum*-analysis of a sunset in the early pages of *Tristes Tropiques*, where I first got a sense of the sort of writerly enterprise he and some of the other critics whom I'd already started reading (with, I'm afraid, till then, not much comprehension) were involved in. There was Lévi-Strauss's and Roman Jakobson's analysis of, first, Baudelaire's sonnet "*Le Chat*" ("The Cat") and, later, of Shakespeare's "Sonnet CXXIX," followed by Michael Riffaterre's rejoinder to the Baudelaire critique and Jonathan Culler's much later critique (in *Structuralist Poetics*) of them both—in which, you might be surprised to learn, almost everyone agrees that Riffaterre "won," hands down.

Still another exciting moment was my first reading of Lacan's "The Insistence of the Letter in the Unconscious" in one of the Jacques Ehrman editions of *Yale French Studies*, republished as *Structuralism*. A short while later there was another special issue called "French Freud," which presented Lacan's seminar on Poe's "The Purloined Letter," along with Derrida's answer to it—"*Le Facteur de la vérité*," which means, incidentally, both "the truth factor" and "the postman delivering truth." These, and the very fine further responses of Barbara Johnson (from still another issue of *Yale French Studies*, "Literature and Psychoanalysis"), Shoshana Felman, and others, have just been collected in a single volume, *The Purloined Poe*, by the bye. And Felman's own contribution to the *Literature and Psychoanalysis* volume (which she also edited), "Turning the Screw of Interpretation," a hundred-page psychoanalytic reading of "The Turn of the Screw" (a text which most of us, I suspect, would ordinarily assume there is simply nothing left to say about), is a breathtaking performance that invigorates the idea of Lacanian psychoanalysis as a tool for literary criticism as much as, or more so than, Edmund Wilson's Freudian approach to the same tale from 1934.

Certainly one of my most exciting reading experiences was my first encounter with Derrida's "Plato's Pharmakon" in Barbara Johnson's translation of Derrida's *Dissemination* (certainly the best place for the careful, but nonspecialist, reader to begin among Derrida's many, but at once meticulous and mazy, texts). The discovery of Julia Kristeva's intensely ideological critique (she was Barthes's sometimes collaborator and for many years editor of the main periodical in the debates, *Tel Quel*) of the early semiotic/psychoanalytic conjunction was wonderfully exciting (*Revolution in Poetic Language, Desire in Language, The Power of Horror*); equally so the critique by Luce Irigaray of Lacan (in *Speculum de l'autre femme* and *Ce Sexe qui n'en est pas un*) and the subsequent outgrowth of the multiple, exciting feminist analyses of reading, canon foundation, film theory, and psychoanalysis.

Once the reader feels a bit more at home within this discourse, I recommend highly the Derrida/Searles debate over the speech act theory of the late English philosopher John Austin. The Derrida side has just been published in book form as *Limited, Inc.*, edited by Gerald Graff—though anyone purchasing it should get hold of Austin's little book *How to Do Things with Words*, and also the full text of John Searle's "Reply to Derrida" from *Glyph* #2 (eds. Sussman and Weber)—and take the time to read them all carefully. It is one of the few places in all this where there are smiles to be smiled and belly laughs to be laughed. And there has been some subsequently exciting literary use made of speech act theory, notably by Shoshana Felman in *The Literary Speech Act: Seduction in Two Languages: Austin and Moliere* (1983), a book whose French title was, incidentally, *La Scandal de la corps parlant*—the scandal of the talking corpse. Also there are Felman's other pieces, collected in *Writing and Madness* (1985), which includes "Turning the Screw of Interpretation," and *Jacques Lacan and the Adventure of Insight* (1987), and still more by Barbara Johnson (*The Critical Difference* [1980], *A World of Difference* [1987]), Gayatri Chakravorty Spivak (*In Other Worlds* [1987]), and Jane Gallop (*Intersections: A Reading of Sade with Bataille, Blanchot, and Klossowski* [1981], *The Daughter's Seduction: Feminism and Psychoanalysis* [1982], *Reading Lacan* [1985], and *Thinking Through the Body* [1988]). With their definite and powerful feminist orientation, these last four—Felman, Johnson, Spivak, and Gallup—are my own current reading favorites in the debates. Along with Jacqueline Rose, Juliet Flower MacCannell, and Alice Jardin, they are the most skilled writers to enter the debates for some time.

If one is still pressed for things to study, there are all the correspondences between these writers and an entirely different school of criticism to consider, the Frankfurt School, which privileges such names as Adorno, Horchiemer, Habermas, and—perhaps most importantly—Walter Benjamin. There are also the early Russian Formalists and folklorists, including Vladimir Propp, whom many cite as yet another origin for this debate. There is the exciting work of Vygotsky (*Language and Thought*, a book that proposes, with overwhelming logic, that the child learns to speak first and only then to think), and, more recently, the discovery of the work of the Russian critic Michel Michelovitch Bakhtin. Jean Francois Layotard's *Driftworks* are brief and elegant; his *Economie libidinal* is a provocative study. Gilles Deleuze's and Felix Guatarri's joint work, *Anti-Oedipus: Capitalism and Schizophrenia, Volume I* (Paris, 1972), which I once heard characterized, amusingly if unfairly, as "Yippie-consciousness for intellectuals," was another explosively exciting response to May '68 and more recently they have written together *A Thousand Plateaus: Capitalism and Schizophrenia, Volume II* (Paris, 1980). Harold Bloom's readings of the misreadings of those he calls "strong poets," especially Wallace Stevens, are elegantly askew and provocative. And the deliriums of Baudrillard are exciting, if ultimately scary and reactionary—those of Baudrillard (*The Mirror of Production, Forget Foucault, Simulations*) characterized by brevity, while Pierre Beaurdieu's tomes (*Distinction* is where one must start) are as massive (and as intelligent) as that of some early structuralist.

Most recently interest has focused on the scandal of the discovery of de Man's collaborationist writings, which he wrote in 1942 as a 21-year-old literary editor in German-occupied Belgium and which only came to light after his death a few years ago, once he had gained the reputation along with Derrida as the most important advocate of deconstruction. A monumental compendium, *Responses*, edited by Hamacher, Herta, Derrida, and others, by a gallery of scholars, such as Gasché and Weber, examines those early de Man texts in the light of past and subsequent history and his work in America at Yale—certainly the most anticipated (in many cases with real dread!) event in the debate.

Some of the names I've cited in the catalogue above no one would think to call "poststructuralist." Yet all—and more—are more or less of interest to those interested in the multiple dialogues so far. But to cite any of these moments, these dialogues, these debates is simply to reiterate what I have already said: Structuralism/poststructuralism has never been a masterable monologue.

SF: New Questions. But this is the moment for the promised return to the "themes" of science fiction: "New Worlds," "The Alien," "Technology," "Time," "Space," and "Utopia/Dystopia." We must note in passing that none of these themes are really ours. Historically, all gain their importance in other fields: "Space" is traditionally taken as the "theme" of nineteenth-century American literature, including Cooper, Twain, and Melville. "Time" is, correspondingly, a traditional "theme" of a slightly more recent current of continental literature, which includes Bergson, Proust, and Wyndham Lewis. "New Worlds" is simply the retelling of another European "theme," the eighteenth- and nineteenth-centuries' fascination with the discovery of America. "The Alien" is a replaying of the European "theme" of endless fascination with the Other. "Technology" is the nineteenth-century "theme" of science and progress. And "Utopia/Dystopia" are just that: In Marvin Lasky's magisterial *Utopia and Revolution*, there is no entry for "science fiction" anywhere in its index. Nor, really, should there have been.

But the unearthing of historical provenances is merely the most passing gracenote in our attempt to displace these "themes." More important than how they got here is what their use has been, since they have been displaced here.

I start by mentioning that the last time I generated this particular list (three months ago), I was in the first days of a class in science fiction at the University of Massachusetts. Having already located those in the class who were science fiction readers, I asked them *not* to respond to the question. Then I asked the remaining two-thirds of the class (the non-SF readers), "What are the 'themes' of science fiction?" A very relieved group of youngsters (on discovery that Professor Delany's questions were going to be so simple), generated my list of "themes" in somewhat under three minutes.

The students were not, of course, familiar with their thematic provenances—*they* came as news. But what I next asked them and must now ask you, is: What does it mean when people who do *not* read in the field "know" what our "themes" are, in some cases substantially better and more surely than people who do? This list of "themes" that so easily comes to the lips of anyone trying to create it is, of course, what the most cursory glance at SF would suggest to those for whom such "themes" were already in place.

And if you explore the use of these "themes" in the criticism of SF, what you invariably find is they are used to denigrate the field. "SF text X or Y should, it would seem, have something interesting to say about Time/Space/Technology/etc., since self-evidently that's what the text is about. But, oddly, it doesn't seem to . . ." This is by far the most common form of the criticism that appeals to any of them. In brief, these "themes" are imposed on science fiction in the mood of legitimization, and are actually employed to delegitimize us through inadequation.

This, to me, however well intentioned, is critical terrorism. In a passing move to depose these themes let me suggest several dispositions of science fiction that can *only* be teased out by reading it. (The Literary Chamber of Commerce cannot glance at a couple of SF-oriented comic books and say, "There. That's what it must be about . . .") These dispositions, as I have already suggested, will only be useful if they serve as places to commence analyses that will move them on to other forms, other figures, rather than as positions at which to stop analysis in its tracks.

First: Much science fiction posits an alternate, technologically constituted space, in which language reaches toward the lyric and death changes its status: Consider Budrys' *Rogue Moon*, Zelazny's "He Who Shapes," or Gibson's *Neuromancer*. (Closely allied to this disposition is the famous synæsthesia episode in Bester's *The Stars My Destination*—doubling is frequently, though not always, a characteristic of this alternate space.) What does this disposition mean, differently, in each case? What does each writer use this disposition to mark politically?

Second: Well before the advent of the most recent phase of the women's movement (1968 on), science fiction had (and still has) an astonishing array of strong female characters. Almost invariably, however, such women either work for the state or work for men with enough wealth at their command to topple states. What is politically marked here? What are the differences various texts bring into play around it?

Third: From Asimov's Susan Calvin through Sturgeon's "Baby is Three" and on, science fiction has been fascinated by the idea of psychoanalysis. Almost without exception, however, SF chooses to analyze subjects-without-fathers. The point that all psychoanalytic transference goes back to in science fiction tends to be the state, rather than the father. (From "Baby is Three," Gerard's free association yields: "I ate from the plate of the state and I hate.") What is marked here? What does it set in motion? And how does it relate to our second disposition above?

Others have noted other dispositions, conventions, and attitudes that fall out of careful readings of a range of science fiction (the generous universe and its disconcerting underside, the profligacy of death; the necessity to leave and return to utopia; the overmalleability of history, etc., already referred to); but very few people have discussed them as politically revelatory dispositions; few critics have tried to dissolve them into their greater problematics.

As an interim strategic inversion, then, I would like to propose that "New Worlds," "The Alien," "Technology," "Time," "Space," and "Utopia/Dystopia" are *not* science fiction's themes at all and can here and now be abandoned to the archaeology of our criticism. And as a longer-term strategy, I propose that what is deeply needed in our field is people to read science fiction carefully, synchronically with the historical and social occurrences (both inside and outside the SF field) around its composition, who are willing to discuss with precision, creativity, and critical inventiveness what they have read. What we do *not* need any more of is people who merely glance at SF and say the first thing that comes to mind—usually something that comes most pointedly from somewhere (anywhere!) else, rather than from the texts read.

To that end, I'd propose, here, before concluding this survey, that we remember both the model of Foucault, as we delve into what it is all too easy to call SF's history, back to its trickles through the penny-dreadfuls which joined to swell into our current inland sea. And I propose equally that, as we work as readers of our own SF texts (which, of course, none of us can own any more than we can master), we remember the model of Derrida. We must read carefully. Equally important, we must write carefully. Is there anything particularly radical in such an exhortation?

Or is such a call for readerly and writerly vigilance always a radical gesture?

Homo Ludens. My last comments, as I move back to our general purpose here, must be about style.

In poststructuralist discourse, style is a topic running from the famously—and sometimes impenetrably—recomplicated language of Lacan's seminars and writings (his *Écrits*, a thousand-plus pages in the original French, abridged to three hundred in the English selection) to the different modes of lyrical precisions (and imprecisions!) of a Barthes or a Foucault. For most readers, at least, structuralism/poststructuralism has been primarily a stylistic explosion (perhaps, for some, a stylistic catastrophe) only matched in English by the explosion represented by Carlyle, Ruskin, and Pater in the nineteenth century. My own response to all these thinkers has been, primarily, as writers. Demanding as their texts can be, for fifteen years now I've simply found them the most exciting *reading* available. (The question of style even covers why I have asked you to listen to a dense and lengthy paper, rather than an informal, impromptu, and even spottier account that this one must, perforce, be.) The several reasons for these several styles are no more monolithic than the various positions put forward in them and by them. But we can cite—and have already cited—a few of these reasons.

One is the pace of thought many of these thinkers have chosen to cleave rigorously to. It is simply a slower and more stately pace than that of the conversational arguments their thematic brothers and sisters frequently favor. And often—as in the case of Lacan or Derrida—what is under discussion is precisely the way certain notions resist articulation.

Two is the analytic vigilance I have already and so often spoken of—which can only be carried out *at such a pace.* Along with such vigilance must go a willingness to problematize radically, as part of their critique, the model—that is language—that still, in these debates, controls so much of meaning.

Finally—three—is the reason those more familiar with these topics have probably been waiting for a while now: Play—play both in the sense of the slippages and imperfect fits that occur in both machines and in language, and in the sense of joy and playfulness, *jouissance* if you prefer, that leads the writer to let the language write him or her into meaning— and even a play of styles that has led more than one critic to comment that any truly intellectual performance is necessarily a comic act.

Critics have written of "the laughter of Foucault"; anyone who reads him long and carefully must hear it. Derrida has said: "I am an intellectual clown."

We are more or less at our conclusion.

What I have done here is told you a story, a fiction, several fictions in fact. I've given them a more or less systematic presentation, held together by certain themes . . . which is to say that they will serve us only if we realize they are too simple: Too many things have been left out, too many questions remain, not enough history and socially stabilizing institutions have been examined . . .

—*Amherst*
1988

10

The *Para•doxa* Interview

Inside and Outside the Canon

P•D: What is the canon? How does it get formed? Does it have value?

SRD: In the two-and-a-quarter columns the OED devotes to some fourteen definitions of the word, from "canon" as rule (from the Greek κανών), through canon as "a standard of judgment or authority; a test, a criterion, a means of discrimination," through canon law, the Biblical canon, and the canon of the saints, to—finally—canon as "the metal loop or 'ear' at the top of a bell," not one of those definitions corresponds to the "canon of English literature," much less to the "canon of Western literature."

The use of the word "canon" that has excited so many of us to so much polemic recently is a metaphorical extension of the notion of canon as the list of books approved as part of the Bible or the list of saints approved of and canonized by the Church. As, in his ovular essay, "What is an Author?" (1969), Foucault reminded us that the controlling concepts of historical, stylistic, ideational, and qualitative unity that held stable the notions of "author" and "authority" are themselves religious holdovers, so is the concept of the canon: The canon is a list of approved books, i.e., books which have been verified to have come from God.

If we are to make any headway in such a discussion, we have to start with a few reasonable statements, however, about what the canon is *not.*

First, the canon is not a natural object. That is to say, if the canon is any sort of object at all, it is purely a *social object.* To use an example from the late Lucien Goldmann, the canon is not an object like a wooden table weighing three hundred pounds. Rather it is a *social object* like the strength required to move a table that is too heavy for one, two, or even three strong men to move without help from a fourth. Largely because they are notoriously unlocalized in space, social objects do not lend themselves to rigorous definitions, with necessary and sufficient conditions. (Does it matter which four men move the table? Does it matter if one, two, or three of them are women . . . ?) At best, social objects can be functionally described (in many different ways, depending on the task the particular description is needed for, i.e., depending on the required function). But functional descriptions are *not* definitions. To speak of them as if they were is to broach terminological chaos and confusion. Along with many forms of power, social objects include meanings, genres, traditions, and discourses.

Second, the canon is not a conspiracy. That is to say, while the forces that constitute it are often mystified and frequently move to heal the breaches effected on it, there is no synod, no panel, no authoritative council, actually or in effect, that confers canonicity on works or establishes their canonical rank. While the history of the canon is full of campaigns, mostly unsuccessful, to bring writers or works into it—or often, to exclude writers and works from it—and while there are often elements of the conspiratorial *in* these campaigns, the canon itself is not one with them.

Third, the canon is not a list. Though from time to time the canon presents itself as a paradigm, this is merely a flattened representation of a complex system, of a rhizome, of a syntagm, or simply of an abstract set of interrelations, too rich to be mappable with any sophistication in less than three—and more likely four—dimensions. The canon's self-presentation *as* a paradigm—or ranked list of works (or more accurately, as a set of contesting ranked lists)—is (1) always partial and (2) part of that complexity. Which is to say, its self-presentation as a paradigm is *part* of the mystification process by which this highly stable syntagm protects itself and heals itself from various attempts to attack it or to change it.

In short, the canon is an object very like a genre. That is to say, it functions (in a way almost too blatant to be interesting, but is thus perhaps more easily memorable) as *a way of reading*—or, more accurately, as a way of organizing reading over the range of what has been written. The astute will realize that, having declared that the canon is not just a ranked list but rather the discursive machinery that produces the many contesting lists involved, we have actually described an object that is nothing less than the historical and material discourse of literature itself.

How is the canon formed? By political forces—in the sense that all social force is political. Traditionally a great many of the forces that we would recognize today as overtly political are also overtly conservative. At this point, one can go back and read the arguments that fulminated over the worth of, say, Edgar Allan Poe—who only just made it into the canon; or

James Thomson—who still hasn't in spite of the campaign launched by Bertram Dobell in the eighteen-nineties to have him included; or the various poets of the Rymers' Club, also from the eighteen-nineties, e.g., Earnest Dowson, Lionel Johnson, John Davidson, William Sharp (aka Fiona McCloud), and Arthur Symons. Or the novel that was, during the nineties, the most talked-about and highly favored work among these same writers: Olive Schreiner's *The Story of an African Farm* (1883). Schreiner's work is as openly feminist a work as James's *Portrait of a Lady* (1881) and later D. H. Lawrence's *Sons and Lovers* (1913) were overtly antifeminist. It is naïve to assume this hasn't at least something to do with the reason James and Lawrence *were* canonized while Schreiner was not. But it is equally naive to assume that such ideological forces *exhaust* the politics of the canon. There are too many counter-examples.

A little book called *The Tourist, A New Theory of the Leisure Class,* by Dean McCannell (Schocken Books, New York City, 1976), is one I would recommend to anyone interested in the formation of literary reputations in particular—and of any sort of social reputation in general. *The Tourist* professes to present a semiotics of contemporary tourism, but McCannell states in his introduction:

> The tourist is an actual person, or real people are tourists. At the same time "the tourist" is one of the best models for modern-man-in-general. I am equally interested in "the tourist" in this second, metasocial sense of the term. (1)

Prompted only a bit by a quotation from Baudelaire that precedes it, we can easily locate in McCannell's "tourist" a descendent of Walter Benjamin's *"flâneur"*—whom Benjamin saw as the privileged subject in Baudelaire's newly urban bourgeois world.

But the strength of McCannell's study is not his meditation on the subject, but rather his astonishingly insightful dissection of the structure of the object: not what goes into making a tourist—but rather what goes into making a *tourist site.*

McCannell states that, naturally, the tourist site must be picturesque, enjoyable or interesting in itself, and worth visiting in some more or less describable way. (See? You don't *have* to say "define" and "definable" every time you want to specify something. Start getting used to it. You'll never develop a sophisticated theory of paraliterary studies if you don't.) But basically what makes a tourist site is the "markers" scattered about the landscape pointing it out, directing us to it, more or less available on the well-traveled road—even when the site itself lies off the path.

These markers, McCannell points out, can be as ephemeral as a word-of-mouth comment. ("Just before we got to the turnoff on I-66, we stopped at this place that served the most delicious, homemade blueberry muffins! Next time you're up that way, try it!") Or they can be as solid as a three-volume history and guide to *Life, Craft, and Religion Among the Pennsylvania Shakers.* They can be as traditional as a brochure in a tourist office or a signboard on the road ("Just Twelve miles to Howes Cavern"). The markers can generate as advertising by those who have invested in the site itself. Or they can generate spontaneously as writings, photographs, or art works from those who have simply passed by and been moved to create these more lasting representations, impressions, and interpretations. At larger and more famous tourist sites, the markers can be intricately entwined with the sites themselves, such as the archways, broadened highways, parking lots, motels, and guided tours that have grown up to accommodate floods of visitors—to the Grand Canyon, say, or to Niagara Falls. Some sites are conceived, created, and built to be nothing *but* tourist sites: Mt. Rushmore, Disneyland, the Epcot Center, each functioning more or less as one of its own markers. And there is a whole set of sites—often the spots where historical events took place— that are sites *only* because a marker sits on them, telling of the fact (so that, in effect, the informative marker *becomes* the site: an apartment house on West 84th Street bearing a plaque: "In 1844, Edgar Allan Poe lived on a farm on this spot where he completed 'The Raven.'"). Without the marker, these sites would be indistinguishable from the rest of the landscape.

Without markers, even the most beautiful spot on the map becomes one with the baseline of unmarked social reality.

And until someone thinks to emit, erect, and/or stabilize a marker indicating it, no tourist site comes into being.

The accessibility of the markers, McCannell notes wryly, is far more important to the success of a site than the accessibility of the site itself. In the case of some sites (various mountaintops, or the like), their *in*accessibility is precisely part of the allure—often pointed out *in* the markers.

Yes, we're talking about advertising and commodification.

But it requires a very small leap to realize that McCannell's discussion holds just as true for establishing "tourist sites" in the landscape of art and literary production as it does for establishing them in an actual physical landscape. For a complex mapping of those literary sites, with suggestion as to what to see now and what to see next is what the canon *is.*

The first, major demystifying and axiomatic claim we can make, then, about the canon, in light of McCannell's semiotic survey of tourist sites, is that the material from which the canon is made is *not* works of literature (and/or art); rather it is made from works-of-literature-(and-/or-art-)and-their-markers.

And the same range to the markers of tourist sites (from word of mouth to the researched historical study) apply to the markers of literary sites.

If the canon *is* made up of literature-and-its-markers (and I believe it is), then to study the canon and canonicity *means* to study literature-and-its-markers. That is the object that controls the discipline. Literature alone will not suffice. The determining relationship of literature-and-its-markers to the canon should be, I suspect, self-evidently clear. If, for example, the major critical markers (or marker sets) associated with *Ulysses* were obliterated and had never existed—*James Joyce's* Ulysses, *A Study* (1930), by Stuart Gilbert, *The Making of* Ulysses (1934) by Frank Budgen, various works on Joyce by Hugh Kenner and the two biographies by Richard Ellmann—*Ulysses* would occupy a *very* different place in the canon.

Positions in the canon do change: We are currently seeing an attempt at a major reëvaluation of Hart Crane—though one could easily argue that Crane has been undergoing "a major reëvaluation" at least since 1937 when the first biography by Philip Horton appeared seven years after Crane's death; and that to be majorly reëvaluated is finally Crane's function, persistent and unchanging, within the canon from his initial consideration period until today. The high modernists launched a fairly strenuous effort to dethrone Milton from his place beside Shakespeare and Chaucer—and failed—while the conflict of values that has continually raged about Walt Whitman since his acceptance into the canon has stabilized his canonical position as firmly as any writer in the history of American "canonicity." (A similar conflict of values has kept Robinson Jeffers from being finally and ultimately excluded.) The canon keeps alive what might be called "the Keats or Wordsworth problem," which memorializes a moment when poetry might be seen to bifurcate into two different sorts of (and possibly even mutually exclusive) verbal objects— as different, indeed, as the work of Auden and Crane; at the same time, through its stabilizing forces, the canon is what keeps us calling both "poetry."

One of the most fascinating and informative examples of canonization is the "invention" of Stephen Crane—by Thomas Beer in 1923. In terms both of the literary texts involved and their markers, at least two aspects to this "invention" are particularly worth discussing: One concerns the young man who wrote the novels *Maggie, A Girl of the Streets, The Red Badge of Courage, The Third Violet,* and the various poems and stories. The other concerns the texts themselves.

Between the two—and the markers associated with both—we have an extraordinarily informative tutorial case in canonical appropriation. Allow me to review it:

Crane became a popular—even a best-selling—author, first with the newspaper syndication in 1893 of *The Red Badge of Courage* (written a year before when he was twenty-one) and then, a bit over a year later, with its release as a novel by Appleton in 1895. Crane's experiences on the *Commodore* in December of 1896 returned him briefly to national attention in January of 1897—and produced both his newspaper account of the ship's sinking and his short story "The Open Boat." But the most interesting literary document to endure from the days of his initial popularity is probably Frank Norris's parody of Crane's impressionistic style, "The Green Stone of Unrest" (1897):

> The day was seal brown. There was a vermilion valley containing a church. The church's steeple aspired strenuously in a direction tangent to the earth's center. A pale wind mentioned tremendous facts under its breath with certain effort at concealment to seven not-dwarfed poplars on an un-distant mauve hilltop . . .

By the time he was twenty-eight, however, Crane was dead in Europe of tuberculosis. And while, in his last years in England, a number of writers, including David Garnett, H. G. Wells, Henry James, and Joseph Conrad, befriended him and his common-law wife Cora and felt that his narrative artistry was well above the ordinary (and in this country, Elbert ["A Message to Garcia"] Hubbard, James Gibbons Huneker and Willa Cather all wrote notes on his passing), twenty years after his death he was as forgotten as any other young writer who had written a best-seller once twenty-five years before.

In the July 1920 issue of the *The Swanee Review* Vincent Starrett published "Stephen Crane: An Estimate," which, a year later, became the forward to the Starrett-edited volume of Crane short stories, *Men, Women, and Boats*, the first book of Crane's work to appear for twenty years. Prompted by Starrett's volume and remembering *The Red Badge of Courage*, in 1922, Thomas Beer (1889-1940) suggested a biography of Crane to the Alfred Knopf publishing company. Beer's biography, *Stephen Crane: A Study in American Letters* (1923), became, in its turn, a best-seller. From its publication we date the rise in Crane's reputation as the father of American poetic realism. Willa Cather, whose novel *One of Ours* (1922) had just won the Pulitzer Prize, had known Crane briefly (i.e., for some four or five days) when, in 1896, the twenty-three-year-old author had come through Lincoln, Nebraska, and had to wait over for money at the

Bacheller-Johnson newspaper office where the nineteen-year-old Cather then worked. Shortly after Beer's book appeared, Cather wrote an appreciative introduction to another collection of Crane's stories, *Soldiers in the Rain.*

To get some idea of how *unimportant* an author Crane was by the beginning of the twenties, however, one notes that James Gibbons Huneker, a well-thought-of critic at the time, a good friend of Crane's when Crane was in his twenties and Huneker was just thirty, and the source of a number of incidents in Beer's book, gives the young writer only the two briefest of mentions (one in each volume, in the second subordinated to Conrad, in the first to Howells) and cites none of his works in his two-volume autobiography *Steeplejack,* which became a best-seller upon its publication in 1920 (three years before Beer, following Starrett, began the resuscitation of Crane), and remained widely read through several editions for the next ten years.

Even with the success of Beer's biography, the growth of interest in Crane was slow. But by 1925, a complete works of Crane began to appear in ten volumes (the final volume of the set appeared in 1927), and by 1936 discussions of the development of the American novel now mentioned Crane regularly. Starting at the end of the forties and blossoming at the beginning of the fifties, what had been a slow-growing interest became a major explosion of scholarly attention. But, with Beer's 1923 biography at its origin, one might argue that a solidly canonical writerly reputation would never be more the product of a single volume until Max Brod's 1937 biography of Franz Kafka.

Almost from the beginning of this surge of interest, however, scholars began to find problems with Beer's account of Crane's life. But, then, Beer's book had not been presented as a scholarly biography; the general trend was to forgive him any small mistakes he had made. John Berryman, a graduate student who had access to Beer's papers, published his own biography of Crane in 1950, ten years after Beer's death. This attitude persisted up to Berryman's 1962 revision of the book.

The Crane letters Beer's biography quotes were the first indication that something major was amiss. Throughout the fifties, working together to collect Crane's letters, R. W. Stallman and Lillian Gilkes found some 230 for their 1960 edition, but *none* of the originals of the letters Beer had quoted in his biography turned up—anywhere!

Finally, thanks to the work of scholars Stanley Wortheim, Paul Sorrentino, and John Clendenning, it is fairly clear that:

(1) All but two of the letters Beer quoted in his biography are fabrications. Among Beer's papers are several sets of vastly differing versions of

what is obviously, in each case, the "same" letter—all but conclusively suggesting a novelist inventing and rewriting the "letters" for effect.

(2) The romance between Crane and one Helen Trent that forms the centerpiece for the first half of Beer's biography is a fabrication. Neither the beautiful Miss Trent nor her guardian existed. A few incidents—including a night spent mooning outside "Miss Trent's" window in the street—*may* have been borrowed from some several other much less intense relations Crane had with a number of other young women, generally beefed up, and attributed to his passion for the wholly fictive beauty. But even that is bending over backwards to be kind to Beer.

(3) In an appendix to his biography, Beer claimed that a Mr. Willis Clarke had preceded him in his attempt at a biography of Crane—and that Clarke had even interviewed Crane in England, taking his words down in shorthand, shortly before Crane's death. Eventually Clarke had abandoned his biography (states Beer's book) but turned over his notes and his interview to Beer. Beer quotes several times from the Clarke interview. But, as far as we can tell (a) Clarke never existed (b) no biography was ever begun, and (c) the quoted interview is as bogus as the quoted letters.

(4) Finally, Beer refers—once in his book, and once among his papers—to two unpublished stories Crane is supposed to have written, "Vashti in the Dark" and "Flowers of Asphalt," the manuscripts of which were supposedly lost or destroyed. "Vashti in the Dark" was supposed to have been about a minister whose wife was raped by a Negro, who then dies of grief.

The story around "Flowers of Asphalt" is interesting enough to merit greater detail in its recounting because it offers a possible explanation for Beer's imaginative flights. As well it poses an all but unsolvable enigma. The details around the writing of "Flowers of Asphalt" were found among Beer's papers by the young poet John Berryman, after Beer's death, and utilized for his own 1950 biography of Crane.

Here is a transcription of an unsigned page, presumed by Berryman to be by the music and art critic James Gibbons Huneker (1860-1921), an older acquaintance of Crane's as well as a fellow journalist during the nineties—before the extent of Beer's fictionalizing had been assessed.

One night in April or May of 1894, I ran into Crane on Broadway and we started over to the Everett House together [a hotel on the north face of Union Square, whose bar was popular with reporters in the 1890s; recently the hotel's old shell was converted into a Barnes & Noble], I'd been at a theater with [Edgar] Saltus and was in evening dress. In the Square [Union Square] a kid came up and begged from us. I was drunk enough to give him a quarter. He followed along and I saw he was really soliciting. Crane was dammed innocent about everything but women and didn't see what the boy's game was. We got to the Everett House and we could see that the kid was painted. He was very handsome—looked like a Rossetti angel—big violet eyes—probably full of belladonna—Crane was disgusted. Thought he'd vomit. Then he got interested. He took the kid in and fed him supper. Got him to talk. The kid had syphilis, of course—most of that type do—and wanted money to have himself treated. Crane rang up Irving Bacheller and borrowed fifty dollars.

He pumped a mass of details out of the boy whose name was something like Coolan and began a novel about a boy prostitute. I made him read [Karl Jouris Huysmans's] *A Rebours* [*Against the Grain*] which he didn't like very much. Thought it stilted. This novel began with a scene in a railroad station. Probably the best passage of prose that Crane ever wrote. Boy from the country running off to see New York. He read the thing to Garland who was horrified and begged him to stop. I don't know that he ever finished the book. He was going to call it *Flowers of Asphalt.*

Written to Garland shortly after Crane moved from the old Arts Students' League building at 143 East 23rd Street into a studio rented by Corwin Knapp Linson (1864–1960) at 111 West 33rd Street, an extant letter (May 9, 1894, *Correspondence* I-68) declares: "I am working on a new novel which is a bird." Berryman took this as possibly referring to "Flowers." In Wortheim and Sorrentini's 1988 two-volume edition of the letters, the editors footnote this, however, as Crane's long-story "George's Mother."

Without a signature, the status of the "Huneker" passage is problematic enough; throw on it the light of Beer's other fictionalizing, and it becomes even more so.

This is not a typical letter from Huneker: It has neither salutation nor closing. Edited by his wife, two volumes of Huneker's letters were posthumously published. Graceful and lapidary communications, they are neither blustery nor telegraphic. It could, of course, be a hastily dashed-off note. But it could also be Beer's reconstruction of an anecdote remembered from a previous conversation or from an early research session with the moribund music critic. But it could also be Beer's attempt—safely after Huneker's death in Brooklyn from diabetic complications in 1921— to ventriloquize Huneker toward a fictionalized Crane that, later, Beer abandoned for whatever reasons of believability or appropriateness.

The editors of the magisterial *Crane Log* (Wortheim and Sorrentino again; G. K. Hall, Boston, 1996), from which I've transcribed the page, in their notes to *this* passage mention a 1923 statement by Starrett of

Huneker's account of "Flowers of Asphalt," in which Starrett says that the work was composed in October of 1898 and was about "a boy prostitute." They note as well that Crane's relationship with newspaper publisher Irving Bacheller in spring of 1894 was just not the sort which made either the request for or the granting of such a loan likely; as well, they note that the date Starrett gives is between unlikely and impossible, as Crane was in Havana at the time. What we can't know is if Starrett's account came directly from Huneker (with the date simply misremembered)—or if it came to Starrett *after* Huneker's death by way of Beer.

A year or so later, once he became famous after the publication of *The Red Badge of Courage,* Crane *is* known to have borrowed fifty dollars in order to help out a young woman accused of prostitution—a scandalous incident reported in the newspapers and which Beer certainly knew about. Perhaps Beer—who was himself gay—was for a while considering introducing evidence into his biography to suggest that Crane was gay . . . or at least bisexual, or at least sexually adventurous.

Circumstantial as it is, there is other evidence to suggest a gay Crane. First, there is Crane's close friendships with a number of the young men living and studying at the former site of the Art Students' League on East 23rd Street of New York City. During his twenty-first and twenty-second year, Crane spent the night there—crashed there, as the sixties would have put it—for weeks at a time. The building rented to young artists. *Some* of the young men who lived and studied at the 23rd Street institution were—probably—straight. Corwin Knapp Linson, the art student seven years older than Crane who befriended the young writer and wrote his own memoir of Crane (*My Stephen Crane,* Syracuse University Press, Syracuse, 1958), *may* have been one such. But there is at least one photograph surviving from the period—a joke photograph taken by some of the boys—that shows Crane, in bed, under the covers, with another boy, asleep with his head on his bearded friend's shoulder. The prankster photographers have filled up the foreground of the room with old shoes and boots—the classical sign for marriage (this is why we still tie old shoes to the back of the honeymoon car today). The usual way the photograph has been read is that Crane, innocently asleep in his friend's bed (we know the boys sometimes slept three in a bed), just happened to snuggle up against his sleeping friend, and some passing art students, looking in on the scene, ran off to get a camera, lights, set them all up, filled the room with shoes, and "snapped" the picture—which, when it was developed, they all had a good laugh over.

The difficulty of taking a picture in the 1890s (there *were* no Kodak moments back then!) simply mitigates against this interpretation—or of Crane and his friend actually *sleeping* through all the preparation. The question here is: What exactly *was* the prank's nature? Was it some straight young men, Crane among them, parodying the relations of the many gay young men around them? Or was it some gay young men parodying themselves—or, perhaps, documenting a love relationship with heterosexual marriage symbolism? Or was it something in-between? The blanket in the photograph looks very much as if it has been painted in later: Perhaps the two boys were originally photographed naked with one another, and then the picture was doctored. There is no way to tell. But if Beer knew of the photograph, it may well have prompted him, however briefly, to elaborate on the notion of a gay Crane.

Of course the "Flowers of Asphalt" account might be one area where Beer actually had the truth and was simply suppressing it; while Berryman, later, revealed it.

The only hint of deviant sexuality that Beer finally allows into his biography comes in the appendix:

It was suggested to me by Mr. Huneker that Crane's picturesque exterior offered a field for the imagination of some contemporaries and that "they turned a little Flaubert into a big Verlaine." The injustice of that romancing was great, however, and inevitably I have concluded that a great spite followed him after his success. Else why did three unsigned letters reach me when Mr. Christopher Morley printed my wish for correspondence in the New York *Evening Post?* All three votaries of romantic love had charges to make and the charges were couched in excellent English.

Some of Crane's friends erred in their mention of him after death. Elbert Hubbard's paper in *The Philistine* contained equivocal statements and Robert Barr's "qualities that lent themselves to misapprehension" is not a fortunate phrase. (Beer 244–5)

After Oscar Wilde, Verlaine and Rimbaud represent perhaps the most notorious gay relationship in the annals of nineteenth-century literature. It is odd to think of somebody like Berryman missing the reference. But in his own biography, Berryman writes: "Homosexuality was the only thing Crane was never accused of." Apparently in the late forties the young Berryman was just not privy to the coded manner in which such accusations were made among twenties literati.

Among Huneker's last publications before his death in 1921 (two years before Beer's book appeared) was a novel, *Painted Veils*, written in six weeks in 1919, published in 1920, and initially available only through subscription from Simon and Schuster. (Liveright reprinted it in 1942— two years after Beer died a destitute alcoholic at the Albert Hotel in Greenwich Village—with an interesting and informative introduction by

Benjamin DeCasseres. For some years it was on the list of Modern Library volumes.) Set in the last decades of the 19th Century, *Painted Veils* details, among other things, a lesbian affair/fascination between a younger woman musician and an older woman, assumed to be a scandalous exposé of the American classical music scene: That is to say, by the time Beer was putting together *his* book, Huneker was known among cognoscenti to be the author of an elegant and immoral gay novel—*and* he was recently dead. He was known to have known Crane. Thus, if Beer had decided to go with a Crane with gay interests, Huneker was a believable person from whom to invent evidence.

But then, *some* of Beer's biography is accurate.

It's understandable why Beer chose not to include the story behind "Flowers of Asphalt" in a biography for the general public in 1923; and while it's possible that the account Berryman saw and I have transcribed was an early draft *by* Beer of something he was once thinking about including—like the early drafts of the bogus letters—it's equally possible that the gay 1920s critic Beer was protecting the reputation of a young writer with significant gay (or at least bisexual) interests—which would also account for the fictive "Miss Trent."

In an April 12, 1962 letter to E. R. Hageborn, Wilson Follett, who edited the ten-volume *Works of Stephen Crane* that Knopf published between 1925 and 1927, admits—even celebrates—Beer's extraordinary capacity to fabricate practically anything: ". . . Things that never were became real to him, once his mind had conceived them, as the rising moon or a drink at the Yale Club during prohibition era. He could quote pages verbatim from authors who never wrote any such pages; sometimes from authors who never lived. He could rehearse the plots of stories never written by their ostensible authors, or by anybody, repeat pages of dialogue from them, and give you the (nonexistent) places and dates of publication . . ." But Follett goes on to say: "[T]he point that always escapes an assailant of his biography . . . [is that Beer] *loved* Crane, humbly idolized him, and was incapable of setting down a syllable about him prompted by any force except that love and idolatry." If Follett is right, and it has the ring of truth, then the page might have been one of the unsigned letters (either actual—or invented by Beer himself) that he refers to in his Appendix. The only way it suggests any homosexual interests by Crane himself is through traditional homophobic contagion: The only person who could be interested in the topic *must* also indulge in it. But what it clearly presents is, whether fictive or factual, the young Crane as an interested champion of gay male prostitutes in New York during the Mauve Decade —a champion turned aside by the exigencies of social convention, represented by Garland's horrified plea to desist.

The fact that the biography that first propelled Crane into the general awareness of the greater literary population turns out to be between 30 and 40 percent fiction—and knowingly so by the author—is, however, almost overshadowed by the textual problems that circulate about the text of *The Red Badge of Courage* itself.

For a moment let us discuss the text.

The twenty-one-year-old Crane wrote a truly extraordinary novel—which he called *Henry Fleming, His Various Battles*. Sometime later, possibly during the rather violent editorial process (from fifty-five thousand words to eighteen thousand for serialization), he renamed the book *The Red Badge of Courage*. But to distinguish the book as Crane first drafted it from the eighteen thousand words of it later published by the Bacheller & Johnson syndicate in newspapers in New York, Philadelphia, and other cities around the country, first in December 1894, then again in its almost full form in July of 1895, we will use the *Henry Fleming* title. And the fact is, *Henry Fleming* has never been published—though a book very close to it was published in 1951 by the Folio Society, and then again by the indefatigable R. W. Stallman in 1952. But even here there were significant differences.

The Red Badge of Courage is a brief novel: In the Library of America Edition its twenty-four chapters run only 131 pages. *Henry Fleming* is thousands of words and a complete chapter longer.

What makes *Henry Fleming* so astonishing is that it is a novel both of poetically rendered action *and* incisive psychological analysis—an ironic comedy in which we are never allowed to identify fully with any of the characters. Rather the young writer keeps a cold eye on them all. It is a novel about young soldiers named Jim Conklin and Wilson and Henry Fleming. All its characters are named, not only in dialogue (as they are now), but in the running narrative of the novel itself.

When the possibility of newspaper syndication arose, Crane—from a commercial point of view quite wisely—decided (or was strongly urged) to omit the ironic psychological analysis. In the course of his cutting, he decided to "universalize" his characters by suppressing their proper names—so that Conklin becomes "the tall soldier" and young Wilson becomes "the loud soldier" that today's reader of the book is familiar with. Later in the story a Lieutenant Hasbrouck loses his name and is referred to only by his rank. And Fleming retains his name only when he is addressed by others. The overall result of the cutting is a somewhat more readable novel—but a *far* less interesting one.

On completing *Henry Fleming* the reader feels that he or she has just encountered a great novel. Its interplay of ironies and associations is masterful. (One suspects that it simply could *not* have been written by a twenty-one-year-old.) Within the superbly orchestrated progression of events, *Henry Fleming* delineates how the characters—especially Fleming—perceive themselves as *unlimited*, and at the same time shows the precise ways in which that perception *limits* their understanding, their actions, and their futures. This is to play the game of the novel on the fields set out by Flaubert, Stendahl, James, and Proust.

By comparison, the reaching after some ill-conceived "universality" through the suppression of specific names (not to mention slicing a great psychological novel down to a more or less colorful adventure) is the single thing about the book that strikes me as a pretentious verbal gesture and the mistake of a twenty-one-year-old: the sort that one constantly has to tell enthusiastic young creative writing students *not* to do.

I say *Henry Fleming* has never actually appeared; when Stallman published his version from an uncut manuscript in 1952, he nevertheless changed the names of the character to the "universal" forms readers of the book were already familiar with (though he indicated the names in notes, so that you can reconstruct the original form). The book as published by Appleton, after its successful newspaper syndication, is an interesting and talented novel. The book as first written (as close as we can get to it is the Henry Binder edition published by W. W. Norton & Co. in 1979) was a great one. But the final and almost inarguable point is that, if the original and better version of the novel had appeared, it would *not* have been anywhere near as popular as it was.

Large, statistical audiences are simply not prepared to do the sort of emotional and moral acrobatics necessary to appreciate an exquisitely crafted book in which there is conscientiously no moral or emotional center of identification. (Slight correction: Very occasionally they will do it if the foreground cast of characters is female; but rarely will they do it for a collection of male characters in a tale of war, syndicated in a weekly newspaper.) This brings us to what is certainly one of the most important factors that goes into securing a book a position in the canon—as it deals most directly with the markers:

The Red Badge of Courage contains one of the most discussed (i.e., marked) sentences in the whole of American literature. I mean of course the dazzling concluding sentence to Chapter IX (in which we also have the excruciating description of Jim Conklin's death: "His face turned to a semblance of gray paste . . . [Fleming] now sprang to his feet and, going closer, gazed upon the pastelike face."): "The red sun was pasted in the sky like a wafer."

Because of its power, its originality, and its orchestration into the rest of the passage, few sentences in American literature have sustained as intense an examination as this one. In a November 1951 article, however, in *American Literature*, XXIII, Scott C. Osborn pointed out that, however inadvertently, the line likely had its source in Kipling's novel *The Light That Failed* (1891), which we know Crane read enthusiastically shortly after publication: "The fog was driven apart for a moment, and the sun shone, a blood-red wafer on the water." In a footnote Osborn went on to point out that the religious overtones of the "wafer" (as in the Eucharist) that had fueled so much of that praiseful discussion of Crane's "symbolism" simply hadn't been available to Crane (or to Kipling) as a writer in the last decade of the nineteenth century. The common use of "wafer" that most certainly controlled the contemporary reading of both lines was the wafer of sealing wax with which letters, at the time, were still commonly fastened. Most eucharistic services before World War I were conducted with locally baked unleavened bread; the "wine and the wafer" did not come into common parlance until after World War I, when, with the gummed envelope, wafers of sealing wax vanished as all but eccentric affectations.

Now if most people had to summarize the elements that militate for entrance into the canon, they would probably produce a list something like the following:

Fame (and/or popularity) . . .

Critical reception . . .

Enduring worth of the work, in terms of its originality, quality, and relevance . . .

More cynical (and/or more conservative) commentators would likely include: what the work had to say, that is, its ideological weight . . .

Those of a more psychoanalytic bent might add that certain figures of desire inhere in the biographical reputations of certain artists and keep pulling interest back to the work—Chatterton's suicide at seventeen years and nine months, Georg Trakl's suicide at twenty-three, or Rimbaud's debauched relations with Verlaine between the ages of sixteen and nineteen, culminating in his abandonment of literature for the life of an African adventurer; Nietzsche's or Hölderlin's ultimate insanity, Novalis's, or Keats's, or Poe's, or James Thomson's sexual love of an early-dying (in Keats's case, unresponsive rather than dying) girl-child, the pansexuality of a Catullus or the homosexuality of a Hart Crane coupled with *their* own early deaths . . .

Well, there are cynical comments to be noted about all of these factors from our Crane story.

Crane's own early fame—followed by his almost total oblivion afterwards—reminds us forcefully that fame alone is no guarantee of acceptance into the canon. What is suggested by the creation of his reputation twenty-five years later by Beer's book is that the fame of the marker

(Beer's biography) is finally much more to the point. As far as critical re-action, it is certainly paradoxical that the most recent confirmation of Crane's canonical position comes from the almost total demolition of the credence given to Beer's initial biography/marker. But rather than dislodge Crane, it has only aroused more interest in him—as I would hope *this* marker does, even while it attempts to demystify the mechanics of the marking system itself.

Indeed, this may be the place to articulate a basic principle of canoni-cal self-preservation. Poets and artists have noted for many years that a too virulent attack is often as great a goad to readerly interest as equally great praise. Heap too much scorn on my grave, said Shelley, and you'll betray the place I am buried. But once the marker configuration has pro-pelled a literary work *into* the canon, the subsequent complete denigra-tion of a primary marker, even when it is revealed to be nothing but a collage of misstatements, fictions, and outright lies, does not alter the ca-nonical position of the literary work associated with it—because that denigration can only be accomplished by the erection of other markers that are effective only as they exactly replace the effects of the former marker. Indeed all such denigration can do is further the canonical per-sistence of the work.

Aside from its fabrications, the aspect of Beer's *Stephen Crane* to sus-tain the most consistent criticism since its publication is its tendency to soft-peddle the various scandals that all-but-constituted Crane's life once he left Syracuse University. (Crane's common-law wife, Cora Taylor, a handful of years his senior and with whom he lived until he died, Crane met within days of his twenty-fifth birthday in 1896 while she was the madam of a Florida brothel—a fact elided by Beer.) Here we mention, with Crane's (Beer's?)—possible—interest in matters gay a prime exam-ple, it is not scandal *per se* that generates markers. Rather, it is scandals that a succession of commentators feel must be reinterpreted (and we may read suppression as the ultimate [de-]interpretation) because their topics represent changing social values: divorce, marriage, prostitution, homosexuality . . .

This is why (to anticipate myself) the canon—and all the textual mate-rial, primary *and* secondary, that constitutes it—is nothing *but* value.

As to the enduring worth of the work, Osborn's demolition both of the notion of Crane's stylistic originality and the religious value of the "wafer" metaphor happens in a textual marker that largely serves to stabi-lize our attention *on* the text, even as it displaces certain values in the crit-ical syntagm. (What was discussed for almost twenty years as a religious metaphor is now historified into an epistolary one. What was a sign of originality now becomes an emblem of influence.) But this is the way the canon constantly functions, destabilizing and stabilizing in the same move.

As to the simple attractiveness of the Crane myth, this is the one thing that is not figured directly by our tale so far—unless our simple inability to see Crane through the various inventions and distortions of Beer in itself constitutes a measure of attractiveness that pulls the modern scholar, the contemporary reader, onward to look harder. Crane's two apocryphal stories ("Vashti in the Dark," *Flowers of Asphalt*) are certainly enticing points for speculative research. But the fact is, they look more and more, the both of them, like Beer's inventions from the twenties rather than Crane's efforts from the nineties.

The early iconography of Crane, left in this mythic margin, *is* fascinating, however; the most common among the early images of our young writer was a photograph of Crane looking serenely out from among the other players on the Syracuse University baseball team. As were many of the men of letters who presided at Crane's early rise in the canon, Beer was gay. It is a paradox that in the early days of baseball, many of those who wrote about it and memoired it and generally exhorted it into the position of the country's national sport were also articulate gay men; and the image of Crane as the pure, unblemished athlete (dying young) had a lot to do with the homoerotic libidinal charge underlying much of his early popularity. This is a paradox because, by 1962, when John Berryman's revised biography of Crane appeared, the situation had reversed to the point where numerous practicing psychologists by now put a good deal of faith, possibly with some reason, into the general rule of thumb; to determine whether an American male was homosexual or not, simply ask him whether or not he liked baseball.

If he did, he was straight.

If he didn't, he wasn't.

We have already mentioned the clandestinely famous picture of Crane (known to scholars but not printed till 1992)—in bed, asleep, with his head on the shoulder of another boy, in a room at the old Art Students' League. Many of the male art students who composed Crane's circle were doubtless gay. The Bowery, well known as one of Crane's haunts, was as famous in the 1890s for its gay life as it was for its more traditional vice—in which Crane so famously indulged. The hint of homosexuality and the vice that surrounded Crane (despite Berryman's obtuse statement that homosexuality was the one thing Crane was never accused of; we've cited a blatant account of several such accusations in the appendix of Beer's biography [pp. 244–45]) very possibly drew not only Beer but other gay men of letters to Crane's cause.

But all these factors were at play in the mythology of the "purest" of American writers—"pure" being the epithet used of Crane by both Berryman and the librarian at the University of Syracuse Library, back in the fifties, then in charge of the library's considerable Crane holdings.

This brings us to the last part of your question. *Is* the canon of value? The canon is nothing *but* value. It is a complex system of interlocking, stabilizing and destabilizing—constantly circulating, always shifting—values. The course of that endless circulation alone is what holds the canon stable, is what alone allows it to bend and recover. We think of the canon as a social object that holds things comparatively stable *in the face of* shifting values. But that "in the face of," with its suggestion of opposition, is only more mystification. The canon is not a passive natural object, but an active social object, and it is precisely the shifting of social values that *fuels* the canon and facilitates its stability. (As an extraordinarily important corollary to our basic principle of canonical self-preservation above: It is the value shifts alone that *produce* the new markers.) Without those social shifts, the canon would collapse. But (within the canon) we can only study those shifts by studying the markers and their history, since they alone memorialize the evidence.

Finally, it is necessary to point out: No one *knows* the canon. And the assumption that other people do, whether those other people be a high school teacher, a professor emeritus, or Harold Bloom, is to grant power to an Other (and to put into circulation a value)—a power and a value that the canon itself might be seen as exploiting.

At best, we can know *something about some of the works (and their markers)* that comprise the canon. We can know something about one part of the canon and/or another. Very few of us would argue, for example, with the assertion that Shakespeare is number one—or, more accurately, in terms of my web model, is at the center—of the canon of English literature. But who is number two?

Chaucer?

Spenser?

Milton?

I have graduate students (under thirty years old) who would be surprised to see Spenser even in the running for that still titanic secondary slot. But, by the same token, anyone over forty who has spent a life in the field of letters would probably be distressed that the same students should *not* know this. Does that mean that Spenser's place in the canon has changed or is changing? No, but it may (or may not) mark a social value shift that will soon begin to emit some stabilizing markers.

P•D: One common criticism of the term "paraliterature" is that it implies a generically constant body of writing that lurks around outside the library of serious or authentic literature, but, in fact, new works—in whatever genre—constantly enter into the "upper" ranks. How would you define—or perhaps, *describe* "paraliterature"? (By the way, are there nonfiction paraliterary genres?)

SRD: The initial criticism you speak of arrives because *literature* implies a generically constant body *within* the library. It's the notion of "constant, stable, and fixed" that has to go in both the literary *and* the paraliterary case. Once we establish a clear view of the circulation of values limned by the range and change in literary markers, the circulation of values in the paraliterary follows pretty directly—though the picture of literary discourse above should immediately highlight the first distinction between the literary and the paraliterary: I mean the relative saturation of the literary *with* markers, and the relative *scarcity* of markers in the paraliterary. (Although one *can* study literature without studying paraliterature, one *cannot* do it the other way around.) And, of course, there is the difference among the *kinds* of markers prevalent in both areas.

Because of the differences between literature and paraliterature— that is, the difference between the saturation and scarcity of markers, the kinds of markers on either side, and the way those markers facilitate the circulation of values (in a word, paraliterary markers generally facilitate that circulation far less than literary ones)—I have suggested that we adopt a different methodology for studying paraliterature: Because we cannot count on the markers the way we can in literary studies, we must compensate by putting more emphasis on paraliterary genres as material productions of discourse. We need lots of biography, history, reader response research—and we need to look precisely at how these material situations influenced the way the texts (down to individual rhetorical features) were (and are) read. In short, we need to generate our own markers—and, even more important, we need to generate them from a *sophisticated* awareness of the values already in circulation among the readership at the time these works entered the public market. Again, let me reiterate: *sophisticated* awareness. If you are going to start with some ridiculous and uncritical move of the nature, "Well, these works were read only for entertainment. They were without any other values," then I throw up my hands and go off to talk with other people. That is simply accepting the literary mystification that still redounds on the paraliterary.

Indeed, anyone who has even the vaguest suspicious that "entertainment value" actually covers all that's of interest in the values circulating throughout the paraliterary, I ask them only to bear with me until I can begin to describe some of the behaviors that constitute the paraliterary, below.

First, however, we must talk about a rift.

The abyssal split between literature and paraliteratue exists precisely so that some values can circulate across it and others can be stopped by it. The split between them constitutes literature as much as it constitutes paraliterature. Just as (discursively) homosexuality exists largely to delimit heterosexuality and to lend it a false sense of definition, paraliterature exists to delimit literature and provide it with an equally false sense of itself. Indeed, since both were disseminated by the explosion of print technology at the end of the nineteenth century, the two splits are not unrelated.

But that abyssal split—that impedes the circulation of values here, while it promotes it there—is as imperative to the current structure of the canon as is the circulation itself.

Now, to say (as you do) that "new works . . . constantly enter the 'upper' ranks" of the canon is, I think, absurd—or rather, it is to speak with very blinkered eyes from the paraliterary side of the abyss with no understanding of perspective on what is occurring on the literary side.

New literary works are constantly being made the focus of attention for more or less extended periods of time in order, as it were, "to decide" if they can enter the upper canonical ranks. (*There* is that illusory synod, lurking just behind the infinitive.) But the vast majority don't make it. Nor should they. Still, it's arguable that once a work is past the consideration stage and has actually become part of the canon, it is harder to dislodge it than it is to get a new work accepted.

Now the vast majority of works easily locatable as paraliterature do not even have a chance for a consideration period. They are marginalized at the outset. But it is absurd to confuse the—admittedly, sometimes very generous—trying-out period with canonical acceptance itself. Yes, by comparison with the attention paid to paraliterary works, which, generally speaking, cannot get any such trying-out period, no matter how well thought of (that is, without some violent displacement from the context and tradition that makes them signify), it might well *look* like "new works" are constantly entering the upper ranks. But that's just not what's happening.

If we may anthropomorphize it for a moment, the canon "puts great trust in" the most conservative methods. The canon "believes in" the worth of the society that has produced it. Thus, any work that both is presumed to be literature and achieves a notable measure of social fame is tentatively accepted into the canon for such a trying-out period, when various people get a chance to generate the particular sort of markers—critical and otherwise—that may or may not go on to stabilize its position. But while a Pulitzer, National Book Award, or a Nobel Prize may

well promote canonical *consideration,* none of the three is enough to assure canonical *acceptance*—as unclear as the line might be between them.

Since World War II, one of the greatest—and, I think, most pernicious—
factors in canonicity has been the *teachability* of works. Whatever criticisms one has of the ability of the conservative notion of general literary
fame to select the best works, the problem of teachability completely
undercuts it. General literary fame is still dependent on the acceptance
by a *reading* public—however sophisticated, however unsophisticated.
Teachability puts a further filter over the selection process, a filter constituted of the popularity of the works among an essentially very young,
*non-*reading population—who are presumably in the process of being
taught to read. But this is a disastrous way to select—or reject—books of
esthetic worth!

We have all heard it many times, from the graduate school T.A.,
through the junior, the associate, and the tenured faculty: "It was a wonderful book. But my kids just couldn't get it. Oh, a few of them did. But
for most of them, it was just confusing." Nor is it a problem confined to
the literary. Those of us teaching science fiction or other courses in popular culture find ourselves with the identical problem. Any work that
makes its point in pointed dialogue with a tradition—any tradition—is
simply lost on inexperienced readers unacquainted with that tradition.
Works that are new and exciting are new and exciting precisely because
they *are* different from other works. But an "introductory background
lecture" cannot substitute for exposure to the dozen to two dozen titles
that would make the new work come alive by its play of differences and
similarities. I don't wish to imply that the problems—not to mention the
insights—of nonreaders must somehow be excluded from culture. On
the contrary. And I am also aware that student enthusiasms can be as surprising as what they reject. I will ponder for years, for example, the
upper-level modernist novel class of mine in 1991 that reveled in Robert
Musil's *The Man Without Qualities,* while finding Julian Barnes's *Flaubert's
Parrot* somewhere between boring and pointless—even after reading
(and enjoying) *Trois Contes* and *Three Lives* as preparation. But young
readers who have absorbed only the limited narrative patterns available
on prime-time TV simply don't have a grasp of the narrative tradition
broad enough to highlight what is of interest in the richest and most sophisticated fictions currently being produced, literary *or* paraliterary.

The discussion (markers, if you like) of people *who read* must generate the canon—not the acceptability of works to people *who don't read.*
But that has been more and more the case for the last fifty years. It's
worth pointing out that this teachability problem is not new: From the

time that it was formulated, the canon was assumed to be a teaching tool. Teaching was precisely what Matthew Arnold and the other nineteenth century theorists of the uses of culture were concerned with. And it was their arguments that promoted the switch from the Greek and Roman classics to works of English literature as the basis for public education. But the difference is, the teachability of works is not being handled today by public discussion but rather by natural selection. And in matters intellectual, natural selection simply doesn't work. (Intelligence would seem to exist primarily as a way to outrun natural selection.) But this is one of the reasons that the canon is undergoing the apparent upheavals that it is. And this is directly behind the growing interest in the paraliterary—which interest, by now, at the ontological level, we can recognize as following a very canon-like process. It is the same order of social object. It's easy to describe it in the same terms.

Which brings us to the second part of your question: How would I describe paraliterature?

While you recall the mystificational notion that the paraliterary is "purely entertainment," let me recount some tales.

Here, from an autobiographical essay written for his therapist, Jim Hayes, in 1965, tells the great American SF writer Theodore Sturgeon about his early encounter in the first years of the Depression with his multilingual stepfather (whom the family called Argyll) over the paraliterary genre of science fiction:

> It was about this time that I discovered science fiction; a kid at school sold me a back number (1933 *Astounding*) for a nickel, my lunch money. I was always so unwary! I brought it home naked and open, and Argyll pounced on it as I came in the door. "Not in *my* house!" he said, and scooped it off my school-books and took it straight into the kitchen and put it in the garbage and put the cover on. "That's what we do with garbage," and he sat back at his desk with my mother at the end of it and their drink. (*Argyll*, 36)

At the time, Argyll was giving his stepson such volumes to read as "*The Cloister and the Hearth, The White Company, Anthony Adverse, Vanity Fair, Tess of the D'Urbervilles,* Homer, Aristophanes, Byron *(Childe Harold), The Hound of Heaven, War and Peace, Crime and Punishment, Dead Souls,* God knows what all" (*Argyll*, 29). And young Sturgeon devoured them. The family even had a regular "reading aloud" session after dinner.

But Sturgeon also continued to read the forbidden pulp stories. He sought for a way to collect the magazines, and he expended a good deal of ingenuity figuring out a way to read them—in his desk drawer, while he was doing his homework, the sides waxed with a candle to keep them from squeaking, when the drawer had to be quickly closed—and to store them: Finding a trap in the roof of his closet, young Sturgeon (he describes himself then as "twelve or fourteen") placed his magazines, two deep, between the beams—starting five beams away. He even went so far as to replace the dust on the beams after he had crawled across them, and did everything else to cover up the traces.

Some time later, however—

I breezed home from school full of innocence and anticipation, and Argyll looked up briefly and said, "There's a mess in your room I want you to clean up." It didn't even sound like a storm warning. He could say that about what a sharpened pencil might leave behind it.

The room was almost square, three windows opposite the door, Pete's bed and desk against the left wall, mine against the right. All the rest, open space, but not now. It was covered somewhat more than ankle deep by a drift of small pieces of newsprint, all almost exactly square, few bigger than four postage stamps. Showing here and there was a scrap of glossy polychrome from the covers. . . .This must have taken him hours to do, and it was hard to think of him in a rage doing it, because so few of the pieces were crumpled. Hours and hours, rip, rip, rip.

It's hard to recapture my feelings at the moment. I went ahead and cleaned it all up and put it outside; I was mostly aware of this cold clutch in the solar plexus which is a compound of anger and fear (one never knew when one of his punishments was over, or if any specific one was designed to be complete in itself or part of a sequence) . . . (*Argyll*, 38–39)

Now *that* describes a room full of paraliterature—and how it got that way.

But here are some stories of a more recent vintage.

A bit over a dozen years ago, around 1980, in my local bookstore, I came upon a young woman in her early twenties standing next to a dolly full of books, shelving them. At the D's, she was putting away copies of Don DeLillo's *Ratner's Star* (1976). Smiling, I said: "You know, you should shelve some copies of that with science fiction."

She looked up startled, frowned at me, then smiled: "Oh, no," she said. "Really, this is a very good book."

I laughed. "It's about three-quarters of a good novel. But at the ending, he just gets tired and takes refuge in a Beckettesque fable. It doesn't work."

"Well, you can't make it science fiction just because of the *ending!*"

I laughed again. "The ending is what makes it literature. But the rest of the book is a very believable account of a young mathematician working for the government, trying to decipher messages from a distant star. It could go upstairs in SF."

Her frown now had become permanent. "No," she repeated. "It really *is* a good book. I've read it—it's quite wonderful."

"I've read it too," I said. "I liked it very much. But that's why I'm saying it's science fiction . . ."

The young woman exclaimed, really not to me but to the whole room: "That's just *crazy* . . . !" She turned sharply away and began to shelve once more.

But when, after a few seconds, I glanced at her again, she was still mumbling darkly to herself—and *tears* stood in her eyes!

Now that too is an account of the social forces constituting paraliterature.

In the late seventies, shortly after receiving tenure in the Pratt English Department, a friend of mine, Carol Rosenthal, was teaching a graduate seminar that year called "Literature and Ideas" and invited me out one Wednesday afternoon to address her students.

Suited, tied, and with briefcase under my arm, I arrived at noon. We had a pleasant lunch at a local Chinese restaurant, and returned to the building for the one o'clock seminar. As we were walking down the hall toward the classroom, another woman faculty member was coming toward us. Carol hailed her, then turned to make introductions. "Chip, this is my friend" (we'll call her Professor X) "Professor X. Professor X is in economics. And this is Samuel Delany—he's speaking to my Literature and Ideas seminar this afternoon."

Brightly Professor X asked: "And what will you be talking about?"

I said: "I'll be speaking about science fiction."

Professor X got a rather sour look on her face, her shoulders dropped, and she exclaimed: "Science fiction . . . ? Oh, *shit* . . . !" at which point she turned on her heel, and stalked off down the hall, leaving an astonished Carol who, after a few nonplussed seconds, began to splutter and make excuses—her friend was *very* eccentric, and probably just having a bad day as well—while we made our way to the class where I was to give my talk.

That *too* constitutes paraliterature.

Paraliterature is also the thousands of people who have said to me, on finding out that I'm a science fiction writer, "Oh, I don't really like science fiction," as though (a), I had asked them (b), I cared, or (c), I was somehow pleased by their honesty.

Believe me, *far* fewer people like poetry than like science fiction; but *far* fewer people, on being introduced to poets, respond with, "Oh, I don't really like poetry." They are much more likely to proffer a socially equivocal "Oh, really?" and change the subject. But the forces that make the one a commonplace of my life (but promote the other in the lives of poets) are precisely the real (i.e., political) forces that constitute paraliterature (and literature).

But only consider the general layout of most medium-size to large bookstores, with the best-sellers in the front, the literature and fiction placed so it is easily available to the entering customers, and the paraliterature—science fiction, mysteries, horror, and romance titles—toward the back (and, yes, sometimes the poetry placed even *further* back!)—for, as countless articles and guides to the running of bookstores have explained: "People who read such books will hunt them out wherever you have them in the store. Thus you need not waste valuable display space on them and can put them in the back, wherever it is most convenient."

That too constitutes paraliterature.

I describe paraliterature by these messy, highly interpretable social tales—rather than by turning to texts to discuss rhetorical features—because, before everything else, paraliterature is *a material practice of social division*. (That's *not* a definition, mind you. But it is a powerful and important functional description.) These tales represent some of the most revealing and informative *social markers* (verbal, informal) that go along with it. And, as we have noted, they are *very* different from literary markers. Paraliterature is a practice of social division that many people are deeply invested in, often at a level of emotion and commitment that many others of us have simply forgotten, as we notice more and more that so many texts developing on the paraliterary side of that division display great intelligence, are produced with extraordinary art, and have extremely relevant things to say about the world we live in. The material practice of social division fuels the canonical/non-canonical split. And the split fuels the material practice of division.

But if paraliterature were really only "pure entertainment," I could not possibly tell such tales about it.

At the rhetorical level, paraliterature is best described as those texts which the most uncritical literary reader would describe as "just not literature": Comic books, mysteries, westerns, science fiction, pornography, greeting card verse, newspaper reports, academic criticism, advertising texts, movie and TV scripts, popular song lyrics. . . . But if contemporary criticism and theory has told us anything, it is that the rhetorical level—the level of the signifier—is the slipperiest to grasp and hold stable.

But that is because, at the level of the signified, things—values, if you will—are *always* in shift.

Are there any nonfiction paraliterary genres? Absolutely. Philosophy has been *trying* to dissociate itself from literature since Plato—and failing. But, for openers, everything in this and any other critical journal is paraliterature. ("Philosophy has no muse . . ." Walter Benjamin comments in "The Task of the Translator." Though Memory's nine daughters who sang on Mt. Helicon represent a genre system far older than our current post-Industrial one, in general it's not a bad notion to check with them and see who was assigned to what. It explains why History—overseen by Clio—is part of literature and why philosophy has, until recently, felt it might escape.)

The paradox is that the vast majority of literary markers are, themselves, paraliterary. Often they are consulted, but rarely are they studied—which is only another reason why the overall process, which includes the literary/paraliterary rift, is so mystified.

You can easily pick out the parameters of the nonfiction paraliterary genres. First and foremost they include any texts not considered literature. They include any texts considered more or less disposable. They include any texts that, if we go back to consult them, ten, twenty, thirty years after the fact, we do so purely for information. They include any text not considered primarily esthetic.

Now of course this is all nonsense. Recently I just went back to reread Leonard Knight's essay, "How Many Children Had Lady Macbeth?" (1933)—in conjunction with Stephen Orgel's "Prospero's Wife" (*Representations* 8, 1984). They are two beautiful pieces, rhetorically balanced and wonderfully rich. But this is a particular view that comes out of the appreciation of the esthetics of paraliterature—which is, in a word, not supposed to exist.

Paraliterary studies can arise only when we begin to historify how this literary/paraliterary split came about (largely in the 1880s when, thanks to the new printing technology represented by the typewriter and linotype, the explosion of printed matter reshaped the informative structure of the world), and examine the absolutely necessary function that rift plays in the persistence of the notion of literature today.

P•D: The focus of the second issue of *Para•doxa* was the mystery genre. In what ways do you think the mystery genre fits into the paraliterary arena? Is there a relationship between paraliterary genres that defines them at the same time that it distinguishes them from non-paraliterary genres? Is there a hierarchy among paraliterary genres? Is there a family tree, a genealogy of genres?

SRD: Literature as we know it is born *with* the literary/paraliterary split that arises when the tenets of modernism are employed to make sense out of the simple and overwhelming proliferation of texts that started in the 1800s and has continued up to the present.

The reason one cannot know the canon is because one cannot know all texts. Because, by the end of the 1880s, there were so many texts, some genres simply had to be put out of the running *tout court.*

The mystery was the privileged paraliterary form up through World War II—when, up until the Hollywood "blacklists," it was briefly joined by the film script. It meant that intellectuals like G. K. Chesterton and scholars like Dorothy L. Sayers—who was, after all, first and foremost a translator of Dante—and literary writers like Graham Greene (generally regarded as one of England's great twentieth century novelists) could offer you "entertainments" in the mystery form, and be accused of nothing worse than slumming. Respected playwrights like Lillian Hellman could have passionate, literary love affairs with folk like Dashiell Hammett, and, in the more liberal drawing rooms of the literary, both could be received.

For the sixties and seventies, SF was the privileged just-sub-literary genre. I think we may be entering a period where that position may soon be filled by pornography.

P•D: "Paraliterature" has become, paradoxically, an academic specialty at many universities in Europe. Is this encouraging or alarming?

SRD: Why should it alarm? To return once more to Lucien Goldmann: Disciplines are defined by their object—not by their methodologies. And the question that must always be tugged around and chewed over at the beginning of any disciplinary speciation is: What are the structure and organizing principles of the *object* we are looking at? A good long wrestle with such questions alone is what lets us know when we are all examining the same object—and when we aren't.

This is just another reason why we must get rid of this incredibly limiting notion of generic definitions. (A discipline is *defined* by its *object.* But disciplinary objects themselves are usually *not* definable. That's why they must be so carefully and repeatedly described.)

We are like the famous blind men with the elephant. And if, at trunk, tail, tusk, and toe we keep trying to shout one another down with quintessential elephantine definitions, we won't get anywhere. We have to be willing to engage in dialogue, present our many descriptions humbly, talk about what they do and don't allow us to do, and only then decide whether we are indeed all talking about elephants, the same elephant, or if, in fact, a few of us have inadvertently gotten hold of crocodile tails or hippopotamus ears.

Let me close off this section of your question with the description of the results of social forces that are very similar, if not identical, to canonical ones—indeed if they were at work in the precinct of the literary rather than, where I shall locate them, in the paraliterary, we would have no problem recognizing them *as* canonical.

Let's consider several books that deal directly with contemporary science fiction: Scott Bukatman's *Terminal Identity*, Damian Broderick's *Reading by Starlight*, Mark Dery's *Flames Wars: The Discourse of Cyberculture*, and my own *Silent Interviews: On Language, Race, Sex, Science Fiction and Some Comics*. Now, which SF writer do you think has the greatest number of citations in the indexes of all these books? In all cases, it's William Gibson—which, today, I doubt should surprise anyone. I can't speak for the other three writers, but I can tell you that for me, the realization that Gibson was, indeed, going to be the most cited writer in my book was an occasion for some concern.

I think Gibson is a fine writer. I don't begrudge him one iota of his fame. What becomes problematic is when we get to (a), the markers that have brought this situation about and (b), the "worth of the work" *vis-à-vis* his fellow science fiction writers.

The major markers propelling him into this position were, first, an extraordinarily uninformed article in a mid-eighties issue of *Rolling Stone* that made the first spurious connection between Gibson's work and computers—a connection Gibson himself began by balking at, until, with his fourth novel, in collaboration with his friend Bruce Sterling (*The Difference Engine*), he decided to exploit it, however ironically. The second (really a marker set) was a series of Big Movie Deals, starting with the proposed film of *Neuromancer* (1984), going on to his scripting an early version of the third *Aliens* film, and finally the 30 million dollar Longo film released in June 1995, from Gibson's fine short story, "Johnny Mnemonic" (1981), for which Gibson himself has screen credit. Add to that the extraordinary teachability of his first and best known novel, and you have the complex of reasons for his prevalence in the indexes of all four books.

Yet these are *not* the markers the books discuss. These are *not* the markers whose values the writers of any of the books in question are interested in either contesting *or* supporting. Indeed, they're hardly even mentioned. Actually, when we step back from it, the whole process looks more than anything like a race to obliterate the first set of markers and replace them by a far more acceptable academic set that, indeed, *does* put into circulation values far more in keeping with what we might find appropriate for a literary text.

Now—do I find Gibson's work of great social and esthetic value?

24   *Shorter Views*

Yes. I have taught it before. And I hope to teach it again.

Do I think it is the *most* valuable work being produced in the science fiction field at the moment?

At this point, I balk—at the whole concept that assumes such a question could (or should) be answered!

What I pose against both the question and the assumptions one must make to answer it either yes *or* no is the incontrovertible and blatant fact that there are more than half a dozen contemporary writers, from the same science fiction and fantasy field that produced Gibson, who are doing extraordinary work, work of at least as *much* social and esthetic weight as Gibson's: Gene Wolfe, Octavia Butler, Michael Swanwick, Kim Stanley Robinson, Lucius Shepherd, Karen Joy Fowler, Greg Bear. . . . Along with Gibson, all have produced work of a very high order. (And this is only to look at the generation after mine, completely ignoring my contemporaries Russ, Disch, Zelazny, Crowley, and Le Guin.) Without any one of them, the current SF field, and our potential for reading pleasure and enlightenment, would be greatly impoverished. They simply lack these all-but-accidental-in-literary-terms markers: *Rolling Stone* and The Movies! (The strength that the *concept* of The Movies has in the realms of the literary is quite astonishing: Sometime in the middle eighties, a novel of mine—*Dhalgren*—was optioned by a movie company. And the people involved sent someone out to buy seven copies of the book— to the same bookstore, as a matter of fact, where the young woman had been so upset about my suggesting DeLillo's *Ratner's Star* might be science fiction—and when one of the clerks asked him why he needed seven copies, he answered: "We're going to make a major picture out of the novel." The next day, when I came into the store, all the copies had been pulled out of the SF section and reshelved as "Literature"—where they stayed for the next four months! The project, as is the case with so many such, never came to anything. But I can assure you, if it had, and the bookstore people had encountered further markers to stabilize their reconception, the novel might well have jumped genres in bookstores all over the country.) To read Gibson with these writers makes Gibson's work much richer. To read any of these writers along with Gibson is to make their work more significant.

Well, with all that in mind, prior to publication, I went through my book and everywhere I could, wherever I'd used Gibson as an example, if it was at all possible I substituted work by another writer. And do you know what the results are?

Gibson is *still* the most frequently cited SF writer in my book.

Why?

Because my book is a series of *dialogues*. And my interlocutors ask more questions *about* Gibson than any other writer! Well, the fact is, any set of critical essays is, on one level, part of a critical dialogue—only the questions are not necessarily articulated as such nor are their attributions always given. But as long as the dialogic process is implicit in intellectual work, it functions to hold the position of various writers stable—even in the face of an active attempt, however local, to dislodge them from that position, such as the one I've just described.

Now—we must make it clear—what's being afforded Gibson in this dialogical process is *not* canonical acceptance. By no means. What is being afforded him is that trying-out period, so rare as to be otherwise all but nonexistent in paraliterature, that may or may not *lead* to such acceptance in ten, fifteen, or twenty years.

But the same forces that work at the canon's edge to stabilize that trying-out period also work—once a piece of writing (through the course of its markers) has been moved deeper within the canon toward the canonical center—to stabilize its position within the canon itself.

Would I like to see similar periods of serious consideration offered to other writers of paraliterary texts? Would I like to see writers chosen for reasons that have nothing to do with *Rolling Stone* and the movies? In the long run, when social values and esthetic values are somewhat further teased apart, at this particular point of seeming canonical upheaval, that's the *only* lasting justification I can think of *for* paraliterary studies.

But again: The canon "believes in" the society that produces it. Thus the canon can only be the canon *of* that society. If we want to displace *Rolling Stone* and the movies as significant and powerful social markers promoting canonical (or pre-canonical) literary (or paraliterary) consideration, we must start producing our own. We must produce social and critical markers that put in circulation values *we* think are important—and we must do that with works (literary or paraliterary) that *we* think are worthy of critical attention. However contestatorily, we must join in our society. We must become (to borrow a term from Bloom) *strong readers* of the paraliterary.

If we do not, then *Rolling Stone*, the movies, and equally extra-literary forces alone will decide what scholars (literary or paraliterary) pay attention to.

P•D: Could you say something about the impulse (either in general, or as regards your particular impulse) to choose to write in a particular genre—whether SF, literary criticism, fantasy, or something else? Where do you begin to conceive a piece of writing? (This is not a thinly disguised version of "Why do you write SF?")

SRD: Well, first of all, it's not an impulse. It's not a decision. It's not a choice *per se.* It's far more like giving in to a habit. When, for a moment, the barrier between what one has been reading and what one might write breaks down, discourse sweeps one up, and somehow absorption becomes emission: And what is emitted is simply going to be controlled by that discourse.

I read criticism; I write criticism.

I read SF; I write SF.

I read sword and sorcery; I write sword and sorcery.

I read pornography; I write pornography.

I read fiction; I write it, too.

Now in my case there's also a desire formally to criticize the genre in which I'm reading—an urge that has something very important to do with obliterating the barrier between absorption and emission. However politely articulated, there's always some element of an oppositional stance. But how that critical desire functions specifically in the process would be difficult to specify.

P•D: You have written that all genres—literary and paraliterary—are "ways of reading." Could you elaborate?

SRD: I'm afraid I must sigh and say, "No. Not here." But that's exhaustion speaking.

Still, anyone interested in such an elaboration as you ask for should, for an introductory view, read the "K. Leslie Steiner Interview" in my recent collection from Wesleyan, *Silent Interviews.* And anyone who wants to see the process elaborated even more fully should read *Starboard Wine* and, finally, *The American Shore.*

The ideas you are asking me to elaborate are counterintuitive ones; thus, to grasp them, they require repeated exposure. Encapsulating them in a single paragraph, no matter how pithy or aphoristic, only betrays them. They require looking at the language in a different way from the one most of us are used to—and they require a constant vigilance against slipping back into looking at it in the old way. Rather than giving a reassuring little summary that sends the reader off with the feeling that the idea has been rendered summarizable, consumable, and that it has (therefore) *been* consumed, internalized, mastered, I would leave your readers with an exhortation to pursue the notion through others of my texts, through some other writerly labor.

For people who are always ready to read another book, literary *or* paraliterary, the canon becomes a far less intimidating concept than it first
appears. And the literary/paraliterary split, while real (i.e., political) and
important, *can* be negotiated.

— *New York City*
July 1995

11

The Politics of Paraliterary Criticism

I

Bright, good-looking, well-read, and socially skilled, Jerry (that was not his name; but that's what we'll call him) was a senior at Columbia University when, in the early seventies, he entered my circle of friends and colleagues, where he was soon a well-liked young man.

In those years, as today, that circle was the science fiction writers, the comic book writers and artists, and the various journalists and editors who made up many of my day-to-day acquaintances.

While Jerry's interests were generally oriented toward what most speak of as literature, like many young people he'd gone through a period in early adolescence, only half a dozen years before, when he'd read comic books and science fiction avidly—so that, somewhat to his own surprise, already he knew the names and work of many of the men and women he was, at first through me, then on his own, meeting regularly: Denny O'Neil, Dick Giordano, Len Wein, Howie Chaykin, Mary Skrenes, Bernie Wrightson, Trina, Alan Weiss, Frank Brunner, Mike Kaluta, Tom Disch, Roger Zelazny, Terry Carr. . . .

Thus, while he did not particularly fetishize the paraliterary would of science fiction and comic books as having any special romance about it at present, it was a world connected to what had once been for him a rich and pleasurable interest.

Because he felt at ease with most people, Jerry was at ease with these people. Because he was bright, outgoing, and well-mannered, Jerry was popular with the people he met. Because his intelligence had once been turned on the products of this world—comics and science fiction—Jerry had enough knowledge, if not expertise, to hold his own, at least to ask informed questions, in conversations with those who made their living here.

One morning Jerry phoned to say that, talking to some comics artists and writers at a gathering the week before, he'd heard some comments about things they'd like to see—or currently disapproved of—in the *Batman* comic as it was then being done. An idea had come to him for a story. To see if he could do it, over the weekend he'd written a *Batman* script. I told him it would be fun to read. Why didn't he bring it down the next time he came by? (I was then living at the Hotel Albert.) When, the following day, he arrived with it, he explained: "*Batman* was always one of my favorites when I was a kid—" (This was years before the Tim Burton movies.) "I realized," he went on, "that I knew the character awfully well. I was listening to what some of the writers and artists were saying, when we went to lunch last week. So, I thought, why don't I just try my hand at a script?"

I read it. It seemed *well* above average in excitement, action, and general plot interest.

"Why don't we show this to Denny O'Neil?" I said. "You've met him—and he likes you. He's editing now for D.C."

"Do you think he'd be interested? . . . "

"The way to find out," I said, "is to ask."

I called Denny. Would he mind looking at Jerry's script? . . .

A couple of days later, after a phone call from Denny, I went with Jerry to the D.C. offices. As we sat in aluminum tubular chairs on the blue carpet, Denny said: "Before I read it, Jerry, I was pretty dubious. We get kids who want to write comics in here all the time. But once I started it . . . well, it's a great story! Also, it's the most professional looking script I've seen go through this office in ten years. It's a fine story breakdown. You tell most of it in three- and four-panel pages. You don't overload your panels with words. Your captions use the nonvisual senses. You've got a real grasp of what comics are about. The only problem is, I don't edit *Batman*. But I'll pass this along to Julie Schwartz." Julie was a senior editor, well-respected at the company. "See what he thinks. He's someone you can learn a lot from. He knows comic book writing's craft inside-out. If he likes what you're doing, and you work with him, you can learn a lot."

That Denny had volunteered to pass the script on to Julie surprised and delighted Jerry. He was vociferous in his gratitude.

A few days later, Jerry phoned to say Julie had called him and asked to meet.

"Come on down here and tell me what happened," I told him, "when you're finished at the D.C. offices."

Eleven o'clock the following Wednesday, Jerry knocked on my hotel room door.

As he came in, I asked him, "How'd it go?"

"He had some interesting things to say." But Jerry seemed pensive. "He suggested some rewriting. He wants me to change the ending."

"So . . . what do you think?"

"Personally, I don't think it'll be as good a story. But he had some points. It won't hurt it that much—though it changes what the whole story's about!" He chuckled. "But I'd still like to see it published. I told him I'd have the rewrite in to him the day after tomorrow."

A week later, Jerry was back from another editorial session. "Julie said he thought my rewrite was a very craftsmanlike job. But now he wants me to make more changes."

"Do you follow his points? Like Denny said, there's really a lot to learn about writing comics scripts. If you can master it—"

"Basically," Jerry said, rather surprising me, "I think most of his points are silly. And, if I do what he wants, it won't be my story anymore. Still, if he wants it, I'll probably try it. . . ."

A week later, Jerry was back.

"I just got through talking to Julie. He doesn't want to use the script at all, now. He says he doesn't think I'm ready—that I've got a mastery of comics craft great enough—to do *Batman*, yet. The thing that makes it so funny, that's exactly what Denny—and you, and everybody else who read it, even him—first said that they liked about it! All the things that made it a good comic book are what he's asked me to take out! Now he wants me to do a whole different script, about . . ." He named another character. "He says if I can handle *that* one, *maybe* he'll assign me some paying work. He says he can't promise. But it's up to me. . . ."

"What are you going to do?"

"I think I'm going to forget it," Jerry said. "The thing is, I don't want to *be* a comic book writer. I got what I thought was an idea for a good story—and I thought I could write a good script for it that would be better than most. That's what I think I did. If it had come out, I'd have been able to say: 'Hey, isn't that neat? I wrote that!' But now it's turned into something completely different—there're all these problems of comics craft that . . . well, I understand them, when he talks about them. But, honestly, they don't interest me. At this point, I think I'm going to forget it."

"Well, you know—" I had a sinking feeling—"you should pay some attention to these questions." Really, I liked Jerry. But no adult enjoys seeing a youngster start something great guns, then not follow through because the going gets a little tough. And because I had introduced him to these people, his failing enthusiasm might even have prompted my own embarrassment. "If you could master it, it might be useful to you later—"

"Yeah, I know. That's what Julie keeps saying. But the fact is, most of what he says, in story terms, seems silly. At least to me. The changes he suggests *don't* make it any better. Now, because he's got the dull script he asked me to write, he doesn't want to use it at all! Really, at this point, I'm not that interested. I've done three versions. He doesn't like them. So I think I'm going to let this one pass."

I remember I said: "But you've only done two—"

"That's what he said," Jerry told me. "But you're forgetting the first version, that you and Denny and everybody else—including Julie—said was so good and so professional."

"Yes, but . . ." Then I sighed, "Okay. But you're a real smart kid. You write well. I hope you're not letting a good opportunity to learn about the craft of comics slip by you."

"Maybe I am." He grinned. "But then, I just have to go by what I feel."

"I guess so."

Jerry called Julie and told him he wouldn't be handing in a fourth script. A year later, Jerry had more or less dropped out of the circle. Shortly, he had a job with a record company. From time to time I saw him. But though he was always friendly, his interests had taken him on, after his graduation from Columbia, in other directions and into other social and professional groups. From time to time, I saw an alternative newspaper article under his byline. Then he moved to the West Coast.

Some time later, in the bar of a science fiction convention, I ran into Julie Schwartz, retired now. When the circle of people around us had drifted away, I asked: "Do you remember, about nine or ten years ago, a young Columbia University student who came to you with a *Batman* script—through Denny O'Neil. I'd brought him to Denny's attention. His name was—"

"Oh, yes. Jerry. A really bright kid. I liked him very much. It's a shame he never followed through."

"What I don't understand," I said, "is that his first script seemed so polished and professional. As well, it had a great plot and was very inventively told."

"It was," he said.

"Why didn't you use it, then?"

"I did with Jerry what I do with every new comics writer who comes to me, Chip. I used to go through the same routine, oh, maybe six, seven—sometimes ten—times a year."

"I don't understand? . . . "

Julie smiled at me. "Look. The fact is, Chip, *anyone* can write a good comic book script. Now, when I say 'anyone,' I don't mean the janitor, or the plumber, or the dry cleaner. But I mean anyone who can write any sort of story at all can probably turn out a decent comic book script—"

"But this was more than decent. It was really talented—it was excellent. I mean, it was up there in Alan Moore territory—"

"Ah, yes." Julie shook his head. "But the craft—"

"I don't understand what you—"

"At this level of writing, talent isn't the problem—which is to say, there's enough of it out there that it will take care of itself. Every new writer who brings me a script (and, the fact is, many of them *are* talented), I tell him—or her—the same thing. I say: 'All right. The first thing I want you to do is change the ending.' We talk about comic book craft. Then, after they bring in a second version, I tell them to change the middle. Then I tell them to throw the whole thing out and write me a new script. Then, I tell them to do still *another* one. . . . And if they do everything I say, then I assign them a paying job on the least important character we have. You see, what we need in the comics industry is writers who will do what we *tell* them to. Doing what your editor says to do: *That's* craft. It's nice when I get a really talented writer, who gets through the whole set of tests. Sometimes they do. But, frankly, what we *need* are writers who have just turned in a wonderful, poetic, brilliant script with a downbeat ending, who, when an administrative decision comes from upstairs that all our stories have to have upbeat endings from now on, will throw that downbeat ending out and substitute a gloriously happy, feel-good ending, sacrificing everything of worth in the story—and who will do it without batting an eye. Like I say: craft. Jerry didn't have what it takes to be a good craftsman. He's probably better off out of the field. Likely he was interested in writing art stories—"

"What's an art story?" I said. "A story that follows its own internal logic, where the motivations make sense, and, after lots of inventive twists, it ends where it's supposed to?"

He laughed. "Okay—sure, that's an art story: *if* you want to make me out to be more of a villain that I am. I could just as easily say: Inventive twists need thought to follow, and thought is not in overwhelming supply among *average* comics readers. But the point is: However you define them, no. We don't have time for art stories. First and foremost, even before talent, we need craft here. And, yes, craft, in this business, means doing what you're told, as best you can—no matter how dumb, stupid, or irrational it is in terms of the material."

"You wouldn't have taken the first script from any writer, then—no matter how brilliant, well written, or professional it was."

"No. I wouldn't." He smiled again. "But that's because I'm interested in the writer over the long haul. I'm there to teach young writers craft—it's too bad Jerry didn't want to learn. But when a young writer doesn't, believe me, stopping then probably saved him—and me—a lot of time and unhappiness. Suppose he had to learn it after he'd already published half a dozen scripts, when he'd already been working as a professional for six months, a year, or more? So, in terms of professional comics writing, I make craft the first priority—before everything else."

We see this concept of craft—where craft is opposed to art—constantly at work. (In a passing, even parenthetical, way, this entire essay is a personal message to "Jerry" so that he, or those in his situation in any of the paraliterary genres, might understand a little of what happened to them—in his case, years ago.) We see it marring the art works we are presented with whenever a science fiction writer or a mystery writer or a writer of pornography excuses his or her failure of taste, of invention, of skill, of insight, or simply of intelligence in thinking through the various ramifications of his or her story by reaching for the excuse that paraliterary criticism keeps ready: "I'm a craftsman—not an artist." We see that concept at work in every incoherent movie in which motivations are absent or unbelievable and nothing makes sense or registers with any import, because, failing to understand the intricate ways in which coherence, believability, and interest must interweave to produce a satisfying story, one or another producer has told a writer, "Do it this way because it'll be more exciting," or, "Leave that out because it'll be dull," all of which basically translates: "Do it this way because I'm paying you." Because the interweave of background and foreground is even more complex in a science fiction movie than it is in a film set in the contemporary world, this is a correspondingly greater problem in SF films than it is in movies with historical or contemporary settings. We see it in almost every attempt to write a story by committee.

Though I retain my personal fondness for Julie Schwartz and have great respect for what he's done in comics, I abominate the esthetic of Craft *vs.* Art. I think anyone who loves the paraliterary genres should abominate it as well. We who criticize in the paraliterary genres should work to unmask it for what it is, discredit it, dismantle it, and permanently retire it. It is not that craft can't mean other things, useful things, valuable and valid things for the construction of art works in narrative form. But wherever craft is presented as a concept *opposed* to art, it will be available as a cover-up for the sort of exploitation in the situation above. Because of the economic forces at work in the paraliterary fields, there's no way to prevent such exploitation.

Two other concepts also hold back the development of paraliterary criticism and provide smoke screens for endless exploitation in much the way the concept of "craft" (and the attendant concept of "mastery") does: First is the concept of "origins." Second is a concept intimately linked with it, that of "definition of the genre." But, as we shall see, all are connected. With strong historical filiation, they work to support and reinforce one another. By the end of this essay, I hope we'll have a stronger sense of how that intersupport functions.

II

Possibly toward the end of the first century A.D., but more probably toward the end of the third, Cassius Longinus (or possibly Dionysius Longinus; *possibly* they were one and the same), wrote a letter-*cum*-monograph to his friend Postimius Terentianus, in which, inspired by a treatise by one Caecilius, περὶ 'ύψους (*Peri Hupsous*—usually translated "On the Sublime," but more accurately "On Greatness" or "On Greatness in Writing," or "On Greatness in Art"), he put forward his own thoughts as to what made writing great. His essay was known throughout the Renaissance as Longinus's "On the Sublime"—Longinus's piece, originally unnamed, having taken *its* title from the now long-lost treatise by Caecilius that was its ostensible topic. The oldest version of Longinus's text is a manuscript copy from the tenth century. Milton mentions it in his 1652 piece, "On Education." But with Boileau's 1674 French translation of the fifty-five page essay, "On the Sublime" became the most influential bit of classical literary criticism in the West for a hundred years or more, briefly surpassing in its influence Plato, Aristotle, and Horace. Indeed, as much as any single text, it is probably the reason why we venerate Sophocles and Sappho as we do today, if not *The Iliad* and *The Odyssey*, all of which it analyzes and praises in terms close to the ones commonly used about these works by contemporary critics.

Possibly in the year or so before 1992, in a phone call to his friend Matt Feazell, Scott McCloud talked about a project he had been considering: "an examination of the art-form of comics, what it's capable of, how it works . . . I even put together a new comprehensive theory of the creative process and its implications for comics and for art in general!!" This is from the "Introduction" to McCloud's extraordinary paraliterary critique, *Understanding Comics*. Reading on in McCloud, we find there is a kind of parent text that McCloud greatly respects, and that his own work is in creative dialogue with, Will Eisner's *Comics and Sequential Art* (and, later, Wassily Kandinsky's 1912 essay, "On the Problem of Form"), which, rather like Caecilius's eponymous περὶ 'ύψους in Longinus, is mentioned a handful of times toward the beginning, then drops away as McCloud pursues his own ideas about his topic.

I would not be surprised if McCloud's *Understanding Comics* becomes as important and influential a work in the development of the whole range of criticism of the paraliterary as Longinus was in the last few centuries of classical criticism. Having said that, let me say also that that is something between an opinion and a hope. I make the comparison with the περὶ 'ύψους in order to highlight a few, limited, particular points—and, more important, to make clear several points that I am *not* making.

In my description above, I've located two tropes—(1) the orientation of a critical study toward the enlightenment of a personal friend and (2) the celebration/critique of a "parent" text examining similar topics—shared by Longinus and McCloud. Because both are writing criticism, doubtless I could find more. But do I believe that Longinus's περὶ 'ύψους is in any way a *privileged origin* of McCloud's *Understanding Comics?* Do I believe that the περὶ 'ύψους, because of the similarities I've noted, in any way lends *authority* to the arguments or presentations in *Understanding Comics?* No, I don't—my answer to both questions.

Do I believe that, directly or indirectly, Longinus's περὶ 'ύψους is in any way a *meaningful influence* on *Understanding Comics?* I would not be astonished to find that McCloud *had* read Longinus. It's available in translation in most large bookstores and is out in a Penguin anthology, an Oxford Classics anthology, and in a critical translation by G. M. A. Grube from the Hackett Publishing Company with an extensive introduction,[1] notes, and a bibliographical index. As well it's been reprinted in several other historical anthologies of European criticism. But though I would *not* be astonished, I *would* be surprised: Today readers of the περὶ 'ύψους are limited largely to those graduate students interested in the history of criticism. For me to suspect *meaningful influence* from one text to the other, I would need internal (some sign in McCloud's text) or external (biographical or historical knowledge) evidence that McCloud *had* read Longinus, or similar evidence that McCloud had read a work by someone known (through similar historical evidence) to have been influenced by Longinus.

The simple use of the two tropes is, for me, just not strong enough evidence to allow me to make any such suggestion. Lacking a direct statement about such reading in McCloud's text, at the very least I would have to find a significant string of words common to the two texts, a string that might have been put there by McCloud to recall the parent text (as when in *Red Mars* [1993] Kim Stanley Robinson recalls Philip K. Dick's novel *The Martian Time-Slip* [1964] by naming the 39.5-odd-minute difference between an Earth day and a Mars day, compensated for by stopping the clocks for 39.5 minutes between twelve midnight and twelve-oh-one, "the Martian time slip" [internal evidence], the source of which is supported by the fact that Robinson wrote a book on Dick, *The Novels of Philip K. Dick* [1984—external evidence]), before I'd venture that such a suggestion carried any critically significant probability.[2]

1. The information about Longinus and the περὶ 'ύψους comes from Grube's introduction. The *Oxford Classical Dictionary*'s account of text and author differs notably.

2. In the past there have been many thematic critics who, considering the two cited figures not tropes but themes, might well have felt that, *as* themes, they were strong enough to suggest an influence. But, as someone who does not consider himself a thematic critic, I am not among their number.

Finally, and perhaps for this discussion most importantly, do I think that what stalls these passages of authority from Longinus to McCloud is that Longinus is writing about literature whereas McCloud is writing about comics? Do I believe something innate to the nature of the different genres—their assumed average quality, perhaps—makes the passage impossible?

Again, firmly I do not. Both McCloud and Longinus are writing criticism—and, in both cases, I believe, they are writing criticism of a high order. Longinus's essay dates from many centuries before the current valuation of genres was in place. McCloud's is from a time—and is at the forefront of the endeavor—when precisely such barriers are coming down. It is the system that tries to preserve such power relations *and* their attendant power exclusions that must be dismantled if McCloud's project (and I hope, with this essay, I make clear that I share it) is ever to see success.

What, then, *is* the status of the relationship between two texts that exhibit such similarity? I believe that for a certain kind of reader who recognizes such similarities, those similarities produce a resonance and richness in the *reading pleasure* to be taken from McCloud's text—and a highly pleasurable book *Understanding Comics* is. But the relation between them is specifically *not* a matter of consciousness or authority. Were McCloud later to inform me that the similarity was, indeed, conscious and in some way ironic (as is Robinson's recall of Dick), I would admit I was mistaken and say, "Fine." But I would also suggest that, were he interested in doing it again, he might leave a clearer trail of allusion (i.e., some internal evidence) in his actual text.

The two tropes shared by *Understanding Comics* and the περὶ 'ὑψους are extremely powerful ones over the range of western criticism. They have introduced many strong critiques. Among them, now, is McCloud's. But does Longinus's use of them in any way lend *power* to McCloud?"

No, it does not.

Having noted the similarities, I note as well that there are myriad *differences* between the content, form, structure, and context of Longinus's letter to Postimius Terentianus and Scott McCloud's phone call to Matt Feazell. Similarly, the uses of their respective parent texts are notably different in many ways. Does *initiating* (in any sense) an essay with such tropes from an earlier classical example, either consciously or unconsciously, in any way *guarantee* the remainder of the text power, insight, or brilliance? As powerful, insightful, and brilliant as McCloud's book is (for it is all of these), the answer must still be: No. Many critiques have begun with the same tropes but have gone on to nothing, save the deadest of academicism. Myriad fine and brilliant critical essays have begun, using other tropes entirely—which is to say, the use of such tropes is neither necessary nor sufficient to produce critical excellence. In no way do such tropes *define* excellence in a critical endeavor.

Because the two tropes have not been used so frequently that they have become deadly clichés, the relation between texts that employ them remains a matter of *resonance* and *pleasure*—in the way that a resonant note, calling up echoes and overtones, might sound richer than one that plunked out devoid of any enharmonics.

The tropes function exactly the way the Homeric parallels do in Joyce's *Ulysses*—adding pleasure and resonance to the reading of those who recognize them. But neither in the case of the likely conscious Joyce nor in the case of the probably unconscious McCloud do they lend, in themselves, *power, authority, persuasive force,* or *greatness. Ulysses* could just as easily have been a dull, boring, unimaginative novel based just as firmly on the *Odyssey*—in which case we would have an uninteresting, boring, dull piece of writing. But what Joyce gave us was a rich and resonant novel, one of whose pleasurable resonances occurs at the level of its Homeric parallels. Even using the two tropes from Longinus consciously, McCloud's book could have been a waste of paper. It is not. It's a wonderful and wonder-filled critical performance.

Tropes are basically formal, and as McCloud himself declares, for a sophisticated discussion of any art, we must separate form from content:

Illustration #1: McCloud, page 199.

Awareness that formal resonances are pleasurable but not authoritative is what, I suspect, led Jorge Luis Borges to write, "The repeated, but insignificant, contacts of Joyce's *Ulysses* with the Homeric Odyssey continue to enjoy—I shall never know why—the harebrained admiration of the critics" (*Ficciones*, 42). This is not an attack on modernism, or on Joyce, or on *Ulysses*. It is an attack on critics who see, in a figure that should produce pleasure, rather a mark of power, authority, or greatness. *That* is what is harebrained.

The first of several places where McCloud's study soars to brilliance is in chapter 2, "The Vocabulary of Comics." The chapter's opening four-and-a-half pages are an awkward discussion of icons; to me they seem an attempt to reinvent, in four pages, the whole topic of semiotics—the study of signs—without realizing that this is what they are doing. But from these unpromising beginnings, McCloud's combination of words and pictures rises to a series of insights having to do with the different ways highly representational art can affect us contrasted to the way the highly reduced and schematic art associated with cartoons and comics can affect us. McCloud argues—and argues convincingly—that the representational portrait of a face is perceived as the face of another, whereas the highly schematic face is perceived as one's own.

Illustration #2: McCloud, page 36

When abstracted from his presentation, the insight may not strike you. But when you follow, in words and pictures, the progression of his argument (from page 28 to page 47), it is highly convincing. It is also delightful. I exhort all my readers to take a look at it, for this is *Understanding Comics* at its best—where a summation, or even the citation of a few panels, is inadequate to convey the force and efficiency with which

McCloud makes his points, a force arising not out of the similarity with any other text—Longinus's or anyone else's—but out of McCloud's own formal organization of his argument.

The next place McCloud shines is in chapter 3, "Blood in the Gutter." Here he introduces an idea he names "closure"—i.e., what goes on between the panels; what joins panel to panel. (I have also seen this referred to as "gestalt perception." But I'm content to use McCloud's term.) As he points out, closure is often at work *within* a single panel as well. This notion of closure allows McCloud to begin an intense discussion of that aspect which is so important to any art: the relation between the shown and the not shown, the stated and the implied, the articulated and the suggested—for here is where all art begins to manifest the complexities that make some formal analysis a necessity for sophisticated appreciation.

Illustration #3: McCloud, page 66

As McCloud eventually says, when he is summing up his findings, "The dance of the visible and the invisible is at the very heart of comics through closure" (205). An earlier comment, however, is perhaps more to the point: "The comics creator asks us to join in a silent dance of the seen and the unseen. The visible and the invisible. This dance is unique to comics. No other artform gives so much to its audience while asking so much from them as well" (92). In an essay on La Fontaine's *Adonis*, the French poet Paul Valéry noted a similar relation between the stated and unstated in poetry: "Follow the path of your aroused thought, and you will soon meet this infernal inscription: *There is nothing so beautiful as that which does not exist,*" italics Valéry's. In a letter to a friend written after the publication of his *Tractatus Logico-Philosophicus,* the philosopher Wittgenstein noted the same relation even in philosophy: "My work consists of two parts: the present one here plus all that I have not written. And *it is precisely this second part that is the important one,*" italics Wittgenstein's. And, of course, so-famously Keats wrote: "Heard melodies are sweet. But those unheard are sweeter," which suggested a similar point about music. This relation between the expressed and the withheld must exist in any art hinging on representation—because one cannot, in any given art work, represent everything.

Something has to be left implied.

If we take McCloud to be saying, by his dance metaphor, that the choreographic *form* of the dance is unique to each medium, comics among them, I have no problem with his assertion.

That the point has been made and made frequently before gives resonance and pleasure. But McCloud makes it well and specifically for comics—and thus makes it his own.

In the course of his discussion of closure, McCloud specifies six relationships that adjacent panels can have to one another: The panels can progress (1) moment-to-moment, (2) action-to-action, (3) subject-to-subject, (4) scene-to-scene, (5) aspect-to-aspect, or be (6) non-sequiturs. What follows this is an extraordinarily illuminating analysis of several comic books, American, European, experimental, and Japanese, as to the number of each type of transition.

American comics, whether they are commercial or underground, all produce the same graphic distribution, with action-to-action transition being far in the lead, with subject-to-subject transitions coming next, to be followed by scene-to-scene transitions. Only in highly experimental work do these proportions change. Japanese comics also produce a different graph: American comics almost never use aspect-to-aspect transitions. Japanese comics use aspect-to-aspect transitions notably more than they use scene-to-scene transitions. I share McCloud's hope that

Illustration #4: McCloud, page 74

pointing this out might inspire our comics writers and artists to try something new.

The third area in which Mc-Cloud rises to brilliance is in his discussion of comics time.

One of the most amusing and effective moments in *Understanding Comics* is when McCloud explodes the notion that a single comics panel shows only a single, isolated instant:

Illustration #5: McCloud, page 95

In McCloud's panel above, possibly for as much as thirty seconds, time runs left to right, intimately tied to the duration of language. His detailed discussion of this is intricate and illuminating. His account of the various lines that comics have used to portray movement (zip-ribbons, as they were once called) leads, through a discussion of "subjective motion," into another fine and revealing section on the nature of the expressive quality and variety of line itself in comics art.

In general, looking back through the several rich and suggestive arguments in *Understanding Comics*, I note that most of the ones I've already pointed out (the nature of faces and forms reduced to lines; the power of the lines separating panels; lines used to signal movement in time and—finally—lines' vast range of expressivity and emotion) tend, indeed, to focus *on* the line. The line and its function in the range and field of comics art are topics on which McCloud is unfailingly brilliant.

McCloud proposes several analytical tools which he uses to help make his points. For example, between pages 48 and 57, he poses a schematic triangle which plots artwork that is still referential along the bottom line, from highly representational on the left to highly schematic on the right. The altitude on McCloud's triangle represents the move from referential

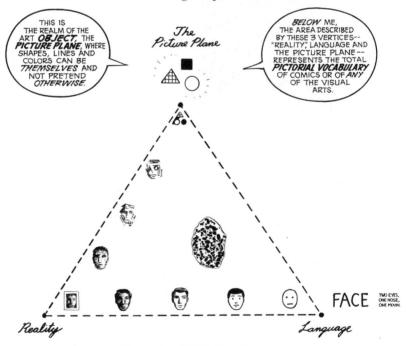

Illustration #6: McCloud, page 51

art, along the bottom, to nonreferential art at the apex—what McCloud calls "the picture plane," and which might be described as that art which, without referring to recognizable objects, instead foregrounds shape, line, color, and even the materials—paint, ink, paper, and what-have-you—for their own sake. Such scales are always provisional. Indeed, had McCloud wanted to open up his triangle's top vertex and expand triangle into rectangle, he could have plotted abstract art along the upper line from (say, on the right) those works that emphasize shape, line, and color to (on the left) those that emphasize the physicality of the materials—ink, paint, paper, nails, string, wood, canvas, masonite, chickenwire, mirrors, or what-have-you—in those abstract works (often called assemblages) that sometimes resemble sculpture more than painting. To date, of course, there's not a great deal of this in comics—though one exception is the more recent work of Dave McKean, many of whose *Sandman* covers are as much assemblages as Rauschenberg's briefly notorious Stuffed-Goat-with-Car-Tire (*Monogram*, 1963).

We've already spoken about McCloud's six different kinds of panel transition—equally provisional.

The third schema that he comes up with is, for me, the most problematic. McCloud calls it "the six steps." This follows upon a "definition of art" that is equally problematic (and which I shall return to). McCloud prefaces his "six steps" with the following statement: "'Pure' art is essentially tied to the question of purpose—of deciding what you want out of art. This is true in comics as it is in painting, writing, theater, film, sculpture, or any other form because the creation of any work in any medium will always follow a certain path."

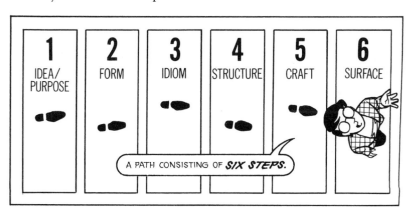

Illustration #7: McCloud, page 170

McCloud goes on to describe each of these six steps:

First [idea/purpose]: the impulses, the ideas, the emotions, the philosophies of the work . . . the work's "content." Second [form]: The form it will take . . . will it be a book? A chalk drawing? A chair? A song? A sculpture? A pot holder? A comic book? Third [idiom]: The "school" of art, the vocabulary of styles, gestures, or subject matter, the genre that the work belongs to . . . maybe a genre of its own. Fourth [structure]: putting it all together . . . what to include, what to leave out . . . how to arrange, how to compose the work. Fifth [craft]: constructing the work, applying skills, practical knowledge, invention, problem-solving, getting the "job" done. Sixth [surface]: production values, finishing . . . the aspect most apparent on first superficial exposure to the work.

The fundamental problem I see with this scheme is that too much is packed into each step, so that most of them have aspects both of form *and* content about them. That might even have been McCloud's purpose in formulating them. But, for that reason, it tends to undercut much of what he has proposed so far under that critically so necessary separation.

It is the quotation marks around "job" in "getting the 'job' done" and the idea of "practical knowledge" in the description of number five ("craft") that holds that description open for my unhappy account of the function of craft in comics art with which we began. The question McCloud sidesteps taking on directly is: Just whose job is it, anyway? (Not in the sense of who has to *do* it, but who *owns* it. It is no accident that this has been such a big part of the nuts-and-bolts history of recent comics.) The comics publisher? The comics buyer? Or the comics creator? The relationship of art and its audience in comics is one classical area of art criticism that seems slighted in McCloud's study—because, especially in comics, that relation, in terms of acceptance, appreciation, and finally money is, thanks to fandom, unique and has had and will have a great deal to do with the development and growth of comics, about which McCloud is so luminously passionate.

Finally, however, I think the most commendable aspect of McCloud's book is its particular combination—manifested in its layout, its draftsmanship, its breakdown of ideas—of intelligence and enthusiasm. Either one without the other would have produced a very different, and lesser, work.

III

McCloud has other things to say about the craft, the origins, and the definition of comics—and because he does not use the pages in which he says them overtly to unmask and demystify the contradictions inherent in all three notions, his overall argument is marred—and marred seriously. But it's a tribute to his critical intelligence that so much of—and certainly the most interesting part of—what he has to say lies outside these three essentialist bogs, and is anchored, rather, on the grounding of his considerable analytical intellect.

At one point McCloud writes (p. 163), "Even today, there are those who ask the question, 'Can comics be art?' It is—I'm sorry—a stupid question! But if we must answer it, the answer is yes. Especially if your definition of art is as broad as mine."

Illustration #8: McCloud, page 164

What makes (or does not make) the question stupid may not, however, be as self-evident as McCloud suggests. As Raymond Williams explained in his book *Keywords* (Oxford, 1976) "art" is one of a number of terms ("civilization" is another, as are "modern," "literature," "poetry" and, most interestingly, "definition" itself) that always have *two* meanings that relate in a particular socially exploitable manner. One meaning is generous, inclusive, and largely value free: "Civilization" covers everything that occurs in the range of life in the developed countries. "Art" is anything that anyone, child or adult, skilled or unskilled, does that is focused on producing an esthetic response, rather than fulfilling a functional role. "Modern" is the adjective for whatever is occurring in the world today.

But each of the terms also has a limited, value-bound meaning that refers, not simply to different objects and materials (which would make it a different word, or a homonym) but rather to a limited (and, because of the fuzzy nature of those values, finally an impossible to define) subset of what the larger meaning refers to. Almost invariably, when the limited meaning of the terms is invoked, it functions in the negative, as a means of exclusion. "That's not art. That's just a child's scribbling," although the scribblings of a child would be easily included in the notion of art under the larger meaning. "People living like that in New York City in this day and age is just uncivilized," though what everyone does in New York, from the homeless to Donald Trump, is part of civilization in the larger meaning. "What do you mean, it's a combination of art and literature? It's a comic book!"

The fact is, until fairly recently for most people "Can comics be art?" was not a stupid question. It wasn't a question at all. Rather it was what the split meanings of literature and art were there precisely to protect against: the serious consideration as art (in the limited, value-bound sense) of *any* texts from any of the paraliterary genres, SF, comics, pornography, mysteries, westerns . . . Indeed, the definition (and, though I use the term rarely, here I mean it in the limited, formal sense of presenting the necessary and sufficient conditions) of "paraliterature" and "paraliterary" is specifically those written genres traditionally excluded by the limited, value-bound meaning of "literature" and "literary."

(One of the things McCloud's analysis points to, though it does not say it outright, is that we need comparable terms, "art" and "para-art," to discuss with any precision the visual genres that are traditionally excluded from the fine arts. As McCloud suggests, historically, in "para-art" and "paraliterature," words and images combine easily [comics, advertising], whereas in the fine arts and literature, though from time to time they intersect [see Mark Varnadeau's extraordinarily informative *High Art, Low Art*], that intersection is much more anxiety-filled for middle-class and upper-middle-class audiences.)

In short, the revolution in the *value system* of contemporary art that McCloud is so passionately pushing for is much more profound, complex, and far-reaching than McCloud's protestation of the stupidity of its central question takes account of. Calling that central question "stupid" is not the way to win that revolution; if anything, it undercuts and even discredits the real advances McCloud has made in the sections of *Understanding Comics* I've pointed out already.

That's a shame.

But let us return to McCloud's "definition" (when people talk about multiple definitions of the same topic, distinguishing some as "broad" and some as "narrow," and when these proposed "definitions" are qualified by phrases such as "to me" and "as I see it," they are no longer talking about formal definitions. They are talking about the broader meaning of definition—some form or other of "functional description." I hope, then, McCloud might accept the less confusing term "functional description") of art, expressed in the panel on the previous page: "Art, as I see it, is any human activity that doesn't grow out of either of our species' two basic instincts: survival and reproduction." One can only assume, especially from the way the argument goes on, that he is using "reproduction" as a metonym for "sex." Otherwise, we would have the immediate problem that *everything* homosexuals did that was oriented toward sex would be art, while *nothing* heterosexuals did that was oriented toward sex would be—even if it involved the same actions. Or: Any heterosexual behavior that led to oral or anal sex would be art, while, if the same behavior led to vaginal sex, it wouldn't be. And so on and so forth. That, as I see it, just doesn't *feel* right.

Readers familiar with a range of esthetic speculation in the West will probably recognize, however, the glimmer of a useful idea in McCloud's formation. Often throughout the history of criticism, the esthetic (not art) has been described (not defined) as those aspects of an object that are in excess of the functional. (I've already used that description above.)

Even though it by no means exhausts the topic, repeatedly this has proven to be a powerful and useful description of the esthetic. Because it is so muddled, however, it isn't, here.

If I may elaborate on that strong form of the description: Anything designed to fulfill a task will have aspects that do not directly contribute to the task's performance. These aspects mark out the realm of the esthetic. Gross examples might include the designs or scrimshaw on the handle of a knife; the paint choice on a car; whether or not a machine, whose cleanliness does not effect its performance, is kept shiny and polished or allowed to get dusty and dull. Fundamentally, these are esthetic aspects. The esthetic is (a further description) the realm in which art (in its large, value-free inclusive meaning) takes place.

There have been powerful and incisive functional descriptions of art that do not so immediately stumble into the sort of problems McCloud's does. One was given by the author of *Ada* and *Lolita*, Vladimir Nabokov: "Art is sensuous thought." One of the pleasant things about Nabokov's description, not accomplished by McCloud's (for who's to say that *Understanding Comics* was not a matter of McCloud's own intellectual survival?), is that it allows us to see McCloud's *own* rich, sensuously visual, and passionate exegesis as art. And, for all my carping, it is.

If, realizing the way in which the two meanings of definition (like the two meanings of art) create an unwinnable game of round-robin chasing-after-one's-tail, critics of the paraliterary could retire the notion of definition once and for all, if they could restrict themselves to the far more modest-seeming task of describing our objects of concern (like comics, SF, pornography . . .), describing never-before-noticed aspects, pointing out the most interesting examples, describing the myriad and fascinating ways in which those aspects react with one another and how they interact with readers and the world, we would produce a far less arrogant, far more interesting, far less self-crippling, and finally far more powerful criticism—as does McCloud at his strongest—than we usually do, a criticism that would go far further toward effecting the revolution *in esthetic values* that McCloud (and I) would like to see.

IV

The idea of "definition," with its suggestion of the scientific, can be associated easily with the idea of "mastery"—which, in turn, can be easily associated with the idea of "origin" and "craft." But the fact is, we do not master an art—and certainly we do not master it through knowing the "the proper definition" or "mastering" its "origins" or simply learning its "craft." (Let me reiterate: It is only the idea of *craft in opposition to art* to which I object; in support of the concept of art, craft is a useful and fine, even necessary, concept: But it is not sufficient to produce art in the limited, value-bound sense—as McCloud himself explains on p. 171.) The more we study and dwell on (and in) an art, the more the art masters us. The clarity with which McCloud reports on the way the art of comics has mastered him is another facet that gives *Understanding Comics* its brilliance.

The people who want to master an art, be it comics, SF, pornography, *or* the various literary genres, are the gallery of administrators and producers, those who sink their money into its creation, its distribution, its sales; those who hope that, through such mastery, they can bend art to their own whims. The results are always broken-backed, limping, incoherent pieces that, to the audience, are laughable and instantly forgettable.

The reason for this is that, regardless of how we like to talk about it, there is nothing there to be mastered. There are only things to be submitted to.

There are at least three reasons to give up the notion of "definition" (and its attendant notions of mastery, craft, and origins). One is logical; the other two are strategic.

The logical reason, first: The one reason to *keep* using the word definition would be if one could form a definition in the limited, rigorous, formal sense of the word—otherwise, to repeat myself, we had better use the term "description" (or "functional description") to avoid confusion. The question then becomes, *can* we create a limited, rigorous, formal definition of a form of art, a mode of writing and pictures, a genre?

Well, there is a certain order of objects—ones that the late sociologist Lucien Goldmann (in his brief book, *Philosophy and the Human Sciences*, Jonathan Cape, 1969) called "social objects"—that resist formal definition, i.e., we cannot locate the necessary and sufficient conditions that can describe them with definitional rigor. Social objects are those that, instead of existing as a relatively limited number of material objects, exist rather as an unspecified number of recognition codes (functional descriptions, if you will) shared by an unlimited population, in which new and different examples are regularly produced. Genres, discourses, and genre collections are all social objects. And when a discourse (or genre collection, such as art) encourages, values, and privileges originality, creativity, variation, and change in its new examples, it should be self-evident why "definition" is an impossible task (since the object itself, if it is healthy, is constantly developing and changing), even for someone who finds it difficult to follow the fine points.

The strategic reasons are more down to earth. Only since the late sixties, with the advent of the schools of criticism known as structuralism, poststructuralism, and semiotics, have some of these limitations of what is logically do-able and what is not become generally known to a fairly large number of (though by no means all) literary critics.

In the 1930s, many American critics wanted to make criticism more scientific. Critical literature of that time abounded in attempts to define rigorously notions such as the epic, the novel, tragedy, poetry, the literary, the lyric. . . . Many of these critics (they were often of a left political persuasion) began to look at the popular arts. Fields such as science fiction, the mystery, and film began to come under the critical spotlight. At the same time, more conservative critics were beginning to dismantle the various proposed definitional projects. These critics (more about them later) were often hostile to the popular cultural aspect of what their fellows were doing. But finally, in the forties and fifties, under the triumph of what was then called "the New Criticism," all but the last of these definitional projects were generally given up.

Often they went out with an ironic flourish: Randall Jarrell, an exemplary New Critic, gave what may be the last "definition" of the novel in his 1965 preface to Christina Stead's *The Man Who Loved Children* ("An Unread Book"), "a novel is a prose narrative of some length that has something wrong with it." George Steiner, in his study *The Death of Tragedy*, ended the search for a definition there, by resurrecting an ancient writer who had noted, about the form, "The best of them are sad." One would have hoped that, in the field of popular culture in those same years, Damon Knight's famous "ostensive definition" from page 1 of *In Search of Wonder* (1956) might have sounded a similarly elegant death knell to the impossible task of defining science fiction: "[T]he term 'science fiction' is a misnomer . . . trying to get two enthusiasts to agree on a definition of it only leads to bloody knuckles: . . . but that will do us no particular harm if we remember that, like *The Saturday Evening Post*, it means what we point to when we say it." For those who need it spelled out, the humor lies in the fact that it's undecidable whether that "when we say it" means "by saying it" or "at the same time as we say it."

One would have liked to have heard a big laugh. Then we might have gone on to more useful critical tasks. Indeed, it could have brought to an end all the attempts to define the other paraliterary genres as well. What that would have accomplished is the first step in putting the *paraliterary* genres on the *same* level as the (now all-but-universally acknowledged to be) undefinable *literary* genres.

We had no tradition of academic rigor, however, to pressure us. Once the populist critics turned away from us, we were left with a general distrust of the academy (that came from our working-class roots), and because there was little pressure on us to *develop* our own criticism (though in the fanzines and through convention panels we have done a great deal of it—and much of it has been powerful and important), in terms of terminology, we've simply gone on using our borrowed vocabulary and talking about definitions for the last sixty years.

What McCloud and the other critics of the paraliterary (e.g., James Gunn, in science fiction) don't seem to realize is that our very insistence that our genre *might be* susceptible to "rigorous definition" functions today as a ready-made admission that the genre *must be* substantially less complex and vital than any of the literary genres. Our adversaries reason: "Since *their* genre is created *only* with craft (and *not* art—note here the two function in distinct opposition), a paraliterary genre can be art only under the larger and inclusive meaning. It can't be art in the limited, value-bound meaning: Science fiction, comics, pornography, mysteries can be considered art, at best, in the way Morris chairs or Wedgwood china (easily definable objects, by the bye) are art, but obviously not in the way that a poem (in the undefinable genre of poetry) is art. The fact that any given one among these genres *is* definable (or that its most interesting critical practitioners, such as McCloud, keep insisting that it is) is proof positive it *must* be simple and second rate!"

Before we leave those thirties/fifties critics, with their desire to make literary criticism compete with science by importing the notion of definition into it, and their openness to the paraliterary field of (especially) mysteries and science fiction (most of them drew the line at comics; but because the comics world had so much social interchange with these other genres, the critical vocabulary and concepts spread), we need to make a final point, which will become important later on. As much as they favored popular art, these critics were also loudly opposed to the new work that is today called High Modernism—the work today represented by Eliot, Pound, and Crane in poetry in this country, and D. H. Lawrence, Wyndham Lewis, and Joyce in the British Isles.

Their reasons were clear and political. While acknowledging the range and vigor of the new collage techniques and anti-narrative structures with which these artists broadened the range of their monologues, they still realized that when, in part II of his first major poem, "For the Marriage of Faustus and Helen" (1923), Crane wrote

> This crashing opéra bouffe,
> Blest excursion! this ricochet
> From roof to roof—
> Know, Olympians, we are breathless
> While nigger cupids scour the stars!

it was not some illiterate southern farmer who knew no other term for black people who was given voice in Crane's lines. Rather it was a trendy upper-middle-class white voice, that had made a choice to ignore the political politeness of the day and whose jazz-age allegiances Crane's poem was celebrating.

When, in a section Pound had excised from *The Waste Land* and that Eliot published two years before the longer poem, under the title *Gerontion* (1920), Eliot wrote

> My house is a decayed house,
> And the jew squats on the window sill, the owner,
> spawned in some estaminet of Antwerp,
> Blistered in Brussels, patched and peeled in London.

(the lower-case "j" there is Eliot's), or titled his poem "Burbank with a Baedeker: Bleistein with a Cigar" ("The rats are underneath the piles. / The Jew is underneath the lot. / Money in furs. The boatman smiles . . ."), he was evoking the most unthinking stereotype of the money-grubbing Jewish landlord, tourist, and businessman. Indeed, the latter poem operates within the most anti-Semitic of models for Jewish "decadence," going at least as far back as Wagner's notorious anti-Semitic article, "Jewry in Music" (1851): the Jew can only receive cultural input but cannot create valid work because of his commitment to trade, money, and (as it is symbolized in the *Ring*) gold.

Pound's years of propaganda broadcasts for Mussolini earned him a conviction of either treason or madness: Pound chose madness. But even the award of the 1947 Bollingen Prize could not erase the sour, treasonous taste of those radio programs.

The fascist ideas of Lawrence (with his love of the idea of racial memory and metaphors of blood and soil) and Lewis were even clearer.

That Joyce's *Ulysses* can be read as the celebration of the daily heroism of an ordinary, working-class Dublin Jew is probably a larger reason than many critics would like to admit as to why it has floated to the top of the High Modernist pool and stayed there. Similarly, Djuna Barnes's astute and finally compassionate analysis of the place of the Jew in European culture that forms the opening movement of *Nightwood* (1936) may well account for why, slowly but inexorably, that novel has risen to take *its* well-deserved place high in the modernist pantheon. What can't be denied, however, is that all these Protestant and Catholic writers were *fascinated* with the place of Jews and the "Jewish problem," all through the course of High Modernism. Whether well or badly, sympathetically or hostilely, they *all* wrote about it.

Though Eliot's brain-deadening work in an English bank and Crane, in his six-dollar-a-week room at 110 Columbia Heights in Brooklyn, lusting after the eight-dollar-a-week room with a view of the bridge, are both mythemes of High Modernism, both Eliot and Crane came from money. Both their decisions to be poets meant a goodly amount of family tension and, finally, financial abandonment. (A candy manufacturer in Cleveland, Crane's father has the dubious distinction of having invented the Life Saver.)

In 1934 Wallace Stevens became a vice president of the Hartford Accident and Indemnity Company, where he'd worked since 1916. Almost Byronically popular in her time (and the only poet of her times, claimed critic Edmund Wilson, whose work felt like that of a major poet while she was alive), only Edna St. Vincent Millay came from more humble beginnings, despite her scholarship to Vassar. She was the most esthetically conservative, and today is the least read, moving toward an obscurity in which she has been preceded by the once extraordinarily popular black poet, Paul Lawrence Dunbar, and in which she is gradually being followed by Jeffers, Sandberg, Robinson—and even possibly Frost. Politically (with the exception of Millay), the American poets of the twenties were the most lackadaisical of liberals, easily swayed by reactionary ideas, and even violently conservative ones, as in the case of Pound.

Among the thirties American critics, sympathy with the popular and a corresponding distaste for High Modernism's politics eventually coalesced into what, sadly, was an all-too-easy argument. Since the working-class audience for popular culture so frequently found the esthetic pyrotechnics in these new works alien and off-putting, *this* was put forward, by the critics, as the major sign of high art's *esthetic* (rather than *political*) failing. It was not a good argument. Too many things lay repressed beneath it.

But I said we'd come back to these critics' critics.

The Nazi persecutions in Germany produced a migration of extraordinary German intellectuals, many of them Jewish, into the United States—novelists like Thomas Mann and Herman Broch, musicians like Arnold Schoenberg, and university figures like Hannah Arendt, Herbert Marcuse, and Theodor Adorno. The situation of contemporary art in Germany and France was very different from that in America. In Germany and France the avant-garde was solidly on the left, and the left academics solidly supported them: A former music student of Alban Berg's, Adorno had already written his book, *The Philosophy of New Music*, in which he defended Schoenberg's atonal works (and castigated the far more popular Stravinsky). Walter Benjamin (though he set out for America, he committed suicide when the Nazis detained him and other refugees at the Spanish border, the vision of concentration camps too much for him to bear) had already written the essays that would make up his *Brecht* book. What those who arrived here found in the American academic left was the vulgarest of "vulgar" Marxism.

In particular Adorno held no brief for popular culture. In German popular culture, the film industry had been among the first institutions to be taken over by the Nazis. But maneuvering the prejudices of the working class and lower middle class to get them to do what he wanted was the name of Hitler's game. All Adorno could see in the American radio shows and films of the forties was patriotic pabulum for the masses, which, if it had any liberal leanings at all, was only because it was not under any particular pressure to be otherwise. (Nor would fifties McCarthyism and the Hollywood blacklists make him any more sanguine. Though he is not cited in their bibliography, Adorno's ideas on popular culture are very close to those found in my old elementary school friend Ariel Dorfman and Armand Mattelart's *How to Read Donald Duck* [Valparaiso, 1971/New York, 1975].) These thinkers and the scholars who were influenced by them began to mount their critique on the American academic populists. Why not try another careful reading of the High Modernists? Perhaps they could be redeemed—as they already were in Europe. But popular culture was lost—a mere puppet of the dominant ideology. At least in Europe it had been.

Under the critique of these newcomers, the American critics began to retreat from the popular. The bad faith at their argument's heart (the use of the *esthetic* as a smoke screen to mask *political* disapproval) was uncovered—though in the realms of the paraliterary, writers, editors, and other folk, left to themselves, still held to the arguments and terminology abandoned, as it were, in their yard, without ever managing to think through (or mount for themselves) the critique that, in the university, had demolished many of the ideas involved.

Often when we look at what critics in the paraliterary fields are doing, even today, we see people going through the empty gestures from the thirties (e.g., immediately trying to define their genre as an opening move, before going on to a discussion of origins), gestures that were determined by a group of critics and ideas that, today, simply don't command much respect. By the repeated attempts to define this or that paraliterary genre, instead of just going about the task of describing what in the genre interests them, critically (I hope I've made it clear) McCloud and others shoot themselves in the foot. Another strategic reason to give up the notion of definitions is because, to the larger world of contemporary criticism, save among the *most* reactionary forces still fighting some last-ditch holding-battle against modernism itself, we look pretty silly, constantly running up and banging into a logical wall that everybody else learned long-ago is not going to go away, then, eyes still dazed and spinning, looking about for pats on the head for our stubbornness.

The second strategic reason is, however, more important than what other critics will think of us. It can be found in McCloud's own passionate thoughts about comics. (I hope he will forgive me for extracting this bit of text from the several integral pictures which, in *Understanding Comics,* lend it an entirely different order of immediacy):

> As comics grows into the next century, creators will aspire to many higher goals than appealing to the "lowest common denominators." Ignorance and short-sighted business practices will no doubt obscure the possibilities of comics from time to time as they always have. But the truth about comics can't stay hidden from view forever, and sooner or later the truth will shine through! Today the possibilities for comics are—as they always have been—endless. Comics offers tremendous resources to *all* writers and artists: faithfulness, control, a chance to be heard far and wide without the fear of compromise . . . It offers range and versatility with all the potential imagery of film and painting plus the intimacy of the written word. And all that's needed is the desire to be heard—the will to learn—and the ability to see. (Ellipsis McCloud's.)

This man passionately desires that comics change and grow. Why should someone with such desires attempt to strait his arguments and observations of his cherished object within the restrictive wall of definition?

Won't careful analytic *description* of what is vital, intriguing, newly noticed, and wondrous about comics (what they are; how they work) finally do the job much better? Why do we need the appeal to that extra, transcendental authority of science that "definition" falsely holds out, but which, as we reach for it, finally and only betrays (and, for certain critics, confirms the truth of) our own inferiority?

Like McCloud, I too want to see comics develop and grow. Like McCloud, I think the seeds of that growth have long since been planted, have sprouted, and, throughout the history of comics, have already yielded fine harvests. But I would also like to see the criticism of comics grow up. And it will not, until it can abandon that galaxy of notions, origins, mastery, craft—and definition. It must abandon them because they represent the several smoke screens behind which false authority has always tried to hold back the development of art. Traditionally "origins" and "definition" are the two that critics have used most widely to impede artistic change: "Because you have not studied the proper origins of the genres, you don't really know what the genre is (its definition) and so are not qualified to work in it."

Two comments.

First: In the paraliterary genres we do not have *enough* critics, or a strong enough critical establishment, for this stance yet to become a real problem. But it has often functioned as a powerful stifling force in the literary and fine arts genres. But, within the dead terminology and empty concepts we can already find, here and there, in McCloud's book, the basis for the problem is already apparent, and it could easily grow into something sizable if those concepts are not clearly and repeatedly analyzed and dismissed for what they are.

A personal example: In 1995, the Museum of Modern Art invited me to write an "Introduction" to the catalogue for an upcoming exhibit, *Video Spaces,* that ran through the summer and autumn of that year, and I discovered a policy of the MOMA's Publications Department: While you can state pretty much any opinion you like, you are not allowed to make a factual statement about art or its history in a Museum publication unless you are a bona fide art critic with an advanced degree in art history. Even statements such as "van Gogh worked on *Wheatfield with Crows* only days before his suicide at the end of July 1890," verifiable from any standard biography, or "The dominant colors in *Wheatfield with Crows* are yellow and blue," verifiable by eye to anyone, are strongly discouraged unless they come from accredited historians. The Museum's editors constantly rewrite such statements from their guest writers as, "To me the main color of this painting appears to be yellow and blue," or, "I seem to remember reading somewhere that van Gogh painted this picture shortly before his death, but I can't be sure." When I asked about this, I was told: "Because this is a Museum publication, we simply can't make mistakes. So we just don't let the kind of sentences occur where factual mistakes might fall." As a nonexpert writing for MOMA, you can have an opinion about anything; but you are not qualified to state any facts—at least about art. The policy extends, incidentally, even to those MOMA curators who do not have advanced degrees and are not themselves accredited art historians. At the same time, when I was writing about science fiction, my own field of expertise, the same editors would blithely insert or subtract phrases that made the accounts of story plots or even genre history bogglingly inaccurate. Also the initial contract offered for the piece was a "work for hire" contract—which was only replaced by a better one when I pointed out the first one was illegal.

Sound familiar, guys? The point is not that MOMA is, somehow, an evil organization. Rather, the same forces are at work in both locations, producing the same results.

Second: There is an inverse of the statement from four paragraphs above: "If you *do* study the always many and complex origins of an art form, you *are* more likely to have a broader range of notions of what that art form might be (i.e., a richer set of descriptions), and thus are more likely to help it grow and change in interesting ways." This statement *is* true—while the earlier statement is false. But I would hope that we could recall our first-term logic classes: Reasoning from the inverse (or the converse) *is* false reasoning. Frankly, I think every day before breakfast every critic of the paraliterary should be obliged to copy out a dozen times:

"The 'origin' is *never* an objective reality; it is always a political construct."

"The 'origin' is *never* an objective reality; it is always a political construct."

"The 'origin' is *never* an objective reality; it is always a political construct . . ."

In the same way that origins and definitions form the usual smoke screen behind which critics hide their lack of esthetic authority, craft and mastery form the traditional smoke screen behind which producers, publishers, and, in general, people with money who have been trying to exploit art since the Renaissance up to the latest incoherently scripted 50-million-dollar blockbuster hide theirs: "He's talented, certainly. His work is very artistic. I just don't think he's mastered the craft well enough to . . ." (note: Again, here craft is being *opposed* to art) which simply means he won't do what you tell him to do because you ask him to, or because you're signing the checks.

V

As I've said, when McCloud's topics are line and its function in comics, or the galaxy of effects that line can produce (unto the colors lines can hold within the shapes they form), he is brilliant.

But because of his commitments to "origins" and "definitions," his arguments that lean on concepts of history are a maddening amalgam of truth and absurdity. The sensitive reader must go through them in full-tilt opposition to much that he says, ready to argue with him sentence by sentence.

Much of *Understanding Comics*'s chapter 5, though called "Living in Line," turns out to be about history, with a discussion of prehistoric cave drawings on page 141, hieroglyphics and Chinese characters on page 142, the development of print on page 143, and a discussion of the relation between words and pictures from the fifteenth century to the nineteenth on pages 144 and 145. On page 150, we find a bit of historical sleight of hand. To untangle it, we have to analyze both words and pictures:

Illustration #9: McCloud, page 150

The picture that the five background characters are commenting on parodies the paintings of Barcelona-born Joan Miró (1893–1983). The grouping around the painting is definitely working class, and their Philistine responses are ironized by the (hemi)head of the child (the least noticeable of the five) in the middle, declaring in his/her small balloon: "Cool." Obviously the little one will grow up to become an alternative comics artist.

Over the next five panels, McCloud tells us: "In fact, the general public's perception of 'great' art and 'great' writing hasn't changed much in 150 years,"³ whereupon he adds a footnote: "Not as much as we like to think it has, anyway."

McCloud goes on: "Any artist wishing to do great work in a medium using words and pictures will have to contend with this attitude," by which I assume he means the *incomprehensibility to the average viewer*, "in others *and* in themselves . . . because, deep down inside, many comics creators still measure art and writing by different standards and act on the faith that 'great' art and 'great' writing will combine harmoniously by virtue of quality alone. The art form of comics is many centuries old, but it's perceived as a recent invention and suffers the curse of all new media, the curse of being judged by the standards of the old" (ellipsis McCloud's). After some examples of a new medium judged by standards of an older one (writing judged as *aide de memoire*, movies judged as plays,

3. The single quotes around 'great' in McCloud above suggest that he knows, or at any rate is willing to suggest that he is aware of, how much of a revolution he is proposing. It is very likely that the idea of *great* art, as we have known it from the romantic period on, will have to be dismantled as well, if the notion of an art that allows the art work from any group, central or marginal, to be seriously considered is to prevail. In what is certainly a too-abbreviated account, the reason *The Iliad* and *The Odyssey* were assumed to be 'great' from the Renaissance on is because it was assumed, in the period c. 800 B.C. when they were written, that they were the first major pieces written for the ruling class, to celebrate the ruling class, and that the ruling class approved highly of the way they had been celebrated. The classic was, then, invented as a model to imitate. (It was assumed that the Romans had assumed the same thing, so that even the attempt to imitate the model, as the Romans had, in Virgil's *Aeneid*, was, indeed, the imitation of an already extant model of imitation—as had Dante in his *Commedia*.) Art becomes great when it becomes endowed with the national spirit, and the national spirit is one with the dominant ideology of the society. This model fell to pieces as soon as the majority of intellectuals ceased to come from the ruling classes and could start to praise art that severely criticized, rather than celebrated, the dominant ideology. The next step—and the reason why it is a revolution—is the idea of analyzing, praising, and celebrating art that simply isn't concerned with the dominant ideology, one way or the other. Through Adorno, it was assumed that all art *must* be focused there, and any art that appeared not to be was secretly, then, supporting it by covering it up. The notion that, within the realm of the esthetic, through a structure of references and ironies, art can simply be doing *something else* (Politically? Certainly. Ideologically? Inescapably. And esthetically interesting) is, I suspect, the gift—some will think it a catastrophe—the postmodern has to give.

Society itself has become too complex for the notion of a single national spirit, bodied forth in the nation's great art, to endure. If any analysis is to take place at all, intellectuals from many classes and areas must begin to look at smaller, subnational units—and that is also, and relevantly, the model for art that McCloud (I suspect) and I (definitely) are putting forward, which allows comics, as well as many, many other kinds of art, till now dismissed as marginal, to be considered in their full esthetic richness. That leaves excellent art and good art and bad art. And interesting art and uninteresting art. And, yes, the level of critical subjectivity and political bias involved in the judgments will have to be, at last, acknowledged as far higher than they have been acknowledged up till now.

TV judged as radio with pictures), McCloud concludes: "Far too many comics creators have no higher goal than to match the achievements of other media and view any chance to work in other media as a step up. And, again, as long as we view comics as a genre of writing or style of graphic art this attitude may never disappear."

Now all of this is such an intricate interweave of insight and idiocy, played out against a set of wildly inaccurate historical assumptions, I don't know whether we *can* tease out *all* its strands here. Unraveling a few, however, might be instructive.

The critical position McCloud's panel dramatizes is one tile in the larger mosaic of the populist/anti-modernist critics' argument of the thirties. The hostility of the working class and middle class to modern art on esthetic grounds is used to support these critics' disapproval of what was often, indeed, these artists' politics.

The historical view that position is based on is right there in McCloud's words, with its 150-year period without basic or fundamental change in the esthetic situation. *Understanding Comics* was written in 1992, so that 150-year period extends back to 1842—the beginnings of what, today, we call modernism, with its three continental giants, Flaubert, Baudelaire, and Wagner. (At one point in *Understanding Comics*, McCloud cites them.)

The transition between the generally figurative impressionism and post-impressionism of the 1870s through the 1890s and up to the abstraction that has come to dominate serious western art in the vast majority of its galleries and museums today (and functions as a sign of the transition between early modernism in general and High Modernism in particular) is usually ascribed to a 1904 trip Picasso took with Derain (some say Matisse) to the Trocadero, a Spanish fort just outside Paris, used at the time as an exhibition hall. That spring there was a large and impressive exhibition of African masks.

The French painters were hugely impressed by the expressive power and the sense of presence gained through the figural distortion and exaggeration in these sculptural forms. They began sending all their friends to see the exhibition as well. From this encounter of French artists with the African esthetic of "significant form" (at least that's what western critics have since called it), in the hands of Picasso, Braque, and Gris resulted in cubism, which led shortly to expressionism and the general turn of serious art to the variety of abstractions McCloud places under the rubric of "the picture plane."

Joan Miró, the painter whose work is parodied in the picture, painted in this particular style in the 1930s and 1940s. The yahoos represented in McCloud's panel evoke working-class characters from the post–World War II period in the forties and fifties—when the transition from representational to abstract had long since occurred. McCloud posits an unbroken 150-year period in which, say, the protests of the upper-middle-class Munich concertgoers in the early 1840s that Beethoven's *Ninth Symphony* was "mere noise"[4] is fundamentally the same phenomenon as the non-art-buying lower middle class's dismissal of the already 50-year-old movement toward abstraction that already dominated the world of art buyers and gallery owners in the period after World War II. But the notion that the bourgeois revolution of 1848 and the equivalent fracases over the rest of the continent in the years around it spurred no changes either in art or in the public's attitude to it would probably leave Flaubert, Baudelaire, Hugo, and Wagner, not to mention Courbet, Millais, and Daumier (all of whom lived through it, all of whose major work came after it and was often in response to it, and all of whose reputations were a direct or indirect result of it) at least a *bit* puzzled. World War I and World War II both had equally pronounced effects on art and the public.

The first thing I want to do is to abstract McCloud's specific statement about comics from all this. As far as I can tell, what he is saying is: The advent of new art (i.e., art forms that have emerged in the 150-year period when nothing changed in the audience response to new artwork) has always been decried at first by the Philistines. Because, however, comics are much older than this 150-year period and go back, rather, *thousands* of years, they should escape this Philistine response. Uninformed about their origins, however, people mistake comics for a *young* art form (i.e., *less* than 150 years old). They dismiss them in the same way as they do abstract art. Indeed, the contemporary academic's dismissal of comics is the same as the working class's mid-century dismissal of modern art—which is, in turn, the same as the haute-bourgeoisie's dismissal of Beethoven's

4. A situation which Richard Wagner, when he conducted the work in Munich in 1846 and again in 1848, overcame brilliantly by preceding the concert with extensive newspaper articles analyzing the piece and pointing out what the audience should be listening for and how the piece differed from music that had gone before, along with extensive program notes waiting for the audience at the Munich Opera House on the Easter eve performance night, and extra rehearsals to ensure that the difficult music was played particularly clearly, and even a new arrangement of the orchestra to foreground the strings and woodwinds and downplay the brasses, as well as a choir of three *hundred* (rather than the seventy-five the previous performance had used) in order to overwhelm the audience with the sheer richness of sound in the final choral movement. It worked wondrously well. For a while the *Ninth Symphony*—dismissed as "mere noise" three years before—became a concert favorite warhorse of the public that rivaled the already stunningly popular *Fifth Symphony*.

late works in the early 1840s. The way to overcome this for comics is to educate people to the age of the pedigree of comics, at which point they will start to respect them.

When it is teased out and displayed in this form, I hope the argument's errors and inconsistencies begin to appear self-evident. The dismissal of comics today has nothing to do, for example, with the presumed length (or brevity) of its historical pedigree. Films are just as much a combination of words and pictures as comics, and, in their talking form, they only go back to 1929. Since the mid-sixties, film has been acknowledged as *the* art of the twentieth century. (*Every* major museum of modern art has a film curator. *None* of them has a comics curator.) The reason comics are dismissed is that, since their beginnings *as we know them today*, in the training strips for soldiers in World War I, they have been conceived of and produced to be the art form for the young children and adolescents *of* the working class. They are academically dismissed not for the same reason the *yahoos* dismiss modern art, but for the same reason as *we* dismiss McCloud's yahoos' *disparaging comments on* Joan Miró. It is not that the working class's positive esthetic judgments are being accepted and their negative judgments being ignored (as McCloud's argument would have it). Rather *all* working-class esthetic judgments, positive *and* negative, are dismissed—because the class is presumed to be uneducated *and* uneducable. No matter whether the art is representational *or* abstract, Titian *or* Picasso, working-class viewers (as a class—so runs the prevailing wisdom) are not going to purchase any significant amount of art anyway. Who cares, then, what they think—unless, now and then, we want to appropriate their uneducated hostility briefly to resurrect a rearguard action in an already long-lost battle against modernism, its political causes mystified behind a smoke screen of esthetic questions.

This is the ugly situation that keeps comics down on the scale of esthetic value—because comics are presumed to be a working-class art form—a situation which, at this point, McCloud does more tacitly to support than articulately to demystify. (Films made it up the scale because they involved more and more money; and the fantasies connected with them frequently appealed across class lines.)

The only way to change the situation is through the education of the esthetic sensibilities and, as far as criticism goes, a clear, constant, and demystifying critique of what the actual politics of the situation are.

One of my great recent pleasures has been to lurk among the galleries of the Whitney Museum on Wednesday mornings when nineteen-, twenty-three-, and twenty-five-year-old art students take student groups from the New York City public elementary schools around to look at the paintings. The youngsters are overwhelmingly black and Hispanic—and, incidentally, working class. The art student conducting the group will often stop before one of de Kooning's swirling, abstract nudes.

"All right," the student leader will ask. "What's the first thing you notice about this picture?"

Invariably, without raising his or her hand, to be provocative some brave nine-year-old will blurt: "She's got real big *breasts* . . . !" or "tits." Or "boobs." Or "titties." From boys and girls I've heard it come out all four ways, now. The rest of the class will snicker.

But the art student (who has been here many times before) will declare, loudly, "*Yes!*—that's right!" then launch into a clear and simple discussion of sexuality and sensuality in art, from its warm and nurturing aspects to the anxieties and discomforts it causes, and even the playfulness about it, demonstrating how all three of these are figured in de Kooning's vigorous brush work . . .

Silent now, the children listen, fascinated.

And they learn.

Usually when I leave the museum, I'm in tears. Somehow to watch what a moment ago was confused, alien, and off-putting to these kids, worthy only of sniggers and laughter, open up and clarify for them, revealing the sensuous thought it represents about the world, is . . . Well, I'm afraid, that's one of my buttons. So is watching kids learn that a response that begins in derision and hostility can pierce through to something fundamental and important that can be accepted and articulately discussed. (The critic's *own* response, Walter Pater noted, was where all criticism starts. Again, to cite it here is a matter of pleasure, not authority.) I can't help it. Nor do I want to. It's probably why I'm a critic as well as a creator. And whatever historic blunders it gets snared into, McCloud's book promotes both orders of experience: I find *Understanding Comics* deeply moving because again and again it accomplishes the same order of clarification.

VI

On the bottom of page 195 of *Understanding Comics,* McCloud gives us a diagram for the communication between comics artist and audience. Any contemporary critic will find it hard not to see McCloud's diagram as resembling both the nineteenth-century Swiss-born linguist Ferdinand de Saussure's famous speech circuit and twentieth-century linguist Roman Jakobson's equally famous refinement of it.

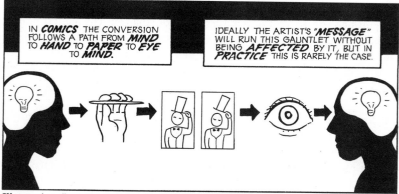

Illustration #10: Scott McCloud's communication circuit for comics (page 195)

Illustration #11: Ferdinand de Saussure's "speech circuit" from the publication of his *Course in General Linguistics*, 1916 (page 11)

```
                    CONTEXT
                  (referential)
                    MESSAGE
                    (poetic)

ADDRESSER    ——————————————————    ADDRESSEE
(emotive)                            (conative)
                    CONTACT
                    (phatic)
                     CODE
                  (metalingual)
```

Illustration #12: Roman Jakobson's language model (from *The Framework of Language*, 1980) that first appeared in 1973

McCloud follows his illustration with a statement of his own perception of his creative process. On page 169, McCloud writes:

The comics I "see" in my mind will never be seen in their entirety by anyone else, no matter how hard I try. Ask any writer, or film maker, just how much a given project truly represents what he/she envisions it to be. You'll hear twenty percent, 10 ... 5 ... few will claim more than 30. The mastery of one's medium is the degree to which that percentage can be increased, the degree to which the artist's idea survives the journey [over the communication circuit]—or, for some artists, the degree to which the inevitable detours are made useful by the artist.

If McCloud says that's how he perceives his own work (not to mention that most of the artists and writers around him also perceive it that way), I believe him.

But I mention in passing that, as a science fiction writer, I have never perceived my own writing in this manner. My own conceptions are comparatively dim, unfocused, and indistinct compared to the finished work. If the finished work doesn't strike me as a *lot* better than the conception, I'm likely to abandon it. Though I plan and outline my work as carefully as possible, in a real sense I write my novels to find out what they're actually about. The bulk of the text always strikes me as a gift from the language. As Lévi-Strauss once put it, I simply happen to be the intersection of a certain number of events which has allowed me to take a certain order of dictation.

My point is not, however, that McCloud and I perceive the creation of art in subjectively different ways. (Actually, I doubt we do.) But the creation of art has been repeatedly described in *both* ways at various times in history. For now, I'd like to look at the part these two descriptions play in the larger esthetic picture into which from time to time they're incorporated.

One might paraphrase McCloud's account: Any given art work is a fallen (or lapsed, or inadequate) version of a grander conception existing in its true form only in the artist's mind.

One might paraphrase my account: Any given art work is a creation of the language/the unconscious (which structuralist psychoanalyst Jacques Lacan said "is structured as a language")/society (among humans, societies are stabilized in their specific forms by language)/God—i.e., in all cases something other than the conscious mind. The artist is only a more or less hardworking amanuensis to this Other.

We find both descriptions from at least the Renaissance on. The poet Dante as well as many artists deeply involved with religious subject matter often described their work as dictation from an Other. (Among moderns, Yeats [and more recently Jack Spicer] is the poet most closely associated with "dictation.") Many great Renaissance painters—Leonardo, Michelangelo, Raphael—often proclaimed their work (rather, critics such as Vasari claimed it for them) inadequate representations of a greater conception.

What happens when these ideas are fitted into larger conceptual schemes? What do they imply about art and the artist? Leonardo (and other Renaissance artists) presented the world with a richly representational, highly finished, virtuoso painterly surface. Their pictures fall far to the left on the base of McCloud's triangle (see illustration #7). For many of us, such painterly techniques (until the advent of the photorealist painters in the seventies, e.g. Audrey Flack, James Valerio, and Richard Estes) *were* the left extremity of that triangle. In their representational intensity, they created awe and admiration, even among the uneducated. Now if *these* paintings were fallen, lapsed, inadequate versions of greater conceptions, then the artists themselves must have been some sort of intellectual supermen, able to conceive of visions far more intense, vivid, rich, and important than the actual paintings—and thus far more intense, vivid, and rich than ordinary human beings are capable of. This indeed fits closely with the Renaissance notion of the great painter, who was at once a philosopher and often an influential courtier/intellectual as well.

If the pictures produced by an artist are located, however, to the far *right* of McCloud's triangle, such as a panel from Chester Brown's *Yummy Fur*, or toward the upper vertex of abstraction, such as a canvas by Hans Hoffmann (the same applies to poetry where verbal skill is not foregrounded by rhyme, meter, or formal stanzaic patterns), so that, in any case, the uneducated response is likely to be some version of, "My two-year-old daughter can paint/draw (or even write) better than that," if it's claimed that *these* works are fallen, lapsed, or inadequate versions of a grander conception, the same uneducated response is likely to be: "You're darned *right* they are! He/she just doesn't know how to *draw!*" (Or paint! Or write!) Regardless of what they actually experience, artists who work at the right and upper vertices of the triangle will likely fare better in the public mind if they espouse some form of the esthetics of dictation: "I did it that way because that's how I received it from the language/the unconscious/society/God. I find it just as surprising and unusual" (and, of course, rich, provocative, and fascinating) "as you do." (Easily this could be a paraphrase of Robert Rauschenberg.)

The esthetic of lapsed or fallen conception tends to separate the artist off from society and posits him or her as intellectual superman. At the same time, it urges the artist toward a glitzy, virtuoso, but (by contemporary esthetic standards) conservative esthetic surface, which must constantly awe the general public.

The esthetic of dictation from an Other tends to democratize the artist, making her or him just another human being, who happens to have a line to the unknown. At the same time, it encourages variation, experimentation, a less virtuoso esthetic surface, a less conservative esthetic, and more acceptance of a greater range of concepts and techniques.

Till now I have purposely stayed away from engaging with McCloud's opening chapter, "Setting the Record Straight," where he presents his definition of comics and discusses what he takes to be their privileged origins among Mayan and Egyptian boustrophedon picture writing, Queen Margaret's Bayeux Tapestry, *The Torture of St. Erasmus* (c. 1460), Hogarth's engraving portfolios of the 1730s (*A Harlot's Progress, The Rake's Progress*), Rudolphe Töpffer's cartoons from the mid-nineteenth century, Frans Masereel's (*Passionate Journey*, 1919) and Lynd Ward's (*God's Man*, 1929) narrative books of woodcuts, and Max Ernst's surreal collage novel, *A Week of Kindness*. Nor will I engage it directly here. In a paraliterary context to say in any way that I believe his definition to be wrong is to suggest that—somewhere—I think there's a better one.

I don't.

My feeling about his discussion of origins is this: I see nothing wrong with comics artists or comics readers looking at or studying as many works of art or historical documents as they want. And if they choose to study them because they have found—or find in them, after they have chosen to study them—similarities to comics, well and good. They should talk about them—and publicize them.

But I believe that, lacking historical evidence of influence, critics must take the relationship between these historical texts and any given modern comics work as exactly the same as the one I set out between McCloud's own *Understanding Comics* and Longinus's περὶ ὕψους. To reiterate: It is a relation that, in the recognition of similarities, can generate great reading pleasure, richness, and resonance. But it is not a relation in which the earlier work lends force, quality, or some other transcendental authority to the latter.

McCloud's argument finally leads to a dismissal of the idea of genre. As I have already quoted: ". . . as long as we view comics as a genre of writing or a style of graphic art this attitude may never disappear," though I hope I have demonstrated that it is the clinging to notions such as "definition" that fosters the reduced and deadening notion of genre for the paraliterary that McCloud wants to escape.

It might be appropriate for me to describe, then (I hope I no longer have to insist, each time I use the word, that—again—I *don't* mean "define"), what I mean when I use the term genre: I mean a collection of texts that are generally thought similar enough so that, largely through an unspecified combination of social forces (they are sold from the same bookshelves in bookstores, they are published by the same publishers, they are liked by the same readers, written by the same writers, share in a range of subject matters, etc.), most people will not require historical evidence to verify that a writer, producing one of those texts, has read others of the group written up to that date. Thus, when E. C. Bentley wrote *Trent's Last Case*, we can assume he had read other English mysteries, without turning to Dorothy Sayers's well-known introduction where she declares Bentley's intent and influences. ("He was sick to death of the 'infallible sleuth' and meant to show him up for what he was." In such a sentence, "infallible sleuth" is a metonym for the assumption of general reading among texts perceived at the time as mysteries.) When Shakespeare wrote his *Sonnets*, we can generally assume without specific historical evidence that he had read other texts of metered lines with (often) end rhymes at the breaks. If I say that the mystery or that poetry is a genre, *that's* what I mean. I use the term as a virtual synonym for a recognizable (not definable) practice of writing. As such, I find it useful and more or less innocuous. Indeed, the notion that writing exists without such perceivable categories strikes me as counterintuitive. Thus, for me, literature is as much a collection of genres as is paraliterature. Though I've encountered a number of arguments against other uses of the term genre (and even, from time to time, accepted them more or less temporarily), I have not yet found an argument that's convinced me my intuitions are, in this case, wrong.

VII

While the academics who had come to popular culture in the thirties were comparatively radical, the academics who first came to the paraliterary genres, specifically science fiction, in the late 1950s (the critical journal *Extrapolation* was founded in 1958) were, paradoxically, comparatively conservative—even though they held many of the same ideas. What made them conservative was the changes that had occurred in the greater field of literary studies around them, the ascendancy of New Criticism, and, a decade later, the influx of continental ideas. Much of what was new and forward-looking in the thirties had been, by the late fifties and sixties, played out.

The academics who entered the field of science fiction in the late fifties and the early sixties loved the genre. But they felt that their major task was to legitimate it in the face of a larger academic situation that still dismissed most working-class art—*not* like McCloud's working-class yahoos dismiss modern art, but the way academics who did not love them and didn't see anything of interest in them dismiss comics. Umberto

Eco, a first-rate scholar whose 1962 essay *"Il mitto di Superman e la dissolu-zione del tempo"* ("The Myth of Superman" in *The Role of the Reader*, by Umberto Eco, Indiana University Press, Bloomington, 1979) is a fine piece of work on a comic book (nowhere in it does it define *anything*), tells an anecdote, which I reconstruct from brief notes and memory, about presenting the piece in translation at a Modern Language Association meeting, a year or so before it was published in Italian. "I was a very proper young scholar in those days, whose field was medieval Latin. The way I prepared for 'The Myth of Superman' was the way I would prepare, however, for any other scholarly paper: In this case, I read all the *Superman* comics ever published—it took me a couple of years. When I showed up at the MLA to give my paper, I arrived with a stack of seventy-five or a hundred of what I thought were the most interesting issues. When I walked in carrying them, people really looked at me as though I were crazy! I couldn't understand it. I kept on trying to figure out what it was I had done wrong . . ."

From time to time, forward-looking critics have involved themselves in the field. Usually, however, they don't stay long. Possibly the reason they've left is because they did not find a *tabula rasa* waiting for the newest critical approaches, but rather an insular field in which all these mummified half-ideas, ill understood—about origins, definitions, mastery, and craft—were in circulation as though they had life and value.

On the one hand, the academics who have given a good deal of their intellectual life to science fiction must be commended for putting up with a lack of understanding from their fellows. On the other hand, there are still forces at work that make the field of science fiction scholarship a haven for—while I will not call it the second rate, nevertheless I will say—critical notions that would be laughed off the floor by a first-rate collection of literary scholars.

Whether it is "in-house" SF critic Darrell Schweitzer writing in a seventies fanzine article that Henry James "had an absolutely tin ear for language, and few people have been able to finish his novels" (in a paragraph that goes on to dismiss *Finnegans Wake* as "unreadable" and "dull") or it is tenured English professor David Samuelson, a regular contributor to *Science Fiction Studies*, commenting in a recent *Chronicle of Higher Education* article on yours truly, that "James Joyce took an awful long time to become popular—if he even is now" (in a paragraph in which he goes on to suggest contemporary literary theory is unreadable), regardless of what the immediate motivations of either man were, you can still hear, behind both, the ghosts of the thirties populist argument against modernism—a battle that, as I've said, was lost forty years ago and which, frankly, it's simply silly to go on grumbling about.

Yes, either by modern standards *or* the standards of their times, the politics of many of the modernist giants was appalling. But so were the politics of Jane Austen and Charles Dickens and Percy Bysshe Shelley and (for all her admirable feminism) Virginia Woolf. And in ten, or thirty-five, or eighty-five years, so will be the politics of Anne Beattie, Don DeLillo, Jayne Ann Philips, Richard Powers, Jori Graham, and William T. Vollman. Doubtless so will be mine and McCloud's. The way critics have traditionally dealt with this problem since the academization of literature shortly after World War I (which, for many people, means the invention of literature as we know it today) is by a critical move that McCloud knows well. Indeed, it is necessary for anyone who loves the potential of a genre but wants to see it develop, change, and grow. I have quoted it once. I shall quote it again:

Illustration #13: McCloud, page 199

The division of content from form is a necessary (but only provisional) critical fiction. The reason it is only provisional is because, at a certain point in the discussion, form begins to function as content—and content often functions as a sign for the implied form with which that content is conventionally dealt. If the critic chooses to focus his or her observations in *this* delicate area for any length of time, the separation of form and content, so useful in other situations, ends up creating more problems than it solves. While an analysis of form apart from content may be *necessary* for criticism, certainly it is not *sufficient*—neither sufficient to distinguish criticism from what is not criticism nor sufficient to distinguish good criticism from bad. Nevertheless, because of the way so much criticism has gone since the New Criticism, it has become, at least in certain circles, a truism for the last forty years: To be a critic one *must* be a formalist.

But return a moment to the critics who entered SF early in the burgeoning of academic interest in "popular culture" during the late fifties and sixties. In 1968 I was invited to give my first presentation at the MLA Christmas meeting in New York City to the Continuing Seminar on Science Fiction (the second oldest continuing seminar in the organization, at that time). When I found the hotel room in which the seminar was meeting, a modest thirty or thirty-five people filled it. The familiar faces were Joanna Russ, Frederik Pohl, Professor Thomas Clareson (who'd invited me to speak), and a couple of fans. Most of the rest—the academics—were strangers. In the milling period before my talk, Clareson pointed out another professor: "That's Darko Suvin—from McGill. Really, he's very sharp." My presentation was an early version of a paper that would eventually be titled "About 5,750 Words." After I'd read it, immediately the pleasantly portly, affable-looking Suvin (he was perhaps a decade older than I) threw up his hand for a question. I called on him. Rearing back in his chair, he said: "I very much enjoyed your presentation, but . . ." here he paused significantly, "I think I disagree with everything you said." Laughter rolled through the room, then stilled. For a moment, I was disconcerted. (It was my *first* academic presentation. I was *only* twenty-six . . .) Suvin went on to make a tiny point, referring to the last sentence or two of my paper, that, really, contained no disagreement at all with anything. I could only assume that he'd seen my confusion and had decided to be kind, rather than present the full battery of his undoubtedly sharp disagreements.

Some years later, Suvin published a widely read volume, *The Metamorphoses of Science Fiction* (1977). In its opening pages, it states that no area of literature can be discussed unless it is first defined, then goes on to propose (as locating its "necessary and sufficient conditions") a definition of science fiction: Science fiction is the literature of cognition and estrangement. Because of the appeal to necessary and sufficient conditions, we must read definition here in the strict, rigorous, and limited sense.

Now, when applied one way, cognition and estrangement produce surrealism about science; when applied another way, they produce fantasies about science; when applied still another, they produce historical fiction about science. A little thought will come up with several others—though any one explodes its aspirations to definitional rigor. Suvin's book was widely discussed for a time and is still, now and again, referred to.

Today my reaction to this type of demand for definition is probably hyperbolic. Turning a book that begins like that loose in the paraliterary communities is the equivalent of telling children that the only way to discuss politics properly is first, before you make any statement whatsoever, to fling up your right hand and shout "Heil Hitler!" These young people may not even know who Hitler was. Some may even have fine and important things to say about a variety of political situations. But as they move out into and through our current world, they are not likely to get much of a hearing. At worst, they will be discussed as nut cases or neo-Nazis. At best, they are going to be thought . . . strange. And they will continue to be thought strange until they abandon what they have been told is "proper"—or until someone takes them aside and tells them to cut it out. When your behavior is strange enough, however, people do *not* take you aside and tell you. Rather, they leave you alone and go off to associate with more civilized people. Finally, all the "Heil Hitler!" people can do is talk to one another.

That strikes me as about how the paraliterary mania for always starting with a "definition" registers today in the larger field of literary theory.

The assertion that you cannot discuss any topic in literary studies until you have defined it is both practically and theoretically untrue—a lie, if you will, and a lie (I hope I've made it clear) associated with a particular critical agenda from the thirties (though Suvin's book appeared in the seventies).

My anecdote, however, is not done.

Ten years later, in 1978, I was no longer a twenty-six-year-old first-time presenter at the MLA; I was a thirty-six-year-old Senior Fellow at a major research institution, the Center for 20th Century Studies at the University of Wisconsin. Annually, the Center hosts a large conference in which often upwards of a hundred scholars participate. That year's conference topic was Technology and Imagination.

Darko Suvin attended.

He was giving two presentations, one on science fiction and one on his central field of scholarly concern, the German playwright Bertolt Brecht. The Brecht session came first.

After Suvin was introduced, I found myself listening to a jejune explanation of the fact that when Brecht, in his writings on theater, used the term "alienation," he meant a positive audience reaction, in which the audience distances itself emotionally from what's going on on stage so that it can better grasp the abstract *ideas* the play is putting forth, and that this alienation is encouraged by various "epic" staging techniques and stylization in the writing; and—this was a completely different meaning from Marx's use of the term, "alienation," which meant the situation in which workers had little or nothing to do with what they were producing, or with fundamental human tasks such as growing food, building shelter, and the like. While I sat there, thinking I'd never discussed either topic with anyone over seventeen who'd ever *confused* the two before, a young German scholar at the Center sitting next to me, a Junior Fellow at the time, Andreas Huyssen, leaned toward me and whispered, somewhat, I think, in awe: "That man is a *fool* . . . !"

Later, in the science fiction session, when a young woman finished giving her presentation (whether it was good or bad, I don't recall) and she asked for questions, Darko's hand was the first to go up. She called on him. Darko reared back in his chair: "I rather enjoyed your presentation. But . . ." and here he paused meaningfully: "I think I disagree with everything you said." Laughter bloomed throughout the room. The young woman looked momentarily flustered—then smiled. Darko went on to make a minuscule point, which only pertained, if it pertained at all, to her paper's last sentence or two. And I understood, then, ten years later, that he was not being kind. Rather, he hadn't bothered to follow the presentation at all. His "question" was a purely comic gesture, designed to entertain the audience, without any intellectual weight whatsoever.

My overall point?

Despite Huyssen's wondering comment, Darko Suvin is *not* a fool.

But though, as he delivered it that day, his Brecht paper might have been informative to undergraduates or to people for whom Brecht was a brand new name, it *was* a foolish paper to deliver to a room full of literary scholars. If he thought that the majority of people in the room would not recognize it as foolish (or if he assumed that most would pay as little attention to his presentation as I now knew he had paid to two others on at least two occasions, so that it did not matter *what* he said), he was mistaken.

The opening assertion in *The Metamorphoses of Science Fiction* on the necessity of "definition" is also mistaken. (It helps to describe things so that people can recognize them; but that's a provisional task, and not definition.) Over the years, I have had many interesting discussions with Darko about science fiction and other topics. As intelligent as he is, however, I can say that he is not particularly attracted to what I feel are the most pressing questions in SF scholarship. Doubtless he would say the same about me.

Finally, however, each of us must decide whether these incidents represent a failure of sensibility or of intellect. The fact is, it's the rare academic who reaches the age of fifty who lacks for bizarre tales. The creators of paraliterature, for all our professed hostility to mainstream critics, are usually flattered by the advent of academic faces. But while it is by no means a general law, it's the case often enough to note: The academics who enter the field of science fiction studies are not necessarily of the first order, even when, in our little pond, they occasionally make a sizable splash. It goes along with their tendency to be mired in outmoded critical concepts.

The most important triumph of the "origin" in SF studies of the last twenty-five years is the sedimentation of Brian Aldiss's proposal that Mary Shelley's *Frankenstein, or, A Modern Prometheus* is the first science fiction novel.

Science fiction writers are as odd and eccentric a lot of readers as any other writers. They have been proposing origins for our genre since the late thirties, when the game of origin hunting became important to the early critics first interested in contemporary popular culture. The various proposals made over the years are legion: Wells, Verne, and Poe, in that order, have the most backers. There were more eccentric ones (my personal favorite is Edward Sylvester Ellis's *The Steam Man of the Prairies*, a dime novel from 1865, whose fifteen-year-old inventor hero builds a ten-foot steam-powered robot, who can pull a horseless carriage along behind him at nearly sixty miles an hour. Out in the Wild West, with a gold miner and an old hunter as sidekicks, they kill *lots* of Indians), and more conservative ones (Francis Bacon's *The New Atlantis*, 1629; Johannes Kepler's *Somnium* [written 1609, published 1634]; Savinien Cyrano's [de Bergerac] *Voyage to the Moon* and *The States and Empires of the Sun* [c. 1650]), and slightly loopy ones (Shakespeare's *Tempest;* Dante's *Commedia*), and some classical ones (Lucian of Samosata's *True History*, from the second century A.D., which recounts a voyage to the moon). There were also backers for Wilkins's *Discovery of a World in the Moon* (1683), as well as Gabriel Daniel's *Voyage to the World of Cartesius* (1692, revised 1703), Jonathan Swift's *Gulliver's Travels* (1726), Daniel Defoe's *The Consolidator* (1750) and—again back on our side of Shelley—Edward Bellamy's *Looking Backward* (1888).

When Brian Aldiss's history of science fiction, *Billion Year Spree: The True History of Science Fiction*, first appeared from Doubleday in 1973 (from page one of Chapter One: "As a preliminary, we need a definition of science fiction . . ."), one might have assumed that the argument filling its opening chapter, proposing *Frankenstein* as our new privileged origin, was another eccentric suggestion among many—and would be paid about as much attention to as any of these others. The irony of Aldiss's subtitle has been noted by at least one critic.[5]

5. "[A] witty, ironic, iconoclastic knowledgeable history of the field that promulgates the theory that Mary Shelley's *Frankenstein*, rather than the works of Poe or Verne, is the first true work of SF, in part because it . . . leads up to him and his friends. The revised and expanded edition (*Trillion Year Spree*) is augmented by many plot summaries but drops the ironic subtitle . . ." (David G. Hartwell, *Age of Wonders*, Tor, 1996).

(If *Frankenstein were* the first SF novel, isn't it interesting nobody noticed it until 1973, while so many people were digging around for so many years among all those other more obscure titles . . . ?)

The problem with all these "origins" of science fiction, even the ones from early scientists such as Kepler, is that, when you read them, they don't *feel* like science fiction. They feel like moral or political parables in which the writer doesn't expect you to take the science even as seriously as you have to take Buck Rogers' force fields and ray guns.

Aldiss argues that there *are* serious scientific ideas in eighteen-year-old Mary's novel, but they're not easily detectable by the modern reader. Claims Aldiss, they come from, among others, Erasmus Darwin (1731–1802), grandfather of Charles. A doctor and eccentric inventor, Erasmus designed a rocket to be powered by hydrogen and oxygen and wrote a long poetic tract, *Zoonomia,* published in two volumes in 1794 (the year Mary's father published his influential novel *Caleb Williams* and Anne Radcliffe published *The Mysteries of Udolfo; Zoonomia* also fascinated the young German writer Novalis) and (posthumously in 1803) a volume called *The Temple of Nature,* in both of which he presented some ideas not wholly unrelated to his grandson's, which may even have got his grandson thinking in the direction that led to the theory of natural selection. According to Aldiss, Mary took them in, along with the ideas from Humphrey Davy, Joseph Priestley, John Locke, and Condillac to give them back to us in *Frankenstein.*

To give Aldiss his due, other than in the title of his chapter ("The Origin of Species"), he does not use the word "origin" in connection with *Frankenstein* in the body of his actual argument. But in the Introduction to the 1986 revision and enlargement of his book *Trillion Year Spree,* he writes:

[O]ne must stand by one's beliefs.

Foremost among these beliefs is a certainty about the origins of SF. Of course it is a Stone Age truth to say that SF began with Mary Shelley's *Frankenstein* (1818). [One assumes that by "Stone Age," he means 1973 when he'd first proposed the idea, thirteen years before.] The more we know, the less certain we can be about origins. [That incongruous admission is the *starting* point of the poststructuralist argument against privileged origins.] The date of the Renaissance becomes less clear decade by decade as research goes on.

Nevertheless, bearing in mind that no genre is pure [another truism of literary theory that had entered Aldiss's argument over the intervening thirteen years], *Frankenstein* is more than a merely convenient place at which to begin the story. Behind it lie other traditions, like broken skeletons, classical myth, a continent full of *Märchen* tales. But Mary's novel betokens an inescapable new perception of mankind's capabilities, as is argued in Chapter One. (18)

There you have his commitment to origins.

I'm sorry. *Anywhere* we begin such a critical story is *always* only more or less convenient. That convenience is determined by what we wish to highlight—or, indeed, wish to cover up.

A careful reading of Aldiss's argument suggests that the "inescapable new perception of mankind" was actually all over the place at the end of the eighteenth century, among people like Erasmus Darwin and others. Mary only reflects it in her novel—which seems to defeat his own claim for her originary newness.

But the main problem with *Frankenstein* as an SF origin is simply that, when you read it, it doesn't *feel* like science fiction any more than the others cited above. In this case, it feels like an early nineteenth century take on the gothic novel, much closer to Matthew Lewis's *The Monk* (1796) and the novels of Mrs. Radcliffe—which were, incidentally, among the novels that Mary read before she wrote her own most widely known work.

My favorite discussion of *Frankenstein* is in Chris Baldick's *In the Shadow of Frankenstein's Monster* (Oxford: Clarendon Press, 1987), which examines the general use of the metaphor of monsters and the monstrous to characterize the working classes between the French Revolution and the 1830s. He relates his examination closely to the scientific *and* political ideas current at the time. As he spells it out, that relation is just not the same as we are used to in what most people today recognize as science fiction. The more one reads about *Frankenstein*, the *less* it feels like a science fiction novel. In his Introduction, Baldick remarks, "I have read that *Frankenstein* is supposed to be the first science fiction novel." In that "supposed," it's not hard to hear a politely disingenuous bemusement.

The academics (and/or science fiction writers) who have accepted the notion of *Frankenstein* as our most recent origin story are not the ones who have gone back and specifically reread Shelley's novel (or E. Darwin's poem) in order to assess Aldiss's argument. Those who do, such as David Ketterer, tend to come down on the other side of the fence.

What contributed more than anything to the acceptance of Aldiss's proposition, however, was a general situation among university critics in the early seventies. Fresh after the triumph of the Johns Hopkins Seminars of 1966–68 on the human sciences, during those years structuralism (aka literary theory) was starting its embattled journey along American university hallways. If literary theory *had* a battle cry at that time, it was: "The origin is *always* a political construct . . ." Many academics felt radically threatened by the Gallic incursion. Still smarting from the New Criticism, too often many thematic critics saw their fundamental job as the tracing of themes "back to their origins." The assumption had been that those origins were not political constructs, changing when one's politics changed, but objective value-free facts. Now this entire plank in literary criticism's platform was being splintered.

In the midst of this ferment, Aldiss proposed his new origin for science fiction. Aldiss was English. Aldiss's argument was reasonably put. At the same time, if you didn't read it closely, it even seemed to exhibit some feminist sympathy—Mary was a woman, after all.

There isn't much, however, if you read the argument carefully. All the elements that figure in the originary importance of *Frankenstein* for science fiction pass from (Erasmus) Darwin and others, through a more or less transparent Mary, to her text; though today most of the people who cite *Frankenstein* as an origin of science fiction have forgotten the pivotal part played by the Darwin connection and her other male progenitors— if they ever knew they existed.

Frankenstein's originary place in the history of SF may be a cherished belief for Aldiss. But to most academics who saw their own fields of literary study rocked by the advent of theory, it was a weighty sandbag on a breakwater against the rising theoretical tide. For the rest, they tended to accept the argument simply because it received a certain amount of attention from these others. Among writers and those not directly concerned with the theoretical debates, there was still a vague presentiment that such singular origins somehow authorized and legitimated a contemporary practice of writing, or that its feminist implications made it attractive.

The way that, since 1973, the anti-theory forces in science fiction scholarship have taken up Aldiss's proposal, along with the "feminist" aspect of the choice (if anything, Aldiss's actual argument does not allow Mary to be the agent of anything significant to SF in her own book, other than that she had the vaguely a-specific genius to put them in a novel), only seems to have proved the truth of the insight that so upset them: "The origin is *always* a political construct." Certainly this one is—as much as the campaign platform of any current political candidate.

What it masks is the situation I've tried to uncover here.

As I do from McCloud's, I welcome the discussion of any aspects of science fiction Aldiss's "definition" highlights, though I insist on calling it a description. ("Science fiction is the search for a definition of man and his status in the universe which will stand in our advanced but confused state of knowledge [science], and is characteristically cast in the Gothic or post-Gothic mode" [Aldiss, 25]; "**com-ics** (kom'iks) **n.** plural in form, used with a singular verb. **1.** Juxtaposed pictorial and other images in deliberate sequence, intended to convey information and/or to produce an aesthetic response in the viewer" [McCloud, 9].) With both McCloud and Aldiss I object only to their attempt to appropriate a position of mastery for those more or less interesting descriptions by claiming for them the authority *of* definitions. It would be unfair not to point out, however, that even Aldiss's commitment to the idea of origins is loosening ("The more we know, the less certain we can be about origins. The date of the Renaissance becomes less clear decade by decade as research goes on . . ." [Aldiss, 18]). There is a playfully self-subversive circularity in that Aldiss's "definition" is a search for a "definition"; and McCloud, before the problem of whether or not cartoons can be called comics art, is willing to allow his own definition to begin deconstructing itself:

Illustration #14: McCloud, page 21

This essay is definitely not intended to fulfill the place of the book McCloud proposes. Rather than validating the *system* of definition by posing one the "opposite" of McCloud's, I would like to step into a different system entirely of intellectual reading pleasure (and power—though we have not yet discussed that directly); and I would like to shrug off the system of authority (the acknowledged claim to power, whether or not power is actually there), purely through generational ties, marked and straited by definition, mastery, and origins.

The pleasure and insight to be gained from formally comparing *Frankenstein* (or Mayan picture writing), either text or context, to any number of modern science fiction (or current comic book) texts or contexts is a pleasure I begrudge no one. (If Aldiss could see his way to comparing *Frankenstein* to a *specific* novel, I think his argument would have been far richer, if not more pleasurable.) I object only to the assumption of the transfer of some transcendental generational force between the two if they can be linked in a familial and genetic (cognate, after all, with genre) relationship.

It is not the concept of category, as carried by the metaphors of family and of genre, that I object to. It is rather the imposition of family values, if you will, that bear the brunt of my critique: the assumption that family or genre members must submit to these generational relations, in a field of fixed authoritative forces. The fixing of relations of reading pleasure and descriptive delirium within a critical oedipal esthetic, conscious or unconscious, too frequently leads to violent exclusions and stasis, when, for the health of the paraliterary genres, those relations should be placed in positions of confidence to welcome and celebrate.

If we read Aldiss's definition of science fiction in the context of the ironies he imbeds it in, if we read McCloud's definition of comics in the context of the restrictions he places around it, we see each writer indicating where his own definition breaks down. From the texts alone it is undecidable whether these self-subversions are more profitably read as reservations only for the specific definition, or whether they sign a more meaningful reservation with the overall system of definition that straits so much of the paraliterary critical enterprise. But if we then turn from these particular self-crippled definitional projects to the discussion each writer mounts under the concept of origins, it's hard not to hear as an originary impulse behind both: "These things are like comics—these like SF. Because their similarities produce a surge of pleasure, I want to write of them."

Above and beyond the insights the comparisons generate, the considerations of these similarities may even provoke belief—a belief the writer comes to cherish—in some vision of the way the world is, was, or should be. If we can find internal and external evidence connecting one of these early texts and one of the later, we can even posit influences.

We *still* don't need a shared identity.

(There is both internal and external evidence for the influence of Joyce's *Portrait of the Artist* [1914] and *Ulysses* [1922] on Bester's *The Stars My Destination* [1956], and of Huysmans's *À Rebours* [1884] on [again Bester's] "Hell is Forever" [1942]: but are these influences—or the evidence for them—less meaningful because neither Huysmans nor Joyce wrote science fiction?)

Often, however, certain of our discussions are straited by a fear that without the authoritative appeal to origins and definitions as emblems of some fancied critical mastery, our observations and insights will not be welcomed, will not be taken for the celebrational pleasure that they are. What can I say, other than that we need more confidence in the validity of our own enterprise?

I am not suggesting that by changing a few rhetorical figures old-style criticism will be automatically rendered new and modern. The rhetorical traces I cite are, in themselves, traces of a discourse—a discourse whose hold on the range of paraliterary criticism, I hope I have shown, is neither inconsequential, nor innocent, nor simple. The argument between McCloud and me over his view of the history of the genre represents a conflict of *two* discourses, one of which (mine) is posited on respect for, and celebration of, difference, and one of which (McCloud's) turns on the dignity of, and, on some essential level, the identity of, the same.

To give an admittedly unsympathetic portrayal, however, of what I take to be the discourse McCloud inhabits, it might be exemplified thus: The Greeks of the fifth century B.C. represented a peak of civilization. We represent a peak of civilization. Thus, because there is an essential identity between the two cultures, the Greek myths can be made to stand in for the Christian karygma. Presented as such, this would probably strike most of us as hugely arrogant. But at the end of the eighteenth century and the beginning of the nineteenth, out of this discourse grew some extraordinary works, e.g., Hölderlin's poem *Brot und Wein* (1803). The way in which this and similar works organize the perceived correspondences between karygma and myth was intended to produce mystical awe. It was assumed in the time when this discourse was a living and vital one that these correspondences functioned as conduits of power, authority, greatness, and that it was the recognition of these power correspondences that produced the pleasure. Our generation has to be satisfied with the pleasure for its own sake.

McCloud's 150 years when nothing changed or the identity he finds between Egyptian picture writing and comics is precisely the sort of conceptual offspring the traces of such a discourse still produce today. They attempt to operate in much the same way as Hölderlin's continuity between fifth century Greece and turn-of-the-(eighteenth-)century Germany. It is a venerable tradition and it has organized much beauty. But with *Ulysses*, as well as the French explosion of comic plays and novels on Greek themes—Cocteau's *La Machine infernal* (1934) and *Orphée* (1925), Sartre's *Les Mouche* (1943), Giradeaux's *Elpénor* (1919), *Amphytrion-38* (1929), and *Le Guerre le Trois n'aura pas lieu* (1935), and Gide's *Œdipe* (1931)—from the twenties through the forties, such correspondences became a site of bathos, opening up the possibility for difference (similarities were sought out precisely to mark a field in which difference could be subsequently inscribed), and the relation was ironized precisely to highlight these differences, so that the Greek parallels critique the modern (as well as the discourse that preceded it) in a way they could never do in Hölderlin.

At the level of the signifier, the way to effect the transition between discourses is, yes, a matter of rhetoric. At the level of the signified, however, the only way to effect it is to do some serious thinking about the respective priorities of pleasure and authority in our current critical undertakings. We must be willing to understand how cleaving to a certain dead rhetoric forces us to go on repeating empty critical rituals associated with past authority and perpetuating the anxiety that what we take pleasure in will not be sufficiently welcomed, the two interacting in a way that does not overcome the problem but only produces a self-fulfilling prophecy.

To all our critics, I offer the assurance: Vision, history, belief, as well as the operationalism of the sciences are all welcome in contemporary criticism. All they require is that, with enthusiasm and intelligence, you have something to say and can put it with grace and insight. And in Aldiss and McCloud, enthusiasm, intelligence, grace, and insight abound. But the thirties' pseudoscientific argumentative form (start with a definition, then go on to origins) is unnecessary and insufficient for criticism today, literary or paraliterary.

Let's lose it.

— New York City & Wellfleet
August 1996

12

Zelazny/Varley/Gibson—and Quality

This essay grows largely from my efforts over the last four years to develop, teach, and refine a course called "Introduction to Science Fiction"
at the University of Massachusetts at Amherst. The notion behind the
course is simply that, today, in 1992, science fiction is such a broad field
that the idea of "introducing" it over fourteen weeks to a group of readers largely unacquainted with it, who will listen to two weekly lectures
and read the equivalent of only some twelve to fourteen books, is simply
impossible—if we try to select readings according to any sophisticated
notion of historical development or any reasonably representative survey of SF themes. Thus, as I explain to my students in the first lecture, if
they come to the SF field as readers more or less unfamiliar with the
genre—and most of them do—it is precisely those SF writers who are
more or less well-known—at least as names—outside the field (e.g.,
Bradbury, Heinlein, Asimov, Clarke, Le Guin, Dick) that we will *not* be
reading in the course.

These are the writers that the general social workings of popularity
and fame have already managed to "introduce" to most people. These
are the writers who, as curious readers, my students are most likely to
pick up on their own and read—and even enjoy. And though students
can all profit from informed study and a more sophisticated understanding of the SF context in which each wrote or writes, it seems unnecessary
to spend an introductory course on them. Instead, we use the course to
read works of writers most of my class will not have heard of before. The
writers we read are writers to whom they can only be introduced by someone knowledgeable in the breadth and history of the SF world. And I
only hope that the things I can add in terms of context will be of use
should their reading then move, on its own, either to more widely known
SF writers (which is likely) or on to SF writers even less well-known in the
SF world than these (which will be a rarer occurrence, but is certainly a
possibility).

Once we have gotten through the barrier of accessibility, my selection is based wholly on a notion of quality. Quality as I present the idea is not an unanalyzable absolute. Quality has to do with a tension between richness and simplicity, as well as the good old fashioned notions of truth and beauty; above all, it is a social construct that exists as a recognizable aspect of any art only through the interrogations and disagreements of educated minds in argument—in short it functions as a process, not a thing. (It is not a consensual construct, but a conflictual one; though it requires an educated, passionate field for that conflict to be at all productive.)

The course is organized as a series of longer and shorter units, some two weeks long, some three. Each term I select between five and six of these units, out of a possible eight—enough to fill up fourteen weeks. There is a two-week short story unit, using two stories apiece by Lucius Shepard, Octavia Butler, and Greg Bear. There is another story unit of three weeks that utilizes two or three stories apiece by Roger Zelazny, John Varley, and William Gibson. Various other units are organized around single writers, usually comprising at least two novels and a handful of stories of each, including Theodore Sturgeon, Alfred Bester, Thomas Disch, Joanna Russ, Algis Budrys, and Barry Malzberg. Much of the material in the following pages is material used to introduce the Zelazny, Varley, Gibson unit.

For many years, I've listened to people—but especially people in the science fiction world of readers and writers—declare that they are not so much interested in "writing" as in "story"—a notion closely connected with that of "craft" and somehow, at least in the minds of the readers who declare it, one that sits in uneasy relation to "art." Stuck with the truism that there's no way to acquire a story off a written page without the medium of language—language, moreover, somebody else has written—finally I find myself having to say that to be concerned with story and not with writing is willfully to ignore what is doing the actual work. And to pursue craft without art is to pursue only those areas of art that produce no problems, contradictions, or tensions between the material and its execution. It is to pursue only that part of art where no risk is perceived, either in terms of politics or aesthetics.

There are readers and writers who are, nevertheless, comfortable reading—and writing—wholly within this discourse of story and craft. But my own analysis marks me as clearly and committedly uncomfortable with it; and definitely outside their number. Some of you will have already figured out what I am saying in effect is that, in terms of a writerly ontology, I don't even believe "story" exists—except as a convenient way to talk about an effect of writing; whereas readers and writers who are comfortable in that discourse are content with a concept of "writing" that makes it one with a notion of "style," which they see as a variable aspect, like color, of a solid, visible, and locatable entity called a story. Whereas for me, words are the solid and locatable elements in a text, and meaning, story, style, and tone are all shifting and flickering aspects to various combinations of words that are, all of them, equally evanescent and intangible, intricately interrelated and inextricable—analyzable yes, but never simple or exhaustible.

Ever since the early days of science fiction in the pulp magazines of the thirties, there have been writers who have achieved a certain order of intense popularity—one that, to my mind, simply cannot be explained with anything like elegance using only the discourse of story and craft. Often the rhetoric that grows up around them suggests the craft/story ontology. But I want to talk about some of these writers in terms that make sense to me. To do so, I will eventually have to talk in some detail about that term that is even more troubling in a populist discourse where "craft" and "art" are allowed to wrangle and "story" and "writing" to dialogize: And this is the aforementioned notion of "quality."

The term is common to the rhetoric of both discourses—but within each it means a very different thing. In the discourse of craft and story, it refers to an important, presumably visible, and locatable aspect that is one with what is good—by consensus—in a good story. But in the discourse of "art" and "writing," quality is not a consensus entity at all; once again, it is a social construct that comes into being through the *conflict* among educated minds.

What Roger Zelazny, John Varley, and William Gibson share as writers is the extraordinary degree to which each, respectively in the sixties, seventies, and eighties, excited the science fiction community of readers, writers, and committed fans.

To speak of "the science fiction community" is to speak of a reading and writing community that, while it numbers in the thousands, is still small enough so that sales or mass popularity is not the only factor broadly meaningful to a writer's reputation. In that community, quality of writing is still—sometimes—capable of generating more excitement than simple ubiquity of copies spread about, which is finally what sales alone mean.

Prefatory essays introduce their stories in the first short story collection by each: Zelazny's *Four for Tomorrow* (1967), introduced by Theodore Sturgeon; Varley's *The Persistence of Vision* (1978), introduced by Algis Budrys; and Gibson's *Burning Chrome* (1986), introduced by Bruce Sterling. In a writing field where such introductions are not at all the rule for first story collections, all three introductions, then, are signs of the greater than usual excitement already in place around each of these writers by the time that first story collection was published.

At the 1966 World Science Fiction Convention in Cleveland, during the opening ceremonies when the names of the various SF writers present were announced, while older and more popular professionals such as Isaac Asimov, Frederik Pohl, and Poul Anderson drew a perfectly respectable amount of applause, when Roger Zelazny's name was read out, it was greeted with a standing ovation in a hall filled with almost a thousand attendees—an ovation which went on and on and *on*! During that same World SF Convention weekend, Zelazny's first novel, *This Immortal*, tied with Frank Herbert's *Dune* for the Hugo Award as best SF novel of the year. When we consider Herbert had been writing and known to the SF world since the early fifties, and that his giant novel had already appeared in serial form as two individual novels, each of which had already been serialized in *Analog* magazine over two three-month periods, and that already, in hardcover, it was beginning to cross over into the awareness of the greater reading public (where it would go on to sell some twelve million copies in paperback and spawn a series of sequels), it's even more astonishing that Zelazny, whose novel had appeared only in a cut version squeezed into two issues of *The Magazine of Fantasy & Science Fiction*, managed to make any showing at all against Herbert in the voting, much less produce a tie.

But all these were signs of the extraordinary excitement that the verbal electricity of Zelazny's prose had generated in the three years since he'd been publishing science fiction.

While he always seemed to enjoy the attention lavished upon him in these years, Zelazny, a slim, dark man of Polish-American extraction, was nevertheless quite humble before that attention. Certainly he never did anything that made him appear to seek it out—outside of producing extraordinarily fine SF stories. The same humorous irony with which he confronted the most intense excitement about his work—from 1963 through approximately 1968—he would use to confront those people who, a few years later, were to declare his newer work not as strong as his earlier production, even as his general popularity grew on the purely statistical level with his various Amber books. Zelazny went on to write more award-winning novels and stories, including *Lord of Light* and "Home is the Hangman." His Amber novels, which began appearing in '69, were unremittingly popular, as the individual volumes came out, over the next twenty years. But the excitement around Zelazny within the science fiction community still centers on the ten long stories ("A Rose for Ecclesiastes" [1963], "He Who Shapes" [1964], "The Graveyard Heart"

[1964], "The Doors of His Face, the Lamps of His Mouth" [1965], "The Furies" [1965], "The Keys to December" [1966], "For a Breath I Tarry" [1966], "This Moment of the Storm" [1966], "This Mortal Mountain" [1967], and—the one where the energy first fails and, somehow, never recovers—"Damnation Alley" [1967]), coupled with a handful of those early novels, *This Immortal, The Dream Master* (an expansion of "He Who Shapes"), *Bridge of Ashes, Today We Choose Faces,* and *Doorways in the Sand*—this last coming to be considered by many his best novel, with *This Immortal* close behind. (Others would argue just as intelligently and just as passionately for *Isle of the Dead* and *Lord of Light,* producing precisely the conflict necessary for the production of the idea of quality this essay puts forth.)

By the mid-seventies Zelazny was deep into his Amber series—commercially successful but aesthetically lightweight. He had publicly stated that he could not afford to write the kind of books and stories he once had. Though his high reputation rested on them, they took too much time for the money they brought in, he claimed. And he was now, by his own admission (reprinted in both fanzines and prozines), too fond of the good life. Sales were up. And there was certainly no fall-off in the amount of fannish adulation he received. But that adulation simply no longer carried the intensity and edge that it once had, when his work had been perceived as exhibiting unequaled writerly invention—rather than the much less complex ability to please a statistically growing audience. Now, in the science fiction field, the first stories of John Varley began to attract attention. By his first story collection, *The Persistence of Vision,* in 1978, the excitement that had been gathered around this tall, quiet West Coast writer, if it was not at the same pitch Zelazny had once commanded, it was in the same ballpark. John Herbert Varley—called Herb by his friends—was a gangling young man, still in his middle twenties when his first story, about life on the hugely hot surface of the planet Mercury, "Retrograde Summer," appeared in 1974. Working as a welfare assistant for disabled people in Oregon, Varley had been assigned to assist a young, wheelchair-bound woman. They'd fallen in love; had married; together, they had three children. And Varley had begun to write.

By the time his first collection of stories had come out in conjunction with his first novel, *The Ophiuchi Hotline,* three things were obvious about Varley. Clearly, he had gone to school at the feet of Russ and the other women SF writers of this period, such as Vonda McIntyre, Ursula Le Guin, and James Tiptree, Jr. (Alice Sheldon). Varley's feminist sympathies were as evident as Russ's, if less analytically honed. As well, he obviously enjoyed the possibilities of technology. Also, he was deeply concerned in all ways with the problem of prosthetics—and, by extension, the dignity and rights of the handicapped. This concern climaxed in his Nebula and Hugo Award-winning novella that gave his first story collection its title, "The Persistence of Vision," a disturbing story—in many ways and on many levels—about a sighted man who discovers a communal society of the blind which has set up its home away from the rest of the sighted world, somewhere in the southwest. Most of Varley's stories ("The Persistence of Vision" itself a notable exception) take place in a more or less coherent universe (the Eight Worlds), in which the discovery of a broadcast band of information originating from the area of the constellation Ophiuchus has allowed humankind to make a quantum technological leap in the next century.

While Zelazny's stories had been the first of his texts to excite SF readers, his early novels had carried that excitement to an even higher pitch. Varley's first novel, *The Ophiuchi Hotline* (1978), was satisfactory enough. But while it fleshed out and added important information to the Eight Worlds series, as a book in itself it did not have the same formal perfection as such stories as "The Phantom of Kansas" or "Overdrawn at the Memory Bank." But now Varley launched into a massive trilogy, the first novel of which was *Titan* (1979). As perceived within a discourse of story and craft, especially as the first volume of a projected trilogy (which, in such a discourse, can always bank on the notion of some later events, or revelation that will make the story move into some particularly satisfying direction), the book was also satisfactory—even popular. And when Isaac Asimov introduced Varley at Philcon in '78 (as "The New Heinlein"), the applause went on and on in the way the SF community had not heard since Zelazny's introduction at the '66 Tricon. And when Herb unveiled his map of Titan, the applause became a standing ovation. But for those people who read *Titan* within the discourse of writing and art, two hundred and fifty pages of writing was still two hundred and fifty pages of writing; and, having nothing to do with where the story was going to go, the micropleasures of those two hundred fifty pages should have long ago begun to cohere into the greater vividness and intensity that marked the shorter works. But what those readers had generally found, however, was a rather lumbering and somehow lifeless job, though all of Varley's concerns, from his feminist sympathies to his scientific interest in prostheses, were further explored in the book.

The excitement around Varley's short stories was, however, still growing. A second collection of earlier stories managed to bear up under the appalling title *The Barbie Murders*; it was, yes, the title of one of the stories contained; that still did not excuse it. Several years later, *The Barbie Murders* was reissued under the title *Picnic on Nearside*—another story from the book: but not much of an improvement! Still, Varley's stories were the most exciting SF being written in those years, with new tales such as "Press Enter ■" clearly ranking among the best he'd ever done. That excitement continued through still a third collection, *Blue Champagne* (1988).

Sometime before this, as fallout from the first surge of excitement, an early Varley story, "Air Raid," was bought for the movies. Varley was retained to do the film script. He expanded his film treatment into a novel, *Millennium* (1983; also the title of the film); what strengths *Millennium* (the novel) had were formal. Like Le Guin's *The Dispossessed*, it alternated chapter by chapter between two points of view: that of a time-traveling woman from a polluted and decadent future whose job is to go back in time and rescue people from air crashes about to occur, and a contemporary airlines crash inspector who begins to realize that something is profoundly wrong in one of the accidents he's been assigned to cover. Though the novel's ending (first) violated its own formal pattern and (second) fell very flat, it seemed that careful scripting might save it. But the movie that resulted—*Millennium,* with Cheryl Ladd and Kris Kristofferson—abandoned any pretense at structure; also, it pulled in several unrelated special effects sequences with no concern for the action; generally *Millennium* (the movie) managed to come in as one of the worst SF films of the decade. (The weakest of Zelazny's early decalogue of tales, "Damnation Alley," had also been turned into an eminently forgettable picture [starring Jan Michael Vincent] of the same name.) Again, the excitement around these writers was initially based on the high skill and craft of their action writing—not the number of sales, the size of their advances, or the success of the movies made from their works. Nevertheless, that excitement has often been injured by a bad commercial choice; and all three of the writers in this unit have made choices perceived by the general community as commercial *and* poor.

By the first years of the eighties, Varley had divorced his wife; neither *Wizard* nor *Demon,* the second and third novels in his trilogy, had done anything to ameliorate the sheer lumbering quality of the tripartite work. While "The Persistence of Vision" was Varley's most honored and awarded story, it was not a characteristic tale. And certain writers, such as Thomas Disch, even found it repugnant.

The year the story took its awards, the country was shocked at the dark horrors of the Jonestown massacre in Guyana, where some three hundred followers of the white Reverend Jim Jones, mostly black American women and children, were brainwashed into committing mass suicide by drinking cyanide-laced soft drinks. Disch's pointed comment about the tale of its self-blinding hero was: "The story made me feel that at any moment someone was going to come up and offer me a glass of Kool-Aid." And, by the middle of the decade, Varley's short stories had all but ceased.

William Gibson began publishing professionally in 1981, with a story— "Johnny Mnemonic"—that a number of readers have since claimed is his best. In Gibson, two of Varley's concerns seem to return, even if in a muted, minor key: forceful female characters (though often in secondary positions)—and prostheses. Molly Millions, the lead action character in "Johnny Mnemonic" and a major figure in Gibson's first novel, *Neuromancer*, seems like a direct rewrite of Russ's Jael from *The Female Man*: Both women are of near superhuman efficiency, both wear black jumpsuits, both have retractable blades hidden in their fingertips, both enjoy their sex, and both—though for different reasons—have unsettling stares.

The correspondence seems so complete, I once asked Gibson if he was aware of the similarity. Though he said he admired Russ as a writer, he claimed to have been unaware of the parallel until I'd asked about it—a sign, I suspect, of just how successful Russ (along with a number of other women SF writers of the seventies) had actually been in shifting the conventions of the genre toward an image of female competence. Both seem to have become shared genre conventions rather than specific aspects of specific writers' work.

By the mid-eighties both concerns had sedimented enough in written SF to affect prominently the second *Aliens* film—arguably superior to the first because of those conventions.

The Ace Specials publishing line had been quiescent for almost fifteen years, but in '82, Ace Books revived the series, again under Terry Carr's editorship. Until his death from heart failure in 1986, Carr was able to publish more than half a dozen volumes. Among the earliest of the new series was Gibson's first novel, *Neuromancer*—which went on to win both the Nebula Award and Hugo Award for best novel of 1984.

In 1982, a writer named Bruce Bethke published a short story called "Cyberpunk" in George Scither's *Amazing Stories* magazine. A few months later, in 1983, Gardner Dozois, the editor of *Isaac Asimov's Science Fiction Magazine*, first used in print Bethke's title to designate Gibson and a number of other SF writers, including Bruce Sterling, John Shirley, Rudy Rucker, Tom Maddox, Pat Cadigan (the only woman writer in the group), and Lewis Shriner: The cyberpunks had been named. (Though Bethke's story had lent them a name and Bethke had occasionally met them socially, paradoxically he was never considered part of the group.) Dozois doubtlessly found the term "cyberpunk" appropriate for these writers because of their hard-boiled and cynical attitude, along with their interest in computers. They were in their middle-to-late thirties, so that the suggestion of youth was ironic, rather than reflective: By the early eighties, the Punk Rock and New Wave Music phenomenon was generally thought to be fast aging, if not over with.

Another thing some of these writers had in common was they occasionally published in Sterling's Texas-based fanzine, *Cheap Truth*, where Sterling himself had a regular, raunchy, even frenetic column under the open pen-name Vincent Omniaveritas—a Latin pun suggesting something like "Truth conquers all." An interesting SF writer in his own right, Sterling had already made some attempts to start a movement among some of these same writers—which he'd first designated simply as "the movement," and later as "the mirror-shades group." As in all such groups, named from the outside, all the writers involved were soon protesting publicly that they had nothing—at least aesthetically—to do with one another, while other readers in other fanzines began to argue whether other writers, e.g., Greg Bear or Marc Laidlaw, really ought to be added to the group.

Cheap Truth, with its fannish energy, had occasionally attacked a number of other new SF writers, including Kim Stanley Robinson, John Kessel, and Connie Willis—all of whom were talented, exciting in their own ways, and generally moving toward popularity. Now another SF writer, Michael Swanwick, in an article that appeared in *Isaac Asimov's SF Magazine*, located another group of SF writers he designated the humanists—a group composed largely of those particularly popular writers whom *Cheap Truth* attacked. To add to the paradoxes, Willis's first collection of SF short stories, *Fire Watch*, contained an early story, "All My Darling Daughters," which, had she not written it in 1979, might easily have been taken as a particularly effective parody, or even pastiche, of an eighties cyberpunk story.

Within the SF community, the general level of debate between the humanists and the cyberpunks—all of whom were busily protesting on both sides that no such groups existed—was generally lively and caused a lot of people to write a lot of pages in a lot of fanzines. To the extent that it caused a number of readers to think a bit more clearly about what was going on within the genre, it was undoubtedly a healthy phenomenon. Outside the SF community, however, people tended to see cyberpunk as some sort of oppositional movement—which ignored the fact that what is generally considered the most characteristic cyberpunk novel, *Neuromancer*, had swept up both the Hugo and Nebula Award in its year, which suggests rather an almost blanket acceptance by both readers (who vote for the Hugo) and writers (who vote for the Nebula). Much of the rhetoric was also silly and self-serving—such as Sterling's claim in his introduction to Gibson's *Burning Chrome* that nothing of interest happened in SF during the seventies—as though there had been no Russ, no Le Guin, nor any Varley. (He was almost immediately taken to task for this by Jeanne Gomoll, in "An Open Letter to Joanna Russ," in her fine and intelligent fanzine *New Moon.*) Sometime in the middle of all this, *Rolling Stone Magazine* ran an article on cyberpunk, centering largely on Gibson—and ignoring any of the writers on the other side(s) of the by-now multi-sided debate.

The result was that Gibson was soon hired to write screenplays for Hollywood—first for his own novel, *Neuromancer*, then for the third film in the Sigourney Weaver *Alien* series. Though Gibson completed both scripts, the third *Alien* film does not use Gibson's, and the *Neuromancer* film has, so far, come to nothing—though I spent an interesting afternoon in Lawrence, Kansas, at the home of William Burroughs, in 1986, brainstorming with him when—briefly—he'd been retained to write a script for the movie.

Gibson's second and third novels, *Count Zero* and *Mona Lisa Overdrive* (like Varley's, continuations of a trilogy) were not able to generate quite the same excitement as his first.

The most unkind characterization of the cyberpunk group that one now began to hear was an anonymous one that, nevertheless, carried a certain weight: "The cyberpunk movement consists of one writer (Gibson), one critic (Sterling), and a lot of hangers-on." Though this slights considerable interesting work, both fiction and nonfiction, by John Shirley, Rudy Rucker, Tom Maddox, Pat Cadigan, and Marc Laidlaw, it nevertheless contained something to think about.

In 1986, Sterling publicly proclaimed the "death" of Vincent Omniaveritas, and ceased to put out *Cheap Truth*. In the same year, he edited a cyberpunk anthology, *Mirrorshades*, that appeared from Arbor House in 1987. With the publication of *Mirrorshades: The Cyberpunk Anthology*, within the SF community the cyberpunk movement was now sufficiently memorialized and monumentalized to be considered over with.

Around this time, the first issues of a new and impressive fanzine, edited by Steven P. Brown and Daniel Steffan out of Washington, D.C., *Science Fiction Eye*, seemed as if it might put some energy into prolonging the movement. The *Eye*, as it came to be called, ran interviews with Gibson and a number of other cyberpunk writers; as well, it regularly gave considerable page space to both Shirley and Sterling, cyberpunk's two most articulate critics. Looking back on these issues, however, the *Eye* seemed more interested in preserving the recently completed history of cyberpunk—rather than propelling that history forward with active intervention.

In order to cash in on the excitement and the term, New American Library publishers contracted Bethke to expand his original story "Cyberpunk" to novel length. When the book was completed, however, they rejected it. (It was, apparently, not enough like the cyberpunk work of Gibson or the work of other writers in *Mirrorshades*.) Eventually, in 1988, it was published by Baen Books. Receiving generally poor reviews, it quickly vanished. Its only effect seems to be that it encouraged certain paperback publishers to start putting clothing and haircuts on some of the characters pictured on their covers reminiscent of punkish styles from the mid-seventies. But since such punk packaging (which continues, by the bye) has never been associated with Gibson, Sterling, Shirley, or, indeed, any of the *Mirrorshades* writers, it finally did more to disperse the cyberpunk phenomenon than to solidify it.

Because of the inflationary excitement generated by the very nonacademic *Rolling Stone* piece—neither an informed nor an insightful article—and facilitated by the documentary evidence preserved in the late eighties issues of *SF Eye*, a number of academics became interested in cyberpunk by 1987/88 and continue even today to speak of it as if it were a living current in contemporary SF production. They are still producing a series of more or less interesting special review issues and casebooks, in which they often try to link cyberpunk with other currents in postmodern life.

Because the cyberpunk phenomenon was always perceived within the SF community as an argument between groups and schools of SF writers—cyberpunks, humanists, feminists (however ill-defined and overlapping these groups might have been)—it doubtless produced more pages of fanzine writing (as well as more articles in professionally published SF magazines) between '83 and '88 than any like phenomenon in science fiction since the New Wave of the 1960s. But it's also arguable that the intensity of excitement produced by the quality of Gibson's work—the writer whose texts were almost always at the center of the debates—while considerable, was not as great as that produced by Varley's work in the seventies or Zelazny's in the sixties.

One reason for mentioning the three introductions with these stories is because each introduction attempts to address the question of high writerly quality, as the three different critics, SF writers all, perceive it for the writer in question. And each addresses the phenomenon from a different point of view.

In English the word "quality" has at least two very different meanings. The first meaning of quality—the philosophical meaning—is assumed to be comparatively "value free" and refers only to perceptible fundamentals: Something has a quality of whiteness, or a quality of largeness, or a quality of heaviness. Here, the word is a synonym for "aspect," without the visual bias (i.e., the visual "quality") the term "aspect" (cognate, after all, with "spectacle") often assumes.

The second meaning of the word—the common meaning—is completely subsumed by the notion of value. Things are considered to be of high quality or of low quality. That is synonymous with saying that things have high value or low value.

But the boundary between the two meanings is never secure. It is precisely the places where quality comes to suggest terms like bias (as it does two paragraphs above), negative or positive, that the slippage is always taking place. But it is, of course, the second meaning that we are referring to here.

Writerly "quality"—what is it? And what is it specifically for science fiction? It's certainly a difficult thing to discuss: And in the science fiction field, as an area of commercial writing perceived by most—both inside and outside the SF community—to lie largely outside the precincts of literature, quality is often a disturbing and even dangerous topic to discuss. "Craft" is thought to be something a writer "learns"—and thus, once learned, is not something that can go away. That is precisely what makes it different from "art," and its sign, quality—which seems to lie somewhere between the notion of talent and aesthetics, without being fully covered by either. But, with a distressing number of writers, both inside and outside SF, their highest quality work is their earliest, or among their earliest, work. Similarly, there are a great many writers whose middle period work is clearly their highest quality production. Both these facts suggest that something like simply energy—associated with youth and/or maturity—may be a factor in that elusive construct: quality. And there are distressingly few writers whose late work is considered to be their highest quality work; and when (outside SF the poet William Butler Yeats is certainly the prime and rare example) a writer comes along for whom that is true, then we must ask whether wisdom also is a factor in high writerly quality.

But all of these anxiety-producing anomalies are conveniently ignored, here in the precincts of SF, through the convenient notion of craft, which is seen as a quality (meaning one) that can only increase or remain stable. You may gather that I suspect "craft" here is—like "story"—a consensus myth that flies in the face of current fact and writerly history, a fiction whose single purpose is to allow SF writers to get a little more sleep at night; or at least to *claim* they sleep. In that light, the intentional statements of Zelazny—that he cannot afford the time, and thus has conscientiously relinquished the pursuit of quality—sound suspiciously as if they may be part of the same fiction.

Though an absolutely necessary part of high writerly quality involves a skillfully wrought verbal surface, skill in writing may manifest itself in styles ranging from the simplicity of a Beckett, Hemingway, or Carver to the recommendations of a Joyce, Gass, or Davenport. Nor does the verbal surface exhaust the concept of high quality. Such quality would seem to be, rather, closer to the concept of a skillfully wrought verbal surface generated in a series of narrative situations that clearly and greatly excite a small number of readers comparatively well-educated in the history, in the traditions, and in the conventions of the particular genre. One part of such excitement must always be subjective—or idiosyncratic—for the excited group, accessible only to more or less historical analysis, and finally of primarily political interest—precisely at the point where the quality ceases to excite *other* readers, *other* groups.

The verbal surface is, of course, easier to analyze than the subjective/historical/political. Surface—or stylistic—elements usually involve at least three aspects. The first is a general economy of expression. The second is a range of techniques for intensifying certain statements—and sometimes techniques that, say, in the case of Proust, James, or Faulkner, seem to contravene all notions of the economical! The third usually registers as an oppositional quality about the text: Another way to speak of this last is the ability of the writer to record (often with economy and/or intensity) things about the world (qualities or structural relations) that other writers have not caught in the past—things that, by implication, have been considered unwritable, at least till this particular writer began to write. The reason this last quality is perceived *as* oppositional is because—often—the most economical or most intense way to start producing such an effect is for the writer to declare that certain things in the world do not conform to the traditional way most people write (or speak) about them—and thus to set him- or herself in opposition to the general movement of his or her own genre. Thus, even when the writer does not employ such a strategy directly, the idea always lingers in the background any time a writer writes something that appears, however momentarily, through its intensity or acuity, to be new; to say something new (or even to say it well) must always be perceived as oppositional to the thrust of common language.

In the literary precincts high writerly quality is often discussed as if it were simply not perceived at all by readers outside the "happy" (read: excited) "few"—as Stendahl characterized them in the eighteen-thirties. Often it's assumed that people other than that few simply do not perceive high writerly quality at all. But the reality of the situation is more complex.

Certainly there are socially limited readers, unused to the range of writerly variation, for whom certain intensifying techniques will simply register as verbal clumsiness or writerly noise. One such intensifying technique is to make a sentence parallel, in its syntax, what it represents in its semantics. Readers unused to this rhetorical intensifying technique—especially if the sentence concerns orders of disruption rather than irruptions of order—often find such sentences clumsy and confusing—rather than vivid and brisk. And readers without wide exposure to the ways written language usually speaks of most subjects are going to have considerable difficulty recognizing a new statement or a new counterstatement—especially when the fact that it *is* new is implied rather than declared.

But there are other readers who do perceive all those stylistic effects and who, still, do not find the work exciting—because of a range of possible complaints having to do with the narrative situations that generate the verbal surface—the whole range of subjective, historical, and political reasons we spoke of before, which are so difficult to pin down, especially in contemporary work. In Alfred Bester's final novel, *The Deceivers*, for example, the repeated and constant intrusion of sex into the narrative, described rather gesturally and without any particular insight or inventiveness, defeats all *my* interest in the book from the first pages to the last. For younger readers, in a society where commercial pornography lies to hand in almost any and every direction, such passages seem (one) pallid and (two) pointless. Older readers, such as I am, find ourselves thinking that the novel inhabits an outmoded fifties sensibility: Indeed, had it been written then (and could it have been published then: For what seem the most absurd reasons today, *The Deceivers* actually would have been illegal to print in this country before 1968), it might indeed have been amusing, by the same codes that made works such as Terry Southern's *Candy* and *The Magic Christian* funny at that time in a world with printing conventions so strict that, today, they produce a chuckle. The fact is, there is much in *The Deceivers*, as there is in all three late Bester SF novels, that is at one with the verbal invention and brio of his two fine earlier SF novels. But the narrative situations that develop that invention and brio fall disastrously prey to what can only be called a kind of historical miscalculation. The narratives of *The Demolished Man* and *The Stars My Destination* were set at a pitch of oppositional tension to the historical forces of their day that still informs their texts with considerable energy for the contemporary reader—and more so for the reader willing to do some historical digging into the time of their appearance. The three late novels seem, for all their verbal (and visual) economy and recomplication, to fall wholly into various narrative paths of least resistance—when they are not busily engaged in opposing historical forces that, for most readers, are just no longer in evidence. As I said, the judgment is political, historical—subjective. But the fact is, the SF community was poised with whole ranges and degrees and orders of intelligence and sensitivity, waiting to read these books as Bester—returned to the field after a fifteen-year absence—wrote and published them. But when they were read, almost no one was excited by them at all.

Because the science fiction community is as small as it is, we can, however, say a few things about it. One large factor in the community is that it contains an extremely high proportion of writers. It also contains an extremely high proportion of editors. And the majority of the rest of the community consists of readers committed enough to the idea of writing—and science fiction writing, in particular—to publish fanzines and to organize SF conventions based largely on their excitement about writing and reading.

At first this seems to suggest a perfectly innocent and apolitically self-justifying *mise en abîme*—the French term for what happens when you look into a mirror when another mirror is suspended behind you.

The writers I have chosen for this essay are the writers who most excited those few people who are, themselves, the most excited about the idea of writing. (The German term for this excitement is *Begeisterung*—usually translated "enthusiasm": It's what poets presumably have for those odd elements that pop up in both life and literature, beauty and truth—or, if you're more comfortable with the terms: high style and right-on politics, however you define them. *Begeisterung* sets off from the herd those who articulately manifest it.) That excitement would seem to be a reason for a general public, looking for quality, to try those works that evoke it.

But those people most concerned about writing are not—politically and historically—really congruent to the general public. The general public tends to be concerned first with success—which, in our society, is a stand-in for the idea of money. Stephen King becomes an interesting—if not an enjoyable—writer precisely *because* he has been as commercially successful as he has, precisely *because* he has outsold Shakespeare and the Bible, precisely *because* so many people have paid so much money for so many of his volumes. (I recall a perfectly serious discussion I overheard between a U. Mass. undergraduate couple coming back on the bus from the Hampshire Mall, where they—and I—had just seen *Pet Sematary*.

(She: "Was that a good movie?"

(He: "Sure it was a good picture. It was by Stephen King."

(She: "But some of it didn't really seem like a good movie to me."

(He: "Of course it was a good movie. I wouldn't have taken you to see a movie like that if it wasn't good. It had all that advertising. You saw all those people who'd come to see it, didn't you?"

(She: "Yeah. Well, I guess it was, then. Maybe I just have to see it again. Sometimes you have to see good movies twice to really understand them.")

What we have here is, of course, a notion even less refined than the idea of "craft"—that is, an idea that sidesteps even more contradictions and anxieties than the idea of "craft," as the idea of "craft" sidesteps so much that troubles in the concept of "quality."

The *mise en abîme* relationship mentioned above actually distracts us from the political differences between the small group of excited people and the rest of us. First of all, that group tends to come from backgrounds that let them *afford* to be more interested in writing than in money.

Most of them are white. Most of them are male. Most of them are heterosexual.

But not all.

Indeed, what is characteristic of such self-selected groups in the *science fiction* community is that they usually contain a higher number of women, gays, and non-whites than there are likely to be in a *literarily* self-selected group—if only because the larger group from which the SF group starts to select itself is itself so marginal. And while this is not necessarily reflected in the social backgrounds of the three writers in this particular packet, it's certainly reflected, here and there, in what these writers choose to write about, i.e., what excites that group: men who are poets rather than adventurers, adventurers who are deeply unsure of themselves, or men who are deeply deceived in what sureness they possess, as with Zelazny; and we have already discussed the range of relationships to be found in Varley and Gibson.

There are often to be found in the science fiction field writers who are more generally loved, perceived to be on more or less the same side politically, and who are more popular than the writers I've chosen to present in my classroom units. Thus, Ursula Le Guin, certainly sympathetic to feminism, a fine craftswoman, the winner of many awards in the field, and far more generally popular and well-known, might seem to be a more likely writer to present than Joanna Russ. I have great respect for Le Guin. Pieces she has published in her book of essays, *Dancing at the Edge of the World*, for example, I feel are powerful, important, and immeasurably brave. Her novels are loved and respected both within and without the field. The recent breadth of her academic acceptance means that, here in the academy, we *must* make special mention of her. Still, let me state it bluntly: Among an admittedly small group of educated SF readers, many of whom admire Le Guin as I do, the excitement that Russ produces through the clarity and invention in her writerly surface and the acuity of her analysis is far more intense than Le Guin ever effected.

Understand, in no way does this denigrate Le Guin. But it is to state a fact.

And, yes, it is certainly a small group, concerned with writing first.

What Le Guin's popularity means, however, is that, because of its more general range, you are more likely to encounter Le Guin on your own than you are to encounter Russ. And if you were able to respond to it, you might well have gained a more intense order of pleasure from her—without in any way denying the pleasure from Le Guin's work.

Similarly, writers such as Asimov, Clarke, Heinlein, and Bradbury are widely popular—and deservedly so. But the intense response a smaller group of readers have had to Sturgeon, Bester, Russ, Disch, Zelazny, Varley, and Gibson is a reason to urge new SF readers toward those lesser-known writers. Through the excitement they have produced, largely among their peers, all of the writers here have, in their decades, changed the face of the field. Moreover, in a field that often speaks about itself as if there were only "craft"—and, more and more recently, speaks as if there were not even craft but only commercial success—it is important to know that high writerly quality can produce the high social excitement that it has in science fiction, however much difficulty we, in that field, have had in discussing it.

If my selection of SF writers by the particular standards I have set were going to be complete, not only would it include Sturgeon, Bester, Russ, and Disch, but also the three writers here. That list would most certainly start with the SF writer Stanley G. Weinbaum, a young man who began publishing SF stories in 1938, electrifying the small world of committed SF readers and writers with stories such as "A Martian Odyssey"—and who died tragically in 1935 at age thirty-three of lung cancer. Even as far back as Weinbaum, we are clearly dealing with a man particularly concerned with the construction of his female characters—at a time when science fiction is generally considered to be almost wholly a "boys' club": Weinbaum produced a whole series of stories about the Black Flame, a kind of future superwoman who has notable similarities with both Russ's Jael and Gibson's Molly.

To move toward completion in its own terms, such a list would almost certainly have to include both Cordwainer Smith and R. A. Lafferty; the first was the pseudonym of an American diplomat, Paul Linebarger, who wrote one SF novel (*Norstrilia*), three novellas (collected as *Tales of Three Planets*), and short stories enough to fill, finally, two volumes (*The Best of Cordwainer Smith, Lords of the Instrumentality*) —only four SF volumes in all. In the course of his career, however, he also wrote books of history, books on psychological warfare, and at least three non-SF novels

(*Atomsk, Ria, Carola*). Lafferty is a southern American writer, a Catholic, whose work is arch, borders on the surreal, and—while almost unknown to any sort of general public—has always had a small but committed following, even among people who do not necessarily share his often eccentric (and rather right-wing) political views.

With a very little adjustment such a list could be expanded to include the best works of Gene Wolfe, a midwestern engineer who has produced an extraordinary exciting tetralogy called *The Book of the New Sun*, comprised of four novels *The Shadow of the Torturer, The Claw of the Conciliator, The Sword of the Lictor,* and *The Citadel of the Autarch.* Wolfe has also written many other sensitive novels and short stories. It would have to include John Crowley whose novel *Little, Big* is extraordinary and whose fictive enterprise is generally astonishing.

By keeping the same standards but only adjusting the variables—expanding the size of the group excited, adjusting both the quality and the intensity to the excitement—we could include Ursula K. Le Guin, Robert A. Heinlein, Stanislaw Lem (a Polish writer), Kurt Vonnegut, J. G. Ballard, Katherine MacLean, Octavia Butler, Arkady and Boris Strugatsky (two Russian brothers who wrote together), Fritz Leiber, Harlan Ellison, Judith Merril, Frederik Pohl . . . But because the factors that generate such lists always have to do with what are finally unmeasurables for any single observer (the education that finally defines the limits of the group, the intensity of the group response), we are eventually thrown back on that last and most troubling non-stylistic criterion: the subjective. But from a list for which there is simply no objective way to situate its end point or, really, to do more than guess at its proper order, I have chosen those writers whom *I* feel best able to teach in the context of a university class, here, today. And that is a factor of my own highly idiosyncratic and eccentric education.

Sturgeon's introduction to Zelazny tries to talk a bit about high quality in terms of the invention worked into the verbal surface. Budrys' introduction to Varley leaves verbal surface "to speak for itself" and tries instead to analyze that aspect of quality unique to SF: the historical relation of the writer to contemporary currents in science. And Sterling's introduction to Gibson attempts to unravel a few of the political strands that also, always, here and now, constitute quality (i.e., meaning two). But all three introductions—all four, if you include this one—are still discussing aspects of one complex and volatile phenomenon.

For the last two hundred years (i.e., since the beginnings of what we call romanticism) musicians, lyric poets, painters, and sculptors have realized something that narrative artists—novelists, dramatists, and filmmakers—have only begun to come to since the advent of high modernism in the twenties: Something in the idea of art judged solely in terms of craft/popularity/commercial success fundamentally and profoundly subverts the idea of high quality.

Even though individual judgments constitute it, such quality is still a social construct: Thus no one individual judgment (such as mine) can confirm—or deny—it. It takes a web of educated/excited responses.

Because signs of craft and popularity can be signs of quality, there is always going to be room for confusion about how these signs—or their absence—can be read. The sign of quality is, of course, how those other signs are deployed within a far more complex galaxy of signs: a skilled verbal surface in terms of the narrative generated; popularity in terms of the excitement the work produces among a limited group of educated (in some as yet undefined way) readers. And since a larger commercial group may contain those smaller subgroups, a small commercial success can either be a sign of a subgroup of excited buyers or a sign of a small scattering of unexcited buyers. These are not the same thing—though marketing departments have almost no way of distinguishing them or of treating them differently.

Then there is the problem specific to the paraliterary fields such as SF and comic books: What of the moderate commercial success within the genre by a high-quality work, a success nevertheless large enough to contain two subgroups, one of which articulately supports the notion of art as craft/popularity/commercial success and vociferously opposes anything that succeeds on any other terms—claiming in the course of its argument special educational privileges having to do with its members' time in, understanding of, and sensitivity to the genre? Attacks of this sort, I am sure, had far more to do with, say, driving J. G. Ballard from SF into the arms of the mainstream than any positive allurements that beckoned from there—though, there, once he arrived, he found a good many rewards waiting. But how is such a subgroup's response to be distinguished from that of another subgroup, claiming equal educational privileges, who claims as well: "We were simply not excited by this work"? The signifiers involved are all ambiguously placed over various signifieds.

Robert Silverberg's science fiction novel *Dying Inside* (about a telepathic man, who, with age, is losing the powers that made his life worthwhile), as well as some of his short stories (e.g., "Schwartz Between the Galaxies"), are as finely conceived and executed SF works as I know of. They are quite exciting enough to merit a high place on anyone's list. But the vast majority of Silverberg's bibliography is not, by the same criteria, exciting—though some of it has been considerably more popular.

Like Zelazny, Silverberg has made occasional public statements—not that he is eschewing the pursuit of quality, but that some of his works are intended to be ambitious and some are not. Silverberg's novel *A Time of Changes* was awarded a Nebula Award by the Science Fiction Writers of America. That could, indeed, be a sign of excitement among a small, educated group. But as one—very idiosyncratic—reader, I find in the book no particular surface skill nor any particular contestatory energy. And a number of the books for which Silverberg has made ambitious claims I find marred by the same surface clumsiness and path-of-least-resistance structure characteristic of his least-ambitious and least serious works. Nor can I see any reason to try and redeem such works by saying—it's certainly not how they strike me—that they are, nevertheless, "craftsmanlike."

Now I am not widely acquainted with Silverberg's many, many SF novels and stories. And part of my particular education involves knowing that often an exciting writer must teach us how to read his or her works before we can really appreciate them: My education is wide enough to make me suspect places where that education is lacking.

Still, I would find it hard to put together a teaching unit of Silverberg as I have done for some of these other writers—two or three novels and a half dozen or so short stories. Again, high quality is not an individual judgment, but a social construct. (And a single person, like myself, expostulating on how he or she perceives it, can only articulate a single thread in the contestatory web that is the thing itself.) It is only the people who have mentioned *Dying Inside* and "Schwartz Between the Galaxies" to me—and the way we have articulated our excitements about them back and forth to each other—that lets me mention them to you. But the greater discourse that has accrued to Silverberg's sprawling corpus, with its occasional commercial popularity, its awards, and its high degree of variation, has not led me on to other of his works—so far—that have facilitated the exchange of like excitements. The discourse has, rather, slowed the process down. Very probably, it means readers other than I will have to do a good deal of the work before I can move in and do what, by temperament, I am certainly inclined to. And it is the discourse of craft/successful/commercial, bolstered by praise and awards, which has obscured a process that, without it, might have led more quickly to greater reading pleasure.

The literary precincts certainly have in place a rule of thumb which moves to avoid these confusions: The writer should do the first winnowing—by never undertaking any project that she or he does not believe to be, at least potentially, of the highest quality. Once, at the height of the New Wave in the sixties, I heard *New Worlds* editor Michael Moorcock express (as an ironic twist on Artaud's great essay of 1938, "No More

Masterpieces . . . ?"): "I can't think of any reason to write anything we *don't* believe is going to be a masterpiece!"

In a marginal field of writing such as science fiction, however, following such a rule may not always be possible, if only because of financial pressures—which the upholders of the craft/popular/commercial aesthetic are so fond of citing and which I can certainly respect. But another reason it may not be possible, which we should not discount, is because of the *temperaments* of those writers attracted to a genre that defines itself so completely in terms of the commercial in the first place. And temperament may also involve matters of education and/or taste.

In some respects—again having to do with the subjective—high writerly quality is a phenomenon brought into being by the very fact of our discussing it, arguing over it, and—most importantly—disagreeing articulately about what texts evince it and what texts do not. In that sense, what is most important about my list, in spite of (or indeed because of) all my analyses, lectures, and justifications for the writers and the works I've chosen, is that some other list, put together with equal analysis and commitment—perhaps, someday, yours—will be different from mine.

SF writers who refuse to speak of work in any terms save the commercial—as I hear them doing more and more on various panels at various science fiction conventions—seriously damage the notion of quality on which, I believe, far more than on popularity, the health—the ability to grow, change, and construct an exciting dialogue with the world—of the genre stands.

If only because the concept of quality produces the anxieties it does in the paraliterary, I think encouraging discussions of quality is particularly important here. And though high quality is a socially constructed phenomenon as much as any other, we must still distinguish it carefully and repeatedly from both popularity and sales—if science fiction is to retain any sort of life.

It's particularly important for young readers (and young writers) to articulate clearly and vigorously, in fanzines, at conventions, in letters to friends, in conversations with all, each other, and sundry—and even in science fiction classes—their responses, their judgments, and their excitement at the writers who produce around them: That means their excitement over new writers, even over brand-new writers—even as these readers listen to, and contest with, recommendations and judgments (such as mine) from a generation or so ahead.

—Amherst
1991

13

Pornography and Censorship

In 1947, a *Life Magazine* reporter interviewing W. H. Auden came up with the question: "But *how*, Mr. Auden, do you know what you're reading is really pornography?"

"That's simple," replied the poet. "It gives me an erection."

In the interview, Auden went on to decry the pornographic. He felt that physical arousal distracted the reader from any rich and complex aesthetic response; thus, Auden felt, the pornographic was to be avoided by the serious writer. It's a reasonable argument and, in this age where license and repression are forever trading names and places, an argument we might review with some profit, even if we don't agree with it—and I don't.

In the early eighties, some years after Auden's death in 1973, in the gay press Harold Norse published a journal account of an afternoon's sex with Auden. I do not have the article to hand. But memory tells me that the encounter involved a pounce by the older poet; the coupling was brief, desperate, and—while, by Norse's description, the encounter was consensual in that he had known certainly that the pick-up was sexual—nevertheless the physical exchange between them verged on rape. The word that remains with me from the writer is that he found the experience "appalling."

My autobiography, *The Motion of Light in Water* (Plume/New American Library, 1988), gives an account of a similar sexual encounter that happened to me about 1960, which, to my mind, has many things in common with Norse's encounter with Auden. When I was eighteen, while we were at the piano bench together, a musician friend in his late thirties, with whom I was collaborating on an opera, suddenly, and clearly in a state of great distress, pounced on me and physically dragged me to his bed. So I know first-hand the sort of thing Norse was recounting.

We shall get back to this in a bit.

I don't believe we really have to dwell on what pornography *is*. It's a practice of writing—i.e., it's a genre; and genres simply do not yield up their necessary and sufficient conditions, i.e., they cannot be defined. But they can be functionally described in terms clear enough for any given situation. And for our situation here (that is, assuming we are all bored with, or unhappy over, or simply angry at the mystifications that have come along with the various pornography/erotica distinctions), we can probably describe pornography as those texts which arouse, either by auctorial intention or by accident—if not those texts that are assumed to be arousing, either to the reader currently talking about them, or to someone else: That is, pornographic texts are generally those that can be organized around some elaboration of the emblem Auden set up forty-five years back.

Arguments over pornography—whether pro or con—seem most intelligent when the critic him- or herself admits to having been aroused (Auden; Jane Gallup on Sade). Those arguments become their most lunatic when the critic, unaroused by a given text, starts speculating on the results of possible arousal in other people—the "general community," "ordinary men and women," "children," etc.—and inveighs against the dangers that might result should someone from one of these groups—to whom clearly the critic does not belong—stumble over an arousing text on bookstore rack or library shelf.

I mentioned Auden's and my musician friend's sexual practices not to vilify them—unpleasant though they were. In either case it might simply have been an anomalous afternoon. But it's also possible that they weren't anomalous at all. And if they weren't, they might tell us something of the context that might cast meaningful light on Auden's disapproval of the pornographic. The context is, of course, the way in which situations of arousal generally fit into the *rest* of one's life.

If such desperate and nonmutual pounces were most of Auden's sex, it might just give us pause.

Though we have no way to know for certain (for such things were not generally chronicled), we can still make an educated guess that up until fairly recently, a good deal of sex—not only homosexual but heterosexual—was much like those precipitous encounters. We have the evidence for it in the date rapes and the marital rapes that still too frequently mar the sexual landscape today.

In a population that basically feels that Sex Is Bad—or at best a necessary evil—often sex will occur, whether within the bounds of marriage or outside it, only at those moments of extreme need, and then in a paroxysm of guilt, so that the sexual incident itself is likely to be infrequent, desperate, brutal, and brief—and satisfactory, if such a word can even be used for an act which, in their different ways, both "perpetrator" and "victim" probably come to dread—for only the most basal needs of the more aggressive partner.

Within such a populace, where this is the basic sexual model and where this is the sort of act arousal leads to, it's small wonder that situations of arousal in general—which include the pornographic—are thought by all concerned to be basically Bad Things.

Straight or gay, most men don't "approve" of this sort of sex any more than straight or gay women—even those among all four groups who are sure that this is the only sort of sex there really is. And though probably not the majority anymore, sadly there are still many of those.

The fear of—or anger at—pornography slated for men that many women feel may well have to do not with any violence-against-women depicted in the pornographic material as such; rather it may simply reflect the fact that many women consider male arousal outside the relationship the first step toward infidelity. And, for many women, male infidelity is a deeply painful thing to contemplate. That pain may be the real "violence" against women inherent in pornography. And if the sexual act is itself associated with the brutal, if not the outright violational, then the violence is even more supported by the reality of things—though I point out that the argument in this paragraph so far follows to the letter my own prescription above for the lunatic, since it involves my speculating in how others regard arousal—in ways I certainly don't regard it myself.

Indeed, I've always suspected that those who get *too* twisted out of shape by what possible arousal means for others (it's "frightening," it's "soul scarring," it "represents a loss of control," it's a "violent incursion upon one's autonomy," it's "confusing and disorienting") are finally revealing all too much about the way they regard sexual arousal in their own lives.

But with all respect to Auden, it is the rushed, the guilty, and the inarticulate that militate against the aesthetic—not arousal *per se.*

Pornography is an important and potentially aesthetically rich and exciting genre.

I've written two pornographic novels—that is, much of the writing aroused me sexually while I was doing it. The first of them, *Equinox*, has been published (as *Tides of Lust*, Lancer Books, 1973). The second, *Hogg* (finished 1973), has been to a number of publishers, legitimate and pornographic. All have refused it.

Only last month, the editor of a commercial house that produces pornography of the sort that fills the racks of adult bookstores approached me and asked me to tell her something about the book. "Well," I told her, "the narrator of the book is an eleven-year-old boy—"

She sat back and laughed. "That lets *us* out right there. The one thing everyone in the industry is afraid to touch today is child pornography. Basically what my job entails is going over the manuscripts we get and changing all the fifteen-, sixteen-, and seventeen-year-olds into eighteen-year-olds and over."

As if—despite Freud's discovery of infantile sexuality—people at every age did not have a real and ever-changing sexual component to their lives!

I go over the above only to point out that there is a real, material, and tangible industry of pornographic publishing in this country that not only has its values and standards (far more conservative today than they were, say, in the 1960s), but also has quite an astonishing set of rich and fascinating classics (e.g., Michael Perkins's *Evil Companions*, 1967; Alexander Trocchi's *Thongs* [the Olympia Press edition of 1965, not the currently available Masquerade edition that has been posthumously editorially rewritten]; Dirk Vandon's *I Want It All*; Pat Califia's *Macho Slut*, 1989; and Alice Joanou's extraordinarily stylish *Cannibal Flower*, 1991)—although these and others such works are rarely discussed.

Despite their possible aesthetic failures or successes, both my pornographic novels, the published *Equinox (Tides of Lust)* and the unpublished *Hogg*, were aesthetically serious undertakings—not in spite of their pornographic aspects but because of them. (One of the self-imposed constraints on the writing of *Equinox* was that I would write none of it unless I was actually in a state of sexual arousal, even for the nonsexual parts—an undertaking I'd advise only for the young and/or obsessive.) And though I respect Auden's warning about the possibly deleterious relation between pornography and art, I still disagree with it. But I am aware that one possible reason for my disagreement is that, despite the autobiographical accuracy I've almost never striven for in my fiction, the overwhelming majority of the situations of arousal I've experienced in the last thirty-five years have been relaxed, friendly (when other people were involved), pleasurable—and largely free of guilt. The vast majority of my sexual partners have basically enjoyed themselves in their various sexual encounters with me—as have I with them. And for me this forms the context that all new situations of arousal enter, even when, from time to time, in specifically pornographic texts, the material is violent or disturbing or generally unpleasant.

But this brings us to the other topic in this discussion: censorship. I would not think to use a term like censorship for the treatment of say, *Hogg*, if only because at various times I've experienced the political niggling and pussyfooting in the name of the commercial that is how a good deal of real censorship is exercised in this country (the editor who rejected a 1967 novel of mine not because he was bothered by the fact that my main character was black, but because he was sure his readers would be—readers who, incidentally, once the book was published a year later, kept the book in print for the next twenty-five years; the print run on a 1985 book, third in a series, slashed in half because the topic was AIDS; and the manuscript of the fourth book in the series returned to me by the same publisher, unread). An editor's rejecting a book because he or she didn't like it—whether the dislike was aesthetic, political, or sexual—doesn't, in a free economy, fulfill my criteria for censorship.

Censorship—for me—requires that someone become deeply involved in deciding whether *other* people will be offended, or dislike it, or be outraged by a work—usually to the point of wholly suppressing his or her own response. (The editor who slashed my print run had gone out of his way, three months before, to tell me that the book was among the most powerful he had ever read in his life, and had left him, in his own words, dazed—however hyperbolic the praise may have been.) It's that repression of the self which creates the dangerous and deleterious field of projections, out of control and wholly away from any possibility of pursuing real profit or even common sense. In this country, the commercial terror of the experimental and the controversial has the same psychological structure—and finally much the same effect—as the hardcore censorship we are so ready to condemn when it happens abroad.

Having said that, I think that in sexual terms, those people who share my basic context for arousal are precisely those who are inclined to say: Let other people do what they want, whether it involves pornography or perversion or whatever—as long as no one is hurt or made miserable. We feel this way because we are under the impression that such a context is pretty much what characterizes the context of pleasure for everyone. Similarly, I suspect that those people for whom a significant proportion of situations of arousal have led to pain, distress, guilt, and unhappiness are the people who are likely to question seriously the advisability of such a liberal attitude toward the arousal of others. But that—as I said— is a question of context, and it may never be resolved until the context itself is interrogated, articulated, and understood in its own right.

I think it is terribly important to have a genre—or genre-set—in which it is possible to say *anything:* true, untrue, or at any level of fantasy, metaphor, violence, or simple outrageousness. And I would rather such a genre-set be the genre-set of art than that it be the associated texts of religion, say (consider the hell-fire sermon in chapter III of *Portrait of the Artist as a Young Man* as an example of a religious genre repeatedly presented to young children from the nineteenth century on, if you want an example of what I consider immoral religious license), or those that comprise journalism (consider the allegations of supernatural happen-ings and the like that are the hallmark of the "popular" tabloid press, *The National Enquirer, The Sun, The Star*). But there are social forces aplenty—and often the same forces that would take away the freedom of speech we vouchsafe for the arts—that, as they would deny that freedom *to* the arts, would redistribute it to religion and reportage—genres whose rela-tion to that troublesome concept "truth" I, at any rate, am fairly glad to see a bit more heavily scrutinized at the more respected levels than, cer-tainly, they are on the lowest and least sophisticated planes. It is not only the freedom to suppress what others say that is wanted, but the freedom to lie as well when necessary—because such lies are assumed somehow to be for "everyone's good."

But we cannot forget those planes. They are always there to grow, to take over, and to swamp what I am perfectly content to call more respon-sible attitudes in religious and reportorial practices.

Art seems the best genre-set in which to allow total freedom of expres-sion (the full range, as Kenneth Koch put it, of "wishes, lies, and dreams") *because* that genre-set is the symbol-making engine for the culture.

If artists who wish to criticize or even shame the country for national acts they consider immoral are not allowed to set up installations in which, say, American flags are burned or otherwise desecrated, then it is precisely the resonance, significance, and luminescence of the flag wav-ing for the country's palpable accomplishments that are reduced by the proscription. (A symbol that is allowed to function only in one context, and that an uplifting one, invariably becomes trite—if not kitsch.) And necessary limitations on the aesthetic presentation of what the body may undergo, either in pleasure or in suffering, immediately and *a priori* re-strict what the mind is allowed to contemplate: For nothing encourages the practice of political torture and sabotages the pursuit of happiness more than blanket restrictions on speaking, in precise, articulate, and graphic terms about either.

—New York City
August 1994

14

The Making of *Hogg*

Harold Jaffe thanks Stephan-Paul Martin and Mel Freilicher for editorial assistance with the questions for the interview.

The nameless narrator of Hogg *[Normal, Ill.: Black Ice, 1995] is a Huck-like eleven-year-old caught in society's most sinister seams. Unlike Huck, though, Delany's narrator passes no judgments on the violent actions he takes part in. Becoming the sexual slave of truck-driver Franklin Hargus (a.k.a. Hogg), he wants only to suck on his master's penis, toes, and fingers, drink his urine, and eat his feces.*

Hogg is no ordinary teamster, however. Various disgruntled men (and women) hire him to rape and brutalize their out-of-favor lovers and wives. Over large sections of the book, the narrator describes Hogg and his gang terrorizing women, sexually savaging them and their families. To relieve his perpetual erection, one gang member, teen-aged Denny, pushes a nail through his penis. Maddened by the pain, he goes on a mass-murder spree. About the same time, a local biker and another of Hogg's gang kidnap the narrator away and sell him (for ten dollars) to a brutal black fisherman on the Crawhole docks. As Denny is about to be taken by the police, Hogg rescues the killer, spirits the narrator away, and the two smuggle the teen-aged psychopath into a neighboring state, where, after receiving the flimsiest of promises to behave, Hogg turns him loose to commit who-knows-what further mayhem.

The novel ends in irony. For the first time Hogg admits he feels affection for his child companion, who has accompanied him on these horrific adventures. But now the narrator has decided to escape, seeking as new masters a pair of sadistic garbage men, Rufus and Red, who operate a scow out of Crawhole and whom the narrator met in passing when he was sold there. As the narrator plans his defection, Hogg asks him what's on his mind. The first he speaks in the book and the novel's last word, the narrator's answer is, "Nothin'."*

FI: You completed *Hogg* in 1973 and published it twenty-two years later. Can you detail some of the problems you had in finding a publisher?

---

* This synopsis is modified from one prepared by Harold Jaffe for the original publication of the interview in *Fiction International 30.*

SRD: In the paraliterary field—e.g., science fiction, comic books, pornography—the relationship between creation and publication is so very different from the relation that obtains in the literary precincts, it might help, in understanding the book's publication problems, if I spoke some about the circumstances under which *Hogg* was written.

In the late 1960s, a company called Essex House began putting out a highly literate line of pornography. Following the model of Maurice Girodias at Olympia Press, instead of exhorting the cynical, if not subliterate, hacks who traditionally provided such textual fare to write for him, Essex editor Brian Kirby approached young poets and aspiring literary writers who were just not making a living, men and women for whom a seven-hundred-fifty or a thousand-dollar advance was a major bulwark against eviction or starvation. Formal parameters were relaxed. The books had to focus on sex—but that's all. What came out was extraordinary. Poet David Meltzer produced *Orf* (1968) and *The Agency Trilogy* (1968); Marco Vassi's works came out of this. To my mind, however, the most remarkable of these books was poet and critic Michael Perkins's *Evil Companions* (1968).

I met Michael just after he'd completed his extraordinary *roman noir* but before it was published. (See my "Preface" to the Rhinoc*eros* edition reprint [1992] of *Evil Companions*.) The energy around these books and writers was immense, pervasive, and infectious. I was twenty-six years old—and it was hard not to be caught up in it.

Within that field of energy and excitement I wrote my first pornographic novel, *Equinox.*

Kindly, Perkins read my book in manuscript. One night in the first weeks of December '68 at Perkins's Avenue A apartment, we had a long, boozy critical session over it that lasted till dawn. As anyone who has read his criticism knows (*The Secret Record* [1992]; *The Good Parts* [1994]), Perkins is an astute analyst of texts.

The session had at least three results.

The first was a four-day hangover. Then, about ten days later, with a New Year's Eve flight, I moved to San Francisco.

The second and third were two new passages I inserted toward the beginning and end of *Equinox*, "The Scorpion's Log." Finally, that spring, I was ready to submit the manuscript to Kirby—only to learn that Essex House had gone out of business.

The manuscript went into the drawer.

The last Essex volumes were, however, still making their way to my wife's Natoma Street flat in San Francisco where I was then living. The energy was still there.

"The Scorpion's Log" had been an attempt to patch up *Equinox* in light of Michael's criticism—criticism that boiled down to: You don't have to sacrifice a rich relationship between character and landscape just because you're writing about sex. As a novel, *Equinox* is largely a collection of set pieces. As such, "The Scorpion's Log" only added some new ones to those already there. At the same time, I was working on a large novel, *Dhalgren*. After having put together a fairly complex outline for it back in New York, I was having some difficulty getting beyond the opening chapter. In that way we writers have, I was looking for things to distract me: One of the things I did was to direct a little-theater production of Genet's *Les Bonnes*—in French. It played in our front hall for three weekends, moved to a church basement for a couple of months, and finally aired over KPFA-FM in Berkeley.

And, because I wanted to try my hand at writing a pornographic work more focused and with a greater psychological density, another thing I did (a fourth result of the session with Michael, back in New York) was to begin *Hogg*. On and off, between March and July '69, the novel's first, handwritten draft filled up two, three, then four notebooks. Next I took some time to co-edit with my then-wife, Marilyn Hacker, four issues of a quarterly called *Quark*. Finally I could turn my major energies to *Dhalgren* again; and this time it began to work.

The *Hogg* notebooks ended up in the back of a closet at Natoma Street.

And *Dhalgren* was taking up pretty much all my time.

In summer '71, after teaching at the Clarion SF Writers' Workshop, I came back to New York City and again got to work on *Dhalgren*.

I'd already sent the manuscript of *Equinox* to my agent, Henry Morrison, who began marketing it around. In the Albert Hotel, where I was living, another project intervened—a film called *The Orchid*, produced by Barbara Wise, which I wrote, directed, and edited on an old "chatterbox" editing machine that was moved into my tenth floor hotel room. The eleven days of filming took place in February. The editing went on up through April and into May of '72.

Prints were ready at the end of June.

That summer's Clarion Workshop had three chapters, one in East Lansing, one in New Orleans, and one in Seattle: I taught at all three. After Seattle's Clarion, with a student I'd met in the class, Pat Muir (grandson of the naturalist John Muir, Pat was an electronics repairman and biker), I rode on the back of Pat's motorcycle up to some Oregon communes, then to Vancouver, where we stayed with Russell and Dora FitzGerald, saw George Stanley again, and met poet Robin Blazer. After the trip was done, I bussed down from Seattle to San Francisco, where my friend Paul Caruso was now staying at Natoma Street.

Between the San Francisco Greyhound Bus Terminal and the house, I stopped at the Empire Theater on Market Street, in the back balcony of which I managed to lose a notebook containing some forty-odd pages of *Dhalgren*, so that when I arrived at Paul's I was rather down. But now Paul asked me: "Do you want those old notebooks you left in the back of the closet?"

I pulled them out, to realize I had the first draft of an entire novel that I'd all but forgotten. It kind of cheered me up.

I reconstructed the lost *Dhalgren* pages. Working on things carefully, sentence by sentence, with lots of notes (the way I'd been writing *Dhalgren*), makes such reconstruction easier. By no means is it fun. But it's only tedious—not impossible. A month or so on, the *Hogg* notebooks went with me to New York.

Later in '72, back at the Albert, I finished a draft of *Dhalgren*—just about the time Henry (my agent), told me he'd managed to place *Equinox* with Lancer Books, a small paperback company—three- and-a-half years after the book had been completed. They wanted to change the title to *Tides of Eros*. We compromised on *Tides of Lust*. Inspired by the sale of my first pornographic novel, on a portable electric typewriter I borrowed from Henry's wife I typed up *Hogg* over the next six weeks.

"I think," Henry told me, a week later, when he'd finished it, "you're going to have a bit more trouble selling this one than you had with *Equinox*." He didn't even want to try Lancer. (Financially they were pretty shaky; a week after they published *Equinox* in '73, they went out of business.) At my suggestion, we submitted it to Girodias at Olympia, which had opened up American offices.

The result was a pleasant lunch with Henry, me, and that urbane and charming old scoundrel. Girodias was interested but noncommittal. Some time later, after he'd rejected the novel, he wrote me: "*Hogg* is the only novel in my career that I have declined to publish *solely* because of its sexual content. Should the book someday appear, please feel free to use this as a blurb, if you think it will help promote sales." Alas, when the book did appear, twenty-odd years later, Maurice was dead. Using that blurb would have confused more readers than not—though I'm still fond of it.

Days before Christmas '72, I flew to England to rejoin Marilyn. During the first half of '73, in our Paddington Street flat, *Dhalgren* went through another—and final—rewrite. Impelled by leftover energy, *Hogg* shot, once more, through the typewriter—and received its final subscription date, October '73, though my agent had been sending around earlier versions for the previous year and a half. In London, editing a string of British men's magazines, American poet Richard Deutch read it and became quite enthusiastic. He promised to publish some excerpts—but had a severe breakdown at about that time. A pleasant young woman I met through Richard, who worked out of her kitchen while her kids played around the table legs, typed the final manuscript. Besides typing, she wrote soft-core stories for British men's magazines. Supportive and enthusiastic about my novel, she was one of *Hogg*'s first fans.

I began to realize the problems to beset the finished book when the London copy shop, where I took *Hogg* to be Xeroxed, phoned me to say that they would not make copies of the text. The office manager had looked at it, read a page or two, and told them to return it to the customer.

At a self-service machine, I copied *Hogg*, feeding in a sheet at a time—and sent it to Henry. Still not sanguine about publication possibilities, he told me over the phone he'd start sending the new version around. I returned from England the day before Christmas Eve 1974 (I was now a father, with a daughter almost a year old), to start teaching at SUNY Buffalo in January '75. *Dhalgren* had just been published, and *Trouble on Triton* was in production. As Marilyn and I were coming through Kennedy Airport, I saw a newsstand rack full of *Dhalgren*s, and—a few minutes later—a sailor in his blues sitting in a tubular chair, at one of the gates, reading a copy. Three days later, Bantam Books phoned me to say the book had already gone through three printings before its official publication date (January 1, 1975). It was scheduled for two more: I had a moderately successful novel on my hands.

A week or so later, Marilyn and I separated for good.

I don't really know *where* Henry sent *Hogg*. I'm not particularly interested in who rejects my work—only in who accepts it. That he tells me only of the latter has always been our arrangement. I know, however, he was sending it somewhere. A year or two on, I picked up a young, stocky Irish-American (complete with red hair, very thick glasses, and freckles) near the city's downtown waterfront, who took me back to his apartment in the industrial streets west of the Village. Our after-sex talk turned to books. At one point, getting up from the futon and putting on a paisley robe, he said: "Do you want to see the weirdest, most outrageous thing I've ever read? Just a second." He went to a drawer, pulled it open, took out a manuscript in a black spring binder, and brought it back to me. "Read five pages of that—*any* five pages. It doesn't really matter which ones—go on!"

I opened back the black cover and began to flip through what was obviously a Xerox of a Xerox of a Xerox—I could only guess at how many generations. There was no title page. It began simply at page one.

It was the manuscript of *Hogg*.

Somehow, to say, "Hey, you know, actually *I* wrote this . . ." seemed absurd.

So I read a few pages. Yes, it was my novel.

"That's . . . pretty amazing," I told him. "Where'd you get it?"

He'd gotten it from a friend who'd gotten it from a friend who'd gotten it from a publishing company, where the manuscript, on arrival, had created a small furor in the office. Before returning it, someone had made a quick and unauthorized Xerox . . .

"I'd like to read the whole thing," I said. "Could I get one?"

"I guess so. Although it's pretty dim to copy once more . . ."

Unfortunately we never ran into each other again. But I didn't really need one.

After the success of *Dhalgren* in '75 (and the smaller success of *Trouble on Triton* in '76), in '77 Bantam Books agreed to buy up all my earlier books, the rights to which had recently reverted to me. Lancer had gone out of business, so the rights to *Equinox* had also reverted. "You know," Henry told the folks at Bantam he was negotiating with, "Delany also has two 'erotic' novels, one of which has been published and one of which is still in manuscript. You guys are doing real well with things like Anaïs Nin's *Delta of Venus*. Do you want to buy the rights to those as well?"

Somebody said, "Sure. Why not?"

So *Hogg* was bought—in a large package with a lot of other books— and paid for—though no one at Bantam had actually read it. Henry felt that was the best he could do. One day at Bantam, however, I asked Lou Aronica if there was any chance of their publishing *Hogg*—not to mention reprinting *Equinox*.

Lou looked at me and laughed. "You know, I just got around to reading them last month. They're extraordinary books, Chip. Both of them. But will we *publish* them?" He chuckled. "Not a snowball's chance in hell!"

Of the twenty-odd years *Hogg* languished in Limbo, Bantam accounts for ten. The book was shown to a few other publishers during that time. Five? Fifteen? I didn't know, because I was working on other things, and (as I said) generally I'm not informed of rejections. Lou said as soon as there was some interest from someone else, certainly he wouldn't stand in the way of our buying back the rights. But as the '80s rolled on, with times becoming more and more conservative, there seemed less and less chance of the books appearing.

But those samizdat Xeroxes were (I guess) still generating rumors:

In 1991, a small publishing collective in Seattle, centered around Ron Drummond, Randy Byers, and the people at Serconia Press (who'd already done a nonfiction book of mine, *The Straits of Messina* [1989]) phoned me. They knew of the existence of *Hogg*.

All the people involved were pretty familiar with the range of my work—including *Equinox*. "The fact is, Chip," Drummond told me over the phone, "we can't *conceive* of a book by you, even if it's about the strangest sex in the world, that we wouldn't want to do. Send *Hogg* to us: We guarantee you, sight unseen, we'll publish it."

"Don't do that, Ron," I told him. "If you're interested, certainly I'll show it to you. If you guys decide you want to publish it, I'll be delighted. But it's unrealistic to commit yourself to something like that without reading the manuscript first. Too many people have found it too great a problem. Make your mind up *after* you look at it."

But I agreed to send it.

Then working at *Reflex Magazine*, my friend Robert Morales volunteered to scan the manuscript onto disk. Five years ago optical scanning and character recognition were not all that hot. Proofreading the text and putting in corrections turned into a far more time-consuming job than I was ready for. Three months later, though, a pristine manuscript went to Seattle.

A couple of weeks later, Drummond phoned again. "Well . . . eh, Chip. Yeah. You were right. We've all got lots of questions about the advisability of bringing it out."

"I'm not surprised," I said.

"What we want to do," Ron said, "is hold a meeting. We want to have a few more people read it. Then we want to have them all discuss it seriously." They decided to put together a discussion seminar of eight people: two gay men, two straight men, two gay women, and two straight women—all people who had read the book and who were familiar with my other work. They decided to record the discussion, and Ron told me they would send me a copy.

About that same time, in his Guest of Honor talk at Readercon, speaking of the problems he'd had with the publication of some of his own more experimental books, Barry Malzberg explained: "Some books are simply never going to be published by a committee."

After seventeen years, I didn't have much emotional investment in *Hogg*'s publication. But on the intellectual level, what I'd heard Malzberg say seemed pretty much to cover the situation.

A couple of months later, at an SF convention here on the East Coast, Victor Gonzales just in from Seattle handed me a copy of the tape. On a walkman in my hotel room I played it that afternoon. One or two of the discussants, at the last minute, hadn't been able to make it—at least one of the gay men, I believe. Other than that, it was what they'd said it would be.

The tape was about an hour and a half.

No writer could have asked for a more astute and sensitive discussion of a manuscript. Listening to the dialogue, I felt that everyone on the panel had read the book carefully and intelligently. They'd all taken in its intentions, its various and several points. None of them had missed any subtleties or major moves in the text. All seemed to have found many sections moving. All agreed that the material was extraordinarily distasteful: It is.

The breakdown as to which people felt the book should be published and which people felt it would be dangerous to publish (not because of legal repercussions, but because of what it might do to unstable readers) was, however, interesting.

The women—gay and straight—felt that, as distasteful as it was, the book ought to be published. One even thought its publication imperative.

The men—gay and straight—felt that the danger to unstable minds was simply too great a risk.

Because the money for the venture was being put up by one of the straight men, however, finally it was decided to forego publication. With many apologies, they returned the manuscript. Randy Byers sent me a fine, thoughtful, and considered letter. I answered him with a letter of my own. At this point, Larry McCaffery became aware of the recent interest in the novel—and the controversy it was causing. I'm not sure whether he actually heard the discussion tape. (At one point, Ron said he was going to send it to him.) Larry asked to see *Hogg* and took it to Ron Sukenick and Curt White at Fiction Collective 2, who were just putting together a new line, Black Ice Books.

Did I want to see *Hogg* published? Yes.

But I was now fifty and the author of more than twenty-five books—most of which had appeared in several editions. The truth is, in more cases than not, publication is painful enough to leach all but the most fleeting pleasure from the printing of a new book. To fixate on the realization of a forthcoming volume only intensifies the pain from the inevitable defects marring its actual publication.

From time to time, yes, I've found myself looking forward to the appearance of a new volume.

But I try not to.

Since Fiction Collective 2/Black Ice are *Hogg*'s current publishers, I feel a certain discretion is appropriate in talking about the problems that I had there.

Most of those problems turned, again, on the committee nature of a collective publisher—and also on the fact that they *are* a small operation. Those problems ranged from some unauthorized last-minute "creative copy editing" that had to be undone, to a delay in the appearance of the book (anyone who looks at the hardcover copyright page will see the book is dated 1994, though it didn't appear until well into 1995), to the obligatory cover-confusion (it was supposed to be white dropout on black; not, as it is, black on blue: It changes considerably the reading of that abstract blob—which is, yes, my significant other Dennis's seminal fluid), to a mix-up in the printing of the first paperback edition, so that the printing had to be pulped: Through dropped or doubled lines, more than ten percent of the pages didn't connect to the page following. It was unreadable.

Suffice it to say, however, that the current paperback printing now out in stores is a fine and largely accurate edition of *Hogg*.

The press and I are proud of it.

FI: Transgressive is a literary category that perhaps has been overused; still one could reasonably fit *Hogg* into that category. It is transgressive in terms of its extensively elaborated scatology; and it is more generally transgressive in that it is narrated from the point of view of the sexual recipient, or "victim," as some might choose to call your adolescent narrator. To what extent were you influenced by the writings of Genet and Bataille, two notable literary prototypes of so-called transgression? Did you have any other artistic models in mind?

SRD: That's a complicated question. First, there *are* victims in the book: the women that Hogg is paid to rape, abuse, and brutalize. But the narrator is *not* one of them. Perhaps that helps make the book as disturbing as people so often find it. We have an overarching sentimental model that says an underage child involved in sex *must* be a "victim"—or, if not (and this is the soiled, nasty underside of sentimentality), then some sort of monster of the *Bad Seed* variety. But *Hogg*'s narrator is neither, though he takes part willingly in rapes, assaults, and brutalization.

When I wrote *Hogg*, the only Bataille I had read was the old Ballantine paperback edition of *Literature and Evil*. Although Perkins was a great fan of Bataille's two pornographic novels, *Madame Edwarda* and *Story of the Eye*, and had recommended them to me highly, neither was then readily available in English. So, no, I *hadn't* read them. In 1961 I'd read *Our Lady of the Flowers* in the 1949 Editions Morihen translation (under the title *Gutter in the Sky*). And, as I said, I was directing Genet's *Les Bonnes* just before I started writing *Hogg*. As it happens, I first read *Miracle of the Rose* in the Frechtman translation *while* I was writing it. But though I enjoyed Genet's second novel immensely, if it was any sort of influence, it was a negative one: Genet's heightened rhetoric a-swirl all through the presentation of a succession of several objects of desire, with whom there is all-but-no bodily contact, is precisely what I *didn't* want to do in *Hogg*.

Guillaume Apollinaire's surreal pornographic masterpiece *The Debouched Hospodar* (Perkins published the first English translation in his magazine *Down Here*) was very much, and conscientiously so, a model for *Equinox*—though I wanted to achieve some of the same effects without recourse to the surreal. (I used drug-induced hallucinations instead.) But for *Hogg* there was no conscious pornographic model at all.

In an article on my several sex novels that first appeared in the *New York Review of Science Fiction* (reprinted in the James Sallis–edited volume *Ash of Stars* [1996]), writer Ray Davis makes a point I, at least, found interesting: *Hogg* is a novel—perhaps, says Davis, the only such novel—that really *is* filled with precisely what conservative forces in the country claim is rampant in *all* pornography . . . violence against women, torture, murder, racism, filth, the exploitation of children, and other acts too perverse to name. The only place it breaks with this (if we can call it such) classical and conservative description of pornography is that it is carefully written, not sloppily hacked out; and it examines those subjects not from the point of view of sociologists and psychologists with their ready-made categories of "victims" and "monsters," but examines them as seriously—and relentlessly—as the *people caught up in such acts* are capable of. That it finds touches of humanity here and there even among murderers and criminal psychopaths is, of course, troubling.

At the end of the book, the reader should ask: What punishment should Hogg receive for what he's done . . . ?

What punishment should Denny receive . . . ?

Is there some unwarranted cruelty in the narrator's decision to leave Hogg for what is a comparatively domesticated version of S/M with garbage scow workers Red and Rufus back on the docks?

And, of course, the final question must be: Personally, how are *you* engaged by these questions?

FI: Among the many atypical aspects of *Hogg* is the fact that it is not "naturalized"; that is, nowhere in the savage goings-on is any norm posited. Rather there is a collective radical deviation from so-called normalcy in which every major character participates. The novel's ending reinforces the significance of the destabilization of all norms, when the adolescent narrator rejects Hogg's plan to domesticate their situation. Would you comment on any of these themes?

SRD: Humbly I'd suggest that you're overlooking, among others, the "normal" couple, Harry Bunim, Mona Casey, and their infant son Chuck, living on the barge beside the scow belonging to Rufus and Red. But there are lots of relatively "normal" people in the novel: the hardware store owner and her daughter, for example; the bartender, Ray, at the Piewacket Bar; the harmonica-playing fisherman, Andy; and perhaps the most important, the director of the radio show. Generally, the "normal" people are the ones attacked and brutalized by Hogg—and, later, Denny. One of the novel's tasks is temporally to normalize a moral frame outside the experience of most readers of the book: The frame that will triumph in the book *is* Red and Rufus's, which the narrator will finally—and sensibly—choose over Hogg's. One strategy the book employs to accomplish this normalization is the metonymic association of Red and Rufus with Harry and Mona.

The prevalence of and the focus on the deviant is high enough, however, that, for the first reading or two, readers are not likely to pay much attention to the strands of normalcy threading the brutality and sexual excess. Nevertheless, those strands are as carefully woven as the "abnormal" ones. If they weren't, the book wouldn't function.

Among the tasks the novel attempts is to mark out a discursive field in which, by the end, the reader can no longer even *say* the words "normal" and "abnormal" without putting them in quotation marks, ironizing them, or somehow or other placing them *sous rature.*

FI: The narrator rarely addresses his own emotional state, yet his description of the other characters and of the frequent S/M and scatological sexual acts in which he participates are exhaustively detailed, always precise, and often stylistically refined. This seeming discontinuity between an adolescent, unself-conscious narrator who is also a keen and even elegant observer/recorder seems central to the novel's impact. Can you discuss your narrator's character and function?

SRD: To begin with, the narrator is not an adolescent: He's *pre*-adolescent—he's only eleven. He is, however, pubescent. That's not the same thing. As a first-person narrator, however—like Huckleberry Finn, like Esperanza Cordero in Cisneros's *House on Mango Street*, like Holden Caulfield—my narrator tells his tale from some indeterminate future age. (Fourteen, seventeen, twenty, twenty-six . . . this last the age I was when, just before my twenty-seventh birthday, in San Francisco, I began drafting it.) This signals to the reader that he's survived the story's events and, like Ishmael, lived to tell them. Yes, he attempts to narrate Hogg's story as it struck him *at the time*—but, of course, there's a fibrillating quality to his sophistication, that registers (to you) as a discontinuity, or set of discontinuities.

Were the material more traditionally associated with children, you might be less aware of those "discontinuities" that of course exist between the character's various levels: the touches that signal the eleven-year-old to whom the events happened, the verbal turns that signal the older personality looking back on the events, and those places where, as it must to those looking for it, the "art of the novel" shows.

FI: In a certain way, Hogg's complexities seem complementary to the narrator's. A sexual torturer and murderer, he performs the most degrading, even bestial, acts with a fiercely relentless exhilaration. At the same time he is capable of astute self-reflection and of discoursing on so-called normalcy and the social construction of desire and identity in the manner of a poststructuralist and gender theorist. Did you have any literary or cultural precedents in mind for the characterizations of Hogg and/or his mentor-protégé relationship with the adolescent narrator?

SRD: Sadism is classically known as "the perversion of philosophers." Presumably when you realize that you gain real and deeply desired pleasure by doing things that *truly* hurt other people, you face the sort of *aporia* that *must* start you thinking about the nature of the social world that defines good and evil and your own place—and the place of other beings—in it.

The same imperative is just not there, say, with masochism: "You derive pleasure from hurting yourself? Go on, then. Hurt yourself—as long as it doesn't bother me."

You call Hogg a murderer. But while he's probably killed a few people before the book begins, in the novel proper, though he threatens many and physically injures many more—injures them to the point they will need serious medical attention—the only *murder* he commits (some readers are surprised when they're reminded of this) is that of the morally loathsome Jimmy.

James Bond, Snake Pliskin, Dirty Harry—all are *far* more lethal than Hogg—in films any eleven-year-old is energetically welcomed by our society to view.

To call Hogg a poststructuralist or a gender theorist is a hyperbole that, I take it, you offer as a compliment. It's a hyperbole still. That he's all but illiterate doesn't mean, however, Hogg can't *think*. Yes, he's smart. (Were he not, he'd have been caught long ago.) Also he's the most active on-stage character in the novel. (When Denny briefly becomes *more* active than Hogg, *he* moves *off-stage* and his actions are only reported indirectly for the duration.) That goes a long way toward needling at the reader's sympathies. Hogg has a specific roster of things he wants to accomplish over the novel's course—and he puts a lot of energy into achieving them successfully, which is, in current narrative discourse, another way of evoking sympathy.

The reader is uncomfortable sympathizing with such a "monster."

But when, at the end, the narrator realizes he can get the same sexual excitement from Red and Rufus, without the accoutrements of murder and rapine, and so chooses to return to the garbage scow and abandon Hogg (a sane, logical decision, which—at the *level* of logic—all of us have to concur with), many readers—if only for a moment—are going to find themselves caught up in the poignancy of Hogg's situation.

That someone like Hogg could elicit our sympathy—that (even momentarily) we should find him poignant, human, and struggling for happiness (rather than monster or victim) — *is* going to trouble.

Well, *Hogg* is a story written to trouble.

It's no more a feel-good novel than *Sentimental Education* or *Good Morning Midnight.*

Davis sees in *Hogg* a combination of Mark Twain and Dashiell Hammett, with a goodly dollop of Sade. But I'd rather let readers—and/or critics—speculate on possible literary models, precedents, or origins than try to untangle them myself. To say that *Hogg* represents something new or unprecedented simply flies in the face of all we know of intertextuality, of the literary. Texts that are readable—and even texts that aren't—just *aren't* new in that transcendent way. I don't mind saying, though, that two dozen years ago when I was writing it, *Hogg* certainly *felt* new. But that's the illusion all writers need to put down words and finish their novels. (To appreciate a book richly, possibly readers need it too.) If it hadn't felt that way at the time, I wouldn't have been able to write it.

—*New York City*
August 10, 1996

15

The Phil Leggiere Interview

Reading *The Mad Man*

Phil Leggiere: In your critical analysis of the subversive qualities of science fiction as a genre, you've emphasized the distinct challenges the language of science fiction (with its built-in conceptual conflict between habitual linguistic frames of reference of the reader's "present" world and those to be inferred in the narrative) offers. *The Mad Man* seems to be a departure to some extent from much of your previous fiction not only in its setting in the chronological present but in its active exploration of other genres, such as pornography, mystery, "Gothic," and the traditional literature of the fantastic and grotesque. Has your work on the novel prompted any new perspective on the subversive challenge of the language of these genres?

Samuel R. Delany: Well, first I have to point out that no genre (or its language) is necessarily subversive—or even challenging—by itself. The challenge—the subversion—is always in the way a specific text is read by a specific reader. That's why readers—and articulated readings, in the form of criticism—are so important.

If anything has given me a new perspective—though it's not a very sanguine one—it's teaching at the university level for the last five years. I've seen lots of texts I considered hugely subversive (some science fiction, some literary) given the most conservative and nonchallenging readings by professors and students alike—readings I would often call blatant and self-evident misreadings. Usually this was because the readers involved just couldn't conceive of a written text making anything except the most conservative statement. Thus, they read them the way they preconceived them—which is conservatively.

Now, I've always felt that the most innocent-seeming haiku, if read properly, can undermine the cherished assumptions of the world's grandest imperialist governments—while the most impassioned diatribe against the exploitative evils of the age can be read as an assurance that such evils will always be with us and thus nothing can be done to change them.

That's why I've fallen back on quoting—and requoting—something that, years before I started full-time teaching, I took from Roland Barthes by way of Barbara Johnson for an epigraph to the final chapter in my novel *Neveryóna*: "Those who fail to reread are obliged to read the same story everywhere."

You've mentioned pornography and mysteries as two genres my new book *The Mad Man* plays with. But the most important genre—or sub-genre—it takes to itself is the "academic novel." And, as academic novels go, it's a pretty scathing one. It's a novel that allegorizes—if you want to read it that way—the situation our contemporary graduate students (who, in most major research universities, teach 50 percent or more of our university classes) have to endure to survive. Jarrell's *Pictures of an Institution*, Amis's *Lucky Jim*, or Philip Roth's *Letting Go* are really the books it contests with. Exploding, or just messing with, the expectations of the academic novel is where it does its most subversive work—and, yes, I still believe that certain genres—especially the paraliterary genres, SF, pornography, comics, mysteries, or newspaper criticism—*do* offer certain possibilities for certain kinds of readings more than certain other kinds.

But *without* the reading, nothing . . .

Language always has two aspects: what you talk about—and how you talk about it. Some of the most nervous reviewers of *The Mad Man* have said they've never seen some of the things I've talked about in that book talked about *anywhere* before! On the one hand, this suggests these critics' reading is pretty parochial. Still, if you're talking about things that are new to most people—what it feels like to be urinated on, what's exciting about excrement to the people it excites, what the life of a homeless chronic masturbator might be like when he's been turned out of a mental hospital onto the streets of New York—you have to talk about such subjects as clearly and cleanly as possible.

PL: How has the relationship between the science fiction community and the cultures of the academic and "avant-garde" literary world changed since you began publishing in the early '60s?

SRD: What the '60s was known for in SF was what was then called "speculative fiction"—which, back then, meant a combination of science fiction, fantasy, and experimental fiction: experimental fiction that used SF imagery, and SF and fantasy that employed experimental writing techniques. Like many neologisms, "speculative fiction" slipped and slid around quite a bit—so much so that, by 1972, most people got tired of that slippage and just dropped it. I was one of those who was happiest to see "speculative fiction" put out to pasture, where it belonged, and forgotten.

But that was because too many people were using it simply to mean "that science fiction I personally happen to approve of." And who needs a term for that? "Oh, but this is not *really* science fiction. It's *speculative fiction*." (Why? 'Cause I happen to like it.) I'd much prefer to see you call it science fiction (or experimental fiction) and spell out your particular agenda.

But, with time (and the term), we also seemed to lose a good number of the conduits between the two social worlds, science fiction and the avant garde. It's arguable that the connection between the world of science fiction writers and the world of experimental writers was maintained, back in the '60s, somewhat artificially—largely by the simple but real affluence of so many art programs back then.

Today, of course, is the era of the artistic cutback.

Conduits between areas like that have fallen away. I was recently at a writers' conference—having nothing to do with SF at all—where I heard a bunch of writers who considered themselves pretty serious about what they were doing decry all experimentation because it alienated readers! They seemed to think pandering to readers (which, in case they forgot, is what the alternative is called) was somehow the way, in an artistic enterprise, to get something of importance done. But clearly their notion of seriousness and my notion of seriousness were just not the same.

PL: You describe yourself in your autobiography *The Motion of Light in Water* (1988) as a young writer preoccupied by issues relating to the creation and portrayal of characters in science fiction. How has your understanding of the creation and exploration of character in non-"realist" and non-conventionally psychological fiction evolved? Has your work in autobiographical narrative and literary theory influenced your subsequent fiction?

SRD: Again, I don't believe—nor have I believed since I was twenty or twenty-one—that even the most "realistic" character is anything more than a learned mode of reading—a mode controlled by a perfectly arbitrary set of learned data expectations; that is, I don't believe there's any simple, transparent, and uncritical relation between "realism" as it's traditionally conceived in narratives and anything we might call "reality."

Most of my characters—those in *The Mad Man*, say—are quite conservatively conceived. But I try to write the conservative character the same way I would follow some mathematically experimental template set out by the OuLiPo Group. And I choose people to subject to this wholly arbitrary regime who aren't usually its focus: a man who likes to stretch his foreskin out to extraordinary lengths with plastic rings, another man with no control over his urinary practices.

Having said that, I think there's something to be said *for* that particular arbitrary mode of reading expectations we call "realism": When I encounter a character in a story, whom I have to live with for more than a certain number of pages, by St. Marx and St. Engels, I want to *know* where the money comes from that buys the character's food and shelter—if the character requires any. And I don't care if it's a wild and wacky surrealist tale by William T. Vollmann or Laurie Moore or if it's the densest sort of verbally rich regionalism by Cormac McCarthy or Randall Kenan. That's information I want from Gabriel García Márquez or Miguel Angel Asturias in their most magic realist modes as well as from James McPherson or Jayne Ann Phillips or Ethan Canin or Grace Paley at their most middle-class or working-class conventional. There's *no* class, from the upper to the lower, that doesn't benefit from learning to ask that question. And there's no writer who isn't made a more aware person by playing with the various ways of suggesting the answer—and suggesting is far more interesting than stating—in his or her texts.

No, it's *not* part of characterization. But it's an expectation of information connected with character initially set up by the likes of Austen, Charlotte Brontë, Balzac, Sand, Dickens, Flaubert and George Eliot—and you mess with the very roots of fiction when you trifle with it . . . notice, I didn't say experiment: I said "trifle."

I'm a poetry reader. And I like experimental fiction. It's not often the kind of fiction I write; but it's the kind I like to read: A new work by Lyn Hejinian or by Ron Silliman and I'm on my ear to get to the bookstore to pick it up. That enjoyment and sympathy informs the more conservatively narrated fiction I do write in comparatively subtle ways. Because it's what I like to read, in a sense it keeps me honest. If I have to put some Greek in my pornographic novel or wrestle with some problem that can only be discussed in terms of Heidegger, I certainly don't say: No, I better not do that; it might alienate the readers!

And, of course, it makes me pay lots of attention to individual sentences.

—New York City
August 1994

16

The Second *Science-Fiction Studies*
Interview

Of *Trouble on Triton* and Other Matters

The following text did not originate as any kind of formal interview. Instead it grew out of an April 1986 session that Chip Delany had with me and my students in a course I was teaching at Concordia University on Utopian and Anti-Utopian (Science) Fiction. By the time this particular class meeting took place, we had already considered Stanislaw Lem's Futurological Congress *and Ursula Le Guin's* The Dispossessed, *and had turned our attention to Delany's* Triton.

Two of the students, Diane Illing and Peta Kom, recorded that session; and perhaps a year thereafter, my former assistant, Donna McGee, made a valiant effort to "decipher" their tapes. Her transcription sat atop one of my file cabinets until April of this year, when I finally found (or, rather, "made") time to verify and edit it. The resultant printout then went to Chip, who subjected it to substantial clarificatory revision.

Except for Chip (SRD), the participants are all designated by an anonymous "Q"; but for the record, the questions not from me come mostly from Renée Lallier (of John Abbott College) and Robert Copp (now a doctoral candidate at McGill).
                                                                    —*Robert M. Philmus*

Q: In *Futurological Congress*, Lem seems to be suggesting that SF is generated from neologisms. How do you react to that proposition? Did *Triton*, for example, in any way arise from the term-concept, "un-licensed sector," say?

SRD: Did it *arise* from the notion or from the term "un-licensed sector"? No.

As far as SF growing from neologisms, however, I do think there's a terribly important verbal side to SF, which your question can be used to foreground. Often, in SF, the writer puts together two word roots, and the resultant term produces a new image for the reader. Take Cordwainer Smith's "ornithopter." To read the word is to know what an ornithopter is—if you recognize the roots: *helicopter* and *ornithos*—a helicopter is a helicopter, of course, and *ornithos* is the Classical Greek word for bird. (In modern Greek, by the bye, *ornithos* just means chicken.) An ornithopter must be a small plane that flaps its wings—like a bird. But even if you haven't seen one of Schoenherr's fine illustrations (that he produced for *Dune* when Herbert borrowed Smith's term), or had it explained to you, it still calls up the image. This verbal side to SF is very important. The range of SF images is governed entirely by the sayable—rather than by any soft-edged concept like the scientifically believable or even the possible.

Consider: "And there, just before me, I could smell the weight of the note D-flat!"

At this point, of course, the "image" (if we can call it that) is fantasy— or perhaps surrealism. Or simply speakable nonsense. But it's not yet SF.

Once we've spoken an image, however, it becomes the SF job of the surrounding rhetoric—especially the pseudo-scientific rhetoric—to make the image cognizable, believable:

> It came from the alternate universe Dr. Philmus's new invention had opened up when I'd pulled the lever—I could smell its weight, ringing out at me, through the glimmering circles of the iridium coil that had opened a portal to a dimension in which such notions, philosophically absurd in ours, nevertheless exist, are common, and make sense . . .

At this point, the image has become acceptable (conventional, hackneyed, even parodic—but recognizable) SF. The image is cognized through a set of codes by which you entail the sayable among a further set of images and ideas that you can visualize and/or conceptualize.

As I've said, the one I just came up with (above) is both parodic and parasitic (parasitic on both philosophy and SF—as well as on our actual situation here, with Dr. Philmus standing right there), and thus brings up a whole further range of questions and considerations. But you get the general idea.

There's often a literal side to SF language. There are many strings of words that can appear both in an SF text and in an ordinary text of naturalistic fiction. But when they appear in a naturalistic text we interpret them one way, and when they appear in an SF text we interpret them another. Let me illustrate this by some examples I've used many times before. The phrase "her world exploded" in a naturalistic text will be a metaphor for a female character's emotional state; but in an SF text, if you had the same words—"her world exploded"—you'd have to maintain the possibility that they mean: A planet belonging to a woman blew up. Similar is the phrase, "he turned on his left side." In a naturalistic text, it would most probably refer to a man's insomniac tossings. But in an SF text the phrase might easily mean a male reached down and flipped the switch activating his sinestral flank. Or even that he attacked his left side. Often what happens with specifically SF language is that the more literal meanings are valorized.

Of course this doesn't happen with *every* sentence in an SF text. Le Guin is an SF writer who uses far less "science fictionary" language than most. But in most SF that most people mean when they speak of SF—i.e., the SF written and released since 1926 that appeared in pulp, or pulp-inspired, magazines and paperback or hardcover books—you have such language here and there all through it; it has a very literal quality to it that, even though we would be hard put to call it referential, is nevertheless quite the opposite of metaphor.

There's a fine novella by Vonda McIntyre, called *Aztecs*, which opens: "She gave up her heart quite willingly." It's about a woman who gives up her four-chambered heart to have it replaced with a rotary blood-pumping mechanism, in order to perform a certain job a person with a pumping heart can't.

Well, this sort of literalization runs all through SF, and is akin to the neologisms you were asking about. Sometimes, when this literalization happens within a single word (between two recognizable roots, say, as in helicopter and ornithos with "ornith/opter"—or "ray/gun," or "visa/phone"), it produces a neologism. But it works at the level of the sentence as well (when disparate words fall into the same SF sentence), and also at the level of plot (when disparate events join in a single diagetic line). If you want to pursue this argument and are interested in a more formal account of it, both in terms of its applications and its limitations, look at section 7 of an essay of mine, "To Read *The Dispossessed*," in *The Jewel-Hinged Jaw*.

Q: Are there any other neologisms in *Triton*? I think there's "metalogic"; but I'm not sure . . .

SRD: The term occurs in the book, only it's not *my* neologism. Or rather, it's another case of philosophical parasitism. In the '60s, with the ascendency of terms like "metafiction" and "paracriticism," philosophers began to ask if there was perhaps a "metalogic"—i.e., a logic of logic. A number of philosophers reached the conclusion that logic *was* the logic of logic. But a few others still clung to the possibility that perhaps there was an extra-logical structure, or "meta-logic," to ordinary logic. Opposing their contention, Quine says somewhere that, really, if you believe you are talking about logic but you assume an extra-logical structure to it, all you've really done is change the subject. I pretty much concur. In *Triton,* metalogic, with its mathematical superstructure (the Modular Calculus), is just general inductive reasoning given a fictive mathematical expression. In *Triton* it "solves" problems I'm perfectly aware general reasoning *can't* solve.

Individual metalogics are designed for different situations. The kinds of problems they solve in *Triton* (always off stage and of a complexity that makes the solution really too hard to follow) are analogous to the following. You're in a room with a door leading to another room. Through the door, someone comes in from the other room, bringing a collection of four or five objects. From a consideration of those four or five objects alone, you now reason out—rigorously and with certainty— what all the remaining objects in the other room must be. Intuitively, we recognize there is no way to find a general solution for such a problem, rigorously and for all cases. The pseudo-scientific rationale (in *Triton*), however, is simply that *if* we had a mathematical reduction whose mathematics were "strong" enough, we just *might* be able to come up with a general-case solution.

The attraction to this bit of logical nonsense is, of course, that we reason our way through similar problems all the time. But precisely the part that can be done rigorously *is* logic. And the rest is hit-or-miss—and produces hit-or-miss results. That's what real experience tells us—if we're honest.

But a real neologism from *Triton?* Well, let's see . . .

Q: "Cybralogs"?

SRD: Cybralogs, yes. I have no idea what cybralogs are or what they could possibly be. But they have something to do with the control of words, obviously. . . . From the context, they're probably some sort of sub-program, either in ROM or RAM form.

Q: The "sensory shield"?

SRD: That would be another one. As would "un-licensed sector." They both pull together two ideas and restructure them, by semantic intrusion.

With "un-licensed sector," the contextual fact that you know it's an area of the city pretty quickly gives you an idea of what must be going on there, what it must be basically like. The rest just enriches it with details. Some others . . . ?

Well, the book was written more than ten years ago, so you'll have to allow for my forgetfulness. But to go back to your original question: Did *Triton* arise out of one specific neologism? No. Did it arise out of several? No. Basically it arose out of some social ideas. The first thing actually written—before I was even sure I was going to write another SF novel— was, oddly, the kiss-off letter that the Spike sends to Bron in chapter 5— or, at any rate, a version of it.

I was sitting in Heathrow Airport, with my then-wife, Marilyn Hacker. A couple of things were devilling my memory, including a recent dinner at a French restaurant not far from our flat in London, where I'd watched some people behave with what had struck me as unthinkable insensitivity to someone else at their table. Marilyn and I were waiting for a plane to Paris, where she was going to purchase some books on textiles and printing for her rare-book business. The conversation between us had fallen off. Suddenly and impulsively, I opened my notebook to a fresh page and began writing this fictive letter a woman might write to tell a truly unpleasant boyfriend it was all over.

That was the start of the book.

From then on, I had to figure out a world—and the events taking place in it—in which this (or such) a letter could be sent. I say "figure out." Actually it all came rushing in on me, almost faster than I could put it down.

Q: Certain parts of Slade's philosophy carry with it radically skeptical implications about the difficulty, not to say the impossibility, of translating system-A, the world of experience, into system-B, the universe of discourse. Also of translating, or transferring, the universe imbedded in one discourse into the universe imbedded in another—which is to say, the difficulty of speaking about *Triton*, for example, and its universe of discourse.

SRD: I should have thought it carried great hope for our eventually understanding such a process—rather than radical skepticism about its possibility.

After all, it happens in the real world. I hope it may even happen—at least in some small part—tonight.

How can one relational system model another? . . . What must pass from system-A to system-B for us (system-C) to be able to say that system-B now contains some model of system-A? . . . Granted the proper passage, what must be the internal structure of system-B for us (or it) to say it contains any model of system-A? (*Triton*, "Appendix B," p. 356 [of the 1976 Bantam edition])

The question encompasses the semiotic situation, since the answer to the second part of the question ("What must pass from system-A to system-B . . . ?") is clearly some form of the answer, "signs"; and the answer to the third part of the question (". . . what must the internal structure of system-B be for us [or it] to say that it contains any model of system-A?") is clearly: It must be of a structure able to interpret signs—i.e., its internal structure must be one that allows it to perform some sort of semiosis.

But the first part of the question sets it in an expanded context that demands an actual algebra of response.

Although we are certainly not going to answer thoroughly such a question here, it's still instructive to look at how the question arose. When I initially formulated it, there *was* no system-C. And my image of system-B was, of course, a living subject.

I (known to my friends as system-B) look across the room and see the desk there, with the globe sitting on its corner, and two pieces of chalk, and several paperback SF novels piled there in the center—the whole complex better known as system-A. Light waves pass from system-A to system-B; those waves are operated upon neurologically, and the brain of system-B now contains a model of system-A.

Or: A computer (called system-B) phones up on a modem to another computer (named system-A) and asks for a directory of all the programs system-A has on file. System-A sends a list of the program names in its directory back to system-B, which then contains a model of (some of) the information available in system-A.

But already the computer version has alerted us to things a bit hidden in the "live subject" version. There has to be an *expectation of information*, which could be broadened to include the general range of familiarity with the possibilities of things system-A may exhibit. That's a basic part of the necessary structure of system-B, for the modular transfer to take place. (That *expectation of information* we might call discourse.)

But the computer version also raises another problem: Once the transfer has occurred, in what sense does the computer, system-B, *know* it contains a model of system-A? The easiest way to resolve the problem is for us to bring in system-C. If somebody else can say she or he knows that the modular transfer has taken place, then it's okay. But what has happened, really, is that system-B has split (or multiplied) into *two* necessary systems: system-B, which "knows"; and system-C, which *knows* system-B knows—the secondary system that can now take the quotation marks from around the "knowing" that system-B was doing, and pin it down, fix it, and validate it.

This splitting of the subject recalls two things: One is the "split subject" that organizes much of Lacanian psychoanalysis. And the other is a famous fallacy that too often stymies progress in the philosophy of mind—the "homuncular fallacy." I'll assume you all have at least a passing familiarity with Lacan. The homuncular fallacy is, however, what too-strict functionalists, or organicists, tend to fall into if they're not very careful when they try to explain consciousness. One assumes a brain, with all its neural sensors—eyes, ears, nose, tongue, skin—is collecting information and sorting it, processing it, associating it with other data. Then, at the very center of the brain, sits this little transcendental human-form who receives it all and actually *is* the consciousness that understands, perceives, knows . . .

And you have to start all over again: Well, how does *this* little homunculus perceive, understand, know . . . ? You haven't really gotten anywhere at all.

What does this all mean? Does it mean that the Lacanian split subject is only another version of the homuncular fallacy? Or does it mean (and this is certainly the way I lean) that the homuncular fallacy is as seductive as it is because it is so close to a reality the Lacanian "split subject" explains *without* falling into homunculism? But this is to move away from *Triton* and to start exploring questions raised in the later "Informal Remarks Toward the Modular Calculus"—i.e., in the Nevèrÿon fantasy series to which *Triton* is the SF prologue.

Q: But the skepticism (perhaps it's all mine)—the impossibility of understanding thoroughly the process by which such transfers work—applies as a *caveat* to anything you are even now going to say in response to our questions about *Triton*—or anything else. Although, mind you, that skepticism perhaps applies least—that's a relative term here—to my next question. On its last page before the appendices begin, *Triton* is subscribed: *"London, November '73—July '74."* Now, it's subtitled "an ambiguous heterotopia." Before writing *Triton*, had you read Le Guin's *Dispossessed*—which carries the subtitle "an ambiguous utopia" and was published in the US in the summer of '74?

SRD: Not before writing the first draft. I believe I read *The Dispossessed* somewhere either between the first draft of *Triton* and the second, or perhaps between the second and the third—so that *Triton* was basically finished before I became aware of Le Guin's novel. Having read *The Dispossessed* after I'd finished a first or second draft—*was* I halfway through the second when a copy of Le Guin's book from Harper & Row reached me in London by mail?—I thought I could probably make that dialogue more pointed by changing a few things here and there—or, better, by clarifying a few things here and there that Le Guin's book directed me to think about. When I first looked through *The Dispossessed*, it occurred to me that the two books generated an interesting dialogue with each other. My added subtitle was an attempt to put the two novels clearly into a dialogue I already felt was implied.

Q: You're saying, then, that to a large extent the dialogue was accidental?

SRD: It began accidentally, certainly.

Q: You're still sidestepping the question to some extent.

SRD: Right [*laughter*]. Some of H. G. Wells's novels were conceived and written as direct answers to other novels by other people, written and published earlier. Dostoyevsky wrote *Crime and Punishment* after reading Hugo's *Les Misérables*. It greatly impressed him; nevertheless Dostoyevsky felt that Hugo, in pursuit of the social dimensions of delinquency, had overlooked some dark and unsettling factors in its psychological dimension that had to be explored. There's a very direct dialogue going on between these books. Indeed, my trilogy *The Fall of the Towers*—like so many other SF novels—is a direct answer to Heinlein's *Starship Troopers*. And that direct dialogue does exist between, say, the treatment of the Freddie and Flossie characters in the men's co-op in *Triton* and the treatment of the Leslie character in the coöperative marriage in Joanna Russ's anti-utopian short story, "Nobody's Home." But, no, that's not the sort of direct engagement that happens between *Triton* and *The Dispossessed*.

Q: Had you written your article on *The Dispossessed* around the same time as you were working on *Triton*?

SRD: "To Read *The Dispossessed*" was written much later—a year or more after I finished writing *Triton*. That essay is dated April 1976. By the time I began it (and it only took me three weeks or so to write), I'd already returned to the U.S. from London, taught for a term at SUNY Buffalo, then moved back to New York City. *Triton* was not only written but had already been published—two months before, in February.

Q: In the dialogue with *The Dispossessed*, if Bron were removed from the book, would the world of Triton still be a heterotopia? Bron seems to be a kind of anti-hero in a critical stance towards the whole world he exists in. If he were removed, would Triton perhaps be a utopia? Compared to Bron, nobody else seems to have too many problems with that world.

SRD: No, certainly it would not be a utopia—though clearly I think its social system represents an improvement on our own. As she or he moves through the novel, I'd hoped Common Reader would progress, in his or her responses, through a series of stages. In the first chapter, when you see the Ego Booster Booths, predicated on the idea that the government is collecting information on everybody, and hear their history, I wanted Common Reader to feel that Bron is a pretty average Joe, but that the society must be hugely repressive. Then, as the book goes on, I wanted Common Reader slowly to shift that opinion: Soon it should become clear that Bron is a despicable man—but the society around him is actually fairly good. Finally, however, with the second appendix, I wanted Common Reader to get still another take on the tale: Since other people from Mars seem to be having problems *very* similar to Bron's, I wanted to leave the suggestion that there is a political side to these problems that the rest of the narrative—at least as it's been told from Bron's point of view—has up till now repressed or been blind to.

The fact is, I don't think SF *can* be really utopian. I mean utopia presupposes a pretty static, unchanging, and rather tyrannical world. You know: "I know the best way to live, and I'm going to tell you how to do it, and if you dare do anything else . . ."

Q: Even an anarchistic utopia?

SRD: Even an anarchistic utopia.

Q: That becomes a contradiction in terms.

SRD: Not really. A problem Ursula makes all but vanish by setting her "anarchistic utopia" in an extreme scarcity environment (and I'm sure it was what she wanted) is the problem of *surveillance et punir*. When the landscape is as harsh and ungiving as Annares' and your laws are set up in ecological accord with it, you don't *have* to worry too much about individuals—or groups—deviating too far from these laws. Those who deviate, the landscape itself punishes—if not obliterates.

In scarcity societies, you just don't have the same sort—or frequency—of discipline problems as you do in an affluent society. In a scarcity society the landscape itself becomes your spy, your SS, and your jailer, all in one.

But if the Odonians had set up their "non-propertarian" utopia on Urras (and Le Guin says as much in the novel), you'd simply have too many individuals—and groups—saying: "Look, since there's all this *stuff*, why *can't* I own some of it?" And the expulsions and disciplinary actions would bloom all around—no matter how anarchistic they started out!

The "ambiguities" Le Guin wanted to examine in her ambiguous utopia are not, I believe, the internal contradictions of a foundering utopia. Rather, she wanted to explore the bilateral contradictions highlighted between two very *different* societies, one harsh and spiritual, one rich and decadent, but each of which considers *itself* the best of all possible worlds.

I've always seen SF thinking as fundamentally different from utopian thinking; I feel that to force SF into utopian templates is a largely unproductive strategy.

Further, I think that possibility is what Le Guin is raising by calling *The Dispossessed* "an ambiguous utopia." It's only by problematizing the utopian notion, by rendering its hard, hard perimeters somehow permeable, even undecidable, that you can make it yield anything interesting.

R. A. Lafferty began the process with his satirical reading of Thomas More in *Past Master* (1968). Ursula and I shared a publisher with him, and we were both sent readers' galleys. In our turns, we simply followed suit.

In a couple of essays and the odd poem, W. H. Auden makes the point that you have four modernist world-views: One Auden called New Jerusalem. New Jerusalem is the technological super-city where everything is bright and shiny and clean, and all problems have been solved by the beneficent application of science. The underside of New Jerusalem is Brave New World. *That's* the city where everything is regimented and standardized and we all wear the same uniform. The two may just *be* the same thing, looked at from different angles. It's not so much a real difference in the cities themselves as it is a temperamental difference in the observers. In the same way, Auden pointed out, you have a rural counterpart to this pairing. There are people who see rural life as what Auden called Arcadia. Arcadia is that wonderful place where everyone eats natural foods and no machine larger than one person can fix in an hour is allowed in. Throughout Arcadia the breezes blow, the rains are gentle, the birds sing, and the brooks gurgle. But the underside of Arcadia is the Land of the Flies. In the Land of the Flies, fire and flood and earthquake—as well as famine and disease—are always shattering the quality of life. And if they don't shatter it, then the horrors of war are always in wait just over the hill to transform the village into a cess-ridden, crowded, pestilential medieval fortress-town under siege.

But once again, Auden points out, fundamentally we have a temperamental split here. Those people who are attracted to New Jerusalem will always see rural life as the Land of the Flies, at least potentially. Those people who are attracted to Arcadia will always see urban life as some form of Brave New World.

For some years, I thought SF could generally be looked at in terms of a concert of these four images: All four, either through their presence or absence, *always* spoke from every SF text. That interplay is what kept SF from being utopian—or dystopian, for that matter. You'll find the argument, at least as it progresses up to this point, detailed in an early essay of mine, "Critical Methods/Speculative Fiction," finished in March of 1969, the second year in which (after fanzines like *The Australian SF Review* and *Lighthouse* convinced me that the enterprise was worthwhile) I was seriously writing SF criticism.

To take the argument a bit beyond that essay, however, I think the post-modern condition has added at *least* two more images to this galaxy—if it hasn't just broken down the whole thing entirely.

One of these is the urban image of Junk City—a very different image from Brave New World. Junk City begins, of course, as a working-class suburban phenomenon: Think of the car with half its motor and three wheels gone which has been sitting out in the yard beside that doorless refrigerator for the last four years. As a kid I encountered the first signs of Junk City in the cartons of discarded military electronic components, selling for a quarter or 75 cents, all along Canal Street's Radio Row. But Junk City really comes into its own at the high-tech moment, when all this invades the home or your own neighborhood: the coffee table with the missing leg propped up by the stack of video-game cartridges, or the drawer full of miscellaneous walkman earphones, or the burned out building of the inner city, outside of which last year's $5,000 computer-units are set out on the street corner for the garbage man (or whoever gets there first), because the office struggling on here for the cheap rent is replacing them with this year's model that does five times more and costs a third as much: Here we have an image of techno-chaos entirely different from the regimentation of Brave New World—and one that neither Huxley in the early '30s nor Orwell in the late '40s could have envisioned.

Junk City has its positive side: It's the Lo-Teks living in the geodesic superstructure above Nighttown in Gibson's "Johnny Mnemonic." You can even see it presaged a bit among those who enjoy the urban chaos in my own *Dhalgren*—or the un-licensed sectors in the satellite cities of *Triton*.

The country landscape polluted with technological detritus is perhaps the corresponding rural image. And there is even a positive tradition growing up within this essentially horrific 'scape; I mean such haunting works as M. John Harrison's "Viriconium" series, in which the polluted, poisonous landscape becomes a place of extraordinarily delicate and decadent beauty, among the "cultures of the afternoon."

But no matter how we cognize and contrast them, the range of these dispositions is what keeps SF from rigidifying into the idealism (in the Marxist sense) and the large-scale social engineering fallacies that characterize utopian thinking—and which, in practical terms, lie in wait to turn utopian applications into oppression.

The problem with this extension of the argument is the problem with all thematics: Themes always multiply, if only to compensate for the reductionism that first formed them. The argument began as a Cartesian space of two coordinates, at which point it was fairly wieldy. For most people, however, a Cartesian space of *four* coordinates (which is where the expanded argument now leaves us) is just too complicated really to see. I suppose, at this point, I'd have to junk the whole thing—however illuminating it was for a while. Finally I have to stick it out on the sidewalk in the Junk City of our own endlessly abandoned critical detritus.

It's always possible someone will come along and find some odd and interesting use for it—or a piece of it.

Q: When you call *Triton* a heterotopia, do you mean it has all four—or all eight—of those images?

SRD: I suppose so. It's certainly one thing I meant.

Q: "Heterotopia" gave me the idea that *Triton* is meant to challenge Le Guin because there's obviously a much greater diversity of choice in the way one lives in *Triton* than in *The Dispossessed.*

SRD: On Urras? I doubt it. But the variety of choices means that novelistically the book can also deal with a variety of problems—can show how they interrelate.

By making her spiritual utopia a society based on scarcity and her decadent society one based on unequal distribution of riches in a very rich world, Le Guin swallows up several problems in *The Dispossessed*— and, while that doesn't hurt it as a story of a physicist torn between two cultures, perhaps it somewhat limits the book as a novel of ideas.

Let me state, by the bye, that though I've criticized it at great (even excessive) length, *The Dispossessed* is a rich and wondrous tale. It's a boy's book: a book to make boys begin to think and think seriously about a whole range of questions, from the structure of society to the workings of their own sexuality. Our society is often described as patriarchal—a society ruled by aging fathers concerned first and foremost with passing on the patrimony. At the risk of being glib, however, I'd suggest that it might be more accurate to say that we have a filiarchal society—a society ruled almost entirely by sons—by *very* young men. Certainly boys—especially white heterosexual boys—are the most privileged creatures in the Western social hierarchy. They are forgiven *almost* everything in life—and *are* forgiven everything in art. Indeed, if the society were a bit *more* patriarchal instead of being so overwhelmingly filiarchal, it might function just a bit *more* sanely. But since it doesn't, there's still a great deal to be said for a good boy's book. And for a woman's writing it. And nothing stops women and girls from reading boys' books and learning from them. I mean *The Dispossessed* is a boy's book the way *Huckleberry Finn* is a boy's book; and, unlike Huckleberry Finn, the boy in *The Dispossessed* is held up to the man he will become again and again, chapter by chapter, beginning to end. (The real tragedy of Huckleberry is that the best he can hope to grow up into, personally and historically, is the sociopathic narrator of Springsteen's "Born in the U.S.A.") *Huckleberry Finn* and *The Dispossessed* are both flawed. (What is it Randall Jarrell said? "A novel is a prose work of a certain length that has something wrong with it.") But all through both, richness flows, surges, sings. Quite apart from any criticisms I've made of it, *The Dispossessed* has beauty and richness.

Q: I find it curious that the utopian possibilities of *Triton*'s social dimension, or the whole dimension of the book that goes along with utopia, seem to be decentered, to be in the background. One of the things that genuinely surprised me was the passage where Sam gets into a dialogue with some Earthlings on the respective merits of their two systems. There one gets the longest and most exclusive passage in the book on the Tritonian social set-up. But what one doesn't get is the sense of Triton's dystopian possibilities. Because, after all, what we're allowed to know is that this perhaps "utopian" social system depends upon something called the "computer hegemony." That term seems, again, to figure as a kind of neologism; but unlike some others, its full meaning is not immediately intelligible. It has to be thought about. And even after one thinks about it, there's a certain vague area, at least in the utopian dimension, for certainly "hegemony" means something more than a trust or a cartel—is something more awful and powerful than that . . .

SRD: I think it's reasonable to suggest that "the computer hegemony" states articulately and clearly—complete with unsettlingly negative implications—the function that computers will play, more or less hidden, more or less off stage, in Le Guin's next book, *Always Coming Home.*

The dialogue, of course, must go on.

Still, you may have hit upon one of the things that makes SF, or *this* SF novel, recalcitrant—I mean, why you have to squeeze it to fit under a uto-pian rubric. To have a term such as "hegemony"—not to mention the surveillance implications behind the Ego Booster Booths—right in the midst of such a "utopian" society, for me, at any rate, leaves the very no-tion of utopia pretty much shattered. These—and many other—linguis-tic turns are used in the book precisely for their negative implications.

This is very different—I hope—from the rhetorical strategy shared by Heinlein and the Stalinists: "These curtailments of freedoms, these mo-ments of oppression, are justified, purified, decontaminated by the greater good they serve." (Either: "The end justifies the means" or "You can't make an omelette without breaking eggs"—it doesn't matter how you articulate the principle.) You asked where the "dystopian" implica-tions were: Well, that's certainly where they start.

You're not going to get the dystopian implications in the discussion from a high-placed political functionary arguing for the superiority of his welfare system. You'll find them, rather, in details, dropped here and there, in suggestions and discrete rhetorical moments scattered about. And I've already talked about the political dimensions to his own problems that Bron himself is blind to and that only emerge in the second appendix. But, again, to look for *any* critique in the book in utopian/dystopian terms will, I suspect, doom you to disappointment and/or distortion.

I simply *couldn't* tell you how Triton, as a detailed political system, functions. But its functioning can be thought about. Its functioning can be interrogated by interrogating—and by manipulating—the text. (Eric Rabkin has pointed out that a fundamental difference between SF and literature is that SF is always inviting the reader to manipulate the text: "Suppose it was different? Suppose it didn't happen that way but this? What if . . . ?" Whereas literature—especially Great Literature—all but demands to be left inviolate. Well, I *want* readers to play with my text in that way.) Even more than the Brave New World/New Jerusalem inter-play, what basically sets SF apart from utopian thinking is a fundamental fictive approach.

By and large, utopian thinking starts with a general political idea, in the service of some large and overarching notion such as "freedom," "happiness," or "equality"; the writer of a utopia then works down and in, to determine what the texture of life might be for the individual in a world run according to such ideas. But what practice often reveals is that, when we start from full-scale politics, the resultant life-texture ends up as far away from the ideal as it can possibly get.

By and large today, in SF, you start with the texture of life around some character. Nor is that texture necessarily conceived of as "the good life." Rather, you say, what would be an *interesting* life-texture? If you have to have bad things, *what* bad things might you be able to stand? You look at the specific texture of the character's everyday world—not the greater political structure his or her bit of life is enmeshed in. Then, in the course of the fictive interrogation-of-the-material that makes up the rest of the book or story, you move—fundamentally—up and out . . . *towards* the political.

What larger structures, you begin asking as you move outward, might produce such a life-texture? But the wise SF writer *doesn't* try to answer those rigorously. Rather, she or he decides: What ballpark would those structures lie in?

Speaking of *Triton,* personally I know perfectly well I can't detail the government that would produce that collection of communes and co-ops, with family units at the outer rim and singles in the inner city, with the social interplay between a licensed and an un-licensed sector . . . but the book makes some guesses. And one guess is that the governmental structure will have to be at least as rich and imaginative and plural as the life-structure of the citizens. But I can't—nor would I try to—specify that political structure in a novel, down to every governmental office and how it relates to every other.

To find such a political structure, we'd have to try things out—and, far more important, be ready to revise our political structure when it didn't work out the way we wanted.

And that, more than anything else, is what makes the enterprise fundamentally anti-utopian/-dystopian. Because a utopia (or dystopia) *starts* with a political structure that is self-evidently—at least to the architect—superior (or inferior) to the existing one.

What I start from is the fictive element, considered in terms of a series of questions. What would you like the *effects* of the government to be? What would you like the world to look like as you walk down the street? What unpleasant things could you tolerate in that world? What others do you simply not want to be there at all? What kind of things would you like to spend your time doing?

Well, the SF writer sets these up and then goes as far outward into the political as she or he can. I can probably extrapolate two or three layers beyond what I've directly described—frankly, I'd hope any reader really interested in the novel would do some extrapolating on her or his own as a matter of course. People often criticize the book by saying, "Well, you haven't told us how the government actually *works!*" True! I wouldn't presume to tell you such a thing. But I hope I've *suggested* a lot about the ways in which it has to function.

No, you're not going to learn which office is on what floor of City Hall and what its official relation is with the offices either side of it—the way you would in a utopia. *I don't know* that; more important, I know the practical political principles that mean *I can't* know that. And if I were setting up the real place, that's precisely why I'd have to keep certain governmental areas open, flexible, and revisable, until we hit on an administrative structure that functioned reasonably in terms of the life of the people on the street.

Q: Thirty-seven politicians reside in a madhouse?

SRD: Certainly Triton is run by sets of committees and individual administrators—somehow. Many of them are elected. But, again, you start from the effects you want. I think that's the politically wisest thing to do. We know that what's wrong with utopian thinking in general is that large-scale social engineering just doesn't work. Everybody who tries it botches it royally.

If you take a group of even 25,000 people (much less millions) and you set up an administration system for them—with offices, housing, various jobs for them and work spaces in which to perform them, all planned out from A to Z before you implement any of it—you can be sure that, once the whole structure has been running a year, a third of your administrative system will be useless and there will be a whole set of new offices, new jobs, and new structures that will have to be set up in their place for the system to function efficiently—or at all.

The new and unforeseen needs will be created by conjoined factors like the frequency of east winds combined with the existing height of the buildings in the Physical Ed complex and the number of people in the population who have hay fever—and the next thing you know, you will (or won't, as the case may be) need a special detail of twelve maintenance men whose full-time job it is to keep the trees to the west of the infirmary buildings regularly pruned.

And the difference between having and not having such a group of maintenance men may make a difference of 10 to 15 percent in the overall productivity of the community.

There's no *way* to predict all such needs that will arise. There's no *way* to make sure similar factors working together won't render some preconceived administrator, committee, or functional group unnecessary. That can only be learned by trial-and-error—along with careful, analytical observation of the real workings of the realized community.

Those needs are going to be different in every case, even when the basic designs and organizational structures have been tried out a dozen times successfully in a dozen other locations.

We now *know* this is how human social systems function—which is why the "good life" simply cannot be mapped out wholly within the range traditionally prescribed as "the political." Indeed, the post-modern notion of the range of the political has probably changed as much as anything else since 1968.

We've got here, of course, the old *bricolage*/engineering dichotomy, first raised in the early days of structuralist criticism. (Critically too, as I've already suggested, we *live* in Junk City—and it's a very rich town.) The difference between the *bricoleur* and the engineer is not just a difference in scale and style. There's also a difference in the movement of the thinking. The *bricoleur* starts with a local problem, then looks around among existing materials for things to fix it with, moving on to more complex solutions only when the simplest ones are clearly not working as well as they should.

The engineer doesn't really feel she's started to work, however, until she's got an overarching principle to apply to the solution of the problem, which she then implements as carefully and accurately as possible by precise technical means, moving in to take care of finer and finer problematic details—until, hopefully, principle wholly absorbs problem. As each moves towards her or his separate solution, the *bricoleur* and the engineer are both looking, here, forward, there, backward. There's always some conceptual movement in both directions with each. But the fundamental movements are, overall, different. And that difference in movement is very much the difference I've noted between the way the SF writer works and the way the utopianist works.

Someone once said: "A politics that doesn't address itself to your particular problems and my particular problems is just not a politics for you and me."

And I think this is not a bad place to start a critique of the political aspect of the situation around us. But it's in Junk City that *bricoleurs* flourish at their happiest and most efficient—though it's often the engineers who provide the junk the *gomi no sensei* works with.

Q: It seems to me that in *Dhalgren* you were after a completely different effect on the reader.

SRD: That's true. *Dhalgren* and *Triton* are two very different books.

Q: Speaking about effects, I'm an average reader. I don't know too much about scientific terminology—about how the sensory shield works, for example, or how to interpret the mathematics of the game-scoring system that we get in chapter 2. What kind of impact do you think such sections in the book have on the average reader—who definitely does not understand any of it? Like me, for example.

SRD: Well, I think it's fair to assume that the average SF reader is going to have *some* kind of popular science background. And if you don't, then—while you may be an average reader—you're *not* an average SF reader. Now, nobody expects the reader to be an expert in *any* branch of science. The science in SF is mostly doubletalk anyway—like the "meta-logics" and "modular calculus" I spoke of before.

There's a passage in *The Dispossessed* where Shevek solves his problem of reconciling the sequency and simultaneity theories of time by assuming that the problems have already *been* resolved, then proceeding as if there were no contradiction between them. . . . You just can't read the passage too closely. If you do, it falls apart into the circular argument that it is. But for better or worse, all the science in SF is ultimately like that. On the one hand, SF presumes an audience who can at least catch the jokes—when they go by. But in general I don't think the science *per se* should go too far beyond what you'd get in most popular science books—most of them by Isaac Asimov and written for bright fourteen-year-olds.

It's the *pseudo*-science that keeps going much further—not the science. But the pseudo-science goes further precisely because it is always assuming that large patches of the unknown are, in fact, knowable.

Q: Does the joke also apply to the math for scoring vlet?

SRD: The scoring modulus is complete gobbledygook. The irony is that the book calls it "rather difficult." The reader is *supposed* to find it daunting. In fact, it's so daunting, you should laugh. And say something to the effect of: "Yeah. Right. '*Rather* difficult.' Sure!" Then you will have appreciated the irony. Now if the reader happens to be mathematically literate enough to realize, after trying to untangle it (for someone familiar with advanced calculus, it takes about ten seconds), that not only is it daunting, it's also meaningless, all well and good. Then there should be a second laugh. But that level is, indeed, secondary—and really just an extension of the first.

Q: Your style of parentheses in parentheses almost has the same effect. Very daunting. What were you trying to do here?

SRD: That's a different matter. Probably I was trying to say too much at once.

Q: I liked the parentheses. I found that the device really helped me understand the way someone like Bron would think, because he's so defensive and he rationalizes everything. He works a thought through before he thinks of some defensive way of worming his way out of the situation. Or justifying the way he thinks or perceives . . .

SRD: That's kind of what I was trying for. But I know—simply because I've talked to enough people—that for some readers it doesn't work. The parentheses only get in the way. Well, they *do* ask a lot of you. Perhaps too much. I write with far fewer parentheses today. But it was my choice at the time—and it may have been the wrong one. Still, *some* people seem to be able to get with it. When you make a stylistic choice like that, this is the chance you take: Some people are just going to find it tedious and balk. Well, they have every right to.

There are two kinds of characters, I think, in most modern fiction: One is the character you're supposed to identify with. That character is like a suit of clothes you put on in order to have the experiences the character goes through.

The other character is, rather, a case study. Though you can feel sorry for—or be amused by—this character (and even recognize aspects of yourself *in* the character), if you identify with her or him beyond a certain point, you're misreading the book.

Q: In *Dhalgren*, which would be the suit of clothes, would you say? Not Kid?

SRD: No. As in *Triton*, in *Dhalgren* you're not supposed to identify. There too, you're supposed to look at the protagonist from the outside. It's amazing, of course, how many such books backfire. Flaubert thought Emma was a pretty, immoral fool—and wrote *Madame Bovary* to expose her. And Tolstoy did *not* want his readers to identify with Natasha or Anna: He felt they were charming, but fundamentally immoral women, who destroyed the people around them until they destroyed, or all but destroyed, themselves; once his books were published, he was horrified when people were "taken in" by that charm and fell in love with his leading ladies. Well, a few people—both men and women, incidentally— have come up to me and confided: *"Bron Helstrom—c'est moi."* [*Shrugs.*]

Q: *Dhalgren* is very detached. It's all from Kid's point of view. But it would be hard to put yourself in his place.

SRD: Right. Although I think it's easier to identify with Kid than it is with Bron, I suspect [*laughing*] it depends on who you are.

When a character is looked at constantly from the outside—when even his or her most subjective responses are analyzed objectively— things tend to go more slowly. In some ways the parentheses were also an attempt to slow down the real reading time of the novel. It's a pacing thing. If you can let a parenthesis slow you down and not lose the first half of the previous clause before you come out the other side, then the parentheses will probably work for you. If your attention is such that you can't quite do that—and there's no particular reason why you should be able to—then they're probably *not* going to work. The reading experience becomes annoying, and you'll spend all your time running back and forth from the beginning to the end of the sentence, mildly confused. It's no fun.

Q: The war which goes on in the book is always in the background. At one point, I think, it's mentioned—twice—that there are no soldiers. It seems to be the pretext for lots of goings-on and restrictions. Is that in any way connected with the perpetual war that goes on in *1984*? Or is that a coincidence? Because it seems there *is* a parallel there.

SRD: In *1984*, it's rather different—and in *1984* there *are* soldiers.

Q: Well, you're told there are soldiers, but you never really know.

SRD: The war in *Triton*, however, is a purely technological war: a war that consists of years of diplomacy—followed by forty-five unthinkable minutes. During those minutes, technicians merely push buttons. That doesn't involve soldiers.

Q: In *Triton*'s final vision, I still can't understand why Bron lied to Audrey. That seems very important in the book.

SRD: Yes, that was very important. But I'd have to go back and look at the text again to explain to you just why.

Q: He concocted the whole story about—

Q: He totally reverses the situation.

Q: He finally realizes he's thinking like a male.

Q: You have to realize that this is a kind of protective reaction on Bron's part.

SRD: Yes. The story he tells is what he wished had happened. You have to remember, what Bron usually does to justify his behaving in the selfish and hateful ways that make him such a hateful man is manufacture perfectly fanciful motivations for what everyone else is doing—motivations which, if they *were* the case, would make his actions acceptable. (In that way, he can ignore the fact that his own motivations are simply and wholly selfish.) Of course, he'd only have to listen to what people were actually saying around him to realize that the motivations he ascribes to them are impossible. But he forgets—or represses—the parts of their conversation that would inform him of that. Or he assumes the people were simply lying when they said those parts.

Well, Freud and Lacan both have brought us the unhappy news that this is, in effect, the way we *all* move through our lives. We hear about a tenth of what is said to us; we repress the rest; and in the resultant silences, we write our own scenarios about what the other person is thinking about us, feeling about us, judging us to be. It has a venerable name in psychoanalysis: transference. And on the strength of our fancied reconstruction of other people's inner feelings about us, we respond to them and the world.

Remember that *"expectation of information"*? One computer calls up the other to get a list of programs . . . ? But that means the information that comes over from system-A is all going to be read *as* program names. If what system-A actually sends (either by accident or design) is telephone numbers or the opening lines of "Jabberwocky," system-B is *still* going to treat them like program names—due to the programming it received somewhere in its computational childhood.

Transference, again.

Unless, of course, it gets something that's just so far from a program name it simply can't handle it at all.

That's what happens to Bron in the final Audrey situation. Bron honestly likes Audrey. And Audrey loves Bron. But in order to maintain his facade, it's not just a matter of repressing things the Spike said and re-motivating others; Bron must actually say that the Spike did things that Bron did, and that Bron did things the Spike did. This sort of direct and overt lie is *not* the kind Bron has told in the past. Till now, a more subtle sort of lie has passed for the truth with him. But his prior programming—the facade—has really been in control. If that facade can *only* survive by a direct lie, it will make Bron lie directly—even while he tries to speak honestly to someone he likes and values. Well, *this* lie he finally hears himself speak. And it's too much for him. He can't surround this one with pseudo-psychological rhetoric about what other people are really thinking and feeling and doing that renders it into Truth for him. The system can't handle it. The whole mechanism starts to break down. And when it does, it isn't fun.

Q: The other thing that goes along with that is that it's not so much that he's lying to Audrey as that he's lying to himself.

SRD: Certainly that's so when he keeps insisting that he never lied before. Because he's suddenly blurting this to someone he actually has feelings for, he's brought up sharp before the fact: "Hey, wait a minute! The machine is coming to pieces . . . !"

In one sense, it's the triviality—more than the directness—of this lie that even allows him to obsess over it as much as he does. *We* know he's told much worse lies, lies that have produced much more hurt—all through the book and without his ever noticing. He lied to Audrey because that was what he would really liked to have happened—or, perhaps more accurately, because that is what would have had to have happened in order to justify what he actually did.

Q: Except that, of course, he never realizes even that much.

SRD: No. But he's still brought up short.

I think I should say, you know, that encouraging a writer to speak this much about his own book is a very odd and awkward situation. I should probably be the last person to talk about *Triton* at all. I'm only one reader of the book—and, in this case, a reader who last read it quite a while ago. What I say about it really is not privileged—as they say in Comp. Lit. jargon.

Q: Or in law courts.

SRD: Yes. I'm only giving one very, very subjective view of the book. And in a way, here, before you, I'm just a bit *like* Bron: What I'm much more likely to do here, under the local pressure of your questions, is to speak of the book *I wish* I'd written rather than the text you—or you, or you— just read.

Q: Are you saying you can't really explain some of the motives behind what the characters do and stuff like that—but you could still defend your fiction?

Q: No, what he's saying is that, contrary to what we might ordinarily suppose, when a writer talks about her or his own work, he or she is talking as a critic.

SRD: More to the point, perhaps, talking as a critic who is not necessarily identical with the writer.

I usually tell people that I live in a world where Samuel R. Delany-the-writer doesn't exist. I've never really read anything he's written. I know a lot about him. I've even looked over his shoulder while he was working. But there's a veil lying between me and his actual texts—it lets me see letters he puts down, but completely blocks the words. All I finally get to do is listen to him subvocalize about a text he *hopes* he's writing—and, when I try to reread it later, again I only hear his subvocal version of the text he wished he'd penned.

When you're inside the balloon, trying to pull it into shape from within, you just can't see it from the outside. All you have is other people's reports—that, yes, you're succeeding in making it look like a camel, or you've got a panda now, or, no, you haven't quite yet made a kangaroo. And those reports, most of them, are pretty inarticulate at that. But it's all the novelist ever knows of his or her own work. Finally, you know, you must take any and every thing I say here with many, many grains of salt.

Q: Granted your *caveat*, what's your subjective opinion of *Triton*'s whole emphasis on "subjective inviolability"?

SRD: I think it's rather a nice notion. I wonder how far you could take it as the major political tenet *per se* of a whole society. But I'd like to see a society try it. But, no, I'm not sure how, in the long run, it would work.

Q: Are we meant to give Bron some credit at the end when he—or she— has the thought that five out of six of the population of Earth have been killed in the *name* of Triton's subjective inviolability?

SRD: What I'd hoped at that point—again, a subjective reaction—is that the reader would have twigged by now to the fact that Bron is just not a nice man. But in terms of whether he is redeemable or not, whether he might someday be able to pass muster as a human being, I wanted to have all the elements on a balance—and I wanted to maintain that balance up to the novel's last sentence. With the last sentence of the novel proper, with the last phrase of that sentence (the one before the place-date subscription), I'd hoped finally to upset that balance, one way or the other—though just *which* way, I wanted to leave moot. I won't tell you which direction *I* wanted it to fall. But I think some people may figure it out.

What's happening at his recall of subjective inviolability is that that political tenet is being problematized. Bron, for a few moments (thirty-seven seconds), has slipped over the wide and muzzy border between ordinary self-deceiving neurosis and *real* psychosis. And it's possible that he will continue slipping. At the point you mention, the surface question raised is fairly simple: How inviolable *should* the subjectivity of the truly mad be—the subjectivity of those who really believe, as Bron does for that long half minute, that "the dawn will never come"; of those who've taken a simple cliché and let themselves accept it as fundamental and revealed truth (which an astonishing amount of madness actually is)?

The world of *Triton* is very different from our world today. I don't know about here in Canada, but I do know about the U.S. And the fact is, a good percentage—even a majority—of the people really don't live in what you and I would consider the last quarter of the twentieth century.

There are many, many overweight people who believe, down to the bottom of their souls, that if you eat two or three teaspoons of sugar, you will put on two or three pounds in the next couple of hours-to-days. And they believe that the weight will generate from the sugar itself. And that it has nothing to do with retaining liquid later drunk, or with the sugar making you eat more of other foods. They believe that "sweets put on weight"; and they believe it not in the metabolic terms that you or I might understand it, but rather in defiance of the laws of the conservation of matter and energy—of which they've never heard. And if you tell them how those laws set an upper limit on their weight-gaining process (so that you can't gain more weight than the weight of the food you actually ingest), they will argue that you are just wrong. It's happened to them, they will tell you, too many times.

There are many, many people who believe that the electricity running along the powerlines is at its highest at the pylons, and that that explains why the grass and shrubbery tend to be thin or die under and around the pylon legs: It's the concentration of electricity at the pylons that kills the grass below it. And they will argue with you for an hour that they know what they're talking about—and *you* don't!

And there are people who believe that lighting a cigarette at the bus stop really initiates a process (a process not in the least mystical, but nevertheless unexplainable) that, often, will make the bus come—and not that starting a pleasurable process makes you more aware of a process that interrupts that pleasure, so that you remember those situations and not the ones where the pleasure continued to its natural completion.

And when it comes to nuclear power, we might as well be dealing with medieval magic. But that's not even to broach topics like astrology, fundamentalism, various forms of spiritualism, and UFOs.

These beliefs are not neuroses.

They are ignorance.

But they are ignorances tenaciously held to, and supported by consensus belief.

These ignorances place these people outside—not the majority, but rather—the *minority* consensus reality of *some* educated people, who happen to include you and me, here in the twentieth century. (You are deluded if you think the majority of the North American population shares what, in many college classrooms, I am probably safe in calling "the consensus scientific world-view." In fact, I suspect, that "consensus scientific world-view" is finally a hypostatization that *no* one fully possesses.) But these are ignorances that are held to the way you and I might hold to the science that contravenes them. And the people who believe them do so because there's a vast amount of folklore that tells them they are right— the same folklore that tells them to bathe in baking soda baths when they get sunburn, or to put calamine lotion on a mosquito bite that itches: folklore that, in those cases, happens to be correct.

Perhaps an example closer to home: Up until my late twenties, I had a real fear of nuclear war. It wasn't obsessive. But it was constant, and it was annoying. I was not afraid of a political decision to start the ultimate war. That didn't make sense. But what if, I used to wonder, something went wrong with the very complex defense system itself: Suppose somebody pushed the wrong switch and started the War by accident? It might even involve somebody going bonkers to boot—as had been dramatized in any number of movies and books. Eventually, when I was talking quite jokingly about my worry to a friend in the U.S. Air Force, he explained to me the difference between a "systems-off" system and a "systems-on" system.

A systems-on system means that you have vast number of processes, all of them functioning all the time, and you only have to flip one switch, say, to bring them all together to make the greater system function. In such a system, an accident mitigates in favor of the whole system's starting to work. Today, for example, human reproduction is a systems-on system. It's terribly complicated. But thoughtlessness and accident are likely to lead *to* pregnancy, not prevent it.

A systems-off system is one in which you have a lot of complex systems, most of them currently not functioning. All sorts of guards and checks are built in against their turning on accidentally: Subsystem-D can only be turned on if subsystem-A and subsystem-B and subsystem-C, all in different buildings, have all been turned on previously—and what's more, they have to have all been turned on in the proper order. If they weren't, then subsystem-D simply won't start up. And without subsystem-D, as well as a whole lot of others, the defense system will not start. The nuclear defense systems of both the U.S. and the USSR are a pair of vast and complex systems-off systems. (On Triton, the universal birth-control system effectively makes human reproduction a systems-off system. Two people—any man and woman who want to—can decide to have a child by taking anti-birth-control pills at the same time. When they then have sex, pregnancy will ensue. But in such a situation, accident, laziness, or thoughtlessness mitigates *against* pregnancy's occurring—not *for* its occurring, as such flukes do in our current systems-on human reproductive situation. Changing human reproduction from a systems-on to a systems-off system, *Triton* suggests, is enough to reverse the current runaway population growth. Is that correct? I don't know. But I'd like to give it a try.) Also, there is simply no place in the nuclear defense system that is so critical that an accident there would make the whole thing go off. If, for instance, the president of the U.S. went batty and suddenly pressed "The Button," a couple of bells and lights would go on in another several buildings, some screening devices would probably check to see what was happening; and not finding what they were programmed to find in case of attack, the rest of the system would shut down—and that's about it. Only when the whole system is operating can it perform its intended job: delivering a nuclear warhead to Russia—or the U.S. In such a system, an accident mitigates for the system's *not* performing, for its shutting down. For the nation's defense system to go on accidentally, you'd have to have 500 to 1,000 very specific accidents, all happening in the right order in hundreds of buildings at hundreds of levels. And any one of those "accidents" happening at the wrong time or in the wrong order would bring the whole system to a halt. Which is to say, the system controlling the bomb's going off is a systems-off system, not a systems-on system.

There's far more statistical reason to fear the defense system *won't* work when it's called on than that it'll go off accidentally of its own accord.

Once I learned this, my fear of a technological accident vanished (though I still don't think the threat of nuclear war is any less serious a *political* problem). That is to say, the fear was *not* neurotic. It was ignorance. And knowledge cured it.

In contrast to this, I have an occasionally recurrent fear of flying. It manifests itself as a simple and vague anxiety about crashing. The engine might fail and the plane might fall. It's likely to come on when I've had to fly a lot, in a brief time, and—as a result—have gotten tired and had my general life-schedule highly disrupted by all the flying I've recently done. This anxiety *is* neurotic; I acknowledge that. And the proof that it's neurotic is simply that (1) it's intermittent, and (2) it isn't relieved by knowing the very reassuring statistics on plane flights or the very simple and almost unstoppable working of the turbojet. Knowledge— and knowledge that I'm quite ready to believe—has no effect on it.

Now this intermittent anxiety has not been particularly debilitating. Never has it prevented me from taking a really necessary flight.

So what has this all got to do with Triton?

On Triton, the first sort of ignorance has been all but abolished. Thanks to childhood education in the communes, the public channel education of adults, and the curtailment of the population explosion, the entire populace by and large really lives in the consensus scientific present—and a consensus scientific present somewhat ahead of ours.

Now, on Triton they have *not* gotten rid of the second sort of anxiety. But because they don't have to worry about the first sort, they can let the people who say, "I'm sorry, but today I just don't feel like flying; I'm worried about crashes," have their way. Or, as the case may be, they can let them have a drug that will banish the anxiety if the person wants it—because most of the populace will be able to recognize a neurotic anxiety for what it is. They can respect the subjective reality of their populace because they've solved so many other problems already. In that sense (like the privileging of freedom of speech), subjective inviolability is an index to the general health of the society.

But the real question about Bron is: Are his problems just a complex and remediable form of ignorance? Or are they something much deeper and less accessible to ordinary social measures of correction?

Q: One understanding I had of heterotopia you not only haven't mentioned but seem to discourage by your remarks about utopia. It seems to me that one meaning the word takes on in *Triton* is something like: "Designer Utopia." Everyone on Triton decides on her or his personal utopia.

SRD: To the extent that—say—there are several sets of laws and restraints and you can choose, by vote, which set you want to be bound by, yes, I suppose that's accurate. But the presumed irony was that these variations are probably *very* slight. The people who vote for tax-system-P, administered by candidate Joey, pay three-quarters of a percent more taxes, but work a quarter of an hour less per day than the people who voted for tax-system-Q, administered by candidate Suzy. Things like that. My assumption was that all these systems came out more or less even in the end. And it was a matter of which was more important to you personally, according to your own temperament: In terms of the choice I just outlined, say, it would be time versus money.

But it could just as easily come down to time versus the amount of greenery in the neighborhood where you live. Or the amount of greenery versus the variety of food shipped to your co-op under ordinary circumstances, when you weren't going out for a special meal. That sort of stuff.

But though such differences might be quite important to various individuals, I'm not ready to designate them as utopian. It's merely a set of social options and minor improvements we haven't as yet been able to institute. I can only call that "utopian" in the most metaphorical way. I meant to *contrast* any social meaning "heterotopia" has to the idea of "utopia," not to absorb that idea.

"Heterotopia" is, after all, a real English word. It's got several meanings. You can find it in the *OED*. If you do, you'll find it has some meanings that, I'd hope, apply quite directly to the book. Would you like me to tell you one?

Q: Tell us one meaning not evident from the etymology.

SRD: Well, a major definition of "heterotopia" is its medical meaning. It's the removal of one part or organ from the body and affixing it at another place in or on the body. That's called a heterotopia. A skin graft is a heterotopia. But so is a sex-change—one of the meanings of the word. So there.

Q: In regard to vlet, I feel as if I'm in something of the situation described in one of *Triton*'s epigraphs from—who is it? Not Quine—Wittgenstein, I think: the quotation about the spectator who doesn't know the rules of chess, watching a chess game. Is that the way it's supposed to be, or is this game already on the market—on the basis, say, of someone's having read the book?

SRD: The name comes from a story by Joanna Russ, "A Game of Vlet" (1974). It's part—or almost a part—of her Alyx series. The game in her story is not quite so complicated as mine; but in Russ's tale, at one point, you realize that the world of the story is actually controlled by the game: you can't really tell where the game ends and the world takes up. The three books I've written since *Triton*, set in ancient Nevèrÿon, are basically the game of vlet writ large. Vlet is a game of sword-and-sorcery. In some ideal future world, with ideal readers, the books might all be considered part of a larger amorphous work, "Some Informal Remarks Toward the Modular Calculus," to which *Triton* is the SF prologue.

Q: Did you intend that business about metalogics to be part of the scientific gobbledygook? I sense that's very important.

SRD: Well, you can go with it as far as you want. During the explanation that Bron gives to Miriamne [pp. 360ff], I really felt I had a point to make about the relation between logic and language. I wanted it to be followable—again, at the popular-science level.

Someone once asked me, "What is the Modular Calculus?" Well, if you think about what it does in the novel (we're really going back, here, to some of what we discussed earlier), you realize that the Modular Calculus is basically a set of equations that will take any *description* of an event, however partial, and elaborate it into a reasonable, accurate, and complete *explanation* of that event.

This means it will take a sentence like "I saw a plane fall out of the sky and burst into flames on the runway," and by arcane deep grammatical transformations, transform it into a full report of weather conditions, mechanical problems, and the pilot's responses that interacted to produce the particular and specific air crash the speaker mentioned. (That is, it can see the objects in the other room.)

This is, of course, magic—another way of saying it's impossible.

Still, that's what the Modular Calculus would be if there were such a thing. (In the Appendix to *Flight from Nevèrÿon* [1985], I have a rather detailed discussion of the Modular Calculus.) It turns any description into an explanation by extrapolating from it. The point, of course, is that some descriptions really do have explanatory force. Others, as you extend them in one direction rather than in another, *gain* explanatory force. This raises the question: What is the *difference* between a description and an explanation. And it asks what sort of elements they might have in common.

Q: Going back to the chronological-geographical subscription to *Triton*: *"London, November '73–July '74."* This is a constant practice of yours—giving the time and place of composition. I'm wondering whether that has some organic significance?

SRD: Well, it's been my contention for some time that SF is not about the future. SF is in dialogue with the present. It works by setting up a dialogue with the here-and-now, a dialogue as intricate and rich as the writer can make it.

The detail you're referring to, at least as it sits at the end of a far-future SF novel, such as *The Fall of the Towers, Babel-17, The Einstein Intersection, Nova*, or *Triton* (or, indeed, at the end of a tale set in the distant past, such as those in the Nevèrÿon series), is also a way to jar the reader. It's a way of saying: "Look, this fiction is a product of a specific place, a specific time." For quite a while I've been a great respecter of history. And I don't think such a historical nudge hurts a story in any way. A published piece of mine that omits the terminal subscription, you can be sure, is suffering from an editorial decision carried out over my objection.

On a less grandiose level, I subscribe my manuscripts so that, ten years later, I have some idea where I was, when. But the reason I leave those dates and places on for publication—and put them back in galleys (when editors have deleted them in the copyediting)—is because I think they serve a real function, not only for the writer but for the serious reader. It's a writerly tradition, after all.

Q: I was wondering whether there was anything from your experience of London that figured in *Triton*. I can't imagine the book's being written by someone who hadn't lived someplace like London or New York.

SRD: When all is said and done, Tethys is pretty much modelled on New York. (Although it's certainly not as large as New York. The population is really closer, at least in my mind, to San Francisco's.) At a certain point, you notice that most large cities do develop areas kind of like the "un-licensed sector": London's Soho, San Francisco's North Beach, New York's Village (East and West), New Orleans's French Quarter (which began at Storyville and more recently has shifted away to Fat City), Paris's *Quartier Latin* (or *cinqième*), or the Freemont in Seattle.

But I was wondering what would happen if urban planners formalized this, even carrying it a few steps further. The paradox about these areas is, of course, that people who do not live there frequently assume, "Oh, my gosh! It must be dangerous there," when there's so much pressure on the place *not* to be dangerous, if only because the areas are such tourist attractions. If the real dangers were more than normal, tourists would stop coming. So constraints on the "dangerous" street life finally grow up automatically.

A successful red light district simply can't tolerate too many street muggings, night or day, because then the prostitution on which the economy of the area is based would be fundamentally endangered. So, while you may lose your money to an over-enthusiastic hooker, you're probably not going to be mugged in an area of the city with a high number of streetwalkers.

Such, or similar, principles, operationalized by the city builders (it's a Jane Jacobs kind of thing), were the basic notions behind the "u-l."

Q: When I was last in London, I noticed that a "micro-theater" phenomenon—particularly in the entrances to the Underground (strolling minstrels, violin players, and so forth)—was more conspicuous than the first time I was there or than it is in New York. Was that a source of inspiration for *Triton?*

SRD: I'm not sure of everything that went into the micro-theater notion. Where we SF writers get our crazy ideas from, we don't really know. Someone once told me there was a good idea shop down on Fourteenth Street. . . . A number of SF writers, in response to the question, "Where do you get your ideas from?," have taken to answering, "Schenectady." [*Laughter.*]

Q: One of these days, someone may open a store there. Your response reminds me of Margaret Atwood's answer to repeated queries about why she became a poet: "I had an uncle in the poetry business." [*Laughter.*]

Q: I want to ask you about the Bruce Cockburn lyrics in *Triton.*

SRD: Well, when I was in England, somebody brought me Cockburn's then-new album, *Night Vision.* And it was dedicated to me; it read something like: "To the author of *Driftglass.*"
    "Well," I thought, "what a surprise! That's very generous of him." I like Cockburn's music. So I decided, "I'll surprise him back," and took some of the lyrics off the album and used them for Charo's songs. I thought: "If he comes across it, he might be tickled by the idea of his lyrics surviving a hundred or so years on."
    Cockburn and I have still never met, though we spoke on the phone once. We've had trouble getting together because whenever he's in New York I'm usually out of town, off teaching.
    Do you have any questions about SF in general? I can be much more illuminating about other things than my own work. The fact is, talking about my work this much in a public setting makes me rather uncomfortable. So I'd like to open up the discussion a bit if I can.

Q: I've read somewhere that you don't refer to your work as *science fiction.*

SRD: On the contrary. With the exception of a period about six months long, starting at the end of 1968, I've *always* referred to my work as SF.

Unfortunately, that was the six months when the manuscript of my story collection *Driftglass* went to press—so that it bears the egregious subtitle, "Ten Tales of Speculative Fiction." (And there was that essay I mentioned earlier, "Critical Methods/Speculative Fiction," dating from the same period.) But on both sides of that six-month anomaly, I've used the term "science fiction" or "SF" and been content with it.

Q: Why *not* "speculative fiction"?

SRD: "Speculative fiction" was a term that had a currency for about three years—from 1966 through 1969.

Q: You didn't coin it?

SRD: Goodness, no! Robert H. Heinlein first used it in a Guest of Honor Speech he gave at a World Science Fiction Convention in 1951: he said that "speculative fiction" was the term he felt best fit what he was doing as a writer: whereupon everyone immediately forgot it for the next 15 years—until 1965 or '66, when a group of writers centered around the British SF magazine *New Worlds* resurrected it and began to use it for a very specific kind of thing. Basically, as these writers—the New Wave—first used the term, it meant anything that was experimental, anything that was science-fictional, or anything that was fantastic. It was a conjunctive, inclusive term, which encompassed everything in all three areas.

I used it for the subtitle of *Driftglass* because that collection grouped a couple of fantasy tales in with the SF stories—the third relevant category, experimental writing, wasn't represented in the book at all. But the only thing the term meant in the subtitle of *Driftglass* was that the book contains both SF *and* fantasy. That's simply what "speculative fiction" meant back then.

By the end of 1969, in the world of practicing SF writers, editors, and fans, *speculative fiction* (like most conjunctive terms) had degenerated into a disjunctive, exclusive term (rather like the honorific "Ms.," which began as a conjunctive term meaning any woman, married or single, but which today, through use, has degenerated into a disjunctive term used [almost] exclusively to mean an unmarried woman who's also a feminist): By the end of '69, "speculative fiction" meant "any piece that is experimental *and* uses SF imagery in the course of it." (By that definition, the only piece of speculative fiction *I've* written is a story called "Among the Blobs," which, to date, has only seen publication in a fanzine. Oh, yes—and possibly *Dhalgren*.) A year later, the term simply dropped out of the vocabulary of working SF writers—except to refer to pieces written within that '66–'69 period, to which (usually) it had already been applied.

At about the same time, various academics began to take it up. Most of them had no idea either of its history or of its successive uses; they employed it to mean something like "high-class SF," or "SF I approve of and wish to see legitimated." Now that's a vulgar and ignorant usage of the worst sort. The way to legitimate fine quality SF is by fine quality criticism of it—not by being historically obtuse and rhetorically slipshod. I deplore that particular use of the term—and though I support your right to use any terms you want, including "fuck," "shit," and "scumbag," I simply *won't* use the term in that way. It's uninformed, anti-historical, and promotes only mystification—all three of which I feel are fine reasons to let this misused term die the natural death it actually came to fifteen years ago.

Q: Where do you see SF going now? I see a present trend toward Sword and Sorcery, a new sort of classicism *à la* Asimov, and what's left of the New Wave.

SRD: I think that any group of writers who could reasonably be called the New Wave had more or less dispersed—as a group—within a year of *speculative fiction*'s ceasing to be a meaningful term for current SF production.

I don't like to use the term New Wave for anything, however metaphysical or material, that might be present in the world of SF today because it obscures the very real, hard-edged, and extremely influential historical movement, called the New Wave, that existed through the late '60s—a movement that included a number of very specific writers (as it excluded a number of others, me among them), who wrote specific stories and novels that we can still enjoy today, who maintained specific relations with one another, and who functioned within a galaxy of specific ideas, which have had a lasting influence on the SF field.

But if you use the term to indicate a fuzzy-edged notion suggesting some sort of undefined opposition to a set of equally undefined "conservative" notions, what you lose is any possibility of retrieving—researching—that so important historical specificity (of writers, texts, readers, and events) actually behind the term. It's particularly deplorable when academics use language that subverts research, that cuts off the possibility for our thinking our own SF history—which is always so in danger of being forgotten anyway.

Certainly one of the most exciting islands of current production in

the sea of SF production is what has been termed the cyberpunk movement, or the Mirrorshades group. It includes writers like William Gibson, whose *Neuromancer* won the Hugo and Nebula Awards last year
[1985]. It's really quite a performance. Gibson has recently published a
second book, *Count Zero*, and a very exciting collection of short stories,
Burning Chrome.

Other writers associated with this group include Bruce Sterling, the
author of *Schismatrix* and several other novels and the editor of the
group's chief critical organ, the fanzine *Cheap Truth*; also Rudy Rucker,
John Shirley, Pat Cadigan, and Marc Laidlaw. But just as (and sometimes
more) interesting are some of the writers the cyberpunks often see
themselves in opposition to: Kim Stanley Robinson, Michael Bishop,
John Kessel, Connie Willis, and Terry Bisson.

The cyberpunks—they don't use a capital c, incidentally—were
named by Gardner Dozois, the editor of *Isaac Asimov's SF Magazine.*
They've been grumbling and growling under it ever since: "We're not a
group. We're each just doing our own thing." But if one may hypostatize
them as a group a moment longer, theirs is a very intense sort of writing;
it's very pro-technology; at the same time, it's very streetwise, very cynical. The writing itself tends to be highly polished—at its best. Which
makes it very different from punk music, where the surface is—well—
not polished.

Q: You've dealt a lot in your writing with the questions of sexual identity
generally, and also with the image of women. Obviously there are many
women SF writers who are doing the same thing. But what about other
male SF writers?

SRD: Well, John Varley is at least as obsessively concerned with the subject as I am. He's done several novels, but I don't find his full-length
works as strong as his short stories. His short works are tremendous,
though; and there are three collections of them. One is called *The Persistence of Vision*; a second was published under the awful title, *The Barbie
Murders* (after the Barbie dolls), but was republished a few years later as
Picnic on Nearside—which is *not* much of an improvement! (I'm going to
be teaching a seminar on Varley's work and Gibson's—Gibson has his
own interesting relation to women, which seems, to me at least, highly influenced by Russ, as well as in reaction to much in Le Guin—this coming
September at Cornell University's Society for the Humanities.) Varley
also has a third collection, as yet available only in hardcover, called *Blue
Champagne.*

Q: What are you working on now?

SRD: Another novel, another novel . . .

Q: That makes two?

SRD: Only one, alas. But sometimes it feels like two.

—Montréal 1986/New York City 1990

Part Three

Some Writing / Some Writers

17

Antonia Byatt's *Possession: A Romance*

Here is a novel of jade, jet, and apricot, in which a number of bathrooms are wondrously described. A fantasy? Not exactly. But two of its major characters, a mid-Victorian poet, Randolph Henry Ash (who, in the world of the novel, had some fame in his day, though his reputation in ours has fallen into the purely academic), and his all-but-unknown contemporary, Christabel La Motte (who managed to publish a few volumes, but who has only just been unearthed by diligent feminist critics), write works steeped in myth, fairy lore, and the supernatural. Christabel is something of a believer in things spiritual. Randolph approaches such topics with the attitude of a debunker in his solid nineteenth-century commitment to scientific rationalism. Scattered throughout the novel's 550-odd pages is a considerable anthology of both poets' poems (and, in La Motte's case, some tales) more than sixty-five pages' worth—through which beneficent and maleficent fairies flitter, knights fare forth to meet enchanted maidens (who come both singly and in triplets), a city sinks into the sea, and a glass key opens a magic coffin releasing a princess from a century-long spell: This novel has enough of the décor and rhetoric of high fantasy to intrigue, if not wholly to delight, any traditional fantasy lover.

Ash's major work is a twelve-book blank verse epic called *Ragnarök*—a Norse-style cosmogony, in which Ash identifies with the slain god Baldur.

La Motte's is another twelve-book epic called *The Fairy Melusina*, based on a horrific folktale from Brittany, in which a beautiful fairy, spied on in her bath by the knight who falls in love with her, is revealed as a serpent-tailed demon, who eventually orders her husband to murder some of their more monstrous children. She is also a fine architect, however (what first attracts Christabel to the tale), who builds her castles "foursquare and solid." From Byatt's description, it's something we might imagine the Christina Rossetti of "Goblin Market" to have written had she not veered off into consolational verse.

Possession begins when a timid but winning research assistant, Roland Mitchell, discovers a pair of letter drafts by Ash to an unknown woman whom he met at a breakfast party and with whom he was clearly taken. The woman is, of course, Christabel La Motte—who has established a Boston marriage with an aspiring Victorian woman painter, Blanche Glover (Christabel's Geraldine?), after the two artists, painter and poet, met at a lecture by Ruskin.

Roland fails to tell his boss, Professor Blackadder (the editor of Ash's complete works), about his discovery, because . . . well, because Roland is *curious*. (It's a word we find a number of times in the book.) He wants to find out what happened for himself. To this end, he seeks out Maud Bailly, a feminist La Motte scholar, who is also a distant relative of Christabel's family. The two begin to compare scholarly notes and set out on a hunt for further evidence. Along the course, the simple—or not so simple—*desire to know* eventually infects most of the contemporary characters and impels both the Victorian tale and the contemporary one to their intertwined conclusions.

En route, an unsuspected correspondence between La Motte and Ash is discovered in a secret compartment in an unopened room in a decaying family manor house; journals—now by Blanche Glover, now by Ash's wife, Ellen, now by a young cousin of Christabel's, Sabine, on the selkie-haunted coast of Brittany—pop up all over the place, each supplying pieces to the nineteenth-century mystery. As well, we get several accounts of a séance, held by Mrs. Hella Lees, at which all sorts of things might have been going on. It all climaxes in rousing fashion at midnight in a rain- and storm-lashed churchyard replete with grave robbers.

The portraits of the various academics (and their bathrooms!) who hunt, or protect from hunters, the various documents which form our center of interest are well-observed and often funny. There are a few moments, however, when the satirical thrusts—at an ambitious American academic (with his "bottomless checkbook") and at an enthusiastic American women's studies professor (who offers herself for a consoling tumble to women and men alike—and always at the absolutely wrong time)—threaten to break out of the whimsical, where they work, into the ugly, where—for me, with this book—they don't. Lady Joan Bailly, in her wheelchair, is wonderfully accurate, down to every over-starched collation she serves her visiting scholars in the frigid halls of Seal Court (sausages, mashed potatoes, *and* turnips). But Sir George Bailly, blustering about and running pushy Americans off his land with a shotgun, is, for all his concern with his wife's health, pure cardboard; and while, it's true, some members of this antiquated English class today really *are* beyond satire, that doesn't free the novelist from the task of making the impossible believable. It's done by showing how a character cares for something *in excess of the plot* (but not of the structure) of the novel—or by showing what has happened so that he or she *can't* care. If we don't see one or the other, what we notice instead is the corrugations on the character's backing.

By *Possession*'s end, however, heroes and villains alike are both revealed to be obsessed with the same *desire to know*, and by its conclusion all have more or less joined to complete the story with their own puzzle pieces.

For such a book to cohere, it must establish parallels between its historical narrative and its present-time tale—as well as between its realistic passages and its fantastic interpolations. Often this is what Byatt does. One side of a most effective parallel is the relation between Roland and Maud, the contemporary "romance" referred to in the subtitle; for most of the book that relation is, while passionate and deep, sexless. And in our sex-obsessed world, the misunderstandings this evokes among both friends and enemies, as well as the confusion it engenders in the two scholars themselves about their own emotions, gives poignancy and quiet comedy to the story. Eventually, we learn that the relation between Ellen Ash and her husband, Randolph, was much the same as that between Roland and Maud—the other side of the parallel. It's an effective—and economical—way to lend believability and sympathy to the Victorian relationship we might otherwise distrust, viewing it through our contemporary Freud-colored glasses. (Who do *you* think is the father in the case of the pregnant servant girl Ellen must dismiss to the unwed mothers' home?) But the book has shown us beautifully how such a relationship can work in present times, despite our prejudices.

Another parallel accomplishes, however, little or nothing. Our modern heroine, Maud, is distantly related to Christabel, and the novel's denouement involves an intriguing twist to this aspect as well as a payoff in inheritance rights (as all good Victorian romances ought to). But Mortimer Cropper, an obsessed American academic, Ash's biographer, editor of Ash's letters, and the closest thing *Possession* has to a villain, is *also* descended from a nineteenth-century American fan of Ash's; and the relation provides us with another important letter, that gives us Ash's attitudes toward spiritualism—an attitude which figures in interpreting that séance. But the ending does nothing with this particular relationship, though all our sense of novelistic symmetry has led us to expect that it will.

Why, then, double the theme—i.e., make this one letter in Cropper's multi-volume collection just happen to be to *his* great-great-grandmother?

It would have been as easy, or easier, simply to make it one letter in the volume, rather than give it this added significance suggesting a plotting recomplication we never get.

This is probably the place to state: Sentence by sentence, scene by scene, Byatt's writing is lush, light, witty, and—sometimes—swooningly lovely. But much of the progression of incident seems provisional; and in passages where we want elegance and exquisitely careful structuring (à la Barth's *The Sot-Weed Factor*) to match the exquisite prose, finally things move on more or less by the seat of Byatt's pants.

Roland Mitchell is characterized as an old-fashioned textual critic, for example, trained in an earlier tradition and generally, if gently, bewildered by the newfangled criticism—deconstruction, feminist theory, and Lacanian psychoanalysis a-swirl about him in an academy he never made—as are many, many literature professors, graduate students, and undergraduates today, some of whom creep timidly through academe's halls, trying not to be noticed in their ignorance, and some of whom bluster loudly, if ineffectually, against the French and Frankfurt tsunami. Maud is presented, however, as comfortable with both critical worlds (as she is, unlike Roland, comfortable with several social levels). Byatt herself is clearly comfortable enough with today's critical trends to give us several pages from a feminist/psychoanalytic paper on La Motte's work that manages, at once (a) to catch the tone of such pieces perfectly, (b) to be funny, (c) to be critically interesting in and of itself; and (d) to relate to the plot—no mean feat of literary ventriloquism.

(Mortimer Cropper's biography of Ash is called *The Great Ventriloquist.*)

Later in the novel, we find, however, a passage where one of the characters reflects on life and history in largely poststructuralist terms . . . I thought I was reading about Maud—and was halfway through it before I realized the character was Roland! Possibly, of course, this represents an irony. But, equally possibly, Byatt simply forgot that, three hundred pages earlier, she'd characterized her gentle textual detective as someone who felt excluded by this sort of rhetoric and who therefore is not likely to have his most profound thoughts using its terms and concepts when surveying his tentative position as a subject in history. It seems to me that, in this rhetorical miscalculation, Byatt's own novelist ventriloquism has faltered.

In the midst of these quibbles, Byatt must be forever praised for having solved a problem that has defeated novel writers from Sir Walter Scott and Novalis up to Nabokov and our own Ursula Le Guin: A major success of *Possession* is that it manages to integrate poetry—great stretches of it, too—quite comfortably in with the narrative. Byatt accomplishes this by never trying to convince us that Ash or La Motte was, in any objective way, a great, or even a very good, poet. Various professors are greatly taken with the personalities of these two Victorian figures. And La Motte and Blanche Glover, at least in the beginning, believe wholly in the worth of their own talents—more than anyone I've ever met, save a couple of really appalling writers. (Such belief allows the artist no room to grow!) But, if anything, this adds a comic piquancy to their characters—and, in Blanche's case, some poignancy. The present-day lay opinion is, however, that both poets wrote over-complicated, highly affected, mid-Victorian clap-trap, and that any interest we have in either one is a case of special pleading. But isn't special pleading what *all* novels finally are?

Still, when we get a one-to-ten-page poesy-passage by one or the other of them, and we find it even readable, it's a pleasant surprise. And the poetic narratives usually reflect pretty directly on the main actions. For some reason, much of Christabel's poetry uses the Erratic capitalization—and Dashes—of Emily Dickinson—as Well as our Dickinson's Favoured tetrameters. Possibly because of, possibly in spite of, this, La Motte comes off better than Ash. And one of her poems, "The City of Is," about the nondistressed Queen of a very distressed town sinking under the waters, really *is* special. But Byatt knows that we all want to discover our own stories (or our own great poems)—and that nothing is duller than being told one about which all is already known.

But to unseat what is already known—that's why criticism exists.

Here and there, especially in the novel's final third, bits of information come almost out of the blue—such as the fact that the box buried with Ash (Box? What box? Never mind. Here we learn there was one) was still intact when his wife Ellen was interred beside him a number of years later. Other things—what really happened, for instance, when pregnant Christabel disappeared from her cousins' for three days on the dour coast of Brittany—could have used some foreshadowing. Without it, it seems as if Byatt got to the point where she needed a revelation, so sat down and made one up—rather than that she had one in mind all along. There's nothing *wrong* with doing it that way. But if you do, you have to go back and do the rewriting that will make it *look* as if you knew what you were up to all along.

On the emotional level where novels are expected to satisfy most, at least one loose end still worries me: What is the fate of Blanche's paintings? I was as concerned about those as about any of the questions over Christabel or Ash. Possibilities are, at one point, speculated on; but, if nothing else, Byatt's own talent as a visual writer, expert at visual set-pieces, makes us *yearn* for a direct sighting by our modern scholars (the point-of-view characters, in old-fashioned pulp terms) of these Victorian visual fantasies.

On the same note, there's a postscript to the novel, whose intention,

I'm sure, was to tie up another emotional loose end and, incidentally, provide a glowingly, dazzingly, mindlessly happy ending (that, nonetheless, remains hidden from our contemporary researchers); but it also makes about a third of the novel irrelevant, both in terms of plot (which may, indeed, just be more irony which escapes me) and also morally—which, to me, feels like an off-note in an otherwise very smartly written book.

One of *Possession*'s finest moments is a subjective description, toward the end, of Roland's reading (in a novel where most of what the characters *do* is read and reread poems, letters, and journals); Byatt sets it in the context of all the things writers usually shy away from describing because they are too personal. By the end of it, in the most gloriously self-reflective moment, however, the reader is no longer watching Roland possessed by his Victorian text, but rather watching her- or himself possessed by Byatt's novel.

Byatt is clearly a lover of Iris Murdoch. (She has published a study of Murdoch's novels, *Degrees of Freedom: The Novels of Iris Murdoch*. Antonia Byatt is English novelist Margaret Drabble's sister.) It's possible that what strikes me as awkward moments are intended to recall some of the semi-absurdist occurrences in Murdoch's intriguing, but finally rather clumsily written, early works, such as *The Unicorn* or *Flight from the Enchanter*. But I just don't feel that such a fragile and—yes—delightful creation as *Possession* can hold up to such intentional false notes. It's as if Wanda Landowska, in the midst of a Bach toccata for harpsichord, now and again turned to the audience and mugged like Anna Russell.

Possession won last year's Booker Prize for fiction in Great Britain. It's certainly a rich, ambitious, and enjoyable read. And it's a book that seems even more interesting a day after you put it down than in the days you were living with it. But it's a book that, truly to live up to the standards it most ambitiously sets itself by page one hundred, would have to have been executed as a wholly committed *tour de force*—something at once a bit more limited than it is and, thus and at the same time, a bit more ambitious. What we have is rather a virtuoso performance with, every so often, some really sour notes. I confess, I can't tell whether the writer is snickering over them or not. But, by the end, there've been enough of them so that I'm not sure if we are to ignore them and try to enjoy the show anyway (it's really rather wonderful!)—or are to take them as postmodern (if not punkish) markings that purposely mar the surface's high luster. I am curious to know the outcome: Will it all seem more—or less—interesting in a year, or five, or fifteen?

— *New York City*
1990

18

Neil Gaiman, I, II, & III

I
A Walk Where the Wild Things Are

Written with Robert Morales

Neil Gaiman's hair is long and dark, his face stark against it, with the stubborn pallor of many Englishmen who stay up late. Sunglasses hide his hazel eyes; and under his leather jacket, he's wearing a black T-shirt. Like an ex-punker turned family man, his bearing is poised between comfort and calculation.

As we walk Gaiman over to his suite at the Royalton, we see a New York cop hassling an ancient black guy who's lying in a doorway, obviously homeless and out of it. "Let's go, man," the cop says, and his nightstick's rap to the sole of the guy's running shoe is notably too hard. Now the cop gives him a extra whack on the shin—then on the other shin—trying to position himself in front, so that this bit of street cruelty might escape notice in the rush hour.

Neil stops, points a finger, and intones loudly: "*You* will go to *sleep—* and dream dark dreams forever!"

His concentration broken, the cop turns to us, frowning, like a pit bull assessing new targets—one with an English accent.

But Neil's already walking on, laughing. "Really, guys," he tells us, as we break away from the cop's rule-book stare, "don't look at me as if I'm crazy: Isn't that *exactly* the sort of the thing people expect the Sandman to do?"

Okay, he has a point: Neil Gaiman is the thirty-two-year-old writer/ creator of *Sandman*, DC Comics' extraordinarily successful adult fantasy title, with monthly sales of over 100,000 copies in the United States alone, right up there with *Superman* and *Batman*. In fact, the Sandman phenomenon is half the reason DC killed off the Man of Steel last year and has recently given the Caped Crusader a crippling spinal injury: because *Sandman* is a comic for adults.

In one of the Royalton elevators, three preteen French girls inexplicably delight in Neil's presence, probably mistaking him for a musician, so we ask what kind of fan mail he gets. "Stockbrokers, witches, ministers, dominatrices—" he nods shyly at the girls; we've reached his floor— "artists, college professors; many, many students." He tilts his head toward the closing elevator doors: "And we get kids, certainly, and they tend to be very bright ones. The average comics reader is between twelve and fourteen, you know—but from the mail I get I'd assume the average *Sandman* reader is closer to twenty-five or thirty."

A *Sandman* story is likely to be set anywhere: the height of the French Revolution, a contemporary Lower East side tenement, Baghdad at the time of the Arabian Nights. The only constant throughout is the Sandman and his numinous siblings, all of whom flicker in and out at the edges of these stories—much like the gods in a Greek tragedy, rather than recognizable, comic book superheroes. The series is a mythic family epic—its human characters unconscious pawns in the service of some mysterious power struggle, presumably to be revealed at the conclusion of its run, in about a year and a half. Much like PBS's phenomenally sucessful *I, Claudius*, then, *Sandman* is perceived as a soap opera for the right people.

The idea of adult comics had been around—as an *idea*—in the commercial comics business since the late sixties. But when Neil (following on another English writer, Alan Moore of *Watchmen* fame) began to write stories that pulled in huge numbers of readers clearly older than the norm, DC realized there just weren't any rules for this game. So writers who crossed over into the adult market—creating that market for the first time, really—have been pretty much left alone by DC and other publishers to do whatever they want.

"I eagerly went into comics straight out of journalism—I was a terrible journalist," Neil admits cheerily. "Inevitably I'll choose truth over facts, and editors hate that. Anyway: In the eighties the field underwent a significant evolution (adolescent power fantasies were, in the main, upgraded to *adult* power fantasies)—you had the revamping of Batman and you had Alan Moore, and there was a then-thriving market for independent, experimental comics as well. So there was a lot of vitality there, and I lucked out. I did some initial superhero stuff for DC—at the time they were spearheading a sort of 'British invasion' which, of course, was vainly all about replicating Alan's genius. When I was given my chance to create a series, I figured what the hell—it'll *fail* anyway, so let's try to do all the things that I've always wanted comics to do, and keep it in the realm of the fantastic."

Stephen King was initially irked by the comic's complexity when his kids presented him the first boxed set of collected Sandman volumes some Christmases back, seeing it as pretentious—but something nagged at him to try again: "Reading modern comics is like reading modern poetry," King told us. "You have to be able to set aside part of your time and be able to go back and re-rig the way you *see* things, because they're laid out in a way that's challenging to an eye that's used to linear progression. Neil's a great storyteller and he's always fun—he puns, he's allusive—" [note the faint echo of Neil's name in *A Game of You*, the latest Sandman story arc] "—he does all the things that serious writers do, because that's what he is, basically: a serious writer who happens to be working this genre."

"He's very brave," Clive Barker says of Gaiman, a friend of Neil's for over a decade, "because what he constantly does is fly in the face of expectation, and in a popular medium that's a tough thing to do." Although he's just been to the dentist, his face half-dead from Novocain, Barker is nonetheless eager to shed light on Gaimania: "You know, he's got a unique vision, and one of the things he's done is prove that there is a life for comics where people don't run around with their underwear on the outside, saving the planet. He brings a kind of intelligence and poetry to his work which is by and large missing in comics; *beautiful* writing—I think he's at the cutting edge."

However, the majority of Gaiman's fans aren't focusing on his technical ability. Tori Amos came upon one of the collections while writing her *Little Earthquakes* album, and worked Neil and "the Dream King" into her song "Tear in Your Hand." ("It really stood out," says Neil, who received an early demo version,"—people usually tend to send me muddled death-metal tapes.") The two met in London, radical classicists both, and fast became pals—she would be the main inspiration for Dream's younger sister, Delirium. Amos is quick to sum up Neil's appeal: "Well, Neil is our subconscious—he goes looking for the dark. And, although he's got his version of a flashlight—whether that be florescent tassels on a belly dancer's melons, *whatever* he takes with him—he has his way of illuminating what we're hiding. I think Neil expresses what we, society, repress. On so many levels, he is trying to tell us who we really are, where we really come from—he's laying it out for us, and he makes us *remember*. So he is much closer to the truth than anything *we* do of the day."

"I didn't *mean* for it to be controversial," Gaiman explains back in his suite, taking a sip of his Royalton martini. (A specialty of the hotel bar, it's blue.) "It" (*A Game of You*), he suspects, has polarized readers by (a) introducing lesbians, abortion, and transgendered folk into the hermetically sealed world of fantasy comics with (b) a story that's as much about *unfulfilled* wishes as it is about the shallowness of the social roles we play and the dream roles we want. "'In dreams begin responsibilities,' Yeats is said to've written; that's largely what this has been about." Neil frowns irritably, and continues: "Untethered to reality, what passes for popular fantasy has really gone soft—by which I mean, become useless in our daily lives." Then what does he make of the fact that *Sandman*'s most beloved character is Dream's older sister, Death—a cocky punkette who comes off as the ultimate veejay in a recent DC Comics AIDS educational insert Gaiman wrote? "Well, she's the only character in the series that's *totally* self-aware, that totally accepts who she is and what the consequences of that are; I think that kind of acceptance makes one all the more vivid."

Roles, acceptance, responsibility, dreams—*Sandman*'s practically a celebration of Gaiman obsessions. That's probably why Neil seems to eschew the inevitable commercialism surrounding the series. There are posters and statuettes, a Death watch; we'll probably see a Despair mug soon and Delirium 3-D glasses. Neil manages a wan grimace when informed an MTV Top 20 Countdown was hosted by a guy sporting a Sandman T-shirt throughout. It's funny, because Gaiman openly idolizes his personal heroes (most notably Lou Reed), yet he can't make the leap toward people's idolizing *him*.

We watched, a few nights before our interview, as Gaiman ran into a Lower Manhattan performance space to give a reading of one of his prose pieces, straight from the airport on a snowy evening. He tore off his leather jacket, yanked off a heavy black sweater—then put the jacket back on, *with* sunglasses—and read. And that's when we finally understood: For Neil, rather than an affected gesture toward image-building, wearing a leather jacket is the *closest* he gets to a security blanket.

— New York City
March 1993

II
Miracleman (Book Four, The Golden Age)

If you read the previous three *Miracleman* collections, you probably felt like me. Where *could* things possibly go? Their inspired writer, Alan

Moore, had upped the ante so far—cleverly, skillfully, and with a writerly craft at once consummate and daring—that surely now it had to be a downhill plummet and plunge. The swing and glitter, of words, images, and plot-strands, that led us through *Nemesis* to *Olympus*—how could you ask anybody to follow the act writer Moore and artist Totleben had just pulled off?

You do it, of course, by passing the torch on to a writer with the same distaste for the formulaic and the easily fashionable. You do it by getting an artist with the deftness of touch, the suggestive line, and the range of textures of Mark Buckingham.

You do it by getting writer Neil Gaiman—

Let me pause:

Gaiman is one of two writers (yes, the other is Moore) who has done more to change the idea of what comics are and can be, among that strange and anomalous group, serious and informed comics readers, than anyone since . . . well, certainly since I started reading them in the 1940s. I've loved them since I discovered them; and in the sixties and seventies I was quick to say I thought you could do things in comics that could be done in no other medium; that as an esthetic form, comics were irreplaceable—not always that popular an opinion.

How have Gaiman and Moore changed the concept of the comics?

Steve Gerber says in his introduction to *Miracleman, Book One*: "Comics are a visual as well as literary medium, of course . . ." But not so very long ago I would have argued with that. For me, till recently, comics were a visual medium—period. As far as I was concerned, in comics the writer worked *for* the artist. Sometimes the writer's job (I felt) was to inspire the artist. Sometimes it was to give words to the artist's vision. Sometimes it was to provide a story if a talented artist didn't happen to have one just then. But it was still the artist's game. When, occasionally, I wrote them, that's the way I wrote comics. That's the way I looked at comics. And that's how I conceived of and criticized comics.

I'd even gone so far as to say that comics were fundamentally *to be looked at*—rather than read. You looked at the panels—in a given order. You looked at the words—and took in what they said. But people who *read* comics were basically as misguided, I felt, as people who went to *see* an opera. No matter how lavish the production, you *still* go to *hear* an opera. And if you *do* go to see an opera, you're bound to be disappointed by what you see. The soprano will be too fat. The tenor will be too old. And while the words—and the stage directions—make it perfectly clear that the heroine is supposed to leap on the back of her horse, grab up a burning torch, ride to the funeral pyre, spur the horse to leap into it, light it, and as the flames rise up, she, the horse, and the corpse of her lover are all finally consumed, what you *see* is a rather heavy woman in a white shift, who, after her final D-flat, picks up a torch and walks hurriedly off the stage.

Who wouldn't be disappointed?

But if you're willing basically to *hear* . . .

I was sure it was the same with comics. To grab the glory of this soaring medium, you looked—and read only in the interstices of looking. Certainly, there had been important comic book writers. Still, there was always a sense that what made a comics writer important was that the writer could lead artists to where they'd really wanted to go all along.

And then—into the world of commercial comics—came Moore, followed by Gaiman. And for the first time, I found myself deeply, consistently, intensely interested in these comic book writers *as writers*.

With that interest came a revision in the idea of what comics could be: They could be *written*—written not just adequately, not just in a clear and coherent manner, more or less adequate to the more or less brilliant visuals. The writing could be brilliant in itself. Here were writers who saw themselves with the range of language, from silence (and where earlier writers had struggled to keep the writing down to thirty-five words a panel, these writers were happy to have three, four, or five panels with no words at all) to song—the whole of language with which to put across their stories.

And the stories themselves . . . !

Neil Gaiman's *Sandman* comic books—well, you all know them; and those of you who don't are going to learn about them soon. (I know the kind of people who read these introductions. You will.) *Sandman* is so far and above the most inventive and most human comic of the decade, I can simply and patently say that, eventually, everyone who loves comics will know it. Then, with his astonishing mythic sense, Gaiman took the age-old idea of *Magic* and, in four "prestige" format books, made it interesting again by rigorously holding it up against the realest of real worlds. And in *Miracleman, Book Four, The Golden Age*, Gaiman has engineered the most delicate and touching tales of some half-dozen very human men and women (and children, and creatures that could only live in a children's storybook, I *think* . . .), all in a world where gods are real—stories of men and women who, once they come to terms with their past, can celebrate the possibilities of a glorious future.

The last movement of the previous *Miracleman* book was a raging panegyric, a dithyramb, a jeremiad dancing, hot and searing, right up off the sizzling griddle of language. There *was* no place to go—so Gaiman threw the whole machine into reverse. His six entwined tales here come like sapphires afloat on a super-cooled liquid, like shards of sea-ground glass, shadow-cooled; these understated stories almost hide their theme: For *Miracleman* is a book that is largely, generously, compassionately about mourning. Their diction is measured. The voices they speak with are real. The tales unfold like haiku. Their endings remain open, still breathing, alive. Their lambent characters, yearning both for bits of yesterday and portents of tomorrow, will linger with you long.

What *could* possibly happen that was true and real in a world like Miracleworld? Go ahead: You *have* to ask it. But Gaiman goes so easily into that world, to overhear the after-love conversation of a young man with memories of a meeting with divinity, or the indiscreet revelations a superbaby might make to her all-too-human mother, that, when the performance is over, the reader can hardly remember why the task once seemed so daunting. We emerge from these six saying, rather, "But of course. Why didn't *I* think of that? The stories I've just watched and heard are real and right—and the way they've set me to thrill, though the vibrations may fade, they'll never wholly cease."

And, friends, *that* takes a writer.

—Amherst
April 1992

III
Skerries of the Dream

When asked to introduce *A Game of You*, a Neil Gaimon *Sandman* series, the first thing I did was turn to the Oxford English Dictionary and look up "skerry," where I found:

> A rugged, insulated sea-rock or stretch of rocks, covered by the sea at high water or in stormy weather; a reef.

It's quite a resonant image, those distant, only partially visible solidities, now and again drowned in dreams—temporarily lost in them. Gaiman plays with it elegantly in the writing; and Shawn McManus (as do Doron, Talbot, and Woch) plays with it equally elegantly in the drawings.

The Sandman is one of the most popular comics of our day—and popular with the oddest lot of people. We're all used to the idea of comic books resonating with elemental mythic patterns: the late lamented Superman, the currently thriving Batman, and Wonder Woman. But, when all is said and done, as such myths go, they're pretty brutal things. *The Sandman,* under the writerly direction of Neil Gaiman, does its work delicately, probing in areas where, often, we might not have even suspected anything mythical lay. It explores always with an ironic cast to the lips. The eyes are narrowed. The approach is always skewed.

Again and again, what it discovers shocks, chills, catches at the heart. It sends us to strange places, to the most distant shores of the imaginative, the mystical, to explore the stuff that can only be figured in dreams . . .

Gaiman's *Game of You*—this particular *Sandman* series—begins in the snow: Need we note that for the comics colorist, depicting snow requires the minimum amount of ink? Take a look: Color there is all but restricted to the shading over the caption boxes. (And that color says: Look at the *language* in this tale . . .) What we have in the opening three pages is two streams of information, all but unconnected, one verbal, one visual. The visual one, by the bottom of the first page, has become shocking: a desiccated corpse . . .

At the same time the words provide a strangely distanced, even elegant, colloquy between speakers named Prinado and Luz about the Cuckoo, the Princess, and the Tantoblin—carrying us right past that shock, into the second page, toward a spot of black: a hole in the snow— a hole, a blackness, that grows larger and larger, till, by the bottom of page three, it engulfs the reader, filling its panel.

Need we note that an all-black panel requires the *most* ink possible from the comics inker? (The only color there is restricted to the shading over the caption boxes: Look at the language . . .). But here two eyes blink in that darkness, to look, indeed, in the direction of the words . . .

What's happening in this three-page prologue is that we are given two simultaneous worlds, as it were, both highly subjective, one represented by words, one represented by pictures. Both are highly formalized—the one represented by words through the deeply conventionalized diction associated with high fantasy, the one represented by pictures through the formal progression from white to black. Both contain violences.

The shocks in one information stream—the starkly drawn ribs of the corpse at the bottom of page one, the verbal shock of "The Tantoblin will not come. I felt him die. The Black Guard found him in the night," even as they fall within the same panel—jar with one another; as we move our attention back and forth between one stream and the other, there is impingement, distortion, and interaction that all but obliterates the distinctions the formalities set in place. And that—in case you're wondering—in spite of the abstract language, is a description of what is going to go on all through the rest of *A Game of You.*

It's our opening example of how the game will be played:

Two worlds—and elements from each will constantly impinge, cross over, to shock and distort what goes on in the other.

Also, we're going to get, just incidentally, a tale that covers just about the range of what comics can do—from panels almost pure white to panels almost pure black.

The way to become really frustrated with *A Game of You* is, however, to read one world as reality, the world of Barbie, Wanda, Hazel, and Foxglove, and one world as fantasy: the world of Prinado, Luz, Wilkinson, and the Cuckoo. If you try to read one as a simple allegory for the other—if you look to one for an extensional explanation of the other—you will not be a happy camper. Clive Barker, in his introduction to the penultimate *Sandman* collection, *The Doll's House*, noted that Gaiman's tales tend to take place not in a world where fantasy invades the real, but rather in what Barker called a "far more delirious" form: "In these narratives, the whole world is haunted and mysterious. There is no solid status quo, only a series of relative realities, personal to each of the characters, any and all of which are frail, and subject to eruptions from other states and conditions." The visual shock that comes as the reader leaves page three of *A Game of You* to turn to page four—the transition from the snow-and-shadow world of the Land, where death is an ugly splatter of ink at the bottom of the page in the progression from white to black, to the sheer *messiness* of Barbie's room (a chaos of clothing and wall photos and rumpled bedding wholly organized around the sexuality of Barbie's buns) immediately suggests this *is* going to be a two-tiered fantasy, of the real and the imagined.

But hold on to Barker's point. He's been there before . . .

Consider: In the world that we—certainly—*start* to read as real, the sullen top-floor neighbor harbors a horde of malignant crows inside his rib cage; the quiet girl upstairs with the oversized glasses who drinks soy milk is hundreds of years old; here, it turns out, the moon *cares* whether or not you have a "y" chromosome, and punishes you accordingly. No, *this* is a fantasy world, too.

The world of the *Sandman* comics finally takes its power from its intense saturation of irony. Here, the Lord of all Dream has a smart-alec crow for a sidekick called Matthew who calls his boss "Boss." It's a world where a stuffed toy animal can scare an old homeless woman into a near-heart attack—or betray you to the point of death. In the *Sandman* a mourner draws the threads of a veil on her face in a restroom with an eyebrow pencil—and, because it's a comic book, we, the readers, can't tell the difference between it and a "real" veil—but all the characters can and comment on it constantly. ("What's that on your face?") It's a world where a "Wundabud" commercial (that's a brand of cotton swab) plays through a storm that all but destroys a neighborhood—in short, it's a world almost as heavily laced with ironies as our own.

The key to this fantasy is Wanda's troubling death (alongside the death of the single black character in the tale)—which drew a whole host of very concerned ideological criticisms, when readers first encountered it in issue 36, part 5. (And, I confess, Hazel's ignorance of the mechanics of female reproduction seemed to me something one would be more likely to find in the suburban heartland, even at the center of Barbie's Florida childhood—rather than on the third floor of a Lower East Side tenement. But the same reading applies . . .) Wanda's initial biological sex is of the same visual status as the aforementioned ironic black mourner's veil at the final Kansas funeral: The biologically naive (Hazel), as well as the forces of religion (Thessaly) and the family (Alvin's) now and again speak about it. But we, the readers, just can't *see* it. (The veil is simply *erased* at the end . . .) And because the comics are a fundamentally visual medium, that ultimate invisibility may finally be the strongest statement the story has to make about the topic to the common (comics) reader. It seems to me, as I was saying, that the key to this particular fantasy world is precisely that it *is* a fantasy world where the natural forces, stated and unstated, whether of myth or of chance, *enforce* the dominant ideology we've got around us today, no matter what. (The dominant ideology is the collection of rules and regulations that includes, among many other things, the one that says that in popular narratives, like the *Dirty Harry* films, say, all the members of oppressed groups, blacks, women, Asians, gays, or what have you, have to be killed off at the end, no matter how good and noble they are—so that we can feel sorry for them, then forget about them. The dominant ideology is what's challenged by, among many other things, something like the ACT-UP slogan: "We're here. We're queer. We *won't* go 'way! Get used to us!") Making the supernatural forces in the tale the enforcers of the dominant ideology is what makes it a fantasy—and a rather nasty one at that.

And it remains just a nasty fantasy unless, in our reading of it, we can find some irony, something that subverts it, something that resists that fantasy, an array of details that turns the simple acceptance of that ideology into a problem—problematizes it, in Lit. Crit.-ese. But, as we said, almost everything in the *Sandman* has its richness, its ironic spin. I'll mention a couple. But look for more. They're there. Taking the time to tease such subtleties out (and the problem with political readings is precisely that the large and general tend to overwhelm the subtle and specific) makes us stronger readers in the end, not because it makes us *excuse* such political patterns, but because we have to become even *more* sensitive to them, if we are to see how they are affected *by* the subtleties (which are, themselves, *just* as political). In life, it will be the subtleties that start to wear away at the major social patterns of oppression, after all. It's the range of subtle subversions that set them up for the big changes that come by as better legislation, economic freedoms, and their material like.

(Notice when major social changes *are* finally legislated and formalized, they tend to surprise everyone *except* those who were paying attention to the details. That's why, in life and on the page, specific details are a good thing to pay attention to.)

Just as George's death (he will be called back to speak by Thessaly) will mirror Wilkinson's death (*he* will be called back to speak by Thessaly), Wanda's death at the end mirrors the Tantoblin's death at the beginning. What—? You don't know what sort of a goblin a Tantoblin is? Well, neither do I. What's more, the OED won't help us: A tantoblin (or tantadlin) is a fruit tart, or a lump of excrement. (And a "tanton" is an inmate of a hospital dedicated to St. Anthony . . .) The point is, as is made explicit in the dream in part 1, Wanda doesn't really know who she is either. And since this has seldom been the problem of most of the would-be transgendered men and women of my acquaintance (if anything, it's quite the opposite), it's simply one more thing that weights the reading of this particular dream world toward a mode of the fantastic.

The question that *A Game of You* puts is: Given a fantasy world in which, among other things, the dominant ideology is not socially constructed but is rather enforced by the transcendental order of nature, what will happen when an even wilder and more delirious order of fantasy is let loose in it?

It's a reasonable question, because, as we all know (1) people like Wanda's family, whom we will meet in part 6, are quite convinced that God *is* precisely what keeps the dominant ideology in place and working, and (2) sometimes very bad things do happen to otherwise very nice, even heroic, people—like Wanda.

So the tale is not without its relevance.

What is to be done?

For one, Barbie will be restricted to a nominal rebellion—which, perhaps, doesn't seem like much. The first rain will obliterate it, and likely no one in Kansas will ever know. But the idea of the nominal (in name only, having to do with names) is a big factor in *A Game of You.* While a name is always something *you* can choose, it only functions socially as long as *I* call you by it. (And try calling people names that they *don't* choose to be called by, if you want to see some real social unrest.) The power to choose one's own name is finally the major playing piece in the power game with which the story closes.

But let's look for a moment at another instance of parental naming in the story. Here's Wilkinson on *his* family's naming practices, during the journey through the Land, in part 4:

> I loved bein' a kid. I was one of seventeen children. We were all named Wilkinson—I suppose it was roughest on the girls, but we all got used to it in the end. I blame the parents, really . . . I would have liked to've bin an only child. That way when someone shouts Wilkinson, you know if it's you or not. Mustn't grumble. Our parents were the salt of the earth. Lovely people. It was just when they found a name they liked, they stuck with it.

In short, the Land is a fantasy world where there *is* no necessary distinction between male and female names for children—but, apparently, parents are just as sticky about preserving the name they pick as Wanda's parents turn out to be in part 6. What we have here is an interesting satirical commentary, given in advance, on the closing moves of the game. (We won't even speculate on what prompted Barbie's parents to name *her* . . . And when she got together with her disastrous ex-boyfriend Ken, wasn't that just *too* cute? . . .) This is not to say that life in the Land is all skittles and Courvoisier. The god the Land is sacred to is "Murphy," which, before we find out his real name, suggests nothing so much as the Murphy of Murphy's Law—that most pessimistic of observations on the Human Condition: "Anything that possibly *can* go wrong, will."

But there're other interesting correspondences between the two levels of fantasy. *Take* the idea of "cute."

In Gaiman's fantasy New York, "cute" is Hazel and Foxglove's "cute frog mug" in which Wanda, utterly against all her own social and aesthetic leanings ("This?" she says to George, passing him on the stairs. "Oh, don't worry. It's not *my* cute frog mug. I'm carrying it for a friend"), must take the milk down for Barbie's coffee.

In the Land, however, being "cute" is the very survival mechanism of the Cuckoo—the principle of evil. Says the Cuckoo to Barbie, in their part five encounter: "I've got a right to live, haven't I? And to be happy? . . . And I'm awful sweet, aren't I? I'm *awful* cute." And Barbie's capitulation comes with the admission: "You're . . . cute . . . as a . . . button." From here, if we turn back to Wanda's encounter in part one with George on the stairs—George, with his crows, is, after all, an agent of the Cuckoo (who, once again, survives because the cute, the kitschy, the aesthetically impoverished and hopelessly sentimental hide her murderous impulses toward the stuff of fantasy that she appropriates by moving into the fantasies of others)—suddenly that encounter is given a second-reading resonance, a resonance, finally, essential to what Gaiman, I suspect, is all about in his *Sandman* stories . . .

For all we can get out of a careful rereading of Gaiman, the immediate pleasures of these stories to the first-time reader are many. It's the rare reader who does not respond to Gaiman's imaginative breadth, coupled with his simple accuracy of observation. The guarded caring with which his characters live with one another ("Don't take too much," Hazel warns Wanda, giving her the milk for Barbie's coffee) is comic and winning—and, of course, wholly recognizable. But this is a largely linear, melodic pleasure. There is also, however, a harmonic pleasure that accrues as detail resonates with detail. It is a pleasure that increases with careful, multiple readings. It is what makes these stories, in a word, art.

Gaiman's delirious world is held together always by relationships. Nor is his a world of relationships between fixed, solid egos, sure of themselves" and clear in their "identity." Each of those relationships, no matter how positive, always has its moment of real anxiety—what relationship doesn't? And all of Gaiman's selves are split, if not deliriously shattered. What he has to say about those relationships is what makes him an artist particularly interesting to our time. The Game of You is, after all, *not* the Game of I. (That's the "me-first" game—most of us know it only too well—where what *I* want is wholly above all other considerations and has to be pursued at any cost to anyone else.) It seems to me what Gaiman is saying, with the help of the artists who draw the pictures, is that, in the rich, complex, and socially constructed world around us, *you* cannot ultimately be what—or who—you want to be without some support from *me*. Wanda supports Barbie at the beginning of the story. At the end of the story, even though posthumously, Barbie supports Wanda. The element of death, however, makes it a much darker tale than that simple and rather Pollyannaish reduction presupposes.

We're not talking simple altruism here. We're talking about something much deeper, that allows individuals to exist; we're talking about the hidden, shifting, undersea reefs on which every individual stands— rocks that so rarely show clear above the tides of illusion and desire. That's the support we mean, and it always begins in something outside the self.

Gaiman is also saying that, because of death—even a fantasy death that allows articulation and information to come from beyond its borders, when magicked up by a centuries-old moon witch—*no* one can win the Game of I. Wanda cannot win it. Barbie cannot win it. (Morpheus tells Thessaly that, for all her longevity, she cannot win it either: Take a look at the various "immortals'" deaths in Gaiman's more recent *Sandman* series, *brief lives* . . .) Nor will I. Nor will you. (Also take a look at Gaiman's moving meditation on the last days of an artist, in his powerful work with Dave McKean, *Signal to Noise.*) Thus, for Gaiman, *A Game of You* is the only game worth playing—because it is the only game where, in the end, there's any chance of coming out ahead.

Even if one wins only by a name written on a stone that will wash away with the next shower, at least that allows something to persist in memory—and thus may lead to something else. But without even the name preserved momentarily in the real world by real action (and here, as I hope we can see, "real" is not the catch-all antonym for fantasy but rather a specific synonym for the political—as it is whenever it's used intelligently), there's no hope at all. Gaiman shows us the *most* marginal win possible in *A Game of You.*

But it's still won by moments, however small, of real social bravery. And that's what, at the end of *A Game of You*, Gaiman portrays. Thus, in a fantasy world whose tragedies are not real (i.e., not political) but are, nevertheless through that fantasy, deeply recognizable (and readable in any number of real ways), he has given us a triumph.

—Amherst
January 17, 1993

19

A Tribute to Judith Merril

This piece was read at the tribute to Judith Merril, sponsored by the Harbour-front Festival of Authors, held at the premiere Dance Theater at 8:00 p.m., on Thursday, October 15, 1992, in Toronto. Other speakers that night in Merril's honor were John Robert Columbo, Katherine MacLean, Elisabeth Vonarburg, Frederik Pohl, Pierre Berton, Spider Robinson, and Michael Moorcock. The Tribute was hosted by Greg Gatenby. It concluded with an interview of Merril by Susan Crean. Judith Merril died in September 1997.

Traditionally, "tribute" is what we pay to those who have conquered. And in the case of art, such conquest is presumed a happy thing.

The first works by Judy I read—and they wholly conquered me—were *Gunner Cade* (1952) and *Outpost Mars* (1952), which Judy wrote in collaboration with Cyril Kornbluth under their collaborative pseudonym, Cyril Judd. Brutal and authority-fixated Cade's transformation, as he learns compassion, to understand human rights and a higher sense of ethics, was as powerful to me as a thirteen-year-old reader as anything I'd read. Then an adolescent friend, more aware of the workings of the science fiction world than I, explained to me that Cyril Judd was, indeed, a shared pen name. Immediately I hunted up stories by both writers.

I found them.

And I didn't like them—what thirteen-year-old reader would? For both writers, on their own, were working in the front rank of the genre, producing the most mature and measured work—and in Kornbluth's case, the most mordantly satirical work as well—of the day. I was, after all, *only* thirteen.

When I came back to Merril's stories, however, as a reader on the slightly saner side of twenty-one, I began to see how extraordinary these stories were and how much—especially Merril's, for all their imaginative material—they clung to the nuance and articulation of the real and recognizable world.

For Merril's science fiction purposely eschewed the luxuriant exotica promising the adolescent mind the longed-for, and often needed, escape for which science fiction is so notorious. Rather, here was a progression of sentences as clean and as balanced as sentences could be in the English of that decade, totally dedicated to the precise evocation of their object. And they were welded together into deeply wise stories, like "Peeping Tom" (1954), and into wonderfully moving ones, like "Dead Center" (1954).

> James James Morrison Morrison Weatherbee George Dupree
> Took great care of his mother, though he was only three.

My own mother had read me that A. A. Milne poem many, many times; perhaps there was no way I could fail to identify, then, with six-year-old Toby, the bright, articulate child who views the desperate action around his father, the stranded astronaut Jock Kruger, and his mother, the engineer, Ruth. But I point out that when it was first published, "Dead Center" was chosen for the prestigious Martha Foley *Best Short Stories of 1954* anthology—the only story from the science fiction community to be so honored. I reread the tale last night. Its accuracy and its orchestration sounded out as truly and as tragically as they did in the year of its writing.

Some time later, Merril would begin a glitteringly incisive essay on the SF writer Theodore Sturgeon, with the ringing constative: "The man has style. . . ."

But one need only read a page of that same essay, or, indeed, practically any of her other works to realize (as an English friend of mine put it when, to his delight, I first passed him the piece): "So has the lady. . . ."

For Merril was reconquering me—like a general who, having swept the land in one direction, sweeps back, securing this or that stronghold on the way, reinforcing this or that border.

Many people have written about science fiction. But few have written about it as continuously and as intelligently as Merril. Because we are writers, our major life experiences are often caught between the covers of a book.

It was my first visit to the Milford Science Fiction Conference (which Merril helped found, with writers Damon Knight and James Blish). Gracious and generous Kate Wilhelm had let me sleep in one of the empty rooms occupied during the school year by one of her adolescent sons, on the top floor of the cavernous Anchorage where the conferences then met. My first afternoon I had walked into the workshop and found myself confronted by more of my fellow SF practitioners than I'd ever realized could occupy a single room. But now both the workshop and the socializing were over. And I was attempting to get to sleep—and, with the excitement of the day, finding it impossible. That year, Merril was not in attendance at the conference—perhaps the only disappointment for me to that extraordinary week. But now I decided, as so many sleepless readers, sleepless writers have done, to step outside and find myself a book.

On a hall shelf, I saw a row of volumes—the Merril *Year's Best Science Fiction* anthologies, unto the first paperback. I was familiar with them—had read in one or two before. Now I pulled one out at random—then two more—and went back to my room. The *Year's Best* anthologies were extraordinary. That the selection of the stories was excellent and imaginative goes without saying. But science fiction, in those years, was a genre with almost no historiography. So Merril had taken it upon herself to create one. The stories were embedded in commentary, forward and behind. These mini-essays were accounts of current politics, science, and the ways the stories responded to both. And that night, somewhat to my surprise, I—among all those writers who prided themselves on never reading an introduction before reading the book—found myself reading along through Merril's commentary to the tales, first to last.

Then I was back in the hallway to get more volumes. I read no fiction that night. But I read the introductions and the commentary and the conclusions from all eight volumes published to that date. When I'd finished, outside the screen window beyond the maple leaves the September sky had gone from black to indigo. But as I finally drifted off, I did so with the troubling realization that, before I had gone through this material, even though I'd had been reading science fiction since I was a child, even though I'd now published a handful of novels in the genre, I simply had not known anything of my genre's history and present reality.

And now I did.

What's more, as I have written many times, and told many students who have come to me to learn about science fiction, and will repeat here: Without reading that meticulously wrought, incredibly economic, and brilliantly ranging commentary from those volumes there *is* no way to know the genre for those years.

A few years later, when I'd met Judy, and we'd become friends, I dropped in on her at the hotel where, with her young then-secretary James Sallis, she was working on the notes to what would be the last of those anthologies, *SF-12*. There I got some idea of the endless succession of eighteen- and twenty-hour days that went into the commentary for those volumes. Merril's criticism of the genre has not been collected. And that means we, who still work in that genre, do so more or less blind to a whole aspect of our history and our reality. And I cannot say how much I hope that lack will be soon mended.

As a writer, Judy had to struggle under one of the greatest curses that can befall you. From time to time she balked at it. More often, she accepted it with humorous goodwill. But let me interject here that when I was taking the local transport service to Bradley Airport this morning to be here in Toronto tonight, I found myself sitting next to a professor far better known in academia than I shall ever be, who explained during our polite converse that she was teaching a course on women and the body. When, to her friendly inquiry as to what I did, I told her I wrote science fiction, she told me: "We use some science fiction in my course."

"Judith Merril's 'That Only a Mother'?" I asked. "Why, yes!" she said. "However did you know?" For—despite the critical approbation of Merril's later works and the fact that, inarguably, other stories have out-stripped it in art, imaginative strength, and insight—her first-sold science fiction tale, "That Only a Mother" (1947), became an instant classic. It was, and probably still is with some readers, her best-known piece—though the upsurge of feminist interest during the seventies and eighties has thrown a warm and luminous light over those longer and richer tales such as "Daughters of Earth" and "Shrine of Temptation." And that's something those of us who love her work can only welcome.

Still, the encounter with Professor Daphne Patai this morning struck me as the fondest of ironies and, at once, only fitting it should take place as I was on my way to this happy, happy tribute.

As you might gather, I have been deeply lucky in that Judith Merril, the name on the spine of the anthologies, the name on the early novel and collection of her own stories, *Shadow on the Hearth* and *The Tomorrow People*, somehow made the transition—one I've found again and again astonishing—to my friend, Judy.

It's my critical position that the best science fiction has import far beyond the borders of the genre—or of the ghetto, as it's sometimes styled—even while a rich and informed reading of it requires a deal of understanding of what life in the ghetto is all about.

Merril's fiction is inchoate to the extra-generic import the best science fiction has established, as her criticism sustains the possibility of a sophisticated access to the genre's richness.

Merril's work after her science fiction and science fiction criticism expanded to an astute exploration throughout society and technology. Two years ago, she came to the University of Massachusetts where she gave the best-attended talk in the Comparative Literature Department we had ever sponsored, on the concept of Gaia and world-ecological consciousness.

I am conquered and—yes—happily so.

Judy—thank you!

— *Toronto*
1992

20

Michael Perkins' *Evil Companions*

Evil Companions is a meticulous miracle of language and observation—an energetic and idiosyncratic vision of the interface between sex, pain, and the quotidian day-to-day of what, at the time it was written, would have been called "bohemian life": the lives of young writers, poets, actors, and people who liked their company, living out of each other's pockets—in which there was seldom more than loose change anyway.

But it can also be argued that this slim, intense volume, which first appeared from Essex House in November 1968 (while its twenty-five-year-old writer was in the hospital, recovering from a stab wound in the stomach sustained at an October party in a small East Village bookstore . . .), is a roadmark at the terminus of an extraordinary moment in history—a document lucid in its imaginative presentation of what had gone before, indispensable for an understanding of what would come after, in that odd phenomenon usually called the Sexual Revolution.

Michael Perkins grew up in Portsmouth, Ohio, a small town overlooking the Ohio River into Kentucky. His first wife, the talented painter Renie Perkins, was from Dayton, where the two met. For five years they had been living in New York. Renie was expecting their second child in months.

The 1960s, when *Evil Companions* was written—the decade of "love-ins," "flower-power," and the Beatles—was paradoxically a decade of extraordinary political violence. The country was at war in Vietnam—and many of our population were furious about it. The decade had been ushered in with a handful of political assassinations, most notably those of black leader Medgar Evers and President John Fitzgerald Kennedy. And in the young couple's St. Marks Place apartment, Michael began the novel—his first—in early March 1968.

On the mild Thursday evening of April 4th, moments before seven o'clock, black men and women rushed out into and through the city streets, uptown and down, stopping others to declare, shocked: "Martin Luther King's been killed . . . !" And at four minutes after seven, the first TV and radio reports confirmed what had been phoned across the country from around the Loraine Motel in Memphis, where the shooting had occurred on the balcony outside room 306 near six o'clock, and from around St. Joseph's Hospital, where King was pronounced dead at seven, in an amazing web of phone calls to all and sundry.

Soon black students were sitting in at New York City's Columbia University to protest both James Earl Ray's assassination of the Nobel Peace Prize-winning leader and their university's racist admission policies. White students joined them. Then, on a mid-April night, a police attempt to end the student demonstration turned into a long night of beatings, brutalities, and riots—broadcast live over WBAI-FM to millions of New York City listeners till five o'clock in the morning. The broadcast was the result of an accident that began when, shortly after nine o'clock at night, the police jammed the Columbia University Radio Station, which the protesters had been using to organize their now campuswide activities. With the communications center out, the police had hoped the demonstrations would fall apart. But the protesters phoned 'BAI, which volunteered its services to them. Thus, when the police became violent, in millions of apartments throughout the city and environs, people heard students phoning in descriptions of the beatings going on around them, heard the thud of clubs on bodies and the screams of protesters, heard the hooves of a police horse smash through the glass walls of a phone booth, from which a young man was trying to describe the mayhem outside it—and the phone go dead. Moments later another phoned-in description from another part of the campus began.

It went on like that for hours.

Violence was still going on after one. Live reports still emphasized the tension and fear that covered the campus after three. At five in the morning, having stayed on the air several hours beyond its usual shut-off time, WBAI-FM finally closed down for the night, leaving millions of numbed listeners questioning what exactly could have caused this in a land that vouchsafed political freedom and freedom of speech.

And when, a few hours later—many people did not go to sleep at all that night—the seven A.M. news on the commercial stations around the city reported, "There was some trouble among the protesters up at Columbia University last night. But police had everything under control by nine-thirty . . . ," one felt the combined bewilderment and outrage of a character in a Kafkaesque dream from which there could be no awakening.

Between a week and two weeks on, Perkins finished his first draft of

Evil Companions—on April 21. (By then there were student demonstrations in sympathy with the Columbia students all over the country—all over the world.) Sixteen days later, on May 7, he mailed the manuscript off to his editor, Brian Kirby, at California's Essex House.

It was probably sometime in mid- or late May that I first met Michael (in that month, across the sea in France, the violence in New York in April had now, along with developments in Tunis, generated a sympathy strike among French students, joined there by workers, whose own violences and glories have gone down in history ever since as "May '68"). As two local writers in the East Village, we were introduced in the recently opened Earley by the Park bookstore by the owner Jack Earley, who was also Michael's brother-in-law. Michael was a tall, lanky young man with a roundish face and a soft-spoken manner. At the time, I didn't know that he had already edited the magazine *Down Here*, which had been the first U.S. publisher of Guillaume Apollinaire's surreal erotic masterpiece, *The Debauched Hospodar*. At our introduction, we smiled and made two minutes of pleasant conversation. Then one or the other of us went on his way.

Sometime in the same weeks, I recall coming home from dinner on Sixth Street at comic book-writer Dennis O'Neils, and having to wait for twenty-odd minutes before the police let me cross Avenue B. When, finally, I and the half-dozen people waiting at the corner with me were allowed to hurry over, we had to hold ashcan covers over our heads, since neighborhood snipers on the roofs were hurling bricks into the street.

On May 20, Renie delivered the couple's second daughter. Two weeks later, on the evening of June 4, Andy Warhol was shot by radical feminist Valerie Solanis—author of *The S.C.U.M. Manifesto*. Only two or three months before, Solanis had called Michael at his office at the small alternative publisher Croton Press, looking for a publisher for her book. Renie and Michael heard about her shooting of Warhol the morning of the fifth on the radio. Both of them recognized Solanis' name—and Renie mentioned that, had things gone differently, it might have been Michael who was shot. Michael went off to his main job—teaching remedial reading in a Catholic school in Brooklyn. That day, the Warhol incident filled the headlines of the city papers; the shooting was not fatal, but Warhol was hospitalized.

And painter Renie, still in postpartum depression exacerbated both by the general climate of violence in the city and this most recent shooting of an artist, went into her studio and drank a can of turpentine.

Taped to the window of Earley by the Park, Michael's sister left a handwritten note:

Mike,
Renie's in Bellevue

Perhaps another sentence suggested that things were under control—
Coming home early that afternoon, Michael went first to the Village
to look in on the Croton Press office, then walked back to the East Side—
to learn of Renie's condition through the note. He has no memory of
the note's last line: The moment he read it, he ran first to his apartment,
then to the hospital.

Later that afternoon, I passed by the store, realized it was closed, saw
the same note, and, unaware of what had happened, jotted down a mention of it in my journal for that month.

Shortly after midnight the same day, Robert Francis Kennedy, who
had announced his candidacy for president back on March 16 and who
had just won the California primary (his fifth win out of six), finished up
a speech in a Los Angeles hotel and was ushered out through the
kitchen—where he was shot to death by a Jordanian, Sirhan Sirhan.
Follow-up headlines on the Warhol shooting were wiped from the front
pages of the nation's papers the next morning by the assassination of the
late president's younger brother.

Renie died at Bellevue Hospital the next day, June 7.

A widower now with two daughters, one not six weeks old, Michael
signed the contracts for his novel three weeks later on June 28.

My first encounter with the *text* of *Evil Companions* came some weeks
after Renie's death. At this distance, my general recollection is that at
least one reason Jack Earley arranged to have Michael read at the bookstore was to give him something to take his mind off the recent tragedy.
Jack asked me to be a second reader with Michael. My then-wife, poet
Marilyn Hacker, had recently returned from San Francisco and came
with me that night. I read a section from my newest science fiction novel,
Nova. And Michael read the extraordinary post-climactic chapter from
Evil Companions, "Blood Country Explored."

When the reading was over and the applause stopped (were there
twelve people in the audience that night? there were certainly no more
than eighteen), we broke up to fill paper cups from the gallon of Ingle-
nook Chablis on the table beside the wall shelf: My memory is that for
the first few minutes there was less talk than is usual on such occasions, as
we recovered from the electric energy of Michael's chapter.

The summer rolled over into warm autumn. And on September 9, editor Brian Kirby sent a letter to Perkins from California:

> . . . And *Evil Companions,* believe it or not, is finally about to come out (in Oc-
> tober), with only very few emendations and an incredible cover by Leonor
> Fini. The attorney was impossible on this but I out-maneuvered him. His main
> objection was that it was too well written!

Evil Companions did not come out till November. Between two and three weeks before copies were available, on October 19, there was another evening wine party at Earley by the Park. There'd been a dinner beforehand at Michael's house, with booze, pot, and peyote. A couple of people had brought their kids. Among those in the bookstore that night was a Ukrainian painter, who played the accordion—to which everyone, including Michael, was dancing. At about ten o'clock, from outside, came the sound of running feet and voices. Michael and Jack, with some of the others, went to the door to look. Some twenty or more Puerto Rican young men were coming down the street, some of them with baseball bats.

Earley, who felt that he'd developed some rapport with the neighborhood adolescents, some of whom were in the gang, started out—over Michael's restraining advice—to talk to them. Earley sported a short blond beard at the time and someone in the gang shouted: "Dirty hippie, look at his beard . . . !" Just then the accordion player stumbled out in front of Jack—and went down with two baseball bats to the head. Earley got the next blow, and Michael grabbed him to protect him—to receive a knife in the side that cut through to his stomach. Describing it later, Michael wrote that it felt like "a soft punch." It was only when they were back in the store, with the accordion player lying in the corner, his skull seeping blood, that Michael realized he'd been stabbed. Children were crying, grown-ups were terrified, and the gang outside was throwing things at the store windows—till a window broke! Repeated calls to the police brought no response for more than an hour. At one point Michael went to the door and, shouting and brandishing a knife at the men now waiting across the street ("I was practically berserk," he described himself, at that point), he broke the last of the baiters up—as the ones with the baseball bats had moved on.

Michael went to the hospital, where he was admitted—and was on the critical list at Bellevue for the next two weeks.

An intern told him that it was only because he had eaten so little that day and had so much alcohol in his stomach that he lived. Michael still carries an eight-inch scar from that night.

Novelist Donald Newlove lived next door to Earley by the Park: His novel *The Painter Gabriel* (McCall Publishing Company, New York, 1970) contains a fictionalized but generally accurate account of that night's occurrences across Avenue B from the southeast corner of Tompkins Square. And Perkins himself wrote an article around it about a year-and-a-half later.

When, in November, copies of *Evil Companions* arrived in New York City (and I purchased my first of several, at Earley's bookstore—for soon the volume was one I was giving away with great enthusiasm to my friends), the writer was in the hospital, recovering. But Earley placed copies in one of the cracked-across bookstore windows, above a sign that declared, for the whole neighborhood to read:

Perkins Lives!

I go into the violence, political and personal, surrounding the writing and publication of *Evil Companions* only to point out that the extreme violence informing the text itself has its correspondences both in the politics of the times—and in the life of the writer.

The fundamental conceit of *Evil Companions* is simple: Suppose the new breed of pot-puffing, longhaired young people—beatniks or hippies—really *were* as perverted and sexually dangerous as a hypostasized American middle class and working class then claimed to fear. . . .

The book was written at a time when long hair and beards on men were far rarer than they are today—and usually confined to a single neighborhood of any given city. And anyone whose clothing or hair reflected that lifestyle often thought twice about the consequences of leaving that neighborhood.

The class divisions that made that aspect of the novel comprehensible in 1968 have, since, shifted decidedly—so that where one is most likely to see, say, long hair on men today is precisely in those working class venues that, in 1968, would have been the source of the imprecations shouted at the narrator in chapter 12: "Why don't you get a haircut?" "They ought to put him in a zoo!" "Hey, pussy face!" Still, the shifting of those social configurations leaves Perkins' specifically sexual vision, if anything, the more intense.

Evil Companions takes its power from a combination of its milieu and its anger. The only place in the novel we must move the suspension of disbelief to a new order is in chapter 14, when the action leaves the East village for the House of the Surgeons on the Jersey Palisades. But its return in the next chapter to the milieu from which the novel takes its strengths registers like Antaeus once more setting foot upon the earth, more than making up for the brief defection. And the novel's finale, fittingly enough on a train that travels to and from the city, is truly frightening—for those who have followed the book on a deeper level than that of a simple sexual picaresque.

The anger in *Evil Companions* is always and unremittingly directed at the "self"—as a necessary stimulus to pleasure. Perkins—along with his narrator's mentor, Anne—never forgets that love is a sensation.

Others of them include hunger, pain, and fear.

One of the secondary messages of *Evil Companions* is that we may learn far more, far more clear-sightedly, about love by looking closely at these others. For it is among these that Perkins' lancet prose always probes for its models and metaphors.

Perkins would go on to write many more erotic novels. The invention in them is constant. Their insights are many. All are shot through with sexual understanding and littered with brilliant passages. And in 1976 Perkins would turn his many reviews and articles about contemporary American erotic writing into that extraordinary survey and critique, *The Secret Record: Modern Erotic Literature,* reprinted by Rhinoc*eros* Books (1992). But there is a coherence and intensity to the first of them—*Evil Companions*—that makes its combination of observation and outrage (if the word existed, "inrage" would be the better term) a particularly powerful amalgam.

Evil Companions is a dark jewel on the erotic landscape that has continually drawn attention back on itself for twenty-five years now—and back to the astonishing and dangerous moments of its making. It is a book that again and again throws into question the boundary between fantasy and reality. ("[I]mitations," writes Perkins in chapter 8, about a pair of would-be bikers, "if they fantasize enough, can overtake their originals in vital aspects.") A quarter of a century after the book's initial publication (for the Rhinoc*eros* edition, the "very few emendations" have been put back), I don't doubt that this generation can still learn something from it—of the limits of pleasure, of fantasy, and the inextricable interweaving of both with human pain.

It may not be a pleasant lesson.

But it is a powerful one.

And throughout, that lesson is strangely, insistently, and vividly close to something we—now and again—must call the beautiful.

—*New York City*
August 1992

21

Now It's Time for Dale Peck

In a hundred-sixty-one chapters distributed among seventeen characters, fourteen of whom speak in first person, *Now It's Time to Say Good-bye* (Farrar, Straus and Giroux, New York, 1998), Dale Peck's third novel, describes a racially split Kansas town, by the end of which description, with lynchings and retributive murders, we have a picture of Galatea (the town's white side)/Galatia (the black side) and have encountered at least one affecting love story between an effeminate black twelve-year-old, Reggie Packman, and a slightly older redneck sociopath, Lemoine Weibe (aka Ratboy). The affair ends two years later when, hustling at the Big M truckstop, the now sixteen-year-old Ratboy is brutally beaten and eventually dies. *Some* symmetrical development occurs: Fleeing urban AIDS, writer Colin Nieman and the twenty-year-old New York hustler he brings with him to Galatea, Justin Time, and local artist Wade Painter with *his* local lover (Reggie P. a few years on, now aka Divine), change partners after the town has traumatized both boys. When white teenager Lucy Robinson is raped and kidnapped, the town tries halfheartedly to pin the crime on Colin. Mysteries, arsons, and murders proliferate; and after a catastrophic Founders' Day picnic, the main question (who raped Reggie and Lucy and beat Justin into psychotic aphasia) resolves. Once, however, minister Greevin's daughter, Webbie, suggests out of the blue someone we've thought dead for the novel's first three hundred fifty–odd pages is alive, for the concluding hundred it's not much of a mystery. Now and again, however, Peck informs passages with impressive narrative life. If it all sounds satisfying, you may well like the book.

I found it rough reading, however. Multiple viewpoints work in Faulkner's *As I Lay Dying* because Faulkner's fifteen narrators (at less than half the length!) aim their observations at one intense and human situation: Addie Bundren's protracted death. They don't work here because Peck's plot lolls over twenty years and as many major incidents

(Eddy Comedy's murder, Noah's Ark's burning, Eric Johnson's lynching, Divine's suicide attempt, Webbie's flight to Wichita . . . etc.) till the shifting viewpoints and narrative voices (from Reggie's jiving to Rosemary's Whartonesque periods to Justin's Fitzgerald-like detachment to Thelma's Faulknerian eruption; Peck is quite a stylistic ventriloquist) only disperse the focus. And because so many of our informants know *so* much, for all its mysteries Peck's novel is without suspense.

A greater problem is, however, that, with plot enough for six novels, Peck's hasn't much structure: In the MFA programs that produce more and more of them, our novelists never seem to learn that the order in which they think up the incidents for their tales is not privileged or even, necessarily, interesting. If handled well, our learning about a character's history *first* can sensitize us to his or her latterly presented injury or pain, if that later injury is rendered meaningfully in terms of the history already given. But (numbed by the notion of the commercial "hook"? It's only a sign of genre and accomplishes *nothing* more) too many writers believe a violence that befalls an otherwise unknown character will subsequently interest us in that character's past life, when, if anything, the opposite is true: In a novel, a violent occurrence to a character armors us *against* further emotional involvement, despite anything of their former life we learn about them later. In brief, if I'm telling you about Joe's adult doings, and I realize things would make more sense with some background on Joe's upbringing, the fact that I (the writer) only *noticed* it then is no reason to put it next in the book. It was already a narrative problem *when* I noticed. It should be addressed in the text *beforehand.*

Had we seen Myra's childhood relationship with Lucy *before* her daughter's abduction (instead of having those memories dragged in later, like the novelist's—not the character's—sentimental afterthoughts), Myra's subsequent breakdown would have *felt* to the reader as human as we all know it is. Had the fill-in narratives about Rosemary, Myra, and the Kenosha fire that produced Galatea's present-day tensions, along with the childhood tales of Eric and Lucy, all of which come in the final hundred pages, been given us instead in the *first* hundred, the ending would have arrived with far greater narrative velocity—and that opening hundred would have been *lots* more interesting. Though, for me, the Packman/Ratboy story was the book's emotional high point, it would have been even more affecting if the half-dozen-odd chapters devoted to it had arrived in chronological order (and in real time), rather than as a random set of disarranged flashbacks scattered throughout the text. Here, however, the mosaic form, rather than generating a clear and vivid pattern, only facilitates the author's telling us, when it occurs to him, what he should have told us fifty or a hundred-fifty or three hundred pages back. Succinctly: Peck is really a short story writer. His most successful epiphanies have always been short-story epiphanies, not novelistic ones. His talent is enough to make one start looking for historical comparisons: Katherine Mansfield, Flannery O'Connor . . . Easily he could leave the novel alone—and lose the cutesy names. When Henry James used them in his early novels ("Isabel Archer," "Casper Goodwood," "Henrietta Stackpole" . . .), it was a dying Victorian affectation. When William Gaddis parodied that affectation in *The Recognitions* (1955), with a literary agent named "Agnes Deigh" and an art critic named "Rectal Brown," it still conveyed a tint of wit by deploying a whiff of the outrageous. Peck's ("Rose Etta Stone," "Norman Never," "Justin Time" . . .) don't work, because the characters themselves feel obliged to *talk* about how clever and wacky their names are (which neither Gaddis nor James would have even considered), knocking us out of the realm of suggestion and nuance by the undergraduate elbow in the ribs, to look, look, *look!*—in case we'd somehow missed it.

Genres, like genders, are to be bent—not mixed. The reason you don't have to mix them is because, as Derrida pointed out, in "The Law of Genre" (*Parages*, 1986), they are never pure in the first place. In terms of practical aesthetics, this means: You'll do better with a mystery that is so well written and cleverly structured it aspires to the level of literature than you will with a literary novel that again and again sinks to the absurdities of your average whodunit. One or two such absurdities may even be forgiven the former. The same one or two—not to mention dozens—cripple the latter.

A skewly doofus humor sometimes surfaces among Peck's horrific happenings. A villainous redneck is eaten alive by pigs. Caught on the top of a forklift in a fire, a seven-hundred-pound mailman falls—twelve feet—to his death. Once Colin burns the retrieved manuscript of his previously stolen novel, Xerox after Xerox turns up and is subsequently presented to him, each copy read by more townspeople, each copy to be burned anew. Peck drags most of these comic/poetic turns in, however, by the seat of the pants. They just don't relate to each other or do anything for the novel as a whole. Climaxes I felt should have been intensely dramatic (Justin's retreat from language; Colin and Johnson's encounter over the still living Lucy) are given in archly fay dialogue. The coy references to Peck's earlier work were better omitted. Characters always arrive at the scene morally paralyzed, so that, unable to respond, repeatedly they fall victim to any ensuing violence. And while larger social motives abound, personal ones remain hazy.

Peck's gay characters include (in Ratboy's words) only "faggots and faggot lovers," which finally seems a distressing parody of the *most* tragically dimorphic heterosexuality—though, I must say here with undiluted praise, the extraordinary meditations from Justin and Divine on getting fucked are, both of them, *each* worth the price of admission. "People don't want to know the truth," says Sheriff Eustace Brown in the book's penultimate chapter. "They just want a explanation" (*sic*). Well, here are explanations a-plenty. Still, *I* said good-bye hungry for some richer ones with greater believability, stronger veracity, and placed more dramatically: Why (just one possible example) would mailman Daniels *want* to read out Divine's letters to Ratboy over the megaphone at the town's annual Founders' Day picnic if he hadn't read them already? And if he had, why didn't he just destroy them—since *he's* among the men the letters incriminate? Some vivid set-pieces aside, for me, finally, things didn't cohere in any satisfying novelistic shape—unless that was the point and, gazing at Peck's ironies with too long a face, I just missed it.

— *New York City*
April 1998

22

Othello in Brooklyn

> . . . let us admit that while Shakespeare was an Elizabe-
> than playwright he was—and now is to us—predomi-
> nantly something much more. Therefore we had better
> not too unquestioningly thrust him back within the con-
> fines his genius has escaped, nor presume him to have
> felt the pettier confines of his theater sacrosanct. Nor
> can we turn Elizabethans as we watch the plays; and every
> mental effort to do so will subtract from our enjoyment
> of them.
>
> —Harley Granville-Barker, *Prefaces to Shakespeare*

Certainly the ultimate compliment to this small but energetic and inventive production of *Othello*, which played through February at the Triangle Theater at Brooklyn's Long Island University, was paid it by my volu-
ble thirteen-year-old. Having come with me to see the play once, when I
was making ready to go for a second evening two days later, she came
running up to me in our apartment hall and demanded, "You mean I
can't go see it *again?*"

Well, she *did* see it again.

And she enjoyed it very much.

I'm sure, if we wanted, we could end this review right here and not
feel we had slighted the play in the least.

But critics *will* go on.

Othello is a particularly straightforward play in Shakespeare's canon.
While here and there it has its comic relief, such as the carryings-on of
Brabantio before the duke, or the jesting of Iago, Desdemona, and
Emilia as they wait at the dock for Othello to arrive in Cyprus, by and
large Othello's tragic deception, which turns him from lover and general
to murderer and suicide, moves at a dramatically breakneck clip. Donald
Lee Taylor's Moor is emotionally clear and hugely committed. The play

can easily turn into a monologue by Iago, interrupted by mere blurts from the other characters. It falls to the actor playing Othello to provide the difficult and complex weight that opens up the play and gives it balance. Mr. Taylor accomplishes this by means of some real actorly strengths: He can be truly charming on stage; he can be believably pained. And he is a very handsome man. But he also has a heavy West Indian accent that made many lines incomprehensible to an American audience. If he wants to continue to do ambitious theater in the U.S., this is something he'll have to work on while acting here. His general stage skills and clear, strong talent suggest that this is a problem that will take only a little time and study to overcome. It would certainly be worth his while to invest them both.

Richard Dent is one of the more technically accomplished actors in the cast. He plays Iago as a dauntingly nasty—and occasionally a really creepy—man. As my thirteen-year-old put it during the intermission, with a small shudder: "He isn't very nice at *all*!"

Yet, because he *is* so good, that may be the reason I find myself wanting even more from him. I would have felt more comfortable if I'd had a greater sense of psychological "core" to the character—or, lacking that, if the absence of core itself had been the character's center.

What does that mean? I'll return to it in a moment.

In this production, Cassio is played with great sympathy, goodwill, and likability by John Duke. Blond, open-faced and openhearted, Duke also is the one in the cast (next to Alison Holt's winning and moving Desdemona) most capable of making his lines sound speakable in contemporary accents. Indeed, the only thing I can chide him for is adding the odd line. I don't believe, "Iago did it!"—which Mr. Duke cried out in the final scene on *both* evenings that I saw the play—is either by Shakespeare *or* necessary! Other than that, he was a joy.

I pose the following to throw light on what may (or may not) be a psychological problem that (only slightly!) mars this production—and that may also clarify what I mean by "core" when speaking of Mr. Dent's Iago.

I never saw the following production. But it was once described to me in great detail by an older actor friend, who, himself, played Cassio in the Paul Robeson/Uta Hagen/José Ferrer *Othello* that electrified New York back in the late 1940s. In this particular production (*not* the Robeson production that my friend took part in), instead of the usual open-faced innocent he is traditionally portrayed as, Cassio was played by a black-haired, weaselly young man, who acted him as a lecherous juvenile delinquent, always in trouble somewhere, who surprised us whenever he was *not* at the root of any problem that came up. In the same production,

Iago was portrayed as the blond, open and aboveboard character—steady, loyal, friendly, efficient, everyone's friend and confidant, the man all people trusted, the man no one would ever think was lying—but who just happened to cherish a tiny "core" (there's that word again) of unexplained, psychotic hatred for his boss. At the same time, while Desdemona was as innocent in fact as she is in traditional portrayals, nevertheless she was played as a hopeless flirt, a giggler and a tease, not only with Othello but with every guard, passing soldier, and visiting diplomat, so that the Moor had good reason to believe in his wife's infidelity, if only from her character—if not from the facts.

"And what did you think of this approach?" I asked my friend.

"Well," he said, "it was certainly a far more believable production than you usually get. It was more believable than we were, back on the stage of the Metropolitan. Iago, whose evil only came out in little psychotic explosions in an otherwise unruffled show of loyalty and goodwill, was particularly chilling. The problem with it, however, was what it did to Othello as a character. Much of what Othello comes to believe is already pretty unbelievable. But when everything is adjusted in the performance to give those beliefs a *reasonable* cause—what T. S. Eliot called an 'objective correlative'—Othello lost all his nobility and grandeur. He seemed, on that stage, like a *complete* dupe of circumstances—rather than one who had 'loved, not wisely, but too well.' Finally, it just didn't seem very interesting—and not at all noble or tragic."

In this anecdote we have, if not a definition of "psychological core," at least a description of what having one accomplishes: believability. And we also have an indication in it of such a "core's" dangers. As it makes the characters more real, it makes them—especially the tragic heroes—less tragic, more pathetic.

Believability and nobility. These are certainly the theatrical poles that pull us this way and that in any contemporary Shakespearean production. Actorly and directorial inventions succeed or fail as they support now this one, now that. Part of the problem is, as Francis Barker has argued so convincingly in *The Tremulous Private Body* (New York: Methuen, 1984), that Shakespeare's world was one "of relentless surfaces, without depth or mystery"—which is to say the whole notion of subjectivity, mental life, and psychological interiority, which is the space in which that "core" must be positioned by the actor (and which space today's actor is so busy making visible on the stage, screen, and tube), simply hadn't been formed to its present state when Shakespeare wrote—before the novel, before Freud. By lack of depth and mystery, Barker only means that characters in Shakespeare never ask each other, "How are you feeling?" "Are you all right?" "Do you *really* love me?" That is to say, in

Shakespeare and his fellow dramatists, feelings are there; they are displayed; they are hidden; or they are—sometimes—lied about. But there is no essential mystery to a shimmering, slippery, uncertain concept of feelings themselves, a mystery there to be endlessly interrogated, as we have had since the nineteenth century and Romanticism, a mystery that has produced, among attempts to solve it, both psychoanalysis and most of modern narrative.

This core, then, would manifest itself in an actor's performance as one, two, or a few carefully considered and repeated signs of personality in a field of largely open interpretive play—those fixed points having been left up to actor and director between them to choose.

This "core" I am asking for in Iago is, Mr. Dent could easily argue, (first) just not there in the text and (second) inconceivable before the nineteenth century—the century that gave us Ibsen, Chekhov, and Freud, as well as Marxism, a score of Republican revolutions right after the War of 1812 through the Dresden Uprising and the Paris Commune, not to mention concepts of social reform and a personal relation of individual distrust of the social, of language, and of appearances that *are* the modern concept of subjectivity, the modern measures of "person-ality."

Well, what is the actor—or the director—to do? Do we try to *be* Elizabethans? Do we play the larger than life "characters" that Shakespeare wrote—which are, finally, for all their poetry, not very lifelike? Or do we add a specific "personality" (a missing "core," whether it leans in traditional or anti-traditional directions), a personality always smaller than the elevation, poetry, and grandeur of the text?

It's arguable that putting the question thus, however real a question it is, just doesn't help the contemporary dramaturge who has to create performances meaningful to modern actors and audiences. It obscures the fact that we miss the core, not because it belongs there, or is more "realistic," or completes something Shakespeare left unfinished, but because it is simply one of the things that lets us recognize what's before us *as* theater. Well, then, let's take another—and perhaps more theatrical—tack.

The nitty-gritty problems with contemporary productions of Shakespeare are of two sorts. The first is simply the difficulty of making the language—which is the English (and the highly conventionalized poetic English) of four hundred years ago—make sense to a contemporary audience. At almost all points the cast and the director in *this* production triumphed over this greatest hurdle. There were only two places where they failed. One was in the aforementioned comedy scene on the Cyprus dock. And all one can say there is that it is almost impossible to make such old jokes understandable, much less make them sparkle, without distorting things with so much business that one is really only disguising them. The other place where there seemed to be some problem was with Iago's famous "Put money in thy purse" speech to young, eager Roderigo. In this production, Roderigo (a whiny, white-haired, and pusillanimous Michael Skinner: Bravo!) has a transparent plastic pouch filled with blue marbles. Each time Iago tells him, "Put money in thy purse" (as he does some half dozen times during the scene), Roderigo takes out a marble or two and hands it to Iago, who pockets them.

It's visually interesting.

It certainly underlines the fact that Roderigo is paying off Iago to plead his cause with Desdemona. But in terms of what Iago is actually *saying* at the moment ("Put money in *thy* purse"—not *my* purse), it's baffling! And, I suspect, because of it, it's a dramatic miscalculation—or, as my otherwise enthusiastic daughter demanded of me after the show: "Why were they doing *that*, Daddy?"

But despite these difficulties, the production was full of truly illuminating invention. The Venetians wore white and transparent plastic, while the Cypriots came in colorful gym pants and print capes. When Iago prompted Roderigo to call up to Desdemona's father's window (father Brabantio was played with wonderful splutterings and ditherings by Tony Kish), Iago got behind him and maneuvered a surprised Roderigo like a giant hand puppet! Bianca was played broadly and adroitly by Janet Geist as an actual—rather than a metaphorical—whore, which gave Cassio, who is indifferently in love with her, a complexity missing in most productions. Clown (a teenage juggler, Greame Sibirsky), Montano (Larry Walton), Lodovico (John Saxton), and the Duke (Joseph [Hussain] Syracuse) were played by actors who clearly ranged from excellent and experienced to new and enthusiastic. But each performed with conviction up to the level of his own obvious skill limits. (In the case of Syracuse's Duke, that's a skill with almost no limits to it at all!) In such a production, no one can ask for more.

The second problem I spoke of is simply the one posed by contemporary acting styles (or, perhaps more accurately, the contemporary audience's expectation of acting styles) brought about by the intimate "realism" of movies and TV. While Shakespeare's plays are full of psychological insights about the human condition, these insights are largely offered as epigrams. Neither the plots nor the characters are particularly realistic or believable. And the *moral* center of his plays—in *Macbeth*, Lady Macbeth, in *Hamlet*, Fortinbras, and in *Othello*, Emilia—is seldom the *dramatic* center. The coincidence of dramatic center and moral center is, of course, what we've come to expect of the well-crafted play after Ibsen. But because contemporary audiences find main characters thin when moral and dramatic problems do not dovetail in one person, we will always, in theaters today, sense a slight emptiness loose amidst all Shakespeare's rhetorical lushness and social range. This may be another reason why actors are so eager to fill up—or fill out—the character with a sense of modern psychological depth and space.

It may be another reason why audiences require them.

I have said Emilia is the moral center of *Othello*. Her unthinkingness in picking up the handkerchief and giving it to her husband brings on the tragedy; and her bravery alone is what reveals the final, ugly truth—and for her bravery, she is stabbed to death most cruelly by Iago. Barbara Wise played her with a wonderful alternation between naïveté and courage; she found just the right emotional directions in which to pitch her aging, somewhat flirtatious, but generally great-hearted Emilia, in order to make that moral centrality sound its proper, tragic note. If this *were* a play by Ibsen instead of by Shakespeare, it would have been called *Emilia*.

If Emilia is the play's moral center, Desdemona is the play's spiritual center. In a world as distrustful of the spiritual as ours is, that's a very difficult position for any actress to command—which is to say, sweet, innocent, sympathetic heroines who die in the end are awfully hard to make come off as anything more than mawkish. Ms. Holt used her considerable sensitivity, in directions very different from her (equally fine) portrayal of Lucasta in last year's *Confidential Clerk*, to hold the play to shape, so that the good can appeal to her with expectations of true sympathy at the same time as the evil baffles her and finally destroys her. She had dignity. She had charm. And her love for Othello was convincing. It was a pleasure to watch her perform.

But a consideration of the spiritual brings us to that problematic area again.

Shakespeare's plays are poetry; they are artificial; they are declamatory; their notions of spirituality and nobility are largely foreign to us; and the style they use to convey those notions is elevated, extreme, gorgeous, and unusual. For all their psychological sensitivity, we must always remember neither their audience nor their author ever saw a psychological state portrayed—well *or* badly—by a movie close-up, or even by a news photograph of a mother weeping beside an apartment building fire, or in a black-and-white half-screen of the numb face of a bystander beside an industrial accident. With the exception of perhaps the upper-income ten percent, most of the audience had never even seen a painted portrait of another person: The Elizabethan age leaves us neither cartoons nor caricatures among its art works. (There were neither museums not art galleries in London at the time.) This means we are dealing with plays from an age when the simple representation of other persons, other places, other times and situations were, in themselves, new and exciting. But there were no audience demands on the richly costumed spectacles for either accuracy or nuance—at least as far as the visual went. Thus, situations perfectly acceptable to an Elizabethan audience simply "look wrong" to us again and again. So many of the assumptions Othello makes, for example, are so hopelessly over-hasty by modern standards that it's surprising just how much of the Elizabethan analysis of the machinery of jealousy *does* ring true.

In an age when pictorial reproductions of one sort or another confront us during most of our public and private lives, postmodern acting is visual, down to the contortions of the facial muscles that create the unrealistic and overwrought speech patterns we have learned to hear today as "realistic" line readings: *visually* real speech—before everything else. What our actors try to convey today by the actorly craft of "showing the emotions" was all left up to the words by Shakespeare and his contemporaries—which may be why the Elizabethan period *was* a period of great poetry . . . and was also such an impoverished period for those arts exhausted almost wholly by outline and ornament. It's doubtful any actor in an original production of Shakespeare (except the clowns) ever crouched, jumped, cringed, or staggered. What the actors most probably did was stand and declaim their lines *very* slowly, in something resembling the heaviest of today's Scottish brogues, which is what linguists have more or less decided a middle-class London accent resembled during the sixteenth and seventeenth centuries. The swordfights were fought by (and watched by) people who had never stayed up late to see an Errol Flynn re-run—or gone off to a Kung Fu movie on Saturday morning. And the deaths were died by actors who did not feel, deep inside, that they had to do *something* to keep the audience from recalling the self-parodying excesses of nineteenth-century grand opera death scenes.

This is not a reason in itself that our postmodern actor shouldn't leap about the set so entertainingly. It might, however, be a reason to find a postmodern "core" that lends itself to a more staid—and less athletic—visual presentation of actorly rightness and theatrical truth.

If we did not mention Mary Alice Miller's glorious costuming of this production, we would be doing it a disservice. Shakespeare's plays were performed, at the Globe and the Blackfriars theaters, with elaborate costumes—and almost no scenery. This is, basically, how Ms. Belgrave has mounted her contemporary production. Wisely, there is nothing specifically Shakespearean *about* Ms. Miller's costumes. But they establish the necessary tension between a parade of brilliantly outlined and ornamented subjects and a shadowy background existing, finally, almost all in the mind's eye—a tension that *was* the visual reality to a Shakespearean spectacle at the time these plays were first written and produced. I confess, I was phoned up a couple of times to make suggestions. And for it, I received generous billing as a "consultant." But Ms. Miller's costume realizations are all *far* beyond anything *I'd* conceived of. Highest praises to you, Ms. M.!

In his famous *Prefaces to Shakespeare*, which he began writing in the '20s (Princeton: Princeton University Press, 1946), Harley Granville-Barker started to wrestle with the problems of producing theatrically vital Shakespeare on the post-Edwardian stage. Granville-Barker was a scholar *and* a man of the theater—actor, playwright, producer, director—at a time when English literature had only been taught at Oxford and Cambridge for less than ten years, and when the actorly problems we've noted above had not been brought to their present pitch by movies and TV. But the precept I've taken from him to head this piece seems to me still very much to the point. Granville-Barker's larger point was that, while we should not try to imitate Elizabethan productions, we should know something about the Elizabethan world and how it—and its theater—worked, so that we can use contemporary theatrical practices to achieve a somewhat historically sensitive, if not a photographically similar, set of theatrical effects. It seems to me this is an idea Ms. Belgrave has followed very much in spirit.

Without eschewing the contemporary demands for a nuanced psychology, she has allowed her directorial invention to shoot off in wonderfully Brechtian and Artaudian directions. She's not afraid of the big gesture on the small stage, when it makes things clear. She brings the audience in close, when her actors have found something at once intimate, meaningful, and appropriate to display. But when distancing effects are called for, she sets them out on the boards with energy and authority.

This is wonderful theater. I can attest that this production has delighted an audience from thirteen to eighty-three, inclusive. But wonderful theater is what Shakespeare (and director Cynthia Belgrave!) has always been about.

—New York City
November 1987

23

A Prefatory Notice to Vincent Czyz's
Adrift in a Vanishing City

Like *every* one of the last three dozen MFA theses I've read, *Adrift in a Vanishing City* (Rutherford: Voyant Publishing, 1998) is neither a novel nor, really, a collection of stand-alone stories. Familiar characters— Zirque (rhymes with Jerk), Blue Jean, the Duke of Pallucca—disappear or are abandoned, reappear or are revisited tale to tale. But equally clearly these are not novel chapters. Our young writers seem unhappy with the strictures of both genres and are struggling to slough them.

If you are a reader convinced of the irrevocable sociality of fiction, I warn you: By and large, the text won't linger on how characters manage to *pay* for their various flights from Pittsburg, Kansas, to Paris, France, from Kansas to Amsterdam, how most of them make their living, or even scrounge up change for the next pint of booze, not to mention make the rent an apartment in Budapest—another trait writer Vincent Czyz shares with many of his contemporaries. In their conviction that the world's socioeconomic specificities are every self's necessarily distinctive background, neither Austen nor Flaubert, Knut Hamsun nor James Joyce, Virginia Woolf nor Henry Miller could have let such an omission by in their successive attempts to delve more and more deeply into some more and more highly foregrounded presentation of the subject. But the clash of micro-class and micro-class, macro-class and macro-class, that makes fiction *interesting*, or even *useful*, to the average Joe or Sue (not to mention to the commercial editors riding shotgun on the stopcock of the smoky trickle of confused tales—overplotted, understructured, and as incoherent and mixed in metaphor as the images within these parentheses, outside these dashes—throughout our Barnes & Nobles, onto our Big Name bookstores' shelves) are simply not in focus on Czyz's screen. They are bracketed along with all notion of labor.

If you feel art is an enterprise in which, when you have found an artist doing what every other artist is doing, you have necessarily found an artist doing something wrong (yet *another* story or poem voicing its appeal to aesthetic distance in that artificial and so-easy sign of the literary, the present tense: *Yawn*...), some of the elements—or absences—I've highlighted here, in a book such as this, might give you pause.

What's extraordinary here, however, what recommends and finally makes such work more than commendable, what renders it a small landmark in the sedimentation of new form in fiction, is a quality of language, a surface that signals that the structure of anything and everything that surface evokes beyond it is simply other than what we have grown used to. Finally such a surface signs to the astute that the reductions our first three paragraphs suggest are, in this case, wildly off the mark. (Czyz is *not* an MFA product.) Such language as we find here projects an aesthetic conciousness, rather, it might be more profitable to read as interested in other things, and not as one merely slovenly, unthinking, or ignorant of the tradition.

Nothing is careless about this writing at all.

Poetry is about the self, as it is defined in the response to love, death, the changing of the seasons... However indirectly, however mutedly, traditional fiction has always been about money. I could speak easily, and easily speak honestly about how much I admire Czyz's considerable talent, his fictive range, his willingness to plunge naked into the gutter, to leap after stellar contrails, his grasp of how ravenously one body grasps another, or of how his impossible apostrophes out of the night are the necessary utterances that make life possible, confronted with the silences of the day. But this is still a more or less rarefied, a more or less dramatic bit of lit. crit. It only becomes a recognizable "story" when I write that Vincent Czyz is a longhaired, newly married taxi driver living in New Jersey, who wants to publish his first book and, as such, has sought my help—a gay, gray, pudgy professor with income tax problems, who commutes to work in Massachusetts by Peter Pan (cheaper than Amtrak), and who has published thirty books over as many years with various presses, commercial and university.... But Czyz's are *not* traditional stories. Indeed, they are part of a counterfictive tradition that attempts to appropriate precisely the substance of poetry for prose: Novalis's *Heinrich von Ofterdingen* (1802), Rilke's *Die Aufzeichnungen des Malte Laurids Brigge* (1910), Toomer's *Cane* (1923), Keene's *Annotations* (1995).... Average Joes and Sues are just not Czyz's concern. He's fixed his finger, rather, on yearningly romantic figures who combine rough American—or foreigntinted—dialect with pristine insight; men and women who, clawing at the evanescent tapestry of perception as it unravels madly from the loom of day, are as concerned with myth and cosmology as they are with moment and the night, and who now and again have more consonants in their names than vowels, many of those names not commencing till the terminal handful of letters flung from the alphabet. . . . Though they fixate on indirectly answering just such questions as Czyz here sets aside, not Proust, not Musil, not Ford of *Parades End* or *The Fifth Queen* is "easy reading" either; and finally for much the same surface reasons. Though the sexuality is more or less normal, the poetic method is closer to Genet's— another writer whose novels tends to ignore those grounding questions, unless the characters are pimps (i.e., living off prostitutes of one sex or another) or in jail (i.e., living off the state).

As an appendix to his 1934 collection of essays, *Men Without Art*, Wyndham Lewis proposed "The Taxi-cab Driver Test" for good fiction. Suggested Lewis: Open the text to any random page and give it to any average cab driver. (Fascist Lewis assumed the driver's first language would, of course, be English; Czyz speaks several—besides working as a cab driver, he's also been an English teacher. He has lived in Poland, Turkey, Lyndhurst . . .) Tell him to read it. Then ask: "Is there *anything* here that seems strange or unusual or out of the ordinary for a work of fiction?" If he answers, "Yes," then you *may* have some extraordinary fiction. If he answers, "No," then you don't. Lewis went on to apply his test to, respectively, a Henry James short story and a banal society novel by Aldous Huxley (*Point Counter Point*, which was thought much of back then because it was a *roman à clef* about the Lawrences and the Murrys—I remember reading it when I was around seventeen. I said, "Huh . . . ?"). James certainly wins; Huxley doesn't. (Today, does anyone read *anything* else he's written other than *Brave New World*, possibly *Island*?) I don't think the Taxi-cab Driver Test is 100 percent reliable. Still, it's a good one to keep in mind; and it's a salutary corrective to today's mania for "transparent prose," even (or especially) among our most radical experimenters. I mention it, because Czyz's work (as does Melville's, Joyce's, Hemingway's, Woolf's, Faulkner's, Patrick White's, William Gass's . . .) passes the Driver Test admirably. The work of the *vast* majority of Czyz's contemporaries does not.

That is to say: Czyz is telling stories many of his contemporaries are trying to tell—and telling them *much* better!

If you are a reader who can revel in language—in the intricate and intensely interesting "how" language imposes on its "what"—then, however skew his interests are across the fictive field (and how refreshing that skewness!), Czyz is a writer rich in pleasures; it's a pleasure to recommend him.

— New York City
May 1998

24

Under the Volcano with Susan Sontag

"I looked out the window. Two of the engines were on fire on one wing. Then the pilot announced, 'We're going to make a crash landing.' He was going to dump the fuel. . . . You felt this animal terror. People were screaming; some people were in the aisles praying; two tried to assault the captain's cabin—get into where the pilot, co-pilot, and the navigator were. As to what they thought they were going to do—take over the plane . . . ? I was in my twenties then, feeling really terrible, because it's so humiliating thinking, 'This is not the way I want to die'—not that any way is nice. It was December. There was a terrible storm and no heat— imagine how cold it was! They had four usable toilets and they were all *unu*sable. And you can't master your terror—all these people are scream- ing. I was sitting next to this guy my own age, and he was screaming: 'Well, when you gotta go, you gotta go! Well, when your number's up, your number's up!' And I thought: 'I cannot believe this crap!' He even called out to one of the flight attendants—who was white as a sheet and trying to help somebody who'd fainted: 'If we all die, do we get our tick- ets refunded?'

"It was Pandemonium.

"It's not that I think it's so horrible what he did to master his fear. But I just didn't want to hear it while I'm doing my best to . . . "

When she paused, I offered: "—maintain what dignity you could?"

"Yes." Sontag went on: "We were over Nebraska, and we ended up in a cornfield. It turned out okay. Nobody was killed."

What changes, I wondered, do such catastrophic experiences pro- duce deep in the soul? Some people report profound changes. Others simply accept them as part of the progression of life. What they *do* do, however, is give a certain authority to what those who've lived through them have to say about the catastrophic: "But there was that fifteen min- utes of the plane on fire and going like this and all that." Her hand swooped and banked above her kitchen table. "And let me tell you, it's really . . ."

"Scary?"

"It's more than scary—it's humiliating."

In Susan Sontag's new novel, *The Volcano Lover, A Romance* (Farrar Straus Giroux), midway through the story, the major characters—the Cavaliere, his wife, and her lover the hero—must help evacuate the King and Queen from Naples to Palermo. The boat is caught in a storm, which yields up one of the novel's myriad fine set pieces—this one a masterly bit of high adventure. "Do not be afraid, my lord," the hallucination of a fortune teller tells the Cavaliere, while he is trapped in his swaying cabin, as the wind and water howl outside. "I'm not afraid," thinks the Cavaliere. "I'm humiliated." Like the whole scene—indeed, like the entire novel—it rings with a certain authority.

Susan Sontag is the author of two other novels, *The Benefactor* (1963), and *Death Kit* (1967), as well as an extraordinarily fine collection of experimental fictions. *I, etcetera* (1979); and her 1987 story about AIDS, "The Way We Live Now," is a moving exploration and dramatization of AIDS anxiety that circles about, but will not state, the dreaded name itself. She's written and directed four films: *Duet for Cannibals, Brother Carl, Unguided Tour,* and *Promised Land.* She directed as well Milan Kundera's dramatic adaptation of Diderot's *Jacques the Fatalist.* And two years ago she received a MacArthur Foundation "Genius Award." But Sontag is generally known as an essayist. Her "Notes on Camp" (1964) was single-handedly responsible for moving the word from the marginal realms of gay slang into the esthetic vocabulary of the nation. And she is the best known of a number of critics who, between them, made respectable the idea of dealing seriously and critically with works outside the accepted canon of Great Art—in her case, works by avant-garde filmmakers, such as Jack Smith in the '60s and Hans-Jürgen Syberberg in the '70s. But rock critics, such as Richard Goldstein and Greil Marcus, who have turned real esthetic insight on pop music, started by taking advantage of the climate of broad esthetic acceptance whose creation Sontag is most generally associated with.

As she wrote of the critic's job in an essay on her friend, the late French critic Roland Barthes ("Writing Itself: On Roland Barthes") a decade ago:

> Though work of every form and worth qualifies for citizenship in the great democracy of "texts," the critic will tend to avoid the texts that everyone else has handled, meaning that everyone knows. The formalist turn in modern criticism—from its pristine phase, as in Shklovsky's idea of defamiliarizing,

outward—dictates just this. It charges the critic with the task of discarding worn-out meanings for fresh ones. It is a mandate to scout for new meanings. *Etonne-moi!*

Viktor Shklovsky was a Russian formalist critic from the '20s who believed one purpose of art was to make the familiar seem strange, weird, and interesting. With that last French phrase, she's quoting Shklovsky's only slightly younger contemporary, the French poet, novelist, and filmmaker, Jean Cocteau: *Astonish me!* But the establishment of "the great democracy of 'texts'" that's been the general critical strategy for helping to bring about that astonishment since the 1960s can be generally laid at Sontag's doorstep as much as it can be laid anywhere.

On a bright, breezy day in late June, in the kitchen of Sontag's West Side penthouse apartment, while her assistant worked at the word processor in the other room, Sontag told me of the origins of *The Volcano Lover.*

"It started with those images." She pointed to the reproductions of eighteenth-century paintings on the front and back cover of the book: a daylight scene and a night scene, across the Bay of Naples, with the erupting cone of Vesuvius. "About twelve years ago, I was browsing hungrily in a print store near the British Museum, on a brief trip to London—I always like to hang out in that neighborhood with all those bookstores and printshops.

"And I saw these images—that I couldn't identify.

"There were a whole bunch of them—some two dozen for sale. Some were of this volcano exploding. Others were just weird rocks—burning landscapes. But clearly they were all by the same person. There were about twenty-four of them.

"I had already begun collecting architectural prints from the eighteenth century (I had fallen in love with Piranesi), so I knew that every time you see an eighteenth century print, you're not seeing a print made to be sold separately. You're seeing a plate from a book which has been ripped apart by a bookseller. He might buy this old, eighteenth century folio volume for five thousand dollars, but it has thirty plates in it, that he sells for three hundred dollars a piece; and he makes a huge profit! But they're just pages torn from a book.

"I asked what the book was. It turned out to be by Sir William Hamilton—about volcanoes. And who was Sir William Hamilton? I couldn't remember. So they brought out *The Dictionary of National Biography,* that they had in the back of the shop. They showed me the entry on Hamilton, and I thought, '*Ohhh,* that Hamilton man!' because I'd seen the famous movie with Laurence Olivier and Vivian Leigh when I was a child, *That Hamilton Woman.*

"That's the husband."

Most of us, if we know anything about him—Sir William Hamilton—we know him because of his second wife, the notorious Emma, Lady Hamilton, and her fabulous—the only word for it—love affair with Admiral Horatio Nelson, that ignited the European imagination and fascinated writers up till (Robert Southey was the first writer to try Emma's biography), well, up till Susan Sontag.

"Then I found out that Hamilton wasn't just a famous cuckold. He was a famous collector and connoisseur of art—and *almost* the first person to write about volcanoes. There had never been a book just about volcanoes before—any kind of scientific book, anyway. Of course there's all sorts of myths and things. But I just fell in love with the images.

"I've had these prints on the wall for almost ten years. But the actual origin [of the novel] is looking at that." Again, she indicated the pictures reproduced on the book cover.

"And because I'm a writer, I thought: I should do something with this. Should I write about somebody interested in volcanoes? First I fooled around with an idea for a story. Then I thought. What the hell—why not write about *him?*"

Hamilton died (in the arms of both Emma and Horatio) on April 6, 1803, in London. Nelson was finally killed at the Battle of Trafalgar, on the October 21, 1805. Always a vain man, he insisted on wearing all his ribbons and medals as he strode up and down the deck of the *Victory*—and so was an easy mark for Napoleon's sharpshooters. After a year in debtors' prison, Emma died in January of 1815, in a seedy hotel in Calais, with her fourteen-year-old daughter by Nelson in attendance. (Emma had two daughters by Nelson; but one, who died in infancy, Sontag elides from her tale.)

Daughter of an English blacksmith, Emma was born Amy Lyon, sometime around 1761. During her teens she may well have been a streetwalker in London's Vauxhall Gardens: She would be accused of that and much worse. A pretty, intelligent, and vivacious young woman, she eventually became a favorite model for English painter George Romney and came under the protection of young Charles Francis Greville, who, in 1786, four years after the death of his Uncle William's first wife, Catherine, sent the pretty, twenty-one-year-old Emma—and her mother—to Hamilton in Naples, where he was British envoy.

Charles sent her quite explicitly to be his uncle's mistress—in exchange for some debts of his the older man had recently paid.

Sir William was already an intimate of the King of Naples, Ferdinand II. Very soon, Emma was a favorite of Ferdinand's queen, the sister of Marie Antoinette, Queen Maria Carolina ("one of Maria Theresa's hellish brood," writes Sontag). But what was shocking was when, in 1791, Hamilton actually *married* Emma: She was now a twenty-six-year-old "fallen woman" of no family or connections, who, though she'd finally achieved reasonable mastery of Italian and French, still spoke English with traces of an East End accent; and he was an English aristocrat and ambassador of sixty-one.

Though they returned to England for the ceremony, it was a very small one. As soon as it was over, they went back to Italy.

It could have only happened to an affair that had blossomed in a foreign land.

It could only have happened in the eighteenth century.

The Hamiltons first met Nelson in 1793. Five years later, after his triumph against Napoleon at the Battle of the Nile (August 1st, 1798), Nelson (who had now lost his right arm and most of the vision in his right eye) was—after Napoleon—the most famous man in Europe, and, amidst the generally rising tide of republicanism that, by the 1850s would become a maelstrom, was the hero of the conservative side. There were Nelson medals, Nelson mugs, Nelson plates, Nelson scarves. And for Nelson's fortieth birthday, Emma—and Sir William—threw him a party (in Naples) for 1,800 guests, complete with food, bands, and fireworks. Somewhere just before or after the fête, the love affair between Nelson and Emma began. In general, it seems to have been carried out with all the privacy and reticence of the marriage of John and Yoko or the breakup of Sonny and Cher.

Sontag: "My original idea was just the opposite of the usual version. I was going to write a novel about a collector. And it was going to be the other view—the reverse-angle view. Everybody else thinks of Hamilton as the husband of Emma, who fell in love with Nelson—the great romance of popular imagination. But in my story that would just be a very tiny thing. Emma and Nelson would be off there in a corner. I'd mention them because everybody knows that story. But I would focus in on the psychology of the collector."

But that's not the way the book turned out:

"Well, I have to tell you, I did fall in love with Emma as the book progressed. Once she came into the story, she took over in a way I never expected."

Though *The Volcano Lover* is Hamilton's story, it gives a pretty complete portrait of the Emma/Nelson affair, as well as Hamilton's life in Naples, from his relations with his first wife, Catherine, his obsession with art and volcanoes, the politics of the day, to his final disillusionment—and even more impressive, his ways of dealing with that disillusioning—when his second wife, a young woman who loves him and whom he loves, finally—

he is forced to see—has found something in the arms (arm?) of another man that there simply is no way he, thirty-one years older than Nelson and thirty-six years older than Emma, can provide.

In that extraordinary essay on Barthes, already mentioned, Sontag locates the two contemporary strategies that control a good deal of what goes on under the current rubric "Literature":

> One is to abolish some or all of the conventional demarcations or separations of discourse, such as chapters, paragraphing, even punctuation, whatever is regarded as impeding formally the continuous production of (the writer's) voice. The other strategy is the opposite one: to multiply the ways in which discourse is segmented, to invent further ways of breaking it up. . . . To write in fragments or sequences or "notes" entails new, serial (rather than linear) forms of arrangements. For example, they may be numbered—a method practiced with great refinement by Wittgenstein.

Sontag's novel manages to encompass both strategies. Reading it, we soon become aware that the prologue, part 1 (with its seven chapters) and part 2 (with *its* seven), do not give us the real partitioning of the book. The prologue is really three sections: in the first, Sontag ("In my jeans and silk blouse and tennis shoes: Manhattan, spring of 1992."), merely to check out "what's in the world," walks into a flea market to be seduced, not by collecting but by the "pure possibilities" collecting has to offer; in the second, the Cavaliere—Sir William—laments to his nephew Charles that he has been unable to sell a much-loved painting hard financial times had forced him to put up for auction; and three gives an account of the last, 1944 eruption of Vesuvius. But all the other macro-divisions of the novel quickly come apart into smaller sections, an array of set pieces, none less than interesting, many of them brilliant.

Now we get a dinner party at which the Hamiltons entertain the poet Goethe, that turns into a disquisition on the arrival of the stone guest in Mozart's *Don Giovanni*, here with a nod toward *The Terminator*, now with a dialogue line cribbed from *Thelma and Louise*. There's the plot of Verdi's *Tosca*, as a gracenote to the Queen's counter-revolutionary activity. Now Nelson and Emma make love in a truly voluptuous piece of writing. Now the trio visits the bizarre palace of the Prince of Palagonia. Here's a fascinating account of the fate of the lost manuscript of Piranesi's autobiography. And there, in passing, is the tale of the student in the British Museum who smashed the Portland Vase. Now we stand with Marie Antoinette herself on the guillotine platform; now we are with Emma, lasciviously dancing the tarantella before her guests in an English drawing room . . .

In a bow to strategy two, it's easy to reformat the novel for oneself into numerous, smaller sections that cry out for numbers. But because the book comes marked only by the traditional parts and chapters, the final sense we have of it is of something rich and crowded with wonders, like the wares displayed, cheek-a-jowl, on a particularly fascinating flea market counter. The formal irony is that a novel, written according to strategy two but presented in traditional chapters and parts—as is *The Volcano Lover*—finally effects the unpunctuated rush of strategy one.

We've mentioned Sontag the essayist. Her achievement in the genre is large enough and generous enough so that it is worth noting the great ones: "Against Interpretation" (1964), "Spiritual Style in the Films of Robert Bresson" (1964), "On Style" (1964), "The Aesthetics of Silence" (1967)—all essays, incidentally, that proceed as a series of separate and, usually, numbered notes or fragments; then, "Thinking Against Oneself: Reflections on Cioran" (1967), "Theater and Film" (1966), "What's Happening in America" (1966), "Bergman's *Persona*" (1967), "Godard" (1968), "On Paul Goodman" (1972), "Approaching Artaud" (1979), "Syberberg's Hitler" (1979), "Mind as Passion" (1981), and "Writing Itself: On Roland Barthes" (1981)—this last is particularly maddening to those academics who study Barthes in the context of poststructuralism, because Sontag goes to such lengths to de-contextualize him from that debate and deal with him purely as reader encountering writer. And there are her book-length meditations, *On Photography* (1977) and *Illness as Metaphor* (1978).

If you have read even a handful of the above, you might wonder why a writer of such extraordinary intellectual strength should want to go back to fiction:

"When I was writing those essays, in the early '80s, I realized I was outgrowing the form. The essays were getting to be like masks. More and more they came to seem indirect, impacted ways of talking about things that I wanted to talk about much more freely and directly. Where I really realized it was the Canetti essay and the long essay on Roland Barthes I wrote after he died. The essays are incredibly hard to write. It's much easier to write fiction. Why was I torturing myself when I could just say all this straight out, front and center—when I could perform it, instead of assume it and argue with it and transpose it and do all these much more complicated things that were *really* hard? Each of those essays took anywhere from six to nine months; but with hard work, I can write fiction much faster. I enjoy writing fiction more."

As a performance, *The Volcano Lover* is as exciting, exacting, and as energetic as *any* of her essays—a judgment some readers, less comfortable with the fiction of ideas (for that has always been Sontag's fictive genre), have withheld from her earlier novels. They will have a hard time withholding it from this one.

Much in those essays is both illuminated by and, in turn, illuminates, *The Volcano Lover*. Besides "Writing Itself," another 1981 essay, "The Mind as Passion," which deals with the writer Elias Canetti, reads practically like a blueprint for the novel finished ten years later.

Sometimes Sontag's novel trumpets its sources, such as Goethe's autobiographical memoir, *Italian Journey*, most readily available in a graceful translation by W. H. Auden and Elizabeth Meyer. But just as interesting in terms of the novel is another Journey to Italy, Roberto Rossellini's 1954 film of that title (also released as *Strangers*), in which George Sanders and Ingrid Bergman come to Naples to spend their time at a villa from whose terrace you can see pretty much everything—Vesuvius, Capri—that you can from the Hamilton's in *The Volcano Lover*. And Rossellini's heroine Catherine, mooning about *her* Charles, sounds a lot like Sontag's Catherine going on about her William.

By the end of part 2, with the deathbed monologue of the Cavaliere, we've finished a very satisfactory novel. We've watched and been, most readers I suspect, mightily moved by the traditional Oedipal drama, only in which all three players are just too civilized to let it spiral down into any of the traditionally ugly Oedipal ends. But the book still has two parts to go—a brief part 3 and a part 4. Another writer might easily have called these parts "Appendices," "Epilogues," or distinguished them in some other way—because they do not take the story forward. Rather, they turn around and look at what's gone on up till now—in a harsher and harsher light as they progress, from a set of diverse and unexpected positions. Part 3 is still a *second* deathbed monologue by the Cavaliere!

And part 4 is four more, posthumous monologues by four of the women characters, including Emma and her mother.

In life, Emma came in for a good deal of criticism. And in Sontag's novel, she gets her share from the other characters. Toward the close of *The Volcano Lover* we have the reflections on Emma by a woman revolutionary, poet, and newspaper publisher, Eleanora de Fonseca Pimentel, who fought for the five-month-lived Italian Republic and was executed for her pains. Says Eleanora of Emma, she was ". . . another talented, overwrought woman who thought herself valuable because men she could admire loved her. Unlike her husband and her lover, she had no genuine convictions. She was an enthusiast, and would have enlisted herself with the same ardor in the cause of whomever she loved. I can easily imagine Emma Hamilton, had her nationality been different, as a republican heroine, who might have ended most courageously at the foot of some gallows. That is the nullity of women like her." The irony, of course, is that Eleanora delivers her pronouncement after having mounted just those gallows steps herself.

Said Sontag, though: "I really liked Emma a lot. But that *is* the one thing wrong with her. All the other criticisms of Emma I think are contemptible: that she's an upstart—I feel, 'Good for her! More power to her.' I love self-made people—I'm self-educated—going someplace that's completely different from where you come from; I think Emma's fabulous. And the way that people sneered at her because she lost her looks, you know, is—it's the Beauty Police. I mean, that's all terrible. But Eleanora doesn't criticize Emma for being vulgar or for being fat or for being a drunk or for being an exhibitionist or for being a vamp. What Eleanora says at the end—well, ideally I'd like the reader to ask, 'What *is* true in this criticism?'"

"Eleanora," I mentioned, as the afternoon drew on, "ends as a very impressive character, and her judgment of Emma and the rest is pretty damning—and a risky thing to conclude your performance with."

Sontag sat back in her chair. "Yes, I know. But I don't want people to think, 'That's the judgment of the book.' I think a lot in cinematic terms, and it's rather like pulling back. A very standard end of movies is the characters going toward the end of the landscape, down the street, and away from the camera; and the camera at the same time is pulling or zooming back, so that you get this wider and wider shot and the characters look smaller and smaller in the frame. But I don't want the reader— I *hope* the reader won't think that's what I, the author—she, the author— really thinks. Of course I think Eleanora's is the most distant view. It's that kind of thing—so it is an end."

Some readers, of course, are going to wish the novel had set them down with the more or less untroubled resignation closing out part 2. For them, the extensions, revisions, and dissociations that intrude, knock things around, and shake things up in parts 3 and 4, however briefly, will seem a bumpy, if not catastrophically turbulent, ending to the flight.

Said Sontag: "How do you end? What's closure? I mean, it's difficult to begin, and it's difficult to end. It's difficult to end *well.* You can do all these pirouettes but you have to—" under the kitchen table, I heard her stamp—"land on your feet!"

For readers who like to use "the tales of the tribe" to think with, however, *The Volcano Lover* will end them up precisely the way it ought to.

It's an elegant, wise, and rewarding novel.

— *New York City*
September 1992

25

Some Remarks on Narrative and Technology

or: Poetry and Truth

1. Science and Poetry are my concerns here. I do not mean the poetry of science. Still less do I mean some mistily envisioned science of poetry. Poetry and Science.

But we must approach the topics cautiously, even circuitously.

It is customary to say, in a presentation such as this, that the following remarks are not systematic. They are not. But I would like to specify here—and narrativize—the nature of their asystematicity: I suspect many readers will see all sorts of relationships among them, some interesting, some troubling. But the status of many of those relationships is—I feel, as someone who has considered them at length and with some care—highly problematic.

2. When this essay was published originally, my university press publisher informed me (I paraphrase): "It's our house style not to use *i.e.* (for *id est*), or indeed to use any other abbreviations of Latin phrases, such as *et al.* (for *et alia*), *e.g.* (for *exempli gratia*), *viz.* (for *videlicet*), *id.* (for *idem*), *ibid.* (for *ibidem*), *cf.* (for *conferre*), or *n.b.* (for *nota bene*). Our only exceptions is *etc.*—which we don't italicize—for *et cetera*." The lack of italics indicates, presumably, that it has been absorbed into English and is now considered an English term.

"But what," I asked, "if the writer *wants* to use them?"

"We explain to him—or her—that it violates house style. As far as we're concerned, using them in scholarly writing is no longer correct."

"Do you know where this house style comes from?" I asked.

"I imagine it's just that we don't want to appear too pedantic and court lots of people not knowing what the writer is talking about."

"But you know what those Latin phrases mean," I said. "And so do I. And most large dictionaries will give you a list of such frequently used phrases and many more besides—should one of them escape you. And there's always Mary-Claire Van Leunen's *Handbook for Scholars.*

"They don't present any practical stumbling blocks. Besides, your acknowledged audience for the sorts of works in which such abbreviations might appear is overwhelmingly academic. That means—at least in the humanities—these works will be read by people used to researching in scholarly texts written before World War II, which means they *have* to know such Latin tags as a matter of course."

There was a moment's silence. "Well," said the voice from the editorial office, that, whatever else one might say of it, was certainly from someone ten to fifteen years younger than I, "that's just not the way we do it."

"I suspect you do it," I said (I paraphrase freely), "as a holdover from the resurgence in the movement just after World War II to remove ancient languages, Latin and Greek, from high-school and college curriculums in order to accommodate the returning soldiers, for whom it was clearly a barrier to graduation—that whole movement itself was a revitalization of the movement just after World War I to democratize higher education by making Latin and Greek take a back seat to the study of English language texts, such as the English novel, which, for the first time had been brought into the purview of university studies via the academic establishment of such then-new disciplines as English Literature. All of this, including, in many ways, the Great War itself, was a response to the rising population and to the growing amount of printed matter that began in the 1880s, when people began to take seriously the recommendations of Matthew Arnold and other educational reformers to bring 'sweetness and light' to the common man.

"But that same rise in printed matter—" (I now paraphrase wildly—) "while certainly Latin and Greek literacy has not kept up with it, has also obviated the need for such retro-pedantic gestures as forbidding scholarly abbreviations in scholarly texts."

My friend on the other end of the phone laughed. "In other words," she said, "it's not very modern at all."

"It's quite modern," I said, "for 1888, the year Arnold died, the year the *New York Tribune* first began using the linotype, and the year the English decided to make their spelling look more sophisticated and up-to-date by Francophizing it, while leaving the earlier and older spelling forms in the first editions of such authors as Dickens and George Eliot to the barbaric, backwards United States."

After another moment, there was a sigh. "If you really want to write '*i.e.,*' I suppose you can."

"Thank you," I said. "I've been doing it for years. It's part of my language. It would be as difficult for me to excise it from my writing and thought as it would be for me to start writing 'different than' for 'different from,' or putting commas before restrictive clauses."

"What's wrong with 'different than'?"

"Today, nothing. But thirty-five years ago, when I was in high school, 'different from' was considered correct, while 'different than' was considered a solecism—and you were marked 'wrong' for it on any English test. Twenty-five years before that, when my mother was in high school, you were marked wrong if you wrote 'X is not as good as Y.' The proper positive form was 'as good as.' But the proper negative form was, 'not so good as.' If you confused them, you were mistaken—though, by the time I was in school, 'not as good as' had become acceptable."

"Now what's a 'solecism,' again?"

"A barbarism considered unacceptable among educated people."

3. I pause here to consider my parenthetical comments: When, in the conversation above, I said 'I paraphrase' (or "I paraphrase freely," or "wildly"), in what way did my words model the situation they purported to describe? In what way was I rewriting or revising the incident (or incidents) I was presumably describing? Well, to begin with, it was not just one conversation that yielded the above, but several—one of which was with someone not involved with the press at all. But my paraphrase involves considerable shortening, as well as condensing the conversations into one. The young woman on the other end of the phone in the major conversation certainly did not have a handle on all the abbreviations I have included—nor, indeed, did I. (I will let you guess in what scholar's handbook I looked them up.) But the anecdote seemed more effective when I cited a somewhat greater number of abbreviations than we had actually first mentioned. And though the outcome of the several conversations was more or less as I have recounted, rest assured that I was nowhere near as eloquent or succinct in my historical rundown, the first time I had to marshal it.

My reason for such revisions?

The historical insight that I took from the situation—and even dare to call its "truth"—is more strongly foregrounded in the more (I confess) imaginative version of the narrative, even though, knowingly and with intent, I violated the letter of the versions one might have retrieved from tape recordings of the contributing incidents, had such tapes been made. And I wanted to stress and give a narrative articulation to relations that, now and again, had been only implicit, and whose status—while they were happening—I was not so sure of; though, with thought, I am surer of that status now. Again: I have called it "truth." Perhaps more to the point, while the parent incidents were occurring, it was a "truth" I intuited and articulated rather clumsily; in the narrated version, it is a "truth" stated—narrated—as such.

(Now even though it holds a place in our subtitle, we will not mention this "truth" again; hold on, then, if you can, to the slippery, imaginative, and generally problematic notion of it presented in the paragraphs above.)

It is interesting that such violation is traditionally referred to as "poetic license," rather than, say, "narrative license."

4. In 1882, Ottmar Mergenthaler patented the linotype that was to revolutionize printing in both Europe and America. Ten years earlier, the Remington & Sons Fire Arms Company took its considerably refined ballistics technology and applied it to a new machine, the Remington typewriter. Along with other technological developments in everything from transportation to papermaking, these were to mean that, by the end of the eighties, something like five times as much material was being printed as had been printed at the beginning of that decade.

The upsurge in printed material in the 1880s has been historicized by many scholars. In her study, *The Origins of Totalitarianism,* Hannah Arendt attributes to this astonishing growth—coupled with the rise of population—the modern forms of both anti-Semitism and (South African and Rhodesian) racism: While both racist and anti-Semitic rhetoric had stayed pretty much the same between the sixteenth and the twentieth century, including the decade of the 1880s, Arendt points out that the referents for this rhetoric changed their form so totally during the 1880s that one could say anti-Semitism was "invented" in that decade. Before the 1880s, incidents of anti-Semitism were small, local phenomena. While, indeed, pogroms, stonings, and virulent social prejudice certainly existed, *vis-à-vis* what was to come they were comparatively rare, with relatively low death rates and damages. Anti-Semitism was the largely theoretical hobbyhorse of a number of eccentric intellectuals such as Wagner, who, throughout the 1870s, even as he wrote and argued heatedly for his belief in the decadence and racial degeneration of the Jews, was nevertheless friends with Jews, entertained them—sometimes royally, as in the case of Hermann Levi, with whom he pleaded (and finally won over) to conduct the premier of *Parsifal.* But when—even at the beginning of the 1880s, it was clear that forces were in place that were changing anti-Semitism from a "theoretical" question into a political movement—Wagner wrote that the Jews were "the only free people in Europe," and wrote to his friend, the conductor Angelo Neumann, himself a Jew, in February 1881:

I wholly dissociate myself from the present "anti-Semitic" movement: An article by me, soon to appear in the *Bayreuther Blätter* [Wagner's own, often self-authored newspaper], will proclaim this in such a way that it should be impossible for persons of intelligence to associate me with that movement.

Arendt argues that it was the growth of print that was to raise anti-Semitism from an eccentric social anxiety, with occasional violent outbreaks, to a major plank in the political platforms of several political parties (not just National Socialism), all with major, material, aggressive plans for action. The quote above is not to excuse Wagner for his anti-Semitism, but simply to point out that changes in the nature of the beast (that Arendt cites, largely in pamphlets and newspapers) were apparent and troublesome—even to a Wagner—as far back as the first year of that decade in which the technological revolution that was to exacerbate the situation really got under way. By the middle of the 1890s (a dozen years after Wagner's death in February of 1883), that movement was to take up and disseminate the Dreyfus Affair, which would polarize the West. Modern comparisons of the Dreyfus Affair with Watergate do not even suggest how pervasive that political scandal was during the years between 1896 and 1900. While it is arguable that the working classes were not deeply affected by the Dreyfus Affair (*viz.* the French peasant who, when questioned at the height of the affair, is supposed to have answered, "*Dreyfus, qui ça?*"), nevertheless the middle classes were exercised over it throughout Europe: Not only were there Dreyfus pamphlets, posters, banners, and books (the best remembered among them, Emile Zola's *J'Accuse*); there were Dreyfus (and anti-Dreyfus) paperweights, letter openers, vases, beer mugs, scarves, furniture, and china service!

5. The rise in the amount of printed material also produced a change, if not a crisis, in the realm of the literary as well: How to organize so much new writing, how to store it, how to treat it both physically and conceptually? The trace of that change can be retrieved from the shift over time in the meaning of the word "literature" itself.

In the eighteenth century, "literature" functioned largely as a companion term for "literacy." Someone who had "literacy" knew how to read and write. Someone who had "literature" had used that knowledge and read broadly over the whole range of what had been written and published. Literature meant an acquaintance with what had been written in the language. In short, literature was a species of knowledge. In the eighteenth century, someone "had broad literature," while someone else "had no literature at all." By the nineteenth century, the word had come to mean the "profession of writing." Someone might be "in literature," in the same way that someone might be "in law," or "in medicine." It is only after we get well into that groundswell of printed material in the 1880s that we find what had formerly been a secondary or even tertiary meaning of "literature" coming to the fore and suppressing these other meanings: literature as a set of texts of a certain order of value.

This rise to primacy of an until-now secondary definition has its underside: the conceptual creation of a vast reservoir of texts outside literature that has come to be called, in recent years, "paraliterature," *i.e.,* centering on the concept of those texts not of that order of value.

Simply in the area of fiction, in order to deal with the growth in the amount of it, categories of fictions—genres—became far more important than they had been before: penny dreadfuls, dime novels, mysteries, Westerns, children's books, adventures, scientific romances, ghost stories, poetry, and literature *per se.*

Literature was, of course, the privileged genre (or genre collection). Meanwhile, other genres were dismissed out of hand: Nor is it innocent happenstance that those genres dismissed tended to be those most popular with working people—the adventure, the Western, the mystery. Nor is it an accident that the genres that actually made it into the category of literature were those that accrued to themselves a certain cachet among the middle classes and their extension, the intellectual classes of the day—the genres that are finally valorized as "literary" *per se:* the novel, the short story, the drama, the history, the epic, and the lyric.

Just as the technological revolution in printing was a cause of the political alignments of the Great War, it was also a cause in the creation of literature, as we know it, during and just after that war. In his survey, *Literary Theory, An Introduction,* Terry Eagleton quotes from the inaugural lecture of Professor Gordon, the first professor of English Literature at Oxford, appointed to his chair just after the start of World War I:

> England is sick, and . . . English Literature must save it. The Churches (as I understand it) having failed, and social remedies being slow, English Literature has now a triple function: still, I suppose to delight and instruct us, and also, and above all, to save our souls and heal the State.

And healing the state, in the first decades of the twentieth century, when these words were spoken, meant specifically proofing the state against the sort of workers' revolutions that had already erupted in Russia in 1906 and 1908, and would explode again in 1917.

6. Reading widely on a daily basis, in the eighteenth century, a Doctor Johnson could consider himself familiar with the range of what had been written in the English language until that time. Nor did he have any need of high genres or low.

Reading widely on a daily basis, in the twentieth century, a Harold Bloom, who claims (however playfully) a Johnsonian range to his reading, must have recourse to the modern concept of literature (and by extension, that which is not literature), as well as—to use terms he has put forward in his most influential book, *The Anxiety of Influence*—"strong poets" and "weak poets." A "strong poet" is a poet to whom we must pay attention; a "weak poet" is one there is no necessity to bother with, even though we may dip into his or her work, and even find pleasure there, now and again. "Strong poets" rewrite the works of earlier "strong poets" in ways that produce new and interesting reading experiences; "weak poets" simply do the same things previous poets have done, however well or skillfully. I do not doubt for a minute that, in the range of the texts he has encountered, Bloom finds criteria sufficient to justify these categories. But the condition of their necessity—what makes them indispensable—is simply that there is too much to read. (Even on first hearing the terms, does anyone need to be told that there are far fewer strong poets than there are weak ones?) Without these categories there would be no way to decide what to read at all, and even more important, to justify what not to read.

While the ostensible purpose of the categories "strong poets" and "weak poets" is to judge an aspect of critical interest (call it quality), its necessity is simply that there are too many poets today for any one critic possibly to give the careful and considered reading to their complete works that is finally and actually what is required to make the quality judgment that "strong" and "weak" imply. And a reader or two away from Bloom, "strong" and "weak" dissolve back into the same unlocatable, rather arbitrary social consensus that constitutes "important" and "unimportant" writers, at least among the writers of today, and more and more among the writers of yesterday.

7. Two models—at least—contest for primacy in describing the humanities' encounter with itself and the world. They contest today. They have contested for years, at least at the rhetorical level. One sees the world as a series of narratives: linear, systematic, more or less rational, more or less negotiable. Technology itself is one conceptual area that is easily represented as a set of highly operationalized narratives about materiality. The operations are called science. Their material fall-outs are the artifacts of technology.

8. When, in his essay, "Epic and the Novel," Mikhail Bakhtin wrote: "By

1900, all genres had become novelized," he was responding to the historical situation of the rise in primacy of the narrative model for generally organizing our experience—and its settling into place by 1900.

9. The model that contests with the narrative model, however, sees the world as a series of poems. This model has never been the dominant one in our culture. But it has never been completely suppressed, either. And there are certain periods when it is far more forcefully in evidence than in others. In the 1890s, again in the 1920s, and arguably in the 1960s, this marginal model moved forward in the general consciousness, and commanded more intelligent attention than it had at other times.

To take the twenties as the most arbitrary of examples, one thinks—at one end of the spectrum—of Cocteau's perhaps glib categorization of all the arts as a species of poetry—*poesie du roman, poesie du musique, poesie du cinema, etc.*—and, at the other end (scholars of the period will realize there is a much closer connection than there is an opposition) Heidegger's enterprise of the period to repoeticize the modern world.

American literature's Beat Generation movement of the fifties and sixties, with its concomitant foreground of the poetry first of the Black Mountain School and then of the San Francisco Renaissance, as well as its privileging of spontaneity in art (with the novels of Kerouac, typed out in the first draft on endless paper rolls) can be looked back on as an appeal to the poem as the privileged model with which to encounter life, rather than the more acceptable and recognizable systematicity of the narrative.

When the poet Charles Olson said, in the first of his trio of 1967 Beloit Poetry Lectures, which shares my subtitle with the title of Goethe's 1809 autobiography, "poetry . . . especially by or in our language . . . is so different from the assumptions that poetry has had in our language . . ." he was citing the fact that the *chose poetique*—what poetry is—had shifted mightily from the 1890s. Yet the *assumptions* about what poetry is had remained remarkably stable, which resulted in Olson's difference.

10. A critical assessment that looked at the relation between Goethe's *Dichtung und Wahrheit,* Olson's lecture trio, "Poetry and Truth," and say, this current paper, and proceeded on the assumption that all the relations ascertained by the critics were signs of a movement through time and of an influential status—with Goethe influencing Olson and Olson influencing Delany (with any influences from Goethe on Delany having to have been filtered through Olson)—would more than likely be controlled by a fundamentally narrative model. A critical consideration that looked for relations not only between Goethe and Olson, between Olson and Delany, but equally between Goethe and Delany, and that assumed that any and all of these relations could run either forward in time or backward in time, and that the determination of their status was problematic, would, most likely, be controlled by a fundamentally poetic model.

I must say, "most likely," rather than "definitely," because it is not the idea of a unidirectional temporal linearity that defines the narrative model, and distinguishes it from the poetic. Rather it is the idea of the problematic status of the relations that defines the poetic model, and distinguishes it from the narrative.

Many critical studies cite relations in which the status of the relations is presumed to be known, even though it is never stated in the critique. Similarly, in many studies the status is presumed to be problematic, even when the status is not stated. Thus, it is often possible to read narrative critiques as poetic—or indeed, to read poetic critiques as narrative.

11. Longinus's *On the Sublime* (περὶ ὕψος) from third-century Greece, whose author was educated in Alexandria, then taught at Athens, and was finally executed (it is widely presumed) by order of the Roman Emperor Aurelian in 273 for having acted as aid and advisor to the rebellious Queen Zenobia of Palmyra, is a critical treatise in which a great many critical relations are foregrounded among a number of texts (Demosthenes, Plato, Sappho, *The Iliad*, Herodotus . . .), and in which the status of those various relations is left more or less tacit. (Are they merely descriptive? Are they fictive? Do they imply influence? Or are they assumed to be at some other level of causality?) It is possible that, at the time Longinus wrote that address to Postumius Terentianus critiquing Caecilleus's monograph of the same name, the status of all such relationships was presumed common knowledge among the intelligentsia; thus there was no need to specify. But because we do not have such knowledge today (nor have we had it at least since the eighteenth century when Longinus first became widely read), we read and traditionally have read Longinus's as the most poetic of critiques.

12. A kind of countercanon of works runs parallel to the canon we traditionally think of as the literary. Often its works are ones for which a more or less massive critical attempt was mounted to enter them at respectable places in the traditional canon; and usually most literary historians would have to say that, for whatever reasons (usually because other critics resisted), the attempts have failed.

These works are in a very different position from those that, for a season or even for a decade or more, achieve a general public popularity because the authors are well spoken and because there is nothing in the works so aesthetically offensive that literary critics feel called upon actively to denounce them. Often these works would appear to have joined the ranks of the immortals, only to be forgotten after still another decade or so, when their simple banality finally subverts all actual critical interest: One thinks of Archibald MacLeish's silly play *J.B.* (1958), Robinson Jeffers's mawkish redaction (another wildly free paraphrase, from Euripides this time) of *Medea* (1946), or even Tony Kushner's AIDS fairy tale *Angels in America, Parts I* and *II* (1993). All three have been declared, in their moments, icons of culture; but, stripped of the artful performances that briefly enlivened them, all three are less than memorable.

Works in the countercanon retain their interest, however. They are constantly being rediscovered. The 1890s is famous for a whole string of such works, though, indeed, to limit the ones associated with the nineties to that decade in any strict way would be far too absolute. It must go back at least as far as 1881, when twenty-six-year-old Olive Schreiner decided to leave South Africa with the just completed manuscript of her mystical—in the best sense—novel, *The Story of an African Farm.* The book was published in England in 1883, when she was twenty-eight. But during the nineties it was the most talked-about novel of the decade, at least among the poets of the Rhymers' Club—and rightly so. Now one stumbles across excited encomia about it in the letters of Ernest Dowson, now one uncovers an account by Arthur Symons, some few years before his final breakdown in Italy, enthusiastically urging it on the author of *Marius the Epicurean* (1885), Walter Pater. Indeed we might even want to extend this line back to James Thomson's *City of Dreadful Night,* which appeared over four numbers of the *National Reformer* between March and May of 1874—a work that grows from the same failure of organized Christianity that produced Shreiner's account of her characters' moral ordeals (with its uncanny, transvestial ending) on another continent in the year before Thomson died from tuberculosis in London, complicated by advanced dipsomania, on June 2nd of 1882.

The poems of Dowson (*Verses,* 1896; *The Pierrot of the Minute,* 1897; and the posthumous volume *Decorations*), with their unarguable verbal beauties, belong to this same line of works—if not the equally delicate tales he produced and published in the volume *Dilemmas: Stories and Studies in Sentiments* (1895) and in *The Yellow Book.* So do the more demanding—for the modern reader: because of their religious weight—poems of Lionel Pigot Johnson and Francis Thompson, if not the works of Alice Meynell. Indeed, the "productions of the nineties" continue on at least through 1904, when "Frederick, Baron Corvo" published his extraordinary novel, *Hadrian the Seventh,* a year after Samuel Butler's novel

The Way of All Flesh saw posthumous publication in 1903. Indeed, Butler's novel, which he began in 1873 and completed in 1884, is a work contemporary with Shreiner's novel. *The Way of All Flesh*, with its iconoclastic satire, was taken into the canon almost immediately, while *Hadrian*, with its far more conservative politics, its wildly erudite religious superstructure, and its barely suppressed fantasy—the writing is simply gorgeous—has led a far more problematic life at the margins of the literary, despite the praise of everyone from D. H. Lawrence to W. H. Auden.

Looking at the range of such counterworks, one notices first the catastrophic lives their writers tended to live: The artists who produced them do not lend themselves to any easy version of the literary myth that art ennobles the artist's life—at least not in any nonironic and socially evident manner. If anything, they suggest that art is a bitch goddess who ravages the creator and leaves a distressing, pathetic ruin behind. It would seem that the canon can absorb a bit of such pathos, but in nowhere near the amounts that predominate in this range of highly talented creators; and it is rare that (with a lot of posthumous critical help) a John Keats, a Percy Shelley, an Edgar Allan Poe, or a Hart Crane makes it across the canonical border. In terms of the reception of all of these, all are poets who, at one time or another, verged on being confined to the countercanon. (How interesting it is to observe the posthumous critical reduction currently going on of W. H. Auden from the poetic giant he was during the last thirty years of his life to a "more or less interesting poet," for no other reason that I can discern—in the half-dozen recent studies and biographies of him I have read—than that [it does not even seem to be his homosexuality] he occasionally neglected his clothing, his St. Marks Place apartment was a mess, and he drank.) As a group, however, the countercanon poets tend toward a brilliance of surface that suggests an excess of aesthetic relations in their texts constituting both their enjoyment and the permanence of their aesthetic interest despite their regular canonical exclusion.

This is why the American writer Stephen Crane joins them. Crane's *Red Badge of Courage* was briefly popular, first in its 1896 newspaper serialization, then in volume form from Appleton over the following year. But by the year Crane died, aged twenty-eight, in 1900, it had been all but forgotten. Despite the fact that, in his final trip to England, he became a friend of James, Wells, and Conrad, Crane was not taken into the canon—nor did he come anywhere near it—until Thomas Beer's (wildly fanciful!—though the extent of that fancy has only come to light in recent years) biography became a bestseller at the start of the next poetic decade, in 1923.

13. Now, to say that science is the theory of technology is not to say very much until we have clarified some assumptions about the relation of theory to the situation it is presumed to be the theory of.

The question is: Is science a set of immutable rules, laws, and universal facts, of which any specific experiment or observation is only a particular manifestation, and often a fallen or inexact manifestation, at that? (Think of all those times in Chem. Lab when our experimental results were so far off textbook prediction.) Or is science a kind of averaged description of experiments and observations that at any moment may be catastrophically revised by unexpected experimental results not fundamentally different from our lab student anomalies? (Think of Einstein's General Theory of Relativity, confirmed by the anomaly of Mercury's inevitably early appearance from behind the sun—finally explained by the idea of the sun's gravity actually bending the light waves of which the image was composed, rather than the sun's considerable atmosphere deflecting those rays—which, till then, had been the traditional, but finally mathematically inadequate, answer.) Indeed, to glance at examples like the ones in parentheses here suggests that science partakes of both. In practical terms, certainly, that is the working assumption most practicing scientists go on—in hope that they will not mistake evidence of a fundamental paradigm shift for a simple measurement inaccuracy (or, perhaps, more embarrassingly, vice versa).

I hold that science is aestheticized technology. However, it is also and at the same time the political aspect of technology—as it is the theoretical aspect. The working part of this suggestion is that science bears the same relation to things in the world as an aspect bears to an object. Thus, though it may be represented as a rule or set of rules governing objects, strictly speaking it is not the rules that constitute science but the explanations for those rules—nor is science, speaking equally strictly, a reduction of an object. (As with an aspect of an object, a representation of that aspect cannot totalize the object, by definition, the way science is presumed to totalize technology.) Thus the relation between science and technology is very different from either of the ones suggested above, even as it explains particular effects or appearances of that relation.

But, yes, the status of that relation is and always has always been problematic.

14. Aspects of objects depend mightily on human biology. It is absurd (*i.e.*, away from reason towards stupidity) to speak of colors that are not colors we or some living creature can see; or of notes and harmonies that, similarly, cannot be heard. That is to say, such concepts do not easily fit into most current logical narratives about the world. (Should we speak of such sounds or colors, because we will be in the realm of metaphor, the status of the relation between word and world will be thrown into question.) And colors and sounds are aspects of objects *par excellence.* Aspects are the ability of objects to excite the biological subject in a particular way.

Science, then, might be called the ability of the object world to excite explanations in the reasoning body that, through their coherence and iterability, allow (or suggest) a greater and greater control over the object world.

15. The object world, controlled or uncontrolled, maneuvered or unmaneuvered, is technology. To pull an apple from a tree and eat it is as much a technology as to hunt through a garbage can, find half a hot dog, and eat it. And there is a science to both.

16. Aspects, to speak figuratively, tend to sit on the surface of objects. That is to say, they are the first things about the objects that interact with us. In a cultural field given over to essentialism, we are very likely to assume that the aspect represents some sort of essence of the object.

I hold that poetry is an aspect of narrative.

I hold that science is an aspect of technology.

But the fact that aspects have perceptual priority explains why it seems to so many of us (including me) that poetry precedes the functional use of language: Clearly, in language, relationships whose status we are not sure of (relationships whose signification/status is unknown or problematic) must precede relationships whose status we believe we know (relationships whose signification/status we can follow). A little thought will show that this makes the historical question: Which came first, poetry or narrative? a chicken-and-egg question. But in terms of the history of any given individual, from infancy to adulthood, poetry must come first.

17. But let us switch topics once again: to narrative and narrativity. Narrative exists as an extraordinary complex of expectations. As soon as we write, "The marquis went out at five o'clock . . ." the problem is not then that we do not know what to write next. Rather, we have an immense choice of things we can follow it with. But there is an equally immense or even greater number of things that would produce a tiny, almost minuscule feeling of upset, violation, and the unexpected: "An anvil fell on his head from the roof and killed him." Or: "At that moment the Titanic sank." To the extent that a narrative is supposed to produce various sorts of pleasure, the sense of expectations violated can be just as pleasurable, or even more so, than the sense of expectations fulfilled. And as soon as one choice is made (whether the writer goes with fulfillment or with violation), a new set of expectations opens before the reader/writer. Which will the writer—say, the writer of what we usually call "narrative fiction" —choose to develop: the sense of violation or the sense of fulfillment? But, like a tree-search lying in front of every writer (and reader), at the beginning (and all throughout, unto the closing sentence) of every tale, the expectations are always there. That tree underlies every text. Any text represents only a specific path through it.

One argument posed by people who claim genre fictions are aesthetically valueless *per se* is that, to be recognizably of a genre—science fiction, Western, horror, mystery—the text must fulfill so many expectations that there is no room for the necessary violations that characterize great literary works. The counterargument is that, first, literary fiction entails just as great a set of expectations as any genre does, and requires just as much conformity to expectations to write it. (People who argue against this often see mundane fiction as simply "mirroring the world," rather than negotiating a complex set of writerly expectations in the same way genre fiction does.) Second, the greater emphasis on expectations fulfilled that indeed characterizes what we traditionally call genre fiction means that, when violations are worked into traditional genre tales, they register more forcefully on the reader than similar violations in tales belonging to the literary genres. Conversely, literary modernism, with its emphasis on violation of expectation, has produced an expectational field where violation is so expected that the differences in effect between expectation met and expectation violated are minimal. Thus, as an effective field, modernism (and by extension, postmodernist writing) is affectively moribund. Well, I believe both arguments underestimate just how rich, complex, and vast the expectational field actually is. They are confining their view to the tiny range of expectations we call "plot," "character," "style," "theme," and "setting." The fact is that there have always been moribund spots at every level: They're called clichés, and they have been with us at least since French printers coined the term in the eighteenth century. (The original "cliché," which means "clamp," was a length of preset type of frequently used words and phrases, held in a clamp and stored on a special shelf, that the seventeenth-century printer could slide into his type tray, instead of having to set that length of text letter by letter.) But the dismissal of entire genres as cliché rests on a blindness to the complexities of what it takes to ignite a genre and make it take life in the first place.

In any genre, literary or paraliterary, texts that go along merely fulfilling expectations register as moderately good or mediocre fiction: the sort one reads, more or less enjoys, and forgets. What strikes us as extraordinary, excellent, or superb fiction must fulfill some of those expectations, and at the same time violate others. It is a very fancy dance of fulfillment and violation that produces the "Wow!" of wonder that greets a first-rate piece of writing—the inarguably wonderful story—no matter the genre it occurs in. The expectations I am talking of cover everything from the progression of incidents that, in the course of the story, registers as plot, to the progression of sounds that, in the course of its sentences, register as euphony. Such expectations occur at the level of metaphor and form, just as they occur at the level of character and motivation, and at many, many other levels besides.

The notion that plot (or character) exhausts what we can say about expectations across the whole range of narrative fiction, among all the various genres, literary and paraliterary, is about the same as the notion that, in music, the most expected note is always a fifth, fourth, or tonic up or down within the same scale; thirds and sixths are also expected notes; seconds and sevenths are less expected; and notes that lie outside the scale are unexpected. Now, with that as our only principle, we must create a rich subject for a Bach fugue, a pleasing melody for a Verdi aria, a satisfying row for a Schoenberg chamber symphony . . .

Taking off from Pater's formalist dictum, "All art aspires to the condition of music," philosophers like Rorty and Davidson are showing us that language is not less complex than music, but more so.

18. Whether fulfilled or violated, each expectation citable in a narrative is the sign of a relationship between what comes before it and what comes after it. Not all of these relationships are necessarily consecutive, nor do they all run only from the past to the future. Something happening on page ten of a text may charge or recharge with meaning something we read on page two. And this can happen at any level. In short, we do not know the critical status of every narrative relation. Often these relations are pleasurable simply in themselves. But what we are doing here is recomplicating narrative itself into a poetic model.

From here on, I am going to try to achieve another level of narrative clarity on top of my fundamentally poetic model of narrative.

19. It is easy to get too caught up in the notion of a tree-search. As early as 1957, in his groundbreaking little book *Syntactic Structures*, Noam Chomsky showed that the "end-stopped" (really, just another name for a "tree-search") model of language was simply inadequate to generate all the well-formed sentences in a language. To counter this model, Chomsky produced the model of "deep grammar," where complex sentences were generated on the surface of layers of vertical development. In terms of current computers, that means a tree-search with a whole lot of loops, flags, go-tos, and recursive features. But the fact is that we still do not have computers that, in a free dialogue situation, can generate original sentences of the range and complexity your average six-year-old speaks easily. That suggests that even the deep grammar model is not adequate to language.

Indeed, it is the notion of language as "well formed" that seems to be the problem. While a lucky few of us may write using only well-formed sentences more or less exclusively, none of us speaks using only well-formed sentences. In ordinary speech, some of us may come up, now and then, with three or four well-formed sentences in a row. But most of us, in actual dialogue situations, generate far more fragments and run-ons than we do well-formed sentences, with disagreements between verbs and nouns and incorrect tense progressions the norm rather than the rule, even though, if one of our ill-formed sentences is pulled out of context and we are asked to examine it carefully, we can usually tell something or other is wrong with it—and often even what it is. "Grammar," even the most carefully constructed spoken grammar, as put together by the most careful linguists is, in most actual speech situations, something that actual language aspires to, something that it approximates, but that actual language is always falling short of, rather than something that controls language in some masterful way. And that goes for the language of "competent speakers" as well as for people just learning it. (Of course the mistakes competent speakers make routinely are very different from the mistakes new learners make. But that is another topic.) Another way of saying the same thing is: A grammar can never be a complete description of an actual language but must always be a reduction of it. One might go so far as to say: If you have a complete description of it, "it" is probably not a language at all but rather a much simpler communication object—a code. Still another way of saying much the same is: It is only after we have an algorithm that can generate both well-formed and ill-formed sentences that we can likely develop a superalgorithm from that earlier algorithm that can distinguish between them (*i.e.*, a grammar); for, contrary to much linguistic speculation, a grammar is not something that, on some ideal or Platonic level, is prior to language, and can be recovered by an examination of specific language situations. If we ask a native informant what another native speaker means by a particular utterance, we will be given some translative paraphrase, or possibly be told, "I don't know." If we ask, "Did the second speaker say what she or he said correctly?" we will be told, "Yes," "No," or, "I'm not sure." It is from the second set of questions, or from the assumption that we know that the speaker was not making a mistake, that we put together our grammar. But it is the idea of grammar that brings the idea of correctness and incorrectness to the language; the language is not founded on this idea. And the native interpreter will be able to paraphrase—that is, to tell us the meaning of—many more utterances than those that, to a later question, he or she may deem correctly uttered: The interpreter will be able to give us at least some of the meanings of the pregrammatical requests of little children, the slurred demands of the drunk, and the heated boasts or the enthusiastic gossip or those speaking too quickly to care about the fine points of expression. The ability to understand a great deal of ill-formed language is not the accidental fallout of linguistic competence (*i.e.*, the ability to speak in well-formed language), but is rather the anterior state necessary to have any concept of the well-formed at all. Rather, grammar always follows language and is generated as an always-partial description of what is actually there (*i.e.*, a description of the parts there that are particularly useful in ways the concept of grammar defines). Thus, by extension, an algorithm that can generate only well-formed sentences but cannot generate both comprehensible (and incomprehensible) ill-formed sentences is simply not a complete language algorithm.

(In terms of science: The ability to generate incorrect explanations necessarily precedes the ability to operationalize our way into correct ones.)

I may not be able to give you an immediate paraphrase of the meaning of these lines from Hart Crane's "Atlantis," which closes his poetic sequence *The Bridge*:

> Swift peal of secular light, intrinsic Myth
> Whose fell unshadow is death's utter wound—
> O River-throated—iridescently upborne
> Through the bright drench and fabric of our veins . . .

But to ask whether, as a sentence, it is well-formed or ill-formed— whether it is "correct," or contains any mistakes of grammar, syntax, or diction—is simply hopeless. And it is still poetry. More to our point, it is certainly still language, and language at a high and (and to me and many other readers) highly pleasurable level of expectational violation. Indeed, the only way to begin talking about it productively as poetry is to read carefully the precise ways in which the language resists the fulfillment of expectations: "Swift peal of . . ." makes us expect, of course, "thunder," thunder being the mythic mode in which the god Zeus traditionally demonstrated his sacred, religious power. But rather than religious thunder, instead we get "secular light." And it is precisely the difference between the expected "thunder" and the violational "secular light" that starts to make the line, and, indeed, other words and phrases in the lines, signify, as it allows us to experience the specific play of differences that is Crane's vision.

An even more extreme example, however, might be taken from Crane's friend, black writer Jean Toomer, who, at the start of the twenties, experimented by writing a poem organized around a single letter ("Poem in C"):

> Go and see Carlowitz the Carthusian,
> Then pray bring the cartouche and place it
> On this cashmere, while I tell a story.
> The steaming casserole passed my way
> While I reclined beneath Castalay,
> Dreaming, ye Gods, of castor oil. . . .

Toomer also wrote, in a wholly invented language, "Sound Poem (I)":

> Mon sa me el karimoor,
> Ve dice kor, korrand ve deer,
> Leet vire or sand vite,
> Re sive tas tor;
> Tu tas tire or re sim bire,
> Razan dire ras to por tantor,
> Dorozire, soron,
> Bas ber vind can sor, gosham,
> Mon sa me el, a som on oor.

To argue whether the first of these is well-formed or not, or whether the second is actually language, is to miss the point: There is no way we can respond to them other than as language. (In "Sound Poem (I)" there is no way to avoid hearing "wind" in the Germanic "vind," the French forms "mon" (my), "tire" (pulls), and "dir" (to say) in "Mon," "tire," "dire"—and a Hispanic form of the same in "dice"; the Latin "basia" (kisses) in "bas," and Spanish and French "el" (he) and "tasse d'or" (cup of gold) in "el" and "tas tor." The English "paramour" and "raisin" linger behind "karimoor" and "Razan," as well as dozens of other semantic conceptions. No, we establish easy narrative relations here neither in Toomer nor in Crane. But that is what Crane's and Toomer's poems have been carefully crafted to do. And they do it not by avoiding language but by maneuvering—in all cases—fundamental language elements.

In all three cases, language expectations are being violated to highlight various poetic effects.

Robert Graves' (1895–1987) delightful poem "¡Welcome to the Caves of Artá!" plays with the English/non-English all travelers in Europe are familiar with from local tourist brochures. ("¡You tell me are you capable to make precise in idiom / Considerations magic of illusion very wide!") And dialect poems from America's James Whitcombe Riley (1849–1916), writing of Little Orphant Allie in the urban Irish dialect of the mid-1880s, and Paul Lawrence Dunbar (1872–1906), writing of Malindy and the effects of her singing in the black speech of the century's turn, to Canada's William Henry Drummond (1854–1907), meditating on "Leetle Bateese" and "The Wreck of the 'Julie Plante'—A legend of Lac St. Pierre" in the heavily accented English of the Québequois, have all forced both meaning and emotion from the tensions in the speech of those challenged by one form or another of what is generally taken to be some form of linguistic failing. Aesthetically (if not linguistically), how does one finally and ultimately distinguish the enterprises of such poets from, say, that of Robert Burns (1758–1796), writing in what is admitted to be a disparate *dialect* of English (rather than in the pidgin of "non-native" speakers—a category put in question by the very enterprise): Certainly the effect on the average "competent English" speakers, who judged him one of the great poets of his century, was much the same—even among those readers armed with a Scottish glossary and thus able to give more meaning than most to specialized terms, "a-glay," "brattle," etc.

Much linguistic work in the past has occurred within a paradigm that sees well-formed sentences as language but ill-formed sentences as, somehow, outside language (work that would certainly place Toomer's "Sound Poems," if not much of Crane, beyond the linguistic border); it sees them as some sort of non-language, when, on the one hand, the most cursory observation of actual language as it is spoken (or, with a poet such as Crane as a prime example, written) reveals that ill-formed sentences are just as much "within language" as are well-formed sentences and are equally a part of the language process, while, on the other hand, the meticulous and careful readings by deconstructive critics of written language (writing: that bastion of the well-formed; but, as well, the classical way to preserve the "ill-formed" for study) reveal that the ideal derived from (but on which, rather, we mistakenly tend to ground) the whole notion of the "well-formed"—the sentence whose logic and clarity precludes all ambiguity, all semantic slippage—is itself an impossibility: that, indeed, if such an ideal were achieved, rather than producing the phantasm of a perfect and mastered meaning, immediately present both to sender and to addressee, it would bring the communication process to a dead halt. The slippages, the ambiguities, the mistakes are, finally, what make language function in the first place. But even with this much of an overview of the ubiquity and utility of "mistakes," some will see that we are back at that very important notion of the violation of expectations, purposeful mistakes, if you will, that must reside in higher-level narrative grammars (even as slippages and ambiguities reside in well-formed sentences), if the narratives are to be in any way richly satisfying.

Both through its exceptional formalities and through its pursuit of "the language used by men," poetry regularly seeks its material "outside language," that is to say, outside proper language as theorized by any number of different grammarians with an extraordinary range of approaches. The linguists—if not the grammarians—might take a lesson: Well-formed language is a subset of a more fundamental notion of language in general. And linguistics should be concerned with language. My suspicion is that a model of language that sees (instead) the well-formed as fundamental and ill-formed as an excess and theoretically disposable supplement is hamstrung from the start.

The much beleaguered project of deconstruction (whose history and elaboration, as much as a view of the range of poetry, certainly suggest the above) can be looked at as a way of foregrounding the necessary and unavoidable "mistakes" (read: ambiguities, slippages) that reside in even the most well-formed sentences—and that must reside there if those sentences are to exist in time—and are to communicate anything at all over the time it takes to utter them.

With the acknowledged failure both of the end-stopped (or tree-search) model of grammar as well as the deep (or vertical) model of grammar, it seems clear that, to describe actual language more precisely, we need another model. More to the point, we need another *sort* of model—one that is looser, more flexible, that allows us to retain the insights of the previous models until someone generates a better technical description, even while our new order of model acknowledges that the ways of talking about those insights, from both earlier models, are now metaphors and, as such and despite their insights, are themselves violations of an expected, more exact model, a more poetic model, *i.e.*, an expectation as yet unfulfilled . . .

But to return to our topic of fictive narrative: No one sits down and teaches you what fictive expectations are, much less which ones to conform to and which ones to violate.

Rarely have I been in a creative writing class that has even mentioned them, much less talked about them at any length.

We learn them from reading other fiction—other truly good fiction; and equally, or possibly even more, from reading bad fiction.

Because violation has as much to do with success as does fulfillment, there can never be one "great work," or even a group of ideal "great works," that can teach you all the expectations at once. The artist, T. S. Eliot wrote in "Tradition and the Individual Talent" (1919), must "familiarize himself with the tradition." In today's computer-oriented world, we might put it (metaphorically): The artist (along with the critic) must, through broad exposure, become familiar with the overall structure of the possibilities of the tree. And the tree (or the tradition), remember, produces not only the good pieces but the bad pieces as well.

We learn those expectations not as a set of rules to follow or to break—though after a while, some writers may actually be able to list a number of them in that form. Rather, we learn them the way we learn a language when we live in another country. We learn its grammar and syntax; we learn what is expected of a competent speaker of that language.

And just to up the ante, languages change, including the language of fiction. What was perceived as a violation yesterday is today a sedimented expectation. What was once an expectation is now honored only in the breach—or people just giggle. The language of fiction is not quite the same today as it was eighteen or twenty-five years ago. It is certainly not the same as it was sixty or seventy-five years ago. And it is almost entirely different from what it was a hundred or a hundred-fifty years ago. So while it is always good to know the history of the language you are speaking, and while that history will often tell you the reason why certain expectations are (or are not) still in place today—where, in effect, those expectations started out—the great stories of the past hold the key to writing the great stories of today no more than an oration by Cicero will tell a modern politician the specifics of what to mention in his next sound bite, even when Cicero and the modern politician can be seen as having similar problems.

All we can ever learn is what the language—of fiction, say—has been in the past. But every time we sit down to write a new text, we become involved, however blindly, in transforming the language into what it will become.

20. As science is an aspect of technology, poetry is an aspect of narrative: It is such an evident aspect of narrative that, from time to time, it has been foregrounded and highlighted and hypostasized, at least on the social level, into a thing in itself, just as, in the same manner, science has been so hypostasized.

21. When poetry is separated from narrative, as it is in much language poetry, *i.e.*, where the coherent narrative units (as in, say, the works of Silliman or Hejinian) are kept down to a sentence or less, the poetic relations foregrounded are much quieter, subtler, and—for the reader used to taking his or her poetry with greater dollops of "argument"—more difficult, at least for a while, to recognize. Yes, it is a reduced aesthetic field that such poets are asking us to concentrate on: But the reduction also represents an aesthetic refinement.

And the fact is, there is simply no way to experience those particular poetic effects (read: verbal relationships of a problematic status) at such an intensity and purity in a more narratively saturated field.

22. The hypostasization of aspects into (conceptual) states that, at least socially and linguistically, are treated as though they were actual objects in themselves would seem to be a constant function of language. We not only talk of "yellowness," "largeness," "smallness" (even "size"), "heat," or "cold" as though they were actual things (rather than aspects of things), but by treating them thus verbally, we allow ourselves to study them and to create explanatory models of them, models that are counterintuitive precisely to the extent that they deny their object status and return them to their aspective states.

It is arguable that such hypostasization is a poetic function of language, and one that, we can easily see, makes science (which is, after all, a similar hypostasization of aspects) possible.

If poetry is cut off too rigorously and permanently from all narrative, in that it represents another such hypostasization, the division may lay out a locus for aesthetic abuse. (At least every time, usually at those historical moments that the poetic model itself has come to the foreground, and poetry itself has taken the occasion to make another lurch away from traditional narrative in order to repurify itself, there have always been critics standing about to shout "Abuse! Abuse!") So can science, when it forgets the complex material world, the technology, if you will, of which it is an aspect, also lay out such areas, and for the same reasons. But I do not think that such hypostasizations are necessarily abusive in themselves, for if they were, we would have to dismiss both science and poetry out of hand. And, myself, I would rather see more of both, conducted at a high and refined level, than less.

— *New York City*
1995

WORKS CITED

Arendt, Hannah (1951). *The Origins of Totalitarianism.* New York: Harcourt, Brace, Jovanovich.

Bakhtin, Mikhail (1981). "Epic and the Novel," in *The Dialogic Imagination*, ed. Michael Holquist, trans. Caryl Emerson and Michael Holquist. Austin: University of Texas Press.

Butler, Samuel (1964). *Ernest Pontifex, or The Way of All Flesh*, ed. with intro. by Daniel F. Howard. Boston: Houghton Mifflin Riverside Editions.

Chomsky, Noam (1957). *Syntactic Structures.* The Hague: Mouton & Co., N.V., Publishers.

Crane, Hart (1986). *The Complete Works of Hart Crane*, ed. Marc Simon. New York: Liveright.

Dowson, Ernest (1919). *The Poems of Ernest Dowson*, with a memoir by Arthur Symons. New York: The John Lane Company Ltd.

—— (1947). *The Stories of Ernest Dowson*, ed. Mark Longaker. Philadelphia: University of Pennsylvania Press.

—— (1967). *The Letters of Ernest Dowson*, eds. Desmond Flower and Henry Mass. London: Cassell & Company Ltd.

Eagleton, Terry (1983). *Literary Theory: An Introduction.* Minneapolis: University of Minnesota Press.

Gregor-Dellin, Martin (1963). *Richard Wagner, His Life, His Work, His Century*, trans. J. Maxwell Brownjohn. New York: Harcourt, Brace, Jovanovich.

Johnson, Lionel (1982). *The Collected Poems of Lionel Johnson*, Second and Revised Edition, ed. Ian Fletcher. New York: Garland Publishing, Inc.

Leunen, Mary-Claire van (1979). *Handbook for Scholars.* New York: Knopf.

Longinus (1991). *On Great Writing (On the Sublime)*, trans. with intro. by G. M. A. Grube. Indianapolis: Hackett Publishing Co.

Olson, Charles (1979). "Poetry & Truth," in *Mutulogos, The Collected Lectures and Interviews*, Vol. II, ed. George Butterick. Bolinas: Four Seasons Foundation.

Pater, Walter (1986). *Marius the Epicurean, His Sensations and Ideas*, ed. with intro. by Ian Small. First published 1885. Reprinted New York: Oxford University Press.

Schreiner, Olive (1939). *The Story of an African Farm*, intro. by Dan Jacobson. First published 1883. Republished London: Penguin Books.

Toomer, Jean (1988). *The Collected Poems of Jean Toomer*, eds. Robert B. Jones and Maregery Toomer Latimer, intro. by Robert B. Jones. Chapel Hill: The University of North Carolina.

Appendix

Some Notes for the Intermediate and Advanced Creative Writing Student

> Write as simply as you can for the most intelligent person in the room.
> —Blanche McCrary Boyd, OutWrite, Boston, 1998

You write simply, we might add, so that your hypostasized intelligent other can more quickly catch you out when you write down idiocies—and, if that intelligence is imbued with enough generosity, so that it can bracket those idiocies and go quickly to what's interesting among the suggestions in your work. From time to time (or again and again) the writer must write directly against that simplicity to enhance and to control just the suggestiveness in which, for such an intelligence, much of the work's worth will reside. This tension between clarity and connotation is why so many writers have two voices—I first heard Dudley Fitts put forward the notion from his wheelchair at a poetry seminar at the Bread Loaf Writers' Conference in the summer of 1960—often in evidence and in tension in the same text. Fitts used Henry Reed's moving poem on Adamic pretensions in the light of World War II, "The Naming of Parts," as a particularly clear example, more than half a dozen years before anyone this side of the herring pond had even considered the Lacanian notion of a split subject.

I have written the following notes as simply as I can. But what use they may have, if any, will be entirely in what they can suggest—as much as if I had written them with the recomplications of some of my examples.

What is literary talent? To what extent should it be treated as a skill?

A skill may or may not be something to be mastered. Certainly the physical ones require strength, muscles, and, in general, those facilities that must be built up by repetition.

My feeling is that literary talent is definitely *not* something that involves mastery in any way, shape, or form. Thus, the treatment appropriate to the mastery of a skill is wholly inappropriate to the training of literary talent. Both encouragement and the proffering of *judgmental* criticism in the early stages are equally out of place—though the student may desperately want one, the other, or both.

As far as I can see, talent has two sides. The first side is the absorption of a series of complex models—models for the sentence, models for narrative scenes, and models for various larger literary structures. This is entirely a matter of reading and criticism. (And, yes, that means criticism of the writer's own texts as well as the criticism of others.) Nothing else affects it.

To know such models and what novels, stories, or sentences employ them certainly doesn't hurt. Generally speaking, however, the sign that the writer has internalized a model deeply enough to use it in writing is when he or she has encountered it enough times so that she or he no longer remembers it in terms of a specific example or a particular text, but experiences it, rather, as a force in the body, a pull on the back of the tongue, an urge in the fingers to shape language in one particular way and not in another. The only way to effect this is to encounter that model or structure again and again in other texts and to experience it . . . well, *through* the body. Clumsy, inadequate, and not quite accurate, that's the only way I can say it.

These models must be experienced through what the early German Romantics called *Begeisterung*—the *sine qua non* for the artist, more important than intelligence, passion, or even imagination and the foundation for them all. Literally "in-spiritedness" and often translated as "inspiration," it carries just as strongly the sense of "spirited," so that it is more accurately designated by the English word "enthusiasm." *Begeisterung*—inspiration/enthusiasm—can alone seat these models in the mind at the place where they can, with like energy, forget their sources, seize up new language, and reemerge.

The training of literary talent requires repetition of the experience of reading, then: But it does *not* require repetition of the experience of writing (other than that required to achieve general literacy) in the same way that piano playing or drawing does. Far too many writers have written fine first novels without ever having written much of anything of particular value before—Jane Austen, Emily and Anne Brontë, J. D. Salinger; but the list goes on. A number of writers who did write one, two, or a handful of comparatively mediocre works before they started producing much better ones—Woolf, Lawrence, Balzac, Cather, Faulkner—frequently tell of a sea-change in their conception of what the novel actually *was* or *could be* that is responsible for the improvement. They realized there were more complex models to submit to. But once they had them, submit to them they did. In none of these cases was it just a matter of the simple improvement or strengthening of a craft or skill.

Which brings us to the second side of talent. The second side is the ability to submit *to* those models. Many people find such submission frightening. At the order, even from inside them: "Do this—and let the model control the way you do it," they become terrified—that they'll fail, fall on their face, or look stupid.

If the body could do it entirely on its own, we'd all be very lucky. But, though, sometimes for a passage or—more rarely—even for a story or an entire book, your body seems to take over and all-but-does the writing for you (it's called inspiration; it's called self-expression—but what it *is* is submission), fundamentally writing is done with the mind. To say it seems unnecessary—but the mind plays an active, complicated, and intricate part in the process, a part *far* more complex than simply thinking up what to write about. *Most* of what the mind does is think about and give instructions for controlling the conditions under which we *do* our writing. This is where, frightened or made anxious by aspects of the writing process, your mind will repeatedly sabotage your writing project. If it does go with the project, probably it's because your mind becomes, as it were, addicted to the pleasure of writing—but that addiction, devoutly to be wished, only happens if you consciously and carefully put writing first before all other responsibilities; which is to say, while the pleasure is there (it's unique, very real; all writers experience it), the truth is, it isn't *that* great. You need lots of it to effect the "addiction" that will keep you at it. Though the practice of writing *has* the structure of an addiction, it's a mild one—one remarkably easy to wean yourself away from, even accidentally or through inattention. Thus, count on internalization of models rather than addiction to the process; addiction without the proper internalized models explains why bad writers often write so much.

Acknowledging that there *are* models to submit to is much the same as realizing: There are standards to be judged by. That you yourself must exercise the first and possibly harshest rounds of judgment on your work is not a situation most of us would characterize as fun. Rather it's a situation most people find endlessly anxiety-producing and unpleasant. But the writer must revel in it and grow. This takes a particular personality type most people just don't have. If you don't get some major satisfaction from such auto-lacerations, however, you might as well try something else which does not demand such constant self-critique. This is (only) one reason why, ten years after every creative writing class, most (often, all) of the participants have given up writing for a less taxing profession.

When people have not internalized the models at the bodily level, often they develop a stubborn streak, usually based on insecurity and fear: While they have a recognition awareness of the models, they're afraid they'll lose something of themselves if they give in to them. This is especially true when someone else with a sense of what might be done to help a piece of fiction makes a suggestion to them for improving it: The writer knows his critic is right—but would rather do anything in the world than follow the suggestion. Well, for them, stubbornness and fear must be taken as one with *lack* of talent. A teacher can do only so much to allay them—although we do what we can. When the writer does have a deep sense of the model that's controlling her or his work, however, and someone makes a criticism that points up where the model has, for a moment, not been followed, often the writer can hardly wait to make the suggested change. (I've seen writers sit down on the classroom floor to correct a manuscript before leaving the workshop.) Having made these points, however, I must also stress: Most criticism is not so dead-on. The writer should respond enthusiastically to that which is useful. Still, most (and often all) of the criticism the writer gets has to be ignored. Though models are rarely referred to directly by either writers or their critics, it is the deep sense of the model that tells the writer what criticism is useful and what is not. For many years, I have told creative writing classes that the writer must be able to *hear* the criticism if it is to be useful. But, clearly, *when* the writer "hears" it, something so much more active than *just* hearing is going on, it would be unfair not to point it out. Similarly, when the writer does not hear it, and there is no deeply internalized model to guide him or her, the confusion, resistance, and hostility is often great enough to note.

To write a novel or a story means that one takes one of these internalized models and adjusts it, often with a good deal of thought, to the material at hand. That, yes, means changing the model somewhat. This is what produces new work. Sometimes it even produces new kinds of work. But it is not an accident that so many of the writers we associate with the production of whole new kinds of writing—Gertrude Stein, Virginia Woolf, T. S. Eliot, Ezra Pound, James Joyce—were articulately aware of the tradition they were developing from/breaking with. (We shall come back to this notion.) The sad truth is, there's *very* little that's creative in creativity. The vast majority is submission—submission to the laws of grammar, to the possibilities of rhetoric, to the grammar of narrative, to narrative's various and possible structurings. And in a democratic society that privileges individuality, self-reliance, and mastery, submission is a frightening thing.

When looked at in terms of the submission to internally absorbed models, only a few things can go wrong with writing. Maybe you've never absorbed the particular model you need. Sadly, that too is tantamount to having no talent—or not having enough talent or the right sort of talent. If that's the case, you have to give it up. Sometimes one has absorbed a model, but it needs time to come forward and take over the material. Time, then, *can* help. But many people read widely and voraciously without *ever* absorbing the models from the fiction they read at a depth that will allow them to *write* any fiction of interest on their own. They might store those models in recognition memory, so that they recognize the patterns that fiction makes and enjoy them immensely as readers. But that doesn't mean they have necessarily internalized them to the extent needed to become creators. We recognize our friends' faces. Few of us, however, can produce a likeness on paper—though we recognize it when someone else does. In this one sense, then, the creative writer is closest to the concert performer playing a composer's score and making it sound out at its most beautiful.

For the writer, the model comes forward in the mind as a kind of vaguely (or, sometimes, very strongly) perceived "temporal shape" that seizes up the "material"—whatever it is the writer is writing about—and organizes it, organizes it rigorously. These models function on several "levels" at once. They are there to organize the words (the sounds and multiple meanings associated with the words) into sentences. They are there to organize the different kinds of sentences into scenes. They are there to organize the different kinds of scenes into subsections (chapters or parts). They are there to organize the chapters or parts into a novel. I say, "They are there . . ." But if they are *not* there, then the novel stalls at a certain point; and unless the writer can summon forth the proper model, the work will get clunky and awkward from that point on—if it progresses at all. Sometimes the model is clearly expressible: "The book will begin with three chapters devoted to the main characters, in the central one of which they encounter or observe some minor characters; then a fourth chapter will be devoted to those minor characters alone; the next three chapters are devoted to the main characters (with, again at the middle of those three chapters, the main characters encountering the minor characters); then, yet again, another chapter gets devoted to the minor characters alone. Then there will be still three more chapters devoted to the main characters (with, again, the middle chapter of those three linking major and minor characters), followed by a minor-character chapter once again; the book will close with three chapters, in the first of which the actions of the main characters will resolve; again the center piece of these three chapters will resolve the minor characters' story in terms of an encounter with the major characters, and, in the final chapter, the emotional fall-out of the whole story is resolved among the main characters. End of novel. That's fifteen chapters all together, with four devoted directly to the minor characters and three devoted to tying them in with the main characters, who in turn command eight chapters by themselves."

Let's look at a chart of this narrative structure where _____ represents a chapter about the major characters, /////// represents a chapter about the minor characters alone, and ----- represents a chapter about the major and minor characters interacting:

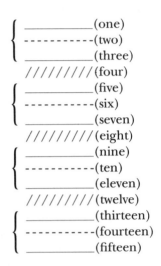

```
    ⎧  _____(one)
    ⎨  ----------(two)
    ⎩  _____(three)
       /////////(four)
    ⎧  _____(five)
    ⎨  ----------(six)
    ⎩  _____(seven)
       /////////(eight)
    ⎧  _____(nine)
    ⎨  ----------(ten)
    ⎩  _____(eleven)
       /////////(twelve)
    ⎧  _____(thirteen)
    ⎨  ----------(fourteen)
    ⎩  _____(fifteen)
```

Charted out, we see that the narrative progresses in four three-chapter units devoted to the major characters, punctuated with three chapters devoted to the minor characters alone. The chapters that deal with the minor and major characters together nevertheless produce an overall structure in which the minor characters are on stage every other chapter, starting with chapter two and ending with chapter fourteen. The chapters themselves, of course, are going to have to be structured, since most novel chapters usually contain more than one scene. The progression of scenes within chapters will also have to be taken into consideration and structured. Possibly every chapter contains three scenes. Or five. Or every other chapter contains three and the alternate chapters contain only two . . . in which case we have to figure out, in the ----- chapters, which scenes get devoted to the minor characters and/or to major characters, etc. At this point, someone may say: "Look, just tell your story." But the sense that you *are* telling a story and not just presenting a random progression of incidents is controlled by (among other things) such patterns.

Rarely, however, does narrative structure (another name for those models we began by discussing) manifest itself even this clearly; and this is already fairly complex.

The all-important social range over which the novel takes place has to be structured as carefully as any other element. (Is the book about a young man or woman's rise [or fall] in society? Do the minor characters move in the same direction, up [or down] the social scale as the main characters? Or do they move in the opposite direction?) At the same time, like a through-composed opera, leitmotivs consisting of repeated phrases, parallel incidents, running metaphors, and the like must be carefully placed throughout this dual story, so that each can recall and mirror one another.

Only a certain amount of this structuring can be externally imposed on the fictive material. The material must call up an appropriate structure, rather, that is already inscribed, as it were, wherever the writer keeps his or her inner feel for fiction. Yes, there can be a certain amount of conscious adjustment. But if the writing strays too far from the model, there may just be no other one there to catch the material up and control it—and the result will be either stasis (that awful thing, writers' block) or chaos.

Notice that not once, in all this, have we spoken of *what* a given novel is about. This is not because the structure *must* precede the novel's subject matter. But the structure certainly *can* precede much of the plot— and also control it.

Our democratic society believes strongly in educational opportunities made available over the range of our country. All people should have the opportunity and education needed to enjoy the variety of art. Another idea, however, has grown up along with this: As many people as possible should be given the chance to *make* art themselves. In terms of writing, we've seen the last twenty-five years' explosion of writers' workshops and MFA programs. But there's a possible built-in failure in this program: While many—or even most—people can internalize a range of literary models strongly enough to recognize and enjoy them when they see them in (some) new works that they read, *very few people* internalize them to the extent that they can apply them to new material and use them to create. Lots of people want to.

But not many people can.

Most of you who read these notes—the vast majority—will discover, sometime fairly soon (that is, in the next three, four, or six years), that you are not really writers. The very few who do not discover this then, will— sometime around the age of fifty-five, sixty, seventy, or seventy-five—discover that, with the general deterioration of the mind that accompanies the second half of our lifetime, you are no *longer* a writer. (So no one escapes.) It is not a pleasant discovery no matter when, in life, it comes. The only consolation anyone can give is: There is nothing wrong with not being a writer—that is, not being one who has, however briefly, been able to submit. It doesn't help that, among people who control the machinery of narrative dissemination, most editors, all publishers, and especially TV and film producers, no one wants to speak of the reality of artistic submission. All "professional" rhetoric about writing is organized, rather, around an illusory phantom called artistic mastery, which involves meeting deadlines, being totally "in control" of one's "craft," and making anything happen in a story you want (or anything that anyone who can pay you tells you that he or she wants), however externally imposed or at odds with any particular model that happening or incident is. These same people are then willing to lie through their teeth (and often pay exorbitant amounts of money for it), declaring that the product is great—when the actual result, visible to everyone in the audience, is that *nothing* either believable or interesting is happening at all in the butchered narrative.

By and large, because she or he must work constantly against this rhetoric of mastery, the writer must be someone who can be more or less satisfied with the pursuit of personal excellence at the expense of personal happiness when the two, as they will again and again, conflict. There are, of course, a few exceptions to this rule of thumb: Most of those are *truly* tragic.

If you're going to write well, you will do a lot better if your prose models are F. Scott Fitzgerald, Vladimir Nabokov, late Dickens, Raymond Chandler, Virginia Woolf, Nathanael West, Theodore Sturgeon, William Gass, Ethan Canin, Guy Davenport, and Joanna Russ (with a few reminders from E. B. White thrown in)—certainly you'll do better than if your models are James T. Farrell, Theodore Dreiser, Pearl Buck, John Dos Passos, Sidney Sheldon, or John Grisham; or even Henry James or William Faulkner. (From the last two you might absorb other, higher-level literary models.)

If your models have come only from the ironic experimenters and minimalists in short fiction of the last thirty years, who run from Donald Barthelme and Raymond Carver up through Ann Beattie and Lorrie Moore, whose work exists only as delightful and graceful—and sometimes poignant—commentary directed in delicate pinpricks against the foibles of the Great Tradition, when you try to write a serious novel about topics of social import, you will come out with a disaster which doesn't even make it to the level of good TV sitcoms or comedy sketches (the best of which are also instructive).

* * *

Things to remember about some common criticisms:

1. If your character is thin, the character is thin *now*. What the character does in the next chapter or scene is not going to help that current thinness.

2. If your plot is incoherent, what happens in the next chapter or scene is not going to make it suddenly cohere. Incoherence is neither mystery nor suspense. (These are *controlled* responses that the writer evokes.) Incoherence is produced by the writer's *losing* control of the material.

3. A bad or incoherent short story will not make a good opening novel chapter. Rewrite that short story and try to make it better. Don't just keep maundering on, hoping that, somehow, later material will repair the damages readers have noted earlier. It doesn't work that way.

4. Stories (and plots) emerge from novels. But novels are not primarily stories. They are ragbags of various discourses (descriptive, dramatic, narrative, reflective, analytic) structured in some inventive and interesting way against a matrix of rhetorical expectations.

5. It is almost impossible to write a novel any better than the best novel you've read in the three to six months before you began your own. Thus, you *must* read excellent novels regularly.

6. Excellent novels set the standards for our own. But bad novels and bad prose are what teach us to write—by setting strong negative examples. You must read both, then—and read them analytically and discriminatingly.

7. Much of good writing is the avoidance of bad writing. (Most bad writing by people who write easily comes from submission to demonstrably poor models.) Get together a list of prose-writing errors that *you* refuse to make any more. Choose them, perhaps, from the most common errors people make in your writing workshop. Before you hand anything in or send it out, read your work over for your own personal list of errors. When you inadvertently fall into them (and you will), correct them. (This is the best example I have, by the way, of what I mean by "submission to an aesthetic model." It also explains why such submission is work.)

8. The novelist who wants to do anything more than paint a portrait of a contemporary character or a more or less limited situation—who wants to show the effect of a situation over a range of social conditions—but has only read the short fictions of the last fifty years with any care starts with four strikes against him or her.

9. The San Francisco renaissance in poetry of the middle fifties and sixties was predicated on the aesthetic principle: "Good art makes great art look even better. Thus, it benefits the great to encourage the good."

10. You need to read Balzac, Stendhal, Flaubert, and Zola; you need to read Austen, Thackeray, the Brontës, Dickens, George Eliot, and Hardy; you need to read Hawthorne, Melville, James, Woolf, Joyce, and Faulkner; you need to read Tolstoy, Dostoyevsky, Turgenev, Goncherov, Gogol, Bely, Klebnekov, and Flaubert; you need to read Stephen Crane, Mark Twain, Edward Dahlberg, John Steinbeck, Jean Rhys, Glenway Wescott, John O'Hara, James Gould Cozzens, Angus Wilson, Patrick White, Alexander Trocchi, Iris Murdoch, Graham Greene, Evelyn Waugh, Anthony Powell, Vladimir Nabokov; you need to read Nella Larson, Knut Hamsun, Edwin Demby, Saul Bellow, Lawrence Durrell, John Updike, John Barth, Philip Roth, Coleman Dowell, William Gaddis, William Gass, Margarite Young, Thomas Pynchon, Paul West, Berthe Harris, Melvin Dixon, Daryll Pinkney, Daryll Ponicsin, and John Keene, Jr.; you need to read Thomas M. Disch, Joanna Russ, Richard Powers, Carroll Maso, Edmund White, Jayne Ann Phillips, Robert Glück, and Julian Barnes—you need to read them and a whole lot more; you need to read them not so that you will know what they have written about, but so that you can begin to absorb some of the more ambitious models for what the novel can be.

The first move the more experienced creative writer can make toward absorbing these models is to realize that "plot" is an illusion. It's an illusion the writer ought to disabuse her- or himself of pretty quickly, too, at least if he or she ever wants to write anything of substance, ambition, or literary richness. (There *is no plot.*) That is to say, plot is an *effect* that other written elements produce in concert. Outside those elements, plot has no autonomous existence.

What there is is narrative structure.

Here is a formal statement of the reason plot doesn't exist:

No narrative unit *necessarily* corresponds to any textual unit. Plots are always and only composed of synoptic units.[1]

I'll try to demonstrate with examples.

Again: What we call "plot" is an effect produced by (among other things) structure. But many, many *different* structures can produce the *same* "plot."

(Structure *does* have textual existence: You can point it out on the page: "See, this comes first. This follows it. This takes five sentences to

---

1. A recent riddle demonstrates what analysis can also reveal—why plot has no definitive existence nor indicates any necessary information about its text:

From the following account of the plot, identify this classic American Depression film:

"An unwilling immigrant to a New Land of Opportunity, a dissatisfied young foreign woman kills an older woman whose face she never sees. After she recruits three equally dissatisfied strangers, together they go on to kill again . . ."   [Answer: *The Wizard of Oz.*]

say. This takes two. This sentence concerns the character's action. This subordinate clause gives the character's thoughts . . ." These are all comments on narrative structure. Structure exists because a given narrative text exists in its actual and specific textual form.)

All of the following: (A) through (G), have the identical plot. All of them have radically different structures:

(A) Joe woke. He tossed the covers back. A moment later he was standing by the bed on the rug.

The plot might be synopsized here: "Joe gets up in the morning." A different type of story—with a different intent, a different focus, and a different development—might take any of the three micro-incidents in the above mini-narrative, however, and atomize one or another of them. One of the most important things that such atomizing does is accent the crispness and brevity of the presentation of the *other* textual units:

(B) Waking assailed Joe and retreated, a wave foaming up and sliding from the sands of day. At its height, there was a sense or a memory of dark green sheets beneath his belly, his knees, the pillow bunched under his shoulder, the quilt across his ear. Rising and retreating at an entirely different oscillation was sexual desire, now an unfocused and pulling emptiness, now a warm fullness in the groin, a sensitivity within his slightly parted lips under the susurrus of breath. Somehow the cycles met. He opened his eyes—aware of the room's silence. (But what had he been aware of before . . . ?) He could feel the dawn moisture drying along his lower lids. Dragging one hand from beneath the covers into the chill, he twisted the heel of his thumb against one eye socket.

Then he tossed the covers back. A moment later he was standing by the bed on the rug.

(C) Joe woke.

Dragging one hand from beneath the covers into the chill, he twisted the heel of his thumb against one eye socket. Then he snagged his fingers around the coverlet's edge. He raised it—and the chill slid down his arm, along his side some eighteen inches. Dragging in a breath, he raised the covers further. Somewhere below, something put two cold palms over his kneecaps. He heard breath halt a moment in his throat. The bedding beneath his shins was suddenly *so* warm. He gave the quilt's rim a toss and began to kick free even before it fell, off below the bottom of the t-shirt he slept in these November nights. One foot made it from the mattress edge, then the other—as the first slid from under the blanket to hang an instant, an isolate entity out in the cold room. He pushed into the pillow with his fist, so that his shoulders rose; his feet lowered.

A moment later he was standing by the bed on the rug.

(D) Joe woke. He tossed the covers back.

He pushed into the pillow with his fist, so that his shoulders rose; his feet lowered.

The shag rug's nap tickled his soles, till the weight of his legs crushed it away beneath. Every damn bone in his feet had to move this way or that a couple of millimeters, it seemed, to get into the right position—and in the left foot, that hurt! He pushed himself forward, the hem of his limp t-shirt swinging over his upper thighs. As his body lifted, a cold blade of morning slid beneath his buttocks and down toward the back of his knees. (Somewhere the springs clashed, muffled below the mattress.) It felt as if someone were shoving at his right kidney with the flat of a hand. He put his own hand there to rub the feel away. He blinked, standing in the silent room, flexing chill toes on the rug, aware (or was it more a memory of something he'd been half conscious of before waking?) he had to go to the bathroom.

A, B, C, and D generate identical plots, but in each case the elements that do the generating are structured differently. (Their content is, of course, different too. But right now that is not our concern.) There are still other effects to be achieved, however, by the use of these *same* structural variants. For example:

(E) Waking assailed Joe and retreated, a wave foaming up and sliding from the sands of day. At its height, there was a sense or a memory of dark green sheets beneath his belly, his knees, the pillow bunched under his shoulder, the quilt across his ear. Rising and retreating at an entirely different oscillation was sexual desire, now an unfocused and pulling emptiness, now a warm fullness in the groin, a sensitivity within his slightly parted lips under the susurrus of breath. Somehow the cycles met. He opened his eyes—aware of the room's silence. (But what had he been aware of before . . . ?) He could feel the dawn moisture drying along his lower lids. Dragging one hand from beneath the covers into the chill, he twisted the heel of his thumb against one eye socket.

Then he tossed the covers back.

The shag rug's nap tickled his soles, till the weight of his legs crushed it away beneath. Every damned bone in his feet had to move this way or that a couple of millimeters, it seemed, to get into the right position—and in the left foot, that hurt! He pushed himself forward, the hem of his limp t-shirt swinging forward over his upper thighs. As his body lifted, a cold blade of morning slid beneath his buttocks and down toward the backs of his knees (somewhere the springs clashed, muffled below the mattress). It felt as it someone were shoving at his right kidney with the flat of a hand. He put his own hand there to rub the feel away. He blinked in the silent room, flexing chill toes on the rug, aware (or was it more a memory of something he'd been half conscious of before waking?) he had to go to the bathroom.

And finally:

(F) Waking assailed Joe and retreated, a wave foaming up and sliding from the sands of day. At its height, there was a sense or a memory of dark green sheets beneath his belly, his knees, the pillow bunched under his shoulder, the quilt across his ear. Rising and retreating at an entirely different oscillation was sexual desire, now an unfocused and pulling emptiness, now a warm fullness in the groin, a sensitivity within his slightly parted lips under the susurrus of breath. Somehow the cycles met. He opened his eyes—aware of the room's silence. (But what had he been aware of before . . . ?) He could feel the dawn moisture drying along his lower lids. Dragging one hand from beneath the covers into the chill, he twisted the heel of his thumb against one eye socket.

Then he snagged his fingers around the coverlet's edge. He raised it—and the chill slid down his arm, along his side some eighteen inches. Dragging in a breath, he raised the covers further. Somewhere below, something put two cold palms over his kneecaps. He heard breath halt a moment in his throat. The bedding beneath his shins was suddenly so warm. He gave the quilt's rim a toss and began to kick free even before it fell, somewhere below the bottom of the t-shirt he slept in these November nights. One foot made it off the mattress edge, then the other—as the first slid from under the blanket to hang an instant, an isolate entity out in the cold room. He pushed into the pillow with his fist, so that his shoulders rose; his feet lowered.

The shag rug's nap trickled his soles, till the weight of his legs crushed it away beneath. Every damned bone in his feet had to move this way or that a couple of millimeters, it seemed, to get into the right position—and in the left foot, that hurt! He pushed himself forward, the hem of his limp t-shirt swinging forward over his upper thighs. As his body lifted, a cold blade of morning slid beneath his buttocks and down toward the backs of his knees. (Somewhere the springs clashed, muffled below the mattress.) It felt as if someone were shoving at his right kidney with the flat of a hand. He put his own hand there to rub the feel away. He blinked, standing in the silent room, flexing his chill toes on the rug, aware (or was it more a memory of something he'd been half conscious of before waking?) he had to go to the bathroom.

Still an entirely different structure (with an entirely different affect) can be achieved by casting the whole "story" so far into the mode of indirect discourse:

> (G) Earlier that morning, Joe had waked, tossed the covers back, and stood up by the bed on the rug. Now he . . .

None of these versions is *necessarily* any better—or any worse—than the others. While each highlights different and particular details, strives after a different sense of immediacy, presents a different pacing of sensations and incidents, with different juxtapositions (all structural qualities), none is more narratively accurate than any of the others. The only thing that will decide which approach you use in a particular tale is what else is going on—structurally, not plotwise (for, again, all seven *plots* are identical)—in the remainder of the narrative.

When we write a story, we often (though not always) start with a more or less vague sense of "what happens" in it. Writing the tale out, however, is a matter of modulating that "what happens" into a specific structure. (And *not* into various other structures!) The structure, finally, *is* the story—even if a reader, asked to synopsize it, can come up with more or less the same "what happens" that you went into it with when you began writing. The overall aesthetic pleasure the reader takes from the story is going to depend largely on how pleasing the reader finds the story's overall structure.

A story or a novel has an overall structure as well as smaller structural patterns. The repetition—or variation—of small structural elements is what produces the overall structure. In general, structure will always produce *some* sort of plot—coherent or incoherent, interesting or dull. Plot is no guarantee, however, of *any* sort of structure, pleasing or otherwise. Be aware of the "plot," sure, in the back of your mind as you write. But be aware of it as you are aware of an *illusion you are creating*. Don't think of it as a reality out there that will somehow write the story for you. The particular problems you write *through*, as it were, while you are actually first drafting a text in your notebook or typing at your word processor, are the structural elements and their relations.

Also, there are a *lot* more kinds of elements to be shaped into a structure than simply detailed observation vs. synoptic account.

Here is another example of narrative structure, in this case juxtaposing a series of sequential present actions with a series of equally sequential memories:

(H) Under a bruised aluminum sky, Joe hurried along the November pavement. Last night, bundled in blankets on the couch, Margery had coughed and coughed, till finally he had been able to pay no attention at all to the TV sitcom.

At the corner, he looked down from the light as it changed to green, then started across for the far curb. Where in the world *was* it? (There was the leather bag store. And the bodega just after it. And down there was the blue and white marquee of the Greek coffee shop.) It couldn't be more than three streets from the house. He'd passed it hundreds of times—only now that he was actually looking for it, it seemed to have moved, or secretly slid further off by a couple of city blocks.

Last night, when, at last, he'd phoned Mark—Mark, his cousin: Mark the doctor—he'd felt like a fool. But Mark, who was basically a good guy, had said: "If it's a dry cough and she's not bringing anything up, then it's just a little flu. Get her some Cloraseptic. It comes over the counter—and it's good stuff. It'll cut the soreness." Waving an arm from her plaid cocoon, Margery had insisted, still coughing, that he not go out for it that night but—it was past eleven and the drugstore was closed—wait till morning.

There it was—at the corner where it had always been! Hands deep in his anorak, Joe hurried by the window, filled with pale plastic shampoo bottles, a bronze pedestal of nail polishes and lipsticks, and a mannequin arm lying across crumpled Mylar, its elbow in an Ace bandage.

He pushed through the door: Warmth puffed against his face—and a bell rang.

The structure of his narrative is:

Present, past, present, past, present . . . where each of the first four elements is slightly longer than the element before. They converge in the final present element in a particularly satisfying way: One of the pleasures of this particular structure is the mystery, very soon resolved, of what Joe is looking for and why.

There are a number of ways we could restructure this, for different effects—again, depending on the rest of the story development. (And if we do decide to restructure the elements, we will lose the micro-pleasure of that little mystery, finally resolved.)

We could, for example, put everything in chronological order:

(I) Bundled in blankets on the couch, Margery coughed and coughed, till finally he could pay no attention at all to the TV sitcom.

When, at last, Joe phoned Mark—Mark, his cousin: Mark, the doctor—he felt like a fool. But Mark, who was basically a good guy, said: "If it's a dry cough and she's not bringing anything up, then it's just a little flu. Get her some Cloraseptic. It comes over the counter—and it's good stuff. It'll cut the soreness." Waving an arm from her plaid cocoon, Margery insisted, still coughing, that he not go out for it that night but—it was past eleven and the drugstore was closed—wait till morning.

The next day Joe woke. He tossed back the covers. A moment later he was standing by the bed on the rug.

From the far side of the bed, Margery coughed.

Minutes on, under a bruised aluminum sky, Joe hurried along the November pavement.

At the corner, he looked down from the light as it changed to green, then started across for the far curb. Where in the world *was* the drugstore? (There was the leather bag store. And the bodega just after it. And down there was the blue and white marquee of the Greek coffee shop.) It couldn't be more than three streets from the house; he'd passed it hundreds of times—only now that he was looking for it, it seemed to have moved, or secretly slid further off by a couple of city blocks.

There it was—at the corner where it had always been! Hands deep in his anorak, Joe hurried by the window, filled with pale plastic shampoo bottles, a bronze pedestal of nail polish and lipsticks, and a mannequin arm lying across crumpled Mylar, its elbow in an Ace bandage.

He pushed in the door: Warmth puffed against his face—and a bell rang.

I've used the initial example, "Joe woke. He tossed the covers back . . ." as a subnarrative within this larger one, to remind us that the material of any subsection can be structured in any number of ways. Note that, structured as it is here, the same textual unit plays a much smaller part in the plot than it would if it introduced the story.

What would happen if we used one of our first six (A to F) structures? Basically, if the remainder of the story is going to focus on the relation of Margery and Joe [and/or Mark], we probably want what we have now or something close to it. That is to say, we want to get Joe back to Margery as quickly as possible, so they can start interacting. If, in the remainder of the story, however, Joe is deflected from returning home from his drug-store mission and the major events happen outside, away from the house, with new characters whom we have not yet met, one of the other more detailed renderings of Joe's waking, throwing the covers back, and standing—depending on the nature of that adventure to come—might work better to focus us on Joe's internal state and prepare us for his responses to these nondomestic happenings; also, the nondomestic story might well be considerably longer than the domestic one, so that it admits of more development all through it. But all of these are *structural* decisions. Plot will depend on which ones the writer makes.

Whether one goes with a story about Margery, Mark, and Joe, or a story about what happens to Joe outside the house while he's going to pick up some cough syrup for Margery, there is, however, another way beginning writers often structure the sort of material in the narrative above. It is one of the *most common* and the *weakest* of narrative structures for the opening of stories or scenes. It should be avoided like the plague:

(J) Under a bruised aluminum sky, Joe hurried along the November pavement.

Last night, bundled in blankets on the couch, Margery had coughed and coughed, till finally he had been able to pay no attention at all to the TV sitcom.

When, at last, he'd phoned Mark—Mark, his cousin: Mark, the doctor—he'd felt like a fool. But Mark, who was basically a good guy, had said: "If it's a dry cough and she's not bringing anything up, then it's just a little flu. Get her some Cloraseptic. It comes over the counter—and it's good stuff. It'll cut the soreness." Waving an arm from her plaid cocoon, Margery had insisted, still coughing, that he not go out for it that night but—it was past eleven and the drugstore was closed—wait till morning.

The next day Joe woke. He tossed back the covers. A moment later he was standing by the bed on the rug.

From the far side of the bed, Margery coughed.

Minutes on, Joe had on his anorak and was outside.

At the corner, he looked down from the light as it changed to green, then started across for the far curb. Where in the world *was* the drugstore? (There was the leather bag store. And the bodega just after it. And down there was the blue and white marquee of the Greek coffee shop.) It couldn't be more than three streets from the house; he'd passed it hundreds of times—only now he was looking for it, it seemed to have moved, or secretly slid further off by a couple of city blocks.

There it was—at the corner where it had always been! Hands deep in his anorak, Joe hurried by the window, filled with pale plastic shampoo bottles, a bronze pedestal of nail polish and lipsticks, and a mannequin lying across crumpled Mylar, its elbow in an Ace bandage.

He pushed in the door; warmth puffed against his face—and a bell rang.

This structure is *so* common among young writers, I've given it a name: "The false flashback." What's wrong with it?

The opening element ("Under a bruised aluminum sky, Joe hurried along the November pavement") is simply wasted, functioning only as a distraction from the far more logical purely chronological version. The transition points—first from present to past, then from past to present—are particularly weak. What's happened, in this third and weakest version, is that likely the writer began to imagine Joe on the street and only filled in the back story in his/her imagination moments later—then wrote it down in the same order he or she thought it up.

(Possibly the writer had some intimation of the possibilities of our first, five-part structure, but lost it while actually writing the opening sentence.)

Well, the order in which you figure out what's going on in your story is *not* privileged.

If you came up with a good twist for the ending of a mystery, and only later figure out how to set it up and make it function, you wouldn't start your story off by telling the end. The same goes for a scene that you suddenly realize needs something before it—even if that scene is only a sentence, or a paragraph, or indeed a page or two, long.

You shouldn't do it there, either.

Generally speaking, it's best to tell your story from *beginning* to *end*—*unless* there's a clear structural reason to tell it otherwise. Make your structural choices because they provide a more economical way to tell the story, and because they add certain pleasures (mystery, humor, suspense [*not* incoherence]) to the tale.

In our first version, there was a clear and distinct structural pleasure to be gained by telling the story in two small flashbacks interspersed among the three sections of present narrative: the creation of a small mystery (what is Joe looking for?) resolved by the convergence of past element two with present element three. Also it's more economical—i.e., it's *shorter* than versions two or three: In version one you don't need the transitional wake-up scene, which would be missed in version two. (If the bulk of the story is set outside the house, without Margery, and is fundamentally humorous, and itself involves a larger mystery to be eventually solved, version one might well be the *best* opening—because, highly economically, it prepares us for what is to come.) But in neither our second nor our third version can the mystery be maintained. So the *single* flashback of version three is purely superfluous. The initial element ("Under a bruised aluminum sky, Joe hurried along the November pavement") is just not long enough or weighty enough to create any sense of fictive presence. Nothing is gained in the third, flashback version that isn't there in the second, chronological version. The displacement in time is unnecessary and confusing.

So don't do it.

Other fictive elements that must be structured into a tale include:

Dialogue. Directly described first-level foreground action. Revery. Indirect reportage of action. Analytic thought. Emotional description of responses. Exposition. Social information. (An action described directly and the same action reported indirectly often generate the same plot—but they produce *vastly* different reading effects!)

One reason structure is so important is because it creates expectation:

If a reader reads a novel, and chapter 1 is told from Joe's point of view, then chapter 2 is told from Margery's point of view, then chapter 3 is told from Joe's point of view again, already there is an expectation that chapter 4 will be told from Margery's. The writerly fulfilling of readerly expectations—especially at the structural level—is pleasurable to the reader. (From one point of view, a novel is nothing *but* a concatenation of structural readerly expectations. The writer's task is to fulfill those expectations at the structural level in such a way that nevertheless lets the text generate an unexpected plot or story.) If the reader is right and chapter 4 turns out to be from Margery's point of view, the reader will experience a bit of structural pleasure. As well, this will strengthen the expectation that chapter 5 will be told from Joe's point of view.

Here is the place to remind the writer of a terribly important reality: Writing takes longer than reading. A novel can take six months, a year, or five years to write. The same book can be read over two to ten hours. In six months, not to mention five years, *you* may grow tired of the structural pattern you have committed yourself to. Nevertheless, if suddenly— in a novel that's been going along in alternating chapters between Joan and Jim—a chapter comes up from Billy's point of view, the reader— surging through the text in an evening—is going to experience a stretch of structural *displeasure*. Plot developments or other things may lay other pleasures over it; but that displeasure is still going to be there. And it's going to mar the reading experience that finally *is* the novel you write.

There are more complicated structures than simple alternating chapters. For example, in a novel of thirteen chapters, chapters 1 through 6 might alternate between Joe and Jane. The seventh, central chapter might be told from Frank's point of view. Then the final six chapters might alternate between Joe and Jane once more—or even, perhaps, between Mike and Milly. You still have a formal, symmetrical apprehensible structure that the reader can pick up on. Nevertheless, to *abandon* your structure in the midst of your story or novel—or to change it radically, without going back and restructuring what has occurred up to that point—is simply to write a badly structured book, no matter how interesting the plot (or plot synopsis: I believe the two are synonymous) is.

Almost as common as the false flashback among young writers is the story or novel that begins by exhibiting a perfectly lucid and clear structure that, after a third or a half of the tale is done, then throws it away. Again and again, when questioned about it, young writers have explained to me: "Well, I just got *tired* of doing it that way. I wanted to try something different."

However sympathetic one is with the tired writer, such derelictions still produce bad work. Your job as a writer is to write a good story, a good book. Don't abandon your structure midway. To think you can get away with it (or that the reader will be just as tired of it as you are and welcome the change) is to confuse writing with reading. It's to forget that a story or a book is to be read—and the much briefer time that the reading takes. (The poet Valéry once remarked, "All art is a disproportionate act." It's the name of the game. If, in practice, the fact upsets you too greatly, it only means you should take up another line of work.) One of the most important pieces of advice a young writer can receive is: Choose material—and work toward a structure—that is rich, varied, and complex enough to sustain your interest, if not your enthusiasm, for the extended time it will take to write the work in question.

If you don't, the writing itself will be painful to undergo, and you will be tempted to cut corners and go off in directions that will only weaken the work. Or, if they *are* actually more interesting than the original conception, you still have the problem of reconceiving the beginning material to bring it in line with where you've decided to go.

Now of course the reader can get tired of a structure too—one that isn't doing anything in terms of the material—alternating chapters, say, that still don't throw new and interesting light on what's going on. But if the reader is going to get tired of it, the answer is not to change it midstream. The answer is to go back, start over again, and choose a different structure that is richer and works better with the material.

Writing fiction *is* work. And hard work, at that.

If you're *not* prepared to work hard, think seriously about doing something else.

Many writers structure their narrative in the following manner or something close to it: a sentence of action, followed by a sentence of emotional response, following by a sentence of action, followed by a sentence of emotional response . . . and they continue on in this way for large blocks of text, now and again breaking things up with passages of dialogue. (An even more prevalent structure is: a sentence of action, *three* sentences of emotional response, a sentence of action, *three* sentences of emotional response . . .) Generally speaking, this is not a very interesting narrative structure. (And page after page of the one, three, one, three narrative structure is *deadly*!) Even if, sentence by sentence, the writing is clean and polished, the overall effect tends to become gray and homogenized because of the fundamentally boring and repetitive structure. Writers can produce more varied and far stronger effects if they will work with larger rhetorical units, as well as structuring those larger units in more interesting and imaginative ways.

We spoke of structure as a way of creating expectation, a few pages back. This may be the place to note that, to the extent that the novel and the short story are forms (that is, structures), each exists as nothing but various sets of structural expectations. These expectations have been set in place by the history of the genre. One of the strongest structural expectations shared by both short story and novel is that, somewhere at the beginning of the text or comparatively near it, the writer will let us know what economic bracket the main character is currently in (and what bracket that character has come from). This expectation has been set up by three hundred years of novels that have answered this question within the first few pages. Because this expectation is so strong in fiction, the ways a writer can answer it have become very subtle. The kinds of paragraphs that are obligatory toward the start of any Jane Austen novel ("A single man of large fortune; four or five thousand a year. What a fine thing for our girls!") need not occur in every novel today. It can be done by the mention of a manila envelope from the VA (Veterans' Administration) or Social Security sticking out from under the coffee grounds in the garbage pail. It can be done by the mention of a bunch of checks stuck in a Savings Bank passbook on the back of the kitchen table. It can be suggested by the clothing someone wears, by the kind of house a character lives in, the mention of a profession or a line of work, or any of hundreds of other devices. But if that information is not stated or implied—and stated or implied clearly—the reader will feel the same sort of structural displeasure as he or she does when an internal set of structural expectations is violated.

The notion of structure runs from how words and phrases are organized within the sentence (even how sounds are organized throughout various phrases), to how sentences are organized within the narrative, to how larger units such as chapters are organized to make up the overall tale. It even covers the larger question of what fiction, what a story, what the novel actually *is*.

Edgar Rice Burroughs, in Tarzan novel after Tarzan novel, adhered to a simple and clear chapter structure: chapter 1 told about the villains of the story; chapter 2 told about what Tarzan was doing; chapter 3 told about the doings of the villains again; chapter 4 went back to Tarzan, who now discovered what the villains had done in chapter 1; chapter 5 went back to the villains, who by now were aware of Tarzan and were trying to trip him up; chapter 6 showed Tarzan again righting what the villains had set wrong two chapters before and going on to find what they'd done in chapter 3; chapter 7 showed the villains at it again; chapter 8 showed Tarzan straightening out the mess of chapter 6 and pursuing the villains, only to encounter the results of chapter 7 . . .

This alternating chapter structure went on throughout the novel, back and forth between Tarzan and the villains, until the last chapter, in which Tarzan gets to fight the villains directly—and triumphs. The structure supported Burroughs through dozens of Tarzan novels—and made him a millionaire several times over. It was simple and effective; suspense was built into it—and the readers never tired of it. But while the *structure* of the novels was the same, the *plots* of all the Tarzan novels—what the villains are after, who they are, the various ways Tarzan foils them and cleans up their mess—are as different as can be.

It's a lot easier to talk about plot than it is to talk about structure. Plot exists as a synopsis that often has no correspondence to text. (Where, among the pages of Kafka's *Metamorphosis,* can you point to the deadening, boring routine of Samsa's work? or to Samsa's character? or to his sister's? or to his father's? or to his family's decisions to take in boarders? But it would be hard to discuss the plot in any detail without reference to all of these.) Structure exists, however, *only* in terms of a particular text, so that to talk about it in any specificity or detail you must constantly be pointing to one part of a page or another, these words or those: Structure is specifically the organization of various and varied *textual* units.

Structures are there, certainly, to be talked about. But if they are to be useful to the writer, they must be *felt.*

(We find out that Samsa's family is now taking in lodgers in the last clause of the third sentence of the ninth paragraph of *The Metamorphosis*'s third chapter—suddenly and without any access to the decision itself, as Gregor must have discovered it: That is to say, the structure of the narrative parallels the *experience* of the Point of View character [*without* directly recounting it]—and as such represents the smallest of structural elegances in the many that comprise that extraordinary narrative performance.)

As hard as structure is to talk about, when actually writing the writer must accustom him- or herself to thinking about structure—and to thinking about it constantly. I don't mean that the *word* "structure" must be in your mind while you write. But, while writing, the writer must constantly be thinking such thoughts as: As I write this section of my story, is there another section that must be more or less the same length (or much shorter; or much longer) in order to balance it? Given the feel of this section, is there another section that, for the story to be satisfying, should have the *same* feel? Is there a section that must have a markedly *different* feel? How does this section differ in feel from the previous section? How should the next section differ in feel from this one? Finally, and perhaps most important, how does a previous occurrence cause the reader to regard the one I'm currently writing about?

These are all structural questions—and are the questions the writer has to ask *while* writing. You have to hold on to the answers, too. In my experience, mulling on these questions during the writing process often precedes any knowledge I have of what, specifically, is actually going to *happen* in a given scene or section later in the tale. (Often deciding on the answers *leads* to a decision about what happens.) These kinds of questions must be wrestled with, usually while the pen is in hand or the fingers are knocking at the typewriter keys, if the story is to come out with a sense of shape, provide readerly pleasure, and project writerly wholeness.

In the canon of great nineteenth-century European novels, the most pyrotechnically structured is Flaubert's *L'Education sentimentale*. The novel begins and ends with comparatively benign anecdotes, both organized around the adolescent protagonist, Frédéric Moreau. The first details of Frédéric starting out on a steamer journey from Paris, a traditional ship of fools, returning to his provincial home, Nogent-sur-Seine. The last, recounted by the now-middle-aged Frédéric, is a reminiscence of an incident that takes place even before that initial journey home—and describes Frédéric and his somewhat older friend Deslaurier's attempt to visit a provincial bordello, a visit that goes awry because Frédéric is too embarrassed and, at the last moment, runs away; and Deslaurier has no money of his own for the adventure so must flee as well. In between, Flaubert recounts half a lifetime of Frédéric's (and Deslaurier's) adventures that carry him through the republican revolution of 1848, during which Frédéric would seem to be an up-and-coming young man, cutting a swath among Parisian women, both in the central light and on the outskirts of French society. Because of his hopeless love for Madame Marie Arnoux, however, Frédéric never gets what he wants. Each triumph is soured at its high point through the interplay of chance, half-understood malice, and misdirection from others. But to speak of the book on such a level is to speak of it in terms of plot—rather than structure. In terms of plot, *Sentimental Education* moves from social success to social success. It climaxes when Frédéric refuses to marry an unbelievably vicious—if extremely wealthy—woman, Madame Dambreuse, and gains his freedom as a man. In terms of structure, it moves from failure to failure, each new one more devastating than the last, each demanding a greater accommodation and deformation of Frédéric's soul for him to endure. Although, by the end, Frédéric is a free man with a good house and a place in Parisian society—and at least some of his fortune intact—one can only assume, from his last encounter with Madame Arnoux, that perhaps his earlier encounter with Madame Dambreuse at the auction house has left him wounded in ways that put him finally and wholly outside the possibility of receiving the benefits Madame Arnoux's love might have given him had he and she been able to come together. If Flaubert had simply *explained* how each social triumph was in reality a failure, the novel would have been banal: Again and again, its structure justifies Robert Baldick's claim at the opening of his introduction to the Penguin edition that the book is "undoubtedly the most influential French novel of the nineteenth century" and makes it the novelists' novel from its time. That structure is what makes the book about so much more than the social adventures of one moderately callow youth and turns it, rather, into the analysis of the dilemmas of an age.

Most people who write novels—that is to say, people who write and publish the workaday novels, the mysteries and romances, the best-sellers or, among the more adventurous readers, the science fiction and the occasional "serious fiction" that, from time to time, falls into the lap of the fiction reader and makes up most of our reading—absorb a few, simple novelistic structures. And they can submit to them. Rarely have they absorbed the range of structures, however, from the possible play of sounds in sentences, to the necessary structures for a variety of scenic resonances, to the structures for the interplay of text and counter-texts in tension with one another that make the novel into the richest of symphonic art forms. Usually the structures they've absorbed are at the mid-range, and are just visible enough to keep us reading through reams of unbelievable dialogue, pointless internal "characterization," and the like, under the illusion we are trying to find out "what happens." We aren't. We are following a mid-range structure that promises that "what happens" at a certain level will be revealed. And, in one form or another, usually it is.

These particular structures can best be characterized as "formulaic." Indeed, the vast majority of fiction that we read *is* formulaic. And formulaic fiction is rarely *good* fiction.

Constructing a new model is always a matter of revising an old model. Certain elements are adjusted. Others are negated. (What happens if, for example, one abolishes the tyranny of the subject [Robbe-Grillet], radically displaces the position of irony [John Ashbery, Kenneth Gememi, James Schuyler], rebels against the tyranny of reference [Hart Crane, Charles Bernstein], the tyranny of narrative progression [Ron Silliman, Lyn Hajinian, John Keene], or even the tyranny of the letter [Richard Kostelanetz] . . . ? In such enterprises poetry and prose, as well as literature and pictorial art, begin to lose their hard and bounded distinctions.) But if, for fiction, say, you were to construct an *entirely* new model, the chances are overwhelming you'll come up, rather, with an awkward (and probably old-fashioned) model for dry cleaning, for archaeological research, or for political lobbying before you come up with one for fiction. The fact that you—and possibly a very few aesthetically sophisticated members of whatever limited audience you might command—

can recognize the results as belonging to the realm *of* fiction (or art—or whatever) in the first place *means* you have retained some signs—if only a label, if only the placement of the object in a context (publishing it in a journal, scrawling it on a wall)—that bespeak it a text. And "text," as most of the readers of this essay will know, already has a distressingly wide interpretation—far beyond what can fit on walls, screens, pages, or stages.

Nonsense is conservative. If your wish is to be radical, think about that. Radicalism resists aesthetic entropy in the same way it resists the formulaic and the cliché. Through irony, there are radical ways the cliché can be welcomed into art. But irony requires more, not less, thought to respond to than ordinary humor, sentiment, or any of the last three millennia's narrative tropes.

To extend our discussion beyond this point, however, where cliché and formulaic structures are distinguished from the relatively neutral structures of genre and the more ambitious sort of good art, we would have to enter a discussion about the violation of structural expectations—a violation which is finally just as important as cleaving to them. (Advice: If it strikes *you* as well, as clearly, or as interestingly structured, go with it. If it strikes *you* as cliché and formulaic, avoid it.) Indeed, it is the combination of fulfilling *and* violating structural expectations that makes fiction not just a craft, but an art. If there is a distinction to be made between good art and art that we think of as great, often it lies in the area of what structural expectations to violate. But the violation of expectations very quickly, over a period of ten or fifteen years, can turn into an expectation itself—one reason it is so hard to talk of, when negativities turn out to be positivities after all. These questions are, however, beyond the scope of such limited notes as these, even though they are just as important—and just as intimately bound up with the idea of narrative.

—New York City
February 1996

continued from page iv

"Neither the First Word nor the Last on Structuralism, Deconstruction, Semiotics, and Poststructuralism" first appeared over three issues of *The New York Review of Science Fiction*, edited by David Hartwell et al., no. 6, February 1989; no. 7, March 1989; no. 8, April 1989, Pleasantville, New York.

"Inside and Outside the Canon: The *Para•doxa* Interview" first appeared as "*Para•doxa* Interview with Samuel R. Delany," in *Para•doxa, Studies in World Literary Genres*, ed. Lauric Guillard, vol. 1, no. 3, 1995, Vashon Island, Washington.

"The Politics of Paraliterary Criticism" first appeared over three issues of *The New York Review of Science Fiction*, edited by David Hartwell et al., whole no. 98, October 1996, vol. 9, no. 2; whole no. 99, November 1996, vol. 9, no. 3; whole no. 100, December 1996, vol. 9, no. 4, Pleasantville, New York.

"Zelazny/Varley/Gibson—and Quality" first appeared over two issues of *The New York Review of Science Fiction*, edited by David Hartwell et al., whole no. 48, August 1992, and whole no. 49, September 1992, Pleasantville, New York.

Part of "Pornography and Censorship" appeared in *Fiction International (22)*'s special issue on Pornography and Censorship, 1992, edited by Harold Jaffee, Larry McCaffery, and Mel Freilicher, San Diego; part appeared the same year in the *Pacific Review of Books*, edited by Ronald Sukenick.

"The Making of *Hogg*" first appeared in *Fiction International*, edited by Harold Jaffee, 1997.

A brief section of "The Phil Leggiere Interview" appeared as "Diary of a Mad Man" in *Paper*, eds. Kim Hastreiter and David Herskovitz, October 1994, New York.

"The Second *Science-Fiction Studies* Interview: *Trouble on Triton* and Other Matters," first appeared as "An Interview with Samuel R. Delany" in *Science Fiction Studies*, vol. 17, 1990.

"Antonia Byatt's *Possession: A Romance*" first appeared in *The New York Review of Science Fiction*, edited by David Hartwell et al., no. 6, February 1989; no. 7, March 1989; no. 8, April 1989, Pleasantville, New York.

"Neil Gaiman": §I was written in collaboration with Robert Morales and appears here for the first time. §2 first appeared as the Introduction to *Miracleman* Book

Four, from Dark Horse Comics, 1993; §3 first appeared as the Introduction to *A Game of You*, by Neal Gaiman, New York City: D. C. Comics, 1995.

"Michael Perkins's *Evil Companions*" first appeared as "Preface" to *Evil Companions* by Michael Perkins, Rhinoc*eros* edition, 1992 New York.

"And Now It's Time for Dale Peck," first appeared in a slightly different version in *The Lambda Books Report*, #12, Washington, D.C.

"*Othello* in Brooklyn" first appeared in the CBA Newsletter, 1987, Brooklyn, New York.

"A Prefatory Notice to Vincent Czyz's *Adrift in a Vanishing City*" first appeared in *Adrift in a Vanishing City* by Vincent Czyz, Rutherford: Voyant Publishing, 1998.

"Under the Volcano with Susan Sontag" first appeared in *Reflex Magazine*, edited by Lou Stathis, September 1995.

Index

Adorno, Theodore, 23, 177
AIDS, 34, 36-39, 43-48, 50-56, 94, 108, 123-26, 132, 135-37
Aldiss, Brian, 263-65, 266-70, and the definition of comics art, 267
Althusser, Louis, 151-52, 157-58, 173; "Ideology and Ideological State Apparatuses," 157
American Shore, The (Delany), 216
Anti-Oedpus: Capitalism and Schizophrenia (Deleuze and Guatarri), 180
Asimov, Isaac, 165
As Is (William F. Hoffman), 94
Auden, W. H., 324-25
Auerbach, Erich, x
Aye, and Gomorrah . . . (Delany), 90
Aztecs (McIntyre), 317

Babel-17 (Delany), 344
Bachelard, Gaston; *Poetics of Space*, 161; *Psychoanalysis of Fire*, 161
Baldick, Chris, x
Barker, Francis, x
Barnes, Steven, 116
Barthes, Roland, 133, 159, 160-62; *The Elements of Semiology*, 159; *The Fashion System*, 162; *Empire of Signs*, 162; *Roland Barthes by Roland Barthes*, 162; *A Lover's Discourse*, 162; *S/Z*, 176-77; *The Pleasure of the Text*, 177-78; *Writing Itself: On Roland Barthes*, 400-401
Bachelard, Gaston, 161
Bakhtin, Mikhail; "Epic and The Novel," 414-15
Baudrillard, Jean, 35
Bear, Greg, 272
Belgrave, Cynthia, 338-95

Benjamin, Walter, vii-viii, ix, 211
Bester, Alfred; *The Deceivers*, 284; *The Demolished Man*, 284; *The Stars My Destination*, 183
Bierce, Ambrose, 12
Billion Year Spree: The True History of Science Fiction (Aldiss), 263, 264-65
Bloom, Harold, 112, 414
Bob (friend), 85-87
Browne, Howard, 93
Browne, Sir Thomas, 14
Bohannan, Laura, 28-35
Brave New World (Huxley), 325
Butler, Octavia, 116, 272
Byatt, Antonia, 353-58

Campell, Joseph, 31
Carr, Terry (as editor at Ace Books), 278
Chaos (Gleick), 149
Crane, Hart, 418, 426; "For the Marriage of Faustus and Helen," 241; "The Bridge," 424
Crane, Stephen, 190-202; *The Red Badge of Courage*, 190, 418; *Maggie, A Girl of the Streets*, 190; *The Third Violet*, 190
Culler, Jonathan, 179
Czyz, Vincent, 396-98; *Adrift in a Vanishing City*, 396

Dahlgren (Delany), 214, 300, 331
Davenport, Guy, 112-14
da Vinci, Leonardo, 3-6, 8, 15, 22, 23; and visual perception, 27
Debouched Hospodar (Apollinaire), 307
Deja, Tom, 115-22
Deleuze, Gilles, 161
Derrida, Jacques, 35, 129, 133, 146-48,

462   Index

Derrida, Jacques (*continued*)
158, 163, 174, 180, 181, 184, 185;
and Foucault, 166–69; *Glas*, 175–76;
Of Grammatology, 141, 174; *The Post-
card*, 176; *Writing and Difference*, 166;
"The Cogito and the History of Mad-
ness," 166
Dick, Philip K., 225
Dispossessed, The (Le Guin), 321–22,
324, 326, 332
Douglas, Mary, 131
Duberman, Martin, 112–14
Dunn, J. R., 8–11, 14
Dying Inside (Silverberg), 289, 290

Eagleton, Terry, 177; *Literary Theory, An
Introduction*, 413
Eco, Umberto, 178; *A Theory of Semiotics*,
162
Einstein Intersection, The (Delany), 344
Eliot, T. S., 241
Equinox (a.k.a. *Tides of Lust*) (Delany),
294, 295
Evil Companions (Perkins), 299, 377–83

Fall of the Towers, The (Delany), 344
Fallopio, Gabriello, 5, 8
Fellman, Shoshna, xi, 153, 179; *The Lit-
erary Speech Act: Austin and Moliere*, 180
Fire Watch (Willis), 279
First Three Minutes, The (Weinberg), 149
Flame Wars: The Discourse of Cyberculture
(Dery), 213
Flaubert, Gustave, 24
"For the Marriage of Faustus and Helen"
(Crane), 241
42nd Street (Times Square, N.Y.), 58,
77–81, 84
Foucault, Michel, 23, 31, 34, 35, 36, 75,
163–73, 175, 183–85; *The Archeology
of Knowledge*, 163, 171, 172; *The Order
of Things*, 163,170; *Madness and Civi-
lization*, 164; "My Body, This Paper,
This Fire," 167; *Birth of the Clinic*, 169,
171; *Discipline and Punish*, 171–72;
The Will to Knowledge, 172, 173; "What
Is an Author," 18

Foundation (series) (Asimov), 165
Frankfurt Group, The, 23
Frazier, Sir James George, 35
Freud, Sigmund, 15, 19, 21, 24, 25, 34,
129, 153–55, 165, 176

Gaiman, Neil, 359–72; Sandman (se-
ries), 359
Gale (friend), 80, 84–85, 87
Gallop, Jane, xi, 153
Gass, William, x, 113
Gay Fathers group, 95–96
Gibson, William, 153, 213–15, 272, 278,
348; contemporaries of, 214; and
cyberpunk, 279–80; "Aliens," 213;
Burning Chrome, 273; "Johnny Mne-
monic," 213; *Neuromancer*, 182, 213
"Girl With Hungry Eyes" (Leiber), 158
Goffman, Irving, 50
Greece: and discursive structures, 31;
trip to, 101; as postcolonial country,
101–6; and homosexuality, 107
Greenblatt, Stephen, x
Guin, Ursula Le. *See* Le Guin, Ursula

Hacker, Marilyn, 80, 87–88, 90, 91–92,
95, 319
Hawthorne, Nathaniel, 12
Hamlet, 28–29
Heidegger, Martin, 141, 146, 173
Heinlein, Robert, 119
Hitchcock, Alfred, 24
HIV/AIDS. *See* AIDS
Hogg (Delany), 294, 295, 296
Holland, Sean, 43
Hopkinson, Nalo, 116
Huxley, Aldous; *Brave New World*, 325
Irigaray, Luce, 155, 179

Jakobson, Roman, 179
JAMA (*Journal of the American Medical
Association*), 50
Jameson, Fredric, 158, 178
Jewel-Hinged Jaw, The (Delany), 317
Joel (summer camp friend), 71–73, 74
Johnson, Barbara, x, 168, 174, 179; *The
Critical Difference*, 180

Jonas, Gerald, 127
Judy (friend), 80, 85, 86, 87, 88
Jung, Carl Gustav, 24

Kermit, S. L., 125
Kristeva, Julia, 155
Kundura, Milan, 112

Lacan, 15, 151–53, 156, 158, 163, 170, 173, 179, 184; on the phallus, 152–56; *Ecrits*, 153; "The Function and Field of Speech and Language in Psycholoanalysis," 155; "Seminar on 'The Purloined Letter," 153, 179
Le Guin, Ursula, 6, 8–11, 277, 286–87, 315; *Always Coming Home*, 327; *The Dispossessed*, 321–22, 324, 326
Leiber, Fritz: "Girl With Hungry Eyes," 158
Lesbianism, 95
Levi-Strauss, Claude, 151–52, 158, 173, 178–79
Literary Theory, An Introduction (Eagleton), 413
Literature and Evil (Bataille), 306
Long, Thomas, 123–38
Lowe, John Livingston, x

MacCannell, Juliet Flower, 153
McCloud, Scott, 224–38; on a definition of comics art, 267–70; *Understanding Comics*, 224, 244–45, 247–51, 252–58, 259
McLuhan, Marshal, 158
Mad Man, The (Delany), 126, 128–33, 136; reviews of, 128; 311–12
Man, Paul de, 112
Man Without Qualities, The (Musil), 206
Mapplethorpe, Robert, 24
Marilyn (friend). *See* Hacker, Marilyn
Marx, Karl, xxx, 157, 158
Merril, Judith, 373–76; *Gunner Cade*, 373; *Outpost Mars*, 373; *Shadows on the Hearth*, 376; "That Only A Mother," 376; *The Tomorrow People*, 376
Metamorphoses of Science Fiction (Suvin), 260

Michel, Jean-Claude, 116
Mine Shaft, The, 49, 50
Mirrorshades: The Cyberpunk Anthology (Sterling), 280
Monad, 8–9, 11
Morrison, Toni, 6, 9, 10
Motion of Light in Water, The (Delany), 87, 313
Myth of Superman, The (Eco), 178, 258

Nevèrÿon (series) (Delany), 127–28; reviews of, 127
Nebula Award, 90, 117
Nemesis Affair, The (Raup), 149
Neuromancer (Gibson), 182, 213
New England Journal of Medicine, 43
New Worlds (Moorcock), 164
New York Review of Science Fiction, 173
New York Times, 43
Nova (Delany), 344

O'Hara, Scott, 136
Origins of Totalitarianism (Arendt), 411
Othello, production of, at Triangle Theater, 388–95

Paglia, Camille, 35
Palmer, Ray, 93
Peck, Dale, 384–87; *Now It's Time To Say Good-Bye*, 384
Peirce, Charles Sanders, 159, 160
Perkins, Michael, 377–83
Plato, 8, 24
Poe, Edgar Allen, 153
Poetics of Space (Bachelard),161
Pornographic publishing, classics of, 295
Possession (Byatt), 353–58
Pound, Ezra, 241–42
Psychoanalysis of Fire (Bachelard), 161
Purloined Poe: Lacan, Derrida, and Psychoanalytic Readings, The (Muller and Richardson), 153

QED (Davis and Brown), 149
Quine, W. V. 57

Rampersad, Arnold, xi

Reading by Starlight (Broderick), 213
Red (street person), 59–65
Red Mars (Robinson), 225
Robinson, Frank; *The Power*, 92–93
Robinson, Kim Stanley, 120; *The Novels of Philip K. Dick*, 225; *Red Mars*, 225
Rose (prostitute), 58–65
Rousseau, Jean Jacques, 174
Roussel, Raymond, 14, 15, 18, 31, 36, 173
Russ, Joanna, 286

Saunders, Charles, 116
Saussure, Ferdinand de, 158–59
Shakespeare, William, 28
Shaw, George Bernard, 22
Shepard, Lucius, 120, 272
Silent Interviews: On Language, Race, Sex, Science Fiction and Some Comics (Delany), 135
Smith, Cordwainer, 287
Sontag, Susan, 137; *Illness as Metaphor*, 403; "Notes on 'Camp'," 89; *On Photography*, 405; *The Volcano Lover, A Romance*, 399–407
Spivak, Gayatri Chakravorty, 98, 148, 169; *In Other Worlds*, 180
Spinrad, Norman, 92
Stars My Destination, The (Bester), 183
Starboard Wine (Delany), 216
Stephen Crane (Beer), 201
Sturgeon, Theodore, 33, 207–8
Suvin, Darko, 261–62, *The Metamorphoses of Science Fiction*, 260

Tale of Plagues and Carnivals, The (Delany), 123–24, 125, 126

Terminal Identity (Bukatman), 213
Toomer, Jean, 425
Tom (street friend), 46–47
Tourist, A New Theory of the Leisure Class (McCannell), 188
Trouble On Triton (Delany), 315–44

Understanding Comics (McCloud), 224–25, 244
Understanding Media (McLuhan), 158
Utopia and Revolution (Lasky), 181

Volcano Lover, A Romance, The (Sontag), 399–407
Varley, John, 272, 348; *The Barbie Murders* (a.k.a. *Picnic on Nearside*), 276; *Blue Champagne*, 277; *Millenium*, 277; *The Ophiuchi Hotline*, 275; *The Persistence of Vision*, 273; *Titan* (trilogy), 276

Wagner, Richard, 22, 131, 411–12
Watt, Ian, x
Whitman, Walt, 134
Wilson, Edmund, 179
Willis, Connie, 120
Wolfe, Gene, 288

Zelazny, Roger, 272, 282, 286; *Bridge of Ashes*, 275; *Doorways in the Sand*, 275; *The Dream Master*, 275; *Four for Tomorrow*, 273; "He Who Shapes," 182; "Home is the Hangman," 274; *Lord of Light*, 274; *This Immortal*, 274; *Today We Choose Faces*, 275

About the Author
Samuel R. Delany is a professor of English at the State University of New York at Buffalo. His many books include the Return to Nevèrÿon series, *Dhalgren*, and *Trouble on Triton*, reissued by Wesleyan University Press; *Atlantis: Three Tales* (1995), and *The Motion of Light in Water* (1987). His most recent books include *Time Square Red, Time Square Blue* (1999), and a graphic novel with artist Mia Wolff, *Bread & Wine* (1999).

Library of Congress Cataloging-in-Publication Data

Delany, Samuel R.
Shorter views: queer thoughts & the politics of the paraliterary
/ by Samuel R. Delany.
   p. cm.
   ISBN 0-8195-6368-4 (alk. paper). — ISBN 0-8195-6369-2
(pbk.: alk. paper)
   1. Delany, Samuel R.—Authorship. 2. Homosexuality and
literature—United States—History—20th century. 3. Gay Men's
writings, American—History and criticism—Theory, etc. 4. Science
fiction, American—History and criticism—Theory, etc. 5. Politics
and literature. I. Title
PS3554.E437Z4756 1999
814'.54—dc21   99-16781